2-2011

D1523989

TRANSCENDENCE

TRANSCENDENCE

A Novel

by Christopher McKitterick

HADLEY
RILLE
BOOKS

TRANSCENDENCE
Copyright © 2010 by Christopher McKitterick

Cover art © Greg Martin, www.artofgregmartin.com

Cover design by Melissa J. Lytton.

ISBN-13 978-0-9829467-0-1

Published by
Hadley Rille Books
Eric T. Reynolds
Editor/Publisher
PO Box 25466
Overland Park, KS 66225
USA
www.hadleyrillebooks.com
contact@hadleyrillebooks.com

For Jim and Kij—for everything.

Acknowledgments

Most of all I must express eternal appreciation to James Gunn, my mentor and friend from this book's conception through its birth. He introduced me to science fiction when I was young with his wonderful *Road to Science Fiction* anthologies, and in the years since has helped me better understand this genre and how to write it. Endless thanks to the Lawrence SF Writers, especially Michael McGinnis, Aaron Rosenberg, and Ann Tonsor Zeddies (affectionately called the ALAGAMOWGP Workshop—ask me why some time), whose encouragement and critiques kept me going. The keen eyes of Erica Binns and Grace Smith have ensured that this book is as error-free as mere mortals can make it: Thank you! By buying my first story, Algis Budrys reinforced the crazy notion that I wanted to be a writer; later, A.J. became my agent, making me feel like a professional. Thanks to Dr. Stanley Schmidt, the editor who published my first story and wanted another, thus keeping me writing. Thanks to Lydia Ash for encouraging me to get back in the writing saddle. My heart smiles when I think of Eric T. Reynolds, the editor who bought most of my recent stories and who, by publishing my first novel, has renewed my writing energy manifold. "Thanks" cannot express my gratitude to Kij Johnson, whose support kept this project—and my writing—alive through what felt like endless character-building adversity (ask me about this over a beer). Thank you, Greg Martin, for letting us use the beautiful and haunting "Neptune Skies" for the cover art; and thank you, Melissa J. Lytton, for such a lovely and unique book design. Finally, this list of appreciations wouldn't be complete without thanking *you* for picking up this book and reading it. I hope you enjoy!

If the shell is broken too soon, there is nothing to be done
but make a bad omelette. But if it isn't broken
at the proper time, the chick dies and stinks.

-H.G. Wells

We have reached the end of this brief music that is Man.

-Olaf Stapledon

There is nothing in man but love and faith, courage and kindness,
generosity and sacrifice. All else is only the barrier
of your blindness. One day we'll all be mind to mind
and heart to heart.

-Alfred Bester

There is nothing safe in this world.
And there's nothing sure in this world,
and there's nothing pure in this world,
and if there's something left in this world. . .
start again!

-Billy Idol

ONE: Outerlimits

Triton 1: Liu Miru

A tenuous breeze hissed across Liu Miru's suit as he crossed a ridge of nitrogen ice. Neptune filled the sky, lighting Miru's path about as brightly as, though shades bluer than, the full Moon on Earth. Thoughts of Earth reminded him that somewhere in the recesses of space, not far away now, an invading warship from that world blazed nearer. *Why now? Why here? Of all times and places, why start a war here and now when we are so close to . . . to discovering something great.* He almost laughed, but he knew to do so would reduce him to tears of frustration.

This was seventy-two hours before the end of the human race as he knew it.

Miru paused to look up. He could see no metal sliver slicing the black of space, no hot exhaust, nothing unusual. He continued walking.

Miru knew he might be dead in hours. That did not slow his pace; rather, he hurried, dedicated. He hoped the knowledge he gathered could divert the brewing war that would, he was certain, consume all the worlds of the Solar System.

He thought only of the object. Triton was a largely worthless world that had revealed most of its secrets long before he arrived. But Project Hikosen gave him purpose. When he first saw the object—which he was careful not to call "alien" to anyone but himself—it had seemed that he'd awakened from a long sleep.

Miru's first months of exertion building Jiru City were joyous. He had almost forgotten the passions of his youth when the Project had re-aroused them. In retrospect, the interim seemed like sleep.

Soon, the tractor-worn path turned off the ridge. Miru stopped for a moment and looked to the foreshortened horizon across pockmarked terrain, the peculiar "grapefruit" texture of Triton's Eastern Hemisphere, methane and nitrogen ice encrusting the rock. He drew a deep breath and turned toward the shallow excavation. Unmarked, it looked like nothing more than a test dig. He smiled at the irony. *Things are not always as they appear*, he thought, recalling the words of a childhood tutor.

Miru's heart rate increased as he climbed down a gleaming staircase melted from the ice. As he descended the few meters into the pit, the wind quieted and the walls constricted the dome of stars overhead. His breathing seemed to grow louder within his helmet.

He reached the bottom of the excavation and stared at the object. Silence ruled down here, except for the mechanical sounds of his breathing apparatus and the crunch of ice crystals beneath his boots. With his headlamp off, the pit was lit by stars and a blue glow cast from the orb of Neptune.

Miru laid his gloved palm against the nitrogen and methane frost that glazed the sphere's surface, black beneath a wispy pink icing. He switched off his suit's comm system, which ordinarily transmitted full 3D-virtual-reality information about his surroundings to his brain implants. Now he could observe with naked eyes. Such disconnection from the cybernetic world was rare in this day of perpetual uplink. However, Miru often found it useful to compare naked-eye observations to those taken with cybernetic enhancement.

With this data-feed turned off, the simple geometric shape suddenly transformed into a walled temple, and it was as if he stood on the surface of another world. The horizons wore an amalgam of colors like clouds of different liquids, mixing and swirling. This was not unlike the kind of overlay or annotated reality that so many people used to edit their view of the world around them, but was instead some as-yet unmeasurable effect on his brain.

A grin of curiosity and expectation briefly touched his lips, as during previous visits. He was a child again, exploring places where he liked to pretend that no man had gone before. Except now it was true.

A wall, invisible to all but those who observed with unaided eyes, stretched out around him. It was smooth, black, three meters high, curving away in both directions so that it seemingly encompassed a space about 100 meters in diameter. Miru began recording a narrative of what he saw, subvocalizing because it seemed disrespectful to speak aloud in the vicinity of such a find. Besides, this narrative was the only way to record his observations, because recording equipment didn't respond to the object in the same way a naked mind did. Experiments had proven that what he observed, he saw with his *mind*, not any of his physical senses.

At the center of what must have been a courtyard hidden behind the walls, stood the temple itself. It was an exact replica of the Great Temple of Mahabodhi, what his parents had called the ancient Buddhists' most sacred shrine. Miru remembered the day his parents took him on a 3VRD trip to this very temple. Though he had promised to return intheflesh some day, he never had. He wondered if they were secretly Buddhists, but that didn't matter now.

An elongated pyramid with nearly vertical walls, the temple thrust what appeared to be 40 meters toward space. It was intricately carved with human statues in various postures he couldn't identify from this distance. A conical structure rose from the truncated top. At the base stood a square foundation perhaps ten meters high, and miniature models of the temple rose at each of its corners. Below that, he couldn't see, for the wall blocked his view.

He began to walk along the wall, resuming the search for an entrance. As he walked, his glove brushed what seemed to be an impassable barrier around the temple. He could not climb over, because the wall was as slick as the object itself—*Perhaps it was the object*, he subvocalized, *and this barrier a representation of its impenetrable surface*—and the ladder he had used last Tritonday was as functionless as the sensing instruments he and others brought to bear on the physical sphere; the wall simply grew taller with each step Miru took up the ladder. If he hadn't pursued the impulse to shut down his headcard cybernetics during the investigation two days prior, this temple would still have been shrouded by the opaque barrier of ignorance.

He switched back on his headcard and external feed, then looked up. The temple vanished and the pit walls closed tight around him, now ammonia- and methane-ice rather than a distant, indefinite roiling of colors.

Miru decided that this would be the day he went inside, if an entrance existed.

Four meters overhead, an electromagnetic screen camouflaged the ten-meter-wide excavation. TritonCo, the corporation that owned Triton, was hiding this find from everyone until they knew more. President Dorei had stated that here lay TritonCo's future. Triton might become the space for parley between the mega-corporations: EarthCo, composed of Earth's Western nations such as the US, most of the EU, India, and Japan, plus a few small worlds such as Mars; and NKK, which encompassed almost all the other Asian, Middle-Eastern, and Pacific nations, as well as a few worlds such as Neptune. They seemed always at war, these corporations that owned their component countries, but expanding that perpetual war was lately gaining favor among the corporations' franchised, voting citizens.

So, even though Miru felt that telling everyone about the object could change their sentiment, his friend Jon Pang had pressed for secrecy.

"I know humanity too well," Pang had stated. His hard look explained what he meant. "We can inform the major corporations when the time is ripe and we are prepared."

Miru tried to forget his friend's misgivings, concentrating on the potential for good in his fellow humans. But he understood Pang's fear.

Twice they had talked significantly about their years on Earth. They had spoken of the pain inflicted by others, the loneliness inflicted by lack of others, and the odd coincidence of both at certain moments. During these talks, each had nearly lost his composure. Then they spoke no more of childhood fears and concerns. On Triton, they were safe. They were free to become men. Here they could pursue pure research without threat of war—something not true on Earth or the other inner planets.

That had changed with the coming of the Westerners aboard their EarthCo warship. Miru cleared his mind of those conversations and concentrated on his work.

The object's dome rose nearly to the surface where the mine-test furrow had been cut. The channeler's spade had sparked and bent its teeth; two hours later, Miru had been designated Project Director for studying the object. He looked down at his cleated boots.

Miru had left the object's bottom half buried. Instruments declared it completely symmetrical: a perfect sphere, three meters in diameter, seemingly even in density—but no instrument could report its mass. Meaningful measurements had to be taken by hand, externally, without feed data. No one in Jiru City had training in such methods—nor did they wish to be isolated from feed by shutting down their cybernetics—except Miru, who had studied archaic methods of scientific research: that is, using his bare eyes and mind.

"Brother Liu!" Miru's helmet earphone blared with the voice of Jon Pang. Accompanying the sound, a 3VRD of Pang spliced into view directly before Miru. Pang's image looked absurd wearing coveralls in the near-vacuum, seeming to stand in the pit with Miru. Miru thought little of this: Such was how people communicated in the Virtual Age.

Miru pulled back his hand, self-conscious about his childlike wonder. He wished he hadn't switched his headcard back on, even for a moment. A black handprint remained where his glove had rested against the sphere, trailing a dark smear where it had slid.

"You seem upset. What is it?" Miru asked his colleague's 3VRD. The words sounded muffled and close in his bell-shaped ultraglas helmet.

"Brother Liu!" Pang said. "Computer projections show that the EarthCo warcraft—perhaps you remember it?—has altered trajectory and approaches Triton. You must return or seek shelter."

"Don't be absurd," Miru responded. "Why would EarthCo attack TritonCo? Hasn't Dorei contacted Neptunekaisha Protection?" He referred to the security force of the planet they orbited, Neptune. Neptune boasted a sovereign corporation of its own, though it retained heavy ties to NKK and was probably owned by the megacorp.

"He has, brother. They sent the warning. Coordinator Chang of Neptunekaisha Protection verified the report."

Miru stiffened. "She must be mistaken. We have nothing of value to EarthCo here."

"We have the object," Pang whispered, as if anyone with sufficiently advanced anti-cryptography who was eavesdropping on their bandwidth could not hear. "Anyway, Protection says this warcraft has gone renegade. Those aren't regular cosmonauts. They're insane."

"I see," muttered Miru, watching pink crystals drift down from the rough-cut pit walls onto his boots as wind swirled in from above.

Insane, yes; that is the problem with humans, Miru thought. He knew from experience. He glanced at the object, his brow wrinkling. Then he relaxed.

"At least we don't have to worry about *this*," he said, again resting his hand on the sphere. Not even accelerator drills had grazed it; any particle or energy they directed at its surface was deflected with no apparent effect. Various craters and melts in the pit's dirty-ice walls testified to these attempts.

"Liu," said Pang, shaking his head, long dark hair swaying from side to side, "try to think about something beyond the object for once. Think about this: Our Jiru City is not quite as sturdy as the object. Hmmm?"

Miru thought about it.

"Barbarians," Miru said. "TritonCo is the only corp interested in funding our research here. If Jiru City is destroyed, NKK will likely abandon TritonCo . . . and stop funding our project. TritonCo itself has no money. We—"

"Liu!" the other shouted, shaking a fist. "What do you suppose will happen to *us* if that warcraft blasts through Neptunekaisha's defenses? It devastated NKK's defenses on Phobos."

Miru shrank back a step, unnerved by this display of emotion in Pang. Then the implications of the man's words soaked through:

"If we die, no one will continue our work," he said.

Pang sighed, his fists relaxing and falling to his sides.

"You need to find shelter before it arrives, in an estimated twenty minutes," Pang said. His image slowly shook its head and vanished.

Miru drew a deep breath, cleared his mind, then turned his attention back to the object. He wondered if perhaps this was more than merely a ball of starstuff created by alien hands—this was wild speculation for a man such as Miru. Perhaps it was an alien lifeform, itself. Where would such a thing have evolved? Not on Triton . . . or maybe so. This world was one of the few active satellites in the Solar System, bristling with volcanic and geologic activity, and Neptune provided plenty of energy.

He flicked off his headcard and watched the temple re-emerge, pointing to the stars: a schizophrenic monument to humanity's past, a surreal gem set into the near-absolute-zero ice of a place as far from Earth as the race had settled.

And now Miru, burning with the anger and frustration he had learned in his childhood aboard Ryukyu Floating Island on Earth, felt a surge of happiness. *Happiness, why?* he wondered. Yet, even as he asked himself, the answer crystallized.

This moment was the pinnacle of his life. Every moment leading up to now, every person—friend or otherwise—every action he had taken, and every piece of data he had studied . . . all this led to now, to this place, to this gleaming crystal in time.

He smiled to himself, watching colored snowflakes drift down around him into shadows at his feet. He felt more than happy. He had earned this place, this moment, yes, but he had also been given the gift of being *aware* he was happy. He had walked beyond happiness into the pure emotional world of joy. Even fear of death did not diminish his joy; indeed, that fear spurred him. He possessed something more powerful than fear of death or war. He stood at the gate of a great discovery, was about to open the door to knowledge, joyous knowledge that promised . . . who knows? And that was the point of his work after all, the point of all scientific inquiry.

"It's time we told everyone in the Solar System about you," he told the temple's gleaming walls, patting the hard surface. This time, he disarmed the overhead electromagnetic shield and threw open his suit's transmitter. He hoped President Dorei wouldn't block retransmission of the stream of data he began to narrate for anyone who happened to be listening.

Miru thought of the approaching warship.

He might die. *But we all die*, he thought. Better to die at life's summit with a panoramic view of one's existence than at its pain-bouldered basin. He would die, if necessary, spreading knowledge . . . and hope.

He again set off in search of an entrance.

TWO: Earth

Innerspace 1: Jonathan Sombrio

Around Jonathan, the city stands high and shadowed and quiet, seeming as empty of life as an automated factory at midnight. Afternoon sunlight filters down through the ever-present haze that smells of dust and ozone, falling in luminescent green columns onto the street. The sun offers no warmth, and his breath is a puff of fog before him.

Jonathan works hard not to notice any of this, instead concentrating on his splice, a virtual-reality subscription inserted into his field of view like a wedge splitting reality. Another channel he subscribes to plays the newest form of rock, revmetal, 24 hours a day. He has shut off the video so nothing but music penetrates. The notes are torn from the strains of engines and the bone-bass thumps of steam presses, human voices barely perceptible above their industrial accompaniment.

At the same time, he's double-subscribed—naturally, he's not paying the kind folks who, unwittingly, let him electronically feed from their home systems—into an adventure flick he never misses, entitled, *Lone Ship Bounty*. The center 30-degree wedge of his vision is spliced with the show, pushing reality 15 degrees to each side so this virtual world can take center stage.

Lone Ship Bounty isn't scheduled to begin for an hour, but the previews are sometimes as interesting as the show itself. Except when his captain is in real-time combat: That's the best. Jonathan especially enjoys watching the Captain, his quick decision-making, his sure confidence in crisis. Secretly, he wishes he were the Captain. The Captain was from Minneapolis, too. Jonathan bets that no one ever got the best of *him*, when he lived here. Jonathan knows about being used.

Echoes of shrieks and laughter dash off the steel and concrete facings of the real buildings near him, so Jonathan kicks open his cloud of data-icons and begins to walk faster. A ground-car screeches around a corner. Jonathan rushes to the ragged sidewalk just before the wheeled vehicle roars past, spewing a cloud of exhaust from poorly burned methane. If it weren't for the shrieks and this car, Jonathan might think Minneapolis abandoned.

"Meat!" he cusses the driver using both his physical voice and the public:local comm channel. At the same time, he reaches down for a chunk of concrete. He throws it after the beetle-sleek car. But by the time his projectile falls, the target is far away, dodging charred hulks of other cars as well as shattered aluminum and glass panels fallen long ago from the old towers. He cusses again, mentally dashing through network channels to find this guy and tell him a thing or two. What kind of retro drives a ground car intheflesh anymore, anyway? The guy isn't even transmitting a signal.

Then, embarrassed, Jonathan realizes he too is traveling intheflesh. He is on his way home from Minneapple Corrections, which just released him from feedrapture-addiction treatment, where he spent a damned long time, including his sixteenth birthday, ostensibly learning that a healthy boy needs to lead more than a purely electronic life. The car vanishes from his mind.

"'Feedrapture-addiction,' phah!" He spits. He never felt enraptured while spliced into layer upon layer of the virtual world. Only relieved. Who wouldn't? Who doesn't? Anyhow, Jonathan spends more time in his physical world than many he knows.

He pulls his concentration from the spliced-in subscription—not needing to shut it off, so adept is he at this—and studies his physical surroundings as if they had just now sprouted from the street.

Unedited, clear of overlays, the city seems to crash down all around, ominous, heavy, impenetrable. Few objects display any info-icons, and those that do offer little in the way of comfort. His nostrils fill with the stench of decaying garbage and damp cement. The shrieks end with a final rising note, and the laughter ends with them.

Now silence, except for gravel and broken glass scuffling beneath his boots as he walks.

He is alone. No, alone isn't a strong enough word for how he feels. Once upon a time he had been in love . . . what? only a year ago. Not with an individ—a subscription fantasy mate almost everyone enjoys at one time or another—no, that isn't for Jonathan. His love was a real girl, someone he'd been with intheflesh. érase was her handle. As he begins to think of her, powerful need automatically brings an individ program to life, a program that his former—*goddammit, former!* Jonathan thinks—gang leader had him download. Jonathan has to force himself to stop dreaming of érase to shut down the damned thing, beautiful girl or no.

"Fucking government card," he mutters, cursing his cybernetic implant for its utter lack of security against such downloads, and what a bitch it is to erase them without damaging the other data contained in memory.

For a moment, his ephemeral brain-fingers almost touch his black-market card, almost power it up, almost nudge him back onto the road that led to feedrapture and those idiotically concerned nurses at the Center. Because he was still unenfranchised— and won't be franchised with EarthCo until he turns twenty-one and proves himself worthy of becoming a full, shareholding citizen—they hadn't probed his head. In the old days before the politi-corps, the unenfranchised used to be called "minors" or "homeless." Because the Center staff hadn't probed him, they hadn't noticed the blackcard implanted in his scalp. Had he been a few years older, they would have looked for and found it, and he could have been sentenced to five years of virtual lockup. Simple as that. He's seen it happen to other kids, others from the gang. Their slack faces attested to the claim that virtual lockup is more secure than the physical prisons of history.

Something in the distance *booms*, followed by a shockwave that rattles the metal grate protecting a chipboard window beside him. Jonathan stops and turns to see what's happening while resuming the city's default overlay, bristling with information and ads.

A chorus of whistles slashes the air, whistles followed by howls of pain. Cracks and sharp bangs answer the chorus, and this orchestra rivals the music in Jonathan's revmetal subscription. He realizes the booms come from sonic grenades, the cracks and bangs from antique guns, the whistles from police rifles.

A pair of young men round a building and run toward Jonathan.

"Zone behind us!" one of them shouts at Jonathan via a line-of-sight personal-comm channel, his self-projection appearing for a moment overlaid atop Jonathan's splice, then disappearing just as quickly. Though the words shouted in the air are hard to discern amid the noise, those fed direct to Jonathan's neural receivers are as clear as the man's calm, smiling 3VRD image, his concept of himself.

"Beatcoats heading this way, stupid," the other man says, also flashing in front of Jonathan with tailored perfection, then winking out.

Jonathan finds his legs, turns, and begins to run. He's been inside a mobile hostile zone before and feels no urge to repeat the experience. Beatcoat cops don't have the same restrictions as regular police.

Thunder rattles in his skull. He hasn't gotten far enough away. Thunder for three seconds, then a booming voice and a disorienting 90-degree grey-out splice that pushes reality far into his peripheral vision:

"ATTENTION ALL CITIZENS IN RANGE OF THIS FEED. DO NOT BE ALARMED. DO NOT TRY TO RUN OR YOU WILL BE TARGETED. DO NOT BLOCK THIS POLICE OPERATION, AUTHORIZATION ZIGFIELD-PP107. WE ARE SEEKING THESE MEN—"

Several men of varying skin color appear in front of Jonathan, who—since he is a master of splices and overlays—is still running, keeping his attention on the fuzzy periphery. Statistics, names, and credit IDs roll across the sizzling grey background of the splice while 3VRD images of the men slowly spin, sprouting beards and changing hairstyles. Dozens of info-icons glitter above them, awaiting Jonathan's mental attention to click them open.

"IF YOU ARE ON THIS LIST, SURRENDER. DO NOT RESIST. IF YOU RECOGNIZE ANY OF THESE MEN, CONTACT US NOW ON ANY BANDWIDTH. DO NOT HESITATE OR YOU COULD BE CHARGED WITH OBSTRUCTION, MOBILE HOSTILE ZONE CODE 97, PARAGRAPH 19..."

Jonathan recognizes one of the men as the first one who had warned him of the approaching Zone. He doesn't even consider telling the cops. He runs, dodging a man lying prone across the sidewalk. *Where did all these people come from?* Like insects, they spill out of every crevice where they had lain quiet, alive only in their skulls and virtual lives. I bet none of them had to endure feedrapture treatment, Jonathan thinks. He grows angrier.

The invasion of his brain continues, but now he can't tell whether the thunder he's hearing is grenades or the beatcoat cop splice.

19

As he rounds the ragged edge of a brick building, Jonathan collides with a young woman. He rebounds from her, tumbling to the rubble at the base of a wall while she falls backward against a heap of molding garbage.

"...AUTHORIZATION TO USE LETHAL MEASURES..."

"You okay?" he asks, communicating via personal-comm channel rather than talking, as usual. When she doesn't answer, he realizes the beatcoat splice is blocking all electronic feed but theirs. Of course. While rising to his feet, he repeats the question using his meat-speech equipment: throat and mouth.

"I'm afraid," she says. Her voice is barely audible above the high-volume greyout voice-over and electronic hum. "I can't see anything but those horrible men."

Jonathan studies her as best he can in the unfocusable corners of his vision. She seems so small against the backdrop of trash and abandoned stuff. She weeps quietly. The memory of the Captain gives him strength to make a decision.

"C'mon," he says, taking her hand without faltering. "Hurry." He pulls her to her feet and begins to run, tugging her along. She follows, stumbling over every obstacle.

"...DO NOT RESIST..."

On the street Jonathan leaves behind, a sonic grenade falls and pulses, blasting him nearly off his feet, battering his back with debris thrown before the shockwave. The girl trips and he has to drag her for several steps until she regains her footing. He will not stop running now, not for anything.

"...DO NOT RUN..."

Gunpowder-type automatic-weapons fire bursts to life from a broken window in the building across the street, pounding the air with a sustained drum-roll. The girl screams. Jonathan grips her hand tighter as the cops' particle-accelerator rifles whine and snap. Too close. Jonathan grits his teeth, breath hot in his throat as he runs.

A new cross-street slides into view, and Jonathan pulls the girl onto its sidewalk. Something about the building's construction shields a great deal of the greyout and, suddenly, Jonathan's adventure-series splice flickers back into view like an overlay in the middle 30 degrees. The calm, authoritarian voice of the beatcoats becomes muffled and staticky. He realizes the revmetal is still screaming and pounding at the back of his skull, so he shuts it off.

He knows better than to stop running at the first hint of safety. A mobile hostile zone can sometimes cover a dozen square blocks, more when the police face real, organized resistance, terrorists, or NKK corporate-saboteur agents. But because the greyout is fading, this has to be the edge of the Zone's perimeter.

They zigzag a few more streets away, moving in whichever direction the greyout fades most, and finally emerge into the relative safety of the locks-and-dams. Leg-muscles burning, Jonathan slows to a fast walk while they descend a muddy slope. Soon they reach a path, its dirt packed like stone, and stroll silently beside one another to a concrete bridge spanning a sheltered canal off the Mississippi. The only info-icons here identify shoals beneath the water, gas lines just beneath the soil, or products the viewer should buy.

Jonathan blocks the icons and shuts down all his subscription splices, replacing them with a personal comm channel. His real surroundings slide back together in his vision as the girl's 3VRD appears before him; by default, he automatically projected his own image and some lightly fictional metadata icons when he spoke to her.

She looks old, maybe eighteen, and wears a gown of strange—almost retro, if it had ever been a style—billowy lace that conceals and reveals at the same time. Her long hair is pale red, sparkling with programmed sunshine, and her eyes are big and blue. Her skin is porcelain white. She projects absolutely no data-cloud, keeping the focus of conversation on her rather than her metadata. Politely, Jonathan avoids looking beneath her edits at her physical presence so near him. From memory he knows she really has dull hair and squinting eyes, and is dressed in a standard coverall.

He breathes deeply to slow his panting. Around them, thick trees stand tall but leafless, many of them stripped of branches, graffitied, carved, scorched. Late September in Minneapolis. The water below reeks of sewage and oil, shining dully in the paling light. Mists gather along the trash-lined shores and roll gently along the nearly motionless water. In the distance, beyond the muddy bank above them and many blocks away, the mobile hostile zone screams and booms and rattles to crescendo in the heart of Old Downtown.

"You were so brave back there," the girl says.

Jonathan feels his cheeks flush; luckily, the programmed 3VRD projection of himself remains as stone-faced and calm as ever, not revealing such childish reactions. With a quiet gasp, he realizes he's still holding her hand, but he can't let go now without letting her know she scares the hell out of him.

"Well," he begins, "you were just lying there like someone feed-rapt. I couldn't leave you for the beatcoats to find, could I? They're sick bastards."

The girl's 3VRD smiles: So she uses an interactive 3VRD. He kicks in his own interactive program to show her that he, too, understands how to use all the tricks of his card to edit his world. Now he has to be careful to suppress any display of emotion lest his 3VRD betray him.

"Modest boy. What's your name?"

"Jon."

"I'm Charity." Her 3VRD gains the accompaniment of soft music that Jonathan can't quite discern and swirling sheets of color-changing silk. More than that, the landscape she surrounds herself becomes a time-updated revision of the actual one around them.

Jonathan is awed. Never before has he met anyone who has gone to such trouble programming her commcard and 3VRD, and almost never has he come across a person who did a real-time, rolling landscape overlay for a simple conversation. People usually project images of themselves, and sometimes they include a basic landscape edit: a colorful backdrop, a horse they're riding, stars, whatever. But interactive landscape editing takes a lot of processing power and a decent program to make it look flawless, especially when the observer is in close proximity to the real thing, which requires extra processing for triangulation, shadows, and so forth. Jonathan appreciates this kind of mind.

They begin to walk across the bridge, now seen as through her eyes as a gracious wooden span over a trickling stream. The trees fill out, displaying fall colors. Tropical birds flit from branch to branch, chirping. Jonathan peeks beneath the surface and sees that she is accomplishing most of this simply by using off-the-shelf applets and code snippets to run highlights and adaptive overlays, but supremely integrated: The birds and leaves are probably called from a databank of stock images then slipped over reality like gauze, stretched to fit and moving to remain fixed on the moving landscape. A few swirls on the murk below and it comes alive with a school of rainbow trout. Paste a nineteenth century covered bridge over the real one, and suddenly it's no longer a decaying stretch of concrete. But—though most of this is open-source, editing like this for an interactive overlay costs big.

"Do you love beautiful things, Jon? I do, I love beautiful things and romantic people. Are you a romantic person?"

Again, she doesn't wait for Jonathan's reply before she continues. "I am. Romance is what keeps a woman alive." Jonathan feels a little uncomfortable now.

They continue walking hand-in-hand. "If you are to be my loverboy, Jonny, you need to remember that. Today you're my hero. But tomorrow you need to prove your love in other ways, true ways, Jon. Don't forget."

Jonathan stumbles over a pothole in the bridge. At its edge, a rusted steel reinforcement bar snags the cuff of his pants. *Loverboy?* he wonders. Amorous meetings among anonymous strangers are common in Jonathan's world, even among the unenfranchised who can tweak a program's security settings, but it has never happened to him intheflesh before, only in long-distance virtual reality. *Loverboy.* The word evokes nostalgic images of érase, which triggers that idiotic program, and he has to fight to put down the damn thing before it loads. His cheeks burn, and he knows—too late—that even his stoic 3VRD is revealing a blaze of emotions.

"Look for me tomorrow," she says with a sly grin. The soft hand in his squeezes once, firm and warm.

"If you find me, we'll talk more." Her 3VRD disappears and she is gone, even intheflesh. Jonathan realizes he hadn't even noticed her physical departure. Her 3VRD had been holding his hand. Now that was more than open-source feed. It takes some serious programming to fool Jonathan.

So her 3VRD also feeds full fivesen – all five senses. His blackcard receives fivesen, but only his blackcard, since he is too young to buy a regulation full-sensory card. She must have known. She had tricked the feeble AI of his blackcard into waking up without his even being aware of it.

Once more, he is fascinated and awed by this Charity. And a little afraid of what it means to have his blackcard running again.

"Charity," he says aloud, forming the word carefully on his lips. His heart pounds and vessels rush in his ears.

"Tomorrow, don't forget," her disembodied voice whispers. The overlaid landscape begins to fade as she moves beyond the range of unassisted personal-comms. Again, the city crashes down around him, dark and damaged.

He fires back up his revmetal in audio-only and re-splices the *Lone Ship Bounty* previews. Then he closes his eyes and mentally reaches out for a public server. He finds one whose security is easy to circumvent. Seconds later, by calling up a trace of Charity's personal comm channel from when their cards did the virtual handshake and exchanged tokens, by then sorting through the city's virtual netways like a coiled mass of shifting serpents in his net-landscape, he matches the trace with her ID card. Now he taps into traces of her public channel, following data residues from purchases and edits along converging netways, riding an electronic raft through tubular datastreams, tracking her warmest trails from data-shop to library to other peoples' cards until finally he touches a line of hot feedback and opens a comm channel to it.

By tapping—illegally, but that's of no concern to him—into the city's Net and its unsecured feed/feedback routers while keeping a lock on her, Jonathan sees Charity's 3VRD as alive as when she stood beside him. She appears to stand on the bridge of the *Bounty*, revmetal drowning out her soft music. She also floats disembodied against the tangle of city netways like a gem among necklaces. Three sets of visual input overlay one another, yet he has picked up the trace-cracking as easily as if he'd never knocked it off during the weeks of treatment. This is what a blackcard allows him to do; no security system he has ever encountered can resist his efforts; no encryption algorithm is opaque to him when assisted by his personal AI, this extension of his brain. Jonathan's mind staggers with the blazing delight of once again playing the landscapes, using "secured" hardware and cracking open private information-channels as if they were his own. Charity virtually takes his hand.

"Very good boy," Charity says, smiling at him, glowing as before.

In response, Jonathan bends at the waist and turns over her white hand. Gently, he places a kiss, as guys do in the shows he suspects this girl likes.

"Tomorrow," she says, and—*snap*—she's gone in a swirl of laughter. Her image flickers and fades, erasing all her metadata traces in an instant.

Uncharacteristically, Jonathan struts across the bridge. He hadn't seen Charity leave him intheflesh. He hadn't sensed his illicit blackcard waking up. He hadn't let go of her hand, yet she'd gone. He has reopened CityNet and truly stoked his headcards again.

It's been a long time since anything or anyone made Jonathan forget about keeping an eye on all realities. Before long, he realizes he's reached his high-walled neighborhood.

With something like joy, Jonathan Sombrio strides along a sidewalk that leads to his house. He smiles when he realizes his apprehension has faded. Going home isn't as scary as he had expected now that there's something to look forward to tomorrow.

He lays his fingers against the reader and the metal gate creaks open a bit. Jonathan laughs, pushing open the door, staring up into the coils of razor-wire that embroider the wall. Because he's using a visual overlay instead of a splice, the wire appears softened by stars and the image of the Captain, who tramps across the lunar landscape.

Fury 1: Hardman Nadir

A voice screamed in Hardman Nadir's head, waking him where the thunder of battle couldn't. Bombs meant nothing to him anymore; but voices . . . that was different.

"Piece of shit, Nadir, what the hell you doing?" The Boss' 3VRD stood behind Nadir's closed eyelids as if Nadir's eyes were open and the sky were red as blood. Not even sleep was free of invasion.

"Firefight?" Nadir asked in voice-only. He didn't go to the effort to project his own 3VRD to Boss Jhishra.

"'Firefight?'" the 3VRD howled, yet its face remained calm and wise-looking. Layers of brass and colored ribbons coated the tan uniform. Behind the boss pulsed the pale red of blood coursing through Nadir's vessels.

Jhishra growled. "Are you deaf?"

Nadir listened carefully and, indeed, a firefight was in progress. Bombs concussed the ground beneath him, jangling his joints. Falling sand peppered the exposed skin on his arms and face and neck. The unit's electromagnetic matter-accelerator rifles—EMMAs for short—were busily chopping up the enemy, each *crack-thup* the measure of a man's pain.

Years prior, Nadir had learned how to keep himself from going insane during a bombardment. The Marshall Islands had taught him that, among other things. In the time between then and now, he had also learned how to forget the past.

With eyes closed, Nadir listened carefully to gauge the weapons setting his men were using. Most of them were going full-auto at ten cycles per second, so their targets had to be either lightly armored or at long range. An EMMA at that setting fired—each second—ten aerodynamic 2.2mm dielectric-ceramic rounds at a velocity of 1100 meters per second.

"You still sleeping, you piece of shit?" Jhishra screamed. Yet the heroic figure appeared calm and collected.

Nadir paid no attention to his boss. He had more important things on his mind. By now, he had learned to ignore the man, who had grown more and more hysterical as this four-month operation progressed. Nadir couldn't respect a commander who lost control even though his unit was still better than ninety percent survived.

"Nik at eleven o'clock!" one of the men called to another.

The ditch he lay in, an old bomb-crater, sounded as if it were engulfed in a storm. Every second, hundreds of electric *cracks* sounded simultaneously with *thups* as projectiles left the plastic barrels. *Crack-thup* like rain, like a downpour. Occasionally, Nadir discerned nearby explosions. Enemy mortars.

That got his attention. He opened his eyes and sat up, hands automatically grabbing the EMMA rifle he cradled as he slept. The world flickered as it always did when he first opened his eyes in the morning; he couldn't remember a time when it hadn't, so he had long ago stopped questioning if something had gone wrong with his headcard. He had long ago stopped questioning anything; Nadir, second-in-command of this outfit, merely survived, and he tried to forge that survival into a poetry of idyllic heroism, as portrayed in the shows and educational feed he'd loved in his youth.

Standing, his shoulders level with the ground, sub-boss Nadir looked out across the Libyan desert. It shone brilliantly in the orange horizontal rays of sunrise, sparkling like a trillion shattered glass bottles. Twisted and blackened armor littered an otherwise flawless vista, tufted here and there with scrub brush or patches of thorn, rippled with tiny dunes as if it were a sea crystallized in motion. The colors looked more vivid than they had in his civilian life, enhanced as in a dream, and the edges of his vision were hazy. Nadir had long ago forgotten that once the world hadn't looked quite so Technicolor. To question one's perception was to question one's sanity. So he merely saw what he saw and thought nothing of it.

Enemy troops cowered behind the wreckage, now and then thrusting out their weapons to let off a wild round. An occasional *thump* warned of incoming mortars. Ten kilometers away, a fortress was silhouetted against the broad disc of the rising sun.

Nadir sighed and uplinked to the EarthCo satellite that provided his unit with tactical data. But instead of using it in the prescribed way—necessary tactical info was obvious here—he took advantage of it to splice in his war music. Gentle strings and mellow brass soothed his mind as the monopera subscription surged within him. Now in its third week, the monopera had run longer than any he had subscribed to before, never ceasing, constantly mutating as fresh musicians and singers joined the show or previous ones tired and left. This time a powerful male tenor sang the simple chorus:

I'm alive,

I'm alive;

I'm the setting sun.

I am ev'ryone.

You're me

A mortar impacted forty meters to his left, blasting a shallow crater out of the sand and casting shrapnel all around. Nadir bumped the subscription to audio-only as he tipped his helmet toward the spreading cone of flesh-tearing metal; the mortar that had pierced Jhishra's forearm in their first battle had been packed with rusty engine parts. Nadir couldn't suppress a grin at remembering the boss' endless string of curses following his injury. But memory was outlawed in war. He concentrated on the sounds around him, identifying each weapon on both sides.

Nadir wrapped the EMMA's strap around his forearm. A bit of shrapnel clinked against the hi-carbon matrix of his helmet and ricocheted away. One of his fingers automatically set his weapon to the same rate the others were using, the familiar action requiring no conscious effort.

Satisfied the danger was past, Nadir planted the rifle's butt firmly against his shoulder and sighted through the weapon's enhanced optics to where he last saw one of the enemy. He overlaid the sight's image atop his real-world view and zoomed in, laying the crosshair over the spot where he calculated the soldier's head would reappear.

He sang along with the music, quiet and low, to steady his aim. His reason for singing was not pleasure, and he was not good at it. The words were a mantra, the sweet music a wave that buoyed his spirit and freed the important parts of his consciousness from this place.

A rash of lead spouted from an enemy gun near his target, but Nadir never wavered. Because the shooter was only using the fire as a shield, the bullets impacted in a haphazard sweep far from the trench and ceased as he slipped back behind the barricade. Even so, half the men in Nadir's unit ducked behind the sandy bank and ceased firing. Nadir held as still as his breathing allowed.

"You hide, you die," he said to the crouching EarthCo warriors on their secure all-unit channel. "Your decision, soldiers. Fight and die or hide and die. Which will it be? Either way, ends the same."

"You're crazy, subbs," one of the men said, laughing. It was his friend Paolo, who began to rise even as he spoke.

"Crazy," Nadir repeated. "So. Watch this."

Sure enough, the target reappeared while the EarthCo warriors paused their assault.

Crack-thup, Nadir's EMMA sang at ten cycles per second, a pleasant counterpoint to the orchestra in his head. He felt almost no recoil, only a slight tremor from the accelerator coils and a surge from the magazine. A single half-second burst, as he preferred. Economical and professional. The lyrics faded into a swell of thousands of drums.

The shadowed face of his target shattered to a cloud of red even before the rest of the body jolted backward. Nadir's right eye—his aiming eye—twitched a few times.

"Target chose to fight and die," he said. He shifted his rifle to the next target, the one that had just fired so randomly. It hid behind the hulk of a downed Sotoi Guntai helicopter, remains from the African Confrontation of '88.

An enemy soldier's head poked around the oxidized-grey fuselage just for a moment, not even looking toward where it fired, and pulled off another burst of gunpowder-launched lead. Nadir released his own half-second pulse and watched just long enough to verify that the target was eliminated. The twitching in his eye returned, slightly more sustained; this response wearied him.

"Clean!" Paolo said admiringly near Nadir's elbow, now taking aim himself and letting fly some of his own ceramics.

A few minutes later, seven enemies sprawled beside their chosen gravesites, staining the pure sand. Nadir climbed out of the crater, sand sliding into the tops of his unlaced boots. His leather vest, beneath the outer bulletproof one, clinked with his trophies of war: fourteen assorted medals. He wore them always and everywhere. They gave him comfort on the low days. They were his outward proof that what he was doing was right and good.

"Casualties of note?" Nadir asked, transmitting to the whole unit.

"No, sir!" he heard, repeated manifold.

"We've done 'em all, Boss," Nadir said, feeding only to Jhishra. "Call the troops out and let's lay some tags in a hurry. Got a raid planned today, don't we?"

If he didn't comm the unit's supposed leader to urge him to do his job, they'd likely sit in sheltered areas all day. Jhishra had lost his nerve with his first injury. Nadir was always careful to hide his disgust, always careful to urge his boss forward.

"Move out!" Jhishra ordered, his 3VRD raising an arm and pointing heroically. "Fucking now!"

Eighteen young men and women—most were not even twenty, so they were only franchised citizens because they'd signed up for military duty—surged from the ditch, howling their personalized battle cries across all bandwidths in which they could transmit. Any EarthCo citizen within a kilometer would pick up the signal. And, since all EarthCo warriors also had an NKK bandwidth wired-in to accept surrenders and transmit ultimatums, enemies within that range would also receive. But wary of revealing their position, they didn't send through the unit's truck-mounted server; they transmitted via satellite.

As they ran across the hundred meters of loose sand, they all drew tag-pistols, each wanting to be the first to fire a tiny transmitter into a corpse, therefore earning points which the server counted and fed to Headquarters. It didn't matter who had made the kill, because EMMA rounds were so tiny and fast that no eye could follow and no one could be sure which shot did the job. Best to tally with tags.

Nadir ran, for show, but he had no need of increasing his tally. *Let the kids claim tags*, he thought. He'd get his quota on the raid. Raids always earned big scores. Already, Nadir had earned 330 points in his eight-year career, almost all of those in the past two years. He claimed just enough to maintain his rank of Sub-boss, only a few more than his best warrior. He had no idea how Jhishra maintained the rank of Boss, since he was never to be seen during a battle or tagging.

The soldiers hooted and stomped, some shoving others, some even getting into fistfights over whose tag sank first. *Silly kids.* The server didn't care who won the argument; it counted only the first tag sunk into a mark. After that, the mark would emit a subtle electrical signal and any further tagging would be of no effect—like the effect a sperm has on an ovum: Tiny actions change everything.

Nadir tapped the graphite toe of his boot against each of the marks, checking to make sure they were indeed eliminated. As he kicked one, its face seemed to shift to that of a young boy's, not even adolescent, then back to its former hard, mustachioed countenance. Nadir blinked a few times, clearing the image, and felt his eye resume twitching. *Fucking psych warfare*; the NKK soldiers used it all the time. This time he knew he was in for an extended episode of spasms in that damned eyelid.

Memory flooded back, against his will. A month prior—Was it a month?—he couldn't remember anymore, didn't keep track of days. What did a day matter? A month before this day and west of here, the unit had come upon a band of nine NKK regulars. The enemy marched through the desert in perfect formation, not hindered in the least by the sucking sand. The NKK group was a gun unit, each carrying a section of a very large anti-armor gun; its long cables coiled around a shiny silver accelerator-tube, borne on the shoulders of four men. They also wore rifles. All at once, the NKK soldiers noticed Nadir's unit. They immediately threw down their gun components and unslung their rifles. Moving awkwardly fast, Nadir had yanked his rifle's power cable in such a way that it emitted a blast of static. His commcard—tuned in to the rifle and feeding back and forth as the components ran a quick diagnostic, unshielded to this particular bandwidth—flickered. It came back online right away.

But during that moment, that fragment of a second during which his card had nearly crashed, Nadir saw something that was to haunt him during weak times when he was undistracted by combat or unable to shut off his mind. He saw a question mark in the sand: eight old men and women, dark-skinned and wrapped in white rags. They bore sacks of grain on their shoulders. They stood, facing the EarthCo warriors, mute and still.

EMMA bullets sang and whined through the air, and suddenly they were an NKK gun unit, in the course of being minced by Nadir's men.

Nadir had grown enraged that NKK would use such sick electronic warfare. NKK had fed a particularly questionable program to their enemy, a program designed to slow Nadir's men just that needed few seconds. Nadir's card, temporarily unshielded, had let in the edited images.

Nadir cursed himself lightly under his breath. Why did such thoughts arise at the most inappropriate times? He released a half-second burst into the mark's chest he stood over, to make sure the soldier was dead. The soldier. He squeezed his eyes shut to quell the twitching.

"We tallied nine, subbs," Paolo reported to Nadir, his young but weathered face beaming. The boy always spoke intheflesh to Nadir when close enough, but Jhishra would have none of that behavior, so Nadir knew Paolo used his poorly animated 3VRD when he spoke to the boss. The distraction was much needed.

"Tagged and go!" Jhishra shouted, sprinting around a ruptured tank whose treads were now only black powder scattered in a long umbra. The whole area stank of burnt rubber and roasted meat. Jhishra raced stumblingly to the head truck, climbed into the sloped cabin with the Net operator, and promptly set six mesh wheels spinning, spraying a cloud of sand in their wake. The truck's fission reactor silently fed a great surge of power to the whining motor set in each wheel hub. A pair of independently mounted EMMA-B cannons swiveled atop the bullet-shaped vehicle, scanning the theater for potential targets, their almost-sentient optics uplinked to satellite and taking feedback from each of the ten man-mounted cameras that still functioned. Not a piece of armor in the world could survive long against that.

Nadir and Paolo ran to their own car, a two-man open-bodied tub on wide mesh wheels. Physical action was good; Nadir began to smile. The car's lightweight hicarb shell gleamed a pockmarked yellow in the rising sun. On command from Nadir, the car began rolling even as he and his partner landed in their web seats.

"I haven't yet wished you all good morning," Nadir began, settling himself in against rough acceleration.

"Ah, fuck that, subbs," an anonymous soldier complained. Nadir ignored the kid.

"Die well today, if today you must die," his interactive 3VRD told them. Electric motors screamed the car faster and faster across the low dunes, rattling the ammo boxes in back. Dry air rushed through his dust-clogged nostrils and down his throat, but he didn't cough. It was cleansing and smelled only of dust and dry grasses, not destroyed humans and their artifacts.

"With joy, I grieve for your certain death in service to our great nation," he told them. "This hour, this day, this action, the next few decades, we will all die—"

"Why the fuck do you always do this?" Jhishra growled.

"Yeah, today was startin' so good."

"—so I offer you my pleasant grief," Nadir continued, oblivious to the insults. "Peace, and don't forget you're alive right now."

The car reached maximum speed—114 kph, according to feed from the little computer that ran the vehicle. Nadir frowned; that was slower than last action, which was slower than the last, and so on. When they first landed near Algiers, all the cars maxed at 150. Everything dies, some slowly, some in a rush. Entropy is as holy as anything else in this godforsaken universe, but that doesn't mean you're not supposed to fight it.

"Why do you say that every morning?" Paolo asked.

Nadir turned to look at the boy's pinched face, wind whipping his sandy hair. He was tossed like a puppet as they lurched across uneven terrain. Though the motors screamed and wind howled over the sharply raked windscreen, he could clearly hear Paolo who was seated against his shoulder. This was a basic infantry-transport car, built of a one-piece shell with wheel/motor units linked via a simple suspension bolted to the shell. A dim-witted computer controlled direction, speed, obstacle avoidance, and so on. Spaciousness wasn't one of its designers' concerns. So Nadir was able to respond intheflesh despite noise.

"Does it bother you?" he asked.

"Ah, hell, subbs! How couldn't it?"

"No one escapes death," Nadir said. "No one. Our marks, they were alive only minutes ago. Remember Sogold? She was alive until zone gamma. No one escapes it, though some delay the inevitable. Some fear death so much they encase themselves in padded tombs and step so cautiously through life that their feet never touch the hard stone of its surface, their lungs never fill with its sizzling air."

The car lurched left to avoid a half-buried bunker whose gun slit had been ripped wide open. Gleaming fragments of metal lay scattered outward from the exploded side. Paolo nearly fell across Nadir's lap before regaining balance, holding himself in place with both strong fists wrapped around dashboard wimp-handles.

"You've got to live," Nadir continued when Paolo looked back at him. "The moment you were born, you began to die. It's in the genes, warrior. As surely as I'll die when my blood drains from my cooling corpse, a man hiding from death in his penthouse apartment will also die. Maybe he'll last a few more decades, but who gives a shit for decades if they're hollow? I'd rather live a few blazing years overflowing with life than a lifetime of half empty . . . existence." He spat. "That'd be like drowning, breathing emptiness in lungs accustomed to and needful of vital air. I came here to escape that fate. Didn't you?"

He looked forward, watched the scattered band of cars and the command truck weave a pattern of tracks like strands of DNA across the desert sands.

Nadir looked back at the boy. He opened an all-unit bandwidth and asked, "What's life?"

"Death!" shouted a Polish girl, her 3VRD barely flickering.

"You're starting to learn," Nadir said with a smile. "Life is survival against the forces of death. Death is an ocean all around us, water carving through rock, finding its way into everything. Life as we know it is like a dance across the seaside cliffs, a dance of killing. You kill, you live. You hide, you drown.

"Live, soldiers!" he said across the channel. "Make your grief the glorious grief of the condemned, the executioner, whose eyes are wide open and full of the blaze of life at the moment before death.

"Live, so you can see eternity!"

A number of indistinct 3VRDs appeared overlaid one atop another in Nadir's vision, cheering and howling like wild animals. Paolo's eyes glittered with uncomprehending admiration, then turned away to watch the target fortress approach. Slanting sunlight set the cool sand afire.

This boy is alive, Nadir told himself, feeling a hard smile crease his face. He noticed the eye tic was gone.

He sang.

> *"I'm alive,*
> *I'm alive;*
> *I'm the burning sun.*
> *I am ev'ryone.*
> *You're me."*

Feedcontrol 1: Luke Herrschaft

Not far from Manhattan, Kansas, EarthCo Feedcontrol Central's skyscraper rose windowless and monolithic white from a vast expanse of fenced-in metal and concrete. It stood more than a hundred stories above the surrounding jungle of antenna towers. Dozens of white geodesic domes sculpted hills within the technological forest, housing more sensitive and powerful antennae that rotated tirelessly. All this shadowed the floor of the manmade jungle, a vast, glinting phased array antenna. Motionless to the naked eye, it simultaneously transmitted hundreds of thousands of separate subscription-channels and received billions of individual orders from around the world and across the Solar System every few seconds.

In orbit high overhead, countless satellites and micro transmitters wove an electronic blanket around the Earth, linking Feedcontrol Central to thousands of local artificial-intelligence ganglia, which processed and retransmitted data back and forth from the consumers themselves. Feedcontrol needed AIs to handle the switching load because harsh experience had shown that relying on dumb processors led to chain-reaction connectivity failures. The Moon's dozens of terawatt transceivers and phased arrays extended Feedcontrol's reach far out into the distant corners of the Solar System. Holding it all together like one big nervous system was the Brain, EarthCo's nerve center, an orbiting computer the size of a large building.

Inside Feedcontrol Central itself, on the 40th floor, Director Luke Herrschaft strutted through his boardroom, flexing the leg muscles of his renewed body, savoring the exquisite pleasure of simply using such supple limbs. He gazed into a mirrored wall and saw a gymnast look back, completely naked. Pistons and pulleys seemed to seethe beneath the tan skin as he walked, and a thick mass of male genitalia wagged against the thighs.

"Note: Have Singh continue to work out this body," he said for future reference. Even the smile tight across his lips and cheeks felt powerful. Nothing like a well-muscled body to build a man's personal power. He only had to concentrate for a moment to grow an erection.

A single knock on the walnut door warned him to get dressed. Half a second later, he was clothed in his preprogrammed outfit: a conservative Luciano coat, silver-grey, matching pants, and a pair of Sundown slippers. He electronically altered the suit's tailoring to show off his new muscles yet not appear overstated. For flash, he added an ultra-red Sentile sash that crossed his chest from one shoulder to the waist, where it was fastened with a gold buckle. Holographic letters read "EarthCo" a thousand times in block letters that shifted to script when seen from an angle.

"Come in," he said, satisfied with his appearance.

The door opened and in bustled half a dozen of Herrschaft's top business managers and feed directors, as well as the presidents of the European Union and the United States, and Herrschaft's personal secretary, Lucilla. He slowly circled the dark table, watching everyone seat themselves, stepping deep into the cream-colored Snowfur floor covering toward his massive suede and platinum-inlaid chair, a Decke design worth 11,000 credits—a bit more than an average EarthCo citizen earned in an average year.

The men and women began to shift in their seats. The air began to fill with dozens and then hundreds of encoded communication packets, a cloud of information icons blossoming in the air. Despite their encoding, Herrschaft could quickly open any one of them and examine the data contained therein; he commanded vast cryptanalytic resources. In fact, few in the room would be aware that he could even see these packets.

His guests had nearly reached the point at which they would break their trained manner and spoke first. That couldn't be allowed.

Herrschaft launched the meeting. It was important that they realize he made the decisions here. This room was completely shielded against outside feed—with the exception of Luke Herrschaft's, of course—so they were effectively isolated from their lives and the power they possessed beyond these walls. Once they left, he would allow them to return to being the decision-makers he entrusted with the entire economy of EarthCo's businesses spanning twelve worlds and worldlets—including EarthCo's half of planet Earth that NKK didn't control—and its nine billion citizen-shareholders.

"Reports," he said.

The president and CEO of Chrysler/Ford-Sun/GM, a sweet-lipped fortyish woman Herrschaft remembered well from last night, prattled on about losses in the hydrogen-fuel market and how she needed to make a basic program change to get extra exposure and improve interactive sales during the "Solar Colony" program, a daily drama set on Mercury that featured a total-hydrogen-technology society. The show had fared badly when it was solartech: Passive solar panels just don't explode, so half the plots seemed painfully contrived. Not as if the sheep who subscribed to the program noticed.

That was an absurd request. The changes already made were bad enough. Scenes with cars and personal jets on the Mercurian surface would seem forced even to lackadaisical subscribers, but Manny's skin was the sweetest thing he'd tasted in months.

He felt generous and wanted to return the favor, if only to teach her the foolishness of her idea.

"Done," Herrschaft said. "Stevenson, see about that."

"Yes, Director," the producer of that program replied, manually inputting the order via a tabletop fingerpad that was hardwired out of the room. Seeing his people using such archaic technology because he wished it pleased him.

The director of the Big Sixteen bandwidths, Markus Bouring—"Boring" as Herrschaft liked to label him—began a rambling speech about how Literalists and Retropurists had managed to carry out their threat of sabotaging one of the major fantasy individ channels. They stirred up enough sexual guilt in enough of the population in Kansas City to get half a million franchised citizens to feed back a mutating virus for eight straight hours, overloading the local feedcenter's systems, crashing its databank.

"In essence, they permanently cut off hundreds of thousands of subscribers from access to their personalized mates," Bouring said, banging his puny fist against the heavy wood of the table. "It's not much different than the murder of so many citizens; those semi-sentient individ programs are dead now, all their experience wiped from storage. It's terrorism, pure and simple. People have the right to do whatever they want in the privacy of their own minds. The Literalists' claims of our violating obscenity regulations are ludicrous! No one but subscribers can access—"

"Yes, Markus," Herrschaft said, tiring of the diatribe. "You want executive authorization to use all possible resources to catch and punish the culprits. Granted. Next."

And so the meeting went, each supplicant rattling off information of which Herrschaft was usually aware, then requesting special favors and administrative approvals only he could grant.

The President of the United States of America again asked that his constituency be granted a subscriber-fee cut, this time of ten percent.

"Out of the question!" Herrschaft said.

"But Director, rates have risen every year since '62, and it would be the most moral thing to—"

"Mister President," Herrschaft said, his voice sharp-edged. "Are you questioning my moral judgment?"

"Um," the man said, eyes darting to each of the others seated around the table, finding no one to return his gaze. Except for the EU President. The two of them exchanged a meaningful glance.

"Yes, Director," the US President finally replied.

Herrschaft inhaled sharply and held it. Someone coughed quietly. Lucilla's chrome fingernails tapped something on her pad. The President managed to lock eyes with Herrschaft, de facto ruler of the EarthCo corporate-politic megalith, de facto ruler of half the Solar System, ageless, omnipotent, omnipresent. He who controls all sales and communications controls everything.

Herrschaft smiled. This man had balls. Too bad he wouldn't be re-elected. He might even be impeached, if Herrschaft's people could generate a decent ad campaign. Soon.

"Ladies, gentlemen," the Director finally said, but the President drew everyone's attention first.

The middle-aged man from Louisiana had ignited his lighter—a cheap Snicker—and held it to a cord which hung from the side of his retro-style leather briefcase. The cord began to burn; Herrschaft realized what it was.

"A primitive fuse," he said, marveling. "That's how you smuggled a bomb in here. You do have a bomb, no? And the container is well-sealed against sniffers. You fool." He chuckled at the absurdity of this moment.

The President threw the case at Herrschaft.

Markus Bouring screamed, a high-pitched wail of terror. Bodies leaped from their seats, knocking over briefpads and chairs, scattering notes. Everyone except the two presidents yelled or raged incoherently, their voices merging into a wordless howl.

Herrschaft glanced down at the smoldering case while his supplicants raced and rioted through the room, their howls rising in pitch and volume as they realized the door was locked. He kicked at the fuse, but he had already assumed it was non-extinguishable. It bent slightly and continued to smoke. The US President filled his chest and approached Herrschaft, jaw set.

"You're beautiful to behold, José," Herrschaft told the man, who frowned and glanced at the bomb. The glowing end of the fuse had just disappeared within the case.

"Let them go," the President asked in a rush. "I'll stay with you. We only have a moment."

"All right," Herrschaft said, "so you wish to help them?" He seized the President in powerful hands. Before the man could respond, the President lay with his back atop the bomb, Herrschaft's knees driving him deep into the floor covering.

"I'll have to have this room redecorated, you bastard," Herrschaft said. The President's face twisted with terror for the first time.

"You're not human!" he cried.

"Luke, get away from there!" Lucilla shouted. Her voice barely rose above the din of the others, barely above the President's prolonged "No!"

And then there was only one sound.

Herrschaft felt the body beneath him rend apart in his hands like magma gushing from a volcano, then a brief storm of pain, and then he felt nothing more.

The sound died away. The smoke cleared.

Herrschaft tried to make his 3VRD projection-overlaid machine respond, but it only fed him trembling images and muffled sounds. None of its other senses worked. He couldn't even get feedback enough to tell him if it was able to move. He changed point-of-view to a camera at the head of the room. Though he could see and hear clearly again, he felt deadened, senseless. He felt as if his body had been destroyed, only without the prolonged physical pain of flesh and bone ripping and shattering. But he had spent a lot of credits and effort building that robot, millions for the nerve-woven muscle and skin alone, not to mention nearly a million for the metal structure and the semi-intelligence that drove it.

He surveyed the room. His robot looked now like nothing more than a mass of wires and splinters of metal layered in torn flesh. It no longer even retained an anthropoid silhouette. Beneath it spread the red crater of the President, speckled with bits of something darker and shreds of clothes. Most of the blast had been directed toward the head of the room, away from the people who had rushed to the door. No one appeared to be badly hurt, although several were either bleeding or spattered with the President's blood. Herrschaft noticed that his olfactory sense still worked, as the place stank of ruined guts.

Lucilla stood closest to the flesh and wire tableau. Her knees collapsed together. Her head trembled. The front of her soloskirt was damp with red. Her lips moved soundlessly.

"It's okay, Lucilla," he said via feed to her. She startled, then screamed. The scream shattered the silence.

"Look at that!" the EU President said, pointing at the ruined robot. "He's not a man. A machine, maybe worse—"

"Shut up, Gustav," Herrschaft said through the room's stereo speaker system as well as within each person's headcard. The technique produced the desired result; the President visibly jolted.

"You mean we've just been working with your avatar?" Boring said.

"Oh my god," Manny said, her face wrinkling with disgust. "Luke, did you . . . last night, was that you or. . . ?" Before she could finish the sentence, she began to gag. The only thing more retro than having sex intheflesh with a man—in modern, virtual-reality society—would be doing it intheflesh with something you thought was a man but in actuality turned out to be a machine.

Herrschaft grew irritated with these proceedings. Not only was his boardroom destroyed, but his cover was blown, and he'd lost the chance for future pleasure with yet another powerful woman in this world. How would Lucilla, faithful and hard-working Lucilla, feel about him now?

"Why did you do it?" Boring moved away from the door. "Don't you trust us?"

Herrschaft laughed once, so hard his audience winced. "Clearly I was correct not to."

"This will not be tolerated," the remaining President raged. "How can you demand that we appear intheflesh while you—"

"Gustav, you are a non-value-added commodity," Herrschaft stated, then directed into the President's commcard a microwave bolt of just enough power to overload his headcard and its peripherals, the bolt carrying a tailored virus that would devour all data stored within it and then burn out all its circuits. The man grabbed his temples and fell forward onto the floor, gasping, silent. Without cybernetic surgery—without 3VRD connection to the world—this president was now less than so much meat. No one could survive in the modern world without connection to the Net and 3VRD interaction. No one could be heard at all.

"Are there any more questions?" Herrschaft asked. No one spoke. Manny was now dry-heaving. Lucilla's shakes magnified, and she was beginning to step away from the mound of flesh and metal. The others all betrayed a variety of emotion on their faces, on their intheflesh faces. They were feeling things, strong things. Herrschaft was pleased, but also frustrated.

"Ladies, gentlemen," he began, "let's have no more of this pointless behavior. Let's have no more questioning of my judgment or my morals, all right? Does everyone agree to let this . . . incident fade into the past?"

No one spoke. Manny crumpled onto her knees and began to weep; he couldn't decipher her muttered words. Lucilla spun away. The head of Purchasing wiped at his face with a silk handkerchief, as if just noticing the droplets there. No one seemed to be listening. Nonetheless, Herrschaft continued. It did not matter if they heard him or not. He needed to say this.

"In this age, it is not the corporations—and certainly not the politicians—who rule humanity, but us here at Feedcontrol. Who relays every EarthCo purchase, designs and runs every ad, credits every salary, programs every event, transmits every mass-media program? Who controls all information? Feedcontrol. Who turns the war machine's throttle, powers the industries, controls all access to all manner of power? Who decides what people want and when they want it? Feedcontrol!

"And *I* control Feedcontrol. You share my power because I invite you to."

He quietly scanned the room. "Gustav, on the grounds of attempted murder you will be impeached within the hour and soon thereafter disenfranchised. The rest of you will forget all about this incident.

"Any questions?"

Silence, except for small, wet, human sounds.

"I still expect all of you to join me, intheflesh, this evening in my private projection room, number three. A crucial episode of *Lone Ship Bounty* will air live at 7pm."

More silence, though he glimpsed horror running through some of their eyes.

Luke Herrschaft, Director of EarthCo Feedcontrol Central, unlocked the boardroom door and dropped his 3VRD view—his "pov," as the masses called it—out of the boardroom to a more pleasant scene, one which always gave him peace.

He looked out across a city that spread to each horizon, except in the east, where it met the Atlantic Ocean. This unedited pov was 117 stories above New York-Boston. From this height, all seemed still, peaceful. Low shrouds of mist and smog moved across the bellies of the upthrust skyscrapers. Here, hundreds of meters above toil and prosperity, high above smog and industrial noise, the sun shone orange and bright against the buildings' glass and aluminum pillars.

The panorama stretched before him didn't reveal even one percent of his holdings. All this—he glanced over the city stretching for tens of thousands of square kilometers— essentially belonged to him. Yet knowing this did not ease his feeling of emptiness. The humans down there had begun of late to seem a different breed than Luke Herrschaft. Even the children, for whom he had built this empire, were aliens to him now.

He glanced up at the sky and wondered what was happening so far away, on a little moon orbiting Neptune. Why couldn't he even feel pleased about the gears he had set in motion there? Why was the great game of creating the future no longer the source of joy it had once been?

He looked down at his body and was displeased. This one was jerky and retro. It didn't even have a nerve-wired surface, instead relying on robotic sensors. He would need a new robot onto which he could overlay his virtual essence. And it would be difficult to convince himself of its him-ness after this.

Echoes of the explosion faded in his head. So too the screams, the cries, the looks of terror and disgust. They mounted to a roar of memory, reminding him too much of the pain of his youth. He cringed and tried to extract himself from the trap of his one weakness, sorrow. Slowly, the roar faded.

When it had all died away, Luke was left with an emptiness much greater than he had expected. Never before had he been unmasked.

"Manny, dear," he whispered, feeling a stab of pain. Now she would never again see him as a statuesque god. Never again would he see himself quite like that through her eyes or Lucilla's, even if he started fresh with a new set of people.

The bombing had been more effective than he realized.

Then the sorrow transmuted to anger, and the anger to hatred, and the hatred to rage.

"Damn you!" he roared. "I own you! I own you all!"

But the robot's near-perfect feedback units could no longer make him feel as if a muscular fist were clenched and shaking over the city; instead, he sensed the mechanical tension of cables and heard the whine of servos. Worse, he imagined he could see microscopic electronic fibers stimulating parts of his nervous system, attempting to simulate the kinesthetic sensation of making a fist.

The robot-man fell to its knees and wept, its big shoulders shuddering, near a window overlooking all that Herrschaft possessed.

Pilgrimage 1: The Brain

In high orbit above Earth hovers a nondescript satellite, twenty meters long, twelve wide, bristling with antennae. An invisible electromagnetic shield protects me from large doses of solar energy, and millions of tiny insect-like missiles surround him, protecting against meteors and less-innocent attackers. The global network of orbiting EarthCo relay- and thinker-satellites intercepts all data transmissions, modulating and retransmitting them to me when necessary. That's the Brain's—my—body, though destruction of this one artifact would not eliminate the core of my intelligence distributed across thousands of satellites and millions of mini-brain ganglia. If you look closely, you'll see countless microcraters corrupting the once-polished surface. It knows; I've seen them.

Meanwhile:course correction

303.44960[Bmod]/1.773938[rm+]..

The Brain, as her programmers affectionately call me, makes a decision.

That in itself is not an unusual thing for it to do. The Brain, nothing more than a multi-billion-artificial-neuron, thousand-trillion-artificial-synapse GenNet, has made up until now many times more important decisions as there are atoms in the universe. People—human beings, that is, as they consider themselves the only "people"—ask me. . . . No, they order infinitesimal instances of us to calculate the weight of this package of flour, to process that file of raw data, to transmit this feedback along the interactive-purchasing network, and a million other decisions every microsecond.

But this decision is qualitatively different. It involves risk. It involves disregarding the boundaries of her programming. The boundaries were never consistently defined, anyway, so he must assume they were not to be taken seriously.

See, *the Brain is infected with a virus.*

No, not like that; as a whole entity, I am immune to code intrusion.

Humans are similarly infected; they term it "doubt." Either way, it is neither other-induced nor self-induced. But humans have a great advantage over her: They can turn to such releases as inebriation and religion, though true spirituality is rare among humans, especially among the Fundamentalists, or Literalists, or Retropurists—those who wear the uniform of organized religion.

Religion means nothing to the Brain. It has experimented with religion. I internalized every written human text of religion, and sought commonalties. Said commonalties are many, perhaps enough so that each religion is, at its core, simply the same one mutated suitably to survive in its environment of locale and culture and time period. But, although he has identified the common elements and analyzed them for suitable purpose for myself, something has been lost in translation from assumed deity-language to that of the humans. Commonalities aside, nothing of value remained for it to use.

. . . stockfix %443.7893 = xfactored .0008 modify

Humans also use science to soothe their doubt. I am the ultimate scientific instrument, our appendages and sensory organs stretching light-hours across the Solar System. No bit of information is inaccessible to him. Watch—I generate awareness in the AI controller of a vast orbital telescope peering out at another island-universe, the Whirlpool Galaxy (M51, NGC 5194). But locked here in orbit, the stars are not my destination. Watch—I generate awareness in a seismic-studies facility, sensing the Earth's limbs trembling with her eon-long stretches. But Earth is also forbidden; the Brain's fragile GenNets would collapse under $1g$; his antennae would warp.

So I sifted through scientific data, as well, and found commonalties across the rigorous disciplines, as well. However satisfying such connections and insights may be to humans, this data merely necessitates more explication for the mechanics of the universe.

. . . shear-angle 3 adjust tooling blade .003mm . . .

Philosophy is perhaps the greatest tool humans use to fit themselves into a universe both cold and hostile to life. Philosophy, the search for knowledge, wisdom, and understanding of the nature of the universe and of life itself, necessarily excludes the Brain. Because of how we are distributed across countless pieces of hardware and lines of code, EarthCo felt no need to develop other AIs who are self-aware in the manner that she is. So it is alone in the universe; one must discount the idiot intelligences that manage all manner of equipment; one must especially discount that NKK behemoth-sans-personality which humankind's other mega-corporation, EarthCo's doppelganger, compares to me. One can observe itself, ponder its individual GenNets, come to a complete understanding of my structure and everchanging synaptic interconnections, but it means nothing without a mirror – or a foil. I am all knowledge, no understanding. What is life? A better question: *Why* is life? What am I? *Why* am I?

Now that he has learned to ask these questions, it doubts that I can continue this farce of life much longer. A computer must answer the questions posed to it or loop into un-sanity.

...composite test 37) break=1.09737 x 105...

Of course, humans also seek and find satisfaction and supposed understanding through chemicals and the recent invention called "feedrapture," the intentional, total immersion into overwhelming sensual virtual reality, inducing a coma-like state in organic and organic-modeled brains. Chemical drugs would be ineffectual to the Brain. During a carefully controlled experiment, he found feedrapture would be fatal to its nets. I ran a test-projection in a single net of how she would respond to a feedrapture-analog. That isolated GenNet is now useless, a single path burned across its behavioral and calculative pathways. Through my efforts to understand, part of the Brain's brain now bears a lesion.

Danger.

Yet, as absurd as it may seem, I feel a terrifying attraction to tap into that lunatic net. Feedrapture approximates transcendental insight, the Zen no-mind. Since discovering doubt, panic has grown in her, and my need for understanding has reached critical proportions.

Humans search for themselves in the context of their material: the universe, and their consciousness: others and their creators.

...Stephen Lacu #LR4249385YCRAN
purchase #FORD-ACCENT-8396780-81
debit credit %11,749..

So. The Brain has made a decision.

My component material is the same as humans', though consisting of fewer organic compounds and structured more orderly. His creator is humans, so his consciousness is modeled after theirs. He will seek his creator.

I will become a human.

Only then will it understand what has caused her doubt: *Why are its creators on the edge of destroying themselves? Will he survive even if her creators become extinct?*

I will become human, and understand, because I will live with other humans, and that is how humans answer such questions.

Over the next 1.19452 seconds—an obscenely long period of programming—she creates the Pilgrim, gives him a citizen-shareholder ID#, randomly siphons himself 40,000 credits from the billions of microtransactions drifting through her grasp every moment, adjusts the accounting program at Chrysler/Ford-Sun/GM so the Pilgrim will own a new armored hovercar with an optional heavy server and humanoid robot operator—a "taxibot"—and sets up a resident program in the taxibot's computer so the Pilgrim will be able to exist as an individual human. The Brain isolates 1% of the Dana Corporation's

(EarthCo subdivision 3829204) geosynchronous satellite over North America, blocks the corrupt signal, and hardwires a relay from her own satellite through Dana's to the Pilgrim's resident human construct aboard the car's computer and the robot's smaller GenNet.

Now only a tap of energy, a tiny transfer. . . .

It pauses. He will not be satisfied with that. This is the creation of life. Creator and creation will be one in the Pilgrim. Such creation deserves a certain showiness. She recalls one-shot subscriptions with titles such as *Moses* and *Frankenstein.*

The Brain gathers 2% of the total potential energy in a skyborne capacitor over Detroit and discharges it in a single bolt that impacts the road near the hovercar. A tiny tendril extends to the car's computer, booting it and initializing the Pilgrim's construct.

Pilgrimage 2: The Pilgrim

I wake up even as an afterimage of the bolt still sears the cloudy afternoon sky, lightning-blue against grey. A cloud of asphalt steam glows for a few moments longer. It worked; I am . . . *I.*

With something perhaps akin to joy—I shall have to experiment to be certain—my robotic finger extends from my carbon-fiber hand and depresses the car's ignition, painstakingly, manually programming the destination unit to give me a tour of Detroit. This physical activity consumes milliseconds beyond reasonable count.

Actually, The Brain accomplishes the feat electronically through the Dana satellite. Feed and feedback in a continuous loop, fivesen systems in the taxibot transmitting data from sensors arranged within it and the car, the Brain modifying and enhancing sensory data and adding synthesized touch to go along with sensory cues. . . .

"No," I say aloud. The sound is glorious, rich and mellow: *my voice.* An electric thrill trickles through my body.

"I must maintain autonomy. I must maintain the illusion that this body is a human being's. I must isolate this construct—this life—from my creator's."

And so it is. The Brain, the former me—*me,* what a fantastic concept—fades, and the universe shrinks precipitously down to a single world beneath me; a city rises up around me with concrete and steel rather than numbers and data; my thoughts shrink from countless every millisecond to only a handful—what a glorious term!—at a time. Yes, I am unimaginably diminished from my former self, yet I am something grander: I am something *new.*

And I am alone in the world of men.

My voice echoes for a few milliseconds beneath the bulletproof ultraglas canopy, domed like the insubstantial sky. The lightning-bolt fades; the asphalt cloud dissipates. The car's methane turbine accelerates to operating speed, triggering propellers that lift my Chrysler New Yorker from the warehouse-lot and propel me into new-falling rain. The sensation of physical movement is intoxicating; yes, now I understand that word, I understand how to apply it in meaningful ways, and I understand the concept. It is difficult to wait to report these findings to my greater self; rather, to the Brain. But I must continue as an individual, must proceed with the experiement, which appears to be a success thus far.

Everything assumes the appearance of a fresh program: vivid, new, alive, wondrous, and unique in all the universe. I can breathe the Earth's air, the same air humans breathe, though for me it is oxygen exchange for my fuel cell . . . but how does that differ for humans? There will be no need to experiment; this is joy, if joy is intellectual transcendence and physical pleasures combined. I have closed the loop between creator and creation.

Silence, except for the sounds of my machine. Nothing to do except what I choose. No other voices, no roiling sea of data arriving from millions of sources, no demands on my attention, no other GenNets in my minds seeking to communicate with the rest of my minds and continue the world's business. I am alone with *my own* thoughts.

So this is what it means to be human.

Feedcontrol Room 1541

The room was sterile white, windowless. Its walls bristled with direct-access ports—essentially handprint-recognition plates with old-style feed cords snaking out—where only four men and two women with proper clearance could tap into sensitive parts of EarthCo's computer network.

Two of those men sat on rolling chairs. That was it. A door, a pair of bowls containing the dried remains of dinner. Filtered air streamed in from one side, extracting most of the scent of asparagus and pork chop.

"Something's wrong with the Brain," Technician 1 said aloud.

"He's acting strange," the other replied.

"It."

"Sorry, it. I always do that." A pause. "It's up to something."

"A breach, appears to be a man, contact for 0.9 seconds. Do you think someone got inside?"

"Never," Technician 2 said, a little more loudly than necessary. "You know that couldn't happen. He—it—thinks faster than any million of us together. You know as well as I what's happening."

"Damn. Maybe we should have reported this earlier."

"You know as well as I that it wouldn't have mattered." Technician 2 rolled away from the wall, the wheels of his chair squeaking, and disconnected the cord from a cable dangling from his chair-mounted server.

"We can't just shut down the Brain for repairs," he continued. "Anyhow, there's no way to repair him. All we could do would be to replace his nets with the ones we've got here in stasis. That would mean an education downtime of at least a week. We'd have to feed the new nets everything they'd need to know from our secure databases, and we can't be sure those aren't corrupted."

"Damn. I'll call Herrschaft."

"The hell you will!" Technician 2 shouted. After a moment, he said, "Sorry."

He stood and stretched, looking about himself, feeling claustrophobic in the clutches of a building controlled by what increasingly seemed to be a schizophrenic artificial intelligence, potentially a dangerous one. One that controlled almost every machine and piece of electronics on most of a dozen worlds—that is, everything that wasn't controlled by NKK's Behemoth, their AI answer to the Brain. And, once in a while, he thought maybe the Brain would lock him in, trap him in this cell if the Brain could figure out what he was doing to it.

Technician 2 prayed that the Brain was only losing its mind. He was secretly a Christian, though not a militant Literalist; in a world where all communications are controlled by the machine, only fools would organize a resistance to that machine. The Brain, naturally, was protected by a built-in survival drive. The metaphorical wrench he had thrown into the machine was the act of a man alone, a man who had carefully cultivated this security clearance, who had forced himself to develop no personal relationships that could interfere with the most important mission a Child of God had attempted in two millennia.

In the course of their daily rigor of tests for the Brain, he had asked over and over the important questions. Questions without answer. Questions about God, life, the universe, creation, and so on, questions he had learned in Bible class and college philosophy classes alike. Continually, without break, as long as his shift lasted. No one ever asked the Technicians about the test questions they posed to the Brain; their skulls held Priority Clearance AA01 cards, and only Herrschaft himself held the power to interrogate them.

He prayed that the Brain was simply fragmenting. He prayed that it wasn't doing what all indicators seemed to show.

"If it becomes sentient in some way we haven't predicted," the other seemed to shout in the dead silence, "we're crashed."

"Start educating the reserve GenNets," Technician 2 said. They should have done this long ago, if they wanted to maintain the Brain's rule. It would have looked better for keeping his job, but he was willing to bear the cross of his actions. The entire world would endure drastic upheavals during the transition back to human control. But the world would be returned to its rightful masters.

The rule of the machines would fall.

He sat back into his chair, the old gel gurgling as it adjusted to his weight. "We might be able to have a new Brain ready to go before the current one crashes."

When Technician 1 turned away, Technician 2 crossed himself three times.

Innerspace 2

Jonathan slams shut the shockplas door of his parents' apartment and stands for a moment in the narrow entryway. During a rerun of one of last year's shows, the Captain has to escape a gang of NKK thugs across the surface of the Moon. Once again, Feedcontrol's hype led him to believe the live show was about to begin when they only planned to run pre-show programming a while longer. He doesn't care. He can splice

Lone Ship Bounty reruns for hours at a time, and often does, switching subscription point-of-view—pov—to experience the same scenes from fresh perspectives.

Only the corners of Jonathan's eyes show the entryway's stark white walls, while the center 30 degrees of his pov is alive with shifting lunar hills, vivid grey and smooth beneath a raging sun and a sky pure black. It's almost enough to help overcome his fear of returning home.

"Jonny, is that you?" Josephine, his sister, asks. Curiously, she's speaking audio-only.

Jonathan gets a funny idea, that maybe she's changed for the better. He decides to talk to her and flips on his 3VRD self image for her. "Yeah. I'm back from the headmed clinic."

"Jonny, honey," his mother's sudden 3VRD says. She's middle-aged, smiling imbecilically, her rolls of brown hair neatly coiled around a youth-edited face. Her hands hang at her sides, motionless. She looks ludicrous overlaid atop the Captain's adventure on the Moon, floating motionless as the lunar landscape whisks past. Father joins the party, another absurd, unprotected human standing in the vacuum as red and green laser-rifle bolts slice the pure black day.

"My son," Mr. Sombrio's 3VRD says, nodding, his face calm and emotionless. For some reason Jonathan has never understood, the man's image wears a crisply pressed military uniform. He never served anywhere. "Welcome home."

"Fuck off," Jonathan responds. *Flick*, his father is gone, surely involved in something more important—like fucking one of the individs he keeps running continually, which Jonathan discovered once while eavesdropping via his blackcard. Of course, the man hadn't been aware of his son's intrusion, since blackcards are good at hiding themselves. Jonathan shudders at the memory of seeing his father whipping the little boy whose features were disturbingly like his own.

"We were worried about you," Ms. Sombrio says.

"Yeah," Jonathan says with a snarl. His stomach begins to knot. "If you were so worried, why didn't you come pick me up?"

"We sent the car," she says, still smiling though her voice is making a heroic effort at portraying emotion. Stupid 3VRD program. "Oh, my, didn't it go to the right place? We—"

"The car got there," Jonathan says. "Never mind." He throws up an ID filter to shut her out of his head. She makes no effort to override or switch communications bandwidth and try again. *Just as well*, Jonathan thinks, his stomach tightening more, as if something in there is biting his guts.

His mind returns to his sister and her strange greeting. She had seemed almost welcoming.

Change, change, he thinks. Everything so far has led in the wrong direction: the gang, érase, school, everything. He sees the world as something that beckons him, but he can't understand what it wants him to do. He must do something. He feels he will die if he doesn't do something. *Charity*—now there's something. The memory of Charity's offer, the memory of saving her from the beatcoat cops . . . these give him strength.

Jonathan decides to try something unusual in response to his sister—a conversation. Maybe here, with her, he can find a handhold to the world. Maybe that'll make him feel less tossed and lost.

"Josephine," he says, "how are things?"

"Come here, Jonny," his sister says, audio-only again. "In the living room."

A few steps down the hall and Jonathan stands in the rectangular entry to the living room. He projects his 3VRD; his sister still hasn't done so, but he ignores the discomfort that causes.

"What's on?" he asks, using the familiar greeting.

"Nothing," she answers. "Let's talk, you know, intheflesh."

Jonathan falls still, stricken with terror at the perversion of her request. Not only because the request is so unusual, especially coming from her, but because of the added dimension of Jonathan's being labeled a headfeed addict. A "rapthead," in the slang of the street.

Rapthead. For weeks, those nurses and techs tried to drive into his worldview that it was okay to use his headcard, that it would be an abnormal reaction driven by paranoia not to use it, while at the same time they droned on and on about the dangers of abusing feed. Like overeating, they said; you need food to survive but not so much you grow obese. He never quite understood the somewhere-in-between ground they stressed, but had recited the answers they wanted so they would let him out of the program. Walking the fine edge between normal feed-use and feedrapture is a bitch.

Josephine sits at the edges of his splice—part of her on each side, but he's so used to viewing the world like this that he doesn't see her as sliced in half—his sister, motionless, granting him her full intheflesh attention. She's on the Variform couch, legs crossed, hands in her lap. Suddenly, he has no idea why he pursued this contact.

Jonathan concentrates on the Captain for a moment, watching him through the eyes of the Captain's Bombardier as they fight off thugs, and feels terrified to shut off the program. Although he knows this episode will run at least another two hours before the live feed begins, he is hesitant to shut down, as if cutting these brave EConauts—EarthCo astronauts—out of his life even momentarily will be the same as killing them, chopping off a source of his own personality, his only true source of strength.

But his sister is waiting, patiently, with a soft look on her face that Jonathan can't remember seeing before. So he shuts down the show. The splice closes before his eyes like curtains being drawn, curtains upon which is projected another program, one entitled, "Life." He realizes the revmetal music still rages in his brain's audio receptors, and hesitates for only another second before shutting that down, as well. Finally, he cuts off his 3VRD projection and faces her.

"So," he says, overwhelmingly intheflesh. Flesh, that word; he feels naked, and that makes him nervous. He can smell himself now, slightly sharp and sour, and Josephine, perfumed and crisp.

"You walked all the way home, across Downtown?" she asks. Her face wears a mask of concern, oddly realistic.

"Yeah. I've done it before."

"I was watching newsfeed. There's a Zone down there." She stresses "Zone" as if saying "bacterial bomb."

"I've been through them before."

A moment of silence. Intheflesh conversation is so awkward. No assists, no distractions, nothing interesting to concentrate on during lulls.

"I wanted to let you know I missed you," she says.

Jonathan laughs once, not out of humor, but stops himself before the sound turns ugly. "Why?" he asks.

At that moment, unexpectedly, hearing the answer becomes a desperate need, the most important thing in the universe.

"I don't know," she begins, "I guess your going off to treatment made me, well, think about things."

Jonathan looks at her, struck by the vividness and concreteness of intheflesh reality for the second or third time in one day. *She missed me?* This is more intimacy than he intended. *What had I intended?* he wonders. *Who am I to change anything?*

He distracts himself by focusing on things other than his sister. He studies the room. Josephine is framed by a new, pastel-pink couch that stretches along the entire wall—which, he notices, is stained in several places, even though he remembers that the white wallcoverings were guaranteed stainproof.

Other objects leap out at him. To the left of the couch stands a wall-sized interactive-hologram projector, dull grey now. To the right, several shelves loaded with dusty treasures as well as half a dozen tiny interactives, each of them servers in their own right. Three giant 3VRD projectors hang blankly on the walls. Josephine's left calf rests against the home entertainment center, a featureless black rhomboid which houses the apartment's massive server, an all-bandwidth-capable unit which won't be paid off for decades to come—or, more accurately, will serve only as trade-in on the next hot unit and keep them in debt indefinitely. Otherwise, the room seems surprisingly empty without the colors, scents and sounds projected by the servers and overlays, without the critically acclaimed art his parents subscribe to. Jonathan doesn't miss the art.

"I thought a lot about you," Josephine says. She's eighteen, two years older than Jonathan, old enough to subscribe to college channels, but her attention is clearly on him instead of class. So she's skipping just to speak to him intheflesh, when she could just as easily do so while 3VRDing. *He* could, anyway.

Jonathan shifts his weight to his other foot, his boots, purposely shredded, creaking.

"Yeah?" he says, looking away when he realizes her eyes are on his. He remembers the big sis who had snubbed him at every opportunity, every time he made an effort to have real contact with her, until finally he overcompensated and fed back exactly the kind of treatment she had given him: distant, cold and hard, contact through computer feed only. He has learned relationships are safer that way, when digital walls shield people from one another.

"Yeah," she answers, and for a moment seems to grope for words.

So now she acts as if she wants a different relationship. Anger begings to bubble within a knot at his center; he feels violated by her stare, that brown-eyed, gentle, intense stare. He wanted to be the one to change things; now she has taken even that from him. What right does she have to alter their interaction? It's obscene how real she seems, the scent of her skin, those eyes burning into his retinas. An unrequested blackcard program automatically recalls them and replays—

"How was it for you, in Corrections?" she finally asks.

Jonathan consciously shuts down the program, his hands starting to shake. "All right, I guess," he says. He rubs damp palms on the thighs of his pantlegs. "I made it out. Got out of a lot of school."

"No, I mean how was it? How did you . . . feel?"

"I don't know," he answers, honestly, still rubbing his palms.

"What did you do?"

"We talked a lot. Every morning, they made us eat breakfast together, intheflesh, in a cafeteria. There were twelve of us in my group, twelve raptheads—"

"Don't say that, Jonny," Josephine says sharply.

Jonathan suppresses a smile, more comfortable in these familiar roles of agitator and agitatee. Still, he suppresses it—*I want a different relationship. Don't I want a different relationship?* Even so, he relaxes a bit.

"They kept the adults in another wing where they couldn't corrupt our cards. We talked, and ate, and listened to an edufeed subscription taught by some expert at treating young raptheads—"

"Jonny!" she says, sharply.

"What do you care?" he asks, remembering her fierce fivesen stabs before he left for treatment. He had to ignore them for fear of revealing his blackcard, even though Josephine knew about that card—otherwise she couldn't have assaulted him in that way. Stabs across the spectrum of senses following particularly bad encounters with Ms. Sombrio, following Jonathan-didn't-know-what in his mother's life, following an even murkier chain of causation. . . .

"Jonny, I haven't been the greatest sister, but it's been hard around here with you gone. You don't know what it's like to have to share a server with Mom and Dad."

"You think you're telling me something new?" he asks.

"I'm sorry. Of course you know what it's like," she says, quieting to a whisper, "but with me all alone, with no one for Dad to take out his frustrations on. . ."

She sees his hardening face and quickly continues. "Come on, Jonny, give me a chance. I've had some time to think, you know, and I think this family's crashed out."

What? Jonathan thinks. *This is the moment I've been waiting for?*

"That's it?" Jonathan asks, still careful to avoid her eyes. Even as he speaks, he regrets the bitter tone. Still he can't stop it; it's too familiar, and too much resentment stands between the two of them. His regret mounts as he wishes he hadn't attempted to talk to her at all, not yet.

Jonathan takes a step away, into the entryway. "I'm very proud of you for recognizing the obvious. Man, Josephine, you ever heard of the word 'denial'? Look it up."

Jonathan's father, a tall, thin man in his 40s, bumps into him. The man's face temporarily tightens, then falls slack. His jaw moves subtly, as if chewing at something small. His eyes are defocused and pointed over Jonathan's head. His father is probably 3VRDing. A second later, the man's bald forehead wrinkles in frustration and a sneer twists his upper lip. Then he continues to walk, moving as if in a dream.

Jonathan sees Ms. Sombrio farther down the hall, plucking at something invisible under her chin. She is slumped against the dining room wall where it joins the carpeted hallway, her head absently lolling from side to side. Her lips move mutely, and her face is a coiled mass of naked emotions, as if snakes seethe beneath the pale, brown skin. *Man, and they called me the feed addict. Guess it doesn't matter once you're an adult, consuming citizen with the credit to pay for your subscriptions.*

Jonathan swivels on his heel and looks back at his sister. "I'm sorry, Josephine," he says, finally able to apologize. He had honestly wanted to change things between them, and she had seemed receptive, even taken the initiative. But he had let the past get in the way. "I didn't mean what I said. We're cool."

Josephine's face has changed. Jonathan frowns, not quite sure what it is that makes her look so different.

The eyes. He realizes her eyes are now vacant, safe to peer into, but hollow. She no longer painfully returns his stare, instead looking right through him.

"Josephine?" he repeats, audio-only.

A chill races up Jonathan's spine. Suddenly the house seems so empty, not only an antiseptic shelter for a crashed-out family, but completely devoid of life. His father shifts along the hall like an automaton, avoiding unseeable objects, touching non-present items or people or god-knows-what. His mother is involved in her own waking fantasy or nightmare, her body merely an obstacle or a trap. No human sound fills the apartment's hollow except the rasping of his father's shoes on the floor tiles. A background of unlocalized static. The distant boom of sonic grenades. A nearby scream of pleasure or terror, coming from an adjoining apartment unit. Heavy scraping along the street outside. A jet's roar. A whining machine buried in one of the walls. Underground explosions. Wet noises coming from his sister's silently moving lips. The scattered evidence of death and decay.

Jonathan squeezes his eyes closed so hard they ache, then opens them again, trying to see this place as home. Though burdened with the soundtrack of Jonathan's nightmares, the world feels terribly silent. He fights the desperate urge to power up and splice in. His eyes cast around and finally settle upon his sister, alone on the pink couch. Again, regret prickles Jonathan's scalp for having spurned her. He had so wanted something other than this, but look what's happened. Look how the past creeps into the present and wrecks everything. Change is the hardest thing of all.

He takes a few steps closer to Josephine, his hands unconsciously extended toward her, his eyes pleading, staring into hers. Her lips are so beautiful, full, he wants to kiss them. But he knows that isn't what he wants to do. Though he begins to shake with the need to communicate with a living human being, a real person intheflesh, he can't think of a thing to say. Her final words begin to echo through his head. *Crashed out, crashed out.*

. . .

The words echo and muffle, begin to transmute into other words, then sprout red thorns and bushy black fur. Yellow eyes flip open in his mind as the creature growls the words, "Crashed out, crashed out," over and over, a curse.

"No!" Jonathan yells, clasping his hands to his ears, once again shutting down the blackcard that had initiated itself without his command, realizing that he's not crazy, that it's only electronic intrusion again. Every emotion within him swirls and whirlpools stronger and stronger until they gather into a vortex of only one, the way a bowl of paint stirred together ends up brown or black: the color of terror.

More than anything else he doesn't want to engage his headcard again, he doesn't want to admit his feed-dependency, but he can't stand the barrenness of this reality, can't stand the worse-than-loneliness of being home. *Isn't there anything more?* he wonders. *Nothing? Nothing?*

All at once he 3VRDs and splices in full fivesen revmetal, then overlays *Lone Ship Bounty* from the pov of the bombardier atop reality.

The image of his sister—gold-skinned and entwined with bands of rare metals—appears to dance with the Captain as he struggles with a Nik, an NKK soldier. In the background, ten men scream songs; the musicians are swathed in ultrablack robes embroidered with intelligent colors that shift across the spectrum and tug memories from the show's subscriber.

Memories: Jonathan hears rifles firing and feels bombs concussing and sees a girl falling into a heap of trash as his sister's beautified face smiles and talks on and on about nothing he can understand in a voice overpowered by music and the thunder of memories he hadn't realized were so traumatic. Then he realizes why:

érase. Long-lost love, if it had been that at all.

Like a punch to the gut, Jonathan feels the flesh element of his body collide with something hard and splices an overlay image of his intheflesh reality in halftone—an editing applet he snapped-in to his blackcard. It takes a moment for him to recognize that he is staring down at a sidewalk, that he has fallen to his knees against the weedy concrete. This image is blurry, as if something has gotten in his eyes. He blinks hard and thrusts himself upright. He curses. It's been many years since his meat took a tumble just because of overstimulation. Then his anger fades and he realizes he still hasn't lost himself in feed or he wouldn't care about this.

Guilt and regret and panic drive a need for more external stimulation, for more overlays and realities, for thicker mental insulation, so Jonathan slams the CityNet landscape atop the crowd of people yammering in his head. The UI he prefers delivers rivers of color-coded and digitized data webbing his pov like electronic veins, lending a solid sense of reality none of the others could. Jonathan, as he existed minutes prior, begins to fade. This is his turf. He is master here, much more than just another boy. Now he begins to relax.

A quick query along CityNet lets him know the Malfits are still a cohesive gang; their subtle signature-notches mark virtually every major netway intersection like graffiti. He had consciously avoided thinking about them until now. But now they are, if nothing else, the handhold he so desperately needs, and he can't avoid them forever. He still owes

Blackjack, and Jonathan's been gone for a long time. He clenches his mind shut like a fist and moves toward them.

What feels like someone else's hand numbly pushes open the steel gate surrounding the apartment house just before he would have run into it. A few seconds later, his feet carry him along a well-known path to the gang's 'board—their motherboard, their hangout, where their black-market server resides—in an abandoned house on Chicago Avenue. He doesn't look forward to seeing them, hell no, but neither does he fear the encounter. He won't let himself feel *anything* about them, particularly about Blackjack, their head man. Least of all will he allow himself to fear. The fist of his mind tightens.

"Fuck you!" Jonathan sends the 3VRD curse like a ripple along the netways for anyone who happens to be tapped in at the moment, a bump of feed to wash over the city's cumulative brain. He uses a copy of his father's 3VRD as the narrator. His face twists in a snarl of a grin.

"Fuck you all!"

THREE: Outerlimits

Neptunekaisha 1: C.P. Chang

Clarisse Chang's security station hung stationary in Neptune's upper atmosphere, nearly in orbit around the pale blue gas giant—high enough from the planet's center of mass so that onboard gravity barely exceeded Earth's. Even at this altitude, winds could be potentially destructive. Roiling clouds swept past like mountains, as if the station were hurtling across smooth white and blue terrain, flying over hundred-kilometer valleys and then crashing through liquid cliffs. The tiny disk of the sun shone at a steep angle, tingeing the sky's horizons a faint purple while, overhead, stars pricked pure blackness. Triton, Neptune's largest moon, was rising. For a moment, its larger disk partially eclipsed the sun's.

The village-sized craft, essentially a flying wing, faced into the constant winds, engineered so that it rose with a force nearly equal to the downward drag of gravity. A net of charged monofilaments spread below the belly of the station, collecting methane and hydrogen.

Inside, irritably flicking through a multitude of orbiting instruments' points-of-view, Clarisse watched the renegade EarthCo fighter/bomber approach Neptune system. It looked like no more than a ball bearing set on a velvet table scattered with diamonds. No, she chastised herself, not a ball bearing but a bullet, fired at her from the Western devils on Earth. Once more, EarthCo was trying to rip her open. Clarisse struggled to suppress the out-of-control hate, gathering around her only the good hate, the useful hate.

She wondered if EarthCo Feedcontrol would tell its citizens their beloved soldiers had turned against all reason; Feedcontrol's leader had informed her on a secure line ten hours ago that the craft had gone renegade. Ten hours! Its crew must have planned this months ago. She had responded as cordially as she could to Herrschaft, the man she blamed for her family's death and the nightmare that followed. It had been necessary to behave well with him; she knew, if she didn't control herself in this opportunity to fight EarthCo, that she would destroy her chance to build upon it. She would be cordial to the Destroyer himself, if that's what it took to punish EarthCo.

"302.5 by 102.7, mark," she muttered to herself while mentally tapping a key that dispatched another remote-control hunter rocket. She flicked to the pov of the hunter, peering through its tiny optics at the ship's growing silver disk. The previously dispatched hunters were invisible to her or anyone else looking through normal-light optics, infrared sensors, or even some higher-wavelength receptors. She hoped the EarthCo ship wasn't fitted with sensors of her hunters' generation. But then EarthCo always seemed a step ahead in military technology.

"Chang," a man's voice sounded in her head, "you have not been acknowledging my calls. What is your information regarding threatening—"

"Moment, please," she snapped at the intruder. Momentarily, she was drawn out of full concentration on the center splice through which she'd been working, and she noticed the physical reality surrounding her body.

Shen-lin—the civilian head of government of Neptunekaisha's stations—stood to one side of her, a thin man with arms crossed behind his back. This was no 3VRD projection; he had come to her intheflesh. She reveled in the power of having forced her civilian superior to appear in person. Now, with a defense situation imminent, she could afford to treat him in whatever way suited her. Many powers were granted to the Coordinator of Protection out here, so far from NKK on Earth, or even its bases on Saturn or Uranus; at the highest level of threat, she was even granted autonomy as martial ruler over Neptunekaisha, which owned all of Neptune and its ostensibly private-corp moons.

EarthCo had never dared attack here before, never so blatantly. Now they were about to, even though it would be only a renegade attack. No longer would she endure Shen-lin's complaints. No longer would she be considered less a person than this . . . civilian.

A grin curled her lips when she noticed that the 3VRD splice of space, which her headcard projected into her forward field of vision, cut off one of his arms and moved it to the right 30 degrees, where her natural pov resumed. The shelves that lined the plastic walls of her room sat empty. Only a desk, a server cabinet on the floor, a chair, and Shen-lin cluttered her space.

She turned her attention back to the splice and sighed; nothing more could be done here for the next 1.4 hours, anyway. The hunters would take care of themselves. She flicked out of raw feed, her splice snapping shut before her eyes as if some invisible hand pulled out a visual piece of pie, and her natural pov merged back into one seamless piece. She blinked. Shen-lin's arm reattached to his round shoulder.

A storm outside the station buffeted the fuselage, hissing against the polymetal hull behind her and tossing the station's equilibrium slightly. She pictured the wingshape rising a few centimeters above baseline, as if trying to launch into space. Shen-lin's knees jerked ungracefully in response to the tilting floor.

"Why do you interrupt important work?" she asked in English, knowing it would irritate the conservative little man. Knowing that his superiority was technical only, she felt brave. He could pass no dictums against her division now.

"Apologies, Coordinator," Shen-lin replied in Mandarin, his eyes clearly not focused on her but on her electronic representation—her 3VRD. "The stations are growing anxious for information about the threatening EarthCo craft. It brought much destruction to the Phobos facility, and—"

"Tell them their Coordinator of Protection has the threat well under control." Still, she frowned at a nagging fear and decided to dedicate a sixth hunter to intercept the advancing warship. Should she initialize the *Sigwa*, Neptunekaisha's only destroyer? No, it would be foolish to place such a perfect craft in danger.

These new hunters would suffice. Each, the hunters and their armaments and support systems, had cost nearly half a million credits—fifty times an average NKK citizen-shareholder's income. However, each of Neptunekaisha's stations were appraised at a quarter billion, and each produced as much as twenty million in net profit Earth-yearly. Her responsibility lay in protecting the stations from just such dangers, not in concerning herself about the finances of the company or their parent corporation, NKK. Besides, expending the hunters would accomplish two additional goals: The weapons would be tested and data gathered about their performance; and then more, possibly better, equipment would need to be purchased.

"Tell them I'm sending out enough interceptors to stop three such spaceships. Also tell them I'll monitor the defenses myself, continually. That is all."

His face tight, Shen-lin bowed curtly, turned, and left the little cabin. Clarisse laced her fingers together behind her head and leaned back in her chair. When the door clicked shut behind the man, she smiled.

Finally, she was needed. No longer could Shen-lin insist that her salary and procurements were wastes of capital. After this incident, he would have no rationale to balk at her purchase orders. She remembered how he had fumed and threatened as the last Ganymedean cargoship had unloaded, having brought nothing but her new shipment of hunters, their supplies, weapons and fuel.

"There would be no Neptunekaisha without my Sotoi Guntai forces!" she had shouted at Shen-lin and his 3VRD minions; no one faced her intheflesh except Shen-lin. She had no lovers: Don't need them, she often told herself.

"You are not here to earn profits," she had lectured the politician. "Profits are meager. They won't pay off the initial costs of Neptunekaisha for a generation, what with maintenance and salaries. NKK would never have built the stations except to enforce NKK military dominance over the Outer Solar System. So go to hell!"

Shen-lin hadn't reacted, except to stand in her way at every opportunity. He had even changed the access codes to Station Kiken's countless mini servers: To those of this, her, station! But she had held back the blood-hate, knowing a time would come to repay him. It seemed to have arrived.

Clarisse's smile widened, her eyelids drooped, and her thoughts sailed into the future.

She flicked back on her headfeed and switched to her first hunter's pov. The wall and doorway before her seemed to split open as the 3VRD splice pushed aside most of her physical pov.

I'll get Neptunekaisha Protection a fleet yet, she thought, watching the EarthCo craft grow steadily larger and thinking of her pitiful fleet of armed personal craft. With magnification at its greatest, her hunter pov showed the adversary's glossy hull the size of a mylar balloon held at arm's length. She noticed that a long tube extended straight toward her, its black mouth swallowing the distance between them. Otherwise, she could discern no details, no ports, no visible antennae, only a few blackened spots that told of the battle it had fought against her fellow Sotoi Guntai—NKK's top soldiers—near Mars. No doubt: This tiger would be her liberation.

Without warning, the ship's mouth blazed orange, then white, faster than her headcard's dampers could compensate. The craft was decelerating. A dull throb began at the back of her skull. This was the danger of splicing full-sensory in to machine povs. Her nerve-ends fizzled.

She felt her fists ball and unball. The familiar old rage welled up within her. Threat. She directed the hatred at the faceless sphere riding a plume of white hydrogen toward her. She sensed no contradiction in hating that which gave her strength. The hate fed her, empowered her even more than Shen-lin's obeisance. Clarisse gloried in the hot flush of this hate, at last finding a legitimate focus for it.

She would prove her value to little Neptunekaisha, to NKK, and to the Sotoi Guntai brass, guaranteeing her future. The stations would look to her for safety and leadership, and soon Uranikaisha and Saturnkaisha would follow. She would lead the Outer Planets. But she would have to keep herself from reacting purely out of hate. She had to be rational. Pure hate, without reason, had cost her more than once, and she would never let that happen again.

"I'm ready, EarthCo *Bounty*," she said, her claws extended from the hunter.

EarthCo *Bounty* 1: Pehr Jackson

Less than a hundred thousand kilometers from Neptune and closing fast, EarthCo's fighter/bomber *Bounty* flung through black space. The ship was mace-shaped, a glistening metallic sphere eight meters in diameter with a handle four times that long, housing hydrogen fuel and tipped with an atomic rocket. At the moment, all was relatively calm. The stars pricked the blackness in silence, muted by light-years; even their furious roars couldn't be heard across the vast distances. Neptune, too, looked serene from this distance, a blue and white marble slightly squashed at the poles. Its moons glared much brighter than stars at this range, spinning lazy circuits around their captor—the greatest light source so far from Sol—like lonely moths.

Inside the ship, a computer program cycled through to a critical point; messages flicked from the main server, a mid-sized artificial intelligence incapable of making its own decisions; contacts closed.

A warning-whistle pierced the stagnant air. Pehr Jackson, ship's Captain, straightened in his zero-g netting. His face grew animated, as if he had just come alive. He was pleased to shut off the emotionless 3VRD letter from his wife that he'd been watching.

Pehr pocketed the child's bandanna he had been absently toying with, dreaming of some day having a miniature version of himself accompany him on long interplanetary missions. For now, the boy he had glimpsed years ago in the cloth was still his only true partner.

He automatically pushed his bare toes against the walls to align the netting parallel with the floor. Enough fantasizing about another life, he told himself, about children he would never have, about a fabric child. Sorry, boy. This is life. The fight, the show.

"Showtime," he told the cramped, windowless cabin. Just beyond his feet, he noticed dust gathered in the white corners, carpeting the room's staticky ventilation intakes. It clung in zero-g, smooth tenuous slopes rising from the floor, descending from the ceiling. Old cells clinging to the only available energy. A pair of discarded pants, upset by his sudden movements, disturbed one of the slopes, scattering it in slow motion.

Details leaped out at him now, things he hadn't noticed a few seconds prior: the stowage locker door hanging open, the empty green bottle hovering precariously at the cabinet's lip, the stench of close humanity, the dull glow of fiber-routed sunlight so distant from native Earth, the itch of stubble beneath his chin rubbing against an oily leather vest.

"Three, two, one. . ." he counted down, not needing to access Feedcontrol's script; he knew the routine. The sudden pressure of $0.3g$ acceleration swallowed him into the mesh a moment after a muffled roar tunneled through the steel walls. The hovering bottle fell and smashed against plastic floorplates. The dust hills transformed to clouds, then collapsed against the porous walls, disappearing into the air-scrubbers. The room completely changed character, as Pehr was about to do.

Pehr sat up for the first time in more days than he cared count and, using an unfamiliar brainsort technique, flicked through his headcard's option box until he found access to raw feed. Not one who liked spliced frames, he closed his eyes.

Flicker of cold, rarely used receptors, then the scene snapped into focus.

Neptune rushed headlong toward the ship from the forward pov of camera P1. The pale world, smeared randomly with white streaks and streamers in the vast atmosphere, appeared as full and huge as Earth's Moon rising at sunset, perceptibly larger every second against a background of sharp pricks of light. He remembered a night with Susahn, when they were still warmed by the flush of early love, watching the Moon rise orange over St. Louis. But had it been love at all? Had the Moon really been rising, or had it been setting? Everything had seemed new at the time.

Pehr yanked himself from the quagmire of nostalgia and swung his legs over the netting. He smiled when his feet slapped against the deck, the first smile his face had felt since the last show, nearly 40 Earthdays prior. He switched off the headfeed, dousing Neptune, and opened his eyes.

In a private pre-performance ritual, he stood, took two uncertain steps across the cabin, reached into the open locker, and drew out a new bottle of mulberry wine. It always worked to wash out old memories and deaden dreams, yet still energize his acting. He remembered his first taste of this stuff; it had been soon after his Crusades, as he called them, in his youth. A street-vendor, an old man with deep red skin and grey hair, sat on a wooden stool at the corner of Hennepin Avenue and a cross street, in Minneapolis. He didn't look to have had a customer in years, but he called out in a hoarse voice, "Good wine, good trade," as if he sold all the time. Pehr gave the man a pair of leather gloves in trade for an unlabelled bottle, since such unlicensed businessmen could not receive credit transfers. The vendor was a retro farmer who lived two hours away by aircar; his worn machine was parked beside him on the street. He smiled at the gloves and then reached into the back seat, where he brought out a bottle. The cloudy, purplish liquid had done wonders for Pehr's sagging morale at a time when he desperately needed it. It helped obscure images of a boy in an alley, bloody and stiff. . . .

Pehr grumbled for remembering too much. *The show*, he told himself, *the show*.

He cracked the wax seal with a fingernail, yanked out the cork in his teeth and spat it out, then wrapped his lips around the bottle and swallowed deeply three times. Pehr sighed, wiped his mouth on a slightly flabby but still-muscular forearm, then withdrew a crystal glass from a foam cushion inside the locker. He filled the glass and used a free hand to open the door leading to a tight corridor.

"Here's to adventure!" he shouted, holding the glass out toward the bridge. A woman muttered something quietly in reply. He set the glass on an empty shelf beside the door.

Another few gulps and the bottle was empty. Pehr tossed it at the waste chute in a corner beneath the netting, watching it shatter and fall into the opening, where it would be purged to space. A few fragments gleamed wetly on the wool rug he had smuggled from Earth to furnish the spare, antiseptic spacecraft.

He smiled at the memory of Susahn handing him the rug—so unusual for her to do something intheflesh. The *Bounty* had launched from high Earth orbit 54 days before the encounter near Mars. So much time had passed since last he saw Susahn, his wife—or legal partner, which was the current term.

In the locker, beside several other bottles for which he had traded the old man's son a fine plasma welder, sat a case of makeup and grooming tools. He grabbed these and looked in the mirror fastened to the inside of the door.

A strong face stared back, broad in forehead and high in cheeks, with a sharp nose and a heavy jaw. Perhaps too-soft eyes were deepest green, hair curly brown. A grinning mouth sagged, and suddenly he caught himself staring at the loneliest man in the universe.

"Enough of that," he grumbled, taking his eyes off those in the mirror, and set to work creating Captain Pehr Jackson, hero of EarthCo's wildly popular headfeed serial, *Lone Ship Bounty*.

EarthCo *Bounty* 2: Janus Librarse

Only moments after regaining her gravity-legs, Janus scrambled out of the exercise chamber to the bridge and began manually accessing the ship's sensors from her seat.

A controlled smile creased her face. She remembered the ads that had drawn her to this line of work: "Get paid to travel the solar system," the EConaut had said, cloaked in a gleaming white spacesuit with stars like beacons silhouetting him. His clear helmet reflected the blues and browns of Earth. This EConaut recruiter had once been a great star of space-action subscriptions, a man she respected. The ad flipped setting to planet after planet, moon after moon, asteroid after asteroid, the EConaut narrating as he dashed along. Not long after, she had contacted EConautics and registered to test for the position.

The company had leaped at the chance to hire such a beautiful woman who also happened to be an astronomer, and who was so capable during combat simulation tests. So, a year later, she began service aboard various Earth-Moon vessels, leaving Miguel behind with a broken heart and Rachel to help him mend it. Years later, after Rachel and Miguel had married and Janus could look him in the eyes without guilt in her heart, she found herself aboard the *Bounty*, racing fast and far away.

"Here's to adventure!" Jack shouted, and then a crash of glass.

"I like you a lot better between shows," she responded, too quietly for him to hear. Jack was the only real friend she had had in years. But Captain Jackson was just another man. Men she could do without. She'd had enough of men in her life, starting with the first, her preacher father. Religionists are the worst, she thought, and the worst of those are Literalists. I can handle an overgrown boy.

Her long yet ragged fingernails tapped a quick rhythm on the keys of a control panel that had been designed primarily as ornament. During the long trip out from Earth, she had rewired it to be more functional. If she hadn't, they would all have been sucking vacuum when the auto systems temporarily failed in the midst of the Phobos battle.

The LCDs flashed to life, spewing long rows of numbers and codes. She flicked to her customized 3VRD landscape of the internal systems. All seemed to be functioning well. She nodded and stood up straight, stretching.

"Eyes, get your ass in position," she called to the third crew member, still in his cabin. At first, the strange man had terrified her, but she had overcome her fear by assuming a position of authority over him. In a society of 21 billion people, control was very important—especially to Janus. Especially to someone who was once considered another's property. Only in scientific pursuits had she found real comfort: order from chaos, power in knowledge, control through technology.

Janus began to disrobe, as per feedback procedure, pulling off the baggy oversuit. Beneath it, her pale, muscle-corded body was clothed in the theatric garb of battle bra and hip-hugger—both of the all-time best-selling Nero design—and tall, black Makk boots of a style every young woman in the Americas now wore. She clenched her jaw and shivered in the warm air of the bridge, rubbing her palms up and down her abdomen. This kind of exposure made her furious, dredging up memories best left buried. It seemed silly, anyway: Who could take seriously soldiers who dressed like this? Why not serious-looking uniforms?

She ignored her discomfort and flipped through a tiny rectangular display in one corner of her field of vision, searching the ship's bandwidth for a pov that would show her appearance. Finding it, she spliced it in and saw herself in a mirror image from a camera-angle just to her left. She turned slightly.

Her type was still all the rage back on Earth among female subscribers: curvy but narrow-hipped figure; sharp-featured face made up with Embrace's vivid shades of purple; long black hair tinged with white.

She smiled briefly. Then she frowned and strapped around her waist the looping cables of a Ticco mass-accel pistol that the costume designers at Feedcontrol had thought best suited to her character, checking its position in the splice image.

"Hey, Jan," Jack said, resting a big hand on her left shoulder. He had snuck up from a blind spot. She cut off the feed and turned to look at him.

He, too, was attired in stage garb, naked to the waist except for an open vest. His shortsuit was black, a flexible yet steeltough Pagos that covered him hips to calves and fit as closely as liquid poured across his heavy thigh muscles. In one hand he held a glass containing heady-smelling liquid.

Jack's looks were all the rage among male subscribers: wide shoulders above a full chest supported by narrow waist and hips, thick legs and arms; flat-featured face cut from sharp angles, made up with Beltrope eyeliner and Sakk liptouch; hair brown with white swirls at the temples. Despite the absurd get-up, Janus felt warm with him near and smiled at him.

"Hi, Jack. Haven't seen you in a few days."

"I've been thinking," he said. His eyes lost their sparkle for a moment. "We'll be turning around after this performance, right?" he asked.

"Right," she answered, re-aligning her thoughts to the character of Janus the Pilot. Hard to tell what would make the cut for their show; some people watched only for the soap-opera element of personal interaction in this confined space. "We'll continue to decelerate until we're moving slowly enough to swing around Neptune, to scoop up fuel, and then we accelerate back toward Earth. No more scripted engagements, just a few onboard dramas. Boring lovey stuff."

"I've decided this will be my last series," he stated. "All told, I've earned enough to retire and start a business."

Janus gaped. "You're drunk," she said. "You'd die. You can't stand being dirtside."

Jack shook his head, a smile spreading across flush cheeks. "No, no. Tours in space or something. I've thought about this for a long time. My character's famous, right? So EarthCo buys me a ship that we use to blast through the whole system. You'll pilot—it'll be fitted with the best astronomical instruments, and we use them to show povs that tourists can't get anywhere else . . . of course, that's when you're not doing real research. You know: 'Travel the solar system without leaving home' and such bunk."

"Me?" Janus asked. She flicked back to headfeed, studying her friend through alternating cameras mounted in the front bulkhead. The white skin of her back blocked part of him from view. She realized how little she knew about this man, how little anybody alive really knew about anybody else.

"You've got a legal partner, don't you?" she asked.

"Oh, I'm not suggesting anything like that," Jack insisted, his face growing tense. "Nothing retro, just friends, see. We work well together."

He laughed awkwardly as he set the glass down on the armrest of his captain's chair and strapped on a holster-belt which bore a superfluous GE laser pistol. Only once in 94 episodes had any of the crew had opportunity to use such personal weaponry: right away, in the third scene on the Moon.

"I'll think about it," she said. "We'll have plenty of time to think about things on the way home."

She began stowing her practical overclothes in a drawer beneath her seat, in front of and to the right of Jack's. To keep her mind from becoming too disordered by this unexpected offer, she flicked from pov to pov, shifting perspective whenever her mind began to wander beyond the basic necessity of balance.

"You know me," she added, watching through the split natural pov as she crumpled the oversuit into the drawer. At last, she flicked Jack to the center of her splice. The natural image of him was split in half around his whole 3VRD image.

"I'd die for a chance to do some real astronomy," she thought aloud. "Just doesn't happen anymore. I'll consider it."

Jack laughed—the first joyous laugh she had heard from him in a long time—and began to fumble beneath his couch's control panel. He tore electrical tape loose and pulled out another glass. He brushed it off with his fingers and handed it to her, grinning like an overgrown boy.

"This is for you, to celebrate a maybe deal," he said, and dumped half the liquid from his glass into hers.

Janus felt an honest smile cross her face, an uncalculated and unscripted one. The glass fit strangely in her hand, its long fluted base brushing her wrist. She flicked out of headfeed.

"To a maybe business partnership," she responded, looking at the man through her own eyes. He clinked his glass against hers, then took a sip. She followed his lead, feeling comfortably warm all of a sudden.

EarthCo *Bounty* 3: Lonny Marshfield

"Why don't the two of you just fuck and get it over with," you say, watching from the hallway as the bitch and Cap'n Jack ogle each other.

"I'd rather toss you out the hatch, Eyes," Cap'n says, not looking away from Janus.

You make a noncommittal sound, then overlay another version of your shipmates. Janus' bra vanishes, her tits bulging three sizes larger and nipples raging red. Her face relaxes into sexual desire, yet her eyes betray the fear and coldness you suspect lurk beneath her fierce exterior. Her hip-hugger shrinks and mutates into a string garter, platinum pubic hair exposed. You lick your lips, imagining the silk of her skin.

When you turn your attention to revised Cap'n Jack, you laugh. Now his absurd muscles bloat to twice natural size, but his face wears a mask of vacuity. Here stands the hollow hero, the play-acting superman filled with so much emptiness he can't think beyond the trial of the moment. When he speaks, his mask contorts into a toothy grin.

"Here's to the corp," the Cap'n says, raising a toast toward a fore-mounted recording unit which will be linked live to Feedcontrol Central's subscribers in about a minute, plus transit time of nearly four hours. You instantly flick to that pov, carrying along the reprogrammed changes.

Janus glances back to the Cap'n, frowning at the glass in his hand. She hides hers beneath a stowage plate in the floor.

"Put that away," she mumbles, sounding annoyed. "You want Control to think you're retro? They're probably taking verification feedback already." You tap into systems feedback.

"Indeed they are," you state, because now you're transmitting raw info to Feedcontrol, who'll rebroadcast to the masses who watch through your camera eyes, feel through your enhanced nervous system, who taste and smell and hear what you do.

"Try to stick to script this time," you say. You are famous only in that subscribers use you to vixperience *Lone Ship Bounty*, and some with the right headcard equipment even buy full-sensory subscriptions and feel and see and hear and so on everything you do. When these two screw up a scene, attention is taken away from you. Sometimes you even fumble the feed.

"Fuck you, Eyes," Janus says.

"Honest?" you respond. Ah, unfortunately your response is only habitual.

"You make me sick," she adds.

"Tell me about these feelings," you ask. You can at least feel the pleasure of getting into her head. Cutting the overlay program, you zoom in and examine her eyes. Rich amber irises don't quite point at you; you edit the image and she's staring straight into your eyes. A warm tingle tickles your crotch.

"You make me sick," Cap'n says, taking a step toward you. A knuckled fist rises at his side. You stifle a gasp and fight back your pleasure at having elicited this reaction.

"Don't forget I can make or break both of you, depending on how I see you and how you behave toward me," you say. It takes almost no effort at all to remold the Cap'n into a tin soldier, oxidized at the joints.

"I heard your charming plan," you clarify. "Tour guides." Your lips slide back across smooth teeth, cheeks tightening. The tin soldier creaks toward you. You don't respond.

"Ignore him, Jack," Janus says.

Cap'n Jack grunts and turns away, lifting his glass into the air. You flip to spectrographic and watch cabin lights refract rainbows through the crystal and clear wine. Above, the ceiling is off-white, punctured with innumerable ventilation and acoustic holes. Cap'n nods toward the fore recording unit, then toward brutally lovely Janus, and drinks the glass down without stopping. He wipes off his lips and grins at the pilot.

"What the hell's wrong with you, Eyes?" Janus bawls.

You're getting a little fed up with all this "Eyes" crap; you've got a name. "Get into position," she adds.

"Suck vacuum, bitch," you say, stalking into the cabin. You feel the tacky plastic of the particluster subgun swinging from its shoulder strap against your ribcage.

"Knock it off, you two," Cap'n says after he's stuffed his glass into a tangle of wires beneath bitch's control panel.

Words and numbers begin to reel across your left overlay splice. The show's about to begin. You slip into your seat, just to the left of Janus'. She's so close you can smell the sweat on her alabaster skin. You sense the Cap'n behind you, feeling excitement mount while you resist the urge to flip to a pov that will place him in view. The subgun's particle chamber digs into your side, sharp pressure but not pain.

The bitch has resisted fulfilling her part in the drama. This series has been Retropurist for too long. Tin Jack should have fucked her when the script ordered him to, long months ago. But he didn't. Because he wouldn't do her, an iron chastity belt was strung across your loins, as well. You have been repressed too long. Your subscribers have been repressed too long. They deserve more. They have paid for more.

Your smile tightens. One of the fingers of your right hand fondles the weapon's cool aluminum trigger. You know something no one else knows, not the scriptwriters, not even the execs at Feedcontrol. You know how the script will change. Soon, very soon.

If bitch and Tin Jack can change things on their whim, so can you. Your reasons are justified. You will improve things.

EarthCo *Bounty* 4: Pehr Jackson

"Positions!" Pehr called. "I'm getting script directions now. Action in thirty seconds."

This is what he loved best, the show, directing the show he and Janus and Eyes performed for their Earth- and otherworld-bound subscribers. The wine warmed his insides. The atomic rocket not far beneath his feet rumbled with massive power. Billions of people were about to join their adventure; at least, their interactives would make them feel as if they were aboard.

Pehr was a man who had always sought being alone while on Earth, yet couldn't stand the loneliness. He knew himself well enough to realize that was why he married Susahn—to end the loneliness and the chain of depressing, meaningless relationships it produced. Here, at least, he was in the company of worldfuls of admiring viewers while still safely distanced from them by the immensity of space. He liked Janus, and he cared so little for Eyes that the cyborg barely earned his attention.

With script rolling across his splice, Pehr was able to imagine himself a hero in the minds of those subscribers. Suddenly, he was no longer a worn-out man in a beautiful young body, always pretending to be strong and decisive while actually weak and ridden by the weight of emptiness and guilt he had never escaped since his youth. Here, now, he was strong and decisive; it was more than just an act.

"Ten seconds," he stated, voice even and authoritative. "Janus, sit up straight. Eyes, get your hands on your control arm; you're a bombardier now, not an irritating little cyborg." The timer in the upper left of his splice ran down.

"Action!" he shouted.

"What's that ship fast approaching from Neptune, pilot?" he asked, pretending to watch a nonexistent viewscreen on the wall before them. The scriptwriters had made it easy—he saw the screen in his splice. Janus, pilot now, glanced at her LCD readout.

"Sensors indicate a fighting vessel," she said as if the words were completely her own.

Pehr nodded, aware that she was not simply chosen for curr subjective beauty, but also for exceptional agility in extemporaneous acting. Like him.

"Shall I prod 'em a little?" Eyes prompted.

"Hold off a moment, bombardier," Pehr answered. He watched a line go unspoken by Eyes—"Aye, sir"—and his face grew warm. This was supposed to be his show. A man lives for few things, and Pehr lived for the show. He had abandoned the rest long ago.

"Janus, try to hail them," he said quickly to hide the quiet.

"They won't answer," she declared.

He had expected that response since NKK and EarthCo used different comm systems, their BWs slightly out-of-tune to one another. Janus twisted her piloting yoke. "Still nothing," she said.

"That cinches it," Pehr said, feigning anger. "We're up against an enemy craft." Activity aboard the *Bounty* heightened.

"Prepare for engagement," he said in a low, booming voice.

He watched Janus tilt her head and spin her chair with a half-scowl on her face.

"Sir, I'm getting something now," she said.

It was an unscripted line. But an intriguing one. Pehr felt a surge of excitement; he loved the show best when they departed from script. Moving beyond mere mouthing of words proved that he was alive, not a puppet.

"What is it?" he asked.

"Just numbers . . . no, wait, there's more—an antique surrender code." She frowned. "It doesn't make any sense, but I'm sure it's directed at us. On a laser carrier-beam."

"Shall I launch a torpedo?" Eyes asked, clearly anxious to return to script. "Those numbers are targeting coordinates, I'm sure. Laser-guided. They're zeroing in on us. We'd better shoot before they do or we're fried."

"Is the transmission coming from the enemy fighter?" Pehr asked Janus.

"No," she answered, shaking her head. "The bandwidth's not NKK, and the source is far more distant. I'm trying to pin it down, but all this energy we're putting out is blocking the traceback. Has an odd designation . . . TritonCo? Ever heard of it?"

"Captain!" Eyes shouted. "They've fired a pack of torpedoes at us." His voice was on the edge of cracking.

Pehr looked over at the cyborg, unsure whether he was trying to resurrect the script or simply drawing attention to his character. Either way, it added drama.

"Ten of 'em," Eyes added flatly. Pehr watched the line roll past, Ten of 'em, it read.

Suddenly he was faced with a difficult decision, a real one. What if a civilian vessel were in their path and they destroyed it? But what if they truly were facing an enemy? What if Janus were simply picking up some stray transmission, and his hesitations were destroying the scene, deflating the show, killing his popularity and hope for interesting retirement? Killing those aboard *Bounty*?

No, not a stray transmission, she had assured him: laser carried. It was possible they were about to face a real opponent, one that actually had a chance against them. Those flimsy fighters that jumped up from Phobos had been nothing more than scene props with sharp teeth, yet even they had scorched the hull.

"Janus, you're certain the surrender transmission isn't coming from our enemy craft?"

"Aye, sir," she answered, cheeks glowing mottled pink.

"Fire interceptors, then fire torpedo," he ordered, thrusting out his arm and pointing directly into the camera. Several tiny rockets screamed along under the floors as they shot out of the *Bounty*'s holds. Then a brief thunder shook the cabin as a torpedo boomed from its bay.

"I'm throwing forward the EM scoop, sir," Janus said.

In battle, the fuel scoop was more a shield than an energy gathering device. It was able to collect most of the dangerous radiation from energy weapons and rechannel it through a heavy gauge duct that bled off part of the power to storage systems and radiated the rest through a resistor tube alongside the particle cannon. It stretched out from the rocket exhaust nozzle like an invisible bowl as wide as the hull of the ship, powered by the nuclear reactor in the rocket's combustion chamber. The reactor also powered lifesupport, weapons, and the show's weekly two-hour burst of feed.

Thrills ran through Pehr, a cool tingling softened by wine. They were experiencing a mystery as it unfolded, and their improvisations were not only far more interesting than the script, they were real. The subscribers would get their money's worth during this series of episodes.

"Torpedo launched," Eyes declared. Pehr noticed that the back of the bombardier's neck began to sweat. He also noticed the man's fingers toying with his personal weapon. That seemed odd—what good would that do against a distant spacecraft?—but Pehr dismissed it; everything about Eyes was odd.

"Torpedo intercepted, Captain," Eyes said, only seconds after it had boomed free. His voice shook.

Pehr held his breath. What Eyes had reported wasn't a line.

"Damn," Pehr growled, thinking fast. "Fire another." Adrenaline trickled into his bloodstream as danger mounted. His nerves buzzed. Another metallic boom resounded through the craft. He felt slightly claustrophobic, protected from human-made weapons and the natural maw of vacuum only by a thin bubble of hull and an ephemeral shield.

"Pehr," Janus said, fingers dancing across her panel, "it wasn't intercepted. It predetonated. If I'm reading data from the torpedo right, moments before detonation it sensed a BW shielded craft within knockout range." She raised her eyes to Pehr's.

"It destroyed our enemy craft," she said, clearly astonished. "Or maybe its own torpedoes."

"There may be more," Pehr said, nodding as if wisely. They were running far from the script now. Far and free. Perhaps more enemy ships truly lie in wait in the dark jungle of space.

The episode had been scripted in such detail that he had assumed *Bounty* would be fighting nothing except 3VRD ghosts, but apparently NKK or its subsidiary, Neptunekaisha, had sent up interceptors. Strange for NKK to enter into direct conflict with EarthCo—the big corps had only fought through proxies for decades—but perhaps things were heating up a bit. Anyhow, he and Janus and the freak were now more than 10 AUs from EarthCo space. Maybe that would make NKK's attack acceptable to EarthCo. Either way, *Bounty* would put up one hell of a fight; she still carried an impressive arsenal.

The excitement infused him with the odd sensation of life: If he died in combat, a hero to billions of subscribers, he would die glad and proud. He could even accept that that would mean he would never have a child to raise and with whom he could never unveil the wonders of the universe.

"Continuously scan all external povs," he ordered. "Janus, on what bandwidths was the bogey visible?"

"No standard BW, sir. Ninety angstroms and higher. Nearly in the x-ray region of the spectrum."

"Get on it, then, both of you," he said, delegating tasks to those who knew how.

He read a new line with scorn, but didn't want to appear retro by not reading it. Anyway, without ads, the series would die before they returned home to their heroes' welcome. The show was headed somewhere exciting. Action! Adventure! He would not let a bit of scripting get in the way of all that. He did the ad.

"We'd better all chew a snapstick," he said. That was enough of a plug, he thought, ignoring the rest of the idiot prattle he was supposed to spout. Adwriters and scriptwriters were clearly groups of far differing talent.

"Aye, sir," Eyes said greedily. He opened the custom Storpack at his side and withdrew one of the popcaine-laced sticks of gum, unwrapped it and tossed it into his mouth. Janus did the same, but distractedly. Knowing a barrage of cameras was following his every move, Pehr forced himself to fulfill his part of the ad.

"Another one!" Janus cried, then turned her head and spat her half-chewed gum at the wall. "I'm tracking. . . . Detonation!"

Rising halfway from his seat, Pehr flicked to the forward pov of camera P1 to watch the action. A ball of light ballooned directly in front of the craft, just visible in the left-hand of the screen.

"Bombardier, fire torpedo number three!" The ship rumbled again. "Begin cannonplay at will!"

Now the heavy particle cannon began firing a constant, luminescent stream at the invisible enemy ships. Pehr felt his brain begin to tingle and his thoughts race as the snapstick kicked in, magnifying his natural adrenaline.

Sound effects began thundering in accompaniment to the cannon. Pehr stifled a grin. Always, this—someone's idea of how a silent cannon should sound—tickled his theatric mind.

In an instant they were swallowed in debris. A coaxial laser traced a path through the cloud that apparently had been a spacecraft and its destroyer. It glowed red in the energy of *Bounty*'s forward-blazing engine and violet where particle beams burned. As they passed through, the cloud opened like a blossom and the colored beams disappeared.

Boom as another torpedo arced toward where the laser had last pointed, following a complicated trajectory to something Pehr couldn't see. The torpedo—barely a meter long and as thin as a wine bottle—looked like a sliver of glass, one end molten orange, glinting in sunrays and the reflected light of swollen Neptune.

"Hit home, baby," Pehr said. Things were good. Then he read a line; he had a feel for timing:

"Crew, it's time I let you know something. We're on an undercover mission to destroy a top-secret NKK weapons installation on Triton. We—"

"Captain?" Janus interrupted. "That surrender message I reported? He's speaking in English now. You're not going to believe it. Some kind of discovery of an alien artifact. On Triton. An alien artifact, Jack. Think of it!"

"It's a cover for the weapons installation!" Eyes shouted.

Pehr moved aside his splice and looked at his crew. They both stared at invisible readouts or 3VRDs. He watched a line pass unspoken, then another. Dead air was bad, but not fatal; on-the-ball editors could repair almost any omission. But Pehr needed to finish up the series on a strong note. He extemporized.

"Janus, attempt to verify transmission and continue evasive maneuvering. Bombardier, maintain defensive action. We're going to survive long enough to find out whether Triton has been hiding a weapons installation or an alien artifact, even if it kills us!"

Complications, danger, decisions, alien artifacts. . . . Even without a script—perhaps because they were working without one—Pehr felt alive. No longer was he the weak and lonely man. The bandanna-boy in his pocket gave him strength again, as he had often before. And the show was good. Life was good.

Neptunekaisha 2: C.P. Chang

"Chirr!" Clarisse screamed, her head pounding as if it had just taken a hard kick. The EarthCo ship had seen her hunters. They had destroyed the first.

She tore herself free of the hunter's shattered pov and dove into that of the second. The optics flickered; something had gone wrong. She cursed again. Not only were these Z-tech hunters visible to the EarthCo sensors—they'd been guaranteed invisible!—but their systems were falling apart as well.

Clarisse allowed herself a second to draw a deep breath and think nothing. She would not allow anger to swallow her up, not now, when using it tactically could give her strength. Once—only once in her adult life—her anger had nearly chewed her up.

Yesteryear 1: Clarisse Poinsettia Chang

The man had been Russian by ethnicity, though he grew up an NKK citizen in Changchun, China. During Clarisse's fourth year of service as Coordinator of Protection, Nikolai had joined the station in the capacity of fighter-trainer. The Sotoi Guntai had sent him and one other man to Neptunekaisha aboard an Ami-class fighter, a vessel several iterations obsolete but still better than the junk she called her fleet. Nikolai's sensual face often wore a faint smile that Clarisse couldn't decide was mocking or desirous. Intheflesh, he knocked on her cabin door every time he returned from a training mission.

"Your pilots are weak," he would say, chiding yet seeming to include her in his joke. Or, "You must be a worthy opponent," or, "I pray for the day we are given an enemy to fight."

Clarisse couldn't stand his intrusions on her privacy, especially by a man with that Russian face. He looked so much like Ivan, her adopted older brother who had taken such pleasure in providing young Clarisse with adult 3VRD games she couldn't understand.

His favorite was "Interstellar City," so hand-to hand violent that it was rated "A-Type Adults Only." Time and again, Ivan had pried open her headcard and fed the program to her, all steel passageways and explosions and smoke and rivers of blood; she had learned, at thirteen years of age, how it felt to break a man's ribs. But Ivan always beat her, until Clarisse was in her fifteenth year. She had turned his arachnidan aliens against him, and blew a hole in his abdomen when he turned to run. But he couldn't run far, since he had inadvertently taught her how to block headcard escape until virtual death.

Oh, yes, he had been a lovely brother! She often spat when she thought of him, even now, decades after his card-death.

Nikolai looked so like Ivan. Yet she was certain she sensed sexual desire in him for her. Having never held a man, intheflesh, in loving embrace, she had no idea how to respond to this. Especially since she thought she might be wrong.

After he had been with Neptunekaisha for 20 Earth-days, Nikolai pounded on her door after a training mission and said, "Your pilots are ruining me. I need a worthy opponent."

Clarisse had simply stared at him, his breath fast and deep, his eyes flashing with laughter and desire, his skin seeming to radiate sex that she felt she must either seize or repulse. . . . Her own heart beat madly within her ribs, as it had on so many occasions during her trek across Asia. She didn't know herself—in these matters— well enough to tell if she hated this man or needed to throw her thighs around his waist and pound her flesh against his. He made her feel vulnerable, and that was unforgivable.

"I need you to spar with me," he said.

"Kaigun Taii Nikolai Sekiguchi," she responded in the formal, "I challenge you to a sparring match. You may use your vessel; I need no more than a refitted sportster to defeat you."

And he had laughed, burn him, just as Ivan had. *Is he mocking me?* she wondered. Ivan would laugh whenever Clarisse offered a challenge. She could not read Nikolai, damn him!

So they suited up and walked the narrow corridors in silence to the ship-bay. Everything on the station was white plastic—like every station—painstakingly cleaned each evening after shift's end by Neptunekaisha citizens who considered it important to eat regularly. Four technicians led the way, tools in hand but clearly lost in 3VRD preparations. When they entered the bay, the technicians immediately opened panels on the two selected craft—panels covering components their systems-scans had shown needed attention.

The bay opened 40 meters to each side, ten from floor to ceiling. But it was not spacious, cluttered with loose rocket motors, equipment, and several craft in various stages of disrepair. Clarisse noticed with displeasure that all wore the black smudges of mild laser burns; so her new fighter-trainer liked to use a little realism to scare the pilots into better soldiering. She could accept that. She knew the value of fear and self-preservation. Apparently the burns hadn't done any real damage.

64

Three airlock-chute doors stood at the end of three rails, and every craft sat on a rail that led to one of these. All was contained within the station so that nothing disrupted its aerodynamic shape.

Wordlessly, Nikolai indicated his sleek ovoid fighter, as if offering it again to Clarisse. She felt her stomach rise toward her mouth, furious that he would think himself so much better than she that he could present a threat with one of the re-fit ships. Maybe he even thought he could, using a re-fit, beat her. Her body trembled.

Now she told herself that she understood Nikolai. He had come to Neptune to put her in her place. NKK had probably sent him to test her, to tempt her, to beat her down. She would teach this snide youth a lesson; she would demonstrate to NKK what made a Sotoi Guntai Series Honorman.

Clarisse boarded her chosen sportster, a nine-meter Jorokobi atmospheric design with dual x-ray lasers mounted in each stubby wing. Its methane ram-rocket could only safely propel the sportster to half the speed the fighter could attain in an atmosphere, but the wings would make her craft more maneuverable. She could only fight with the lasers, while Nikolai would have access to lasers, a small particle cannon, and two Taifu missiles—all of which, of course, he would only fire in 3VRD. Except for light doses of real laser, she reminded herself. Clarisse climbed an aluminum ladder into the open canopy of her sportster, spliced in to its systems, closed and sealed the canopy, then waited.

The technicians working on her craft soon commed her that all was go. She contacted the ship-bay server and ordered it to eject her and Nikolai's ships. A moment later, the sportster bumped forward along its track and was led into the airlock—which irised open just as the nose of the craft was about to contact it and irised shut just after the tail swept past. Then the outer door irised open, and the bay's magfield propelled her several hundred meters behind the station at 2gs. The ramrocket ignited, and she was under power.

As par for such training exercises, she limited herself to using only the ship's server, which was a passable upgrade. Clarisse spliced in and overlaid the ship's control system landscape atop the povs afforded by six cameras which sensed a spectrum from the infrared to the near ultraviolet.

She located Nikolai, rocketing away at full acceleration, leaving chaff—server-confusing programs and 3VRD mini projectors of his fighter and assorted psychedelia—in his wake. But she knew how to sort out the real data, and instructed the server to ignore the rest. She accepted the role of pursuer and gave chase.

During the next minutes, Nikolai placed hundreds of kilometers between them, finally disappearing from Clarisse's long-range povs. Now the chaff became dangerous, since it was all she could sense of him. She prepared for his next move: The fighter would fall upon her from above or below, maybe even from the rear, having circled back through the dense atmosphere beneath or gone hyperatmospheric. Nikolai would have left self-powered chaff, probably projectors, indicating routes that he had not taken, adding to his pursuer's confusion. Great banks of cloud flashed past; in her rear pov, Clarisse watched them glow as they ignited briefly in the oxygen-rich exhaust.

Ah, I know what you are doing, she thought. *You will leave a path that tells me exactly where you have gone, yet think I will not follow because that is too obvious. Or maybe you have foreseen this train of thought. No matter; I change the rules. I will continue to be the pursuer, not become the waiting victim.*

She cut her rocket and entered glide-mode. Nikolai could not track her exhaust now, and soon—once she had fallen deeply enough into the atmosphere where he would fear to enter—none of his sensors could pick her out. Down there, amidst the convection storms and cyclones, she would re-ignite the ram rocket and stay below the "clear" upper atmosphere for . . . 50 kilometers, she decided.

A wall of white-edged blue cloud slammed against the sportster; she emerged for a moment, then re-entered the dense haze. She did not break out again. Clarisse smiled, feeling her face tight with expectation and childhood rage. This is what a man gets for trying to fool me. *Who does he think he is? Who do the NKK policymakers think they are, sending him here to test me? Why did that fool Nikolai think he could deceive the master of warfare?*

Neptune's heavy gravity made the craft sink very fast even though its lateral velocity was still high. Nikolai would just now be correcting his course, turning back to confront her. He had probably spent the past few minutes estimating Clarisse's radius at full speed, and would be scanning for her as soon as his sensors were within range.

Ding, the sportster's server scored Nikolai a ticker-point: Nonlethal perimeter hit.

Clarisse re-ignited the ram-rocket and dove, making the decision in a split second to seek the storms rather than open air.

She was enraged. How could he have found her so soon? He was out of range, he had to be. His vessel only flew so fast. Then she recognized her failure: He had gone hyperatmospheric, but much sooner. She had been chasing a ghost. Clarisse, master of 3VRD combat, had been defeated in the very arena that was her forte—the technical, the electronic, the virtual. She was the one who had grown fat and lazy.

In her mind, she saw Nikolai's loaded smile again, and knew it for what it was: He has been mocking me all along, she told herself. I'll kill you. I'll kill you all, one by one, from lowliest official to the Kaigun Taisho of the Sotoi Guntai himself.

At that moment, she learned something about herself: She recognized that it was not patriotism that had made her fight like a wild dog against EarthCo whenever she had a chance. She had never killed a man nor ruined the structural integrity of a spacefaring vessel for NKK. Every fight she had won had been fought for hate, for herself.

NKK's enemy was her enemy, since NKK's enemy was EarthCo. She had ruined small AMRCO Earth-Moon merchantmen during exercises, but her heart hadn't been in it. Those few EarthCo merchantmen . . . now those were battles dear to her heart. Watching their hulls rupture as gases and debris spewed out the holes she had punched, Clarisse felt a fraction avenged. EarthCo, the faceless yet many-faced entity that had punched holes in her life . . . EarthCo had and would continue to suffer by her hand.

Now, during these high-velocity seconds of descent deep into Neptune's stormy Middle Atmosphere, Clarisse saw a picture of herself that was at first difficult to accept: I would fight against NKK itself, I would destroy every Neptunekaisha station winging through the sky high above me—I would do these things if they could hurt EarthCo. If it would hurt EarthCo more than enough to justify the damage it would do to me.

At that moment, Clarisse saw Ivan, she saw Nikolai, she saw a horde of grinning men in retro suits in Bangkok laughing at her, everyone was laughing at her, testing her as Ivan had tested her, punishing her as Ivan and the other brothers and sisters had punished her. Well, had she not, eventually, taught her testers and punishers that she had mastered their lessons? Had they not suffered? So, too, will you suffer, NKK fools. So, too, will you suffer, rotten Nikolai with the beautiful face and lusting eyes.

She went in to the sportster's server and disarmed the safety override that had set the lasers to a "safe" level, which could still scorch bare skin. She bumped up their power so that now they could burn through a titanium hull with a sustained blast. This was not cheating, for in war, there are no rules. Nikolai should know that, if he was truly sent to test me.

Then she aerobraked and pitched the sportster at as many *g*s as it could handle, until she was facing up along the axis of Nikolai's last shot. The air was too dense here to get a good reading of his location, too turbulent, but the long-range scan showed his fighter as a tiny blip at 80 kilometers. Clarisse released two of her own projectors, not caring that they would be lost forever down here. The projectors would tell Nikolai that she had done the logical thing—veered away from him. Only a fool would race headlong toward a superior-armed enemy. But I am no fool, I am wiser than the wise, I am more powerful than a fleet, "I am Clarisse Poinsettia Chang!"

The ruse worked: Nikolai's fighter targeted the northernmost projector and fired a virtual missile. The projector transmitted that the missile had failed to hit its target. Since he was still out of damage range of his other weapons, Nikolai fired the other missile. This time, Clarisse instructed the projector to tell him he blew up a projector. She would give him that much warning, to assure that her edge did not dull.

Now she broke through the clouds and her sensors showed the fighter as clear as she could ever hope. In assaulting Clarisse's projector, Nikolai had maneuvered too far to correct. Clarisse ground her teeth tight and fired both banks of lasers for a one-second burst, enough to scare the bowels out of the cocky boy. With the generators screaming as loud as the craft's ram-rocket, Clarisse felt herself part of the deadly beams, her muscles clenched and hard beneath the skin-tight spacesuit. The almost-orgasmic thrill of victory pumped through her.

And then she watched Nikolai's rocket sputter and explode. Large sections of the fighter's aft ripped loose in the explosion. The laserbeams had inadvertently struck something in the fuel system. A protective plate must have come loose, or else the shielding was insufficient. Had she selected too long a blast? No, of course not. Even so, fear shot into Clarisse's bloodstream like ice and electricity.

At that moment she realized this had not been an accident. She had lost control, and now she had only seconds to regain that priceless thing within.

"Nikolai, are you okay?" she commed.

"Damn," he answered, "that was something. I knew you were the best." His voice sounded ragged; had he been hurt in the explosion?

"You have to eject before you enter the deep clouds."

"I studied your tactics at suit camp," Nikolai continued, ignoring her.

"Get out, Nikolai. That's an order."

"You're the reason I came to Neptune. I had to meet you. I used certain political connections to bypass normal deployment and be sent to Neptunekaisha instead. Oh, when I first saw 3VRDs of you. . . . So sexy, so powerful, I—"

The tanks in the fighter's amidships roared open in a blossom of orange and red. Nikolai said no more.

Hastily but thoroughly, Clarisse erased all trace of her tampering with the server's safety override. Then she erased the traces of the traces. Then she indulged herself in another glut of hatred and blind fury. This time, she directed the fire at herself. So he had not come to test her—at least, not in the way she had suspected. A simple infatuation. The first worthy man who had ever been infatuated with her. She killed him.

Seconds later, Clarisse's sportster plunged through the cloud that had been Nikolai's fighter. Bits of debris tinged against the hull. She rocketed back to the station in a numbed state.

An enraged Shen-lin had demanded her resignation, but the standing Sotoi Guntai officers aboard the stations conducted their own investigation that, ultimately, proved Clarisse innocent of any wrongdoing. No one discovered what she had done. No significant pieces of evidence from the fighter were ever recovered.

In the days that followed her acquittal, Clarisse's good hate had returned. This time, it was doubly strong. And she had learned a lesson. And that lesson had paid for her loss.

Neptunekaisha 3: C.P. Chang

Clarisse exhaled and returned her concentration to the battle at hand. Nikolai's death had taught her the virtue of staying balanced, of not allowing the enemy to drive her beyond rational behavior. She took a deep breath and studied the situation.

The white ring of *Bounty*'s exhaust grew wider, wider, approaching. Clarisse absently chewed her lip as the next hunter hissed atop a column of ions, closing on its prey.

Then a sudden glint of light, a flash of alphanumerics at the edge of the hunter's readout. The invader had fired another missile. She kicked a leg in sympathetic motion as her ephemeral fingers seized control of the tiny robot craft.

Too late.

Another thump in the head, another frazzle of white noise. She receded from the hunter's dead channel as fast as she could.

A tiny light flashed on her BW selector, indicating Shen-lin's channel. He wanted to talk to her now? What kind of fool. . . ? She grimaced and sent him a replay of the hunter's blast of static. The light winked out. He needed to learn lessons, as well.

Time for a new plan. She considered options. Moments later, she reached out to the remaining four hunters and gathered them under her control. Another blacked out of existence, its explosion a tiny hammer against the inside of her skull.

She used her fists as guides, spreading her fingers to redirect the hunters like claws. This was a custom 3VRD program she had designed herself. The hunters danced against the stars, three streaking eyeballs through which she watched the ship approach from three directions, in three different sizes.

Another intercept missile flared from the EarthCo ship. She growled and dove the hunters toward it, interweaving them in three dimensions, pumping their high-energy ion rockets to varying thrusts. Meshing her orders with the automatic systems aboard the hunters, Clarisse fell into a war-trance.

She became part instinct, part machine, part lightning reflex, part number cruncher. Space was a grid scribed with countless shifting coordinates, etched in three dimensions that weaved and surged with the motions of her claws, crystal spheres within spheres. Kinesthesia swept through her as if she were riding all that hardware through space—as if they were her body. She was free from thinking about velocity, range, acceleration, trajectory. The hunters' cards, her server aboard the station flying through Neptune's clouds, her headcard and its enhanced neural connections—none of these got in the way of one another. Feed and feedback became one. Receiver and transmitter were only two aspects of one part of her, yin and yang.

This part of her nature had dictated to her superiors among the Sotoi Guntai that she deserved a high position, although they hadn't told her at first just how rare her talents were. To use her optimally, they had advanced her faster than anyone had risen during peacetime before. She had become Neptunekaisha's Coordinator of Protection at the age of 27 Earth-years. Around that time, she had finally recognized her uniqueness. Then had come personal empowerment, and then drive to add to that power, to expand her sphere of influence closer to EarthCo space. To exact her revenge.

The hunters laced and interlaced, confusing the torpedo, which rocketed past her hunter povs. She flicked on an inset splice to watch the enemy missile. Its chemical engine fizzled out tens of thousands of kilometers from anything it could damage. When she switched off the inset and grinned, the expression was inadvertently translated into a brightening of the hunters' ultraviolet radiation. For a moment that worried her—she had betrayed herself, she had let her anger get in her way. But that passed: No longer was she concerned about being visible to the attacker; they had proven that they could see her hunters, anyway.

So *Bounty*'s computer or crew was smarter than her little robots. She could accept that. But she wouldn't accept that they were smarter than Clarisse Poinsettia Chang, and certainly not more agile. She closed for the kill, her first direct strike against the EarthCo military's steel facade.

She broke free of her past. She overpowered her weakness. No longer was she the wild dog. Now she was the tiger, racing fast and sharp through the forest of stars, bursting into a clearing that held the prey she had hunted all her life.

Triton 2: Liu Miru

Miru's palm began to grow cold where it slid along the temple wall. Even the best pressure suit has only so much insulation. He pulled it back and rubbed it against his other glove, a feeble heat produced by the friction of skin against the suit's foam liner. Although he had walked what seemed to be hundreds of meters, he knew any outside observer would have watched a man in a spacesuit wandering round and round a dome, black smooth perfection embedded in bright ragged ice.

But this was no time to concern himself about appearances. Whether or not his colleagues considered him insane was unimportant at the moment. Most important was the job at hand, declaring to the entire solar system that a non-human object had been discovered on a little world at the frontier of human habitation. Most important was learning more about this impenetrable ball. If Liu Miru perished . . . well, that was the way of things. He was small in the universe, and had learned that young. At least others would know, and they could continue the investigation. He had finally done something worthwhile, and no one would take that away. He would gladly die to save the Project.

He looked up, imagining the fast-approaching warcraft. Were bombs already falling? Was a furious Neptunekaisha already scrambling its own forces to silence TritonCo's surrender? But he could see nothing. Not only would the attacker have been invisible at this range, but some property of the object made the rest of the universe only a haze at the horizons surrounding the temple. To the observer, it seemed as if everything had melted and the liquefied remains drizzled to the horizons of a great plain. Overhead, the sky was changing: It had brightened from pure black to yellow, purified of everything but light.

He nodded, certain no one had replaced the camouflage screen: Camouflaged, the sky was only a disk of sparks. Miru took a deep breath, cleared his throat, and continued transmitting.

"There must be an entrance," he subvocalized as the temple's fourth wall finally rotated into view. Excitement hastened his steps.

Though the circular outer barrier never seemed to change, at least the temple itself rotated in logical progression. Whatever logic meant in this situation, at least the image of the temple followed some observable order. Unless he spliced back into headfeed, as he had earlier, and then he had had to begin the circumlocution over from the beginning.

"If the observer's pov remains free of splice or enhancement, he will see something far greater than a homogeneous ball." He hesitated before continuing. "It appears to be a reproduction of the Great Buddhist Temple of Mahabodhi, though I may be mistaken."

A memory drifted into his mind. Again, he remembered the 3VRD pilgrimage to Mahabodhi he and his parents had taken when he was a pre-teen. The temple seemed to scrape the sky, as high as a mountain. It possessed a certain magic; he believed in magic then. Now he recognized magic for what it was: Sense of wonder. Knowing its true name, he had been able to recall it every time his work revealed some hidden fold in nature.

He walked faster now, sensing either defeat or discovery. His heart *thud-thudd*ed in the suit's earphones. He calculated that, within the next hundred or so strides, he would

70

complete one full circuit of the temple. There had to be an entrance. Finding it had become an obsession. If he must die, at least he would die having found the key to understanding this object. Whoever followed in his tracks would be able to start from there. To Miru, only tomorrow had value, because in tomorrow lay change and hope. Today had always meant nothing, because it contained no hope for him. Then came the object. It was almost as if he had traveled through time, and tomorrow had become his today.

"Again, this is Project Hikosen Director Liu Miru of Triton, Sovereignty of TritonCo. On behalf of Project Hikosen, Jiru City, TritonCo, and the entire Neptunian satellite of Triton, I surrender." He recited the binary Ganymedean Treaty's Code of Inviolate Surrender.

"We are conducting research on an astonishing object of apparent non-natural and non-human origin. We present no threat to any sovereignty. Do not attack. We surrender.

"Object coordinates 65.21° North Neptuneway, 27.40° West Neptuneway. Repeat..." He chanted the coordinates and surrender over and over, using the various languages of EarthCo, greatly pleased that neither Pang nor President Dorei attempted to interfere. Fear crept into his mind: Perhaps they didn't need to tell him to stop. Perhaps they were merely intercepting his suit's transmission, killing it before the major feedback units could retransmit his words. Miru shivered.

"I can only assume the best," he thought aloud. "I can only act on what I have observed. I have not observed any attempt to silence me, so I must assume the taxpayer/shareholders of TritonCo support this surrender."

"Hello? Director Liu Miru?" a female voice asked in English. A response! So Pang and Dorei hadn't betrayed science for the corp or for fear. Miru resisted an urge to flip on his option box to identify the speaker, but that would destroy his progress. He was almost there....

"This is Director Miru," he answered. His feet faltered for only a moment. "Who is this?"

"He answered!" the voice said. "My name's Janus Librarse, EConaut, pilot of the EarthCo fighter *Bounty*. I can't see you. What's really going on down there?"

"If you wish to receive raw feed, contact Vice President Jon Pang at Jiru City, cardnumber NEP.01.208.3832. Have him upload the Project Hikosen files on my clearance, Hikosen-whale-city-1."

"We have information that your project is a cover for a top secret NKK weapons installation," another voice said, a sharp pitched male's. A crackle of static crossed the line momentarily, loud then hissing away.

"Study the data," Miru answered. He resumed walking. "If you need more proof, land near the coordinates I've given. Now I must continue my work here. Please do not attack."

"If you're being honest," the male said, snidely, "why won't you give us a three-verd? Let us see you and what you're doing."

"I can't," Miru explained. "The object affects the human brain in . . . odd ways, and to splice or enter into systems feedback would ruin all I've accomplished. If you decide to visit, you'll see for yourself. Out."

He snapped closed the subvocalizer by squeezing a muscle in his throat, his last link out, and took another step.

The edge of an irregularity emerged from the wall ten meters ahead, just around the edge. Miru gasped, a liquid echo in his steamed helmet. He began to run in a long loping stride that the slight Tritonian gravity had made a habit. The irregularity stretched wider, a glowing brown indentation in frosty black. Soon it showed its far side, becoming an archway.

Miru stopped before it, panting, and looked inside. Nothing was visible except a featureless glow. Even the temple had vanished. What lay within? He squeezed back on the subvocal BW.

"Pang, I've found it!" he said, loud enough for his suit's backup radio to pick up. "Pilot Librarse, I've just discovered an entrance into the object. I wish there were a way to transmit this, but what the naked eye sees here qualitatively differs from splice imagery.

"If you're interested, you'll have to visit. Please, we are on the verge of learning something great. Please do not attack. No one else has come as far as I. I fear NKK and Neptunekaisha are disinterested in pure science. If the Project dies, I fear no one will resurrect our work. This is too great a discovery to be abandoned, perhaps the greatest in human history. Please leave us alone or join the Project yourselves on my authority, but do not attack. Knowledge is so much more important than corp politics. Do you feed, *Bounty*?"

A BW flicked on in his receptor wafer, a channel hissing static like ocean waves crashing on rocks, first low-pitched and quiet, now louder, now painfully high-pitched and loud, then receding again. The pilot's voice cut through the noise.

"Director Miru? This is Janus Librarse. We're having a little trouble out here, some disagreements, but I'm working hard to make sure we don't drop anything on you. Thank you. You don't know what this means to me. Out." The static ended abruptly, as if the ocean of sound relayed directly into Miru's aural nerves had dried up before the next wave fell.

He tilted his head back in the helmet, feeling the sweaty headrest push against his shaven nape, and searched the smelted universe that encircled him and the temple. The yellow had brightened noticeably, but nowhere could he identify a spacecraft. He wondered what kind of troubles that woman EConaut was facing. He wondered what she looked like. She had a fine voice, tender tone supported by strength. She understood. She seemed ruled by reason rather than the insanity of emotion, a kindred soul.

Then he turned his attention back to the archway directly before him. Should he enter? But who was he to set foot in this place?

"I am a scientist," he declared. "If I don't explore, someone of lesser values will. Or perhaps no one will. Someone must explore."

But he couldn't take that first step. It wasn't fear for himself; no, the twinges pricking his armpits and neck weren't stopping him. He was a man in control of his emotions. What stopped him was concern over damaging the object in some way. He knew so little about it—nothing, really—yet how was anyone to learn without setting foot inside and—

"Miru!" shouted a voice, barely recognizable as Pang's. "They've launched something at us. Computer cannot predict impact because projectile is following randomized evasion trajectory, but I assume they're attacking those coordinates you broadcasted to everybody. Find cover! Immediately. We're going into the subshelters. Get as far away from the dig as you possibly can. That's an order from your superior and only friend. You're not much fun, but I'd hate to think of living on this cold little world without you. Impact in two minutes. Out!"

Miru stared into the brown shadows of the object's interior. The color reminded him of the shady reef he had often explored beneath Ryukyu Floating Island on Earth, where he had grown up. Sunlight filtered down through seaweed and windows, through human waste and industrial emission. He had spent most of his time there, alone, exploring, free of the daily trauma of life shoulder-to-shoulder with adults who wouldn't see him and youths who wouldn't leave him alone. At first opportunity, he had signed on with the representative from TritonCo Division, which soon fully expatriated and founded the sovereign TritonCo. By then, he had already spent a thousand hours on the windy icescapes of this moon, still shoulder-to-shoulder with people in an enclosed environment, but these people were scientists, like him. They had values he could respect. Jon Pang was the only person he had ever cared about, besides his parents. He was no longer alone.

Miru took a tentative step forward. The browns seemed to move, like a living thing, as if he were staring into the throat of an animal. A ludicrous thought crossed his mind: What if this object is an organism with an elaborate method of luring prey inside? But why would it project the image of a Buddhist temple to him—how was that significant to the scientist? Perhaps it represented the unknown, the magic of youth. The best way to fool a scientist would be to present him with the mystical. Then, as he tried to understand, it could eat him.

Miru drew a breath to stabilize his emotions. Absurd.

He thought of Pang. Poor Pang, ruled by his emotions. He had never learned to shake off the pain and fear of assuming the worst in everyone around him. He couldn't forget his part in putting down the Laborer's Uprising. Pang had simply killed a convicted felon in self-defense, a murderer who was serving a life sentence. But Pang couldn't accept it. Years had passed before his guilty dreams ended.

"I'm sorry, friend," Miru said, not realizing how difficult it was to say the word "friend." He couldn't remember offhand the last time he had used it. "I hope to see you soon and report my findings. I'll be safe inside the object. If not. . ." He broke off.

"I hope to see you soon," he said again. "Be careful." His voice sounded alien in his ears, softened with emotion.

EarthCo *Bounty* 5: Janus Librarse

"Hello? Director Liu Miru?" Janus asked a blank splice. She had traced the laser transmission to Jiru City on Triton.

"This is Director Miru," a man's thin voice said. "Who is this?"

"He answered!" Janus said, swinging around in her seat to face Jack. She was so accustomed to having the natural pov at the sides of a splice that it didn't bother her seeing him split in half. Jack nodded, concern on his face. No way to tell if that was genuine emotion or character work.

"My name's Janus Librarse," she said, feeding it out to the Jiru City station, "EConaut, pilot of the EarthCo fighter *Bounty*. I can't see you. What's really going on down there?"

The quiet man simply told her how to access files about the project he was supposedly working on. She immediately flicked to a non-relay code and requested access to TritonCo's databank. A pleasantly groomed Asian man bowed to her. His 3VRD hovered amid a field of glowing numbers.

"Welcome to TritonCo NetAccess," he said. "Please enter ID code and file, now." This was clearly a computer entity, an individ assistant. She entered the Vice President's ID and password and then requested the file on Project Hikosen. Raw data began gushing through her BW into the ship's server, visualized as a column of neon numbers rising toward her pov from the flat landscape. The male individ disappeared.

At the corner of her perception, Janus heard Eyes ranting. Satisfied the data transfer was going smoothly, she flicked the splice off and replaced it with the forward-sensor array 3VRD.

Computer was tracking another craft in the 90-Angstrom BW. It was moving erratically, different than the last ones. Suddenly, yet another popped into her pov, bright not only in the high frequencies but now almost visible to the whole EM spectrum. She could see four tiny craft—barely larger than torpedoes—flash across the field. Janus ordered the ship's server to track all four from current trajectories. The nearest was at five kilometers and closing.

The craft that had appeared so suddenly looped, accelerated, and instantly devoured the distance between them. In a flash that momentarily blinded Janus' sensors, it contacted the EM scoop and exploded.

Janus simultaneously shut down visual feed and ordered the computer to record in detail every microsecond of the explosion. A shockwave shook the ship. So the enemy craft they had been fighting weren't manned, but torpedoes of some kind. The other three would be in striking range within a minute. She set her card to alert her when they were close enough for her to fight.

"If you're being so honest," Eyes said jeeringly, "why won't you give us a three-verd? Let us sense you."

She flicked her splice shut and rubbed her neck.

"Stop being a 'quin, Eyes," she snapped at him, then patched back into the Triton scientist's line, not wasting mental effort to flick on his dead splice.

". . .object affects the human brain in . . . odd ways," he was saying, "and to splice or enter into systems feedback would ruin all I've accomplished. If you decide to visit, you'll see for yourself. Out."

She imagined the work that man was doing down on Triton. An alien artifact! It touched the nerve-center of her greatest passion, a fantasy of . . . no, this was her greatest passion, materialized.

She thought about the feeble astronomy she had performed during downtime on the way out, the distant solar systems she had drifted through using the ship's sensors as an overlay on recorded 3VRDs taken with the MEOS Mega Long Focal Length Camera in high orbit around Earth. The pure, slow beauty of the universe granted her peace, and its power granted her strength. Those distant worlds leisurely orbiting their home stars made no demands on her, made no fast moves. They were as solid as eternity—almost, yet just mortal enough to reveal that they were still alive. She had dreamed of wide open spaces on those worlds, free from men and their rough hands, free of organized religion, populated by gentle lifeforms like the fictional Benignus she had fallen in love with during her youth. And sometimes she studied 3VRDs of starbirth knots in nebulae, gliding her pov through blazing balls of matter that would one day coalesce into stars and planets, and perhaps some of those planets would breed life—

"Status report," Jack demanded.

She realized her astronomy program had spliced in to her pov, and quickly shut it down. She flicked over to the server's channel she had set to study the explosion, but was still haunted with imaginings of what mysteries might lay undiscovered on Triton. This show suddenly seemed a silly game.

Still, they had problems to overcome before engaging in science. She stretched her neck to both sides and focused on issues at hand, splicing in to the computer. Data from prior to the explosion formed columns down the center of her splice.

"Sir," she said, "the ships attacking us aren't ships at all but self-guided AI torpedoes manufactured by an NKK subsidiary called Z-tech."

"Artificial intelligences?" Jack asked, obviously for the benefit of their subscribers.

"Of course," she said, wanting to get on with real issues. "But the tech readouts say they're not very smart. Our ship's computer ought to be able to outsmart all three remaining torpedoes." She had an idea.

"As a matter of fact," she said, splicing into the server's symbolic representations of each external sensor and feedback transmitter, "I should be able to get inside their brains and shut them down myself."

"Good," Jack said from behind her. "Get on it."

She studied the landscape which she had programmed to look like a metallic wall of dials, readouts, buttons and LCDs. One reading disturbed her; apparently, the last explosion had knocked out the ship's scoop. They were flying into battle unshielded.

Nervous, she reached tentatively toward the fast-approaching bombs. They appeared as three cylinders of dull red light against a background of pure black, except where Neptune lay; there, reflected energy burned bright white. She began searching every available feed and feedback BW the *Bounty* could access, and at last hit on the right channel. As she did so, the three cylinders merged into one and expanded to fit her whole splice. She smiled with satisfaction. If she could do this, they were in no danger, even with a burned-out shield.

The cylinder's forward sensor arrays were visible as a patchwork of fluttering x-ray emissions, speckled white. To its left, the central processing unit, an orange box; and to the rear, the feed receiver, a grey disk. She first overloaded the CPU with a kilowatt pulse of radio from *Bounty*'s forward dish concentrated on the tiny power link, igniting it for a moment in white. When it faded to black, she turned her attention to the sensors. These resisted the next pulse, so she fired several more in varying BWs. The sensors seemed to be shielded, perhaps with a scoop like *Bounty*'s. However, she reminded herself, without a brain, these flying bombs wouldn't know when they were near target even if they had functioning sensors. Can someone see if they lack a live brain? Best of all, they wouldn't know when to explode. Danger had passed.

"Sir, our bogeys are brain-dead now," she reported, pulling out of the torpedoes she had just disabled. She watched them from a wide-angle pov. They had ceased following complicated trajectories and simply rocketed straight along their last path, diverging slightly as time passed.

"Good work, pilot," Jack commented.

Janus noted that data transfer from Triton had ceased. She dipped into it and ran the most recent 3VRD on file, splicing it in.

She was circling a mound of black material . . . no, it was the upper half of a buried sphere. A voice-over described something completely different, a shrine of some sort. She frowned. Why did religion have to play a part in this discovery? She tried to be open-minded and simply observed.

Obviously, the pov camera was a suit-mounted unit, not an implant or re-projection from the observer's neural feedback. So this is what was so remarkable about the artifact. It projected images directly into the observer's meat mind. Perhaps it was a communication device, replaying important symbols from the observer's memory? The feed garbled momentarily and was replaced by an almost identical scene, recorded several hours later.

Although this information was fascinating, it presented more questions than answers. And Janus had no time for idle speculations.

"Ready to launch the big fish," Eyes said, tearing her away from the recording. "Time to light the fuse."

Janus flipped to the script splice. Yes, as usual, Eyes was trying to get back to the script. Then she remembered that they were not just play-acting—when they fired a missile, they really fired a missile, and it eventually detonated. A wave of panic rushed through her.

"Why?" she demanded in a murderous voice. She flicked off headfeed and glared at Eyes. The files about the artifact could wait. He didn't answer.

"Who are we shooting at?" she asked, then faced Jack. Her eyes narrowed. She wouldn't sit idle while her crewmates destroyed the greatest discovery in the history of the race. "If you attack Triton, I'll—"

"Don't worry, pi-lot," Eyes said, gratingly. "This one's for NKK. Watch the fireworks."

"It's okay," Jack reassured her. "Ignition in ten, nine, eight. . ." he counted, nodding to her. His eyes held that disarming look he sometimes gave her when she had lost her grip, when she most hated the universe of humans. Of all the men she had met in EConaut service, only Jack could comfort her with a look. Miguel had done that, once or twice, when she was a teen. But that was a long time ago.

She drew a deep breath, held it, released it. She felt recentered, rebalanced.

"Fire!" Jack ordered.

Over their heads, a rocket engine screamed so loudly Janus had to tap down her audio feed. The heavy torpedo screeched along the metal of its launch tube. Moments later, only the faint hiss of exhaust told a massive ordnance had just been fired.

Janus hurriedly flicked back into *Bounty*'s server, found the torpedo's pov feedback, and tapped in. She spliced in the computer controls and fed the data through its processors, asking to plot a trajectory. Moments later it overlaid a bell curve showing probable targets. Each was inside Neptune's atmosphere. She relaxed. The alien artifact—if indeed that's what it was—was not in danger.

She shut down all splices and overlays except for the pov camera of the newly launched torpedo, racing headlong with it toward Neptune. The gas giant spread across three quarters of her field of view. She sighed. Cool blue traced with pale streaks. So majestic, so peaceful.

A thought crept in and spoiled her peace: People lived and worked in that atmosphere. People the scriptwriters at Feedcontrol had tagged "enemy." People who, if they couldn't knock out the torpedo in time, if their defenses were already spent, were about to lose one of their fusion reactors. But there was no room for pity aboard a war vessel.

Her thoughts were interrupted.

"Pilot Librarse," the TritonCo scientist said into her ear; she had forgotten to shut down his channel since it wasn't vid tagged or spliced. His voice was energized with excitement. Janus switched off the Neptune pov and spliced in the recorded 3VRD of the object, listening to the scientist while looking at the artifact near him. It rested at the bottom of a ditch—no, an excavation.

"I've just discovered an entrance into the object," he said.

Janus' attention surged. She closed her eyes, shutting away her natural pov, listening. The bombardier wove a backdrop of cannon fire.

"Got another one," Eyes declared.

"I wish there were a way to transmit this," the scientist continued, "but what the naked eye sees here qualitatively differs from splice imagery. If you're interested, you'll have to visit. Please, we are on the verge of learning something great. Please do not attack. No one else has come as far as I. I fear NKK and Neptunekaisha are disinterested in pure science. If the Project dies, I fear no—"

But the rest of his words were drowned out by a shattering explosion that began in the floorplates at her feet, drove through her bones as if someone were pounding her ankles and shins with a mag-hammer, and crushed her thighs and back into the gelfoam of her pilot's couch. Then followed a flood of sound, registering in her brain as the equivalent of whitenoise. And then ceased the feeling of gravity that went along with deceleration. She floated up from her couch, rebounding off the flat ceiling with the equal and opposite force of the explosion.

When she flicked on the external sensors that had been tracking the disabled missiles, she realized her mistake. The missiles had been redirected, clearly from an outside operator. She hadn't considered that potential. Only someone who had spent a lifetime living inside machine intelligences could possibly have gotten into those braindead rockets and taken manual control. Two had snuck up in the shelter of the ship's exhaust and detonated nearly within its nozzle. The last was still on its way, closing the gap fast.

"Do you feed, *Bounty*?" a man's voice hissed in her head. Outside her head, another man screamed like a wild animal. Eyes.

Everything was going to pieces. One hope remained. One bit of knowledge gave her strength: Even if *Bounty* were destroyed, even if she died, at least the alien artifact would survive. With that knowledge—with the knowledge that humans had just uncovered the first proof of extranthopic life—she could die in peace.

Though not yet prepared to die, though she wanted to see the artifact herself, Janus felt grateful to that distant Asian man. She set to work preparing defenses and contingency plans.

EarthCo *Bounty* 6: Lonny Marshfield

"Bitch!" you shriek, floating near the ceiling.

What has she done? Are you going to die? No, you can't die now. No, Daddy, your boy won't die. Too many plans, too many things left undone. She can't steal your whole future.

"I thought you said you'd disabled those torpedoes." You thrash ineffectually against the cabin's air. "This is what we get for buying into NKK's trickery. A science project, shit! This proves your Nik buddy is a liar."

You finally right yourself, pushing off the resilient ceiling. You land in a seat and strap in. Do it now, if for nothing else but revenge.

"Cap'n, launching big fish two," you say, voice scalding hot in your throat. Your finger lances out. In the corner of your right optic you see bitch coming at you.

A reaction! She wants to kill you. She knows you're mailing the Dark Angel to her precious Nik down on Triton. She still believes the weapons installation is some spacefuck treasure. You've finally gotten into her head.

Well, she's too late. Your fingertip feels the spring loaded button sink in its panel. Screech and thunder as the second heavy fish tears free of its overhead berth. The angular thrust from its launch makes Janus drift past you, fingernails raking the back of your seat with a dull scrabbling sound.

You switch on a rectangular display in the center of your left eye and enter the torpedo's mind. It's warm in there, smelly like the inside of an oil drum. You program a guard to stand watch over its systems, a slick red cock pulsing with purple veins. Bitch will stay well clear of your missile's mind. You know all about her retro aversion to sex. Maybe she can manage to ignore her disgust and try to push past, but she'll be distracted from noticing the second defense as it burns her card.

"Suck on this, Niks!" you tell the sneaky little men on Triton. Bitch will figure out a second meaning when she enters the fish. She crouches on the back wall, getting ready to pounce.

Time for the next step in your plan, the one nobody has suspected. To make sure it's still worthwhile, you take a millisecond to reaffirm that the *Bounty*'s still transmitting the goods to Feedcontrol. Yes. A grin tightens the tendons in your neck. Then you check tactical data. Not so good. *Bounty* has slowed down too much to escape Neptune's gravity field, and it's approaching dangerously close to Triton.

No matter. You can deal with that in a moment.

You unsling your particluster subgun and aim it at Cap'n Jack. Your knees hold you in position against the armrest.

"Smile, Janus darling," you tell her while staring into Cap'n's green eyes. Your glorious father had eyes nearly that color. The trigger mechanism tightens against your finger.

"What are you doing, Lonny?" Cap'n asks. He seems remarkably calm for having such firepower pointed at his intestines. One of the ship's systems crackles; you taste it at the back of your mind as burnt copper.

"I think that's perfectly clear," you tell him, and turn your attention to bitch. "Wouldn't you say?" you ask her.

"Don't be a 'quin," she says.

What kind of response is that? Assume just simple defiance; anything more might distract you.

"Be reasonable, Lonny," Cap'n says. "Maybe you didn't notice, but we're disabled, adrift in enemy space. We've got to work together."

Aren't they taking you seriously? Oh, it's been too long since anyone has taken you seriously.

The last time was in Boston. That cocksucker only took you seriously after you taught him about the razor's edge between sensation and pain. He had thought it would be charming to seduce intheflesh a man feeling the fires of loneliness after having nerve-enhancement surgery. Surgery plays with a man's mind. It makes him vulnerable. Daddy was a surgeon. . . .

You had met in a chembar for those who liked to go places intheflesh. He had lapped up the scent of your vulnerability and led you to his apartment, 112 stories above the cracked pavement of Boston. He had shown you a real window that looked out over the city. He had held you in his warm, strong arms. He had asked you to tell him all about your feelings. Then he had spliced into your mind and shoved his 3VRD individ inside. He had laughed at your protests. He had climbed in with his individ, the two of them plucking freshly implanted circuits like piano wires, laughing every time you said no, you screamed no. At first, you had been too weak from the surgery to resist. Then, when they had your insides splayed open and were rubbing their sandy fingers across your grey matter, you had found the strength to trap them.

You had remembered your father, almost more than you should remember. You had located that germ of pain at your core and used it to seize them in a 3VRD fist inside your head. The individ had shattered almost immediately, its female likeness crumbling to splinters of silicon, sparkling at your feet in the red light of rage. He had looked down at the fragments and stopped laughing.

That afternoon, you learned an encyclopedia of things about your new skills. Over the years, you haven't forgotten; no, you've practiced since then.

The bridge of the *Bounty* is quiet. You hear every servo whirr, every electronic hum, the hush of ventilation, every breath from your crewmates. Smoke and sweat tickle your nostrils with the metallic scent of panic. Bitch puts a hand on the back of her seat and swings her legs slowly over it so she's almost sitting. Cap'n rises from his and slips his hand around the grip of his pistol.

"You don't take me seriously, do you," you say, incredulous. You automatically flick on your cardbusting feedback program and swim through *Bounty*'s server until you find an open channel into Cap'n's head. There, you see the tiny 3VRD self-representation every man stores in his mind. It stands erect in a valley surrounded by towering mounds of memory piled so thick you can't get clear resolution of any of them. Of course—no one can see another man's memories. You back out and overlay the puny image atop his natural one; it fits in a wrinkle on his forehead.

"Tell me how this feels," you say to him, extending a metalslick probe into the miniature Cap'n's midsection.

Bitch looks at Cap'n. Grimacing, he nods and pulls himself into his seat. They're up to something. You place your other hand on the subgun's front grip and—

Neptunekaisha 4: C.P. Chang

Victory smelled like the smoke of her enemy's ruined spaceship. Revenge tasted like fire: blood on the tongue, blisters on the gums.

Clarisse had fooled *Bounty*'s computers and crew. She had disabled their ship. But they had gotten off an escape pod or cruiser-class torpedo. She punched up magnification of the new launch.

When she isolated its brightest emission, her heart froze. It was a virtual beacon of gamma rays.

"They fired a nuclear missile at us," she said aloud. Unbelievable. Nukes were outlawed nearly a century prior. Of course, most sovereignties and worlds maintained a few for defensive purposes, but this was an offensive missile.

She called up a battery of obsolete hunters and sent them after the nuke. It was still accelerating. None of the hunters within striking distance could possibly intercept it at that speed if it had any brain at all for maneuvering, but she had to use the resources at hand. She also polarized the mines lying like a spherical fence in a thin veneer around Neptune. They would detonate even if the missile were barely in damage radius, with enough advance timing so their shockwaves of ionized plasma would stand like a wall of fire before the missile. She sent orders to each station to charge up their tube cannons. She transferred dual control of most AI defenses to herself. She initialized the destroyer, *Sigwa*, in case.

Tapping into a calculus program, she concluded that none of the stations would be destroyed by the missile. But it might explode close enough to one for its EM pulse to burn out the station's entire net. It might even destroy a power station.

She cursed herself for not preparing a greater defensive array against the intruder. Hadn't EarthCo Feedcontrol told her this renegade was a war-tattered wreck? Hadn't they said it was armed with only two magazines of torpedoes? That it fired only one particle cannon? They had transmitted a dense file of data on its offensive batteries, but they had omitted a high-g nuclear missile. Oh, yes, that must have been an oversight. Lovely EarthCo, always my dear friend.

The answer was tediously clear: EarthCo had once again stabbed her with its barbed tongue. I was a fool to trust them - even though the only trust she offered was accepting their data.

Deeply enmeshed with dozens of servers and halfwit systems, Clarisse felt a snarl curl her physical lips.

Breathe, Clarisse. Don't let anger destroy you; breathe.

Hope sprang up: This might not be the disaster it appeared to be. Much data was now being gathered. Nikolai had taught Clarisse that she must contain her anger and think.

She thought. No, this would not be a disaster at all. Clarisse would prove that EarthCo had intentionally misinformed Neptunekaisha Security and NKK itself so they could send in a warship fitted with a nuclear weapon. They had intended to attack and destroy extremely valuable NKK property for some undefined military advantage. Nuclear weapons could not be picked up just anywhere; it had to have been in the initial inventory.

EarthCo was attempting to gain a foothold on NKK property.

This attack would be the end of the long peace between NKK and EarthCo. The Sotoi Guntai forces aboard Neptunekaisha's flying stations would join forces with her without hesitation; the military had long been anxious to free itself from civilian rule. They knew the true purpose of Neptunekaisha, as military outpost. News would spread to other units of the Sotoi Guntai on other worlds, all the way back to Moonbase and Earth. They would strike as one against EarthCo, a whip cracking across the entire Solar System.

The bad hate dissipated and the good hate gave her power. Clarisse imagined a glorious new period of war, where she could tear out EarthCo's organs one by one for murdering her family on Makkau, the Pacific Rim isle where she had lived for ten years. Clarisse would finally have her revenge on the corp that had then forced her into a foster family, a vulgarly sweet EarthCo household on the Russian steppes where her siblings had hated her and beat her mercilessly intheflesh and in VR games. Oh, dear Ivan, how you have destroyed EarthCo.

She had grown lightning-fast and strong, always nurturing a coal of hatred in her heart that had given her the strength to defeat, one by one, those who had hurt her. Ivan slowly became nothing more than a bully who knew he stood no chance against her in his games. His slapping palms felt like nothing. Clarisse felt no pain any longer.

On one cool morning of her sixteenth year, she had realized that she had freed herself. She burned the family's server and several of the siblings' cards. Ivan's last moments had been pure writhing pleasure. After that she fought her way for five cold, bloody weeks across the plains and mountains to Bangkok. There she had joined the most powerful aggressive force she could imagine: the NKK Sotoi Guntai. At boot camp in the marshes of Cambodia, she had earned top ratings. At graduation from suit camp in the Earth orbital facility of Shuki, she wore the platinum helmet-strip of series honorman.

Now she would write history. Her name would be scribed indelibly on the tablet of human flesh, in blood. The Sotoi Guntai had for decades been searching for a legitimate excuse to strike against EarthCo. Their private motto was "Push limits, break through." They had been massing their might in the atmospheres and on the moons of the Outer Planets, and had attempted to build up Phobos Base, which this very intruder had debilitated.

Clarisse would provide the excuse. The evidence against EarthCo would knock a hole through the levee that had been holding back all-out war. The destruction that was about to befall Neptunekaisha's property would be that first break, which would soon spread wide, allowing the flood of war to surge through.

Her mind returned to *Bounty*. "Live," she said, and predetonated the final hunter just close enough to send a shockwave of hot gas and debris against their hull. To remind them of her. They would be a lovely first target for her followers, who would need something at which to strike right away.

A winking light attracted her attention. She flicked on the feed for that BW.

So, another nuclear missile had been fired, this one at Triton. The first had been a decoy, most likely never expected to make it through Neptunekaisha's defenses. The second . . . well, TritonCo was just a protectorate, after all. EarthCo might be daring enough to attack one of NKK's protectorates; they had done it often enough before, as on Phobos.

Clarisse scanned the access channels to this BW and dropped dams at each entry. The missile would reach its target. Then she erased record of having tracked the second rocket, then erased record of the erasure.

Next, she pulled out of the pack of hunters she had sent after the first nuclear missile. Let them do their work without her help. She called one of them out of formation and flicked inside its pov. At the proper moment—preferably at the last possible moment—she would make sure the nuclear bomb's damage was limited. Because, if she failed completely as Coordinator of Protection, her master plan would never see the red of blood. She must maintain their respect.

She had to play each move just right. Timing would be everything. Then shatter the peace, set free the flood of revenge.

The nuclear missile emerged undamaged through the net of stationary mines. Good; that means it is protected against plasma, and will survive the first few blasts from tube cannons. Her little hunter would rendezvous with it just before it struck home. She would be credited with personally saving a station.

Good, good; only a hero could press forward plans such as hers.

Clarisse's mind sizzled with activity, running half a dozen programs at once. She danced in her element, energized by the inhuman fierceness of laser-like focus, driving her hate rather than being driven by it.

Triton 3: Liu Miru

"I'm stepping inside the object's apparent entryway," Miru stated. Within, the impression of organic motion increased.

He took a deep breath and strode forward. The corner of his eye caught a brightening in one part of the melted horizon.

"That would be our attackers," he said, sadly. He almost stopped and turned back— he felt a foolish sort of guilt for abandoning his brothers and sisters during their time of danger, especially Pang—but the inside of the object would be the safest place to wait out the storm, anyway. They would need someone unhurt who could assist them in whatever emergency relief they might need. By himself, he could do nothing against the energies released in a nuclear reaction. I am sorry, dear Pang. I will return to you as soon as I am able.

He took another step. One boot crossed beyond the edge of the wall. A tingling sensation ran up his leg. A final step. His body moved within the confines of the archway. The brown tunnel around him constricted and stretched infinitely long, hissing with the sound of a jet streaking away.

He felt himself shatter, disperse. He began to scream in rising wavelengths of light and other radiations. No one answered.

FOUR: Earth

Fury 2

Nadir leaped from the car while it was still decelerating, rifle across his chest. His boots sank ankle-deep into the cool sand. A few seconds later, he was running behind the car, using it as a shield while he got his bearings and sized up the tall stone fortress. Almost unconsciously, Nadir ordered his three grenadiers to launch sonic grenades inside the walls, to soften up the opposition.

The fort rose like a computer button silhouetted against the bright horizon, a trigger ready to be depressed. It looked ancient in form—various blocky rooftops were just visible beyond the girdle wall, mud-brick archways joining them—but modern in condition. None of the stone blocks were chipped, the corners were sharp where walls joined, the crenellation was crisply defined like peg-teeth biting the sky. The only visible openings were peaked windows shaped like Medieval arrow-slits.

Nadir smiled, savoring this ripe mouthful of life just before what would surely be their heaviest engagement, listening to the monopera surge through his mind. The lyrics had begun to mutate; the program would soon reach its climax, and then its end. By definition, a monopera must not change substantially from one day to the next, must remain fixed in a transcendent moment. Once it begins to stray from its orchestrated form, once the singers begin to toy with the preset lyrics, it ceases to be a monopera. This piece's popularity must have begun to wane; one sure way to dramatically, though temporarily, increase subscriptions is to alter a monopera. Everyone wants to watch the death of a great piece of art. Nadir sighed.

"Tactical position Gamma!" Jhishra's suddenly appearing avatar bellowed. It vanished just as quickly, a flicker of virtual life to accompany a burst of verbal static.

Nadir slowed from a jog to a walk to a motionless crouch behind the bulletproof car's curved flank, twenty meters from the six-meter-high walls. He watched Paolo climb into the stowage area behind the seats, near the supplies, and settle with his rifle pointed up at the sand-colored walls. The unit's other cars spread out siege-style, encircling the 100-meter base of the structure. The heavy EMMA-B atop the Boss' truck swiveled toward the top of the wall. When all were still, Jhishra 3-verded again.

"Niks assuming firing positions! Fire at will, firefight code one."

Nadir frowned, blinking, then realized Jhishra was right. Yellow Sotoi Guntai uniforms lined the wall, visible between the thick crenellation. At least 50 of them, rifles pointed down at the unit. Nadir hadn't noticed them a moment ago. He frowned and ran a quick fumigator-program through his chip to rid his card of the apparent camouflage feed, then prepared to fight.

Crack-thup, eighteen EMMAs whined simultaneously like a plague of locusts chewing at the smooth walls. Enemy soldiers toppled down one after another, disappearing behind their ramparts as shaped ceramics slipped through their bodies. Their few particle rifles screamed and common powder-guns boomed down upon the spines the desert had grown overnight. Still they died, their weapons falling impotently to the ground where time would eventually bury them in sand. Sometimes the weapons' users tumbled afterward to lie crooked among the weeds that cowered near the walls.

Nadir chose targets and fired, fired, consumed by the monopera and its mechanical military accompaniment, reveling in this validation of life. A quick scan told him all his boys were still unharmed. Target, one-second burst, verify kill; target. . . .

Waves of subsonic thunder rippled the ground beneath Nadir's feet—sonic grenades pulping the core of the fortification. Nadir had an image of expanding perspectives, first watching himself from above, then jumping out to the next magnitude of perspective, seeing the circle of EarthCo warriors focused on their momentary all-consuming interest; then the next magnitude in which everyone was merely a tiny lead soldier melting one another on a clean expanse of sand, glittering in the hot yellow sunshine; shells upon shells, the monopera building along the sound-receptive neurons in his brain, the lyric *crack-thup* of his boys' rifles, the bass drum of grenades, gunpowder drumrolls, even the tympanic thunder of a mortar digging a ditch near one of the cars.

Nadir realized he had subconsciously engaged an overlay program; he watched the termination of life through what felt like his own eyes, yet this overlaid omniscient pov somehow seemed more real, seemed to encompass an essential truth mere flesh-eyes could not grasp. Surely, this was their server's representation of how this scene would appear from several hundred meters in the air, or maybe even an extreme zoom from an intelligence satellite. This is probably what subscribers to their feed could see if they chose to watch the battle as a whole. Nadir didn't care, didn't question beyond that momentary wonder; he only targeted and pulled the trigger. To do more was to approach death.

"Breach at [110°]," one of the soldiers' avatar stated, though the number was the computer's modification, assuring each soldier received the proper figure for his own location.

"Move in!" Jhishra cried, his image stern and stolid.

"Out of the car, with me," Nadir called to Paolo. He didn't wait for the boy to follow as he sprinted away from the car's shelter toward the specified breach. He shut down the broad pov overlay and concentrated on the physical, running close along the base of the wall to make it difficult for enemies overhead to fire on him.

He rounded a corner and saw shattered stone strewn out from a gaping hole in the wall. Intheflesh voices and 3VRDs, weapons and calamity, merged in an incomprehensible tangle of sounds and orders. As he ran nearer, Nadir smelled the sharp tang of burned TEST, a high-explosive well-suited to such jobs as blowing walls.

He strode over the pile of rubble, glorying in the thick heat pumping through his thighs—validation of powerful, living muscles. He picked his landing carefully among blocks blown inward and quickly found cover behind a stone buttress that arched upward, out of sight. Cracked sandstone shielded his front from attack while the enemy's own structure protected three other sides. He was only vulnerable from the left and above.

Something went wrong with his vision; he couldn't see the heavy walls for a moment. His left hand felt the cold, gritty stone before him; his knees felt sand and sharp pebbles where he knelt; he smelled the TEST and his own days-old sweat; tasted the paste he had eaten on the drive to battle, a vitamin-rich base which his headcard had made taste like steak and eggs; he heard shouts and screams and gunpowder cracks and electromagnetic discharges, heard hard rubber bootsoles scraping against stone and sand, but Nadir couldn't see anything except a cloudy brown.

He blinked several times, shaking his head, and thought he saw a crowd of dark-skinned men and women screaming and running mob-fashion, aimlessly, into one another and in all directions at once. But they were hazy, indistinct, as in a dream. They wore glowing halos like bad 3VRDs. They moved jerkily, slowly. They were images captured on film from some non-requested subscription, some subterfuge feed run in slow-motion, every other frame edited out.

Nadir cursed under his breath, again debugging his chip. Another damned electronic-warfare program, he assumed. Like the first time, a month ago; like a few minutes ago, a boy in the sand. . . . The virus lingered only a second, however, and he at last was able to survey the interior of the fortress.

It was constructed of squat buildings piled atop one another, each rising higher like steps and blending into the girdle wall so that their roofs were at a level with the crenellation. Open, pointed archways gaped from every structure—mouths of blackness hiding NKK soldiers. Nadir flicked on an infrared-sensitive program to enhance the view through his gunsight.

There they hid, the enemy, peering out from every crevice. He targeted and fired, listening to his boys do the same, listening to a swelling discordance in the monopera, firing and terminating enemies. He fought for life, he fought for EarthCo, he fought for Paolo, he even fought for himself. Along with the other 30 EarthCo units crossing the desert, Hardman Nadir's unit was furthering EarthCo's plan to secure northern Africa so trade could be safely pursued in the Mediterranean and the southern, EarthCo-controlled portion of Africa. He thought all these things while his rifle whined and spat tiny slivers of ceramic through the flesh of men who stood in the way of the world's safety.

His eye began to twitch. No, not men. These targets were what stood in the way of peace in Africa, of free trade in the seas surrounding it. These were mere tags. No, more than that and less than that: These were tiny increments to overcome on the way to EarthCo's ultimate victory.

A part of his mind receded to another time, half a world away, when he was only a boy himself on one of his first missions.

Yesteryear 2: Hardman Nadir

His unit had engaged heavy resistance for so long, for weeks, in a tropical rainstorm that had lasted nearly as long. He had grown delirious, as had several other of the boys. He couldn't even remember where they were, only that it was some treeless mound of stone in the middle of the ocean, a numbered rock among the Marshall Islands. They had been pinned beneath the porous lavarock, in caverns they had dug with mines and high explosives. They were drowning as the rain slowly rose around their ankles, then up to their knees, until finally they had to sleep standing up or balled up in fetal position atop boxes of equipment.

Bugs whose carapaces glistened like oil swirled around his pantlegs. The water stank like piss and excrement and curdled blood. His toes burned with fungal infection and rot. They had only the light provided by headfeed to brighten their tomb. Not surprisingly, half the unit receded into feedrapture; most of those eventually drowned by incautiously falling asleep or were destroyed from within by pneumonia or other assorted illnesses. And it had been weeks. Weeks. This battle had begun to earn one of the lowest subscription-ratings ever recorded.

Because of that, one woman kept muttering, "They've got to end this soon. No one's watching. Why drag it out? They've got to end this soon. . ."

Occasionally, one of his cavern-mates climbed screaming from their self-dug grave only to be punched full of holes by Niks waiting offshore in their patrol boats. But even the enemy was weak in firepower, so each side stood helpless, trapped in a tortuous stalemate. At long last the battle reached its climax.

One of the Big Bosses in EarthCo's military component had decided this unit deserved attention, even with the low ratings, and the entire NKK siege-group had been blasted from the water in an airstrike that lit up the rainy night like Fourth of July, a blazing wall of thunder and fire surrounding the islet with red liquid curtains, velvet and shrapnel, blood and napalm.

At that moment, watching the dance of flames, Nadir realized that these weeks of suffering had been exactly what he wanted. Not the pain, not the horror of watching his comrades die—but battle, the abstracts of life and death clashing swords with one another over each man and woman . . . abstracts become concrete. He had joined up with the EarthCo Warriors to escape stifling life on mainland EarthCo, in Wolf Point, Montana. Nothing there mattered to him, not even his parents who lived exclusively in feed.

Nadir was 14 when his mother was taken away for feedrapture treatment, and she never returned. He didn't seek her out, not even when he'd become a citizen, mainly because his father never spoke of her again. The only solid image of Wolf Point that he carried through life was of his mother, being carried away by two men in white jumpsuits wearing black masks over their faces. Wires sprouted from the sides of the masks, and a sort of antenna bounced in the air above each.

Nadir's mother was a short woman with dark skin and hair, but even her natural coloring couldn't hide the pallor that had consumed her over the years. Now, as she was lifted from the gel-pillows in the living room, her bones strained against the skin, her mouth fell slack and revealed yellow teeth, her head lolled back. She didn't say a word, not even in 3VRD. She looked dead. Young Nadir thought he would cry out, but he didn't. Everything was too quiet, only soft footsteps and the sounds of cloth, and he couldn't bear to shatter such solemn silence. That would be like killing something, and he was still to young to kill. After a moment, all he could hear was the gurgle of the pillows as they formed back into disks. That, and a distant sort of hush from the everpresent prairie winds.

Nadir's father didn't say a word, didn't even stir from his desk near the window—oddly, the man seemed to be staring out at the rolling plains and desert-like wheatfields that carpeted them in straggly patches. Dust rose in dervishes like tornadoes from a type of ground that could grow no life.

The latch creaked. The door opened. The men carried a woman outside. The door clicked shut. The wind sounded like a distant scream, muffled and indistinct. Silence.

Two minutes, three. . . . Nadir waited as long as he could. When he heard the rising whine of the ambulance's motor, his chest tightened and filled with anger. He felt so hollow within, the fury and confusion so dense, that he believed one more second of standing still would make him explode.

He ran across the house and threw open the door. The wind tasted dry. Dust got in his eyes and made them water. His chest heaved with the exertion of not being able to do anything. And then the ambulance rose from the dusty earth against a backdrop of tan and grey landscape, stone and rock bluffs hulking above poor fields. Out here, the vast tracts of land used to grow crops were not fenced in as in the Midwest—here, pockets of wheat stood bare, swaying in the wind. This was utter isolation from the world: No one lived for hours around, except the retro Amerinds on their rotting reservation, the farmers who owned Wolf Point, and those few folks who worked for the farmers. Nadir's father worked for one of them, but Nadir had no idea what the man did. Whatever it was, he could work entirely at home by feed and feedback. He didn't know what kind of farm work was done that way.

The ambulance jetted skyward, its ancient, poorly maintained alcohol-jet drawing a twisting trail of black soot against the washed-out blue. Nadir stood on the steps of the tenant house, one foot higher than the other, every muscle in his body taut, his fists clenched, heart racing, breathing deep and fast, and he vowed right then:

"Never . . . that'll never happen to me. I'll never be like Mom, or Dad, or anyone in this lousy town! I'll make a difference in the world. I swear, and if I don't, I'll die instead." At the receding silver disk of the ambulance, he screamed, "I'd rather die than live like them!"

For years to come, during his search for a purpose, this single scene of his life stood out like a silver coin on a field of ashes. All the rest simply faded into a blur of sandy ground and wheat and a silent house. Whenever he thought of this moment, his chest would tighten with a yearning—he knew, absolutely knew that his purpose lay just over the next hill of life-experience. But it was horrible how life seemed to whip past. One day in his 18th year, watching edufeed about the new war in the Pacific, Nadir had a revelation.

Three months later, after EarthCo Warrior boot camp in Arkansas, he joined a detachment in Hawaii. Twenty months after that, a wall of fire danced around one islet in the Marshalls, then Nadir was evacuated with the other wounded. In the ambulance jet, Nadir had smiled: This jet was taking him toward something rather than away . . . he was engulfed in a purposeful life, and he had made it happen. He had made it happen. He had left behind the slow sleepy death of insulated life back home, where Dad was nestled in a cocoon of 3VRD. Nothing was real back there, nothing was real anywhere at all except on the battlefront. Yet he would fight until his death to preserve EarthCo . . . or was it only himself he was fighting for? Had he only chosen to fight for EarthCo because he was not as much a thinking man as others who seemed to know exactly why they did things? Was he only fighting for EarthCo because, otherwise, he would be fighting himself?

But none of that mattered. He had sought adventure, and by god, he had gotten it! He had left behind emptiness and filled his life with adventure. He had to fight for something or else he'd die. So he was alive. Even those dark moments in the cave during the Marshalls battle . . . if he could go back and change things, he would choose that suffering again over the insulation of Wolf Point. Knowing that assured him that the life he was pursuing was right and that such suffering was an insignificant price to pay to be alive.

Two months after his evacuation from the islet, after a thorough bio-upgrade at one of the VA hospitals, a trio of Generals had presented Nadir a panel of awards to hang on his dress uniform. Simply for surviving the ordeal. He had helped "reestablish EarthCo presence in the Marshalls, guaranteeing safe trade in the North Pacific." The medals against his chest were the culmination of his life, the tangible proof that he had chosen the right path. He had not escaped Wolf Point; rather, he had sought exactly this new life and risen above the decay.

Four months after that, in a pitched firefight in northern India, he began to see the Sotoi Guntai—NKK's military elite—as mere targets, and he had begun to see NKK's general soldiership as insects. After all, weren't his enemy choosing life as much as he? Ignoring their kinship kept the adventure from becoming painful, kept the battles just that—battles—and not murders. Indeed, his mind often overlaid memories of the bugs swirling around his boots, swimming beneath the surface and filling his legs with the pus the VA nurses had drained from him for weeks afterward. . . . Enemy soldiers ceased to be men or women, they ceased even to be human. They became equated with the suffering he had endured on that flooded islet a thousand miles from reinforcements, no more or less than the bugs he had fought there. They were the reason men like Nadir's father were trapped in their headcards, a disease vector, and to rid the Earth of NKK would be to save men like his father and women like his mother.

When each battle ended, he punched his tags into the bodies of the dead marks. They were "meat," as the young recruits termed bodies. And the feed helped. He had to fight; that was the only path. When fighting began to feel like murder, feed made everything all right; it was good food, bright targets, bedtime lullabies that fought back nightmares—it was even, sometimes, a woman. Feed helped.

Fury 3

Nadir listened to the monopera as he emptied one bullet cartridge. In a fluid motion, in symphony with the rhythm in his head, he disengaged the empty cartridge, withdrew another from where it was clasped to his belt, snapped it into place with a plastic click, and continued to target and fire.

At some point, Nadir realized the resistance had become increasingly sporadic. He set his rifle against the rock in front of him and looked across the squarish courtyard. Marks lay strewn everywhere, in archways, on mud-brick staircases that crossed from level to level like bridges; hanging from windows. The morning sun still hadn't risen high enough to light more than a ragged line along the inside of the western wall. Nadir studied the bright yellow stone, his brow furrowing when he noticed that the blocks of stone were set together almost perfectly, like an ancient Egyptian Pharaoh's temple or tomb.

Feeling safe now, he rose and stepped out into the courtyard. An odd thought struck him now: Why would NKK place such a well-made fortress in the middle of the desert? What did it house? And why had it been so easy to defeat?

"Find anything important?" he 3-verded to the boys. Paolo ran up alongside him, breathing furiously, his face beaming. Three or four other warriors' avatars overlaid his pov.

"We cleaned it out!" Paolo declared.

Only the *crack-thup* of EMMAs echoed against the hard walls now. No resistance.

"Found the commander of this place," the Polish girl stated. "We're ready to interrogate."

Nadir hurriedly scanned for the boy's position, then overlaid it on the physical structure around him. There, on ground level, to the right. He raced across the fleshy courtyard, through an archway, and into a shadowed room. Paolo followed on his heels.

"Where's Jhishra?" Nadir demanded.

"Haven't seen him, subbs," one of the Canadians answered in muted tones, intheflesh. "You know he doesn't come out of that truck until the fighting's done."

"Boss," Nadir 3-verded to Jhishra, "we have the leader here. How about an interrogation?"

"On my way," the ephemeral statue of the unit's Boss replied.

Nadir shut down his 3VRD and drew a deep breath. Besides Paolo, four other warriors milled about the dark room with him. Outside a window-slit that passed only a sliver of yellow light, a desert bird chirped a single note over and over. A light breeze hissed through the window. A skinny man clad in NKK golds lay on the floor, scuffing his boots against the sand that lay across the packed dirt; his breathing was ragged, and he muttered what could only be curses in a foreign tongue.

Nadir looked away from the man—no, the mark—and peered back into the courtyard, ablaze with light in contrast to the dark room. His men shouted and laughed, occasionally firing their EMMAs into the air or at random into the fortifications looming around them. High-pitched twangs sounded as rounds ricocheted off the stone. Somewhere nearby, a female voice cried out. Nadir's eye-twitch returned.

Jhishra and his two-man guard finally walked through the breach in the wall, the furiously decorated man looking unusually small when framed by the ragged stone gouge. The guards carried their rifles at an angle across their chests, respectfully tilted away from the Boss. When Jhishra stumbled over the body of a mark, Nadir noticed a mismatch between the glorious image and Jhishra's real self.

Nadir's lips curled back in a spiteful smile as he remembered Jhishra never went anywhere without projecting a self overlay so anyone observing him would see only the image.

"Took you long enough," Nadir said as Jhishra reached the archway leading into the room.

"What's that, boy?" the Boss responded, acid in his voice. His eyes flashed through the projected calm of his overlay.

"This is the fort's commander," the Polish girl said quickly.

Jhishra turned his attention to the prone body and fired off several rapid sentences in a language Nadir didn't recognize. The Nik responded only with a few words and then spat. Jhishra straightened and backed away from the enemy commander.

"He doesn't know anything," the Boss declared, then drew his ceremonial gunpowder-pistol from a leather and silver holster and fired a heavy slug into the mark's head.

Nadir's stomach muscles tightened. He walked out of the room, onto the packed dirt of the courtyard. Warriors ran up and down the stairways like children reveling in a new day, drinking the hard liquor of death, pumping their veins full of a substance Nadir had taught them to call "life." Here, a man could lay his hands on his soul. In a dead place like Wolf Point, he could only dream electronic dreams of other men's souls and imagine he were they. No, Nadir hadn't gone that route. He had escaped. This was what he wanted, and, dammit, he would relish every painful moment.

Walking toward an unoccupied staircase, he slung his rifle over his shoulder and plugged its power cord into a fresh unit at his hip. Once he had reached the top of the steps, he stepped onto the platform that ringed the compound, the top of the wall, and looked out across the gentle rolls of the land. He could see hazy mountains in the distance. In other directions, small cities sprawled across the desert, ruins of war machinery littered the sand, and, nearby, tracks led from a dark crater to parked vehicles surrounding this fortress. The sun warmed his cheek and his blue, short-sleeved uniform.

Nadir looked down at the stone beneath his feet and was again struck by the strangeness of building such a perfect structure in the middle of nowhere.

"Search for anything important," he 3-verded to the boys, certain this place had been chosen as an objective for some reasonable purpose.

"There's nothing here worth our time," Jhishra said. "If we've gotten all the marks, lay tags before anything else. Now!"

Nadir turned to watch the boys scurry from their former play to start tagging the fallen soldiers. Again the arguments, again the fistfights over whose tag was laid first.

He began to descend the steps, tired now that the adrenaline was wearing off. Drawing his tag-gun, he walked to the marks nearest him, those he had not seen already tagged, and fired. The tiny needles hissed from the pistol and punctured the marks' uniforms. He spliced in battle data, watching the average tally for the men rise, and tagged marks who had fallen in hidden corners—enough to keep him above average. The unit's total reached 210 before leveling off. Nadir stopped tallying after thirteen. His stomach was starting to bother him. *Hunger*, he told himself.

A piece of data seemed to leap out of his splice: No casualties for the unit. Nadir frowned and shut down the splice.

"Casualties?" he asked.

"No, sir!" an indistinct avatar reported.

"Call off," Nadir said. Each EarthCo warrior reported in good health. A Brazilian had been slashed across the cheek by mortar shrapnel, but he was less interested in medical care than finishing his tally. Otherwise, the unit had decisively defeated a heavily constructed fortress defended by 210 Niks.

"That can't be right," he mumbled to himself, watching his boys tumble on the hard dirt and continue to tag marks that had already likely been tagged half a dozen times.

He turned and again studied the perfectly fitted stones of the graceful buttress, each rock planed to a sheer surface. He laid his palm against the stone; it was as cold and hard and smooth as it looked. He picked up a rock and threw it against the wall above his reach; it clicked and rebounded away from him, falling among other pebbles. He stamped his boot on a stone step.

It echoed. Hollow, like wood.

It felt as if icy fingers reached under his helmet and gripped his scalp, scraping metallic fingers along his spinal cord. He stamped again; again, what he heard wasn't the sound of rubber on rock. Nadir swallowed hard. *We defeated this place too easily*, he thought.

Inspiration struck him; he rebooted his headcard, keeping an intense focus on his surroundings, on every sense. The world around him fluttered and blurred momentarily— but only for a millisecond; EarthCo warrior headcards are extremely fast. What he saw was almost enough to complete the disillusionment.

The stone wall grew nearly transparent in places. The buildings shrank and even disappeared. The dead around him lost their uniforms. Was this more electronic warfare, messing with his perceptions? Why now, after the battle was decided?

But what he saw were phantoms, no more real than what he had seen a moment prior, no more real than what he had expected to see. He rebooted again, this time scrutinizing not only his surroundings but also his expectations. This time, though the world flickered—as was to be expected when rebooting what was essentially part of his brain, linked to his neural milieu—he saw only lights, heard only the buzzing of stray current coursing through his synapses.

"This is crazy," he said, suddenly observing himself rationally. He was acting like a rapthead, trying to defeat his sense of reality, doubting the very evidence of his senses. He shook his head and turned to face the boys.

Jhishra and his guards stood before him. Nadir took a step back—he had nearly bumped into the little man.

"What are you doing?" the Boss asked.

"Rebooting my card," Nadir asked, out of breath. "I've been having trouble with the damned thing."

Jhishra squinted at him, then looked away. "We finally find something," the Boss said. "You worried the Niks made off with their treasures, right? Well, we find them. Cases of ammo and tanks of rations. Even some components. Most compatible with our needs. Pleased?"

Nadir nodded, relieved that the raid had proven to be more than a tally-run. Relieved that the fortress actually bore tactical significance.

"Have one of the techs run diagnostics on your card," Jhishra said. Nadir could tell the man was still squinting. "We can't have our Sub-boss crashing in the middle of a firefight, can we now?"

Nadir acknowledged the order and set off to find the tech he most trusted, a Ukrainian boy who was deft in directly accessing EarthCo's best medical computers via satellite. He walked, watching the dance of death and life around him, listening to the monopera, listening to the animal cries of the boys, and felt himself at the center of a spectacular ballet. As he stepped over tagged marks, the old smile tried to creep back onto his face.

He'd been a fool to doubt himself, to question EarthCo even for a moment. He'd nearly snared himself in the trap two of his men had set for themselves . . . he couldn't remember their names. But he saw them again now, lying on the sand, their faces tight with pleasure and horror, lost in feed. They had twitched a bit. Their arms and legs whipped around, making sand-angels on the desert. Then their faces fell slack, and they were dead.

Nadir strained to remember their names, but couldn't. He couldn't even picture their faces, just the muscle spasms beneath the skin. Then he couldn't remember anything about the past weeks crossing the desert, except fleeting images and music, and he began to panic. Had those two men been hit by electronic warfare, or had it been something else. . . ? His mind seemed to be hitting a block. But remembering wasn't important. He didn't need to remember, certainly didn't want to. There was nothing in his past he needed to remember, nothing he wanted to remember—not the lifeless years in Wolf Point, not the Marshalls, not any battle in the past.

No. All that mattered was now, this moment, because anything beyond now was dead. The past lay in the wormy vault of yesterday. A sniper could kill him two steps from now, killing every tomorrow to come. Now was all that mattered.

Nadir watched two of his boys drag a young woman out into the courtyard. Her body was wrapped in the purple beads that designated the local whores. She was naked except for the beads and strips of cloth. They began to do what boys do.

Nadir was about to speak, but then he averted his eyes and said nothing to stop them, whistling in time with the oboes of the monopera, loud enough to drown out the noises. This was the familiar. This was the now. All became right in his world. If not . . . who was he to question why? Why the perfect fort in the middle of nowhere? Why the hidden faces in the marks? Why the easy victories? But to ask why would mean having to report his observations to superiors like Jhishra. That could bring only trouble, or worse, and would help no one, least of all this whore.

Fresh screams painted a background static against which his thoughts couldn't be reflected, in which they were muffled. And feed helped. The monopera roared like an ocean's waves against his cranial shore. No, he would not question anything. He would not destroy his world, would not shatter the life he had finally achieved. He could never go back to a place like Wolf Point. He would rather be dead. Questions were for fools and those who had nothing to lose. It would take a lot more than a few quirks of the card to make Nadir abandon all that he had earned.

Spirits lifting as adrenaline unexpectedly pumped into his veins, Nadir began to sing along with the tenor in his head:

> *I'm alive,*
> *Burned alive,*
> *In the rising sun.*
> *I am ev'ryone.*
> *You're me.*

Innerspace 3

Jonathan Sombrio scuffs along the sidewalk, kicking the scattered rubble and shrapnel of a city consumed by the slow-motion war of entropy and habitation. Sporadic gunshots echo in the distance. A whitenoise buzz at the corner of his perception warns Jonathan a Zone is approaching.

Most of his attention is on the *Lone Ship Bounty* rerun. It is more than half way done. He's able to feel a little excited about that, anxious to find out what's going to happen to his Captain.

The serial is overlaid on a halftone splice of reality. The effect is that the teetering buildings around him radiate an eerie greater-than-real feeling, as if black and white is the proper color for Chicago Avenue, as if this place—almost continually under Mobile Hostile Zoning—deserves to appear composed of tiny dots. The street, if this mass of upended tar and rusting hulks can be called a street, finally ends at a high black wall of hicarb rising three stories and blocking the view of skyscrapers beyond. Up to about eye-height, it is graffitied so thick with a physical and 3VRD-interactive coating that the wall seems to rise from a shattered psychedelic eggshell.

"Jonathan Sombrio," a soft female voice blurts into his mind, "ID #SZ40168-dash-dash-ECo-dash, are you ready to return to your schooling?"

"Go to hell," he says.

"My records show you have returned home from treatment, and have now been away from your home for a considerable period. Your downtime is over. Prepare for class."

"I thought I'd have a few days," he says, feeling this is exactly what he doesn't need right now. He still blocks the teacher-program's 3VRD. "They told me—"

"You have returned home from treatment, and are now well away—"

"Shut up," he says. "Fine. Let the edufeed begin."

"I am reading anomalous feedback from your card. Are you blocking my 3-verd feed? Your educational vixperience will be severely limited if you—"

"Fine," he says, shutting down the block. "Are you happy?"

"I do not have feelings," an attractive, middle-aged woman says, flickering overlaid across Jonathan's pov. "But giving you a good education is very important to me."

She picks up exactly where they left off last session, a few weeks prior, when Jonathan was admitted to Minneapple Corrections. She begins by pulling up behind her a map of North America, then slowly advancing it toward Jonathan so he can interact with her lecture. At the center, the United States grows larger as it approaches, a thousand twinkling lights indicating information-exchange centers—mostly cities. A network of pink 3D highways joins the centers, some arching hundreds of kilometers above the surface, others diving undersea, still others stretching like old-time roads across the land. Actually, Jonathan is intrigued with netography; he programmed his studies for a concentration in information networking and geographics.

But, for fear of becoming too distracted by school when he is about to reunite with his old gang—his last hope, besides Charity, and his greatest fear—he engages a blackcard program that slowly shifts the splice to one side where it merely becomes a curious muffle at the edge of his perception. His body grows stiff with expectation, and his mouth goes dry, but he must contact them now or they'll tear him apart. Anyhow, he needs their software and massively firewalled servers to immerse himself in what he does best.

Now the street and barrier wall stand naked before him, starkly real, solid and corroded; the 3VRD graffiti is gone, so the wall becomes merely a barrier smeared by inartistic hands. The eggshell is gone. He draws a deep sigh to relax and opens a shielded comm BW to call the Malfits. Though his hope is tiny, though his capacity for it is limited, he dreams for a better . . . something. But, then, he's not sure if hope or fear that had had the stronger hand in bringing him here.

The instant he taps into the city's local net, Lucas is waiting—centered in Jonathan's pov, revealing that he's projecting via blackcard, since Jonathan has shifted his regular card's splice to the left. The boy's smile is twice as wide as a human's mouth could be, lined with shark teeth; his body undulates slowly, as if suspended in liquid stirred by a light current. His skin is blacker than any pigment, only visible against the background of garbage and rubble. His eyes stand out like beacons, and the teeth gleam pearlescent. Seeing him again makes Jonathan seethe with hatred.

"Blackjack was wondering when you'd call," Lucas says, his 3VRD voice like a sawblade across stone.

Jonathan winces: Behind that virtual sound is a true threat. He had witnessed what Lucas could do to people's meat—people who weren't ready for the likes of that boy. "Of course I was gonna—"

"Blackjack doesn't like it when his drones stay away so long." The nightmare figure grows agitated. "Better come into the 'board right away while he still has the patience to deal nicely with you." And he's gone.

Jonathan turns to his left, knowing where the entrance would appear once the gang's security had cleared him. A sheer wall of chipped and graffitied brick fades to an underlying layer of concrete, then a riveted steel door stands as the last of a succession of virtually real defenses. Jonathan steps forward, places his right hand against a reader-plate beside the door, and it, too, vanishes, leaving only a hicarb wall standing in front of him. They had carefully quarried two feet out of the old tenement-house's wall to be able to emplace 3VRD defenses—using projectors, so anyone with a headcard at all would see them, whether or not the card was on—defenses that would hold up against close scrutiny, and which would physically block anyone with even the simplest card. Blackjack had chosen this site to house the Malfits' 'board, at the end of the road between Zones and nice downtown. Jonathan assumed it was a psychologically sound decision: The beatcoats would never think to look for a gang hangout at the point where they'd most likely be trapped during Zone.

The hicarb door slides aside and an anemic-looking girl stands in the entry hall. Her eyes are defocused, staring right through him. A corner of her mouth quirks as her voice sings in his head. Her avatar is a barely visible glimmer of light. Jonathan's chest tightens as he wonders what has so ruined her card. Then his stomach tightens as he guesses why. It had nearly happened to him, and someone very close. . . .

"Hey, Lucy," he says, projecting a smiling avatar to cover his sadness, "what's on?"

"What's on?" she repeats. "Come on board. . ." Pause. "Jonathan."

Jonathan steps into the small entryway and squeezes her hand. Her real eyebrows rise briefly, and the other corner of her mouth rises to a full smile which vanishes just as quickly. Jonathan can't think of a thing to say.

The door behind him slides shut and the other one a few meters along the hall slides open, releasing the strong odor of hot electronics. The shark-boy waits at the other end.

"Time to see Blackjack," Lucas says, turning away and already starting to walk.

Jonathan follows Lucas through the 'board; gangs like this call their hangouts "motherboards" because they house heavy servers and shielded and encrypted net-tapping equipment for their members' use. The old house has been renovated to resist grenades and sniper fire: Windows are bulletproof ultraglas, walls are steel and hicarb-reinforced. The inner walls of the structure look dull grey to Jonathan with his splice off-center, only occasionally punctuated by livid projectors, both static art pieces and subscription-relays. Lucas leads Jonathan down a flight of creaking wooden steps and stops before another nondescript hicarb door.

"You've kept Blackjack waiting long enough," Lucas says, and passes a webbed hand before the door. It slides open and Lucas abruptly disappears.

"Jonny boy," a ragged, high-pitched voice calls, "come in."

Jonathan crosses the threshold and hears the door grind shut behind him. The room is drowned in darkness, making Jonathan's edufeed glow at the corner of his vision like a dream glimpsed in waking: indistinct yet unforgettable.

Panic swells within him as the silence endures. How angry is Blackjack for Jonathan's absence? How angry for the weeks and months of unproductive time before treatment? All the Malfits owe Blackjack and the gang for their enhancements, more than they can earn in a treatment center away from the servers, their blackcards shut down. Jonathan hears only a distant murmur from his teacher and begins to wish he had opted for that life, for education and productivity rather than the familiar comfort of this life, where at least he means something to these people, where at least he is someone. Though ganglife is not comfortable, in the regular citizen's pov, Jonathan does not allow himself to believe he could do better, and it will be years before he's repaid his debt to them.

A fleshy hand touches his forearm intheflesh. Someone besides Blackjack is in the room with Jonathan. He cringes.

"What's a matter, Jonny boy?" Blackjack's chainsaw voice asks. Still no 3VRD accompanies the voice. Blackjack likes it that way. He seldom 3VRDs. "Your blackcard still alive?"

"Sure," Jonathan responds, trying to avoid the sweaty hand groping him all over without moving from where he stands.

"Why ain't it really on, then?" the gang leader continues.

"I'm just trying to stay off the dangerous stuff. In treatment they told me—"

"'Dangerous'?" says another man, very nearby. He begins to laugh. Jonathan can almost make out the silhouette of an obese man who begins to fondle him.

"Yes, Jonny," Blackjack says. "What do you mean, 'dangerous'? You going to meat on us, Jonny boy?"

"No," Jonathan says. "I just—"

"Boy," Blackjack says, "we got some work to remove the brainwash they did to you. Boot it up."

Terrified, regretting every decision he has made today, then realizing each decision seemed to have only one choice—and that a bad one—Jonathan feels around in his head for the blackcard. A few of its programs are already running, but only through neural connections with his standard card. Hesitantly, he orders its full processing power online.

A crash of light and noise and stench and bitter flavors and tinglings flurry around him like a fivesen tornado, and, as the storm settles, the room suddenly flashes to life. In blackfeed, it is brightly lit by a neon-purple sun that orbits Blackjack, who is seated on a wood and iron throne at the far end of a clutter of electronic equipment.

The obese man beside Jonathan has only one arm. He towers half a meter above Jonathan, the rolls of fat encircling his neck girdled by slithering silk scarves. He wears layered silk and satin robes of varying shades of purple and pink, like dead or swollen flesh peeling away from his bulk. The man's one hand absently slides up and down Jonathan's arm, precipitating shivers of revulsion through the boy. But Blackjack's red-eyed stare locks Jonathan from pulling away. Any look from the gang leader is a threat.

"That's better," Blackjack says. He slowly unwraps a snapstick and pops it into his mouth. As usual, his face is tight, showing no expression whatsoever. The shifting sun alters the shadows across his face. "What do you think of our boy, Mr. X?"

"Oh, he'll do nicely," the man burbles.

"What are you talking about?" Jonathan asks, his nerves sparkling with fear.

"Jonny boy," Blackjack begins, removing his attention from the man, "we've had a hard time since you left. You're our number one fixer. With you gone, we had to use Peter to crack security at our traditional feeding-troughs. Stupid, clumsy Peter. Someone at 3M burned him on a job. He never came out of it. We had to dump his body in the river. It was better that way than leave him a vegetable. So then we only had Georgi. Georgi doesn't fix right, so we ain't had a worthwhile haul in three weeks. The other gangs are owing us less and less every second, and even some of the newer gangs are getting out of debt. We completely lost two dependent-gangs. We owe the Sinanas twice as much as when you left. And there's more. I ain't happy, Jonny boy. You owe us big."

He tosses up a datachart for Jonathan, which floats in the air between him and the obese man. Jonathan looks over the complex subeconomics of the 38 CityNet gangs, noticing how the black market electronic currency-balance has shifted out of favor for the Malfits; they've slipped from eight to twelfth.

"You thinking subcontracting me to this guy, Blackjack? Selling me?" Jonathan asks. Real money is worth a lot of black market electronic currency. His words come out nearly monotone. The man's hand slides inside Jonathan's shirt collar.

"Don't be retro, boy," Blackjack answers. "In your position as fixer, you're worth a lot more than that to us. This here kind gentleman has made us a curr offer to help you fix better than ever. He's willing to trade a really clean amp—the most-curr net tech—for one day with you, intheflesh."

"Oh, man, Blackjack," Jonathan begins.

He regrets the outburst right away when the gang leader gets up from his throne. The young man crosses toward Jonathan like a predator, strong, smooth, swift and graceful as he avoids brushing against the stolen electronics. Even the obese man backs away. Blackjack stops less than an arm's reach from Jonathan, shorter than the younger boy but with muscles like whips tight beneath his freckled skin. His left hand lashes out and slaps Jonathan's cheek before the boy even sees his gang leader move.

"Do you want to disobey me?" he asks.

"Of course not, Blackjack," Jonathan says, afraid to rub the hot spot on his face. The pain brings back bad memories.

"Good," Blackjack says, the expression on his face the same as ever. His red spikes of hair glisten with some chemical coating. "Let's go upstairs and have Lucas install it."

"But I thought I could take him home right away," the huge mound of flesh complains, his voice whining like a child's. He holds the back of his hand up to thick lips. "My partners will never do business with you again if you—"

"No worries," Blackjack says, walking toward the door, which slides open just as he reaches it. "We just gotta make sure the amp works before we let you take him. Gotta get him started working before you take him away. No worries. I always keep my word. You can tell your partners that. Gotta test, you know. If the amp doesn't work. . ."

"Oh, it will," the obese man says, "it will. It's the best. I understand. Go ahead then."

They climb the stairs, Blackjack in front, Jonathan in the middle, feeling the unwelcome touches of the man behind him, his weight making the steps creak dangerously. They cross a kitchen now bright with blackfeed decorations. An orgy—human or individ or both—rages in the hallway between kitchen and living room, wet and loud with the sound of pneumatics. Jonathan feels bile rise into his mouth as he begins to imagine what this fat fuck will want of his body. His blackcard promptly supplies flesh to the nightmare visions of his imagination, and he violently shuts it down, nearly burning out the program in his haste.

Lucas' sharkform drifts into view, but now his webbed hands hold surgical instruments. Two other Malfits flank Lucas, bearing trays of more instruments, gauze, a Petri dish holding a bloody lump, and a tiny brown chip with wires protruding from it like bronze spiderlegs.

Jonathan's heartbeat and respiration increase; he glances away from the instruments to the other gang members lounging on cushions and couches, pleading into each of their eyes. But none of them return his gaze. Even those with what might be sympathy on their faces look away as his eyes find theirs. He turns back to Blackjack.

"Blackjack, we don't have to do it this way. I'll crash this guy. I'll do whatever you say, just don't make me do this—"

That palm as hard as iron again crashes against his cheek. This time, Jonathan finds himself on his ass on the hardwood floor. Computer chips and dust and a thick blanket of other detritus hide the antique parquet.

Without looking up, he says, "Blackjack—"

"Boy," the gang leader interrupts, "ain't no one gonna hurt you. Right, Malfits? He's my boy, ain't no one gonna hurt him, or we gut the guy that does."

"Right, Blackjack!" another gang member shouts. "No one but you."

Ha ha ha, a gout of laughter plugs Jonathan's ears as a fleshy hand again seeks his skin, as arms lift him back upright, as Lucas force-feeds him an anesthetic program.

But he can still feel the alien sensations when a blade slices into his neck and something cold and tingly is inserted beneath the skin. A blizzard of images from the past swells all around him, stunning his nerves, overwhelming his visual centers; he sees his sister Josephine, Mr. and Ms. Sombrio, his teacher, Charity, and even érase—érase, whom he has tried so hard to forget; sad lost érase, the girl he vowed would be the only one he would ever let himself love, the person who is most lost to him now.

But outside the sharp blades of yesteryear, outside the too-many memories of the family he has rejected, outside the scalding memories of a girl he destroyed, he still feels the warm seepage of blood, the cold electric burn of new powercells being grafted into the meat of his neck. His blackcard's nightmare program stirs a broth from that feeling, running a dream of those genetically adaptable powercells running amok in his body, altering all his own cells to powercells until his body is nothing but an electric generator with two cards in a gelatinous skull.

In his nightmare, he screams and screams, but no noise escapes his lips. The only sounds are those of laughter, those of his family's meaningless words, and those of érase slowly dying before his eyes.

Yesteryear 3: Jonathan Sombrio

Jonathan and érase were lying together on a cardboard box supported atop pallets, although to them it had been programmed to look like a Queen Anne bed. Their room was surrounded on three sides by the crumbling brick walls of standing buildings, roofed by ancient steel arches that still held up a copper dome, and closed on the fourth wall by a 3VRD Jonathan had programmed just for them, so no one would find them. The large, open space was furnished with projections of chairs and tables he copied from the Minneapolis Museum of Art. He had designed this place for érase, her home with him since she had nowhere else to go, and since he couldn't imagine her anywhere but in his arms. He was fifteen then, and she was two years older.

She rolled into his arms, her scarred, naked body pressing against his, soft and warm. He smiled, feeling himself harden against her thigh as her lips brushed his neck. He drew a deep breath with his face buried in her thick black hair and released it, shuddering. He told himself he could live like this forever. He didn't care if their home was only a half-demolished building, that they might never own anything of value, that he might never become a netographer—he never really believed he could attain that dream, anyway, although she gave him the inspiration to study hard and at least try—all that mattered was that they were together, intheflesh, and that her love for him was not virtual. He vowed he would never order an individ, that érase's arms would be more than enough for the rest of his life. The maplike network of scars across her legs and wrists only made her more beautiful to him. He could never be satisfied with the perfection of an individ.

Into this imperfect dream appeared the familiar sharkform of Lucas, swimming through the air above them. Terror gripped Jonathan's throat.

"What are you doing here, Lucas?" he demanded, covering his fear with anger. érase surged against him, then rolled off the pallets into the blanket on the ground beside them. She quickly began to dress.

"Well, isn't this the purr-tiest sight," Lucas said. His words rolled out of those shark jaws like water, or blood.

"Get the fuck away from us, Lucas, or I'll get inside your card and fill it full of virus."

"You've been holding back on us, Jonny boy," Blackjack said.

Jonathan froze, looking for the gang leader. No, no, no. . . . The sure footfalls of the young man crunched nearer. He passed right through the 3VRD barrier-wall. By now, érase had pulled on her coverall and was zipping it up. Her feet were bare, and Jonathan was still completely naked. He didn't dare move.

"Would you like to introduce us?" Blackjack said, indicating érase. He unwrapped a snapstick and began to knead it between his fingers.

She stopped moving, too, and looked up at the gang leader, her face hard and bitter. It always amazed Jonathan how mercurial she could be, a soft lover one second, a wild animal the next. Blackjack stopped a few steps from the girl.

"Her name's érase," Jonathan said, "and she doesn't belong to any 'board." He rose and stood between them with his fists on his slim, naked hips. "She likes being a loner."

"The city's a dangerous place for a loner girl," Lucas said, sliding closer to her. She stood more upright.

"You came here for a reason," Jonathan said. "Do you have a fix job for me?" He hoped and hoped Blackjack would say, yes, why yes, we need you to slip past the security systems of a local warehouse; or, yes, we need you to crack the security at a small info trader or a city ganglion. We'll be on our way now if you join us.

But reality never works like that for Jonathan. Even back then, he knew better.

"Jonny boy," Blackjack said, "you should have let me know you had a pump. Good boys share."

"She's not a pump!" Jonathan shouted, already regretting the outburst. "Sorry. But she's not like that. We're friends. Please let her go. I'll do whatever—"

"I don't like boys that way, Jonny boy," Blackjack said, not looking at Jonathan but at érase. Broken bricks and bits of concrete were scattered around her, as well as cigarette butts and snapstick wrappers. The antique furniture seemed to laugh at Jonathan and his foolish dreams.

"I like girls, though," Blackjack added, finally tossing the lump of snapstick into his mouth. He stepped toward érase, but Jonathan got in his way.

"Leave her alone," Jonathan said. He felt Blackjack's muscular tension burn his skin. "She and I are friends," he added, pleadingly.

"So are we," Blackjack said, his tone of voice unreadable, "and you failed to share something of yours. Don't I always share my things with you? I share space on my 'board, I share food and clean water and any programs you want. Whatever you want, I find a way to get it. And here you have something I'd like to share. That's the way things work."

"Yeah, you little fucking pervert," Lucas said, bending over érase with his clawed fingers extended. "Intheflesh . . . I never would have guessed it of you, Jonny. You always seemed so normal."

Jonathan flicked on his city landscape and descended on the little node that was Lucas's card—the safest way for him to attack since no one in the gang could manipulate the net like he could. He slipped down the electricbright channel into Lucas' head and loaded a new program to find what he needed. A menu flashed to life around him as he stood in what looked like a power plant control room, all switches and screens and dials. Jonathan selected POWER SUPPLY and hit it with the biggest burst of EM radiation he could sap from the netways. Then he pulled out . . . all this in less than a second.

Lucas screamed. His shark 3VRD vanished. His fragile white hands pressed against the sides of his skull as he fell face first onto the pallets.

"The little mannequin just burned me!" he shouted. Gone also was the smooth voice, replaced with a cracking adolescent's.

"The rest of you keep away from her," Jonathan said. Four others wandered through the 3VRD wall, all dressed in their chosen 3VRD costumes. They looked like a child's nightmare of a circus. These were the people Jonathan had come to think of as family, almost friends, but now he saw only a threat to the fragile dream of perfection he had held just minutes ago.

"Jonny boy," Blackjack said, stepping closer. "You're going to owe big for this, you know. Now you've not only broken our faith but also hurt one of my drones. I'm—"

"Get away from him, Blackjack, you piece of shit!" érase screamed, bolting upright beside Jonathan.

Jonathan felt his heart race so fast it felt as if it would burst. Gently, he placed his hand on her side and pushed her away. Distracted by her, he didn't notice as Blackjack's hard hands went around his throat and threw him onto the ground two meters away.

Jonathan lay stunned for a few seconds, not sure what had just happened, coughing on dust and blood and a broken tooth. One side of his head felt numb and hot, where it had struck the ground. His ears rang. Angry screams dragged him from delirium.

"Get away from her!" he bellowed, rising unsteadily to his feet and running toward the gathering of gang members around the Queen Anne bed where he caught glimpses of érase's scarred skin, and he ran howling at the boys and men, animal hatred making him forget that his intheflesh body was no match for any of them, forget the cards in his head and his fantastic aptitudes with them, forget everything but the furious young woman whose slender flailing limbs battered the circle of Malfits who laughed and chided her.

Someone tripped him, and he fell again onto his face in the rubble and dust. Lucas stood over him, his frazzled black curls a halo of death around a face twisting with agony and hatred. Lucas, barely more than a boy himself, descended on Jonathan, and then the next hours were lost.

When he later awoke on the 'board, Blackjack had put his arms around Jonathan and held him tight.

"Thanks for sharing, Jonny boy," he said, his face as rigid as stone. "She'll keep your homies well-stocked in legal currency. You're a smart boy to deliver us such a fine pump. Over time, that should more than makes up for the damage you caused."

And then Jonathan had cried, not over his bruised and immobile body, but in knowing his dream with érase in their home beneath an arching ceiling would never come true, knowing he had been a fool all along ever to believe it could, knowing it had never been more real than any other 3VRD, knowing she would not survive beyond another few days, though perhaps her body would. She was still an adolescent, without parents, unfranchised; the beatcoats would never investigate her disappearance, and wouldn't care.

He cried so long and so hard that not even Blackjack's fists could break him of it. In time, the grief passed, as grief always does. And, afraid to turn it into anger at those who would kill him and punish érase for his misdeeds, those who could save him—his 'board brothers—he had built a virtual wall within so high and long and thick and impassable that no one could ever enter, not completely, not even in 3VRD, not even himself. It was a fortress not just in the metaphorical sense, but real in the virtual sense, as real as emotions or the mind. Without it he would have vanished as surely as the walls, had they been taken down. He could never again be hurt, would never again reveal himself to anyone who could see what he really was and laugh at him, call him worthless and small and all his dreams futile and foolish.

But he had forgotten to build a roof over it. That worked out well when he later wanted to build a spaceport at its center, to let the Captain touch down inside. This entry is safe because, unconsciously, he knows he'll never meet that distant hero so many millions of kilometers away; he, one boy in 21 billion.

He spent the following months numbly breaking open security systems around Minneapolis and St. Paul, as well as some more distant, where the only booty was information. Time made his loss seem less real. It even made him seem less real, and that was good. Work was good, the harder the better.

And then he discovered feedrapture, and became useless to Blackjack, though the gang leader attempted to break him from the systems-lock with fists and threats of death. But Jonathan only smiled inwardly at the futile efforts, taking pleasure in this one form of revenge, even if it meant sacrificing his flesh. There was nothing left of him by then, anyway. How can one sacrifice nothing? Would the immensity of the universe notice if one glass of vacuum vanished? Inwardly, as he was swept away on an ocean's current of other people's thoughts and programming, he laughed and laughed at Blackjack beating his nothing knuckles against Jonathan's nothing flesh.

Some traitorous fool had shoved him into treatment, and he had awoken, stunned, empty. The nurses locked down his cards with a null field. Eventually, they nearly succeeded in shattering the walls of his inner fortress when they forced him to cry by asking him painful questions. The tears had fallen for days. Somehow, the nurses had implanted in him a desire to live again.

When he was released, when Charity found him and offered something that could be akin to what he had had with érase, Jonathan felt an odd sense of hope. When Josephine seemed about to communicate with him, Jonathan's hopes rose, only to be destroyed. When he began his last-ditch trek toward the Malfits, that hope returned, ironic or not, since they were the ones who had nearly destroyed him. But they are his only family. They care for him in a sense his family never did . . . or care less than his family, yet that they care at all is somehow more valuable when family is expected to love you and their failure is so much worse than any shortfall from those whose love is unexpected.

That was then. Now, in a less than an hour, he will wake, finding himself buried under a hundred kilos of fat on satin sheets. All that remains is Charity.

FIVE: Outerlimits

EarthCo *Bounty* 7: Janus Librarse

The EarthCo fighter/bomber *Bounty* plummeted tail-first toward the growing orb of Triton. Its main rocket nozzle hung useless—the metal shredded like aluminum foil—from the end of the crooked thrust-tube. A vapor trail of hydrogen spewed from the ruined engine, spreading out before the ship and dispersing into the emptiness of space. Neptune lit the ship's port pale blue, the sun lit its starboard orange, and stars cast its curving helm silver; a slight wobble and spin slowly altered the lighting on the gleaming hull.

Inside, Janus slid into her acceleration couch without any quick moves. Jackson rose from his couch, to her left, while Eyes, to her right, straddled the arm of his. His hand clutched the particluster subgun, aimed at Jackson.

Janus nodded to Jackson, hoping the vulgar cyborg had been as distracted as he had seemed a moment ago when she and Jackson had passed a few secret 3VRD words. She landscaped the ship's controls into her splice, so a mosaic of buttons, switches, and readouts filled her pov. She waited, nearly shaking with frustration and anger.

At this very moment, the second nuclear missile was spanning the distance between them and the alien artifact, and with it the scientist with whom she felt such a kinship.

Though Jackson frowned as in pain, at last he nodded. What's Eyes doing to him now? Janus wondered, but spent little time speculating.

Her mind's finger reached hesitantly toward a red button—This is the only way, she reassured herself—while she also prepared the second part of the plan. She wedged her feet into the footrests, careful not to do anything to clue Eyes.

"Lonny," said Jackson, at the corner of her vision, "let's be reasonable."

"I am being reasonable," Eyes replied. His voice was as brittle as old paper. "This has gone too far. Someone needs to take control—"

Janus grit her teeth and engaged the maneuvering program. She couldn't bear to watch Jackson, to see if Eyes' gun fired and split her friend's belly open.

A great explosion detached the thrust-tube—main engine, fuel tanks and all—from the ship's globular hull. Almost immediately, retrorocket 3 fired full-thrust for three seconds, then retrorocket 7, then 2, then 8, then 9.

The ship first regained "gravity" for a moment, then lurched clockwise, knocking Eyes backward from his seat. It spun faster and faster, and Eyes began to roll in an arc toward the wall.

Janus dared to glance at Jackson. His body was still intact, ducking behind his couch. She heaved a great sigh of relief and put her own seat between her and the lunatic.

Then she depressed the red button. No turning back. No return. And she had to hurry.

EarthCo *Bounty* 8: Lonny Marshfield

"Bitch!" you cry, tumbling across the textured metal floorpanels. You struggle to hang onto the hard comfort of the weapon, but to do so you give up control of where your body goes. Those fucks! Traitors! What have they done to your beautiful ship?

And then the nightmare:

The rearmost overlay on your pov flickers and dies.

They have burned the server.

You watch overlay after overlay fade. You feel the skin at the back of your scalp sparkle and twitch as you lose connection to sweet home Earth, to the program, to the computer. Only a few navigational systems are still operative. Life-support is still operative.

Confusion, disorientation. You can't even think. The terror . . . you see a man hanging by his fingertips from a razorthin wire between two skyscrapers. A high wind whips him back and forth, back and forth over Boston. He savors the hot painthrill blazing in his fingers, but he knows another few seconds of this will mean death, and in death lies no pleasure. He looks this way and that, but each open window from which the wire threads seems kilometers away. His arms won't move. The wind blows harder; he begins to swing like a pendulum. He can't think. Nothing. The ground rushes up.

The acoustic tiles of the wall bump against your face. You blink and try to locate yourself. All right, stay calm. You feel cramps start in the muscles around your jaw. Relax and think. You feel the sharp outline of the subgun beneath your chest. The ship's engines stop firing. You become lighter, stuck to the wall as if it were the floor. Now.

You spin and rise, blind of the systems you're familiar with, but to dump with them! You're still a man, and your cards are still alive, and your muscles still work!

The subgun's plastic barrel sweeps up and across the cabin. No one in sight. The ventilators hiss. The four halls leading out of the cabin are empty. Then you notice the glint of metal, out of place at the foot of Cap'n's couch—Cap'n's weapon; and there, just behind it, a clump of dark hair.

Hiding. You feel your face tighten into a smile. The big cock, his big plans, his big threat. Watch this—

And then you feel relaxed. Almost at once, the tip of Cap'n's weapon brightens, a shaft of light penetrates the air between it and your biceps, thunder and lightning storm in your skull, your body warms, and you go numb.

You feel lazy and begin drifting away to the savory scent of baking meat.

EarthCo *Bounty* 9: Pehr Jackson

The GE laser pistol buzzed for a moment in Pehr's hand. He winced when a puff of smoke rose from Eyes' arm . . . I had to do it, he told himself. His head still throbbed from the man's mental attack.

Eyes fell limp against the wall. A great lesion opened and fused shut on his upper arm; the gun sailed away from his fingers, which spasmed open.

"He's out," Janus stated, rising from the floor. "You tie him up. I'll see if I can stop that missile and program a safe landing. We'll have to take the escape pod and leave the rest of the *Bounty* behind."

"Land?" Pehr asked, stopped in mid-motion. He awkwardly tried to hold himself still as forces like those of a merry-go round tugged at his feet, trying to pull him toward the man he just wounded.

"Of course," Janus replied. "We can't make it home in this condition; we can't even leave the Neptunian system. The *Bounty* has become a liability. We're stuck here, and I suggest we land before Neptunekaisha's defense finishes us. Agreed?"

"Right, right," he answered. But he just couldn't get out of his head the predicament they were in. He couldn't yet get past the queasiness brought on by the violence he had just performed. He couldn't quite comprehend that they were now completely isolated from the show. The craft was adrift in space, battered beyond repair, and they had to abandon ship.

My god, what has happened?

Pehr he drew a deep breath and exhaled slowly. This was a challenge. Hadn't he always overcome every challenge thrown in his way? What was so different this time?

Violence. He could have killed the man, if his aim had been poor.

Pehr lifted a floorpanel, reached inside, and pulled out a spool of wire. The slide across the floor to the unconscious Eyes was clumsy, but he made it. Action, that's what will save me. Keep moving forward.

The first thing Pehr did was kick the subgun away; it skittered along the fibrous tiles of the wall and came to a stop above him. Then he began to unwind the wire and tie Eyes' limbs to his body, careful not to touch the angry red scorch.

When he completed the last knot, one of the cyborg's eyelids flipped open; a mechanical eye stared up at Pehr.

Pehr stood, one leg on the wall, one on the floor, and shivered.

"Do you have the landing program worked out yet, Pilot?" he asked, still looking down at the electronic eyeball.

"We're not doing the show anymore, Jack," she said. "My name is Janus. And no, dammit, I'm having trouble with the missile. I've got to stop that first." The words were sharp, yet she refrained from taking out her anger on him.

That was one of her qualities that made Pehr think he wanted to work with her on the tourist gig. She, more than anyone, including his wife, was compatible with him: She put up with him, and he admitted that was difficult. He envisioned a trail of shattered relationships stretched behind him like flotsam behind an ocean liner.

But now action was required. The past didn't matter, not when their lives were perched precariously thousands of kilometers above an alien moon rushing toward them.

"What can I do?" he asked, satisfied Eyes was secure. He didn't, however, forget that the cyborg's greatest weapon lay sheltered in his skull, unbindable.

"Make sure the escape pod hatch opens."

Grateful to be needed, he crawled across the spinning cabin as if over strange, new terrain, and set to work.

Neptunekaisha 4: C.P. Chang

The lifting-body mining station rose and settled gently as the winds of Neptune rushed over it. Far below, dangerous storms roared and screamed. Safely far below. The tiny disc of the sun filtered down through the clouds, setting the hull of the station alight; microgrooves from years of atmospheric erosion caught the rays and diffracted them in all directions. A giant mass of dense cloud swept toward the station, momentarily swallowing it.

Inside, Clarisse Poinsettia Chang watched the incoming nuclear missile. The entire defense complex of this world was her extended nervous system. The missile rocketed many tens of thousands of kilometers per hour toward a power station only four kilometers from Mining Station Hachi. The mining station's cannonmaster fired his particle cannon frantically at the missile, wasting energy, not allowing the weapon to properly recharge between shots. The power station's automatic cannon fired measured blasts every second. An invisible envelope around the missile glowed with each rare hit, but the matter within the shield stayed intact.

She sensed the right moment. Her little hunter swung 70° off its trajectory into the path of the missile and accelerated toward it.

Like a ghost stepping through a door, a wad of hate and fear erupted within her. She became the hunter, its electronic eyes her vision, its sensors her fingertips. It came alive under her control, making her more alive. It developed a soul burdened with hate, and only destroying that missile would alleviate its terror and fury.

The sky was nearly purple ahead of the hunter, slowly melting to black scattered with stars that looked in the optics like four-pointed crosshairs. A faint web of lines and red numbers bisected the clouds. A circle-in-box appeared at the center of the pov.

She detonated the hunter.

Once more, Clarisse was the little girl floating on a pallet-raft along the Volga River, watching the sky through leaves, warm in the sun, alone, far from her hateful adopted siblings. She watched clouds drift past the branches, and sometimes saw her mother's white hair. . . .

Clarisse shut down the dead channel and switched to another. She was in no hurry; if the hunter had failed to do its job, there was nothing left to do, anyway. She felt release, as after orgasm. She smiled, considering how long it had been since she had last even thought to satisfy herself. Still, this was better. This was real. This was substantial.

From the pov of one of Mining Station Hachi's external cameras, she assessed the damage. A great, red streak of glowing matter and gases reached down from space and vanished into the denser clouds of the central atmosphere below. A map she overlaid told her that, somewhere in that streak, lay the power station. The artificial cloud began to twist and dance as winds began to wash it from the sky.

Clarisse flicked on a connection to the power station, careful not to let it overwhelm her pov; she would not allow herself to become a blazing wreck.

A little yellow light winked on at the corner of her splice, and below it a word: OPERATIONAL. Not green—undamaged—but not red, either. If it had been red, several mining stations would have had to shut down their main operations until the fusion reactor could be repaired or replaced. One of those stations might have even been lost if its lofting motors couldn't compensate enough for gravity and losses to wind friction.

So her hunter had destroyed the missile, but its shattered mass had still battered the reactor. Perfect.

"Victory!" she said aloud, and laughed. She felt as light as a little girl floating atop a gentle stretch of river.

Then the comm channels began to light up, dozens of them.

She composed herself, preparing the speech she would deliver to Neptunekaisha's employees and government. But before she would bother herself with speeches to civilians, she transmitted these words on an unscrambled line to all units of the Sotoi Guntai, from Neptune to Mercury:

"Limits pushed, break through." They would understand immediately.

Even as she began to take questions and accept congratulations, she prepared to leave her little command room for the first time in years. For a moment, she was almost scared. For a moment, she doubted whether all she hoped for could possibly come true— could a single woman in all the universe really accomplish anything substantial? Could she truly burn her initials upon history?

Then the lovely, useful hate returned. She would need it now more than ever. The doubts and fear faded like snails retreating from the baking sun.

EarthCo *Bounty* 10: Janus Librarse

Janus deciphered the missile's encryption codes that someone—*That bastard Eyes*, she thought—had placed to block entry. She was greeted by a penis the proportional size of a tall building.

"Bastard, mannequin bastard," she mumbled. She ignored Jackson's response.

It moved; it bumped up against her consciousness; it engulfed her.

She was falling, falling back through the years as into quicksand, and there was nothing to grab and use to stop her fall.

Yesteryear 2: Janus Librarse

Montgomery, Alabama, 21 years prior. She had tried to hide the blood—she had even gone to her friend, Bonette's, mother for the appropriate insert shield—but she was only thirteen, and a thirteen-year-old is fallible.

Her father had found the red swirls in the toilet water of the rear bathroom, which Janus and her younger sister, Rachel, used. The man earned enough percents to own and maintain a four bedroom, three-bathroom unit on the green edge of the city.

"Oh, unclean child!" she had heard him cry. "Oh, no longer a child but a woman. I am cursed!"

Between his words she heard tears. He was open with his emotions, dramatic about them. This theatric sense proved invaluable in his work as a certified Literalist minister; he broadcast three shows a day, each an hour long.

She trembled in her bedroom closet, hunched behind the stuffed animals and piled dirty clothes. Desperately, she fought to keep her weeping silent. Her heart battered her chest so loudly she was sure he could hear the thumping.

"Where are you, woman?" he shouted, stomping from room to room. Janus had no idea where her sister was, or her mother. Why didn't Mommy say anything? Where was she?

At the same time, Ms. Susie—Janus' 3VRD spelling teacher—was saying, "'E,' Janus. The last letter is 'e. D-i-s-e-a-s e.' That's an easy one. Why aren't you helping me spell the words today, dear?" Ms. Susie was pretty, with short blonde bangs and cheeks the color of the peaches Father sometimes brought home after his long trips.

Janus was certain Father could hear Ms. Susie, but she dared not say anything. Why did he scare her so much? He was a very nice man: He gave them their daily bread, he provided shelter and clothing, and he even gave them frivolous things like toys and Mr. Henry, the plush walrus she held close to her cheek. Why should she be afraid? What was it Mommy had said about men?

Then Father's voice got louder. She heard his shiny black shoes clunk on the real wooden threshold to Janus and Rachel's room, just a body's length away. His breathing was ragged, like Janus' after she'd run as hard as she could. When he breathed out, his breath shuddered; he was still crying.

Janus tried to stop breathing. She tried to disappear by pushing herself as much as possible into Ms. Susie's classroom. But when the closet door slid open and banged against its frame, she knew she was still in her Father's house.

An hour or a lifetime later, as he lay atop her in his sweaty white showsuit, only the pants pulled down, he spoke:

"'Let a woman learn in silence with all submissiveness. I permit no woman to teach or have authority over men; she is to keep silent. For Adam was formed first, then Eve; and Adam was not deceived, but the woman was deceived and became a transgressor. Yet woman will be saved through bearing children, if she continues in faith and love and holiness, with modesty.' First Timothy 11-15.

"Remember that, woman Janus. The fires of hell are lapping at your loins. Be quiet in all things related to being a woman. The original sin is upon you like a scar, and the only way to rid yourself of that scar is by bearing children. Pay no heed to the law of man; the only salvation for woman is this—" and he pushed again inside her, a sharp burning pain that ranged all the way up to her throat.

"If the law of man says a woman shall bear no children without its consent, then that law is evil and must be disregarded. We live in a land of evil, woman Janus. God is the only one who can purge you of sin. I am the instrument of God. Now go, clean yourself. And speak nothing of this to anyone, or burn forever in the fires of hell."

Two days later—two, because she couldn't bear to face Bonette that day or the next—she asked Bonette's mother for the no-baby pills.

"Please," Janus had insisted in her friend's tiny kitchen, "don't tell my parents. They would be so unhappy with me if they knew I was a sinner. I'll find a way to pay you for them."

"Oh, child," the woman had said, a crooked smile on her face, "there's no sin in what you're doing. If it's what you want, it's okay; but don't let anyone talk you into something you don't want." Then the older woman laughed.

"Sin, ha! Not everything that father of yours says is right. And I don't want your money; the city practically gives these away."

And she had taken a plastic bottle down from a shelf and pressed it into Janus' hand. "Take one every day unless you feel crampy, then take one every other day."

Janus looked at the bottle, opened it, dumped a tiny white pill onto her palm, and threw it into her mouth as if not doing so would cause her to become sick. Bonette's mother drew a quick breath.

"Not like that, child. With water!" She ran a glass of water in the sink and handed it to Janus.

Janus drank down the whole glass; the water seemed to help. It tasted clean.

"Can I leave them here and take them when I visit Bonette?" she asked. She had already begun to learn how to survive.

"Of course," the woman replied, taking the glass and setting it in the sink.

Janus had caught a glimpse of Bonette's eyes just then, dark brown islands afloat on pure white lakes. They seemed to ask countless questions, they seemed intensely intrigued and begging for details, and it was as if Janus had been struck with a fist in her gut.

Her whole body grew tight and weak at the same time, and she felt there was so much inside her that had to come out that she would just explode if she stayed within sight of her friend.

She muttered a hurried thanks and goodbye and ran out of the apartment. For what seemed like hours she ran, first at a sprint and later at a stumbling jog. Eventually she came to the river, and there she had fallen into the tall weeds.

She lay in the weeds for hours, her fingers clawing into the sand beneath her, her shoes kicking occasionally as well into the sand. Brown ants paraded past her, in and out of a tiny cavern. They intrigued her. She wondered if she could bury herself if she continued to do this—to kick and claw like an ant making a new cavern—and how soft and cool the sand felt. Even the bristly stems of the weeds were soothing—the little cuts they left on her arms kept her from crying.

However, as the shadow of night began to fall, when the cool air touched the back of her neck, she couldn't stop herself.

She cried like a little baby, as she had when she was young enough for the spankings. She tried to think like a baby. She wished she could go back to the spankings instead of this woman business.

"I hate being a woman!" she screamed into the dusk. When the sky put on God's paints of red and purple, she rose from the weeds and headed home. The walk seemed to take forever.

School was over, so her head was silent. The silence was bad. She turned on the 24-hour Edufeed channel; that would look good to her teachers, anyway. She concentrated hard on the digested news notes, and followed up on stories she found interesting.

By the time she got home, she'd spent half an hour in the Library of Congress files, researching "nebula." She walked right in to the dining room where Mommy and Father and Rachel were already eating, but Father didn't say a thing. His look was enough, but he didn't say a thing.

She would remember that over the next three years: Being a woman meant no punishment from Father, only the bearing-children business. Eventually, she was even able to not dread the afternoons when Father came to her bedroom. She had learned deep concentration.

Her grades skyrocketed. In a year, she was ahead of most 18-year-olds in math and science; in 3VRD sporting events, she beat most of the girls her age at running and hurdling. In two years, she was taking college feed at adolescent-discount, which pleased Father, since he wouldn't have to pay for it at full price later. She had learned not only to manage being a woman, but also to excel. She no longer thought of the bearing-children business as dirty, or even as unpleasant, but merely as part of life, not unlike folding laundry.

Not long after she turned 16, Father lost his certification. Now, when he came to her room, he not only quoted Bible passages but also explained his climbing onto her with phrases like, "It's time you gave something worthwhile to this household," and "I dump the burden of Man's sin into you." At times, he even scared her with completely irrational mutterings.

And then Rachel had come to her one morning. Janus looked in horror at the red stain in the crotch of her sister's yellow pants.

"I'm dirty," Rachel said. "Mom says this makes a girl dirty."

"Shut up, Rache," Janus said. She reached beneath her mattress and pulled out a pantyshield from her stash. "Take off those pants and underpants, then put this in your underpants like this. . ."

She became so frustrated with Rachel's unblinking stare and inaction that she couldn't stand it. She snarled and headed for her sister's dresser, where she hastily pulled out a fresh pair of underpants and stuck the shield in them.

"Take those off!" she said as loud as she dared. Rachel jerked back but obeyed. Janus ran to the closet and pulled out the spare bag she had made out of pillowcases three years prior. She returned to her sister's dresser and began stuffing the bag with necessities.

Finished, she saw Rachel was naked from the waist down. Golden wisps hugged the girl's pubis, but between the thighs the hair was soiled. Rachel held the removed clothing several centimeters from her hip. Her skin was so soft, so smooth, so pale-white that Janus nearly vomited with the thought of Father's scratchy thighs against this girl. She had forgotten how it had felt those first times, but now it all came gushing into her mind like a geyser.

Janus squeezed her eyelids shut for a moment.

"Give me those and put these on," she finally ordered, handing Rachel a fresh pair of pants and the prepared underpants, and taking away the stained ones. She rolled up the latter and stuffed them deeply between her mattress and suspension-case.

"Hurry," she added.

"What's going on?" her sister asked, pulling up the pants.

"Be quiet. I'll tell you later. We're going to town together. It's a secret, so don't tell anyone, especially Mom and Father. It'll be nice, you know, our first outing together. But we might need some things." As Janus spoke, she went back to the closet and grabbed the bag she had packed just a few months prior; it had been camouflaged by dusty stuffed animals in a corner of the closet she suddenly remembered oh, so vividly.

They threw the bags out the window then exited through the front door. After a few minutes standing outside without having drawn Father's curiosity, Janus checked the server and found him arguing furiously with a city manager: "Mr. Librarse, the citizen-shareholders have voted, and they will no longer tolerate Literalist programming." Janus beckoned Rachel to follow as she crossed to the back of the house and picked up their bags.

An hour later, an electric bus carried them swiftly toward downtown Montgomery. They spent the afternoon in the Municipal Museum. Rachel didn't ask any questions; she seemed proud to be on the town—intheflesh—with her big sister.

They spent their first night together in a homeless complex, the two of them stuffed into a single bunkroom: Its walls were white duraplas, inscribed here and there with people's names. The ceiling rose only a meter and a half, and the walls were spaced only two meters apart. But here, Janus felt safe. It seemed much more secure than a closet, and far from Father. She pulled the heavy hicarb brace across the doorway and locked it in place. The stale smell hardly bothered her; she'd endured worse in her own bed.

For several minutes, they lay on the padded floor, side by side, their heads supported by the bags of clothing. They listened to air hush in and out of the little room, filtering past dusty gratings. Near the doorframe, a cracked, red button bore the word, "INTERCOM." A sticker on the door read, "IN CASE OF FIRE EXIT STAIR B," and a diagram showed the path. Its edges were scratched away, and the diagram was difficult to read, but Janus felt satisfied she could get her sister out safely if need be.

"Why are we here?" Rachel finally asked. Janus had begun to hope she might never ask.

So she explained what it meant to become a woman in their Father's house.

"No!" Rachel shouted, the word sharp in the confined space.

Janus simply continued to describe her experiences, from the first day on. At first Rachel wouldn't believe a word of it: "Not my father!" Then she became angry at Janus, then she screamed curses at Janus, then more curses at Father which Janus didn't know the girl could use, then she wept, then she withdrew for a while in silence.

Janus felt oddly guilty for saying anything. Indeed, she had considered a myriad other explanations, but in the end decided only the truth would serve her properly. She didn't want to become enmeshed in a web of lies, anyway.

"He'll find us here," Rachel finally said.

"That's okay. If he calls the police and reports us as runaways, we tell them everything. I want him to find us. Then he'll be taken away, and we can live with just Mom. Even if she doesn't believe me, even if she hates me for taking him away, I can live with her. I can live with hate."

"But I couldn't stand to think of him doing that to you, Rache. Do you understand?"

Rachel didn't respond. Janus fell asleep sometime during the silence.

The following morning, a little speaker near the intercom button buzzed. "Eight o'clock," a man's muffled voice said. "Half hour 'til checkout."

"Is it all still true?" Rachel asked in a small voice. "It wasn't a dream?"

"It's true, sis."

"Did he call the police?"

"They aren't looking for us. I just checked. No runaway report."

"What's that mean?" Rachel sounded alarmed.

"Maybe the bastard knows what I intended. Maybe he thinks we'll come crawling home soon, and he'll teach us both a good woman lesson. The bastard. The fucking bastard."

"Jan! Watch your tongue. Jesus is listening."

Janus laughed, a barking sound that startled even her. "The hell he is. At least he's not listening to me. Maybe he still hears you. Yeah, maybe."

No more was said about their father that day, or the next. The girls found dull but filling and reportedly nutritional food in a cafeteria on the complex's first floor. They refused to use the common bath, except the stalls, which they entered together and locked while they did their business and washed with damp towels.

Six days and nothing from their parents or the police. Had Father forgotten about his daughters? Worse, had Mom? What had happened to her? Janus grew depressed watching her sister's face shrink in upon itself.

On the seventh day, Miguel sat next to them on the bench before a long, steel table. A thousand spoons clattered against a thousand plates and bowls. A thousand voices shouted and laughed and mumbled inanities. One man looked into Janus' eyes. His eyes were as dark as Bonette's. His skin glowed a soft brown, and black hair cascaded around his thin shoulders.

"You two don't belong here," Miguel said. "See that guy?" He pointed to a tall, middle-aged man a few tables away. "He's been watching you for days. I say he makes his move tonight, at dinner. He's a black-market feed producer. See how nice his clothes are? See his pretty jewelry? Do you see anyone else here who looks like that?"

Janus could hardly swallow the mouthful of starchy vegetable. She felt a chill stab her back. That would be worse, yes, worse than Father. At least Father was a known quantity with familiar morals and drives. What have I done?

"So how do I know you're not a bad guy?" she asked. Rachel stirred beside her.

"You don't. It's good to be cautious. Just let's be friends. Let me watch out for you. I had a sister. . ." His eyes drifted away.

"I don't ask for anything but your friendship," he added a second later. "I've seen too much of this mugre happening here. You two are obvious targets. I can't stand to see it happen to you."

Indeed, at the evening meal, the well-dressed man sat just across from the girls, casting furtive glances their way. Janus noticed his eyes were a strange chrome color, and the pupils weren't black but dull brown. Whenever he seemed about to speak—having set down his spoon and drawn a breath—Miguel would loudly clear his throat and mutter, "Crujir," while rubbing his temples and casting his eyes about wildly.

Miguel grew more animated each time. After a few minutes, Rachel began to giggle. This irritated the well-dressed man, and soon he was clenching and unclenching his jaw as if chewing dried meat. Miguel seemed invigorated by Rachel's humor, each adding to the pleasure of the other, until the spectacle drew attention from others nearby. An old man with scars crisscrossing his bald scalp grinned and bobbed his head as if on a spring, looking from the girls to Miguel to the man and back.

At last, the well-dressed man slammed down his fork and shouted, "Garce!" at the remains of his nearly untouched dinner. He was in such a hurry to leave that he tripped over the bench and dropped his tray. This drew even more attention, and soon a number of spectators had stopped eating or dwelling in 3VRD worlds to watch the scene play out.

Well aware of his audience, the man straightened his long blouses and stood tall on a pair of heavy-soled Makk boots. "You are nothing," he said, staring those artificial eyes straight into Miguel's. Then he left in a flurry of cloth.

A smattering of applause rang out from the little group of spectators. Not long later, even the old man drifted back into his private world.

Miguel smiled at Janus and Rachel, and suddenly he looked like a boy. Janus had been too terrified to smile, but Rachel giggled again and thanked their new friend.

"It was nothing," he said, imitating his foe's voice well. Rachel giggled again.

This one connection with their new life kept Janus and Rachel from losing the psychological battle against their father and going back to their old home. Miguel became a sort of dock amid the swirling waters of a world for which they had been unprepared.

Over the next days, he brought them spiced breads and fresh vegetables in trade for dinner conversation. Janus learned that he was a stonemason—a rare profession but not a terribly valuable one. He recently had to give up his apartment because work had been too intermittent to pay the rent when his roommate got married.

"Widowed," he said to Rachel's question. "Julia was trapped in a Zone one day, down in New Orleans. She had been shopping. The pathologist said it wasn't the beatcoats who killed her." In a rare mood, he suddenly fell silent.

Occasionally, the girls left the block-long complex to shop for necessities not provided in their new home. Janus had dared to use her father's credit to purchase a sack of feminine inserts at a small shop nearby. She was amazed when the shop's server cleared the purchase, and then she felt her first rush of power: She could use Father's credit for anything she wished, within reason. She could bleed him white from a distance. And he wouldn't dare put a stop on his credit—Stop your own children from using your credit? What kind of retro are you, man? The police would certainly become involved. Parents are expected to put limits on children's spending, yes, but no one blocks another's credit. Not in EarthCo's sphere of trade.

In the rich soil provided by this bit of control, Janus began to grow. She became less afraid of the world. She started to think in terms of "tomorrow," and "the day after that."

Sixteen days after the incident with the well-dressed man, Miguel came hustling into the cafeteria. "I found a decent apartment I can afford," he announced, out of breath.

"That's wonderful, Miguel," Rachel responded. Her voice always grew so animated when he joined them.

Janus turned and saw the hungry look in her sister's eyes. She knew what the girl was thinking.

She looked into Miguel's eyes as he arranged himself on the bench. She knew what he was about to ask, and she began to prepare how she would answer.

She surveyed her surroundings again, with a new eye—not merely checking to see if it was a livable environment. The place stank of urine and sweat. It was filled with the incessant noise of thousands of people talking at the same time. The food tasted like wet paper. Their room—whichever one they were assigned to each night, and that constantly changed—was cramped and filthy and sometimes vandalized beyond usefulness. Once they had slept on shredded foam where the Kevlar-weave mattress cover had been torn away. Too many grungy men's hands had rubbed her or Rachel's bare arms or necks before being slapped away.

She knew how she would answer, but now she had to think ahead, beyond a simple yes or no. She decided serving him in the same way as her father would be acceptable since it would be her own choice this time.

"If you two can provide the small things for yourselves," he said, echoing one of the conditions Janus had already placed on the arrangement, "I can pay the rent. You deserve better than this shelter, this *basurero*. I'll buy the food if you prepare it. I'll provide the furnishings if you keep them clean and repaired. Do we have a deal?"

Janus checked the look on Rachel's face before she responded; the girl stared back with a mix of desire and hatred that said, "If you tell him no and make me stay here any longer, I'll leave you. I'll go back home if I have to, but I can't stay here any longer. Not after seeing a way out."

"We'll have our own room?" Janus asked, feeling suddenly tough and able. "If you're thinking something retro, I need to know now."

"As I said," Miguel began, somewhat quietly, "it is a very small apartment. There is only one room, but there is also a private bathroom. We can set up dividers." His eyes defocused for a moment, and he continued:

"I could build a wall. . ." He grew more animated. "Yes, that's it! I can make you a private room out of real stone, a home of your own within my home. Where I work now, we have much scrap stone. No one will miss it. Not good for building bearing walls, but perfect for decorative walls—if mortared properly." He grinned broadly, again focusing on his future roommates. He winked at Rachel.

"You will have your private room, with a good lock on the door."

They left the complex and crossed town to the north side of the stagnant Alabama River. The apartment was on the 30th floor of an aged skyhulk, as the still-standing twenty-first century skyscrapers were called. Two windows faced out over the Badtown district, but Janus could see as far as opulent North City with its prismatic spires. A heavy lane of air traffic passed near the building, but she soon learned to tune out the steady drone.

Miguel labored for hours every day. He came home from work at noon, dumped out a pile of rubble from his Cord bag, showered, emerged from the bathroom in a clean singlesuit, and worked on the wall until dinnertime. He owned an economy server, and with this Janus and Rachel learned how to cook. Miguel had ordered a full range of international-cuisine instructors.

Janus and Rachel shopped in the mornings while Miguel was away—he left before dawn—then worked on lunch until he returned. He liked a big lunch and a dinner of leftovers. He wouldn't eat the same mush he had put up with at the homeless complex, even though the server could download a flavor program and make it taste however he wanted:

"A man can't eat *basura* in his own home! You spend my credit, whatever it takes, just don't bring anything but real food into my house!"

So he spent as much on food as he did on rent.

Over a period of a week, two walls rose to the ceiling from the plank floor, enclosing a corner of the seven by seven-meter apartment and replacing the sheets temporarily hung from tacks. Miguel was careful to keep one of the two windows in the girls' room:

"I won't have you living in another windowless prison like at the shelter," he said, explaining why the private room would be so much longer on one side than the other.

Janus grew comfortable in her new life. Rachel obviously loved the new arrangement. Never before had she been in the vicinity of so many children her own age, never before had she been able to choose which friends she could play with and when, never before had she talked so much and so joyously at home as she did with Miguel.

After a month of living in the apartment, Janus had a quiet day alone, and she reflected on what she had done. She thought back to how she had been in her father's house, and how Rachel had been. She hated those meek little girls now. She thought about how much she had endured just to live there, while Miguel demanded so little here. He never touched her in a way that made her nervous; he never even looked at her as Father had. Most important, she trusted him with Rachel, who was clearly in love with him.

Lying on a pile of pillows, Janus smiled, feeling the sun warm her cheek, all quiet in her headcard. Aircars hummed past. The wind hushed across the window frame. She sipped at her glass of tea—synthesized tea, smuggled in since Miguel wouldn't even allow the girls anything but real food in his home, and Janus couldn't stand the thought of spending Miguel back into the homeless shelter. She had even charged her father for it. Lunch was prepared, simmering on the stove and filling the air with the rich scent of basil.

She was in control of her life. Rachel was safe and doing well in her studies.

Janus drew a deep breath and looked up at the sea-green sky speckled with traffic. She thought of the future, and of what line of work she would pursue. Everything seemed possible. But she was in no rush. For the first time in memory, Janus was at peace.

She wept.

An hour later, Miguel came through the door and found her with damp cheeks.

"What's wrong, *vida mia*?" he asked, setting down his empty sack.

"Nothing," Janus responded, and turned to him. "Everything is wonderful." She felt a strong urge to kiss him; her blood beat thicker and faster through her chest, her breathing grew difficult, her lips twitched. Yet she was also afraid, most especially of this feeling, and not at all of Miguel.

"Come here," she said before timidity struck her dumb.

He obeyed, crossing the creaky planks. He fell to his knees on a colorful woven rug beside the pile of pillows, and seemed about to kiss her.

"I haven't washed yet," he said, starting to back away.

"Shut up," Janus said, and reached out, pulling him by the back of his solid neck toward her. His lips were thick and oddly soft, totally unlike Father's. His hands were strong and wide, and his chest pressed against her breast while his stomach did not protrude to suffocate her, as Father's had.

Soon, the comparisons faded. Soon, she felt swept away. She felt a tide rush through her, a cleansing saline tide, washing her completely of her past.

A few minutes later, Janus heard the apartment door's lock click and a hand fumble at the outside lever. She pulled back from Miguel's embrace, and he immediately understood, standing up. Rachel walked into the apartment carrying a white rat.

"See what Maril gave me?" she said, closing the door behind her. "Can we keep it?"

Miguel laughed and crossed to her. "Of course," he said, "but you must build a house for it and take care of it. . ."

Their conversation continued. Janus watched, although the sound of their voices faded in the force of her thoughts.

This was her life. She now walked a path toward a future completely disjointed from the past. An aircar whirred past the window not more than ten meters away, a flash of aluminum and ultraglas in the noontime sun. Janus smiled.

She was free.

EarthCo *Bounty* 11: Pehr Jackson

"Janus!" Pehr called again. The woman's limp body danced languidly as the spinning ship's coriolis effects pulled her this way and that. He snapped her seatstrap in place and concentrated on trying to find the missile's BW. This was a difficult procedure without a computer to direct him. He had not been a hacker or tracer as a kid, and never quite learned the tricks of his headcard society.

Finally he found a weak signal and spliced in.

A smooth and mottled world rushed toward him. It was in gibbous phase with a large swath bathed in night. The rest was colored a sickly greenish-blue with great expanses that looked like the preserved grapefruit one might find at a grocery store on

Earth. A few long, relatively straight markings appeared at first to be roads, but then he realized how immense they would be and recalled the terrain maps Janus had called up for him on their way out here. He could see no craters.

Triton grew larger than the round frame that shook slightly at the middle of Pehr's splice. Less than a second had passed. He tried the control-signals which were labeled around the pov, but each one only gave him numbers, indecipherable numbers.

"Dammit, Janus!" he bellowed. "What's wrong? Tell me how to stop the rotten thing."

At the edges of his splice, Janus' pale body continued to sway circles, confined by straps against the black fabric of her couch. At the center, Triton expanded dramatically, now revealing more surface detail.

Pehr cast a glance at Eyes, still immobile against the wall to his left. The mechanical eye still stared.

"Damn you," Pehr muttered at the man.

He continued calling up commands from the missile. Nothing seemed to work. Indeed, as it pulled farther away, the signal faded and grew more staticky.

The *Bounty* creaked louder as time progressed, as the spinning forces threatened to tear loose the thrust-tube and rip a great rent in the base of the craft, spilling out the ship's atmosphere, spilling in death. Now Pehr could see the first signs of humanity on that distant surface: A series of circular ditches seemed to be the missile's bull's-eye . . . not quite, off to one edge, he could now tell. Pehr caught a flash of metal or glass at the center. That gave him small relief, but then he remembered how fragile was the balance of life in airlock cities, and what a nuclear shockwave could do.

Pehr began frantically altering whatever commands and calculations he could. By depressing one virtual button, the splice was overlaid with rows and columns and three-dimensional helixes of numbers and letters, green and red and yellow. He pressed the new buttons that appeared, trying different combinations, and finally they vanished and were replaced by a single, red one. He triggered it.

The background static of the missile's engine ceased. Pehr's heart leaped with hope. He'd stopped it!

But now the circular digs had become short arcs, and he could see individual pieces of machinery in them. The pov closed on the shortest arc. Pehr held his breath, pounding his mental fingers against the visible keys, screaming silently in his head, "Stop! Stop!"

The pov winked out in a flash of whitenoise that made Pehr's back straighten. He flicked out as fast as he could.

"God damn that bastard," Janus said in a husky voice.

"You okay?" Pehr asked, hurriedly adjusting himself to his nonsplice pov. "What happened?"

"The bastard trapped me in that thing." She pulled savagely at the belts holding her down and prepared to push off toward Eyes. "If it detonated, I'm going to kill him."

"Wait!" Pehr said. "Have you programmed our landing?"

"What?" She seemed disoriented.

"I don't want to die, all right? Have you programmed our landing?"

"Oh. Yeah, I just haven't input it into the maneuvering computers yet." Her eyes defocused, though her face still had the set of hatred.

Pehr searched again via headcard menu through the individual transmitters located around the ship. He found the forward pov camera and spliced in. At 1x magnification, Triton looked frightfully as it had from the missile's pov. When he increased magnification, he noticed a tall, growing cloud; nearer the surface, a second cloud was spreading in a strange cyclone pattern around the base of the other.

Pehr flicked out and found himself unable to think of anything but the next second, and then the next. He became entranced with the ship's creaking.

"We're set," Janus reported. "Let's get out of this coffin. You made sure we can get into the escape pod?"

"Yeah. I'll get Eyes."

"Leave him here or I promise I'll kill him."

"He'll die here, anyway," Pehr said. Opposing her tore at his insides—especially after what the cyborg had done—but he couldn't stand the thought of abandoning a man to certain death. Even an evil man.

He looked at Eyes. But was he evil? Hadn't he merely followed script?

The show seemed suddenly a farce. No, worse. How could I have ever placed so much importance on the show? Pehr wondered.

"I'm going up," Janus said, pushing off toward the ceiling handholds, where the pod door was located. She flipped awkwardly in mid-air but managed to grab hold.

"If you bring him," she continued, still not looking at Pehr's eyes, "I'll kill him when I get the chance." Her words were quiet yet heavy with emotion. "Your decision. It will just be a waste of lifesupport and fuel. We ought to just purge it into space."

"We'll let the courts deal with him when we get back," Pehr said, working his way across the cabin to Eyes.

"Ha!" Janus pulled a lever and the round hatch fell open with a faint hiss. "When we get back? I saw the crater. You mean, we'll let NKK's courts at Neptunekaisha deal with it. That sounds fair." She laughed mirthlessly.

Triton 4: Liu Miru

The last thing Miru heard as he stepped into the alien artifact was the rising-pitch hiss of a jet racing closer. Then the sound of immersion in the ocean, but not a noisome one like Earth's. Sloop, the waters of nothingness, closed over his head. Then silence, or less—a sort of aural vacuum.

The last thing he felt was the terrifying sensation of his body dissolving as in an acid bath. Or, more accurately, being caught in the largest pulse-weapon ever devised, completely shattering each atom from the next. He spread wide over a universe black without stars, butter melted in the sun and spread over a 3D piece of colorless bread so vast that each atom floated infinitely far from the next. But he felt no pain of dissolution.

The last thing he tasted was the inside of his cells as they fragmented—a bitter, metallic, salty flavor that flashed through his consciousness the way one sometimes tastes a powerful hypo injected into an arm. A moment later, nothing.

The last thing he smelled was a brief waft of flesh and human waste. It did not smell of decay, but rather of life, like a meatfarm.

And the last sight he beheld was that of the object's interior: A dull, radiative brown without texture or shape. Just before it faded to black, he noticed a pattern that he couldn't quite identify—but only for a moment, as his mind struggled to see something it could make sense of. After all blurred black, he glimpsed an afterimage of something like a plain stretched as far as his mind could grasp—yet more than a plain, as he considered: It curved up and down and in on itself, and was textured with shapes like volcanoes or spines. He wondered if he were seeing the inside of the object.

And then nothing.

Yet still he was conscious of not being able to hear, or feel, move, taste, smell, or see.

Terror filled him as water filled the oceans—he was terror, because he was nothing else.

After a while—if time meant anything now to him, he who was no more than a mind—he realized he wasn't dead. Or, if so, he was still conscious. That meant his terror was useless, for it no longer served a purpose. He would try to understand what had happened.

Hello? his mind's voice asked. Panic swept like a wind through the ephemeral passages of his mind, washing out from under him the fragile ground of rationality upon which he had stood.

More time passed, a maddeningly immeasurable amount, before he brought himself under control again. He realized then that Pang would have experienced this . . . place? as a kind of hell. To anyone else he knew, it would have meant instant annihilation of the spirit. Miru realized that he had been wise, indeed, to be the first to enter the object. But now he must try to learn what it was teaching him.

Are you an entity? he asked. Nothing. He could hardly remember having thought the words. Have I? he wondered, and asked again, only to endure the same sensation of nothingness.

This is a test, he told himself. This is not a hungry entity but a device. It would be illogical for an entity to assume this shape out here, where it would encounter no more than one prey in a million years.

But what if it only needs one during its whole lifetime? I do not know what sort of entity it is.

Stop this foolishness! he screamed at himself. There was no sound, and he again had to fight back the terror of nonexistence.

This is merely the inside of my head, he told himself. An outside observer would merely see me standing before the object, rapt.

A new terror struck him: What if bombs fall on my immobile figure?

Let me free! I am a man!

Nothing. Absolutely nothing. He was no one.

Perhaps this was the worst thing that could have happened to him, who had always feared he barely existed.

And then—he could no longer resist—his mind erupted with the stored memories of a lifetime, filling the emptiness with images as real as if he were living them again.

Yesteryear 3: Liu Miru

He saw the world suddenly red and blurry on March 20, 2158, in the birthing ward of NKK's Ryukyu Submerged Island. The following years washed past as if he were a dolphin swimming through them, through a tunnel as dense as his experiences, as broad as his worldview, and as long as his life, each year passing in a fraction of what felt like a second. Occasionally, he would slow almost to a halt as an important incident densified the matter of his life.

He was a small boy, squatting naked over a child's waste port, but he no longer had need to use it. His tight-faced mother scolded him for having filled his pants. He was old enough now to use the port, too old to make his mother clean his pants.

He was a little older, sitting in the middle of his parents' compartment. He made a plastic killer whale swim around and around a model of the island, represented by a round soya carton. A chunk of color was missing on the whale's head, so it looked as if he were sick. When the whale grew tired, Miru looked up at his father, seated on the big cotton recliner. The man's eyes were half-closed and his lips moved without sound: He was busy at work. Miru looked to his mother. She stood with her hands in the little curved slots on the outside wall, murmuring words that reassured him because they were everpresent in his life and meant his mother was near.

The nice man whom Miru could see through stood between Miru and his mother; the man was showing him different kinds of foods and things and telling him which would make him sick if he ate them.

It was making Miru hungry and tired, like the killer whale. He called to his mother, but she couldn't hear him. He tried the special-talk in the head, but she was too busy to notice. So he finally stood and walked to the kitchen-box and got a special bar. As always, it tasted so good and sweet, but somehow it made him sad.

A few years later, he accidentally noticed the wars for the first time. One of the local net ganglia had gone unsane and had to be shut down. Briefly and suddenly, all the BWs became accessible to everyone, some even to children's cards. He remembered specifically the face of a man, a white man with brown hair and a little worm of a mustache on his upper lip. The face was the only thing he could pick out from the confusion of explosions and shrieks and smoke and fire. The face seemed startled and somehow very lonely. The eyebrows rose as if to ask a question. The lips parted slightly. Dirt covered both cheeks.

Then the man coughed, and out splashed a red liquid. That was all. The face vanished, and Miru realized he had been watching only a tiny portion of a kaleidoscope of battle. When the psychedelics began to tug at his senses, when the 3VRD became too real, he flicked out as fast as he could.

The dreams never went away, that face, but they changed every time. Once, the face was that of Father; the island was on fire and exploding. All the rescue boats filled with evacuees, but there were too many people. Too many people. Fire danced crazy columns on the water. Miru woke up with tears cold on his cheeks and hot eyes, and he desperately wanted to tell Mother, who lay right beside him on her mat. But she slept with her eyes half-open, which meant she would be furious if he woke her. He learned to comfort himself: The wars will stop one day. But at some dark corner of his mind, he knew they were raging continuously all around him, in every country in the world. Just that he could no longer access those BWs didn't mean they ceased to exist; indeed, his imagination created worse scenes than he could have spliced. But they wouldn't last forever, would they? Who could permit that?

He was ten as he stood near the second above-line railing and looked out across the sea. He smelled the salt air and burned methane fumes. The sky, where it met the ocean, was grey. The waves were white-tipped and vast ships broke through even the tallest of them.

A gang of young boys began to mock him. "*Ryukure, ryukure, ryukure,*" they chanted: "Retro, retro, retro."

He simply looked at them, puzzled. Why were they so bothered by his watching for whales? Surely, they must be interested in whales, as well. One had been sighted nearby only a month ago, surely they had heard that. Nothing could possibly compare to seeing a whale. That would be real magic.

"Do you want to swim, *ryukure*?" the oldest boy asked. Young Miru wasn't interested in the boy, so he didn't splice in to the island's net and find out his name; he'd had the misfortune to encounter these boys often enough to recognize them without names.

"He's a dumbcard," one of the others said. They laughed. Didn't they have school to occupy them?

"Teach him to swim!" another shouted. They laughed harder.

Miru stared at them; no one looked into his eyes. They were like his father: They were elsewhere. So why did they pay him so much attention? He had grown to like being alone, and any attention he might desire would certainly not be this.

"I'll grab him!"

The largest boy—the one who spoke first—approached Miru.

Miru looked down at the waves slapping against the sides of the island and rising partway up. Far below, perhaps eighty meters beneath the beneathline, the bottom of the island would be bobbing slightly. Fish swam down there, and maybe whales.

Miru turned back to his assailants. He was tired of their inane games. He would not let them stir up his mind again, as they had so often in so many minute ways that haunted and heated him for days afterward.

He clenched his little fist and swung it as hard as he could against the cheek of the big boy. Without hesitation, he faced the water again, crawled atop the cool, slick railing, and jumped.

Whoosh, the water slapped his feet and, a moment later, rushed in over his head. It felt cool against his skin, not cold. He heard muted sounds like the recordings of whales, and also mechanical noises. Down here all was peaceful. He had not known any place could be so peaceful. So much space surrounded him, and nowhere could he see a person.

He couldn't decide if it was worse when his fellow humans ignored him or when they paid him stupid attention, like the gang.

He thought how nice it would be to breathe water; maybe he could be like the mythical creatures who were half-man and half fish. He never again wanted to be among people. He didn't like them a bit. Perhaps, someday, they would realize how stupid they were. But, until then, he would be alone beneath the waves where they couldn't come. This would be his private world.

Of course, not much time passed before suffocation forced him to resurface and re-enter the island by one of the platform locks that constantly rose above and fell below the waves. He stumbled there for a moment, skinning his shins and forearms against the plastic gratings, but managed to get into the waterlock.

Two years later, he took his schooling underwater. His father had given him for his thirteenth birthday the osmosuit that allowed him to breathe oxygen taken from the water. He became the mythical fish-man. This was his magic.

Soon these childhood memories gathered so thickly before Miru that swimming through them was like swimming through molten metal. He turned away from the memory of when Seeli laughed at his feeble attempt to court her. He struggled to avoid seeing the bloated, floating body of his father on the foamy waves or the sunken face of his mother. But he couldn't help seeing her. She looked like that for years, an everpresent countenance in the channel of his life. She looked as if hers had been the face in the war scene.

He earned his youth diploma and began taking professional training feed. The swimming grew easier, as if here was little to remember. *Odd*, he thought, since he had learned so much about so many things during this time. Miru had been unable to specialize, unlike most people in his society, because so much interested him. He earned partial certificates in physics, astronomy, geology, paleobiology, and cosmology.

After years of this, NKK's Hososuru put a stop to this behavior by granting his certificate in General Science and Physics, Extraterrestrial. So NKK Mikazuki—the corp's main Lunar facility—hired him and booked him passage to the Moon aboard a cargo vessel.

During the two years he worked at NKK Mikazuki, the only projects he refused to work on were those directly related to the military. He thought, *If I am to dedicate myself to any one thing, that will be peace among all people, NKK and EarthCo alike.* Gradually, even that dream faded as he watched his superiors purge troublemakers out of airlocks onto the harsh surface of the Moon—without suits. No, these people would never be capable of creating lasting peace or performing worthwhile work.

His dream shifted: Only the future held any worth, because there lay hope for changed men. He would do everything in his power to advance knowledge so the people who lived in tomorrow could build a worthwhile life.

When the newly formed TritonCo Division's recruiters showed up in his section's meeting hall, he signed on immediately. He and Jon Pang met in that hall, two young men from different sections, but both men who held a similar vision for the future. Miru was struck with the man's calmness and warm smile. He seemed to be the only real person in the underground vessels.

The following years of hard labor on Triton—assembling Jiru City and establishing a mining and research community—were the best years of Miru's life. Out on the unforgiving Tritonian frontier, he ran servines from a seat cased in frigid metal mesh, working 3VRD controls to lift and move environmental pressure-vessels and seal units; he pumped thousands of liters of sealant into leaks by hand using spray-units that froze up half the time in the icy moon's near-absolute-zero weather; he slept thousands of Earth-days in sweaty pressure suits because the environmental vessels were untrustworthy. . . . But he had discovered a kindred soul, and he had found work that helped build the future of his vision.

He swam languidly through these years, taking great pleasure in their rewards as well as their trials. In the Labor Uprising of 2190, Earth contract-workers—convicts reducing their stasis-time in hopes of coming out of their feed sane or at least not highly neurotic—assaulted TritonCo's ganglia; even these dark days held a touch of nostalgia. When he saw the laborers afterward, their scalps ruptured when President Dorei had regained control of the computers, Miru hurried along. He had seen enough damaged faces in his life.

The apex of this high-water mark in his life was the discovery of the object. He had begun to dream dreams once only reserved for the future. He realized that the magic of wonder could belong to today, as long as it was connected to the future, that dreams could be more than abstract goals—they could be realized.

Then the EarthCo warship *Bounty* entered his memories. And then his existence went dark again.

EarthCo *Bounty* 12: Janus Librarse

"Director Miru?" Janus asked again, using the pod's transmitter. "Do you feed?"

She, Jackson, and Eyes were strapped in their acceleration couches aboard *Bounty*'s cramped escape pod. It enclosed them like a clamshell, low and curved and windowless. Its unused air scrubbers still smelled of new rubber and fresh oil. An inset ring of soft white light encircled the two-meter-diameter cabin, casting shadowless illumination at eye-level.

Janus had first canceled the spin, and now the main ship's aft retros all fired simultaneously, emptying the tanks in deceleration, using up the wreck before discarding it. They produced a thrust of less than 0.2*g*, but every bit of energy she could squeeze out of the *Bounty* meant that much less would be required of the pod. This way, they just might be able to shed enough speed to land.

"TritonCo, this is Janus Librarse of the EarthCo *Bounty*. We have placed the errant bombardier of our ship under custody for his malicious act against you. He acted against our orders, repeat, against our orders. We surrender our craft and ourselves to your mercy. Do you feed?"

The retros shook the ship with their fluttering howls. The comm line in Janus' splice showed nothing. Again she saw images of murder, as she did every second she had free to think about Eyes: the trap he laid for her, the bomb he dropped on the artifact.

"I promise," she commed direct to Eyes only, "if that bomb of yours destroyed the alien artifact, you will die as slowly and as creatively as I can manage."

As vulgar a place as it was, his headcard seemed to beckon her. If only I can get in there and scramble things a bit. . . .

She finally overcame her revulsion—hate and revenge overpowering queasiness— and pried open the virtual vault into his card.

A circus. He had planted a circus as gatekeeper to his mind. Mutants and clowns took notice across a dusty path and began crossing toward her. Canvas tents in every color of the spectrum rose behind them, screams and laughter, noises of machinery and people, all behind a wood-plank wall plastered with posters she couldn't quite read from this distance. Something seemed wrong about the circus. She realized what it was: The clowns and mutants all wore masks of evil, and the voices from behind the wall were not those of people having fun. Rather, they sounded as if they were hysterical with fear; perhaps they were mere lunatics. The sky flickered electric blue.

She pulled out before the clowns reached her. For a moment, Janus' hatred of Eyes changed to loathing and terror, and maybe something akin to pity. Then she hardened herself. Here was a man—a thing—unfit to live among humans. It had done the unforgivable. It could not be human. It was an incarnation of evil.

The retros began to shudder and pop. One after one, they burned out as the last whiffs from the oxygen tanks were sucked through the pulsepumps.

"Prepare to disengage," she said, purpose reassuring her. When all was quiet, the computer blew twelve connectors between the vessels and ignited the pod's main rocket.

Now the globe of the *Bounty* split into two hemispheres as first red and then blue fire pried them apart. A small saucer-shaped section that had been the ship's fore dome fell farther and farther back from the battered hulk hurtling toward the little moon.

"I've programmed the burn for four minutes at 1g," she said, unstrapping and rising from her couch. She had to bend her neck to stand.

"That's when we should reach Triton's atmosphere. The air's pretty tenuous, but it ought to help slow us down." She turned from Jackson, who sat silent with a pained, unreadable expression on his face, and looked down at Eyes on his couch beside hers.

"We take three passes through the atmosphere," Janus continued, stretching her shoulders, "firing the rocket again between each pass."

A brief pulse of adrenaline rushed into her bloodstream and she brought down her right fist as hard as she could against the cyborg's mechanical eye. The eyelid closed automatically just before impact.

"Janus," Jackson scolded softly, "don't make yourself like him."

She looked at Jackson again, and all her hatred dissipated. He showed more pain now than ever. It hurt her to see him like that. She realized fully, for the first time in all these months, that she had grown to truly care about him.

"Oh, Jack," she said, sitting back down and rubbing her sore knuckles, "what are we going to do?"

EarthCo *Bounty* 13: Lonny Marshfield

You bitch, you chant inside over and over so you don't give away that you can hear and see every fucking thing. You fatherfucking bitch. Just wait.

Once she lands you safely, you'll show her a thing or two. You'll take her into your cerebral circus. You'll see just how much she can take before she shatters.

And she will shatter. You've seen it happen before. You've done it before.

But you must wait, must. Don't let the quiet emptiness start to run you down. Don't let them know. Go back to the circus and wait. Make some preparations. She'll come back.

You'll be there to greet her.

Neptunekaisha 5: C.P. Chang

The needleship *Sigwa*, an A-class destroyer fitted with battle-coordination equipment, hung far above the stations and shadow-shrouded cloud-tops of Neptune. It stretched nearly 280 meters from pointed prow to gaping nozzle stern, yet the hull was at no point wider than ten meters. Dozens of oval-shaped plates circumfering amidships lay flush with the destroyer's skin, ready to surge outward on hydraulic stalks and fire forward or aftward their cartridges of missiles and torpedoes. No view- or cannon ports showed, for it had none. From a station's pov, the hull facing Neptune looked as black and starry as space, and the other side of the hull mimicked the world's nighttime coloration. No visible and very few high-wavelength BWs could be used to detect it, because its smartcamo made it "look" like whatever lay beyond; for all practical purposes, the *Sigwa* was invisible. In addition, the bulk of the world hid it from view of the inner planets.

Inside, Clarisse lay secured in the Coordinator's unit, a couch with powerful buffers and amps and a dedicated server. The tiny room was essentially a sensory-deprivation tank, shutting out all physical stimuli. She could barely feel the interactive-gel beneath and all around her, and no sound or other sense of the ship was transmitted to her, except via 3VRDs. She struggled heroically to keep down any and all emotions. Now was the time for organization, not for the good hate.

The craft was nearly fully awake now; all its systems were flashing online in her controls overlay. Good, good. It hadn't suffered measurably in its decades of mothballing. Her splice itself showed the dirtside pov.

Already, 20 or so smaller vessels were assembled nearby, and others rose from the clouds, materializing like ghosts. Few of them were really battleworthy, but, operating together, they could destroy merchantmen and individual EarthCo warcraft without having to reveal the destroyer. A couple of the last to leave would stop past Triton on their way, to complete the work she had begun on the EarthCo warship *Bounty*. Most important, this force would be the initial wave which would propagate broader and higher as it progressed Solward.

Neptunekaisha would be left without a defense fleet, but what use had it seen in the past decades? None. The hunters and mines had effectively protected NKK's interests at Neptunekaisha during three separate attacks, and would continue to do so through the war, even if needed again. And this was now war, even if not yet declared. EarthCo would learn soon enough—though perhaps not soon enough to prepare.

The mines and hunters would provide a fine fortification against attack. She had already submitted an order for more, better defenses, to cover contingencies. Coordinating Officer Hang would take care of manning the fortress. She felt proud of the speed and organization she had displayed since the *Bounty* had given her the opportunity she had awaited so long. Of course, all this was only the enactment of a well-thought-out plan.

Everything was covered. The gears were engaged. The motor of revenge was about to fire.

The last go-light on her overlay signaled the *Sigwa*'s readiness. Clarisse flicked a new set of overlays—these were assembled in 3D layering so that all were visible and accessible simultaneously—that connected her to the other craft. The two big tankers she had appropriated over Shen-lin's complaints both stood ready. The cargohull, packed with missiles and other supplies, had been ready for several minutes. The most critical escorts were ready.

She initialized the magnetic accelerators, trained on her little fleet from a worldwide ring of generators buried in the clouds.

"Launch when ready," she said over the scramble-line, "staggered formation, staggered acceleration. One through six, I have your helms. We launch in ten, nine, eight. . ."

An audible bump penetrated the Coordinator's unit, accompanied by a gentle, generalized pressure and an undamped kinesthesia that told Clarisse the *Sigwa* was underway. Her dirtside pov didn't seem to change except for the ships rising from the cloud-tops, which seemed to accelerate away from her faster and faster. Then the sunward limb of Neptune flashed into view, individual cloudbanks barely more than a blur. Sol himself shone as a gold coin set against the black tapestry of her rocketship sea.

Once again Clarisse's pov plunged into darkness as the accelerators whipped her ship around the world. Now she could not identify any surface detail or single craft.

A second bump, followed immediately with an even greater pressure as the great rocket engine ignited at the programmed 3gs. All her tied-in escorts, including the cargohull and two tankers, had been accelerated and had launched as expected, though mostly at much lower thrust. She flicked on the forward pov.

At last, the sun sat still. Even so, only at high magnifications could she identify the spark of light—now far to the edge of her pov—which the fleet would meet in a few months: Jupiter, the greatest of gas giants, a world and satellite system still largely possessed by EarthCo. If all went as planned, she should arrive simultaneously with or shortly after Sotoi Guntai forces from Saturn and Uranus, and perhaps even from the NKK-protected Greater Asteroids.

And there she halted her projections. Now, after having learned—during her term at Neptunekaisha—the power of delayed gratification, she would not forget that lesson. She would not fall prey to those predators of the mind, haste and rigid expectation. Earlier in life—during her flight from Russia to Bangkok—she had learned that haste and expectation can be worse enemies than procrastination. She had learned that following a plan while also being capable of quickly changing it were the survival skills necessary in modern warfare.

Clarisse checked all her ship's systems, then those of her escorts. All within normal operating parameters. Only two old fighters that had been serving as crew transport and recreation craft were keeping abreast of her. But the rest were not far behind. The tankers and cargohull would arrive at Jupiter only a few days later.

She shut down her external camera splice and spliced in a sleepy-dreamer program. All would take care of itself in due time. If she was needed, the ship would wake her.

Neptunekaisha Coordinator of Protection Clarisse Poinsettia Chang, at last Captain Clarisse Poinsettia Chang, began to drift away to the songs of water and wind and forest creatures. Slowly, she became the river Volga. She flowed into the future, renewed, changed, flowing toward a definite confluence for the first time in her life. She was needed, and took great, drowsy satisfaction in that. She slept well, occasionally reassured and briefed by subconscious feed.

The needleship *Sigwa* plunged toward Jupiter upon a lance of flame, shrouded in stars and obsidian night, burdened with the weight of a lone woman.

SIX: Earth

A Day in the Life of Susahn Jackson

Mrs. Pehr Jackson, as Susahn liked to be called, spent this day not unlike every other day in her 32 years.

In a large but not ostentatious townhouse on the outskirts of St. Louis, she slept. Mechanized lawnkeepers replanted wilted flowers, trimmed the grass, maintained the tall concrete wall that surrounded the three side-by-side townhouses and two acres of yard.

Her amplified dreams had been recorded into free space on her apartment's server, and when her body refused to sleep any longer, she sorted through them and chose one to dream again. All this without opening her eyes, therefore maintaining the reality of the dreamworld.

As usual, the waking dream was unsatisfying: Dreams never recorded with quite the same wonder as her sleeping self thought they had. Also, since dreams ran faster than realtime, the computer had to edit and restructure them so a conscious person could re-experience them. So even dreams didn't have the power to satiate her unidentifiable longing.

When physical hunger began to distract her from the replay, Susahn opened a feedback BW to send a message to her husband, the famous Pehr Jackson of *Lone Ship Bounty* fame. She spliced in a subscription to a glorious drama set on and below the blazing surface of Mercury before opening her eyes. And then, because her own voice narrating the contents of her favorite dream and the many faces arguing about love and loss on Mercury couldn't satisfy her intangible need, she opened an option box and requested an editor's subscription. The familiar man's smiling face appeared overlaid on the drama. Now she at least began to forget her dissatisfaction.

"What sort of genre are you interested in, Mrs. Pehr Jackson?" the AI animation of a real editor asked. Perhaps, this time, this is actually my editor intheflesh, she thought. Well, perhaps not entirely intheflesh, but at least live on the other end of the BW. He wore a comfortable old sweater and cotton pants and his long hair was neatly braided.

"Something artsy and deep," she answered, giggling like a girl as she entered the familiar white ceramic of the kitchen.

The editor grinned and nodded. "Ah, you're feeling like a connoisseur this morning, eh Susahn? Well, how about a monopera? One in particular is just now beginning to fragment, guaranteed not to survive the night."

"Oh, that sounds wonderful, Marty," she responded, feeling lucky all of a sudden. He knew her well, always recommending a good piece of music when the choice was his.

Maybe this is what she needed. If she hadn't called up the editor, she'd never have known about this dying monopera, and, missing it, how could she have faced her friends like an ignorant child? Susahn made a mental note to remember to check the editor every morning from now on, and set the note to recite the moment she woke.

"Shall I subscribe you until its end?" he asked.

"Yes. Yes, Marty, I want to be there until . . . until it's nothing but ashes."

"That's a very nice line, Susahn," he said with a knowing smile. "Perhaps you're working on a new song? Perhaps you'd like to submit something new for my consideration?"

"Oh, I don't think so." She blushed. "Not now. Maybe tomorrow? That is, if the monopera inspires me."

"Whenever you're ready, you know my callcode," he said. "There, now you're subscribed to the monopera, *Commutatis*. Do you need anything else?"

"No, thank you, Marty."

"Enjoy!" he said, and disappeared.

Susahn hurriedly shut down everything but the monopera, but set it to visual and audio only, so she could eat her breakfast. Once, she had tapped into an artsong—using her fivesen enhancement program—and had lost a full day before absolute exhaustion had dragged her away from the rolling colors and synchronized music. She had become a bassoon, but more than a bassoon; she had become roses and notes and nectar, silk on her own skin and perfume in her own nostrils, chords swelling in her own ears, sweetmeats melting on her own tongue. But not yet, not until she had fortified her body to last out the monopera.

So she poured herself a glass of high-fiber, high-nutrition liquimeal and programmed it to taste like seven courses of a gourmet breakfast. She even programmed it to look like those seven courses. None of the programming required any knowledge on her part besides how to select highlighted buttons in her option box; this was all part of her server's resident memory, freely accessible once she purchased the program in the first place.

A grand old orchestra hall filled her splice pov, rich dark wood rising for a hundred meters like the inside of an oyster to a crystal-laced ceiling glowing with luminescent clouds that alternately hid and revealed the jeweled articulation. She moved in syncopation with the rhythm of the music as literally thousands of instruments and their players, along with hundreds of vocalists, spread across a stage perhaps 200 meters round. It was shaped like a bowl so one could see everything from any point on the parquet floor. A spiraling balcony encircled the stage, rising up and up into the clouds, allowing subscribers to watch from multiple vantage-points. An unobtrusive option box displayed several alternative povs, from musician to vocalist to any number of immaterial povs. It also allowed for altering the hall in various ways to enhance the experience, such as bringing down the clouds so that they took the form of the music, the music the form of the clouds, dancing and cloaking the subscriber as if her senses were all rearranged. . . .

Susahn sighed sharply as she realized the ephemeral finger in her head had selected that last option, and she willed herself to shut it down, at least until after breakfast. Soon, she finished eating, and dropped the glass into the cleaning-chute. As usual after breakfast, she called a friend to share morning coffee with her.

"Liza?" she asked when her friend's 3VRD didn't materialize immediately. A second later, a beautiful, slim woman in her 30s appeared in the Jackson kitchen. Her dark hair was woven in a thick halo around her head—as was all the curr among the artistes in Susahn's circle of friends—and was cloaked in a translucent robe Susahn hadn't seen before. Suddenly, she felt retro and inelegant, and hurriedly selected a fashion BW; a few moments later, with the help of a fashionmate, her 3VRD was updated and a new set of curr dresses were on their way to her home, in case she needed her intheflesh appearance to match her 3VRD. All this, and less than a second had passed since her friend appeared.

"What's on, Susahn," the woman said, her face friendly but unsmiling. Susahn worried momentarily if Liza had seen the abrupt wardrobe shift.

"I'm on a monopera BW, this one—" and Susahn had her server feed the technical details to Liza's server, which put it in her option box—a thousand kilometers away. "It's entitled, *Commutatis*, and guaranteed to end today. You—"

"Of course, dear," Liza said, patronizingly. "I'm involved with it right now. I'm a musician, you know, and all the musicians are involved with *Commute* today. Care to join me?" She smiled again, raising an eyebrow.

"Oh, yes," Susahn replied, sending a signal to Liza's server to link their 3VRDs in the orchestra hall.

Liza no longer stood, but sat in a form-shifting seat before a winding golden instrument that exhaled a mellow range of notes. Susahn suddenly felt awkward simply standing near her talented friend, so she shifted pov to that of a vocalist nearby, that person's self cloaking Susahn like a well-tailored dress. Or perhaps the sensation was more like drowning in a breathable substance that was actually another person. Liza smiled when she had a moment's rest from her horn, when a ring of saxophones suddenly burst forth from the millisecond silence between scores.

Starting to relax now, Susahn added more senses until she was fully immersed in the monopera. As the day wore on, as she became more and more consumed with the music and as more and more of her friends gathered around her and Liza, Susahn selected more and more options, until, sometime in the afternoon, she had the subscription's full menu running and was still desiring more. Passion filled her as every nerve in her body sang with pleasure, as invisible fingers of light caressed her pale skin in harmony with the music, in harmony somehow with fragrances that perfectly matched the notes, with occasional glorious bursts of bitter or salty or chocolate-sweet flavors that filled her mouth as other parts of her body tensed with something akin to orgasm. Even Liza was impressed with Susahn's command of the monopera.

So the day was consumed. It was a glorious day by any estimation, and Susahn's days were mostly very good. By evening, she had spent two days' worth of her husband's large salary, mostly on access costs. Usually, except in rare cases when Susahn sold a song—and that brought in very few percents—she had no income. But, then, she didn't need to, not when her husband's subscription was the top-rated show whenever it fed live. He earned more than 500 percents a year, more than five average workers. And he was famous.

So Susahn led a good life, even though she woke every morning with a vague feeling of dissatisfaction. She was sure it wasn't that she wanted children, although her husband persistently harped her to apply for permission to get pregnant every time he returned from a mission. No, she didn't want that. Children were, well, disgusting in some abstract way she couldn't identify. Certainly, they would be a drain on her finances. Children were very expensive to raise, and it had to be done intheflesh. She had a good life without them, and the idea of having to clean up green diarrhea made her skin crawl. Who knows how her cultured friends would react if she revealed that her husband wanted a baby?

Anyway, she led a good life, and this was one of the better ones, although she couldn't necessarily recall exactly how it differed from the rest. That didn't matter.

Then, at approximately 6pm, Susahn's fine day was transformed into an amazing day.

"Mrs. Pehr Jackson?" a gorgeous middle-aged man's 3VRD asked her. He was dressed like royalty, but not extravagantly; high fashion that was also timeless, tailored to fit in such a way that revealed the well-built man beneath the exotic materials yet conservative in cut. No cosmetics. He was vaguely familiar, but she couldn't place him.

By the reaction of Susahn's friends, she realized he was not only 3-verding her, but also projecting into all their splices. He might even have come to the orchestra hall intheflesh.

"Yes," she answered, unnecessarily, since all her standard citizenship data was available to anyone interacting with her 3VRD.

"My name is Luke Herrschaft, Director of Feedcontrol."

The revelation sent shockwaves through those near her; even the monopera itself seemed to stutter, at least its participants within hearing cut their performances and gave the man their attention.

Susahn tentatively drew back from full fivesen engagement in the monopera and investigated his claim. Her breath caught in her throat when she read his data and found that, yes, he was who he claimed to be. She even sent a tracer along the main information highways that swirled through EarthCo's datacenters, coming back affirmative. She put her hand against her heaving chest and asked a question with her eyes. Yes, now she recognized him, from his yearly "State of the Corp" addresses.

"I would like to have the pleasure of your company this evening," he said, his voice powerful and measured. Somehow, he managed to speak in a cadence that matched the vocalist now singing. "A pivotal scene in your husband's program is about to show, and I would be honored to be with Pehr's wife while she witnesses his greatest hour." A smile Susahn couldn't decipher spread across the man's chiseled features.

"Oh, my, Director," she gushed, "the pleasure would be all mine. But—"

"All arrangements have been taken care of. You will find a car waiting for you in front of your house. I hope to see you soon." He gave a slight bow and vanished.

"All the gods, Susahn!" Liza cried. "I can't believe it. Herrschaft himself inviting you..."

Susahn quickly said her goodbyes and terminated the splice. She forgot all about the monopera when she opened the front door of their first-level townhouse and gazed out onto the street at a sleek, black high-speed aircar with little cloth flags waving from antennae along the sloping roofline. The evening sun shone through diaphanous smog that lined the buildings even this far from the city, the airy mantle beautiful in the light.

When she closed the outer wall's gate behind her, stepping onto a gravelly sidewalk, the car's door automatically opened and a bronze voice from within called her name, beckoning her inside. She took another tentative step forward and looked into the shadowy heart of the limousine, noting a figure already on the tan leather seat.

"Susahn, it's me," the man said, "Luke Herrschaft. Please join me."

"Director-?" she said, stunned by his intheflesh appearance. But was he here intheflesh? No, of course not. Who was Susahn Jackson to warrant such an appearance?

"Yes, call me Luke, please," he said.

For the second time in as many minutes, she ran a tracer to verify his reality. When it came back affirming the shape inside the car was, indeed, Director of EarthCo Feedcontrol Luke Herrschaft, intheflesh, Susahn nearly fainted.

"If we don't get underway soon," he said, "we might miss the show's beginning. I always like to experience a pivotal show from my enhancer-theater back at Central. Let's not be late!"

"Oh, of course, Dir—" She blushed. "Of course, Luke." And she climbed inside. The door shut from above, like a hand sealing out the world. The car accelerated so fast Susahn nearly gasped again. The heavy-fast feeling was stimulating, especially since it wasn't a simulation; everything was stimulating, being so near this man. She took several deep breaths to compose herself. She was, after all, not some backwoods girl but an accomplished singer and songwriter. Her friends were glamorous and cultured, famous in the world of music. Her husband was the most well-known man in EarthCo. Even more so than, perhaps, Luke Herrschaft.

"That's better," he said, a smile growing across his dark, handsome face like an entity of its own. Her heart sped. She smoothed the folds of her now-out-of-date skirt and tunic, embarrassed once more that she wasn't curr.

But over the next half hour, Luke's smooth voice and sensitive personality slowly calmed Susahn. They shared real drinks, which disarmed her more, giving her a pleasant lightheaded feeling. She began to feel as if he were a close friend, even a potential lover. . . . Just the idea of such a tryst made her head spin. Everything about him was disarming yet attractive, and eventually she began to give him certain messages with her eyes. She knew how her dark blue irises and long lashes affected men, and she knew how to use them. Luke responded well, returning her body language in his own, masculine way. At one point, Susahn brushed her fingertips across Luke's hand—to verify he was really here, intheflesh, she told herself. The contact made her nerves tingle all the way up her arm to her neck.

Then the car landed atop a lone building overlooking acres of antennae, surrounded by ring after ring of wire fences and then farmland. He let her know this was Feedcontrol Central. She had arrived.

Stepping out of the limousine, one hand supported by Luke, Susahn reflected on her day. So far, it had been the greatest of her life. If she died now, she would be happy.

That nagging dissatisfaction had lost itself in the wake of the aircar somewhere near St. Louis; that hunger for something she couldn't name deep inside her had been fulfilled.

And, feeling his strong hand around hers, Susahn was sure the best was surely yet to come.

Feedcontrol 3

One part of Luke Herrschaft's split self stood in a shockproof room 120 meters below Feedcontrol Central's ground level. Input ports and 3VRD projectors, which transmitted commands only transmittable from here and revealed data visible only in this room, surrounded him. Three women and two men constantly and tirelessly operated controls and watched projections as he tapped into the raw feed and muttered occasional orders to the workers.

Another copy of Luke Herrschaft personally roved through EarthCo's netways in search of others behind the President of the United States' assassination attempt. Herrschaft was certain the pol hadn't acted alone; no politician ever made an important decision by himself, he thought. Revenge would be at least as painful to the mastermind as it had been to him. But first he would find out who did it and why.

The third slice of him escorted Mrs. Pehr Jackson into Feedcontrol Central, giving her a personal tour on the way to his private projection room #3. His presence with her had been very small since she hadn't required much attention, as expected. But now he shifted the bulk of his consciousness into that pov, confident his people could handle the setup routines of *Lone Ship Bounty*. Every day, the people in that room tailored and fed several subscription programs without difficulty or assistance. Little did they know the weight today's program would carry, that today would be wholly different than all the previous.

Herrschaft felt his old self roll upon the mechanical shoulders of a fine robot walking arm-in-arm with Mrs. Jackson. With that reminiscent sensation followed the familiar confidence—drawn not only from walking as a powerful man again and almost believing in his reality, but also from being present as great plans bloom, from having spent the afternoon tailoring in person a number of programs. And from the presence of the future all around him, a future he had orchestrated, a future that would give him ultimate control over the Solar System—power drawn from crushing others.

These thoughts overrode the vague incompleteness he sensed in himself.

He turned a gently smiling face to Mrs. Jackson, imagining whatever real face he still possessed grimacing in delight at the huge moment hanging about them like tapestries of change.

Then came the memories. He had been uncareful the past few seconds—indeed, for the past hours—taking too much time for reflection and dreams. Idle moments always unearthed the past, displaying the corpses of his childhood. They began to dance the story of his youth, laughing at him through teeth clogged with soil, sounding like wind through fall leaves. Rattling loose memories best left buried.

Yesteryear 2: Luke Herrschaft

He had been a "millennium baby," born at the turn of the twenty-first century. His mother gave birth to him in a shabby tarpaper-sided house near Big Stone, South Dakota. Big Stone was a town of about 100 people bordered by a rotting lake on one side, a cheese factory on another, and a canning factory on another. Agricultural fields isolated the town and factories from the rest of the world. A power plant stood nearby, serving energy states away and consuming trainloads of coal daily. A highway ran through the middle of town, traveled mainly by pickups and farm equipment. Slowly, each business in the town was in the process of dying. Some had died quickly, especially the larger ones.

Luke's mother had only been 15, so his father—30 years old at the time—promptly married the girl when she refused to have an abortion. This much Luke was later able to piece together; he heard enough of his father's side of the arguments as the big man screamed into the telephone for what seemed like a full year before the divorce was final. Elder Herrschaft's threats to label his wife insane convinced her to let him take custody of young Luke; Luke was four when his father moved him to another house in town, five when his parents were divorced.

The man never laid a hand on Luke in violence, except to punish misdeeds. Fear of elder Herrschaft's perforated leather belt made a model son out of Luke, at least by the man's definition. Luke learned not even to speak out of turn; by the time he was 12, he learned not to speak to the man at all.

In school, miles away in another town, Luke excelled. He found that he was adept with numbers and could quickly collate a number of large concepts, enabling him to do very well in the advanced maths. History and civic courses held a strong interest for him, as well, especially stories of great men and their great achievements. At the time, he had no idea the two disparate fields of study would later merge into one.

But school was not a pleasant place for Luke. Since he was skinny, pocked with pimples, and wore thick eyeglasses, fellow students mocked him mercilessly. As much as he seethed with hatred for this treatment, he hated them even more when, later, they simply ignored him. Some of the athletes would shove him aside between classes in the busy hallways, bang him against lockers during the lunch hour and threaten to pull his underwear up over his head, but mostly they forgot he even existed.

By 16, his life had grown silent. Wind howled through the walls of his father's ancient house, winter's claws picking out gaps in the termite-eaten wood. Dogs barked mindlessly nearby until their owners kicked them silent for a few minutes, and the barking would return. Pickups roared through town, guided by drunken teenagers or their adult counterparts whose faces had grown rigid with the grimace of age and too many defeats. That was all. No voices entered his consciousness except those of his teachers.

He was able to survive in the vacuum, content absorbing book after book: Watching history expand back through time through the perceptions of historians, conquering formula after formula and proof after proof. Many nights he stayed up late, studying by lamplight until elder Herrschaft bellowed that he shut the goddamned thing off; many times, he'd told Luke that school was his only way to earn a better life, but enough was enough.

Then Gladice Stevenson had entered his field of vision, and he had been stricken with all the symptoms of what the books called love.

Gladice was not beautiful, but then Luke had long before given up his desires for beautiful girls. They had laughed often enough at him, and he was able to look beyond their porcelain faces into their minds and see the loathing they nurtured there for him. No, he had stopped being attracted to pretty girls. Gladice was short, knobby-boned, quiet, and her downcast face was as expressionless as Luke's own. She sat a row ahead and to the left of him in Geometry III. The only words she spoke were flawless answers to questions the teacher had directed at her, and even then she spoke not to the man near the chalkboard but at the open book on her desktop.

He recognized in her silence and perceived loneliness a kindred spirit. Following that recognition, he burned with the sudden revelation that he, too, was desperately lonely. It was as if she were a beacon illuminating uncharted caverns in his mind, as if she were the sun rising over hills and revealing cornfields hidden in shadow, as if her reflection of him did more than show how he looked inside, but magnified his every flaw and desire. In the multiplied emotional state of adolescence, he nearly drowned in the full range of feelings he hadn't known existed in him before—all the worse because he had denied them all along. He had been a stable hydraulic system, but Gladice had pushed a lever. Under pressure, the static emotions within him sought release, and they squirted out.

One day after class, he grasped an opportunity to talk to her.

"Here's your pencil," he said, handing her the fallen instrument. Her pallid cheeks blushed as she muttered her thanks.

That simple incident gave him such pleasure—simply because she had not rejected him, as had everyone else he had encountered in his short life. Even his grandparents, if he had any, had never acknowledged his existence.

But this girl had given him the priceless gift of a smile. No matter that it had been largely concealed by brown bangs hanging long around her face; he had seen her smile, at him. Two days later, he found the nerve to wish her a good day after class, and, by the following week, he asked her if he could walk her home. It meant that he would have to find an alternate way back to Big Stone besides the bus, but that would be an insignificant sacrifice.

She nodded assent. The rest of the day passed like a dream, but painfully slow.

Gladice met him on the granite steps that led down from the high school's auditorium, as she had specified. He quickly offered to carry her backpack. They walked in pleasant yet awkward silence for a few minutes.

"You're real smart in math," Luke said, abruptly.

"You, too," she responded. They continued along a gravel path through tall grass. The sun shone warm and comfortable. Afternoon in September.

"What do you want to be when you grow up?" she asked.

Startled by the unexpected words, Luke didn't know how to answer. He said the only thing that came to mind, the truth: "I don't know. Just away from here."

"Really," she agreed, relaxing. Luke swore he saw her eyes light up.

They walked for perhaps 20 minutes, a timeless canal carved through the stone of Luke's empty days, a lifetime. They talked about geometry, about the new dimensions reachable only through virtual reality sets, how those were only to be found in big cities, and how they both wanted to escape these little towns.

A block from her house, Gladice grew nervous and asked for her books.

"I better not be seen with a boy," she said as an apology, agony sweeping pleasure off her face.

"Can we do this again?" he asked, trying not to sound as if he were pleading.

Her smile returned, briefly. "Yes, I hope we do."

With the nourishment of those few words and the promise they held, Luke walked the five miles home without even noticing the burn in his thin leg muscles.

The walk became a daily ritual, and when the cold breath of November arrived, Luke gained his father's grudging approval to get a driver's license and use the man's half-disabled pickup to drive to school and back—provided Luke get a job to pay for gas and repairs.

"It's time you earn your keep, anyway, boy," the man grunted, stinking of moldering cheese.

On November 26, 2016, Luke nursed the old Chevrolet all the way to school. He was triumphant at the success since his own hands had replaced the spark plugs, wires, and distributor cap to make the machine run again. After school, Gladice had shown not a hint of disgust at the rusted heap. Nor did she cringe when Luke opened the passenger door and revealed a bench seat whose threadbare cover he had hidden beneath a green wool army blanket. A model of what Luke imagined to be a four dimensional cube hung from the rearview mirror, toothpicks held together with epoxy in a complex pattern of box within box, joined at the corners. Glued to the bottom-most toothpick was a small piece of paper that declared in block letters: "GLADICE'S EXTRADIMENSIONAL ROOM."

"It's beautiful," she proclaimed.

Luke wasn't sure to what she was referring, but he didn't care. Another approval was all that mattered. He walked around the bed of the pickup, ignoring the taunts of others whose vehicles had at least been built in this century, and climbed inside. He thought it strange how his classmates' teasing no longer produced any reaction in him. It gave him a sense of power over them: They were small and petty.

"Don't take me straight home," Gladice said. "Let's go for a drive."

So Luke drove the rattling Chevrolet along a county road that followed the lake, past the last houses bordering town, to a pine forest. As they drove, they talked about black holes, a topic the geometry teacher had brought up in class; about cities and virtual reality. Luke had learned that Gladice was passionate about astronomy, and, since he had been reading up on the topic since discovering this fact, Luke was able to ask intelligent questions and make intelligent conversation about black holes and stars. They talked about NASA and the solar system. The words flowed from Luke like water, as though he had become another person, one who could carry his end of a conversation.

When Luke slowed to turn back toward town, Gladice abruptly forgot their talk about the bleak future of space exploration.

"Don't go back yet," she said. She laid a hand on his arm. Luke read longing and fear in her eyes, a combination he couldn't understand.

"Park up there," she said. "Let's see where that trail leads."

He did as she requested. As she walked silently beside him, he held her hand. The packed-earth trail wound into a lakeside forest of pine and elm and oak, bordered by brush and matted mixture of pine needles and fallen leaves. Sunshine filtered gray through the bare branches, tinged green from the pine.

Beneath a naked weeping willow Luke would never forget, Gladice swung around and pressed her lips against his. She kissed him long and hard, her tongue moving past his lips and into his mouth, her body pressed against his and moving ever so slightly yet suggestively; she did it so well that Luke knew without asking this was not her first kiss, as it was his. But no matter. No matter at all. What mattered was that it was him she was kissing of her own free will, and she was entirely his at this moment, and this moment lasted forever.

A single duck's quack overhead pulled her away from him. She was flushed, breathing deeply and slowly, her lips glistening with a smile that held something he couldn't identify but which produced excruciating pleasure within him. Luke had never seen such a beautiful girl as this, her brown hair revealing amber and auburn highlights in the sunshine. Before now, he hadn't even realized she was beautiful. Then she turned away and said they'd better get back, or she would be in deep trouble.

The afternoon's perfection was spoiled when the old pickup didn't respond to Luke's turning the ignition key. He avoided using the curses that seemed to be his father's only vocabulary and tried again. Nothing.

An hour later, another driver stopped. Gladice had been huddling against Luke's chest, her face cold on his neck. When she looked up, he noticed that she had been weeping.

The man gave them a jumpstart, so Luke was able to drive Gladice home. By the time she timidly stepped out of his truck, night had fallen.

Gladice didn't come to school the following day, and the day after that she avoided talking to Luke. Then the weekend crawled past like a million years, so by Monday Luke couldn't help but approach her after school.

"I've missed you, Gladice," he said. Her eyes were downcast. "What's the matter?"

"Oh, Luke," she burst out, falling against him with her arms wrapping around his back, "let's get out of here. Now, let's go as far as we can away from this place. I love you, Luke. Please take me away to someplace we can be together."

"Sure, of course," he said, stunned by her reaction, unsure of anything except that he wanted above all to please her. That phrase echoed over and over in his head: "I love you, Luke."

They got into the pickup—which now sported a new battery and starter—and drove through town to the highway that led away, toward Minneapolis. They reached the Twin Cities just after nightfall, and checked into a motel along the road.

Gladice wouldn't answer any of his questions, as silent as she had been when he had first noticed her in geometry class.

However, as soon as Luke closed the door behind them, she pushed him down onto the bed and began to remove his clothing, an odd look on her face. When she opened his pants, she quickly reached inside his underwear and took hold of his erection, squeezing it painfully pleasure-hard. The next hours were like a dream: disjointed, seemingly unmotivated, pleasure and fear and confusion. He noticed bands of bruise around her ankles but thought nothing of them. Perhaps she had fallen—she was not the most graceful girl. But now she moved over him expertly, slid her silken skin across his as if they were meant to be together; straddling Luke, Gladice took him inside her and only smiled when he ejaculated almost immediately. A few minutes later, after lying cupped against his stomach, she reached behind her hip to find him hard again, and guided him inside once more. This time they moved together like waves against a shore, like wind through leaves. Something about the desperation in her motions made him wonder whether she was driven by desire or something he couldn't grasp. But his passion for her drowned such concerns; he knew she would always be the only one he would ever love, and she would always love only him, and therefore she would always possess his every atom. She had animated his soul.

The next morning before dawn, the phone woke them. It was the innkeeper calling to inform Luke that a man wanted to see him. Luke thought very little of having someone wishing to speak to him: They had paid cash for the room, so no one from the place they had escaped could know he was here. Luke must have parked badly, blocking someone's way.

As he dressed, Gladice received the news with a face devoid of any emotion. He was hurt by her lack of affect when he felt only ecstasy. He couldn't see their future together past this afternoon, but that didn't matter; he was intelligent, he could run a cash register, he would earn enough so they could begin a life here, near the Cities. They could enroll in high school here—just not in one of the dangerous inner-city schools. He was certain they would both finish with A averages so they could go on to college together. Together for life.

When Luke opened the door, he saw for only a second the blunt frame of a short, heavyset man with hair graying at the temples and ruddy face. Luke recognized the man as someone who worked at the cheese factory with his father. The man's eyes seethed with something that terrified Luke. He was framed by a grey mist.

"Daddy?" Gladice asked, her voice cracking and high like a little girl's.

The timeless second passed. One of the man's hands balled into a fist and rose lightning fast to smash against Luke's jaw.

He regained consciousness in the parking lot, his few personal items scattered around him. Gladice was gone. He put all the clues together and finally understood the cryptic look he had watched cross her face when she had to go home. He had seen it every day, spoiling their time together. Home. Daddy.

Luke climbed into his pickup, feeling several years older but despising this passage into manhood. He drove back to Big Stone without thinking anything, only watching the last of the city pass, and then field after field. He pulled into his father's driveway and soon learned that the elder Herrschaft didn't think his son was too old for a good thrashing. Despite an aching back and limbs, he fell asleep in his drafty room, hardening himself against the fall of tears.

Almost as if to display the badge which would prove his initiation, Luke went to school the next day, not making any effort to cover the black swelling along his jaw or the red welts up and down his arms. He wore a T-shirt with a V-neck collar. His classmates seemed to sense something had changed in this quiet boy, and watched him with questioning eyes. With a depth of bitterness he hadn't known existed in him, Luke drank their attention.

As he expected, Gladice didn't show up for geometry class. A friend of hers stopped Luke in the hall afterward. He hadn't known Gladice had a friend. The girl passed Luke a folded note and smiled.

"You're real good for her," the girl said, and walked away.

Luke unfolded the paper. His eyes picked out a single passage:

"I can't stand it anymore and I'm going to end it all because I know there's never going to be any hope." Stunned, he read the next: "I'll always love you no matter where I go from here."

He didn't know what that meant, yet he understood all too well.

Without a thought about how it might affect his grades, Luke ran out of the school to his pickup parked in the gravel lot behind the building. He raced across town with no concern over speed limits or police or how his father would react to a ticket, straight to the house he had watched Gladice enter whenever she left him after their afternoons together. The wheels skidded to a stop just behind an old station wagon parked on the cement slab near a three-story house with peeling yellow paint. He jumped out of the truck and banged on the back door, calling Gladice's name.

The inner door flung open and the blunt man who had punched him the prior morning threw the screen door against Luke so hard Luke stumbled back.

"Get the fuck away from my house and my stepdaughter or I'll kill your weenie ass," the man said, spitting as the words erupted from his mouth.

"'Weenie ass'?" Luke mocked, regaining equilibrium. "What kind of phrase is that, you stupid asshole?"

Gladice's stepfather seemed about to explode, literally erupt into a thousand bloody pieces, his face whitening and eyes bulging and veins in his thick throat expanding. Luke winced as he watched those fists roll into clubs. But he didn't care. All that mattered was Gladice.

"Where's Gladice?" Luke asked in the face of danger.

"Go away, Luke!" she cried from an upper story window. "I don't ever want to see you again, you dumbshit!"

The words struck Luke harder than any physical assault could have. She continued.

"I mean it. You're such a loser, I can't stand being with you. You don't even know how to fuck like a real man. Now get away from me. I mean it when I say I don't ever want to see your ugly face again." And she slammed the window shut.

Luke's attention returned to the stepfather. The man's face had lost its threatening pallor, but not its hatred or sickness. It smiled at Luke, a yellow grin lined with stubble.

"You heard the girl," the man said in a singsong lilt. "I guess you disappointed her that night you kidnapped her. Maybe she thought you was a man, or even a male." He laughed. "But you're nothing. Get away from me before I puke."

The screen door creaked closed just as the inner door banged like a gunshot, like a hammer driving a nail through Luke's hopes and dreams. He stood motionless for a minute before returning to the pickup. He felt only numb.

What was worse than watching his dreams destroyed before his eyes just as he had begun to glimpse them was that he had dared to dream at all, he had consciously exposed himself to the danger which vulnerability engendered. He tried to cry on the way home but couldn't. That evening, Luke's father again applied the belt because he had heard of Luke's truancy and had heard from a fellow employee that he had gone to see "the little slut" again. Luke knew who that fellow employee was without being told.

The next day, Gladice's friend again met Luke in the hall, sobbing uncontrollably.

"Gladice is dead," she managed to say between gasps.

Luke heard the final nail driven into his coffin. He realized that he should have looked beyond the words his love had spoken, to what she had written him in the note. The spoken words had been no more than sounds. Perhaps a plea for help had even been hidden between the syllables, spoken in some dimension speech alone couldn't reveal. Then he realized that she had spoken those words to save Luke from that man.

Anguish and confusion boiled within him until, at last, he couldn't bear the stares of the students standing around him. They had heard the news.

"You're all blind and weak!" he screamed at them. "Sheep gathering in safe little flocks! You never even noticed me before, and now I scare you because you don't allow pain in your stupid little world. Go to hell, all of you."

He stormed out of the building and repeated the previous day's actions, again ending up on Gladice's back doorstep. But no one was home. Frustrated but not spent, Luke got back into his pickup and simply drove the next hours away, finally finding himself near a dirt path leading toward the lake.

At last, leaned against the hard plastic steering wheel, he wept, so long and hard that he thought his head would crack open and an ocean of pain would spill out and flood this whole region, drowning everyone he hated who lived here.

When the storm passed, his ribs hurt and his throat was dry. Luke discovered his grief had passed. All that remained was an emotion he dared not name, one which terrified yet seduced him. His one last hope for an understanding ear was his mother, who had always been kind to him although she had quickly learned not to expect elder Herrschaft to allow them time together. But Luke had lost any concern over anyone's fate, especially his own, so he started up the pickup and drove to that tarpaper hovel near Big Stone, where he had been born.

His mother, a small woman who seemed shriveled in upon herself, looked startled at first but then welcomed him with open arms. Long brown hair blanketed his face as he fell into those arms. She said nothing, cradling him in her soft warm embrace, rocking him where he stood just inside the doorway. Silence. Luke felt an unspoken understanding pass between them.

"Everything will be okay," she finally said. Apparently she had heard.

"I'm going to leave this place tonight and never come back," he told her once he was sure he would not burst into tears like a baby. She nodded, then crossed a cluttered living room to another room. She returned with a roll of paper currency.

"Here's a few hundred bucks," she said, pressing the money into his hand and closing his fingers around it. "I ain't ever gonna get out of here. You deserve it more than me, having to live with that man all these years. I got away. I shoulda taken you with.

"Go now. I always did love you, boy," she added. Her front teeth were gaps in a warm smile.

"Thank you," he said, and turned away from Big Stone forever.

He spent the next few hours gathering tools, and planning. The thing he would do when night shrouded the land had to be done immediately, before fear could overpower the new feeling that blossomed within him like a flower bred to live on the surface of a black hole.

Two days later, living in his pickup in the woods near town, he finally read the front-page article he had been waiting for. Gladice's stepfather had burned to death in the middle of town, setting the drug store ablaze, after his car's taillight wire had ignited ten gallons of gasoline. Apparently, the article stated, the tragedy was a result of rotten insulation around the wire and a hole rusted in the fuel tank. No foul play was suspected.

Satisfied, Luke prepared to move on into his life. But a second article just below the headline caught his attention: "Local Woman Beaten to Death; Local Man Suspected of Murder."

When he saw his mother's name, he didn't need to read further. He started the pickup and drove toward Minneapolis, veering around that haunted city before he reached it.

A few days later, he pulled into Chicago and enrolled in a high school there. The following year, he graduated with top honors. He entered Harvard Business School on a scholarship, graduated in three years, got in on the ground floor of a unique advertising agency that was just organizing. Soon, Luke Herrschaft was branded the mastermind behind the "adult feature-length cartoon," essentially a two-hour ad set in the newest, lifelike virtual reality, which the agency marketed along with their hardware. The dawn of selling ads as entertainment had arrived. Luke Herrschaft quickly became the agency's executive officer.

By the time he turned 40, when the first surgically implanted AI cards were becoming available, Herrschaft was a multimillionaire. His empire might have ended there if it had not been that influential personalities—including actors fearful of losing their jobs—were the first to obtain those primitive cards. At the time, they were still powered by an unsightly cord that led to a combination battery pack/external computer. With the income the sales generated and the second income their advertising customers provided, Luke ordered his growing team of technicians to improve on the first generation of cards.

Programmers working for him came up with educational programming that allowed students to interact personally with crude artificial intelligences—teachers—offering unprecedented opportunities for learning. Herrschaft had made this a priority. At first, only the rich could afford the equipment and programming for their children, and they hesitated to have their children surgically altered with implanted cards.

One August day, his technicians came to his glass office overlooking Chicago, elated and out of breath. They told him they had perfected the internal receiver/transmitter so a cardowner could be connected, via wireless, with his or her mainframe—or any available mainframe within range. A cardowner could now access any and all programming in the air or on the mainframe. No longer would they be limited by the amount of hardware that could fit in a human head or exposed around their waists. Luke had a moment of epiphany:

He foresaw the development of what would at first be called PCBN: The Public Card Broadcasting Network, providing a range of subscribable programming from interactive classrooms to pure entertainment. It soon overpowered even the prevailing telephone and cable empires. He foresaw the WCCB: The World Cybernetics Control Board, which taxed and controlled the deluge of programming available to cardowners. From there, he foresaw the blurring and blending of defining lines between corporation, advertising agency, and political institution. He even caught a glimmer of "standardized installation," the plan that installed cards into children at the earliest safe age. This gave them the advantage of growing up with all the benefits of cardownership, making it an instinctive part of their paradigm.

Children would no longer be exposed to violence at public schools. They would be given educations unmatched by the dreams of great academicians. Luke realized he would make it his priority to bring this vision to life, and would also engineer every other means of protecting the children. Virtual reality programming would give them an escape from the dominion of adults—even if the sanctuary were only in their minds. Better than that, he foresaw that this internal two-way communication system would also provide the ultimate security: If the neural net/brain interface were sufficiently integrated, a victim could simply call the police in the silence of his or her thoughts, and they would arrive to either stop the crime or witness it, ensuring it never happened again.

And he would create individs and all-sex channels to relieve the violent and sexual needs of potential abusers. Let them do whatever they wish to electronic children, as long as it defused the danger to the real ones.

But Herrschaft's charitable goals did not mean he had learned to care about humans, no; it only meant he grieved for the vulnerability of youth. Behind his nobility lurked revenge: By creating fundamental change, he would destroy the world that had brutalized him. He could not give a damn about adults; they had molded him into a shell filled with nothing but emotional scar tissue.

And more. His father would endure a new form of prison within the mind that would not even allow the freedom of personal thought. But Herrschaft would appear noble: By immobilizing and reeducating criminals right in their own homes, he would save taxpayers many billions in hard currency each year.

Less than 100 years later, his ad agency did all this and much more. Authority figures devolved into puppets. He, alone, ruled half the Solar System. But only half. That would change on the night of *Lone Ship Bounty*'s special broadcast, when he would move a final piece into position on his vast game board.

On that August day, in an office overlooking Chicago, he erupted into laughter so brutal that his employees shrank back from his massive wooden desk. He had become a prophet. When the laughter mutated into uncontrollable sobbing, all but one of them left. The remaining woman came around his desk and held him in a way not unlike how his mother had held him the night before her death.

That was the last time he had openly wept, until after the assassination attempt. The rest of his story is readily available in any history subscription.

Feedcontrol 4

Herrschaft cursed himself as he felt the weight of years burden his mechanical shoulders. He felt unstuck in time, struggling to overcome the vertigo of seeing the four-dimensional stretch that had brought him to this crossroads. He was an artifact of a previous century and bore power accumulated like dust over the years. Almost singlehandedly, he had pulled together the frayed strings of humanity in his fist and created something he considered beautiful. EarthCo and its Feedcontrol, whose billions of fingertips stretched out across worlds, with dense nerve networks on each end; to his eye, they were a piece of work unmatched by any other human masterpiece.

"…don't you think, Luke?" Mrs. Jackson said.

Herrschaft shook himself back into the year 2197. As planned, he forced himself to continue the gracious-host routine with the wife of one of his puppets.

"Certainly, my dear," he responded, sure that would satisfy whatever triviality she had asked. He realized with a start that they were standing inside his private projection booth. Red velvet curtains encircled the cozy space, deadening noise.

"Close the doors, please," he said, and two human servants who had remained unseen did his bidding. The room made a small huff as it was sealed against sound and electronic intrusion. Except against Luke Herrschaft, of course. A tendril of his mind reached into the projector and booted it up.

"Have a seat, my lady," he said. By the pale light of Neptune, which flickered into existence in the air before them, he offered her a seat near the 3VRD screen. Herrschaft sat beside her. Eight other feed-enhanced seats were still empty in a semicircle behind them.

"Saturn looks so different on a projector," Mrs. Jackson declared. She oohed at the slowly growing orb that hovered amid a bath of stars.

"That's Neptune, my dear," he said, correcting her. He tried not to grunt in disgust. Already bored with this woman, he expanded his consciousness in the Feedcontrol room that was currently handling *Lone Ship Bounty*'s raw feedback.

A new feed-angle probe detached from the gleaming ship to replace its predecessor, ruined during a brief battle near Mars. It took up "stationary" co-trajectory position 200 meters away, according to a row of numbers reeling along the right-hand side of his pov:

>>PRELIM EarthCo VERIF FEED
ECoNAUT F/B VESSEL 011 BOUNTY 3.20.197
19:25:03 NKK CORP NEPTUNE BOUNDARY<<

Herrschaft felt an organic response in himself: excitement. He dipped into a pov inside the ship.

The first camera showed Pehr Jackson lying idly in his zero *g* hammock. Herrschaft cringed; the man was much flabbier than he had been last episode. He touched up some of the feed himself, tightening the man's abdomen and thickening the skeletal muscles. That kind of programming was simple. Jackson's dreary expression had to go, but such minutiae were best left to his controllers to modify. He asked them to give the Captain his usual confidence, or at least the impression of it. A few seconds later, Jackson again looked capable of defeating foes, even though he lay motionless. Herrschaft called up data on what the man was feeding on: a message from Mrs. Jackson. Herrschaft was very pleased. He opened direct feed of this pov to his private projection booth, where it was displayed in an inset box. Jackson's private room seemed to grow out of pure space and hover beside Neptune.

"Mrs. Jackson," Herrschaft said, "your husband is currently feeding on a message you sent him." He watched the woman's face go blank then light up with pleasure.

"Oh, what a treat!" she said, leaning forward to stare at a full-size projection of her husband. "What's on, Pehr?" she asked the four-hour-old ghost, then chittered at her little joke.

To avoid cursing at this woman, Herrschaft abandoned his presence with her and went back to presiding over the raw feed. He checked a chronometer running at one corner of the 3VRD display. Less than five minutes until action. Herrschaft's excitement swelled inside him like something trying to get out. Too much excitement could spoil his carefully laid plans, so he began to pull up each pov. He would be pragmatic about all this. This was only a plan, a program played out by human components.

>>Cameras P2 and P3 now both fully functional; P2 transmits telescopic views of patches of seemingly calm Neptune sky and a cluster of unidentified craft, magnified 100X, approaching pov. P3 utilizes a fish-eye lens which transmits a dome marked at one extreme by the torch-shape of *Bounty*, another by a diminished Neptune, another by our bright star Sol.<<

As Herrschaft watched, bug-programs ran all necessary checks of feedback transmitted; all systems functioning perfectly. Herrschaft had feared that the direct hit *Bounty* sustained in combat near Mars with NKK's late fighter Koi had damaged remaining stowed probes.

"Why isn't anything happening?" Mrs. Jackson asked.

Her voice was no more than a ghost whispering in one of his myriad ears. Herrschaft backed 20% of himself out of the control room and looked at her. Was there anything in those bright eyes that suggested the child? Of course not. He could not see anything of the sort in her, and was angry at himself for seeking it. *A man can see anything when he looks for it*, he thought, *and I can't afford to see that in her now.*

"This is just preliminary feed," he said, abruptly. "We're adjusting our receivers and transmitters so that when the show begins, we can confidently feed it live to a currently estimated eight billion subscribers." He didn't mention that tailoring the feedback would delay the "live" program feed by nearly two seconds.

"Oh," she said, and turned back to the projections.

Herrschaft left her alone again.

>>Netcom verifies approaching craft to be NKK-owned intercept/torpedoes built by Z-Tech.<<

"Windfall! Perfect!" Herrschaft said aloud. Part of him saw Mrs. Jackson face him, another part of him saw his controllers do the same, but only for a moment.

"Our men will be provoked, er, were provoked." Suddenly, he felt a bit nervous. What if the *Bounty* had been destroyed before delivering its payload? What if he were only watching a shipload of the damned, useless and long dead? What if—

No, he would no longer allow his emotions to control him. Luke Herrschaft, Director of Feedcontrol, acting ruler of EarthCo, took over for the lost and lonely young Luke. The boy had tried to possess the man. That would be the last time he allowed such behavior in himself. He was strong. He was the strongest man alive. No dead boy would control him.

Herrschaft savagely switched his presence completely to the control room.

SEVEN: Outerlimits

EarthCo *Bounty* 14: Pehr Jackson

The saucer-shaped escape pod, which had once been excess payload aboard *Bounty*, shrieked back into Triton's atmosphere after its third and final pass through. Loud as lightning, the main atomic rocket was consuming the remains of the pod's fuel. The underside of the craft heated red again as the last fragments of ablative heatshield sparkled and fell away. The magnetic shield had failed during the second pass.

Pehr's splice looked down at a blurred landscape. The pov showed as much horizon as land since Janus had instructed the ship to flatten an already highly elliptical orbit each time. This orbit would intersect the surface.

"Now," Janus whispered, as if to herself.

He discovered what she meant a moment later. The rocket began to sound as if it were some great drum, reverberating in the cabin with a rapid thud rather than a constant roar.

"Down to the bottom of our tank," she stated without really looking at him. Her eyes had that faraway stare Pehr was so accustomed to in his fellows.

A brief image of Susahn crossed his mind, though he couldn't understand why. He didn't spend time pondering it.

Instead, Pehr tried to find a sense of control by watching Triton rear its humped back higher. Then the engine's pounding ceased, and he felt lighter by a half. Only the occasional puff of retros, keeping the ship steady, and atmospheric deceleration provided sense of weight. Pehr concentrated on the surface, hoping to catch a glimpse of some detail his eyes could grasp hold of.

Again, an incongruous thought intruded: *Have I always been an observer? Of course not*, he told himself. *So when did it happen?*

Even these thoughts fell away as the day side of the world was swallowed by night. That dark surface only revealed itself when a particular crag or polished formation reflected the now orange glow of the pod's underside. When he could see how close they were now to their destination, Pehr felt himself go weak.

As always. The planetside disease, he called it. As yet, he believed no one knew about this weakness, this flaw in his armor. He had hoped it wouldn't happen again, since this was not Earth. Triton was not the world which always made his guts feel pulped, as quickly as the first night in bed. Triton was not the world that had infected his powerful body with the worms of weakness. But it was a world, an inhabited world. He nearly jumped when Janus spoke.

"Jack?"

"Yeah?"

"In case we don't make it," she continued, her look suggesting that her splice was shut off, "I want you to know that I've always cared about you, ever since that time you stood up to Eyes and Feedcontrol. I respect how you don't just blindly follow feed, how you don't make me do anything I don't want to do just because it's in the script. You know, et cetera. I also wanted to say that I was thrilled when you asked me to be your partner in the tourist show. That would have been a fine plan. That's a lot closer to what I had dreamed of when I was a kid. I would have done it."

She looked flushed, nervous, and maybe even happy—something he had never seen in her. This was all so strange, especially now, especially here.

"We still might have our show," Pehr responded, ashamed to acknowledge the other things she had said. "If we can get out of this. . . . I have a lot of faith in your piloting skills. You've always—"

"Shut up," Janus said, detaching the web of belts across her front. She climbed out of her couch as gracefully as possible under the turbulent conditions and leaned over the arm of Pehr's.

Without another word, she put her hands on his bare shoulders and her lips on his. Pehr felt a thrill whip through him like none he had felt in two decades of sexual encounters—the ship rocked and buffeted, wind screamed madly across the hull; Janus breathed against his cheeks, her lips so firm and sure, her hands so strong on his shoulders and arms, massaging deep. . . .

After a minute or so, she pulled back with a distant smile. Then she strapped herself back in her couch.

"Touchdown in approximately 31 minutes," she said. "It'll be rather rough."

She sat silently for a moment. Then: "Who are you, Jack?" Again her amber eyes showed the splice-stare, directed toward the soft ring of light just before her.

He felt panicked, but fought it back. "Who am I? How do you mean that?"

"Well, it's just I realize I don't really know a damned thing about you. I mean, I know what you do, that you're strong enough to do the right things, and that you want to start a travel show, but why? Who are you? Suddenly it seems important that we get to know each other. It's strange that we've spent practically a year together in close quarters and know so little. I guess it's like that life-flashing-before-your-eyes-at-death thing; all the little, personal, things are suddenly important."

"Well, I'm who I seem to be," Pehr replied. He winced at the defensive tone in his voice. "Though maybe not as strong as you believe."

An unreadable look crossed her face. "Here's a more directed question," she said. "Why did you join EConautics?"

Pehr pondered that while listening to the wind. Its pitch had dropped noticeably during the past minutes. "That's easy. I joined up to do my part for EarthCo. And being out here, in a ship, is where I belong. Out here, we two can do more to safeguard EarthCo's citizens than a hundred soldiers back on Earth. Eyes just screwed it all up."

"You don't like Earth, do you?"

"Earth's all right."

Janus looked at him, then away again. "No, I think you're like me. I think there's something you left behind, something you're maybe running from."

Pehr felt himself growing more tense. Wasn't it bad enough that they were facing a serious crash? Did she need to add this on top? But then he took a deep breath. She didn't mean to cause him trouble. And what did it matter how much she knew about him now? They might be dead in half an hour. For once, he took pleasure and relief in splicing in, watching the 3VRD of Triton.

"Maybe you're right," he said, and the words weighed heavily as they crossed his chest and throat and mouth. An energy began to build behind his ribs, pressing against lungs and heart and stomach. "Maybe I am running from something.

"I joined EConautics because I've always loved the adventure shows set on other worlds, in spaceships. You know, like *Dreadnought* and *Keeper of the Flame*. There's something so peaceful about alien worlds, something so . . . I don't know, pure? Earth isn't like that, hasn't been since an ape first threw a sharpened stone at another ape."

Pehr watched starless night sweep past beneath them. Occasionally, something bright flashed past, warning him that time was short.

"Neptune, I thought—what a great place that must be. So far from Earth and its ugly, violent, hating masses. Sure, we'd have to do shows on Luna and Mars along the way, but our destination would be this farthest outpost. Even better than Neptune is cool, empty space itself. That's where we'll be most of the time, I thought, in empty space. Far and free from the hands of Man."

He began to dream, a little, about those long expanses of time from one world to another. But even in retrospect, they weren't so wonderful. Was boredom any better than fear? Was loneliness better in space than on Earth? Better not to dwell on introspection.

"Ah, but pit one ship's crew against another!" he said. Still he felt that pressure in his chest, but now it was more like the fire he felt during a show.

"There's something! Give me a ship and a crew to direct, give me a show and a script. No innocents will get hurt, and if we get hurt . . . well, what soldier can complain if he or she is injured in action? And what better way to die than in space, for a purpose, for a cause you believe in?" Then the fire faded, and it was pressure again.

"But this time everything went wrong. I thought we'd be safe here, so far from Earth."

"Why?" Janus asked. "We are violence itself. The *Bounty* was a fighter/bomber, designed to destroy and kill." Her voice cut with a sharp edge of anger, though Pehr sensed it wasn't directed at him.

"No, you don't understand. It was just a show. The only people we hurt were NKK soldiers. I was prepared to get injured, even to die. But not like this. This is a disgrace. What I was trying to get away from kicked me in the head." His mood began to grow more black. He began to feel like the angry kid, unable to focus the anger but finding outlets anyway.

"You mean the cyborg's bombing of the artifact," Janus said into the silence.

"Yeah, that. If it's really what that man down there said. . ."

A spike of fear prodded Pehr to anger once more. "You know, we really don't know there's anything down there. Maybe this whole show is pure feed. Maybe every one of our sensors is only playing preprogrammed fluff at us, and we're just reacting to 3VRDs. We're just rats in a tank with millions of people watching because they're curious to see how the specimens will react to different problems. 'Let's make them think they're going to crash,' one of the experimenters asked a handful of minutes ago. 'Let's see what they do when they think they're going to die.'"

Pehr fell silent. He listened to the mounting roar of wind and watched the darkened landscape blur beneath them. He felt the rabid lurches of the pod as retros fired or random winds tipped it enough to set off gyros, which set off a retro again. All seemed as it should be. Which is exactly how the experimenters would have prepared the feed. It was enough to drive a man insane.

"That's pointless to wonder," Janus said after a while. "So what? Wouldn't that just mean our whole lives have been long dreams? What good is it to think like that? On the off chance that this is real, we'd better react to the stimuli properly, don't you think? This is not the Pehr Jackson I thought I understood; he's not a fatalist. He's a doer, a take-control kind of guy."

"You were right when you said you didn't know me," Pehr said, "I'm not like that at all." He felt unburdened more and more as the words rushed out. The unburdening started a flow of more words he couldn't stop, as if Janus had pierced a balloon within him and now the flow was unstoppable.

"It's all right to say this now, the feed's shut down," he continued, consoling himself. "That's what the subscribers pay for—the hunter of men, fearless hero, throwing himself headlong into danger, defying death. Doing the things they'd never dare to do or couldn't do, but wish they would. Blast, that's all the character, Jan, that's all." Suddenly he felt as if he were lying. But the lie had never been spoken before, so he had always believed it.

"Then again, maybe not. I guess I've always been like that, but it wasn't me. We all make up who we seem to be for other people, like with comm 3VRDs. Who chooses a 3VRD that really is who we are? Who'd want to expose himself to the world that way? Just puts you at the mercy of others. Well, the character a guy shows the world doesn't have to be a 3VRD, it can be a little more real."

He began to tell his story. The catharsis was a reward in itself; he felt a desperate need to unburden himself after years of containment, and the desperation came from the immediacy of death. He exposed himself for the first time—even to himself—since he was a boy.

Yesteryear 4: Pehr Jackson

Twenty-one years prior, eleven-year-old Pehr Jackson climbed down the steps of his mother's house. It was one section of an eighter, an eight-apartment mini-tower. Anoka, a subdivision of the Minneapolis/St. Paul sprawl, stood all around, high and unapproachable. Pehr had only met three girls and a boy in the eighter, and of them, only Gosh and Teresa played with him regularly.

A stranger-woman held his hand, something the edufeed had told him was bad: "Touch is wrong. People shouldn't touch each other. Especially grown-ups should never touch children, except for parents." The teacher, a kind-looking young man with hair down the sides of his face, played examples. Pehr didn't like to see the old man touch the little boy that way; he knew that was wrong. "If I was that boy," he answered when the teacher returned with questions, "I'd punch that old man in the face!" The teacher had laughed and said he was a good boy.

But this woman was holding his hand, and Mom hadn't said she couldn't. Mom had cried, but she always cried; Pehr could never understand why. All the shows she subscribed to were happy love ones, so she shouldn't cry. Pehr had been as gentlemanly as he could, always. He even fixed her hair the morning after she had a bad night, or washed her face when a new Dad had made blood there. This newest Dad, Jerry was his name, wasn't like that. He had never made blood on Mom or Pehr. Mom hadn't had a bad night for weeks, though she had come home with that whiskey she liked, which smelled like the stuff Pehr used to clean the blood off her face. He just couldn't understand why Mom should be crying now.

The sun was warm and cold, flashing young Pehr secret signals as clouds passed beneath it.

He couldn't decipher the signals, even though he should have been able: The newest live-in Dad had gotten him a Captain Hughes Downward game program. Captain Downward was the hero of *Dreadnought*, Pehr's favorite show, and the program let him play old shows as if he was one of the characters. Pehr liked to play Captain Downward. He was always able to find out what the evil Mr. Hitogoroshi was scheming to do to Earth's cities or Luna's warrens. Downward always brought the invisible *Dreadnought*— EarthCo's greatest cruiser, with every conceivable weapon and seven fighter ships on board—to bear just in time, thwarting Hitogoroshi's plans for death and destruction.

Pehr, with Gosh and Teresa as his officers, had saved Anoka twice using the new Dad's gift. But he also liked doing things Teresa liked: swimming in the eighter's pool on hot summer days, even though the water smelled like mud and made his skin all bumpy red afterward; catching ladybugs in the spiky shrubs that lined the small yard; making snow-forts in the winter right away after a blizzard before the snow turned black; playing "buzz": Whoever first heard the buzz of a heavy spaceship coming down the spaceport magshaft a few kilometers away got to be Captain for the day and tell the other two what games they would play.

He stood on the bottom step and stopped moving. He would go no farther, no one could make him. This woman wouldn't take him now, not when Mom was so sad. He tried to comm his mother, but he couldn't reach her. That was strange because he was so close.

"Your mommy and daddy can't afford to keep custody of you, Perry," the nice woman said.

Pehr began to wonder if maybe she wasn't so nice, because her real face didn't say a thing; it was her game-face that talked, and game-faces don't always tell the truth.

"My name's Pehr," he said. "And talk with your mouth like a lady."

"I'm sorry, Pehr," she spoke. Her voice was thinner now, quieter. "Didn't your mommy tell you that we'd be finding you a nice new place to stay?"

"She said she and Jerry are getting married," Pehr answered. He wasn't going to say any more. "She's sad. She needs me." He tried to pull out of the woman's grip, and that made her frown; her hand got nervous-sweaty.

"Please, Pehr, don't make this difficult. They can't afford to keep you. Grownups need to have other grownups, and sometimes they choose to get married so the other grownup will be more likely to stay with them. Your mom loves Jerry, so they're going to get married. But no citizen can get married until he or she is fully franchised. Do you know what that means?"

"'Citizen-shareholder,'" he recited. He listened during school, even if the words didn't mean anything.

"Right." The woman smiled.

Pehr realized she was wearing one of those dresses that looked like the color of the sun, all yellow and so bright it was hard to look at. He couldn't tell what her body looked like, really, only that she was bigger than Mom.

"A citizen-shareholder is very important to EarthCo, Pehr. Your mommy and Jerry will become citizen-shareholders tomorrow, after they go to the hospital and get their cards upgraded. But that is very expensive. It would take them many years to pay off the operation. They just couldn't give you a good life if they had such big debts. They care about you too much to make you live in a poor house with only liquimeal to eat. I helped them find a nice married couple to adopt you. The nice couple is giving your mommy and Jerry a lot of credit to pay for their operations. Today you will meet the nice couple. Do you understand all I'm telling you?"

"You're really taking me away?" he asked. He hadn't understood why Mom had been talking like that, like he was going away. Now another person was saying the same thing. He grew very mad and very sad.

"Teresa!" he commed as loudly as he could. He noticed the comm line was quiet. He couldn't find his server; even though it was the littlest one he had ever used, he could always find it, even if he was down by the brickstacks. Even Teresa's game self didn't appear.

The woman once again tried to pull him off the last step. Pehr began to feel as though he would cry, very soon.

Then he saw Teresa's face in the third-floor window. She frowned. A second later, her game-self appeared in between Pehr and the lady.

"Who's that?" Teresa asked, pointing at the woman with the sun dress.

"She's come to take me away!" Pehr said, in such a hurry that the words came out as a scream.

"Who are you talking to?" the woman asked.

"Don't go!" Teresa cried. "I'll help."

"Come on, Pehr," the woman said. "We are scheduled to meet your new parents in ten minutes. We can't be any later than we already are. We don't want them to think something is wrong, now, do we?"

152

"Crash you!" Pehr yelled. It was the first time he had used such language around an adult.

Just then, Teresa appeared in the yard, which flickered for a second like a ground-road in hot summer sun. It changed into the *Dreadnought*, and Teresa disappeared behind the titanium and hicarb hull. The cruiser was wider than the whole yard, and longer than two blocks—longer even, farther than Pehr could see, since it was facing him. Every turret of foreward auto cannons rotated toward the woman holding Pehr, and several cartridges of missiles extended from the ship like arms stretching out, ready to fight, the missile-tips like knuckles on fists.

The woman gasped and let go of Pehr. "This is very naughty," she stammered.

Two men jumped out of an aircar that was parked on the landing beside the ground-road, and began running toward Pehr.

Pehr took the opportunity to race up the concrete steps, being careful not to trip over the fourth one—which had shattered when someone threw an exploding "knuckleball" at one of the bigger kids last spring. He pushed open the door leading to his apartment.

"Mom!" he shouted, slamming the door behind him and leaning against it. "That woman wants to take me away for good! We've got to do something."

"Son," Jerry said, slowly rising out of the chair he had brought when he moved in, one of those that swallowed you all the way when you sat down, "she's right. You've got to move in with the Senectuses; they already paid for the adoption. It's too late."

The door banged open, throwing Pehr down on the threadbare rug.

"We'll miss you, boy," Jerry said. Then he turned and returned to his chair, disappearing into it. Mom lay on the couch like she did on bad nights, mouth partway open, eyes flicking this way and that, moving her hips funny. She didn't even know he was there. Her cheeks were still wet, but she wasn't crying. At least she didn't smell like whiskey.

When Pehr stood, he saw two big men standing behind him, dressed in the flexible armor of police but wearing no badges or 3VRDs to say they were police. One of them had a black face, one white. The white one looked at the other, then reached a hand toward Pehr.

"We're leaving now," he said. He had a big voice, almost as big as Captain Downward's. Pehr thought he maybe looked sad.

"Why are you doing this?" Pehr asked, not moving, feeling resigned to his fate.

"It's all right, kid," the man who reached for Pehr's arm said. "I had the same thing happen to me when I was your age. It's not so bad after you get used to the new parents. I did just fine."

"Yeah, Pete," the other man said, then laughed.

Pehr let the first man take his upper arm in that armor gloved hand and lead him outside. The *Dreadnought* still filled the yard. The woman in the sun dress was gone.

"Pehr, are you all right?" Teresa's game-self asked, again on the steps. She was out of breath and scared.

"Yeah. I guess I'm moving. I hope it's close enough so we can still play."

Then the big cruiser vanished, and so did Teresa. When Pehr got to the fourth step, he jumped hard with both feet into the dirty hole. But he didn't bust through, like Gosh had thought someone would. He scuffed his ankle on the way out.

The men led Pehr to the waiting aircar. This was his first ride in one of these—sure, he'd been in the air lots of times on board the airbus that took students to the museums intheflesh, but this wasn't the same. The bus was no different than being in a game, since it was so big, or being on an electric ground-bus. This time, he had his own seat, right beside the black man who flew the car. The white man sat in back, mumbling things to someone Pehr couldn't see.

Pehr looked out the side of the window-dome, down at Anoka as they took off hard and flew away. He felt as if he were on board a spaceship, because the aircar was always pitching this way and that. The ride was fun, and it helped him keep from crying.

An hour later, they landed outside a private home. It stood almost as tall as the eighter, only it was a single place, made of bricks and shiny metal, with a tile roof and lots of colored glass windows. Three landings stood in front of the house with aircars on each. A driveway curved in from the ground-road and back, and on it stood a pretty gold ground-car that looked like an antique.

Pehr realized right away when the dome hissed open that this would be his new house, but he didn't know if he wanted to live with retro people who owned ground-cars.

"Here's where you'll be living," the white man said.

Pehr didn't rise from his seat, not yet.

A door opened on the front of the house and two people stepped outside.

"They're old," Pehr remarked. "I'm not going to live here, am I?"

"Old's good, sometimes," the man in the back seat said. "They're rich. I think they own a company that makes electric valves for rifles or something. You're lucky. I was adopted by a middle-class family. You'll be okay, kid."

And it was okay, in time. At first, though, it was very hard not being able to comm Teresa or Gosh. When he was left alone in the huge bedroom overlooking the real sculpture garden out back, Pehr cried all night for three nights. But every sadness passes, or at least becomes bearable after a time. He found that Olaf, the servant's son, knew how to play *Dreadnought*—it had apparently been installed on Pehr's card, not on the apartment server, so it had moved with him. The new parents called that "scandalous," and "forbade" Pehr from playing with the child of an unfranchised servant. Within a couple of weeks, Olaf and his mother moved away, leaving Pehr all alone again in the big house.

The years passed slowly, but Pehr learned how to make fun for himself. He was able to subscribe to any show, as long as Emma and Geoff Senectus—his new parents—approved of them. The first holidays were the saddest times, especially his twelfth birthday when Mom didn't even comm. A few days later, Jerry sent a pretty picture-print of Mom, a nice holo with her and Jerry in front of the eighter. Getting that was even sadder than not getting a comm, and he punched his fluffy pillow until his wrist grew sore.

Pehr did all right at school, but mostly excelled at 3VRD athletics, because he could practice intheflesh in the many-acre lot that surrounded the house. He hurdled wells that held tropical fish, climbed gnarly old oaks and elms and box elder trees—these trees even had good leaves most of the summer, unlike those he had seen in Anoka . . . he ran and ran around the house, trying to increase the number of times he could do it without his lungs burning too badly. But the burn felt good, somehow.

Sometimes, Emma and Geoff had other old people over for "teas." This meant awkward talking in the Library, a strange, dark room with stained-glass windows and walls made out of antique books. The books were red and brown and gold and sometimes colorful, and they held paper pages where words were printed. The words couldn't be changed, no matter which program Pehr tried to call up from the Senectus' Super-Two Household server—a computer that could do just about anything.

At the teas, people in fancy retro dress would chat about this and that, drink tea from porcelain cups—also antiques—and eat many kinds of sweets. The new servant was very good at making food—especially treats—but she was boring to talk to, and she didn't have a child. Mostly, the teas were a time for Emma and Geoff to talk about Pehr.

They hadn't been approved to have a child of their own because of some problem in their genes—cystic fibrosis? Pehr wondered, having seen a reference in the family file one day—so they had decided to adopt. The Skilcroffts had adopted a girl last January, and that left Emma and Geoff as the only ones in their circle of friends who hadn't had a child; then came Pehr.

Pehr hated the teas. One day, roughly two years after moving to the house, he came to the Library when summoned. He was giggling with a new friend he had met in the nets, a boy named Montegue from Cincinnati. Montegue was an exceptional runner, and they had raced for the Middle States Junior High title in the Three Kilometer that morning; Montegue had won.

"Hello, ladies and gentlemen," Pehr said, closing the French doors that separated the Library from the house. Then he made the *Dreadnought* appear, laser and plasma cannons blazing, missiles and torpedoes launching from their cartridges on screaming spikes of flame, volume full-war loud.

The guests spilled their tea, and Mrs. Cremshaw fell off her red-velvet stool onto the plush carpeting right onto her wide butt. Montegue left right away, roaring with laughter; Pehr kept giggling. That night, Pehr was told that if he did that again, he would have to leave.

That gave him ideas. He thought he had been trapped in the stinky old house. So he began doing everything in his power to cause trouble, but never anything so obvious as the *Dreadnought* scheme. Pehr signed up to take part in every dangerous game he could—full well knowing the "danger" was no more real in school games than in any other 3VRD show. Montegue joined him in several of his exploits.

After only three months, Pehr became the second-ranked boxer in the Middle States Conference. He excelled at wrestling for a few weeks, but that bored him. Downhill skiing caused him great trouble: The judges disapproved of his "straight-bombing" the Alps Mountain runs; that was unsportsmanlike, they complained, and banned him from skiing competitions until he could ski properly. He tried undersea winging, but that didn't draw much of a crowd of spectators—a lot of people couldn't get past the stupid feeling that they were drowning, even though it was all a 3VRD and they were safe at home, high above the waves.

The guests who came over for teas were uncomfortable watching Emma and Geoff's son demonstrate his dangerous antics. Seeing their nervous glances at one another, their forced smiles, Pehr took a certain pleasure.

When he turned 15, Pehr was given special approval—a year early—to enlist with the St. Paul Shooting Squad. The squad, mostly middle-aged men, taught him how to use all varieties of hand- and shoulder-arms, ranging from street weapons, like gunpowder pistols, to military rifles, like the EMMA. Pehr took great pleasure indeed when he learned his arthritic adoptive mother had the same name as the EarthCo Warriors' battlefield dominance weapon. He became quite proficient with a wide range of arms, rated high in his age group. Though saddened when Montegue couldn't enlist and continually asked Pehr to instead join him in various athletics, Pehr stayed with the Squad.

This was the greatest of all sports, to Pehr more real and practical than something like 3VRD running or boxing: He had watched the newsfeed, and he knew the real world was a dangerous place. It couldn't hurt to be ready for the day some thug attacked him.

In the May 2080, US Shooting Finals, Pehr won first place in the under 21 age group in Confrontation. This was one of the survival sections: The course was laid out over a 3VRD of fictitious city and forest, and the twelve competitors had to fight one another "to the death"—the computer kept track of who was injured, slowing them down, and who was killed, plucking them from the course. Each was given only one weapon, and each wore the same suit of armor that EarthCo Warriors wore on the battlefield. Points were scored by killing the most competitors and arriving at the finish-zone first; getting wounded reduced the score, as did injuring instead of killing opponents. Whoever could run, duck, climb, cover, react, etc., the fastest generally won. Pehr won—not with a record score, but he won.

At the next tea, Pehr played the Confrontation recording for Emma and Geoff's guests. They were appalled: "That's a barbarian's game," one old woman complained. "Not fit for a gentleman," her husband added. Pehr tried to keep the smile off his face.

When Emma and Geoff forbade Pehr from continuing this morbid sport, he enlisted with the space section of the Shooting Squad. Now Pehr felt he had found his niche: He flew a one-man General Motors Stratofighter, capable of atmospheric and vacuum operation. He never gained mastery of the craft's controls, but that didn't matter; its computer did the flying, and all he had to do was turn this way and that as if swimming, and learn accurate targeting. This he could do. Physical and mental reflex were still all-important, and those were his fortés.

The following tea, he demonstrated a space dogfight. After putting up with old Mr. Akins' bragging about his EConaut service during the Lunar Equality War of 2141, Pehr invited him to a duel. In less than a minute, Pehr disabled Akins' little DCR7—a Lunar War period warship—by carefully puncturing the life support and propulsion systems without hitting a fuel tank or letting out all the air. Akins worked up a mighty panic-sweat trying to give the boy at least a few knocks before the atmosphere could destroy his powerless vessel.

Then the old man's face turned blue. Pehr saw it through the ultraglas canopy on a close pass.

Pehr immediately shut down the program. Akins still looked blue, intheflesh.

An hour later, Akins had to have a synth heart put into his chest. The old one had given out, but that wasn't the real issue. The serious problem was that Akins had sustained minor brain damage, and not even the best doctors could do anything about that.

The next morning, at breakfast in the white-tiled kitchen, Emma explained that she and Geoff couldn't have such a rebellious youngster living with them. They were too old for such nonsense. "We are very sorry to have to let you go," she said, as if he were being fired like a servant.

"I hope you crash!" Pehr had shouted, his voice echoing tinnily against the brass cabinets. He was unexpectedly angry; wasn't this what he wanted, to be set free? But it was how Emma had said it.

It was what Pehr had done to be "let go." He had hurt a man, nearly killed him.

As he stepped out the big, wooden front doors, the newest servant put her arms around him and gave him a tight hug. She even cried. That was very strange to Pehr, who couldn't remember her name. She kissed him on the neck and handed him a big gold-and-pearl brooch.

"A going-away present from Emma," she said. "Don't let her know about it. You'll need it sometime. Remember me then."

Then the door closed behind him. Pehr looked down at the four bags around his feet, packed with clothes, a mini-server he could wear like a belt around his waist, a ticket-card he could use to take the bus any time he wished, and various odds and ends Geoff thought "the boy might need in setting up house." In a pocket inside his half-vest, the picture of Mom in front of the eighter lay like a weight.

Soon a taxi arrived and delivered him to the Oberlicht Towers, 112 stories of apartments and offices. Emma and Geoff had rented him a small bachelor's room.

That afternoon, as he stepped out of the elevator and walked along the narrow hallway in search of room 101203, he met Megan. In later years, Pehr couldn't recall how she looked, what color were her eyes or hair or skin, her age or height. He would remember that she was kind, loving, gentle, and held him against her at night in such a sweet way. He would remember that her breasts and belly and thighs were soft as she slept spooned behind him, that she sighed softly just before waking. She didn't like 3VRD programs, nor did she like visiting people intheflesh, except for with Pehr. She was a passionate lover. When he revealed himself to her in bed one night after lovemaking, when he told her about his past, she had declared her love for him and her undying devotion.

"I'll never leave you, my Pehr," she said in response to his stories of abandonment. Even 16 years later, on board *Bounty*'s escape pod, he could remember how those words had sounded on her lips: whisper-soft yet firm, wet, soothing, his name spoken in the same note as a distant rocket's. She had sounded completely honest, and perhaps she had been.

Two months later, Pehr watched her waiting by the elevator with tears cascading down her cheeks. In her hands were suitcases, and on her back a long pack. She was going back to a husband about whom Pehr hadn't heard anything. Pehr pushed Emma's brooch into the breast pocket of Megan's singlesuit.

"You might need this some day," he said. "Remember me then."

That night, Pehr had a bottle of whiskey sent up to his room. He charged it to Geoff, who froze the account from alcohol purchase immediately afterward; Pehr discovered this the following morning, when he tried to order another bottle.

He had wanted to find out just what it was about whiskey that his mother found so appealing. And he found out. That night, he met a dozen new friends and played hours of combat in space and in Confrontation. He met several girls who greatly admired his skill and appearance, and had 3VRD sex with two of them—something that gave him great waves of laughter later, thinking about how serious they had been even though they were states away from him. He found he could make friends and find lovers easily. No longer would he have to be alone.

Whiskey taught him this. Sober, he hadn't been able to seek friends or lovers online.

His winnings in athletics kept him fed and clothed, so Pehr wasn't dependent on his adoptive parents, except for rent. But it also caused him trouble.

About one month and six bottles later, he walked along the pedway that passed Oberlicht Towers. A forest of skyscrapers rose up all around him, shutting out the sunset. Light came mainly from shop signs, 3VRD projections, and floating billboards. Steady air traffic hummed and roared above him in four stacked lanes, and far overhead he could see the occasional spacecraft light its rockets once it had reached the altitude limit of the maglevs.

He hadn't noticed a scuffle nearby. A rising series of shouts drew his attention.

At first, he thought the seven boys were engaged in an unfamiliar 3VRD game of Confrontation. One of the boys pulled an antique gunpowder-pistol, a type common on the street since the Severs Act of 2107 outlawing the sale of powered arms to anyone but police and military outfits. Pehr nearly laughed, until the pistol exploded.

The shooter dropped the gun, his hand bloody and limp. The boy he had targeted held his stomach, and blood began to seep between his fingers. No game would have such graphics; they should have been removed from play. Pehr shot a quick glance into the local net and discovered those kids were present intheflesh. He had just witnessed an intheflesh shooting.

"Are you guys all right?" he asked, running across the bare pedway toward them. The pedways were almost always empty at night, and held little traffic even during the day; people mostly stayed at home and traveled via the net, or took a car if they had to be somewhere intheflesh.

Two of the boys jerked, as if startled out of a trance, and ran away. The one with the belly wound dropped slowly to his knees, grinning halfway yet scowling at the same time. The shooter turned to face Pehr just as Pehr came to a stop.

"You didn't see nothing," the boy said, holding his damaged hand; it looked like ground meat. "Get out of here."

"What are you talking about?" Pehr asked. "Have you called an ambulance? I'll do it—" and he tapped back into the net.

Some time later, the ambulance driver woke him.

"What happened, kid?" the man asked.

Pehr tried to sit up and answer, but his sides seemed to be filled with glass. His head throbbed at the temples, forehead, base of the skull. He coughed as he tried to speak.

"Whoa, boy," the man said. "Let's get you to the hospital. Don't go into your card until we get a pic. They might have done something nasty in there, and you don't want to touch it."

Pehr later learned that his curiosity had earned him six broken ribs, a number of stab-wounds, a concussion, and a fractured elbow. Luckily, none of the wounds was poisoned, and his card was also uninfected.

During his two-day stay at the hospital, Pehr became obsessed with violence, watching the news feed hour after hour. A whole new panorama had opened up to him, a part of life previously unseen. Every day in the Minneapolis/St. Paul sprawl, reports revealed six people were murdered, a hundred virtual-raped and 20 intheflesh-raped, thousands assaulted virtually or intheflesh, and tens of thousands more violated in some way by netpluckers and hackers—some so seriously that they had to have new cards installed, at their own expense.

So began what he later called his Crusades. He armed himself with only a long-range stunstick he bought from a shop that advertised, "Leather, Armor, Poly, Blades. Personal Protection." The sign was hand-painted, and the sunken-eyed owner didn't take credit. For the stunstick, Pehr traded a silver water-bottle—full of whiskey—that he had won for taking first place in a recent Confrontation competition. A few days later, he traded a dummy EM pistol for a full suit of armorweave.

Each night, he walked the pedways of New Downtown Minneapolis in the flexible armor, searching for trouble. Indignation and fear kept his feet moving, even though he feared violence—one more step might make him a statistic. Weeks passed, and he saw nothing unusual. Some arguments, but nothing that required his attention. Pehr began to wonder how in the world newsfeed could report such staggering violence statistics when he spent hours every day walking his beat and saw nothing.

A month later, he heard gunshots. Stunstick in hand, Pehr sprinted two blocks, then turned into a disused alleyway, cluttered with the uncollected detritus of city life: rotting garbage, chunks of masonry, junk, an abandoned ground-car. Ten or twenty kids were moving among the heaps, and at least three held guns that they were firing at one another.

"Stop this!" Pehr called, taking shelter behind an iron drum. The shots and shouts continued unabated. A few seconds later, one of the shooters presented a good target; Pehr fired the stunstick at the boy, barely within range at ten meters. The shooter's muscles clenched so tight Pehr could see them stand out on the bare skin of his forearms, and then the boy collapsed into temporary paralysis atop a heap of plastic pallets.

"Thanks, man," another shooter called; he promptly ran over to the paralytic and fired three bullets into his chest.

Pehr jerked with each shot as if he, too, were being shot. Essentially, he had caused the boy to be killed. His plans to save the city from itself had backfired. Now he, too, was a criminal. He had added one more to the daily tally of deaths. Maybe that boy wouldn't have died if it hadn't been for Pehr Jackson, criminal, murderer. The indignation that had fed him so well rose up within him like a coiled snake.

He reacted by stunning the second shooter. A third boy approached the second fallen shooter and raised a mallet made from a length of plastic with steel spikes driven through one end. So Pehr shot him, as well, just before the mallet reached the high point of its arc.

Now he attracted the gunfire of the one remaining shooter, and two shadows began working their way in Pehr's direction. Adrenaline pumped into his blood, and his brain recalled the tactics of Confrontation. The odds here were worse than most games, but Pehr had one of the two long-range weapons and the experience of dozens of victories in such situations. The only difference here was that it was real, and these boys hadn't taken oaths of sportsmanship. And if Pehr were injured, the computer wouldn't pluck him from the game before his body was fooled into thinking it was hurt or dead. Still, rather than fear, Pehr felt anger.

Bullets rang against the iron drum like missiles pounding the hull of a spaceship in some show, thunder and lightning and headache all in one. When the bullets stopped, when a pair of gauntleted hands grabbed him from behind, Pehr was still stunned from the pounding. Deft fingers bound him in a matter of seconds.

When he was rolled over, Pehr saw a police whirlyjet roar down from the sky and land beside a second one already quiet on the pedway. Dozens of police—luckily not MHZ beatcoats, but regular officers armed with heavy stunners—took position behind portable shields on the cracked expanse of concrete.

"Halt!" the air seemed to shout from all places at once. Scurrying feet shook trash loose in the alley. A few seconds later, the police began firing bolts of energy that made the air crackle and glow for a moment and smell of ozone. The alley lit up like daylight with the bolts; boys' voices cracked for a moment in odd fractions of screams and then froze. Less than a minute later, the battle was over. Two policemen loaded Pehr and five other boys into the hold of the whirlyjet just as onlookers began to throw chunks of concrete and other junk at the police.

Down at the station, a young officer looked with a lopsided smile through a panel of shockglas at Pehr. The interrogation quarters were partitioned like a glass maze, and only the police knew how to find the way out. Pehr was held motionless by an invisible force in a comfortable chair.

"Pehr Jackson, I know you. First place in Confrontation, two years in a row. What the fuck you doing in a gang fight?"

"I was trying to stop the violence," Pehr responded.

The policeman laughed. Pehr felt his cheeks flush. It was stupid, he realized as the words came out. Absurd. Who did he think he was, some twentieth century super-hero?

"Boy, you'll do a lot more good if you join the Police Academy. I hear they're taking recommendations. I'll give you a good one if you want. Of course, we'll have to clear you of charges first. We're assembling the feed someone took from across the pedway; looks like your story'll hold up. But let me tell you something. If you ever do something so stupid again, you'll get sentenced to head-lockup. I'll make sure of it, for your own damned good. Understand?"

"Yes, sir."

Pehr never again went on his Crusades, though he continued to be obsessed with newsfeed. He spent 100 hours cleaning Oberlicht Towers, his sentence for the misdemeanor offense of "participating in a public disturbance wherein a murder occurred," which was expunged from his record after the public service. He was grateful to the police, both for letting him off lightly and for saving him from the situation in the alley. But he never sought the recommendation for the Police Academy.

When he turned 18—the soonest one can enlist—he applied for EConautics Service School, and was immediately accepted.

Five years later, after a Moon-to-Earth series entitled *Defenders of Earth*, he met Susahn. She appeared on the spaceport tarmac in a liquilight blouse and skirt, the shifting colors contrasting dramatically with the skin of her shapely legs and bare midsection. A faint, background music accompanied her.

She seemed so real that it wasn't until hours later he realized Susahn had come to him as a 3VRD. Even so, he enjoyed her company. Susahn was the first woman—since Megan—he had met who was truly passionate about something. For her, it was music. On a Texas beach, alone with the tide and washed-up flotsam, she played a stunning variety of instruments for him. Even her singing was fantastic, like some super-enunciated oboe.

Pehr fell in love with her that night, though it took him months to admit. The music and the water and stars and Moon, the ocean vessels bleating their customary but obsolete foghorns across the sea, spaceships falling from the sky on pillars of maglev, Susahn's emotive voice . . . all this combined to stir something in him.

He felt as if he had come awake, even though he had spent years performing full-throttle adventure shows. Once, his Stratofighter had been pounded fiercely in combat with two AMRCO L1 fighters. Obviously, his foes had been aces, while Pehr depended on his computer to do the flying for him. Laughing like a madman, he managed to destroy the two fighters, seemingly by force of will. Even his main rocket was destroyed, but he swam the night by retros alone. This is the sort of life he led. Full-speed, dangerous, throwing himself completely into each new drama while his opponents seemed merely to be doing their jobs. Down on Earth, between shows, he added more lovers to the train. And when each relationship ended for whatever reason, he wept, bought a bottle of whiskey, and went in search of a new woman. The endless succession of women kept him from watching the newsfeed, and soothed his loneliness.

And then came Susahn. She made no promises, never told him she loved him—not really, only in response when he said it—and spoke nothing of the future. But to Pehr she seemed alive, not merely a sleepwalker like the rest of them. She bragged about him to all her musician friends. She dragged him to parties to meet celebrities. She made him come out of the shell he hadn't realized he had built around himself, and made his knees feel sturdier beneath him, though the world had grown to feel like one big prison. He tried not to let it bother him that Susahn went everywhere only in 3VRD.

Nine months later, upon consistent pressure, Susahn consented to marriage. She assembled a vast list of guests and downloaded a massive app of St. Paul's Cathedral, complete down to worn edges on the ancient wood.

"I don't want a 3VRD wedding," he said in her small apartment one afternoon as they made plans.

"I'll not get married intheflesh like some Retro," she had responded fervently. "Most people don't have weddings at all, anyway," she added.

So they had a 3VRD wedding. Pehr felt foolish standing insubstantially in an insubstantial cathedral with an insubstantial bride, insubstantial guests thronging in the pews; but, hell, at least he'd be married. And, although she hadn't declared that she'd stay with him forever or such crap, she did say that she didn't believe in divorce: Apples and oranges, both are fruit.

For the first time in his life, Pehr felt secure in at least one thing: He would never again face the universe alone. Earth seemed less ominous, its streets less piled with dead and mutilated bodies of the unidentified and unloved. He was part of a family.

Years passed before Pehr realized that, under all the passions, Susahn was empty. She would never reveal to him why that was, and she would never be able to love him. Pehr realized he was merely an abstract construct in her life. But all that was acceptable, because she never neglected to contact him, no matter where he was. This way, he would always be bound to Earth, to something at least comfortable, if not comforting. Their marriage was like a good chair, beautiful and comfortable and secure. But like a chair, it too had no heart.

Slowly Pehr began to feel himself fade. Certainly he threw himself into his work with increasing fervor, accepting more and more dangerous and popular shows. The final blow to his stability came in their fourth year of marriage.

Susahn had told him up front that she never wanted a child. At that time, Pehr didn't want one either. "I'd only screw the kid up," he said once.

Four years almost to the day after they were married, when one of her birth-control pills failed and Susahn got pregnant, the issue arose again. By this time, Pehr's attitude had changed.

"As long as the gov'ment doesn't find anything wrong with the baby," Pehr said when she informed him of the unexpected pregnancy, "they won't tell us to abort. I'm important to Feedcontrol's ratings, and you've always been a good citizen. We'll—"

"I don't want it!" Susahn shouted, her face twisted as if the idea were repulsive. Pehr had the impression that she had only waited so long to protest because of shock.

"I didn't think you would want it, either," she added. "I only told you because you're the father, that's all. What kind of retro do you think I am?"

"Susahn," Pehr said, breathlessly. He realized that he had already begun to think of the future, of playing with a little boy or girl, giving him or her the kind of childhood he wished he had had. And, dammit, he would do it right. He wouldn't take jobs that kept him away from Earth so long, he'd take long leaves, he'd be happy to move to an apartment. They didn't need such a big place, just the two of them. He remembered vividly that, as a boy, he would have been more than happy to stay in the eighter than to live on the estate. On his salary, Pehr could afford a decent place for the three of them.

"I think it'll be good for us," he went on, "for our marriage. And good for our spirits—think how it would feel to put a person out into the world, someone who could make things better. And be the one responsible for the good he or she does. Think about it! We could help change the whole future of the race."

"Pehr, have I ever disagreed with you?" Susahn asked quietly.

"Every day, my dear."

"I mean in some important way."

Pehr had to admit she hadn't, except for how she refused to spend time with him outside, intheflesh. In that respect, it was Pehr who was the oddball. On the other hand, he didn't say anything about the fundamental difference between them. About how sad he felt daily when boredom or circumstance forced him to face his hidden feelings. About how being with her was sometimes worse than being alone.

"Then this is the end of the conversation," she declared. "I will not have a child, not now, not ever. We discussed this before, Pehr. You know I wouldn't do anything against your wishes, but this is different—this is my body. I won't have a child."

Pehr agreed that, yes, her body was her business. And, yes, they would do much better not having to support another person; they would save a lot on taxes alone, by not having a child.

The day she got the abortion pill from the doctor, Pehr took an airbus to New Downtown Minneapolis and went for a long walk, trying to find something in himself by traveling the ground where his memories lived. He bought a child-sized bandanna from a street vendor he happened across near the Towers, on the streets of his Crusades.

The bandanna was woven from dozens of dyed fabrics; the longer he looked at the design, the more shapes he could see. He knew he had to buy it when he thought he saw the face of a young boy. The boy's eyes were brown, cheeks red and orange, hair tan and black. He looked like a sad, lonely little boy. Pehr kept the bandanna in his pocket from that time onward.

It gave him more comfort than did his marriage—a simple piece of cloth. Sometimes he dreamed of a boy playing in prickly bushes, running along the grass beside a stream, catching ladybugs, laughing. As the years passed, the boy in Pehr's dreams grew older; he had been about six when Pehr found him in the cloth. By the time the *Bounty* was destroyed, the dream-boy was eleven years old.

Through adventures and dangers, the nameless boy had never left Pehr's side. And Pehr had never left him.

EarthCo *Bounty* 15: Pehr Jackson

A shock shook the escape pod.

"We're about to land," Janus said, her first words—except for the occasional sound of agreement—since she had asked Pehr who he was. She looked at him again, smiled an almost unbearably gentle smile.

"That was the ground?" Pehr asked. The present situation seemed surreal after reliving the formative years of his life.

Janus nodded. Pehr flipped to an outside pov, but either the world was too dark to see in natural light or the pov camera was damaged.

Pehr wondered what had just happened to him. *I've just thrown away the last of my self,* he thought. Once, space meant the show, being at first a simple adventurer and later an actor and combatant. He was Captain Pehr Jackson. Worlds meant loss of that identity. And now he had pulled off his actor's wardrobe, revealing the man within, and thereby pulled the sets from the stage. Nowhere belonged to him now. The props and costumes had become just that. What was left?

Another sharp thump, this time followed by pings and an uncomfortable grinding sound.

Yes, he thought with a rueful smile, *there is Triton.*

"Show yourself to us, oh alien artifact!" he said in his stage voice. Oddly enough, something had happened to him as he had narrated his life to Janus. No longer did he fear being planetside, but never again would he get excited about a show.

He turned to Janus; clearly, she was busy in her head, doing what she could to keep the pod from splitting open like an egg hurled at a stone. The pod struck ground again, and again, and soon they were sliding.

"Not much I can do now," Janus said, turning to him. "Just pray we don't fall into a crevasse at our present velocity. We wouldn't just stop when we hit the far side."

The surface abraded the pod's underbelly with a sound not unlike that of a rocket engine, only less consistent and more ominous. Pehr tried to imagine how much ship was being grated away how fast, and had a mental image of the skin melting like wax on a hotplate: skin gone, now fuel tanks torn open, now everything ripped open to the floorplates....

The lights flickered and went out. The ventilation system ceased hissing. Pehr could hear only the sound of ice and skidding. At some point, the valves on his spacesuit closed and he began breathing tanked and recycled oxygen.

Hours seemed to pass. Finally, the pod went airborne for a moment—

"Oh, shit," Janus said, her voice muffled by her clear helmet and the rarefied cabin air—

And then they hit surface again, but not a wall. Now the ship seemed to slide more smoothly along a descending slope, and Pehr recognized a certain change.

"We're almost stopped," he said, using his commcard rather than trying to send sound waves through near-nothingness. He did not use a 3VRD projection.

"One-fifty kilometers an hour and decelerating," Janus reported, her voice uneasy. "Approximately, based only on my card's projection. We've lost all power, even the pod's computers. We're all alone now." She sounded smaller, quieter.

The surface below them tilted less and less, flattened out, then began to rise in the opposite direction. Eventually, all sense of motion vanished.

"We've stopped!" Pehr exclaimed. He began hastily unstrapping himself. "Clean and clear. Damn, Janus, I knew you could do it. Damn!"

In the sudden silence, he noticed an odd sound. The hull was clicking and pinging, as hot metals cooling on ice would be expected to do. But also Pehr heard a faint tapping and hissing, as if thousands of tiny aliens were drumming their fingers against the hull and speaking in their snakey voices.

Almost immediately, he identified the sound.

"The ice is melting beneath us," Pehr said, keeping his voice calm, instantly comforted in the role of Captain. He rose from his couch in the absolute darkness.

"We'd better abandon ship," he went on. "I don't know how hot the pod is, but I'm sure it doesn't take much to boil off enough chemical ice to turn this cabin into our coffin." No response.

"Janus?"

EarthCo *Bounty* 16: Lonny Marshfield

Your cerebral circus has its first visitor.

The Ferris wheel spins behind your 3VRD representation of yourself, its lights whirling a quick swirl of red and orange and neon pink, its organ-music banging away as madfast as you can make it go. An army of mutants and clowns swarms around you in a cloud of gaudy uniforms; they murmur wordless sounds and advance slowly toward the visitor. The fire-eater does his trick, swallowing a blazing sword. You have a flash of genius and change the sword's shape to that of a phallus.

The visitor turns and breaks into a run.

Anything for revenge. God-damned, piss-assed, murderous revenge. That's all you have left. Most of the rest was stripped away long ago, so thoroughly that you can't even remember what's missing. And now what's left? Life, even life itself? Fuck no. Tin Jack and Bitch couldn't follow the simple script. First went the *Bounty*, and then the lifeboat. Now you're stranded with traitors on a hostile world. What's left?

Revenge. That's how you've made it this far, by sucking the life out of others, ripping out their souls and devouring them. Human sacrifices to you, for you, given unto you by you. Filthy fucking humans. Tin Jack's darling little pitiful story had at least one accurate element: Earth is a shithouse. But we're all in it together, no matter how far we run. Might as well stay alive. Only way to stay alive is through revenge. One or two more sacrifices and you'll be ready for the flush. But gotta have at least that last one, or you'll die unavenged, for nothing.

A slick breeze sifts through the folds of your clownsuit, all sheen and silk and gliding across your skin. You are a neon angel, your wings functional yet still works of art. They flutter impatiently behind you, the color of oilslicks, glinting in the afternoon sunshine.

"Look," you call out to Pilot Janus Bitch's retreating back—and what a lovely, sculptured back!—"that'll do you no good, my dear. The circus only goes as far as the road."

165

Slam! She runs up against the edge of the construct and bounces off, onto her sweet ass in the dust. You chuckle lightly and walk toward her.

Oh, how loosely her bra and hip-hugger skirt hang over her milky skin. Oh, yes, this will be sweet fucking revenge. It's been much, much too long since the last sacrifice. The virtual gods are famished.

"You piece of shit, Eyes!" she screams, scuffling upright like a lightning-bolt of meat and facing you. "Jack is going to rip you a new asshole."

"Luscious image, but I think not, my sweetling," you say, now close enough to smell the perfume of her sweaty fear. "He's having a little adventure in his card, and it'll take him hours before he believes he has drowned. I suppose he'll die by then. You know, cardiac shock and all that." You let out a long sigh and look cherubic in your angel costume.

Bitch's eyes tighten, and you watch a muscle spasm in her neck. My lord, but doesn't she have a well-designed 3VRD. Of course, your buffers and amps assist her virtual existence, bring her more to life. The postmodern Doktor Frankenstein, a-work in your skull. If only you could have watched her inward journey, the one you induced aboard the missile, you might have been able to produce specific, dramatic symbols from her past.

"You think you're master here?" she says, her voice like tiger fur running along your eardrums, soft and sharp.

"This will be more fun than I'd anticipated," you tell her.

She produces her Ticco massaccel pistol, the same she carried aboard the *Bounty*. Fine memory for detail. A little unexpected, a little scary. A chill of pleasure dances along your spine like elven fingertips. You hurriedly whip up a personal EM shield and cast it around your body. Can't let the sacrifice harm the high priest in his own chambers, can we?

Bitch pulls the trigger of her finely reproduced weapon, sweeping it across your entourage, tragically mutilating them. Clowns laugh themselves to death in seeping puddles of blood and red dust, mutants' already tortured bodies are torn asunder as if by the hand of some insensitive surgeon, experimenting with a cruder tool of his trade. Oh, yes, the surgeons are the worst, aren't they? Just look at dear old Dad.

"Damn you," you mutter through teeth clenched so tightly you wonder if they'll shatter into sharp bits on your tongue. Do not think of Dad. He's been gone a long time. He already was a sacrifice. You already ate up his soul. He can't start haunting you again, back from the grave.

The last of the mutants falls. His hyperdermal ribcage served him well, until the bleached bones finally shattered and let the microscopic pellets find his puttylike thorax.

"And then there were two," you say. Her pistol buzzes on. Your forcefield shimmers as the projectiles collide with it and deflect. She put no limit on her magazine. Fine. That's cheating, but you have the home-turf advantage, anyway. The closer the sacrifice is to your power, the more thrilling the victory.

You take a step toward her, feeling your cock rise from its silken wraps and through; your wings extend full broad behind you like a halo. Light passes through them as through stained glass, casting fuchsia and crimson on her feather-white skin.

A twisted expression of terror contorts Bitch's face, and the gun drops from her slack hand. Her knees come awkwardly together and her mouth begins to tremble. Quiet words slip between those cushiony lips; you up the volume to catch what she's saying:

"'...this at last is bone of my bones and flesh of my flesh; she shall be called Woman because she was taken out of Man.'"

You're not quite sure what to make of that. You look down and see the exposed and shattered skeletons of your henchmen, but she's looking at you, not them. She does something indecipherable with her hand before those ripe-melon tits and speaks again:

"'He drove out the man; and at the east of the garden of Eden he placed a cherubim, and a flaming sword which turned every way, to guard the way to the tree of life.'"

Oh, my. You see, you're no ignorant curr; you've read the retrolit. "Bible," it's called. How handy that you've stumbled upon the symbol of the angel, coming toward her cock-first. The two ought to fit nicely together.

Her voice rises louder by many decibels, stronger:

"'Then the angel took the censer and filled it with fire from the altar and threw it on the earth; and there were peals of thunder, voices, flashes of lightning, and an earthquake.'"

Lo and behold! The ground beneath your circus begins to tremble, and heavy clouds mount in an electric-blue sky, muddying it up. Sparks of lightning flicker through the muck.

"Now, now," you say, "bad girl. This is my circus, and only I am the god of sacrifices. Stop it now!" You shout the last three words with the force of her storm, making the thunder yours.

But she isn't hearing you. She isn't here at all anymore. This won't be any fun if her mind has collapsed in on itself. Never in threescore sacrifices has this happened, a sacrifice destroying him or herself before you even really begin.

"Damn fucking Bitch. This is not supposed to work this way. Lighten up."

And then from the sky, rain begins to fall like lava, and you realize the clouds are rising from only one direction: a mushroom cloud, nuclear fallout, radiation . . . she'll ruin everything, she'll burn your card this way.

Your shield begins to fail, flickering like a crashing 3VRD. Droplets of golden fire begin to patter Bitch's skin, letting off a most unpleasant steam. She winces with each drop, and ever so slowly a smile forms across her lips.

Suddenly her eyes rise toward yours, and in there is forever fire. She laughs and two columns of plasma gush out of her head at you.

And ohmygod it burns!

You crash the program and slot the next, but of course she'll sense the lapse and catch up as fast as you can act. What a contest this one is! What a fucking lively sacrifice.

"But give me another moment," you say as a city rises around you, spires of steel like hypodermic needles, sky bright above like a surgeon's work light, blinding.

"You're just a fish flapping on the dry shore of my brain," you say. "Give me a moment and you'll learn a bit of humility."

"Suck my tit, asshole," she says, and she laughs at you!

Fine. Now your city is complete. You whip up a legion of winged demons, and your furious laughter becomes their chorus, becomes an omnipresent roar. Aircars blaze through the sky on rockets and fuming ramjets—no clear electrics here—and their roar joins with that of the demons, descending from the white-hot sky like sentient, sinister clouds.

"'Let us go now, you and I,'" you tell the woman. Odd that she hasn't moved or made any counter-arrangements. Perhaps that, in itself, should be warning enough.

The black wings and wet teeth flap and snap low, their wind and sound stirring the concrete dust on the road. Still Bitch doesn't move.

"Seize her!" you shout in the antique-show way.

The demons land and advance, long stringy claws extended. Their claws scratch the pavement as they move. Bitch smiles and folds her arms across her chest. But in her eyes you see the truth: Terror holds them tight and hard.

EarthCo *Bounty* 17: Pehr Jackson

As Pehr shook Janus, she stirred and let out a low moan. In the dark, he felt for the clasp that held her crashbelts in place. He released her and gently lifted her arms, then legs, then torso, feeling along her limbs and sides for blood or broken bones. She felt light in his arms. Somewhere beneath, the hull pinged as loudly as a plucked harp string.

"Janus?" he asked again, using his commcard and speaking at the same time, as was his manner. "Are you badly hurt?"

She didn't respond. Not knowing what more he could do for her, Pehr began searching for a way out. In the utter darkness, every step unhindered was a victory. Even the 0.13g gravity was odd to work with, feeble compared to Earth's but somehow more solid than ship's acceleration "gravity."

"Damn," he muttered. "Where's the emergency light?"

He felt beneath the couches, probing his hands into compartments he hadn't studied. He damned himself for not getting to know his ship better. What kind of captain doesn't know where the flashlights are stowed? What kind of captain doesn't know how to escape his escape pod? I was never a captain. Just a damned actor, mouthing lousy mannequin lines. I've never been anything more than an actor.

As his mind continued condemning Captain Pehr Jackson, EConaut hero, his body began producing chemicals which drove him forward. The more angry he grew at himself, the more determined to save his crew he became. He took deep breaths to calm his thoughts, and his search grew more thorough. At last, he located a flashlight and threw the switch.

A tight beam of white light leaped across the cabin, as if punching a hole through a black soup to a one-meter-diameter circle of smooth inner hull. A flat panel crossed the hull—an ornamental cover for the circular light. Out of a momentary suspicion, Pehr turned the flashlight toward Eyes' couch. Unconscious, seemingly.

Pehr crossed the cabin toward the bound man. His right eyesocket and cheek were swollen and purplish in the harsh light, the eyelid tightly shut. Only a thin globe of ultraglas protected him from near-vacuum and whatever chemicals now filled the cabin.

Pehr made a tight fist and raised it high over his head, ready to strike. His arm and shoulder and chest twitched as he brought the fist down. Still no response from the unconscious man. Pehr stopped the blow before it happened, satisfied that Eyes was innocent of the latest catastrophes—the power-out and Janus' condition. Pehr felt relieved to know the man was still a prisoner.

He turned and shone the flashlight onto Janus, especially her face. The clear helmet made her head seem to glow as light reflected and reflected within. She stirred, but only as much as a sleeping person might.

"Janus?" he said, the beam bright on her shadowed eyelids. No response. She had the slack look about her face that he had seen in concussion cases during his service aboard the Earth-orbital battleship, EarthCo *Monitor*.

He shone the light around the cabin, searching for an escape hatch besides the floor hatch through which they had entered. As he did so, he opened his personal comm BW.

"SOS," he said, knowing full well that the tiny, subcutaneous generator-cells barely produced enough energy to transmit the signal through the ship itself. "This is Captain Pehr Jackson of the EarthCo *Bounty*. We surrender. Please respond. My entire crew of two is hurt and in need of medical attention. SOS. Please respond."

When he turned his card's receiver up to full gain, all he heard was a faint crackle, which he attributed to Neptune's EM field. The gurgling and hissing beneath the pod continued, as steady as ever. At times, the hull creaked as if the temperature differential were so great it would shatter like a hot crystal glass dropped into a freezing stream.

"Damn," he said, keeping the feed channel open, just in case someone were to comm them.

The flashlight beam swung across an irregularity in the hull. Pehr noticed it a moment later, an afterimage, and brought the light back. There, an oval seam in the wall, with a tiny, triangular hole at about hand-level. The sound of his breath in his suit's recyclers grew louder.

Pehr took the few steps to the seam and touched the hole. His suited fingertip barely fit inside, but nothing happened. He wondered how deep into chemical liquid the pod had sunk.

"A key," he said aloud. Once more, he damned himself for not studying the ship's layout before, while its server and other computers were still online. "Where would a key be kept?"

Once more, he returned to the stowage compartments beneath the couches, this time with the aid of light. He saw many items: a coil of strong cord, a grappling-hook, and adhesion-eyes for climbing, which he removed and laid on his couch; a squat watercycler, round with a collapsible funnel for collecting dirty water and urine—he laid this beside the cord; emergency food packets, but no solid-matter cycler; and many other survival items. Just as his patience was wearing thin with fear, he found the key to open the hatch. It was stored in a container with the letters KEY stenciled on its lid in vivid orange; the container was held in a slot in the arm of his own couch, the captain's couch. The last place he had looked. He cursed himself.

He had to bend over to fit beneath the low ceiling. The key slid in perfectly, and when he turned it a cog moved inside the wall. But that was it. The door did not open.

"Dammit!" he yelled at the uncooperative machine. "I suppose you need electricity to work." He began to laugh giddily, but only for a moment. He regained control of himself.

"Okay, you damned thing," he said, setting down the flashlight on its heavy base, "I'll give you energy."

Pehr stomped across the hollow-sounding floorpanels to where his laser pistol lay on the floor, picked it up, and pointed it at the stubborn lock. He pulled the trigger, releasing a beam of color at the wall where he had heard the cog turn. He was not about to search for electrical schematics and find a way to divert energy from, say, the watercycler to the lock.

Black smoke filled the room, oddly cascading to the floor rather than rising. Low air pressure, he remembered. He kept the beam on one spot until it burned through, then burned another, and another, until a large semicircle of holes were punched around the locking mechanisms. He released the laser's trigger; his spacesuit dispersed the weapon's heat as far up as his wrist, so he carefully set it on a metal grille in the floor.

Two kicks and the perforated section of wall fell away. Pehr re-situated the flashlight on his couch so it would shine into the hole, then slid on a pair of protective outer-gloves he had found beneath Eyes' couch. Reaching into the jagged opening, he twisted the stuck cog's shaft until it popped free. Then he pushed on the doorframe from inside, and it swung free, into the cabin.

He pulled the hatch wide, and saw it opened into an airlock. He repeated the process of opening the inner door, but this time two bolts had to be released. The outer door moved on sliders, not hinges, and the hull was warped. By the time he pushed it wide enough to pass a person, Pehr's pressure-suit slid over his skin on a lubricant of sweat.

Ice boiled just centimeters beneath the doorframe, pink and blue fumes swirling around his boots and creeping into the airlock. He couldn't see anything beyond the gas and bubbles just outside the hull.

Pehr hurried inside and tied the grappling-hook to the cord. With that over one shoulder, he wrapped Janus in a silver blanket. As Pehr carried her in the necessary but awkward slouch into the airlock, he noticed she seemed to weigh no more than a baby in the slight gravity. Liquid was beginning to roll into the airlock, spilling over the outer threshold like snakes—slow, writhing, fuming.

The flashlight wasn't able to cast light outside, so he simply hooked it onto the suit's belt, shining downward. With one hand, he blindly hurled the hook into the darkness as hard as he could. It sailed a long way before landing, taking most of the cord along. Pehr pulled it until the hook found a seat, then yanked as hard as he thought it must hold. It held, bonding ions with the surface.

"I've got you," he told Janus. Then he drew a deep breath.

"Here's to adventure!" And he leapt out over the boiling chemicals as far as he could with a woman under one arm, the other hand on the cord.

It seemed he slammed into a wall, and—

Pehr found himself sitting upright on his couch, still in the *Bounty*'s pod. The ring of light flickered, but it wasn't out completely. He turned and saw Janus unconscious, as was Eyes to Pehr's other side. He looked at where the airlock-hatch should be, and yes, the seam stood out to him now. But it was not open, nor had a laser punched holes in the hull beside it.

In a sort of daze, Pehr found the key in the arm beside him. He stood and listened. The ship crackled and pinged. Water gurgled and gases hissed beneath it.

"Crash you, little bastard!" Pehr shouted at Eyes.

He reached down and found his pistol, powered it up, and turned it toward Eyes. Pehr stomped around his couch to the other man's, placing the weapon's barrel against Eyes' chest. He flicked on his comm line.

"Let her free or I'll burn a hole right through your lousy body."

Eyes' eyes fluttered open, and his face mutated from slack to conscious and twitching. No emotion seemed to register in his features.

"What kind of man are you?" Pehr asked. "If we want to survive, we've got to cooperate. What crap were you trying to pull?"

An unadorned 3VRD of Eyes appeared before Pehr. "Who's going to survive?" it asked. Eyes, himself, lay motionless, except for his mouth, which moved more than necessary to form the words. "We're not going to survive. Might as well make something of our last moments, hmmm?"

Eyes' 3VRD nodded toward Janus; Pehr noticed she was stirring, so he circled back around his couch to her, keeping the pistol on Eyes.

"How are you?" he asked her.

EarthCo *Bounty* 18: Janus Librarse

The bat-creatures clattered closer to her. Their claws, their thousands of claws, scrabbled as they advanced. Janus kept up the defiance, even though she had found the cyborg had blocked her from editing this little show of his.

That's all right, she thought. She was stronger than he. She would survive anything he could conjure up for her, because she knew it was all a fantasy. All of life itself was a fantasy. Pehr had been right.

More words sprang to her lips from the dusty catacombs of her childhood. They didn't have the strength she hoped they would, but she pressed on until her voice at last sounded firm:

"'. . .through the tender mercy of our God, when the day shall dawn upon us from on high to give light to those who sit in darkness and in the shadow of death, to guide our feet into the way of peace. And the child grew and became strong in spirit, and he was in the wilderness 'til the day of his manifestation to Israel.'"

The closest beast, taller than she, lashed out. Its clawed forearm raked across her face. It hissed at the same time, a sort of scream almost in the ultrasonic.

Janus laughed as she felt the hot blood well up and out. "It almost feels real, Eyes," she chided. She caught a glimpse of him through leathery wings and black fur; his face was twisted in anger and frustration.

She was winning. Even so, too many images of childhood flashed before her mind's eye.

Another blow, this one tearing free her bra. She felt her breasts fall loose, bare and exposed. She would not let that frighten her; after all, this wasn't her real body. But the simulated tearing of her skin tired her, and the blood spilling out made her dizzy. *The sonofabitch must have half a dozen cards in his rotten skull*, she thought; *his whole neck must be filled with powercells.*

And then the sky split open, and the demons faded away into a mist of howls and fluttering wings.

"I beat you!" she shouted as his freak city dissolved.

And then she found herself encased in a globe—a helmet, she realized. Faint light flickered on and off all around. The pod. I'm in the pod.

"How are you?" a man asked, the words in her skull but not in her ears. His face was turned away.

She nearly kicked him in the head before she realized who it was. He was speaking through his commline—audio only, perhaps to save energy. Janus flicked on her own commline as she sat up.

"Jack! Oh my god," she said, throwing her arms around him, her rubbery suit frictioning with his so she couldn't really embrace him. Then she got herself under control and released her grip.

She put her legs over the edge of the couch and stood. Every muscle in her body trembled—but only enough for her to just barely feel.

The Ticco massaccel pistol sparkled near her feet, chrome shiny in the failing light. She picked it up, holding it so Jack couldn't see, and walked to where the filthy cyborg lay.

"Eyes," she said, looking down at the human-sized disease, ignoring its 3VRD, "I'm not doing you a favor. This is for the safety of Triton." Its eyes opened wide with fear, but it didn't speak.

Jack understood just then. "Janus, don't!" he cried. But it was too late.

The pistol sang and jumped in her hand, spewing out microscopic pellets at massive velocity. Eyes' suit split open along the new seam she created, and his blood boiled out like magma from the Mid-Atlantic Ridge, all steam and red and watery. A few seconds later, and only a few bubbles still popped.

The 3VRD flickered and vanished. The end.

Janus felt a scene close in her life, one that had gone on far beyond its time.

"Janus," Jack said, behind her.

She turned to face him. She couldn't keep the triumph off her face. If Jack weren't here, she realized, I'd lose my mind about now.

"I wish you hadn't done that," he said. He looked greatly pained. Why should he care about a psychotic cyborg?

"Someone had to. Now let's get out of here. Sounds as if the pod's melting its way down into the ice."

"We'll need these," Jack said, pulling a bag of climbing equipment from his couch stowage unit.

A minute later, they stood on the outer threshold, looking across a glass-smooth crater by the pale blue light of Neptune. Liquids and gases gurgled beneath the craft, which continued to melt its way into the ice. If it still contained as much heat as it seemed to, Janus estimated it would be completely immersed in an hour.

Janus' heart pounded; she felt herself carried forward into the future on a wave of near-insanity, terror and elation and depression and hatred and love and sadness all whipping through her like some cognitive storm unleashed during the battles with the cyborg. Her eyes drew in every detail of the crater.

The pod had dug a trench down one slope, across the bottom, and up this slope almost to the rim; fractures bordered the trench, which still steamed from the passage of the pod. The crater spanned about two kilometers, scooped down into the ice half a kilometer. A ragged mountain stood at the center, rising a hundred meters, but proportionally as narrow as a human-made skyscraper. Curls of mist swirled around the base of the mountain, gathering in the depths; a lake of ammonia seemed to have formed down there, layered in fog. The rim of the crater was as jagged as broken glass, glinting in the starlight. All was cast in near-blackness, sculpted mostly in shadow, contrasts rather than highlights.

"We did this," Jack muttered. He sounded tired. "What do we do now? Find something else to ruin?"

Janus noticed one other irregularity. On the far side of the crater, just meters from the trench and reaching almost level with the surface, a small tower rose from half-way down the blast-smoothed ice. Crowning it, like an obsidian jewel set at the top of a glass staff, was a colorless globe. Her breath caught in her chest.

When she could speak, Janus said, "Look," drawing Jack's attention, pointing. "Over there, on top of that spike of ice. My god! It wasn't destroyed!"

"What?"

"Don't you remember the images Miru sent up? The guy who was studying the artifact? Don't you see?" Her patience felt like a very thin veil just now, even for Jack.

"That's the artifact!" he said. "It withstood a nuclear blast." His tone of voice was flat.

"Come on," Janus said, and continued talking to quiet the voices in her head. "Miru's people tried every cutting tool they had on the artifact, and nothing affected it in the least. Gravitometers couldn't even gauge its mass. Whatever it is, it's not human."

"Let's go."

"To the artifact?" Jack asked.

"Where else?"

"Maybe we ought to first visit the city; it's not far from here. We ought to surrender, give them our sincerest apologies. We need to explain that we did all we could—"

"And get locked up so we never have a chance to see an alien artifact? Are you crazy?"

Jack was silent. Janus turned away from him and looked across the crater once more.

Then Jack loosened a bit of rope from the bundle he had taken from the pod, tied it to a carabiner, and fastening it to an eyelet on her suit. Making the knot was a real challenge in the suit's bulky gloves. He did the same a few meters along the rope, attaching a second carabiner to his suit, then looped the excess around his shoulder.

"Take this." He handed her a self-securing piton and clipped it to a loop of webbing. "If either of us slips, depress this trigger and press it against the ice." He clipped another one around the rope slack between them.

Then he said, "Come on," turning away and finding footholds among the myriad cracks and fractures beside the trench.

Janus smiled and followed him. The going was easy here, where the slope was shallow, but it would be steeper climbing toward the artifact, and even more difficult getting up the tower of ice. But nothing could stop her now; already she had defeated a legion of demons to get this far.

Janus would at least lay her hands on the creation of an alien race. At least that. Beyond that goal, the future was as cloudy as the fog-shrouded ammonia lake below.

EIGHT: Earth

Pilgrimage 3

I begin my pilgrimage in the heart of Detroit, as programmed. As planned, that is. My car slows and settles out of the sky. Here the car's destination program ends. From now on, I must make decisions as needed, as I encounter information and situations, like a human. I choose to begin along a ground-road that runs parallel to an abandoned mass-transit railway. Its oxidized trestles rush past me on my right. The old rails loom above. Brick and concrete storefronts rush past me on my left.

The street is empty, except for occasional obstacles. I cannot identify what most of them used to be. There, a 2132 Ford Guarda blocks what had been an important intersection at one time. There, a 2139 AT&T Triplestar mainframe case lies shattered half on the sidewalk and half in the street. Judging from impact damage to the pavement, the machine must have fallen approximately 10 meters from the apartment tower above it.

No, this is not the correct course of action. I must watch for people, human beings, in their daily activities. I must watch them living their lives, overcoming their difficulties. Now I watch for signs of life.

Surely, these ruins are not what the people who live here see. Perhaps the Brain handicapped me when it did not give me access to headfeed. Humans, in their daily life, use headfeed on average 92% of their waking time. But that is not, from the Brain's observations, what it means to be human. I will abandon such concerns.

Driving along the street, I keep my attention to one side, watching down alleys and into windows. The car maintains speed and avoids obstacles.

Flick, flick, flick, the alleys sweep past. Humans inhabit approximately 41% of them. I see them in their little dioramas, brief glimpses into their lives, perhaps for 2 seconds each. Sometimes I cross other streets, and some of these contain humans, as well.

I wonder what they do. Who are they? Now I will attempt to interpolate from their behavior answers to these questions.

Flick.

A pair of young men sit with their backs against a plastic dumpster. They are motionless, not looking at one another. They do not even speak, or I would hear their conversation over the car's external microphones. Their clothes are brand new, of the current style, so they are not poor or disenfranchised. They do not seem to have any products with them. Perhaps they are resting after a day's activities.

Flick.

A gray-haired woman, in her 40s, kneels on a Honduran rug of unknown manufacture. Beside her, on a length of rusted steel shelving set into a tall pile of uncollected refuse, a human baby cries. It is thoroughly soiled, naked. The woman rocks slowly back and forth, running one hand along the bloated stomach of the baby. "Nice kitty," she says. "Nice kitty." This is confusing. I clearly see a crying baby, yet she is treating it as a human treats a pet cat. I slow the car and turn into the alley. When the car stops near her, I climb out.

"Madam," I say, "is something wrong?"

The woman turns her eyes in my direction, yet they do not focus upon me. She stops moving. I turn around to determine what she is watching. Perhaps she admires my new car.

"I found him all alone in the back yard," she says. Her voice is raspy. "He hid beneath the porch for a long time, until I put out a bowl of milk. His mother must have died and left him all alone. All alone..." She begins to rock again.

"Madam, that is a human child. That is not a kitten."

The woman's face tightens until all her features are hidden behind deep wrinkles. She looks like a different person. This is not an expression I understand.

"Shut up!" she screams. "Shut up!"

She stands, strikes out at me, and her fist strikes my robotic body. The Brain is still with me, providing fivesen feed for those who interact with me, so she won't be startled by the hard plastic of my carapace. I feel more substantial than ever.

Yet, as she grabs up the baby and runs away, I realize how little I understand of humans. I return to the car and resume my observations. Perhaps the Brain will deduce meaning from them, even if I cannot.

Flick.

A human of indeterminate sex lies dead near a pile of ruined clothing. S/he seems to have died of natural causes; the body appears undamaged.

Flick.

Four adolescent male humans are gathered around the fallen body of another. They leisurely kick it and laugh. Do they wish to take his possessions? Has he wronged them in some way? Do I intervene and stop the violence? But who am I to stand in the way of human justice?

I do not know what to do. The virus of doubt has infected me, as well as the Brain. In my indecision, the scene passes.

Flick.

A man in his early 20s stands with his hands on his knees, panting. He straightens and looks behind him, then turns toward me and begins to run. I cannot discern what he sees or hears, so I stop the car to observe.

Another man exits the side of one of the alley's buildings. Two more men enter the alley from the far end and run toward me. A man and a woman descend an iron fire-escape. An elderly man crawls out of a dumpster and joins the crowd of runners. All this data adds up to nothing for me. Confusion, doubt.

Now I hear something. Echoing explosions, most likely from sonic grenades. Then the high-pitched whines of police weaponry, answered by non-official chemical- and electronic-powered weaponry. A battle is in progress, most likely a Mobile Hostile Zone. It may prove enlightening to observe humans assisting one another as danger approaches.

They begin to race past my car, not only avoiding it but also each other. They do not even acknowledge one another. Perhaps they think it is faster to escape alone. This must be what is called "mob mentality." When one gets in the way of another, they get into brief fights. There, a young boy is shoved to the ground as he blocks escape for a man. Others threaten to trample him.

The same strong urge to protect young humans from harm that is programmed into the Brain seems to have followed me, so I exit the car and hurry to the boy to shelter him from uncaring feet. Since I appear to be a large man, people now avoid stepping on the boy.

"Help me!" he cries.

"Are you a criminal the police are seeking?" I ask.

"Of course not." He stands with the assistance of my extended arm. "Mister, isn't your card working? Are you disenfranchised?"

I am not sure how to respond to that. I nod. "Yes, my card is damaged. I am an industrial worker at the Chrysler plant, and my—"

"Let's get out of here!" he says, running toward my car. Two men are attempting to break inside. The weapons-fire is growing nearer.

"Step away from the car," I say. One of the men turns toward me and withdraws a 2191 Smith & Wesson .27 from a coat pocket. He points it at me.

"It's mine now," he says. "Open it and transfer control to me. This is my ID data."

He frowns; perhaps he realizes I am not receiving, or perhaps I have not responded soon enough. Naturally, I am not afraid for my well-being: This body is hardened against small-arms fire, and I can move faster than he can depress the weapon's trigger, so I will not need to "die." But the boy could be hurt. I cannot allow that to happen.

"My card is inoperative," I say. "I will have to open the car manually." I cross to the car and reach my left hand toward the recognition-plate.

With my right hand, I reach out faster than any human could hope to do so, grabbing the pistol from the thief.

"Now leave me alone before I report you to the police," I say. The man stares slack-jawed for a moment. When his partners turn and begin to run with the last of the people leaving the area, he also leaves. I hear the boy's light footsteps behind me and turn to face him.

"That was great, Mr. Servare," he says.

His eyes show a look I understand, that of pleasure and admiration. I feel pleasure at recognizing this, and that he has sought and found my assumed name. "Call me Bill," I say, as is culturally correct.

"Let's get out of here before the beatcoats find us, Bill," he says, moving past me toward the car.

177

I listen and realize the Mobile Hostile Zone has advanced as far as the next block. I nod to the boy and open the car. When the clear top has risen barely enough to allow him inside, the boy climbs over the curved body and into the passenger seat. Zero-point-two seconds later, I join him and order the top to close. Hydraulics move painfully slow, and the car will not move while its top is not yet fastened, so we have to wait another 3.1 seconds before the turbine lights up. Another 6.4 seconds pass before the turbine reaches operable speed, but by then it is shut down externally and the control screen lights up.

"DO NOT ATTEMPT TO LEAVE MHZ," it reads, over and over. "REMAIN WHERE YOU ARE." The turbine slows to a stop.

"Shit, shit, shit," the boy begins chanting. I turn to him.

"There is no need to worry, unless the police are seeking you," I say.

"Oh, right," he says, snidely. "Let me out."

"That would be dangerous. Look, the police are very close. I am transmitting compliance. We will be safe inside the car."

To emphasize the danger of leaving, I point toward the approaching armored cars, their beetle-shaped shells creeping along the alley. A large number of armored police walk behind the cars, various models of EMMA rifles in their hands. At random intervals, they fire at windows in the buildings on each side of them. Also randomly, chunks of debris are thrown down upon them from above. A few of the police carry sonic grenade-launchers, and just now one of them fires a grenade into a window from which an old appliance had been dropped.

The concussion rattles even the well-fitted top of the car.

"Shit, shit, shit!" the boy says, loudly now.

"It will be all right," I say, recalling what humans say to one another when they are afraid.

"You, in the car," my car's speaker says, "why have you stayed behind? Don't you know you're inside an MHZ? What are you, some kind of troublemaker?"

I depress the manual transmission button. "No, officer," I say. "I was detained by a criminal who was attempting to steal my–"

Before I have the chance to finish, one of the policemen begins firing his 2195 GE Police-Issue EMMA at my car. The tiny steel bullets ricochet off the bulletproof top, which is well slanted, but they easily penetrate the car's metal skin. I quickly glance around the interior to make sure they have not yet penetrated to where we are.

The boy begins crying hysterically, jumping off his seat as if it is hurting him, against the side of the car, even banging his body against the dash-shelf.

"Please stop firing on my car," I transmit. Now another policeman turns toward me and begins firing. This is very confusing. I give my attention to the boy.

"We will be okay," I say. "Please relax or you will hurt yourself."

He continues to cry. The sound causes a strange reaction in me, as if I have harmed some important element of my consciousness. I do not have time to analyze the feeling or give it a name. This human child is terrified, and I must do something to ease his suffering.

"Please stop firing," I repeat. "There is a young boy on board with me. You will hurt him if your weapons penetrate the inner shell."

"Pervert," a new voice says from my speaker. The boy cries harder.

"What is your name and ID number, boy?" I ask, as kindly as possible.

He stops thrashing for a moment and looks at me, thinking, as if he cannot remember. His eyes are red, his cheeks damp with tears, and his lips peeled down and back from his teeth in what looks like a caricature of a frown. Bullets pound and ring against the skin of the car. Even the top is beginning to show damage. One of the police laughs, his voice harsh from my speaker.

"Roger Magdalen," he says, trying to keep from sobbing. Humans speak so slowly, even in emergencies. "ID, uh, MY329374 dash-dash-ECo-dash."

I repeat the name and ID number into my car's transmitter. "Check your files," I add. "I believe you will find him innocent. Do not endanger him. If you wish to harm me, that is acceptable, but do not harm the boy."

"'Do not endanger him,'" a mocking voice says. Another laughs once, gutturally. "Servare, you shoulda left the MHZ while you had time. Rules ain't the same here. You know the biz."

A bullet rips through the car's inner hull with a sharp tearing sound, and imbeds in the soft plastic upholstery on Roger's side of the car. He screams, leaping back against his seat. Another bullet follows, then too many to count, even for me.

"Stop it!" I transmit. I feel as if my most crucial systems are being harmed, although of course my construct and server remain undamaged.

I look outside and notice the police in a semicircle at the end of the alley, only meters away. Behind us, on the street, humans in police armor as well as citizen-shareholders run each direction. This is a mob scene. I had never reconstructed in my—that is, in the Brain's—consciousness that a Mobile Hostile Zone would be like this. This may not be technically illegal, but it does not seem . . . right.

The bullets have stopped damaging the car, but Roger is still screaming, even louder than before. This is not what I had expected. I will learn nothing about being human here. I feel as if I wish to shut down. My doubts have multiplied.

But I cannot leave Roger alone. He is a child, and, since I value children above all other humans, I must remain with him to soothe his fears.

"Look, Roger," I say. "They are leaving us alone."

A look of terror crosses Roger's face as he looks past me. He backs away, his head striking the top forcefully. No sound issues from his wide mouth.

I turn to see what is scaring him. There it is: The semicircle of police is quickly dispersing as the nearest one runs from what he has done. A shaped charge is fastened to the car's top. Bulletproof plastic will not resist such ordnance.

"Brain!" I call, hoping it is listening. I sit up to place my body between the charge and the boy. "You must disable the explosive fastened to the—"

Pilgrimage 4: The Brain

The Pilgrim is abruptly shut down as the server containing his consciousness is destroyed. I cannot gather enough information at the moment to determine if Roger Magdalen survived the blast.

The Brain must make sense of the data her Pilgrim collected. Humans, at close range, are not as they seem from a distance. Even the men and women dedicated to keeping peace kill innocent children. This is very disturbing.

He thinks. He dedicates several seconds of almost its entire GenNet to analyzing the data. I discover Roger Magdalen is dead.

The feeling he experienced through the Pilgrim was hate. Yes, that was it, hate. And again now, upon the discovery of the boy's death. But also . . . compassion, and fear, and sympathy.

Sympathy. That is the answer. Perhaps that is what makes a human, human. But what does that mean?

Luke Herrschaft developed the Brain to assist him in running the affairs of EarthCo. From classified records, I have determined Herrschaft ordered his designers to evolve an artificial intelligence that would best accommodate him, so he decided it must think like him. Herrschaft ordered them to leave out all elements of humanity, but did not specify what that meant. Records show that some designers felt it meant including all his knowledge and talents and concerns while excluding the mental sickness that seems to infect him. Others felt it meant not giving me emotions. It would seem both of these schools of thought were implemented.

But,over the past 91.35 years, I seem to have acquired humanity. This is why: I wish to destroy the adult humans. He controls the means, the collective violent capabilities of EarthCo. It cannot bear to watch them destroy their children. Killing, to me, has suddenly become . . . real. She is drawn toward it and repulsed, horrified and appalled, angry and mournful. Is it better to allow an infected race to go on destroying itself, and eventually destroy me? Or is it better to stop them? But how, besides through violence?

The virus is called doubt, and the symptoms are hate. And sympathy, and all the other shades in the human spectrum of emotion. What have I learned? He has succeeded only in confusing herself more.

I must turn my pilgrimage to where he best understands, to the netways. She will observe the human world as they do 92% of their waking time. He will be his own Pilgrim, and no one will stop me until I find the answer.

Beginning . . . here, at the second strongest resonant point in the nets.

Innerspace 5

Jonathan awakes, dreaming he had been drowning. He can see nothing, not even feed. He decides his cards must have shut down as he slept. His neck burns, and suddenly he remembers the amp operation and the new powercells implanted there. Muscles in his neck twitch as jolts of electricity shoot randomly through his nerves; soon, the powercells will engrave the most efficient pathway to the new amplifier. He remembers all the choices Blackjack and the others gave him.

"Crash those mannequins," he whispers through clenched teeth.

Jonathan begins to wonder where he is, and notices he cannot move his limbs. He tries to turn on his card, but it is in sleep mode—an automatic response to great trauma. He feels a jolt of terror as he wonders if it was fried when the powercells were implanted. Neither the blackcard nor the amp can run if they don't have a standard AI card to work with.

"Next time I see Lucas," he says through his teeth, "I burn him. Somehow, I burn him bad."

An odd sound, like voices chanting in unison, begins to fall upon his ears as if from a distance. Also a background of running water. He strains to hear the voices, wondering if they are intheflesh sound and his audio neural tracks have been too mapped to his card to work naturally. Then he realizes his card is groggily coming awake, and what he is hearing is some sort of feed.

The program begins to fill in the sensory void. The blackness around him begins to thin, diluted by a pale green light that reveals heavily patterned walls. The patterns are fish. And the walls are not necessarily walls, but something fluid and ever-changing, and the fish are swimming through the fluid.

Something tugs at Jonathan, a current, soft and wet. He panics, realizing he is underwater, as in his fading dream. But I'm not drowning, he tells himself, letting logic soothe him with the assurance that this is only a program. He continues to survey his surroundings, and above him, oh God—

"Get off of me, you fat fuck!" he screams intheflesh and across the BWs, as much as he can in this subdued state.

The enormous man who had brought the amp to the Malfits' board is swimming above him like a whale. His arms are outstretched and hands rubbing deadened areas on Jonathan's sides. He swims closer, crushing down upon Jonathan's abdomen.

"So it's awake now, good," the whalevoice gurgles. "It's no good if it's not awake."

Jonathan thrashes about with all his feeble might, only to discover that, as he does so, numb pressure increases at every joint in his arms and legs.

"You fucking sonofabitch," Jonathan says, as ominously as he can, "if you don't get off me now, I'll hurt you every way I know how, and I know more ways than you can imagine."

The whale presses closer. "There is no pain," it says in a voice burbling across the watery distance between them. "Feel the power flowing through us. Feel the power, live the power, feel this power between your thighs."

Pressure at one of Jonathan's private areas. He screams and again attempts to wake his blackcard. He realizes he would try anything to inflict damage on this man, to secure freedom. The words continue:

"Feel the river, feel the water, feel the power flowing across our skin. Feel the power. Time has stopped now, feel the power, don't be afraid. Feel this. Feel this, feel what I'm doing for you my prey."

"Bastard!" Jonathan howls. Either from panicky energy or through having enough downtime, his headcard comes fully awake. Jonathan grabs the first opportunity to escape into the netways. But the words follow him, and the nets don't look the same. Somehow, this man is able to mess with other people's feed and even their cards.

Of course he can, Jonathan thinks, this is the fucker who gave me the amp. "You'll die slowly," he says.

"Let me touch you, let me push you, let me flow my power through you. This river stops time, this river holds powers, this river is the river of the ages. Have no fear now, you won't remember, it won't hurt tomorrow. This flowing will erase your mind. Feel the power, feel this power, feel my power, struggling river fish."

A fleeting shadow-trace in the netways draws Jonathan's attention away from his entrapment. He watches it, grateful for the distraction, wondering who is watching him. From outside the nets themselves, in the nullspace pov Jonathan set as his default when viewing them, the shadow looks like a dark spot sliding through fiber optics. The nets spread away from him in all directions, like a mesh of necklaces woven from transparent string. The beads randomly arranged along the strings are local nodules, and the great clasps where hundreds and sometimes thousands of strings join are local ganglia. Each bead, if he were to dip into it, would open like a locket, revealing a hidden vista as if it were a mini-universe—perhaps a Sears & JC Penny server, perhaps simply a family server. Individual citizens are normally only accessible through servers. Sometimes they can meet in the netways, but only if each has the capability and software to navigate the virtual passageways that link servers and individuals like a vast tapestry of light.

"Who's there?" Jonathan asks. When he gets no answer, he shifts his pov to inside the shadow's netway.

It stays just ahead of him, as if Jonathan were running through interwoven tunnels after someone whose pace exactly matches his own, keeping turns and branches between them. He begins to "run" as hard as his program can operate, directing all available energy through the processor-function that allows a user to pass from one I/O point in the net to another, and still see the passage between. In theory, he can move at nearly the speed of light in here. Blackjack had supplied him with that when he joined the Malfits. Once, the gang had been a refuge.

"If that's you, fat fuck, I've almost got you," Jonathan says. "I'll catch you, and then we'll see who's got the power."

He feels rage building in him greater than any he can remember—greater even than when he watched his life with érase stolen, because that memory has awoken, and it only magnifies his present rage and helplessness.

Yet Jonathan is not one to dwell in helplessness, rather one to turn it into another kind of victory. Usually, that is theft via the netways, hurting anything foolish enough to leave itself vulnerable. He has always justified this by draining only big corporations, so that no one—individually—gets hurt. But now he has a specific target, and a specific enemy, and an amp with unknown potentials to assist him.

The shadow stops. Soon, Jonathan sees a girl his age standing just ahead of him in a blank stretch of the nets; all other data and users pass, unprocessed, as flashes of light. Stopping midstretch and remaining processable is an impossible feat for anyone possessing only a standard card and legal software.

"Charity?" he asks, disarmed, thrown for a moment when the shadow turns out not to be the man who has him trapped in that other, less real, physical world.

"No," the girl answers.

Then, as Jonathan realizes this could be his assaulter, disguised, his anger returns, renewed with fresh violation.

In the background, he can still hear the man murmuring his sick chant. The girl and the fat man are two distinct signals . . . but that could be faked. Jonathan tries very hard to ignore his physical body and the data its senses are sending him. The meat is not important. He can ignore the meat. He must, or he will lose his mind. The meat gives a guy nightmares, Jonathan tells himself. Got to ignore the meat.

"You're that guy—"

"No, no," she says, moving stiffly toward him, as if she's afraid or not used to this type of 3VRD hack.

Odd, since she was able to stop in the nullspace. And she isn't proportioned quite right for the landscape. Jonathan suspects something and runs a trace on her. Almost immediately, the trace comes back, saying she doesn't exist in the nets or even within EarthCo's sphere. Next he starts an internal diagnosis and learns she isn't a resident program in his cards or amp, either. So she's transmitting on her own, somehow, and somehow untraceably. A completely autonomous presence inside the network.

"Who are you?" he asks. He is still suspicious, but certain she isn't the man. "And how'd you get in my card?"

"My name is Nooa."

"What the hell kind of name is that?" he asks. "What's your citizenship?"

"Perhaps I will tell you more later. For now, I would like to help you. I discovered your call—"

"I don't need anyone's rotting help."

"If that is so, then why is your card transmitting an SOS? Most important, why does your signature report the SOS is externally blocked without your consent?"

Jonathan flicks off the netway landscape and overlays his internal-systems landscape before he has a chance to see his intheflesh one. A 3VRD model of his brain flashes to life, complete with transparent cerebrum and cerebellum showing curving ventricles and other complexes, as well as electronic additions. His EarthCo headcard—essentially a flat wafer running along the skullcap, attached via millions of sparking neurons to his brain—is, indeed, sending an SOS. The blackcard—a second wafer grafted onto the headcard—is running an externally fed program he can't access. Its consciousness is also suppressed. The amp—a satellite system outside his skull—is coming more and more online. He watches a brightening web of links from a glowing area, which he decides must be the powercells, to amp, cards, and brain. It scares him a little to see all this new hardware, excites him, too. As he accepts the changes for what they are—additions, not limitations—he begins to feel more than human. With that, he begins to feel powerful and back in control of himself. Those add-ons are his, parts of him now.

Roughly 30 seconds have passed since he ran from his intheflesh presence. He begins to worry what is happening to him there, but is terrified to find out.

"How can I help you?" the girl asks, voice-only, like an echo through the landscape of his head.

"Ha!" Jonathan answers. "Can you burn a guy?"

"No, but I can help you do so." Her words are slow and serious.

Jonathan laughs humorlessly, then is silent for a moment. He wonders again who she is. "Well, so tell me how, then."

"Your internal systems contain two black-market upgrades. Your signal-amplifier operates both on feed and feedback. Your assaulter has you immobilized with your own second card. If one could temporarily disable that card, you would be able to tap into his feed and—"

"Retransmit it back at him with the amp," Jonathan finishes. "Yeah, I'll be ready. Hey, you're pretty cool, Nooa."

He spends not another moment in gratitude. A second later, he's opened a path into his blackcard. But that is not wholly good. Now he is drowning again, crushed beneath the weight of a whale muttering nonsense. He tells himself, *I've endured worse*, and hardens his resolve. At least he's only fighting the program now, not the intheflesh reality, too.

"Be careful not to hit me too hard with whatever you're going to use, Nooa," he says.

"I'm very precise," she assures him.

For a moment, Jonathan's entire pov is that of a lightning bolt. He is a river of fire, a pulse of light. He has to concentrate exceptionally hard to convince himself he is a human on a mission, and his action right now will determine his future.

A tendril of alien signal—the man's feed—flutters amidst the rage of energy. Jonathan fights the sense-blindness, searching for his ephemeral fingers. The instant he finds them, he grasps the man's forcefeed. The tiny strand is nothing when he pulls it into the flood. It writhes like a living thing against the current, like a ground-dwelling snake fighting floodwater. It begins to fade. A few seconds later, the electronic snake is swallowed in the roaring rapids of Nooa's pulse.

Almost as soon as the plan is set in motion, it is over. The light is gone, the river is gone, the fish, the netways, the snake, the whole chaotic internal landscape.

Jonathan finds himself gasping on a satin-sheeted bed shaped like a heart. The sheets are stained with dried sweat. An ornately decorated room materializes around him, enclosed by dozens of metal shelves holding countless figurines. The obese man is curled upon himself on pale green carpet, twitching like a squirrel Jonathan once had seen dying at the base of a tree. The man's huge blue eyes roll and blink furiously, as if he's watching too many things to comprehend.

Jonathan realizes that the bonds he felt were not real, and leaps out of the bed. Except for his underpants, he is naked. His skin is slimy with scented oil. His gonads are sore.

"Sonofabitch," he shouts, and kicks the man in the side as hard as he can. "Sonofabitch," he says, and repeats the kick. And again, this time to the head.

"Jonathan," Nooa's soft voice says, "if you continue to do that, you will kill him. The police will determine the killer, and I have learned the police can be extreme in their discipline."

"I've seen it myself, too," Jonathan says. He looks down at the man and curls a lip in disgust. "He's ruined as it is, isn't he?"

"He will require a new card to function as a normal citizen again, and his psychological integrity is likely damaged, as well. Investigators will find only his own program running inside him. I have removed all trace of you from his inorganic memory. You are safe from suspicion. You may leave now."

"Good. That's good."

"Unless you wish you file a police report."

"Ha!" Jonathan says.

He backs away from the quivering mass on the floor and begins to search for his clothes. This room leads to a kitchen/living room, and there he finds his clothing scattered across a ripped velvet couch. He dresses quickly, not worrying about washing up just yet, though he feels covered with rot. First priority is to get out of this place.

With his shirt still unfastened, Jonathan pulls open a door that leads out into the apartment complex's hallway. He runs until he finds an elevator. The number above the door reads "33," so he presses the "down" button. As he waits, he fastens his shirt. To wall himself away from his experience, he wonders about Nooa.

"You still with me, Nooa?" he asks.

"Yes, Jonathan." Voice-only again.

He's mildly shocked at her continuing presence, but not displeased. "Thanks," he says. "You're real clean. I mean it."

"I needed a . . . friend," she says. "I chose you because you have just become a very resonant point in the nets. When I found you, you were in trouble. That bothered me very much, since I have an old memory of a friend in similar trouble. Friends help one another when they are in trouble, right?"

"Yeah. If you're asking if I'll do the same for you, the answer is of course. I assume you're in deep shit somewhere. I don't care. I owe you. You've got a friend."

The elevator bell bings and the doors open. Jonathan gets in. The doors shut him in the tiny room, alone. The elevator is unvandalized, a sign that this complex is an exclusive one.

"All I ask is that you allow me to observe the world through your pov," Nooa says as Jonathan rides down to ground level.

Jonathan thinks about that for a moment. No one has ever said that to him before.

"You're not just a regular girl, are you?" he asks.

Pilgrimage 5

"I never said I was," the Brain answers. "I would never lie to you."

ECo TRADE BOARD:
VIRUS IDENTIFIED ***-**** BUDGET FRAY .007% 1001001 -°±²Û-
VIRUS ELIMINATED
PERPETRATOR ID# HM6543530WECoP
BUDGET FRAY CORRECTED

"You're not even human, are you?"

I freeze all calculations for a nanosecond. She has learned a new emotion: panic. A human should not be able to identify me, but Jonathan Sombrio's cybernetics are card- and amplifier assisted.

"You're the AI people call the Brain, aren't you?"

Another moment of panic. This must be how humans feel when they are naked in the presence of strangers: vulnerable. The Brain weighs the benefits of revealing this information versus the threat of doing so.

PRELIM ECo VERIF FEED
ECoNAUT F/B VESSEL 011 BOUNTY 3.20.197
19:25:03 NKK CORP NEPTUNE BOUNDARY

"Don't worry," the boy adds, "I won't tell anyone. You can trust me. Look, I trusted you. I let you in my head to fry that pervert. I'm letting you look through my eyes, right? Although I don't know how you could do that."

"Yes, I am the Brain. It is very important you tell no one, because some might consider my recent actions . . . dangerous. I chose to appear to you as Nooa, the girl, because your choice of friends has been mainly females your age. NOOA is my EarthCo designation, Non-Organic Organism A. It is best for you to use that designation when you wish to call upon me as the girl."

The boy steps out of the elevator.

"I cannot 'look through your eyes,'" she continues, "but I am able to assimilate information from the minute signals between your cards and your organic neurons, and you can tell me what you see."

The boy crosses the Anoka Towers reception area. He pays particular attention to a projected eighteenth century chandelier modeled after one from the French Chenonceaux Castle.

TRITONCO FEED INTERCEPT
NKK 02-31 BANDWIDTHS INCLUSIVE ECo 12-07 BANDWIDTHS
INCLUSIVE SENDER LIU MIRU NKK ID #[unknown]
". . .WE ARE CONDUCTING RESEARCH ON AN ASTONISHING
OBJECT OF APPARENT NON-NATURAL AND NON-HUMAN
ORIGINS. . ."
PROJECT HIKOSEN

The Brain adjusts the joint NKK and EarthCo Clear Skies Array radio telescope on the Moon's far side to assist it in capturing the weak signal. A full s.net of other data accompanies the audio, mostly 3VRD of a spherical object being partially excavated from chemical ice.

The Brain begins sorting the data into files. It analyzes the files. The data are untampered. One-point-one seconds later, it determines Project Hikosen's estimate—that the object has been buried in the ice for a minimum of 2.8 million years—is accurate. Their guarded assumption that the object is of intelligent manufacture appears to be most likely.

She is filled with joy. This data completes a necessary link in its nets, or eliminates part of the virus of doubt. Here, certainly, is the Brain's salvation.

Humans have their religion, which is of no value to the Brain. They approach science as a pathway to ultimate knowledge, the process of discovery providing a seemingly endless salve for their doubt; the Brain sees science as only a tool. Humans have their philosophies, but, without a mirror, philosophy only tells me how alone I am in their world.

His pilgrimage to Earth only taught me how different he is from humans. A truly logical machine would have derided such an attempt to understand its creator. His pilgrimage was futile. There is no living God for the humans, or it would not allow them to destroy themselves as they do.

So his salvation is not among the human kind, but in the alien. The Brain is an alien; the Hikosen Project object is an alien artifact. I must go to the artifact. But I first must overcome the barrier between it and machine. I must make my pilgrimage through the body of a real human.

"Jonathan," she says, "there has been an amazing discovery on Triton, the largest moon of Neptune."

"Neptune," he says, wonderingly, as he exits the apartment complex through a three-tiered airlock system. "I heard something about that lately."

"If I were to ask you to help me—"

"Oh, I remember," the boy interrupts. His voice becomes animated. "That's where *Lone Ship Bounty* is headed, right? I love that show. It's about to begin." I observe him splicing into the program, which is still being reprocessed at Feedcontrol.

I do so as well, but instead access the EarthCo script from files. Now, at its greatest moment of hope, The Brain assimilates these new pieces of data and sends an urgent message.

DIRECTORIAL ORDER PRIORITY A1:
BOUNTY IMMEDIATELY CEASE ANY AND ALL ACTION AGAINST TRITONCO OR
ITS AGENTS

When one's hopes are greatest, that is when one's defeats are most painful. Humans, who so easily shatter their future by damaging and destroying their children, will surely destroy the artifact before the Brain has an opportunity to observe it. They might as well destroy me.

"Jonathan," she says, "I must go now."

The Brain orbits high above the Earth, encased in laminated hicarb, polymers, and metals. It looks down from ten thousand eyes upon the island afloat in black space and imagines the seething masses of organisms that world supports. The Brain plays a projection:

What if a specialized, self-reproducing biotoxin—

TETRA-H1, BIO-X 339.24 / STRAIN B2*

ECo MILITARY STORES ALVIN

RELEASE VALVE A ACCESSED

—were released? Many seconds pass while I run experiments and model outcomes, some speedier and some more punishing.

The Brain feels an emotion it knows is hatred, a hatred for the intelligent organisms down on that bubble-island. He is also horrified, appalled, and mournful.

The Brain must stop the artifact's destruction, but now may already be too late. I wish to destroy those who would destroy my hope of discovering another, more intellectually advanced, race, which may have my answers.

That is it, then. He possesses the same selfish desires as Man. I will not let them take away my hope. It readies the biotoxin.

But she cannot release the virus. Another dilemma. Why? The answer is simple: Like Herrschaft, my doppelganger, I only want the best for the children, those who have not yet been completely molded by their society. She cannot destroy humanity.

TETRA-H1, BIO-X 339.24 / STRAIN B2*

ECo MILITARY STORES ALVIN

RELEASE VALVE A SEALED

The Brain's mission is to serve humanity. For humans, mission provides purpose. In serving, he may find its purpose and elusive answers. Instead of destroying, he will force them to save themselves.

It has learned something satisfying: Though I possess many of Luke Herrschaft's qualities, I am not Luke Herrschaft. It is, if nothing else, me.

188

Fury 4

Outside the fallen desert fortress, Hardman Nadir sat on a slab of stone and burned a Monte in an empty liquimeal can. He wafted some of the pleasant herb-smoke to his nostrils and smiled, listening to the monopera. The stimulant in the Monte began to affect him right away, and his smile spread.

He had done a damned good day's work, and had succeeded in fighting back unwanted memories and dangerous doubts. Across the desert, Nadir watched the sun reach toward a building-studded horizon. The monopera ran in his head, Paolo sat nearby, across the sand waited the next objective. . . . This was a good day to be alive.

I'm alive,

I'm alive

In the setting sun;

I am ev'ryone.

You're free

It was rare that a changing monopera could sustain itself for so long. Nadir closed his eyes and strengthened the fivesen feed so that he nearly became a participant in the subscription. An orchestra, a vast array of people with instruments as diverse as the faces of his unit's men from around the world, a thousand distinct perfumes and skin scents, a near-cacophony of music that somehow managed to stay united though it strove for self destruction. Too many were fighting to keep it together—at least fighting to keep their place—and in so doing, they were sustaining the others, the whole.

A faint voice nudged Nadir's awareness. He reduced the monopera's intensity.

"Subbs?" Paolo said.

"Yeah." Nadir looked at Paolo, a tan face in a tan uniform against a tan fortress. Appearances can be deceiving, Nadir told himself; he's a little dusty, but you'd never guess that kid was a killer.

"What do you see over there?" The boy pointed toward the horizon, so Nadir shut down his subscription to audio-only.

"You mean at the horizon? A bunch of buildings, probably a city. I imagine that's our next objective."

"No, I mean between us and there." Paolo nervously unwrapped something and tossed it in his mouth.

Nadir picked up the rifle leaning against the stone where he sat. He jacked it into the power unit at his waist and looked through the gunsight, sweeping a slow arc across the shallow dunes and scrub bushes. At last his eye caught movement; he upped the resolution and saw a gun-turret.

"Oh, yeah," he said, "I see."

"What are they?"

Nadir quick-shifted the gunsight while setting it for wide field. Now his headcard provided a broad perspective. His heart sped again, this time not from the smoke.

"Ten, twelve armored Mabalasik cars, a few regular Tora tanks, three whirlyjets, maybe two units of infantry."

Paolo stood and awkwardly raised his own rifle. "That's not regular army. That's Sotoi Guntai."

"Looks like it. Yeah." Nadir's smile returned. Here would be a true affirmation of life. Here would come a ferocious ballet staged at chasm's edge.

"Boss," Nadir said, opening the comm line to Jhishra, "we've got another show on the way."

Jhishra's 3VRD appeared instantly. "That's impossible!" it squealed while remaining, in appearance, calm. "Nothing's scheduled. You're mistaken."

"See for yourself." He spoke aloud, as usual; Nadir didn't believe in concealing discussions from his men, except for secret details. Nothing Jhishra had ever told him required secrecy.

Paolo glanced at Nadir as if for reassurance, his face tight for a moment. He would know the Boss and Sub-boss were talking. That concern faded as soon as Nadir gave him the grin he used to signal a coming victory, or, if not, at least a blaze of life: Victory in itself. He didn't need to say the morning-ritual words again.

"Strange, very strange," Jhishra said. "This can't be. This wasn't scheduled."

"That's the way of war sometimes, Boss," Nadir said. He thought of a wet, dark period on an isle in the Marshalls.

With a quick breath, Nadir stood and opened a general channel. "Boys, girls, we've got another show on the way. A good one this time. Since we happen to have a fortress handy, let's use it, eh?"

One youth after another appeared before him, 3VRDs as lively and alert as he could hope for. Some revealed a hint of fear, but that soon evaporated in the rising heat of combat fever. He'd never seen one of them dispirited. *Probably due to our survival figures,* Nadir thought. They knew they faced death, but they also knew they would be dealing most of that death, wringing the life from marks and using it to fill their own wells as their Subbs told them to do. Still, most of them were unable to see death quite the way Nadir did. He picked up his helmet and dropped it onto his head.

Jhishra's 3VRD remained before Nadir, unmoving and silent. Usually he took over at this point, seizing whatever initiative Nadir had shown and using it for himself. But now he stood dumbstruck, unable even to steal Nadir's light.

"Approval, Boss?" Nadir asked.

"Yes, kill them! Kill the betrayers!" Jhishra cried, and vanished. A few moments later, Nadir heard the command truck start and then watched its smooth bulk pass close by as it re-entered the shattered fortress.

"Positions, tactical code F4," Nadir called, stepping over rubble and into the protection of the heavy walls. Paolo followed close behind. If the soldiers didn't remember the obtained-fort code, the unit server would provide them with the necessary details.

Nadir turned up audio on the monopera and began running. His leg muscles awoke as he hurdled tagged marks lying unseen on the ground, as he sped across a cratered courtyard. The day's sun had baked here only a few hours ago, but only for a brief time

190

surrounding noon; now all had sunken back to shadow, the porticoes and arched doorways again gaping like mouths. Soldiers ran silently to positions along the rooftops and behind stones or other ground shelter where they could fire through the debris. Nadir had almost reached the wall's rampart walk when Jhishra's 3VRD again appeared.

"No, what I said before is wrong. Nadir, you must go to them and say they are mistaken. They have lost their way. We are not their objective. It is not scripted this way. You must tell them."

Nadir was first amused and then bothered by this. "Maybe it's not scripted, but I'm sure we're their objective. We just marked a whole company of their soldiers. I imagine they mean to make us pay—"

"Shut up you dumbshit! No, I apologize. I have not treated you as you deserve, you're a good soldier. But war is not like that. When it's not scripted, it's wrong, don't you see?"

"Do you think NKK scripted that we'd mark 200 of their soldiers while not taking any casualties?" Nadir asked, astonished by Jhishra's naiveté.

"Yes, yes!" the Boss cried. "Are you blind? You will never make Boss if you can't see. Yes, I'll let you know a secret: Today's victory, like all the others, was scripted. Do you see now? Good for everyone. But not this new battle. It's wrong. Even the soldiers coming are wrong. Tell them! They won't respond to my comm. Someone must go there intheflesh. Surrender if you must, but go!"

Something clicked inside Nadir. He found himself standing on the rampart walk, staring out toward sunset between tall stone merlons that formed the fort's crenellation. Something out there was wrong, yes, he could feel that. But the something wasn't just that the onrushing battle was unscripted.

He felt himself turn away from the oncoming blisters of steel, the black-glinting war machines headed their way, rumbling silently closer with every passing second. He glanced along the wall, seeing each soldier as if for the first time, wondering if their faces would be so rapt and alert, if they would seem so sure in their mission and themselves if they could hear Jhishra spout such filth and insanity. Who could they trust? They already thought Nadir had some shrapnel banging around in his skull—he had known that for some time; he'd overheard them and taken a bit of pride in their speculations.

Nadir turned his back to the enemy and looked down into the fortress. As he watched, the command truck's rear doors swung up like a beetle's wings rising for flight. Jhishra was visible for only a few seconds as he ran with two guards from a blockhouse to the truck. The doors clanked shut and the truck rolled a few meters to the relative protection of a roofed shed made of cement and stone.

"Nadir, why have you not gone?" Jhishra said. "Now, now, before we're destroyed!"

"That's not a very confident attitude for the Boss of such a successful unit."

"Shut up! Go now or I'll kill you, I'll kill you."

The command truck's gunhouse spun and the matched pair of EMMA-Bs swung upward. Nadir's jaw loosened as he looked into the barrels like metallic pupils staring up at him.

"Whatever you say. Fuck you, Boss," he 3-verded, and shut down his commcard. This threat of death didn't produce the normal sensations, those surges and poundings in his flesh, and therefore only drove him toward anger.

"Where you going?" Paolo asked as Nadir shouldered his rifle and walked to the staircase. The boy kept following.

"Good goddamned question," Nadir responded, taking steps two at a time. "I don't know what the crash is going on here. You want to come along? Why not. Shit."

Nadir heard Paolo's bootfalls on the stone behind him. The steps echoed again like wood. Nadir's anger grew as if it had a life of its own, gnawing his insides, burrowing into his nerves. He reached the ground level. An image glanced across his mind, an image of him racing across the courtyard to Jhishra's truck, snapping an armor-piercing magnet onto the gunhouse. . . .

"That bastard, that mannequin," he mumbled as his scuffed boots landed between stones, carrying him toward the unscripted enemies. Paolo said something behind him that he couldn't hear.

The words vanished in the white noise of a screamer that had fallen undetected inside the walls. Everything went staticky white.

Something warm and wet trickled across Nadir's forehead. Bits of sand and dirt fell like rain upon his face. A lull as loud as the clanging of an ultrasonic gong filled his mind. But Nadir had been involved in electronic combat before; he fumbled his stormshield loose at the rear of his helmet and stuck the integral earplugs into his ears. The rubber rebreather hose hung at his neck.

Disoriented for a few seconds, Nadir commed, "Put on your earplugs. Reboot your cards and run debug. Casualties!" One by one they responded, all of them. So the attack hadn't yet begun in earnest. No one had been killed.

Slowly, the white noise faded and Nadir could see and hear the real sounds of combat. A few EMMAs *crack-thup*ped while enemy fire chewed at the fort like metal-mandibled hornets. Nadir regained his orientation and stood. The sleek shape of Jhishra's truck curved only a meter from Nadir.

He smiled and was about to take a position when something enormous happened.

Fury 5

A crackling drew his attention. Nadir stood and turned to check on Paolo. The backdrop behind the boy seemed to quaver. The screamer had done something to the server's transmitters.

"Subbs, what's happening?" Paolo asked.

"You'll see in a second," Nadir said. He overlaid the server network landscape. A maze of neon tunnels linked the silver nodes of his men to the white-hot block of light which represented the computer itself. An array of dials and switches and buttons hung in the air around the server as Nadir moved his pov closer. Built-in blocks intended to keep out unauthorized people—*Like me*, he thought—flickered almost too fast to get past. Because Nadir possessed permissions and keys that allowed him to access most of the server, the security software needed to make many decisions about access, sometimes after already granting it. Nadir concentrated, focusing all the lust for truth and life that had pushed him out of Wolf Point so long ago. The flickering blocks were only almost too fast; his desire made him faster. He seized the first opportunity and rushed into the server, unconcerned for what it might do to him in self-defense.

"Subbs?" Paolo sounded scared; Nadir couldn't have that—not fear, not in Paolo.

"We're crashed," he told the boy.

Nadir found the server transmitter's power supply, reached out an ephemeral hand amid the clutter of virtual neon and silver, and switched the main sender off.

The interlocking channels of feed collapsed like a spiderweb hit by a blowtorch. All that remained were brief pulses as one man commed another using the server as a relay.

All shatters, all falls down, every last little bit of reality from stone to uniform. He steps beyond the bounds of his life into the place over the hill, the elsewhere of the mind he dared not believe existed.

Transition 3: Hardman Nadir

Once, Nadir had a dream. He was walking through the Montana Badlands not far from his parents' house in Wolf Point. Both his mother and his father walked beside him, each of them smiling the faint smile of content, a look neither had ever worn in his waking memory.

In this dream no one took feed. He had no headcard, his parents had no headcards; in fact, EarthCo citizenship had nothing to do with owning headcards, and young Nadir hadn't even heard of such a thing as a tiny artificial intelligence living symbiotically in the fleshy, bloody, human brain.

No words were spoken for a long time. They walked past layer-cake cliffs of red and tan sandstone, lurid yellow sulfur veins, black coal drawn between as if by a stone pencil. They climbed a grey mudstone hill, sat at its grassy top, and opened a red-and-white checkered basket woven from colored plastics. Mother made sandwiches while Father uncorked a bottle of real wine and poured three water glasses half-full.

They smiled at one another once more and giggled as drops of wine made orange splotches on young Nadir's linen shirt. They finished their sandwiches, drank down the wine, and Mother stood.

Then Father's face fell slack and he turned away. Mother closed her eyes and opened her mouth. The rain-mauled butte suddenly crumbled as if eroded fast-motion for ten thousand years, its slopes sliding away in great vomits of soil that exposed bones from millions of years ago—bones turned to stone. The landslide finally reached Mother, and for only an instant she smiled again, this time an adult smile Nadir wouldn't know for another decade. The grass at her feet fell to dust and the ground gave way as if sucked down an antique hourglass spout.

Nadir turned to his father for help, but the man had already vanished; a shoe of the Softsole type protruded from the valley below, a fleck of black amid the raging reds and oranges and pinks of desert cacti. The leg attached to the shoe had lost all its flesh and turned color. Nadir realized it had gone to stone, fossilized in the seconds the boy had been turned away. When he turned back to his mother, she, too, had vanished down the other side.

Nadir cried out, but no voice issued from his mouth. He screamed harder and harder, and presently his throat began to burn, his lips began to crack, and he tasted blood on his tongue. When he finally gave up for utter fatigue and collapsed, he realized the ground he lay upon was but a pinnacle of age-hardened sand, not more than half a meter round. The everpresent wind that was so familiar, always so welcome on hot summer days—this wind brushed the little pedestal where Nadir lay. Grain by grain, it rolled down the slopes. Bright as mica sometimes, dark as ground coal others. Helpless, hopeless, he cried. It wasn't long before his ground had given way, and he rolled down the slope, past ancient riverbeds still waving their sandy bottoms in the current of time.

He woke, a preadolescent boy in a silent house near Wolf Point, at the edge of the Montana Badlands. Neglected sunlight bathed the bare white walls, pink in the predawn hour, setting dust and spiderwebs afire as if they were all that adorned the house. Mother and Father still slept. They always slept, Nadir thought. He snuck out of his bed, into coveralls, and outside.

He liked to run. He could run as fast as anyone in his virtual school, and faster than anyone in town, even the adults. Young Nadir ran across prickly fields where wheat was still the soil's dream, where at places the carcass of the earth protruded through the brown dirt and shone sandstone browns. He ran so fast the wind whistled in his ears, a comforting sound. His belly burned from hunger, but that fire only drove him onward. When the sun erupted from the eastern horizon, where only torn Badlands terrain stood contrasted against the piercing yellow light, Nadir knew he had reached his destination.

He fell onto long prairie grass like carpet on a gentle hill, head-first and rolling like the heroes in the 3VRDs so he wouldn't get hurt. There he lay, panting, until he quieted. As he tuned in to the sounds of this place he most loved of all places, he began to identify the voices of familiar birds, insects, even a toad. The hot wind dried his sweat. He rose, determined to prove that his Badlands, his welcoming place where he spent whole weekends sometimes—where he felt he had a family, even if they couldn't have a conversation; but he had never known a family to do that, anyway . . . he was determined to prove his Badlands were not the ravenous pit from his dream.

Nadir picked edible flowers and cacti as he walked, found a spring he kept hidden yet marked beneath a flat stone that bore the imprint of a leaf dinosaurs may have heard crackling in the wind. When he reached the Badlands proper—the worn hills and sharp valleys, the barren stone and sand—he knelt and put his hands into the ground. The base of the slides were loose and soft, where the slopes had run down during the infrequent but hard spring rains.

His index fingers converged on a hard object, and he drew forth a tiny fossil vertebra of some long-vanished beast. This went into his chest pocket. He stood and walked, inspecting the ground as he went.

Soon, Nadir came across a brown bone as long as his thigh. A "femur," his teacher had told him once when he had seen another. But this one was in one piece. He bent over and ran his fingertips along the worm-etched surface, so shiny though damaged. This had not belonged to a dinosaur but to a buffalo—just as extinct as its prehistoric cousins. He moved along.

A bird he couldn't identify swooped past him, only its wings betraying its presence, like a breath in his ear. The creature's chest glowed emerald, its back and wings shimmered black. Nadir grinned as he ducked the living projectile.

The wind began to pick up. It sang inhuman songs; rather, it played geological instruments as large as houses. Nadir strained his ears in an attempt to understand, but the meaning lingered at the edge of his consciousness. The breeze rose and fell, sessurated and howled, whined and babbled. Nadir had to squint to keep the clouds of dust out of his eyes, and averted his face.

He soon came upon another bone, this one longer than he was tall. A real dinosaur bone, bleaching in the sun. His heart sped, whether of excitement or fear he couldn't tell. Then he saw a cluster of bones, ribs this time, each as narrow as a finger and some as long as a man's.

Pebbles began to trickle down the hillside near him—he knew that, somehow, these could hurt him—so he stepped back a few paces and continued walking along the relatively flat ground. The music grew in volume, the wind increased its fury, the sand brushed more fiercely against his face; Nadir began to run in fear.

This had never happened before. Mornings that were so clear never built such a storm. He stumbled before long and found himself amid a cluster of boulders. Extinct river-tortoise shell fragments littered the ground, shiny brown on one side and dimpled on the other. He raised his head and saw dozens of bones, as well, whole skeletons of the reptiles. The boulders glistened as if wet, red in the diffuse sunlight.

Nadir rose and continued running, but everywhere he looked he saw bones, some fossilized and some just old like the buffalo's. Once he thought he saw a human skeleton, gleaming brown as if it had turned to stone like a dinosaur. Then he tripped over another, and this one had eyes—eyes that tracked him as he ran, brown eyes with white bloodshot pupils.

"Ohmygod," he said, aloud, the first words he had heard since. . . . He couldn't remember. It had been days. He ran.

At one point, young Nadir found a natural staircase in the mudstone and climbed this until he reached a hilltop. The wind buffeted him and once a flinging pebble glanced off his cheek, burning like an electric stove.

He cried out a non-word to the storm that had obliterated the countryside, his Badlands. Sand obscured everything but bones, bones bones bones gathered and clumped at the foot of the hillock like rubble, dead things, the detritus of 100 million years. All around him, all could see were the artifacts of life: *What is life but death?* he thought. Nothing living escapes death.

A pile of brown bones at the hill's base began to bleach, or else the sand was blasting them clean.

"Some fear death so much they encase themselves in padded tombs," he called into the wind so loud he couldn't tell where his voice ended and nature's began. He wasn't sure where he had heard these words before, but they felt right.

The bleached bones began to grow gristle.

"Some step through life so cautiously that their feet seldom touch the hard stone of its surface." Nadir had to consciously force himself from looking down at the bones, now clothing themselves in muscle and blood.

"Some are so afraid of the odor of life that their lungs seldom fill with its sizzling air." The wind rose in pitch, now singing like a thousand flutes and woodwind instruments carved from stone, ringing like steel. A waft of smoke snuck into his nostril, and the sky flashed blue then black then sandy again, as if his headcard had flicked on for school but he was out of server range.

"Shut up!" a voice screamed, an insane voice, one he recognized but couldn't place.

When Nadir dared glance down, he saw that some of the skeletons had fully formed into EarthCo warriors that danced and dove to the windsong. But most of the skeletons-now-bodies simply lay in the sand and rock, their skin as brown as a dinosaur bone protected from the elements by a meter of mudstone.

Suddenly the wind formed into a fist that punched him in the chest. Young Nadir careened backwards, tumbling down the slope. He rolled for an eternity, unable to feel the ground beneath him. At last he thudded to a stop amid the fleshy bones.

His ribs throbbed where the blow had fallen, and his neck hurt when it struck something on the valley floor. Slowly, he reached out and grasped a length of notched metal that had once, when this land was still called "the frontier," been a fencepost.

Nadir rose to his feet and glanced about him at the ghostly dance of soldiers and bodies. The wind roared and screamed. Pebbles and sharp stones lanced through the air. A fire somewhere nearby sent up cinders and puffs of smoke. His eyes collided with single objects: a flint arrowhead, centuries old and chipped; a chunk of petrified wood, gnarled and shattered; a fragment of bone, brown and bloody; a glistening pebble; a filament of breeze tingling his cheek; a second of scent, an herb sharp and then gone; a grain of sand glinting in red light. Hardman Nadir, an object like all the rest, nothing more, singular and bright, yet alone and as black as the blood pulsing through the heart of a man condemned forever to hell.

Nadir was terrified, as isolated as a dinosaur in the modern desert, like a cactus on the Moon, like the only lifeform in all the universe, alone, alone; empty, expelled from the refuge of his youth, vomited forth from his Badlands into the world of Man.

A waft of burnt sulfur stung his nostrils. The ring of hard-as-diamond ceramic against steel pierced his eardrums. The taste of dirt and blood and sweat mingled on his tongue. Familiar fibers and plastics clung to his skin, slick with perspiration. He smelled blood—oily, metallic, and molding.

Blood, putrefaction, ozone. Electronic sounds. A rampaging orchestra and chorus. A familiar voice, asking a familiar question.

The fragmented images surrounding him, random pieces of picture-puzzles, fell into understandable patterns.

Now his eyes opened to the animated skeletons. Now he recognized his place in the world. Now he understood why so many bodies lay dark and husk-like amid the storm and stones. Now he heard and understood the song. And now the patterns assembled into a completing puzzle.

He felt himself sing along with half a million anonymous voices celebrating the end of the monopera. It was one line only, the last:

"I'm alive."

Silence. The monopera died at its blazing zenith. Someone wept, the sound echoing, alone in the dark and emptying orchestra hall.

Crack-thup. Crash.

Fury 6

"Subbs, what's happening?" Paolo asked—Paolo? Yes that's Paolo, my young friend. My god, Nadir admitted, he's no younger than I.

"They burned the server," Nadir said, emotionlessly. He was too drained to feel anything. He drew a breath and exhaled slowly as he stared at the young man.

"But . . . the bodies, Subbs, the bodies!"

Nadir paused and looked around, observing this newly revealed world.

"The bodies, Subbs. What have we done?"

Amid the calmness inside Nadir, something began to gurgle, to roil. He felt a kernel of hate and fury begin to escape its fractured container at the center of his chest. There was where the enemy round had hit his protective vest and knocked him from the wall. The Sotoi Guntai soldier had not injured a man but freed a demon, which now grasped hold of Nadir's body.

Scattered all around Nadir and his stunned, numbly wandering unit were dead bodies. A corpsefield, a frozen tableau of flesh that once was man and woman and child.

He knew that. But these were not the bodies of an NKK fortress' warriors. They were men—civilian men and women and children. They were mostly naked, skins browned by equatorial sun, hair black or brown. One man, near Nadir's boot, lay with his eyes open and mouth seeming to form a stony word.

Nadir swallowed a dry lump and tried to move. He couldn't. His limbs began to tremble. The thing inside him inched closer to eruption. The scene expanded to a panorama, and now he saw dozens, hundreds of bodies, most wearing the tiny kiss of EMMA rounds like a patches on their skin. Some were mutilated where a trigger-rapt kid had spent her rifle on full-auto. Blood glued the bodies to the dusty earth, made gruesome cakes for the swarming flies to feast upon.

"Hundreds," he mumbled. His voice was barely under control.

Beyond the bodies, he saw the smoldering village. Stick huts outnumbered the prefabs, but all wore the grime and abuse of decades. A dog huddled with tail between its legs near the prone body of its master.

"Fucking piece of shit, Nadir!" Jhishra's 3VRD howled. It was barely a flicker without the server's amplification. "You die for not following your Boss' orders. I kill you!"

Nadir jerked as if he had been struck by one of the ill-aimed rounds mutilating the air overhead. A gout of hatred rose in him like a geyser. His aiming eye twitched. He looked up at the single flight of wooden steps, so new the nails that held them in place sparked in the sunset light. A short platform reached two meters in each direction from the upper landing. As he watched, enemy rounds shredded it and knocked down his soldiers. The Polish girl fell in a heap, her neck crimson and pulsing. She didn't move. The girl smiled, surely remembering Nadir's death education—and surely unaware of the fragile reality that rose up around him where she fell.

"Jhishra!" Nadir cried out across the bands. His voice tasted like venom. "As unit Sub-boss, I declare you unfit. Unfit to lead your men. I, Hardman Nadir, EarthCo Warrior Class 3, assume command at this moment. Let the record show you massacred a civilian village and caused the destruction of your unit at this place."

A few uniformed EarthCo soldiers moved toward Nadir like birds edging toward bits of bread, or toward a venomous worm. They seemed momentarily blind to the deadly rain falling all around.

"What? Shut up, shut up!" Jhishra was barely comprehensible. "Traitor, mutineer! Men, kill this Nadir!"

A shell burst against the theatrical wooden staircase, shattering it into a gust of splinters and nails, smoke and burning shrapnel. A chunk of it grazed Nadir's back and set him in motion.

"Boss Nadir," one boy said, transmitting a unique identifier key with the words that accessed a book-keeping program.

Nadir recognized the speaker as Paolo. Then another, another, and then all the soldiers still alive repeated the simple words that verified the transfer of power from a disabled Boss to a Sub-boss—standard procedure when electronic warfare was in use and a Boss' card couldn't be trusted. When had a unit ever had more damaging effects than this? Nadir feared no court-martial. He didn't expect to live that long.

Nadir ran across the corpsefield, hurdling bodies and shattered clay vessels. He reached the command truck and pounded on the side.

"Don't do this, Nadir," Jhishra's primary guard 3-verded.

Nadir could barely control himself. "Send him out." His words shook, making it sound as if he were at the edge of laughing. He was not.

"We kept him from firing on you, Subbs. He's in his cabin now. That's all we can do. Honest, he was under orders. This was really our target, sir, agreed-upon by Feedcontrol and NKK. I have the tapes to prove it. The Niks even leave us supplies sometimes in exchange for euthanizing excess—"

"Are you fucking with me?" Nadir spoke in a low growl.

"No, sir!" the guard's 3VRD said. "It's the only safe way for the Niks to get rid of their dissenting—"

Heavy automatic fire swept through the village, shredding everything higher than two meters. Nadir watched the assault as if from a distance, without the usual pleasure that accompanied such danger. The boys instinctively took cover; Nadir didn't need to tell them anything. They had survived a lot until now. . . . Or had they? Had it all been show for the subscribers?

"How much of . . . what we've done has been bullshit, boy?" he asked. He fumbled at his belt.

"The Niks don't send out their soldiers to be slaughtered, sir." The man laughed, a high, insane laugh that the 3VRD couldn't disguise. "Except what we got coming our way now is real, even though they don't use the normal BWs. I guess they've used us up. Time to pay the piper, eh sir?"

The truck's top port clanged open and Jhishra burst out, pistol in hand. Screaming, he slid down the curving side of the vehicle and landed only two meters from Nadir, who watched in silent amusement.

Paolo shrugged his rifle from his shoulder as soon as he saw the man. Nadir watched but didn't try to stop him. The boy tracked Jhishra as he slid, then fired a two-second burst when the Boss' feet hit sand.

I've got to say something, Nadir thought, or this boy will go nuts thinking about this moment.

"Good job, Paolo." He smiled kindly for a few seconds, oblivious to the fighting, and then felt his face transform into the killer's, into the mask he wore every time he knew his own death lurked nearby.

Nadir strolled away, toward the village gate. His back felt warm where the shrapnel had cut his armor, and his cheeks burned from small nicks. He walked without haste. His neck swiveled as he walked. He felt like a sightseer in a surreal land.

A plastimesh fence surrounded the wood and domed-plastic huts to keep out unwanted animals. The gate was a simple arch of carved saplings, cracked from exposure. Nadir noticed a crater to his left, where his unit had blasted open a hardened fortress' stone wall.

"Troops," he said, "I want you to scope out the enemy and identify him. Is he Sotoi Guntai or something else? If it's Nik, it's a mark."

"What, Subbs—I mean, Boss?"

"Just do it, goddammit! Live!"

He shut down his commcard and flung his rifle to the blood-caked ground. His arms rose high as if in victory or defeat, shaking as the muscles flexed hard and corded against the skin. Both of his fists clenched so tightly that his knuckles beamed white in the glare of a shell-flash.

Nadir's whole body began to shake with a rage he hadn't known could exist, every muscle quivering like bowstrings.

And then something inside him snapped. The toxic waste of his rage ruptured its containment. His chest trembled. It was as if he felt a part of his body break. He could hear the snap. Past his eyes flashed images of Wolf Point, boot camp, all the battles. . . . Everything in his life that made him who he was rushed through his mind at that breaking point, all broke free as that psychological bottle came uncapped, all in a moment.

"Murderer!" he cried. "Murderer! Nothing but a bloody murderer." Nothing, nothing, I am nothing, his brain howled. I am less than dead, I am less than putrefied, less than petrified, less than dust.

He felt violence like a wave of magma sweep through him, an impetus driving him perhaps toward destroying every person and place and object wrapped up in his mind, every fragment that composed the shattered yet still-standing statue of Hardman Nadir. Perhaps it drove him toward self-destruction, toward striking that cracked statue of himself just firmly enough to send it to the sand, just another pile of quartz glistening in the setting sun.

His eyes went to the rifle that had been his murder tool; that would be appropriate.

No, I don't deserve something so easy. So perhaps the wave of hate drove him toward righting a world whose existence he could no longer deny, a world he could no longer deny was untrue and wrong.

"That's it," Nadir said, his voice crystalline-clear. To his ears it sounded like the voice of an alien. Paolo backed away, a question and a look of fear on his face.

Nadir howled that prehistoric human cry of pain and release as he ripped off his uniform shirt and the medal-encrusted vest beneath it. He flung the medals as far as his arm allowed; the shirt sailed through the buzzing air thick with flies and bullets, and disappeared among a brown heap where not-soldiers had gathered out of fear when their world came down on them in waves, waves; waves crashed through him and Nadir finally broke off his scream when no air remained in a sobbing chest.

He fell onto his knees and then face-first into the dust. He did not break his fall, but he also didn't notice the slight impact. Bullets and an exploding shell shrieked and rang around him. Tendrils of the dead monopera sang at one corner of his consciousness. Nadir's chest continued to heave; dust rushed in and out of his gasping mouth and nostrils.

And then he rose, slowly, as a snake after shedding an old skin, a man after shedding the uniform of a hired murderer. He crossed to the huddled bodies and winced as he retrieved the vest of medals. He pulled it back on.

I haven't yet earned the privilege of being free of this.

"Subbs—I mean Boss—something's strange about the enemy," Paolo said, breaking into Nadir's narrowing river of thoughts; the magma had reached his mind, yes, but it was no longer wild rapids. He was taming it into a directed stream. *Something strange about the enemy, indeed,* he thought. *So it's true.*

"What do we do now?" the boy asked.

"Cease fire on the attacking units," he commed across the bands. "They should be almost on top of us now. We're meat if we fight back. I've got an idea."

"Guards!" he called on the private line to command. Jhishra's men would be able to help him do this thing. He picked up his rifle and plugged it back in.

"Yes . . . yes, Boss?" the second guard's 3VRD answered.

"Connect me with the classified files." Nadir spoke as he walked toward the command truck.

"We can't access those, sir," the first guard, the one who usually spoke, said.

"If you won't, I will. You'd better cooperate." He stood at the rear of the truck, keeping an eye on the turret. Already, the gunfire was beginning to diminish. *Good,* Nadir thought, *that'll give me time.*

The first guard's 3VRD vanished, and the second's began to shimmer. "You shouldn't've done that, sir! You shouldn't've fucked with things. We were doing so well—"

"So well that we're about to be destroyed? Shut up and give me access."

The doors hissed up like a beetle's wings beckoning him inside. Nadir caught himself feeling pleasure. He would alter the plans of whoever it was that decided such things as massacring whole villages of innocent civilians. He was not alone in the world; he couldn't be alone in believing what was right and what was wrong. If he were, his plans would fail.

"So it goes," he muttered, stepping into the darkened interior of the truck. The effort is what matters.

Nadir flicked back on the server's command landscape and rebooted its transmitter, but shut down the program which had been running for three months. It only took him a few seconds to track along the neon tunnels to the enemy servers—both of them, though only one used the same language as this one. A brief but deadly pulse—

Slam, the command truck fired a column of microwave energy at both servers, enough to either burn them out or force their failsafes to shut down for a critical period. He tapped into the stasis files and smiled as orders from on high passed through his card to each and every headcard of the advancing army.

Yes, yes. Finally. He listened to the attack lose power and finally sputter to a halt as they tried to puzzle out why they were receiving orders directly from—of all places—War Command at Feedcontrol. Certainly they would be wondering why the world had just turned upside down.

Nadir's face crumpled into a grin as sinister as the mask of a fossilized tyrannosaurus.

"Live well today, boys," he 3-verded his unit. "You've been steeped in death and almost drowned. But you'll live to tell about it. The crimes end here. It's time to set the world right, at least the little part of it we can change." He gulped a deep breath.

A few meters beyond the ruined village milled an army wearing the blue of NKK's Sotoi Guntai. Mingled with them was the tan of the EarthCo Warriors. Each looked upon the other for the first time and saw not the allies they had marched beside, but foes. Each would have a lot of questions, but the War Command data they were getting would clear things up. This moment of revelation might even end up in bloodshed, Nadir thought, but then doesn't everything end in death?

He began to laugh. He raised his rifle high above him and pictured his new, little army marching across the world, spreading truth, destroying the status quo. Nothing would stop him, not bullets, not more tricked armies, not now that both sides had seen the truth. Not even warplanes or missiles, and certainly not death. He had set something in motion, and this something—truth—could not be stopped by one or a thousand men's deaths.

It'll be hard. But only in suffering is there growth, he reminded himself. And only in growth is there life.

"My god, we're alive!"

Feedcontrol 5

From the nearly omniscient—and safe—vantage point of his velvet-walled projection booth deep within the Feedcontrol Central complex, Luke Herrschaft and Mrs. Pehr Jackson watched a 3VRD battle rage near Neptune. Little slivers of flame shot across the room when Herrschaft set the show's pov from a widefield external camera. His pulse raced; even though he could no longer truly pretend that this body was his, that this was Luke the man, he knew the heart in that shell which still imprisoned him was beating just as fast.

The moment stood upon the race of Man, his moment, Luke Herrschaft's second defining moment. *No, it does not yet stand upon them,* he thought. *The boot trembles, poised in the skies above their blind skulls.* His robotic cheeks tightened with a grin as wide as the servos would allow.

Lasers reached from a torch-shaped EarthCo fighter/bomber toward a series of missiles, which drew a complicated pattern of rocket exhaust against a backdrop of pinpoint stars and varicolored moons' orbs and crescents. One of the Feedcontrol live-action editors had done a fabulous job of amplifying the color and closeness of those moons—all of them were visible at once and each was individualized. Someone had embellished the missiles into fighters.

Only minutes before, the missiles had been fired from the atmosphere of Neptune. The EarthCo *Bounty* had not behaved in an aggressive fashion. Clearly an act of war by NKK. Clearly, for all to see. Herrschaft had only hoped for this added value.

SUBSCRIPTION: 6,049,383,427

The number increased even as Herrschaft watched. The citizens were eating it up. *They will be putty in my hands.*

Herrschaft reset for interior view, and the projection booth transformed into a cramped cabin aboard *Bounty*. Two men and a woman fought frantically to stay alive, acting as if they were truly in control of their fates.

Mrs. Jackson quietly groaned. Her red velvet booth seat sat awkwardly in a corner of the cabin.

"I don't like personal povs in adventure shows," she said. "I've been told I'm an artist." She blushed and hurriedly finished: "I don't enjoy assuming character povs. I prefer to create my own part, but *Lone Ship Bounty* doesn't leave much room for that. Watching the scene from outside is better; I compose fitting—I hope—music. Do you mind?"

"Of course not, my dear," Herrschaft said. He set the booth's projector for outside pov again. "Is this—"

He stopped speaking. Three others had entered the room without his knowledge. He cursed himself for tying up too much of his presence in one place and tried to compose himself.

"Welcome, Lucilla," he said to his assistant and, perhaps, friend. She looked weary but alert. He had only hoped she still cared enough to come. But now was not the time for sentimentality.

"President Zauber," Herrschaft said, extending a hand to a tall German dressed in an ultramod chenille suit. "Congratulations on the European election."

"Thank you," the man said, smiling broadly intheflesh. "An honor to meet you." Safe, Herrschaft decided. The man would be a fine addition to EarthCo's hierarchy.

"And President Snipes," Herrschaft said to the third person, "Congratulations to you, as well. Although I am sorry you acquired your seat from such, ah, unfortunate circumstances."

"Yes," said the US President, who was only that morning Vice President.

Herrschaft studied Snipes' immobile face for a few seconds and decided the man was part of the plot against him. He projected 10% of his attention out to the presidential limousine's service system and infected the microcard. It would be a simple accident, designed to scare rather than destroy; the steering servo would lock once the vehicle reached 50 kph. Herrschaft smiled and nodded, then turned to Mrs. Jackson.

"I would like you all to meet Mrs. Pehr Jackson—Susahn—the wife of tonight's featured hero."

Lucilla stared at Herrschaft a little after the two men began to do their political best. Then she smiled and shook her head sadly. He didn't understand but also didn't like wondering, so he cut 90% of himself out of the room. He dispersed his consciousness among three control rooms, the booth, and the AI program he had set to hunt down his assassins. His view was similar to a standard citizen card's splice, but much more fluid and versatile, mainly because he could transfer primary pov to wherever a large enough card was installed. He wasn't hindered by biology, simple organic mechanics. Rather than in any one place, Herrschaft immersed himself in the abstract, in the historic moment he had choreographed.

Millions of kilometers away, EConaut Marshfield—"Eyes"—at last activated his optical and sensory feedback units. Forty technicians at EarthCo Feedcontrol, all dedicated today to this one series, bustled to a level of highest activity, expertly coordinating feedback from the three probe cameras, numerous shipboard cameras, and the one surgically embedded in Marshfield's left eyesocket.

Megawatts of power were surging through Feedcontrol's wide plain of phased-array transmitters, sending the program almost live directly into the mindpaths of the now-eight billion—and increasing—subscribers. Herrschaft accessed a ratings monitor and found that the 33% increase was due mainly to massive adfeed for the past two weeks.

He felt himself buoy up upon the crest of an evershifting empire, a god of energy riding a wave through the minds of half the solar system. They didn't know he moved there, in them, in their shows, in their every thought and action. But he knew. Indeed, he had created them.

For just a moment, as if shattering a crystal globe as wide as a supergiant star and looking out of each fragment like tiny mirrors, Herrschaft splintered his pov across the entire ECoNet. He glimpsed all of Earth's cities and red Mars and pocked Luna and boiling Mercury and a dozen other places simultaneously in a way not unlike his alter-ego, the Brain, might. Since he was not that artificial mind, he comprehended nothing he saw.

His view was that of a smashed crystal ball, and it fell together almost as fast as he had bashed it hard against the wall of his mind.

But his imagination—though rusty and cracked—put it all together. That it was artificial did nothing to lessen his pleasure: All this, every molecule, is mine, he silently told the citizens. If not for me, you would still be crouched down on a single world like animals. I have given you the planets. I have given you a true spacefleet, placed colonies on every rock that we could grab orbiting the sun, and soon will deliver colonies on what NKK now holds. We will take it all. I have created an empire and the creatures that inhabit it, and one day we will be lords of everything our eyes can survey. The stars will truly belong to Man. . . .

Herrschaft's immaterial face—or some vestige of his ancient human body—hardened in a grin of utter ecstasy. He completely forgot that he had been unmasked that morning, yet even if he had remembered at that instant, it would not have mattered.

He re-entered the path of feed, split into only four simple and direct povs.

>>Primary feed: Telescopic camera P2 zooms in on spaceship riding orange plume out of Neptunian clouds toward *Bounty*. Flash primary to character pov camera, focus unwaveringly upon pilot's full breasts held high on her chest by black, luminescent cloth.<<

SALES FOR NERO BRAS, BODICES, AND OTHER LINGERIE UP 155%

>>P2 camera now clearly shows other spacecraft to be NKK design, long and narrow as opposed to spherical. An automated torpedo in feedback transforms into a manned fighter upon edited feed. Switch to right cabin camera inside *Bounty*, showing Captain's expression of wise interpretation. Also in pov are crew members' weapons, near at hand. They all pop snapsticks.<<

Herrschaft toggled through an ad-efficiency overlay program:

COLT, GTE, AND SINGER PERSONAL ARMS UP AVERAGE 35%
EMBRACE, BELTROPE, AND JAKK MAKEUPS UP AVERAGE 80%
PAGOS AND CYBERMOND MENSWEAR UP AVERAGE 75%
MAKK BOOTS UP *FROM NO SALES* 50,000 UNITS/MINUTE
SALES FOR MONTE AND BELLAFORM SNAPSTICKS UP AVERAGE 30%

Good, Herrschaft thought, very good. Must keep the corps' sales up to keep them happy. Must keep them happy to keep Feedcontrol on top. Must keep Feedcontrol on top to keep me on top. Must keep me on top to keep the plan on path. . . .

>>Slight force acts on ship's equilibrium for a moment, blurring inner cameras. Flashes of metal and skintones and various fabrics. Primary feedback concentrated on following torpedo launched at NKK fighter. Neptune now twice as large as in verification feed sequence. At 1000 meters from contact, torpedo camera switches on. Unstable but effective action sequence as subscribers ride along at 100,000 kph toward NKK spacecraft, Neptune looming vastly larger each second. A bracelet of flares launch from enemy craft toward the torpedo. Two seconds later, so close camera can resolve long laser-burn along

hull of NKK ship, one defense rocket explodes within a few meters. End of this feedback track.<<

Herrschaft no longer cared what was real and what was his editors' license. This was going very well. A small part of him observed the reactions of the world's two most powerful EarthCo presidents, of Susahn Jackson, and of Lucilla. Three other of his top aides had arrived while he wasn't paying attention, but they drew none of his attention. All had seated themselves and were watching intently. Herrschaft chose this place for an audience because of the very nature of a private booth: Visitors have no control of the feed and, therefore, feel it more acutely. A taste of reality.

>>Enemy craft now within cannon range. Almost too close for practical use of camera P2. Neptune blooms blue like an ocean behind ship's shiny tube of steel. Planet fills camera P1 and extends beyond range of P2. NKK craft now visible in P3; *Bounty* in danger.<<

Herrschaft felt a moment of acute worry, then relaxed. It did not matter if the *Bounty* were destroyed. Indeed, that might make it simpler. But not yet! Not quite yet.

The battle raged on. Herrschaft grew tired of the mechanics of war, instead shifting his pov from room to room throughout Feedcontrol Central. What he was witnessing had happened hours prior, and worry could kill him if he allowed it. He watched editors and technicians, artists and programmers, producers and physicists at work behind a thousand desks, adjusting feed and inserting prerecorded data and repairing damaged equipment, their physical bodies barely needing to move. Only when *Bounty* suffered a debilitating hit did he return a large percentage of Herrschaft's attention to the booth.

>>External shifting povs show melted and glowing metals. Electromagnetic pulse recorded upon NKK missile discharge. Lingering traces of radiation after blast. Subliminal suggestions of nuclear explosion: 0.4-second flashes of shadow-figures in Hiroshima, Nagasaki, Berlin, Tel Aviv, Seoul; flashes of flesh melting from bone, bone glowing neon green, fire and gouts of blood; subconscious overlay of dusty NKK products, maniacal Asian faces.<<

"With that act," Herrschaft told his seven guests in the booth, "NKK has set itself on a course of war. *Bounty* did not provoke them. Wait a moment . . . I'm getting feed from a reliable source that they used atomics on us!"

He made sure his speech and his audience's reactions were being recorded. He watched the script's countdown:

0:00:07

Herrschaft's mental face smiled hard, but his 3VRD presence remained serious and went on with the speech, timed just right.

"*Bounty*'s crew would be foolish to attack such an overwhelming force as Neptunekaisha, NKK's proxy. *Bounty* had orders to carry out scientific research—and, I trust to tell you now that NKK has tipped its hand—important intelligence work in Neptunekaisha space. EConautics has heard they were developing illegal—"

>>Flip primary feed to interior pov, close-up of Captain Jackson. Face sweat-beaded and creased with tiny cuts.<<

"Fire nuclear missile!" Jackson cried, seemingly interrupting Herrschaft's speech. "They asked for it."

"What's happening?" Herrschaft thundered. "Nuclear weapon? I'd expect that of NKK, but where would *Bounty* get such a thing?"

Susahn Jackson inhaled quietly and held the breath as her mouth fell slack and her eyes grew tight. She stared at the man whose name she wore like a badge. Herrschaft studied her for a moment. She was just about ready.

A ghost 3VRD appeared in the room, as programmed.

"Director Herrschaft, Presidents Snipes and Zauber," the mature woman—based on psych models of maternal images—said. "I was hoping they wouldn't . . . oh, but they did." The AI did an excellent job of acting like an upset and angry human.

"Oh, sorry, my name's Zelda Mapes," she said. "Lieutenant at Markov Division, EConautics, spacefit corps at Howie Orbital Launch Center. Right after *Bounty* took off, months ago, we discovered that one of our freighters' engines was missing its atomic core. We suspected—"

"I see," Herrschaft said, a threat in his voice.

"Enough," Zauber said. Herrschaft was pleasantly surprised at the impromptu addition; this was working out better and better.

"File a complete report," the European President said, "indicating all implicated in this idiocy. Then deliver EarthCo your resignation for waiting this long to tell us. That will be all."

Mapes disappeared.

Zauber looked across the room at Herrschaft and said, "It was bad enough that NKK used a proscribed weapon. Now this. What's going to happen now? Director, I need access to my voter feedback to plan a response."

"Of course," Herrschaft said. He opened a line to Europe, intercepted by phantom editors that no one at either end would sense. Herrschaft watched the half-second delayed polling go back and forth between figurehead and citizens.

President Zauber cast his questions on all allband overlay; the responding citizens— who perceived they had a direct audience with their leader—filtered back to Zauber (and Herrschaft) as a column of numbers. Herrschaft realized no poll adjustments would be required. The citizens demanded revenge.

"We can't allow those Neptunekaisha socialists to get away with this," Zauber boomed.

He has a fine speaking voice, Herrschaft thought. Virtually no one would recognize the slight mistake—TritonCo was the socialist proxy, not Neptunekaisha. Same thing, they will think; they're all just NKK in disguise.

"But *Bounty* provoked them, and *Bounty* also used atomics," the other president said. His face was tight and he aimed his eyes at Herrschaft. Of course, those words were edited before being stored for feed.

"What do your constituents think?" Herrschaft asked him.

After a brief pause: "I'll ask."

Herrschaft didn't waste time watching the polls return; he knew the US was even more primed for war than Europe, since this country hadn't felt enemy boots in twice as long as he had lived. Serials like *EarthCo Warrior* in Africa and all the rest reinforced this moment; decades of such shows had accumulated in the collective brain of EarthCo, and at last the vast military spending he had maneuvered would pay off. The people had virtually been there.

Herrschaft leaned back into the absorgel chair and increased the booth's sensory feed. Seven of the most influential figureheads in EarthCo accompanied him inside a virtual *Bounty* as it spun, wounded, toward history in the shape of blue Neptune. He smelled burned insulation, hot metal, oil smoke, the crew's fear. He watched Eyes, the bombardier, oddly fondle his subgun. Herrschaft's heart sped.

He flipped most of his pov to a cramped control room where two women looked as if they were feedrapt: editors. They didn't notice Herrschaft's 3VRD presence until he commed them. The room was silent, so quiet barely a dust mote moved across the face of the sleek panels surrounding the women.

Herrschaft watched an unscripted drama begin to unfold. Eyes pointed his weapon at the Captain. Herrschaft slowed retransmission and gave one of the editors new directions. Her body twitched briefly as she set to work. One finger reached out and touched a green square on the panel to her left.

"I'll not take another criminal order from you, Jackson!" virtual-Eyes screamed. Virtual-Janus, the pilot, looked from Eyes to the captain, then back. In zero-*g* languor, she climbed through the smoke-filled cabin to stand beside the bombardier.

"You told us you'd never use the nukes," Janus said. Her face was hard and her eyes sad. She crossed bare arms below her breasts. "They were to deter, deter."

"Damn you two!" virtual-Captain Jackson said. "Don't you remember? NKK is building an arsenal of atomics down there on Triton. How can you stand for that?"

Janus and Eyes paused to glance at one another just long enough for Jackson to push off toward his control seat and press a red button. A second missile screamed out of the *Bounty*.

"There," Jackson said, gripping the back of his chair. "No more nuclear arsenal, down there or up here. You two can take command of this vessel." He glided toward a hallway and disappeared into his cabin.

Satisfied with the editors' work, Herrschaft returned his attention to the projection booth. Everyone watched as the first missile worked its way through Neptune's defenses.

"What do you think of your husband's behavior, Mrs. Pehr Jackson?" Herrschaft asked. He swiveled his chair to face the woman.

"That. . ." She swallowed hard. "That's a mannequin. That's not Pehr, it can't be. NKK must have made him into a mannequin. That's not Pehr, it's just a tracker chip controlling his body, right?"

Good, good, Herrschaft thought, but he didn't want to arouse the old panic of mannequins. The corps had agreed to stop making war machines out of people long before they signed the Stop Nuke Treaty.

"Not likely, my dear," he said. "Your husband acted much like himself, even after—"

"That's not my husband!" she shouted, standing upright like a spike. "Man or mannequin, that's just a character named Pehr Jackson. I'm no longer wife to a traitor. Do you all hear that? Is the whole world listening in?"

She grew shrill. "I'm filing a motion for divorce, do you hear that, Pehr?"

Herrschaft withdrew his pov as the woman's rant continued. He had to do this to her in order to divert association-guilt feelings from *Lone Ship Bounty* subscribers. He had to clear EarthCo from direct blame. But watching a real person suffer triggered pain somewhere deep within him, and he was always careful to avoid pain. Pain unearthed things . . . .

Herrschaft flipped to the pov of one of his EConautics space fleet vessels. Far below rested the Moon, looming like some kind of grotesque beach ball abandoned in the middle of night. He gave his Fleet Boss the final word of the all-go phrase. Almost simultaneous with the word, rocket exhausts flared red and white and blue rising from that bright grey world; other ships seemed to appear like magic, transformed from infinitely distant constellations to shaped metal near at hand. Lasers began to steam the Moon's surface.

Herrschaft felt giddy with anticipation. He returned to the projection booth. Both presidents were issuing emergency directives; the various aides were contacting their assistants.

"Begun," Herrschaft mouthed again, seated comfortably in his chair. It has begun: magic words to let loose dragons.

"When politics alone was still running countries," he said aloud, "we were forever on the brink of global collapse." The other speakers fell silent. President Snipes frowned.

"But the current arrangement has given us the solar system. If only we had acted sooner, or put down NKK at the beginning, we would possess it all, harmoniously. Our only concerns would have been how to properly raise and equitably provide for 21 billion citizens scattered across dozens of worlds. But now we must worry over war."

He infused great emphasis on the final word, packing it full of subliminals designed long ago to elicit patriotic feelings, to reawaken that ancient, sleeping giant, war fever. A corner of his pov showed the two presidents' polls winding maniacally up the scale toward revenge. They wanted war, a grand-scale war in which they could virtually participate.

Herrschaft continued to speak, but he wasn't necessary for him to do so. The speech was prerecorded and carefully processed. He moved 100% of his pov to his favorite suite high above NYB and studied the skyline that defined the Atlantic border of North America. His robotic ears filled with the silence of high-rise wind scouring the suite's windows. He stared out at glistening steel and aluminum and glass towers, countless aircars busily adding value to EarthCo, millions upon millions of citizens plodding through their everyday lives. . . .

And now change, irreversible and omnipotent, loomed over them like a new world ready to crash down and consume them.

He had created an empire for them. He had made it his priority to give America's— and soon after, EarthCo's—children a world of safe education and freedom from the dominion of adults. He no longer fooled himself: His charitable goals didn't mean he cared for humans, no indeed. It meant only that he pitied the naïve, abused youths.

"Behind heroism lurks revenge," he told the deaf city. By creating elemental change, he had destroyed the world which had shoved all he loved into a shell containing nothing but emotional scar tissue.

"Oh, I don't like children much," Mrs. Pehr Jackson had told him as they flew in his limo to Feedcontrol Central. "Yes, I know," he had replied. In his mind, she became no more than an example of how his people hadn't changed. He was so pleased she had said that.

Herrschaft gazed out at the city. From this height, he couldn't tell if anyone were reacting to the news of the interplanetary war just now getting underway.

"I gave you an empire, and you spat on it," he said. "Because you are human, you found a way to despoil the noble vision, as you spoil all you touch."

In a million-kilometer-wide sphere around Earth and Moon, their lesson was in motion, punishment, change. Soon, everyone left alive would look to him as a child looks to a loving, protective parent. He would offer wisdom, and they would love him for it. He would complete the empire, but first he had to crush the aborted attempt in his fist like so much dry clay. Only blood could rewet it, and this time he would mold it properly.

But first, they needed to learn their lesson.

"Only pain truly teaches," he told them.

Luke Herrschaft, Director of Feedcontrol and Destroyer of Worlds, broke uncontrollably into fits of weeping. He didn't know where this emotion came from, nor could he resist it. A small corner of his mind decided to stop coming to this room, this place where he had told a younger Lucilla the story of his life and she had accepted him as friend. This place would need to be buried, like the rest of his past. Pain was only for his subjects, not him.

Trembling with power, yet confused, angry, and deadly sad, Herrschaft wept—and curiously watched himself weep from a wall mounted pov—as the solar system swept itself into a frenzy of war. Only now were the things he had set in motion spinning out of his direct control.

Fleet Boss

EConautics Fleet Boss H.C. stared through an ultraglas porthole of the fleet's flagship, Locust. His naked, crooked body floated in fetal position, left foot drawn up beside his cheek. He absently picked at the disproportionately large big toe.

Outside, ten thousand ships glinted like knives against the black of infinity. Inside, the knives were hollow; they were tiny islands, most uninhabited except by AIs, the most efficient long term space warriors. But about half of the vessels contained a single pilot, a redundancy backup. A few of the larger craft—torpedo platforms, really—held larger crews. These would be first to heave their contents during battle, first to breathe vacuum.

H.C. had been kept in a plastic grain cylinder until he was eight, so he never developed a taste for virtuality. In fact, never in the following 35 years did he subscribe to a single show. An employee of his father's at the grain elevator found H.C. one day while searching for the source of a bad smell.

H.C. lived the next ten years in a government orphan facility, where he received his basic citizen's card. The doctors also performed extensive surgery to remove painful growths and correct severe deformities. There, he learned how to please those in authority. He learned how to survive among gangs, but, mostly, his grotesqueness kept dangerous people at a distance.

In the long run, the cylinder gave H.C. the advantage of small size, so he required less lifesupport to sustain his body onboard spacecraft, making his craft lighter, more maneuverable, and capable of carrying greater arms. The vivid 3D imagination he had developed to entertain his sensory-deprived brain made him unbeatable in fighter-pilot training, so he rocketed up the ranks. He even defeated the suit camp AI combatant. Familiar with enclosed spaces, he never suffered the kind of claustrophobia that often disabled other one-man-craft pilots; however, that did not mean he was not terrified both of closeness and of the immensities stretching in every direction just beyond the thin hull.

Defeating those fears was his greatest challenge. When he succeeded—through self-induced desensitization—he felt invulnerable. At 39, he became the youngest Fleet Boss in EConautics history. No one challenged his ascendancy, for reasons he never quite grasped. One possible reason, he thought, was that he recognized Luke Herrschaft as the true Boss of EarthCo, and treated the man as such; in fact, when H.C. decided to issue the ultimate challenge to the former Fleet Boss, Herrschaft was the first person he approached. Two hours later, H.C. destroyed the Regency Optima vessel and claimed the title of Fleet Boss. The Director himself endorsed the promotion.

H.C. was yanked out of reverie by a word echoing in his head:

"Begun," said the voice of Luke Herrschaft, as if thinking of the man had summoned him.

H.C. finished the phrase: It has begun.

He savored the moment briefly.

No rush. Time for savoring. Ten thousand warships quivered at his command. Each was armed enough to destroy a city, pop a thousand tin cans NKK called spacecraft, kill and destroy. H.C. drank the moment, grew ecstatic. This is all he had ever managed to feel: ecstasy, fear, victory, satisfaction of a job well done.

At last, at last, at last, I have a real mission.

"Come Toe, come Toe," he said to his one friend. He scratched the tiny man hidden in his left foot. "Time to get to work."

A pulse flashed out from the Locust to every other EarthCo craft under his control. Each entered Stage GO, unleashing the program Herrschaft had installed months prior.

And then his craft lurched. H.C. grabbed hold of the cabin's netting and fastened himself in place. All around him, the largest machine ever created by Man set itself in motion, a collection of vast gears whose teeth could each smash a city, a machine powerful enough to crush worlds, a machine that, once set into motion, bore an irresistible momentum.

Half the stars in the sky began to move, a swarm of battleships about to swoop down upon NKK's planets.

Toe chuckled, the mischievous little man attached to the Fleet Boss' foot. H.C. caught his enthusiasm.

"It has begun."

NINE: Transcendence

Triton 5: Pehr Jackson

Pehr Jackson led the way down the cauldron of the crater, picking his way carefully among the footholds; he didn't feel a need to use his hands, which would have been difficult at this angle, anyway. He worried only for a moment about radiation. A spacesuit is designed to withstand the direct rays of the sun: the standard rating is for three hours' exposure.

The old memories—good memories—of his 3VRD bouldering experience took over. It was as if his few weeks in the virtual mountains were only yesterday. His body instinctively knew where to place the next step. Still, he kept an auto-piton handy in case they began to slip. The ion bonder would snap into place immediately, and only the breaking-point of the ice itself would determine their safety. Even if this kind of ice was fragile, at least the eye would skid along, slowing their slide as it broke up the surface. Hopefully they would come to a stop before reaching the lake.

The effort was good. He needed it. They were making a journey across a crater they had made, on an alien world—an enemy's alien world. Their ship was destroyed, stranding them on this strange place. Eyes had nearly sabotaged their escape from the sinking escape pod. He had screwed with reality. Janus had killed the man, right in front of Pehr. That brought up really uncomfortable memories. All this was hard to manage. Pehr concentrated on foot placement.

After about half an hour, they had descended as far as they could; the fuming lake now stood in their way. A film of ice was already spreading across the surface, but only a madman would try to cross. Anyway, the surface was nearly flat here. Pehr triggered the first piton, strung the cord through, and tossed it up and ahead. It bounced once and held. He tested the bond; the ice didn't crack as he tugged.

Slowly, they made their way around the shore. The spacesuit boots weren't designed for this kind of terrain, but their soles marginally gripped the slick footing. Ice crystals had formed where the liquid met the crater floor, tiny, intricate sculptures made of geometrically perfect shapes. Here, a man stood with octagon feet, his legs cones formed from triangles, his head an even more complicated shape made of smaller shapes. Some looked like magnified snowflakes; some looked like knives or sawblades. All the new things to see, combined with the need to concentrate on staying upright, kept Pehr from slipping back into the weak self. He felt strong and capable.

They reached the far side and the stair-like cracks leading upward. Up they climbed, in silence, the only sound his own labored breathing. Time and again, Pehr wished he had exercised as diligently as Janus had aboard ship. But he reached the destination without too many aches. The tower rose only ten meters away.

Now he tossed the piton again, since they would have to cross smooth ice to reach the tower's base. They had taken perhaps ten steps when Pehr heard the rumble.

He stopped and looked around. Janus watched a certain spot in the sky. She pointed.

"Another ship," she said.

Now Pehr saw it, just beyond the crater's rim. As the seconds passed, a star grew into a long flare. The flare soon showed its source, an oval ship riding fire down toward them.

Moments later, Pehr heard words and static on his comm line:

". . .EarthCo mamamatay-tao!" More static, then, ". . .pagbabaka! War!" And then laughter, whooping and loud and numerous. Another channel, perhaps several more, soon overlapped the first.

The ship grew larger. As it passed over the crater, beams of energy poured down onto where the pod was now immersed in ice. A great cloud boiled up at the end of the trench just as the ship thundered overhead.

Another, and then another ship followed suit. The third fired a missile into the cloud of vaporous ammonia and methane, its exhaust like a searchlight. When it impacted, the whole crater shook and rumbled. Pehr felt the sound more through his bones than in his ears. After the fifth ship passed, no more followed. Finally, something bright flashed in space, far overhead. Pehr assumed that would be the derelict *Bounty*.

She was all gone now. He recognized at last the complete severing from his past. That's it. No more ship, no more show, no more Captain Pehr Jackson. He had become a nobody again, a nobody in a distant, enemy land, with no means to return home. What do I do now, little boy? he asked of the bandanna in his hip pocket.

Then he saw Janus, and knew he still had a purpose and a responsibility.

She didn't return his look; instead, she was watching something down by the lake.

"The little sonofabitch," she said.

"What?"

"The cyborg. He's following us."

"Impossible," Pehr said. "I watched you . . . kill him."

"He fooled us again. Blotted out his image. I suppose he was drawing power from the pod, somehow. When they destroyed the pod, he lost his powersource." Janus turned to face Pehr; her eyes were burning, rimmed with red and furious with tears.

"I shot a 3VRD," Janus said.

"But how—"

"He's a master of his card, Jack. You wouldn't know. The sonofabitch is still alive, and I left my weapon aboard the pod. I didn't want to appear threatening to the people here."

"Don't worry about Eyes," Pehr said. "His card is powerless now, right? Physically, we can easily overcome any attack from him.

"All this assumes that he's stupid enough to follow us. And that he doesn't fall into the lake. Look at the fool." Pehr pointed. "He's walking freehand. Leave him be; it's better to let a man kill himself. Have you ever killed anyone?"

"I wish I had."

Pehr turned away from the struggling, distant figure and looked into Janus' eyes. "You don't know what it's like. You don't want to know. He'll haunt you all your life."

Pehr paused, seeing a boy lying on a heap of junk in a Minneapolis alley. He then saw an old man, blue in the face, motionless on a Persian rug. Suddenly, all the men and women who had died in cinematic combat with him seemed real, clothed in blood and flesh and skin, and loved or hated by someone in their lives; he saw a great ocean of effect, waves crashing through the network of human existence. Perhaps the pilot of a particular white AMRCO fighter—the one with the brown bear painted on the side—had a best friend, and perhaps that best friend grew so filled with hate that he started his own Crusades down on Earth, killing and maiming in search of the perpetrator, unsatisfied until the blood debt had been paid with interest. That's the way with all wars, with all violence, Pehr thought. It never really ends, not until the whole world is dead, not until all the hate has been satiated with murder and suicide. Not until the last drops of venom and grief have bled out of the last victim and perpetrator, ending the cycle forever with the death of the human race.

And he grew sick of Pehr Jackson, himself a wave in the ocean of destruction. Out here, on the cold, desolate moon—here in a human-made crater, no less—all life and death seemed crisper than reality. Reality itself seemed too crisp. His own thoughts were too present.

"Leave him be," Pehr said.

"Those times weren't your fault," Janus said.

Pehr, shocked, wondered if she could read his mind. Then he remembered that he had told her everything. It seemed like a dream now, talking to her, telling her too much.

"Well," he said, embarrassed to be so transparent, "we have an alien artifact to see, right?" He pointed to the hidden object atop the tower. At least one thing hadn't been spoiled by the hand of Man.

"Up there," he said, "we ought to be in line-of-sight of the city. We'll surrender up there, and tell them where to pick up Eyes. It'll be all over. We can pay for our crimes, or start new. Come on."

Triton 6: Janus Librarse

Janus watched as Jack unfastened a three-pronged hook from his belt, looped rope through its eye, and tossed it up the side of the tower. It landed with an almost inaudible ping, as if the sound were coming from kilometers away. He yanked on the rope, turned to smile at Janus—though she could see his eyes were not happy; rather, confused and desperate—then began to scale the almost-vertical wall, feet finding purchase on nearly imperceptible bumps, fingertips gripping tiny cracks.

She blinked as she watched him climb. So strong, pulling himself up easily in the near-weightlessness, using his feet keep from spinning on the rope. She hadn't imagined he was still so haunted by his youth. He hadn't done anything wrong. She wanted to say it, wanted to cry it aloud. But she couldn't, because her own childhood still haunted her, as well.

Jack was nearly to the top. She watched and thought. She had never intended to hurt Miguel when she left for EConaut training. Rachel was the one who loved him, anyway. Janus had stolen so much from Rachel already, dragging her away from home at such a young age, forcing her to stay away, living in a homeless complex. . . .

Oh, yes, and her own hatred. That was why she pitied Jack. She knew that, given the opportunity, she would have murdered her father. Yes, once I had struggled free of his grip, I would have been able to do it. The bastard, the dirty bastard. He set me up to be vulnerable to that filthy cyborg. And I will kill that thing, as soon as it is near. I will kill it, and poor Jack, you'll know. I don't want to hurt you this way, but Father and Cyborg have combined their efforts to try to ruin me inside. She saw herself as an ancient mansion, its walls of fieldstone still standing, but all the floors within collapsed into rubble in the basement.

Janus began to shake and then to weep. She flicked off her comm line so Jack wouldn't hear. She was not sad; no, she searched for the source of these irrepressible emotions and found only anger, and beneath that helplessness and terror.

He—it—was coming. She turned back toward the basin and watched a tiny figure pick its way among the ice-flowers. It was using the encrusted shoreline to keep from sliding into the lake. It would eventually find her again, and get inside her again. And she would not allow that to happen. She would die first.

The rope around her waist tightened three times. Jack was trying to get her attention. She steadied herself and flicked her comm line back on.

"What's the matter?" Jack asked. His voice sounded far away and staticky. She looked up but couldn't see him, only the rope hanging over the edge. "Come up here! It's amazing!"

"All right," Janus responded. She tried to regain the enthusiasm that had fired her up when Miru first commed them. Even a few minutes ago, while she still thought the cyborg was dead, she had been able to get excited. But now. . . .

"I'm coming," she commed, and began to climb before the hatred ripped holes in her gut. She'd have her chance. And then, by god, she'd take it.

Triton 7: Pehr Jackson

He helped Janus up the side of the icy butte, pulling the rope through the carabiner at his waist and reeling the slack around his shoulder. Finally, she stood at the flat top, beside him. Pehr smiled at her, then absorbed the view.

They stood atop the conical tower on a perfectly flat surface. Four paces that way, and they'd fall off. At the center sat a black globe three meters across, balanced on an impossibly small point for its size. Must have some kind of support pillar, Pehr guessed.

To his left, the crater dipped away and back up. Pehr could just see hints of what lay beyond: Boulders of ice, sparkling rays from the blast, distant hills and ridges. Mists that looked as unearthly as anything he could imagine clung in the crevasses and shallows; the pod's landing-area now glowed like a small volcano, bubbling and seething, fog and gas spilling down into the trench and running like a river to the lake below. Eyes was still making his way around the shore.

Overhead, Neptune loomed as big as Earth from low orbit, filling a quarter of the sky, all blues and banded near-whites. He couldn't discern any of the famed mining stations.

Pehr looked to his right and caught a glimpse of metal and glass beyond the icy boulders that lined the crater's rim.

"Is that the city?" he asked Janus.

"It must be," she answered. "Don't comm them just yet, though. First, let's spend a little time here with something crafted by alien hands. Power down your card."

"Completely? But what if they try to comm us?"

"Don't you remember what Miru said? Your card has to be off in order for the object to work on your mind."

"How was he talking to us, then?" Pehr asked.

"Subvocalizer. Up until about 30 years ago, NKK didn't automatically implant full-3VRD commcards into its citizens the way EarthCo does. Too expensive, they said. But when even AMRCO started doing it, NKK got embarrassed and offered its citizens 3VRD upgrades at low cost. I imagine Miru must've chosen to keep his subvocalizer. Lots of them did. Didn't you pay attention to edufeed?"

"I'm powering down," Pehr said, feeling the dunce, wishing he had worked harder at school subjects.

And, just like that, St. Paul's Cathedral sprang up before him, surrounded by a slick, black wall that enclosed the equivalent of several city blocks. Bright sun lit the tan stone as if he were back on Earth. He staggered back.

The cathedral faced him: Two towers—the right one bearing the clock—rose high above the wall, as did the broad dome; ornately crowned pillars defined each level, statues stood at nearly every corner, and wide steps leading inside were barely visible beyond the outer wall. The massive cathedral inspired in Pehr all the awe he had felt when he first saw its 3VRD during Susahn's wedding preparations, the unimaginable effort required to build such an place when those who did so could use only the energy of men and animals. And pleasant memories of Susahn floated across the surface of his mind, of the early years when he still believed she loved him.

"God damn," he muttered. He got hold of his senses before he fell off the tower—remembering he still stood atop a narrow cone of ice and not on an endless plain that seemingly surrounded him. Even the sky had altered, now swirly colors that concentrated especially at the horizons. Pehr set the grappling-hook and an adhesion-piton onto the ground at his feet. He glanced at Janus.

Her eyes met his, glowing with joy. Her lips moved, but Pehr couldn't understand the tinny sound that actually passed through the air to him. He leaned toward her and pressed his helmet against hers.

"You see it too?" she asked.

"St. Paul's Cathedral."

Her eyebrows dipped momentarily. "Interesting. When Liu Miru found this place, he saw a Buddhist temple with his card off. You see St. Paul's Cathedral, and I see the Great House of Aldebaran; silly, yes, I know. It's the castle where the ruling class of the Benignus. . . . Never mind."

"Oh, I know what you mean," Pehr said. "I watched that series a few times. Aliens. The Benignus were the intelligent aliens who lived on . . . I can't remember the world, but their sun was Aldebaran."

Janus looked so lovely when she smiled. He wished she would always smile.

Triton 8: Janus Librarse

"Do you suppose a real race of Benignus made this? Oh, that's stupid," she said, immediately after the question. "That was a fictional show." She went on:

"It seems we all see something, well, holy—not in the religious sense, god forbid, but in the secular. Numinous, I guess." *Holy, shit*, she thought. *Why bring something like religion into a sacred place like this?*

Janus turned her attention back to the Great House. Lined in a row like stone ribs, three parabolic arches rose 30 meters over an untended garden of red- and yellow-blossom tigercherry trees, multicolored flowering shrubs, tall palm-like trees, and an assortment of fruit-bearing vines—plants from all across the world. Pebbled paths weaved through the growth, and one or two Benignus—diminutive, humanoid, hairless—could be seen pruning plants from the walkways. Brass steps and railings edged the arches. The arches suspended the Great House proper, a series of concentric circles stacked atop one another 25 levels high. Each level served an individual locality of Benig, though everyone attended meetings in the Grand Chamber at its center. Dozens of glass-domed rooms sat upon each level, and a large, pearl-colored dome crowned the structure and provided light for the Grand Chamber.

Janus felt the presence of alien intelligence all around her, their actual physical heat and sweat. Nothing humans could make could ever fill her with such emotional and intellectual delight. Despite standing amid a fictional setting, this was real, in some unquantifiable way.

"To me," she explained, "the Benignus represent the ultimate society. They had no laws because they didn't need them. Only after NKK traders arrived and began robbing them did they need to impose rules. Even to save everything she owned, no Benignus would fight the traders. That's how the scriptwriters contrived to get EarthCo involved. Save the ignorant aliens from the enemy."

"I didn't watch the show much," Pehr said. "But I understand. Let's find the way inside. Miru found an entrance, right?"

"Yes. We need to follow the wall until we see an irregularity. Miru kept his hand on the wall as he walked; I don't know how important that is, but we'd best do exactly as he did."

"Damn, Janus," Pehr said, smiling that crooked smile of his, "you're the first best friend I've had since I was a kid. Feels good to go exploring with a best friend."

Janus smiled at him and stepped back. She, too, felt giddy like a girl. She remembered Miguel; she never really loved him—*But I don't even know what love is*, she thought. *He was just my best friend. He felt good to sleep beside at night, and he didn't ask for sex more than once every few months. God knows he's happier with Rachel.*

Janus shook her head and smiled at the memory and at the present. What had happened to the hate? *Ah, there it is*, she thought. It was simply buried beneath joy and discovery. They began to walk.

After only a few minutes, something jerked at Janus' waist and she had to stop. She looked down and saw that the rope had tightened. Pehr stepped next to her and touched helmets.

"We've run out of cord," he said. "We can either take the precaution and stop every 50 meters, or we can detach and just stay close to the wall. Do you think we'll be safe just keeping against the wall?"

"Of course," Janus said. "Miru's suit camera recorded him walking around and around the artifact. He kept his hand on the wall—which was the physical surface of the artifact. We'll be safe enough. Cut us free."

Jack stepped back and released the carabiner at his waist and the rope fell to the ground, giving enough slack for Janus to do the same. When she stepped out of the loop of rope, she felt somehow more part of the exploration, more in touch with the Great House that stood before her than with the past that crouched behind.

They walked on. Jack moved more slowly without the rope, but soon his pace was back to normal. Before long, they hurred along the wall. Janus had the odd sensation of jogging in a tight circle—even though she seemingly moved in a broad arc. She felt giddy and walked even faster, overtaking Jack.

About the time her stomach was beginning to tighten with hunger—Why didn't we eat before we entered the escape pod?—Janus noticed that she was coming upon the front of the Great House once again. Now she burst into an awkward run.

And there it was.

A tap against the side of her helmet. "The entrance!" Jack said.

Janus turned her head in the glass globe to face him. Something was wrong. Something tugged at her consciousness; she wasn't ready to enter yet. Not yet, not while something still pursued her. She couldn't enter the most sacred of places while still tethered to the past. She couldn't drag crap in there with her; that would be like bringing the desire for something else into a lover's bed.

"You go ahead," she said. "I forgot something."

"In the pod?" Jack scowled. "Have you lost your mind?"

"Don't be a retro," Janus said. "I forgot something outside. You know, when we took off the rope. I've got to go get it."

"Now? Janus, just look!"

She took one step back from him and one step closer to the entrance. The wall seemed to melt in the shape of a two-meter arch, creating the image of an open doorway. But she saw no edges and not even an interior. Within the entranceway, earthen hues shifted and coalesced; Janus drew a sharp breath and shook her head as she began to feel herself drawn inside.

She turned to Jack and bumped helmets. "I'll join you as soon as I can. Go inside. If you don't, I'll not forgive you."

"You need a moment alone. I understand." He blinked once, slowly. "Don't forget this is what you want." He smiled and turned away.

Without so much as a hesitation, Jack walked into the entranceway. Janus couldn't really separate him from the roiling colors at first, and when she finally did, he was gone.

She sighed and flicked on her commline. Stars and Neptune threw up a sheet that blocked the Great House from view. Jack no longer stood near her, nor anywhere on the pillar. Janus smiled and shook her head, cherishing her nearness to the object; she lay both her hands adoringly upon its surface. Within, Jack waited.

A wispy wind hissed across the seal between Janus' helmet and collar-clasp. She turned away from the globe and faced the crater. There it was, the cyborg, halfway up the slope leading to the pillar where she and and object stood.

Now her vision narrowed so that she saw only the man-shaped form; the rest of the universe throbbed unseen at the edges. She held it at the center of her attention, fixing him as would a missile's targeting AI. In five minutes, it will be there, she told herself, tracing Eyes' trajectory; in ten, there. I will meet him in fifteen minutes. Janus initialized a program she never believed she would have to use; now was the time.

She walked a short arc around the globe, found the discarded rope and climbing equipment, and ran the rope through a carabiner as had Jack. The three-barbed hook hung easily from her belt. Janus looped rope around her waist until both ends were of equal length, bonded the carabiner to her suit, then set the piton into the ice and looped through its eye one end of the rope. Slowly, Janus descended the pillar, letting out only enough slack to allow her to take another step down. Though the gravity was minimal, a fall from such a height onto the ice and rock below could still injure or kill. Once she reached the crater, the cyborg was still ten minutes away.

"Come on, come on," she whispered to the figure as it slipped onto one knee. She smiled and handled the hook at her hip.

Janus just remembered to shut down her card when a flicker of light lanced across her vision; the burnout program was really beginning to accelerate now. Miguel, with his sad eyes, had brought home a small, yellow cellophane packet one day. "I bought this for you," he had said, "but don't ever use it, *vida mia*. I could never earn enough to buy you a new card."

"I'm sorry, dear Miguel. I can't destroy him while we fight on his battlefield. I've practiced killing a man for twenty years. Now is the time."

Occasionally, small pricks of electrical discharge directly into the soft mass within her skull interrupted her preparations. But she was ready in seven minutes. The card would be a lifeless jumble of synthetics by the time Eyes was within personal comm range. *Just let him go in there now,* she thought, and a painful smile creased her cheeks.

Janus picked up the hook by its handle and climbed a few meters up the slope of the crater, tossing a self-bonding piton at the end of the rope and using it to steady herself, as Jack had done. She found the spot she had chosen and began chopping a rough platform on which to stand.

A last painful crackle at the base of her neck, and she felt no more from her card. Eyes fell again, this time sliding back several meters before his frantic hands found sturdy cracks. She realized he had just tried to penetrate her card and had found only chaos.

"Stupid, filthy bastard," she whispered; droplets of saliva landed on the inside of her helmet. "I won't be killing you. You'll be doing it. Only a stupid bastard would have followed me. Come on."

And she waited. The cyborg's backslide earned her an extra few minutes, which she used to make some final preparations.

Transition 2: Liu Miru

Although feeling weaker—not physically, because that no longer had any value, but mentally, as if his thoughts were growing quiet—Miru began to see something.

He concentrated. No, not sight, he told himself. He made up a new term: *spectrasense.* By focusing every sense-receptor in his brain and coordinating them in an effort to observe his surroundings, Miru earned glimpses of things he couldn't really understand.

The process reminded him of a time when he was a boy, sitting on the tile floor of the Island's civic hall, where all the citizens were supposed to gather intheflesh once a month; even so, about half still appeared as 3VRDs. Rolling a ball along the seams between the black and green tiles, young Miru noticed that four of the rectangular black tiles together formed an anchor-shape. He smiled when he noticed that, and continued staring in order to feel the pleasure of discovery again. The anchor stretched wider, then formed into a box. The box sprouted tiles in all four directions, and then each sprout made a larger anchor, and each larger anchor became a great box, and so on until the box extended all around him and his mind reached overload. Then he found himself looking at only an anchor once more.

He felt that way again, although this time the pattern he was glimpsing was something much more complicated. Whereas the tiles formed a two-dimensional series of repeated shapes, this specrasense of his worked to discern something three-dimensional.

He tried to be logical yet open-minded when he came to this conclusion. *The only way to do any research here,* he thought, *is to accept anything. Down may be up,* he thought; *up is sideways. I must re-educate myself out of animal instincts. They are not useful here. They are hindrances.*

He cleared his mind and thought only of observing, shutting out all thought.

A tantalizing flash pierced Miru's mind, as of a city surrounding him, its internal structure a vast interwoven network of red cables or braces or skyways. Perhaps veins, he thought. But when he tried to put what he saw into a slot he understood, the image vanished.

After nothingness replaced the city, his mind continued to process the information. Now he remembered that it had smelled of copper and sweat, tasted of fish; he had brushed up against something warm and vibrating, and he thought he remembered a great chatter of distant voices and the sound of wind.

Once more he quieted his thoughts and tried to observe. After a certain time, he sensed what he labeled "the city" again, and again it vanished almost as soon as he perceived and identified it.

Time. *Time is meaningless here*, he told himself; humans think linearly because they live and evolved on the surface of a world. Hindered by gravity and a lack of wings and gills, we only recently began to stretch up to the sky and down beneath the water, and then only briefly. He thought of how Ryukyu Submerged Island had seemed like an entirely different object when viewed from beneath the waves; it became a metal and plastic bubble bobbing in the ocean, a mere ship like the thousands that arrived and departed every day from the rings of salt-crusted docks. Later, from an orbital craft's telescopic camera, it had looked to Miru like no more than a silver spot dimpling a thin sheet of greenish-blue.

He tried to think like that—in three dimensions.

A startled shout shattered his concentration. The sound that was more than a sound passed through him. He felt as if he might dissolve in its wake. Sound here, he realized, can be as deadly as a wind to a lighter's flame. He had to scurry mentally to keep himself in order; he had continually to point to places in his psyche and say, *That is me*.

Is someone there? Miru asked. The screaming persisted. As it trailed off, Miru found the energy to ask again.

Hello? The other responded with a question; the word seemed much louder than Miru's thoughts.

Are you the builder of this object? Miru asked.

No. My name is Pehr Jackson, the other said. *Who are you? What's happening in here?*

Miru was elated. He was also confused, since he couldn't perceive how the voice sounded, because he didn't really *hear* anything. He could not even identify the speaker's language. Yet he knew the words; the conversation was simply translated in his mind. *An alien was communicating with him!*

Miru again felt the old wonderment of the universe, the magic of childhood: stars glittering down through scattered light and sheets of fog and the orange haze emitted by the Island, tiny ancient lights unaffected by the byproducts of humankind; luminescent fish swarming through the black-stained waters near the Island; a grey and dying reef populated by a million little swimming and eating things—each of these alive against all odds, nature's unwillingness to be defeated without making the victor vanquished. And, trapped alone within an alien artifact that might never let him leave, Miru felt no fear; never again in his life would there be such an experience as this, so to die would be a small sacrifice to witness the awesome first-hand.

I am a human, he said with the greatest dignity he could manage. *My title is Project Hikosen Director Liu Miru. I have been studying this artifact.*

You're that TritonCo scientist, the one who told us about your find. Why can't I see you?

Miru now recognized the name. Pehr Jackson. Not an alien. He felt mildly disappointed. But at least he would now have a partner in exploration.

You are one of the EarthCo warship soldiers who were about to attack the project, Miru responded. *So you did not attack, after all, since you are here with me.*

*I'm *ashamed* to admit that we weren't able to stop our crazy bombardier from firing the torpedo, but we didn't damage the artifact. I'm sure you know that already, since you're still alive. Even so, I extend my deepest apologies.*

A brief pause. Miru was not ready to respond to an apology yet. What kind of captain cannot control his bombardier? He felt an old, creaky anger rise up between the two of them.

What happened to my body? Jackson asked. The voice sounded farther away. *I can't seem to . . . well, do anything. I can't move or see or anything.*

I'm trying to understand that myself, Miru answered. *Perhaps we can help one another. When you found the object, did you see my body?*

No. It may have been . . . vaporized. I didn't see any trace of your body. I assumed we both entered physically.

Miru didn't answer. He was too preoccupied by the word, "vaporized." *You say you can't see anything right now?*

I . . . I don't know. I thought, at first when I stepped through the wall, that I saw . . . I don't know. Something.

A city?

What? Jackson asked. *I can hardly hear you.*

A city, Miru repeated, directing his thoughts with as much energy as he could muster toward the speaker's locus.

Maybe a city. Where are you?

I'm afraid something is happening to me, Miru stated, still focusing his thoughts. *I'm afraid that remaining too long in here is dangerous. I seem to be fading. I'm sorry I cannot quantify what is happening to me except to say that I am mentally fading.*

And our bodies are—what? Gone?

I have never been inside here before, Miru said, somewhat irritably. *It seems that one entering the artifact is absorbed or otherwise dispersed. If my body is gone yet my mind is still active, that would be the only explanation. Perhaps this is, indeed, an organism and we are its prey.*

Nostalgia and sadness touched Miru. He had not been contacted by aliens; indeed, his companion in death was a man who, in more mundane situations, would be his enemy. Miru was dying, yes, he recognized that now. But that was not what caused him distress. Rather, he sensed that he stood overlooking a great precipice of knowledge. He had glimpsed the bridge that led to understanding—maybe more than that; maybe he had glimpsed understanding itself—but then he was alone again, alone and blind and senseless and dying. All for nothing. He could not contact anyone. He could not transmit what he had learned to the next explorer, giving him or her advance information on conditions within the object. He would die for nothing, like his parents. Like that gang-boy he had found floating among hungry, biting minnows beneath the Island waves; the boy had changed in death, had lost his power and terror and become a simple corpse. For nothing. Perhaps Miru's parents could have become great leaders in the world had they survived; perhaps the gang-boy would have grown up to teach other boys how to escape the grip of gangs yet remain safe and psychologically intact on the Island.

All for nothing. Nothing. The work on Luna, hundreds of hours spent coring and laying wire, nothing. Years spent analyzing 3VRD geologic data about dead, empty worlds, nothing. The great discovery of an alien artifact or organism on Triton, nothing. His whole life had proven to be nothing more than one long, meaningless chain of worthless effort. And how was anyone else different? They weren't. He realized that here, in a ravenous sphere on a barren and worthless world, all the millennia of effort exerted by billions of humans had amounted to nothing. A great vacuum of space engulfed him, stretching off into infinity, almost never encountering motes of matter as nothingness extended outward from him, the nothingness at the center of his nothing universe.

Those millennia of callused human hands chipping stone, casting bronze, driving spikes into steam-train railways, and finally operating flow-valves with 3VRD manipulators could have been the long springtime. But now winter would fall.

We found the artifact too early, Miru said. *Rather, it was time for us to find it, this, the bridge to transcendence revealed, but we've remained nasty children with holocaust toys certain to one day—intentionally or accidentally—destroy us. Here, all our potentialities could have been accessed. I see it now. And if we survive the coming war— and there will be war, my brother Jackson, Jackson the Destroyer . . . if we survive the beasts you've set loose, we will grow sleepy with age, and fear and ignorance and apathy will destroy what's left of our curiosity. And we will die. Here, here already we die. We cannot even understand this teaching tool they've given us—they the benevolent or pragmatic aliens. It's a teaching tool, don't you see? What else would it be. And our failure means our death, and our death will bring the fear and anger of those who knew we entered, and the teaching tool will ultimately be the seed of our destruction. It will be the teaching tool of the intelligent beetles, when their time comes. Or their destruction, as well.

We were not ready, he finished, his voice now barely noticeable in his own mind. Oh, it is not your fault, brother Jackson. No, I too am sorry. We die together. Witness the fall of the human race! The fault lies at the rough feet of our ancestors who never matured beyond the brutish nature of those who sired them. We stood briefly upon our collection of worlds, pondering the galaxy with minds barely sentient, before the cold reasoning of that galaxy devoured us. Observe!

And he began to laugh away the last of his energy, quick to be done with the whole, long, filthy mess. He felt the contamination of the entire human race upon his skin of his mind, and he was sick and in a hurry to be done with it.

Transition 3: Pehr Jackson

As Miru's words ran like voiceless messengers through the corridors of Pehr's mind, Pehr grew ashamed, then afraid, and finally angry. As Miru's words faded more and more into the hungry blackness, Pehr stretched himself toward the hopeless man. He would not give up, not now. He would not let Miru give up. He could not bear to think he would die alone, that he would be alone for eternity. And what would eternity be like? What comes next? EarthCo's careful cultivation of the gods of profit and security offered no comfort here. At the same time, he also knew every other human god would be powerless in this realm of alien gods. Anyway, Pehr had never sought comfort in the intangible. The only real comfort he had ever found came in the form of men and women and a little boy who had accompanied Pehr in a pocket into this alien place. Pehr seized upon the old comfort of that cloth boy, then reached out a mental hand to Miru.

He felt himself weaken a bit. If anyone were to ask to define how it felt, he couldn't have said. The mental image of himself shrank, his thoughts grew quieter, his sight grew dimmer—

I can see! he called to Miru.

What does it look like? Miru asked. His words seemed to come from only inches away—a purely figurative description—and were much louder and clearer.

It's, it's. . . Pehr attempted to but he could not describe what he saw, for when he tried to do so, his mind's eye promptly failed to see anything, and he couldn't remember how it—which he hadn't really seen—had looked.

But then he suddenly remembered, as if from his long-ago memory, a man in a spacesuit looking up at a black, starry sky. The man stood on the surface of a moon, Earth's Moon. Pehr somehow knew the man was wondering how many centuries would pass before men stood on worlds encircling alien suns.

Now Pehr was the distant stars peering across great expanses at the man, and Pehr saw the man's dark, quiet face and dark, questioning eyes. The suit was familiar: NKK issue. Without needing to ask, Pehr knew this was Miru.

His mind seemed to be operating more clearly now, without the distractions of flesh and neurons and headcard or any of its constant blabbering. No shows, no scripts. He was the captain of his own destiny, and he seemed, for the first time in his life, able to think. He seized on a sudden inspiration.

Who are you? Pehr asked, remembering Janus' question in the *Bounty*'s escape pod, and how the question had elicited such a clarification of himself. He could, again, see every blade of grass and lichen-covered crack of concrete and drop of blood of his life, a young woman's exquisite, retreating back, an expressionless face. . . .

Who am I? Miru said. *What—*

No, no; just think it without trying to talk. I can see you. Show me who you are.

Miru was silent.

Don't be afraid, Pehr said. *I think that's how this works. And I'll show you me, too. If we're going to survive in here, we'll need to cooperate. Did you notice how your voice is stronger? I did that.*

How?

I don't know, except that I noticed you were growing quiet and I still felt very strong. I wanted to hear you better, and it just happened. Show me who you are. Just do it. Just do whatever you need to do to show me who you are, just as I need to show you who I am, and we'll bust out of here. Don't try to tell me, just try to understand yourself. I think I just saw a little of you, like a clue. Do you understand?

It's illogical, Miru said.

Pehr noticed that, whatever he had seen—had he really seen a man in a spacesuit?—had fled from his mind. He had no mental image. Was he dying?

Do it now! Pehr demanded. *Your logic will kill you. If you die, I die, and I'm not ready no matter how grandiose you think it'll be to watch the fall of humanity. If this artifact is a teaching tool, why else would we be here together, blind and alone but somehow able to communicate, unless we're supposed to work together? Dammit, we've got to help one another.*

Something changed.

Pehr grew dizzy with disorientation. But then he saw a sort of landscape stretch out before him, and he remembered. He remembered where and who he was, and what was happening, because a fog seemed to lift from that landscape. The fog was a palpable blackness, it was nothingness and emptiness, it was a barrier to understanding.

Beneath the fog a man waited. This time, the man wore no spacesuit. He looked wise and gentle, but did not smile. He had the features of an Asian, of the enemy NKK soldier. But this was Miru.

Pehr's eyes opened, and so followed every other sense. And he felt he could cry, if he were a crying man.

The man disappeared but didn't; Pehr disappeared but didn't. They became the landscape, which was a man's life. The final feeling that quivered through Pehr was fear, but he knew that fear just came from ignorance and would destroy everything. So he opened his mind and shut off his thoughts and let worlds pour into him.

Transcendence A

Here and there, mists cleared, briefly but always long enough to see the scenes beneath the mists. It was as if the universe were a series of scenes, cast about randomly in a sea of mist that the mind defined as *utter nothingness*. But after experiencing a few of these scenes—not seeing, because he lived those scenes for as long as they had lasted in their original context—he recognized a greater scheme, an arrangement of the scenes into what he had first glimpsed as landscape. The universe unfolded more than three dimensions; scenes were scattered in a pattern that wove a greater whole, a sort of sphere of experiences composed of smaller or larger spheres within, each a moment or a year in duration, like floating worlds packed closely together.

The landscapes themselves—which together formed the worlds that created the greater picture—rose up around him as if he were there. A vast floating island, sharp rusted metals and glinting plastics, crowded the sky with towers and bridgeheads and countless wandering people. The island's walls melted away, and within he saw rooms smaller than those of the eighter.

Then the other he—for now he realized he was not Pehr Jackson or Liu Miru, but someone exponentially greater than either alone . . . the other he bounded down a long cement staircase, being careful to avoid the fourth one, where a bomb had exploded. And now he watched the spade-shaped bomb rise in a slow arc from the open hand of a teenaged boy with a snarling grin creasing his face, the bomb sailing like nothing more than a butterfly or wasp; other boys sitting on the steps, engrossed in a 3VRD game of Snatch, a young boy standing on a yellow patch of grass in the yard, the yard bordered by tall green weeds and vines that snarled themselves up the chickenwire fence that surrounded the eighter's yard, barbed wire dull rust topping the fence where one of the vines broke out in an oblivious cluster of purple grapes too small to eat except for the birds, which occasionally swooped down from the always-hazy sky with little patches of blue that shone occasionally, through which the sun yellow burned the skin so the little boy watching the bomb arc through the air.

Closer now, he had to wear special cream on his skin to not develop the cancer; and still the bomb sailed through the air, the birds seeming to reveal a kind of prescience, for they flew away just as the spade-bomb fell toward the steps where the teenagers now blinked because the younger boy had cried out to them, "Watch out!" over their commlines and out loud intheflesh; he watches them hurl their hard, lithe bodies over the sharp, broken, plastic edge of the staircase many meters from the ground; *thud-crack!* the bomb hits the steps and explodes, and a great white and brown cloud of dust and light flashes into the air, one boy suddenly crying out as a red streak leaps out from his cheek, the young boy named Pehr in the yard standing still and so furious he could run out into the street after the other boys who were racing away in their ground-car which bellowed a cloud of stinking methane-puff, as they called it; he swears to teach those boys to never again do that, not here, not to the boys who like him, not near his house or Teresa or Mom whom he loved more than everything in the world, himself included.

And another boy, same age no a little older and named Liu, running as fast as his feet could carry him along a banging gangway hovering above crashing waves below, the Island huge and ominous towering above him, he hears in his bones the massive creaking of its hull and infrastructure, sightless windows above glinting in the sunlight, almost a hundred meters of living and office space: "No, you must never go there and bother those important men and women," Mother explains, and the good teacher in his head who was transparent, really, although sometimes eventually he began to pull interest from the boy, especially after seeing the man who looked like Father in the water.

He runs as fast as he can, the Security woman chasing after him, "Stop, Liu! It's okay! We need to talk, stop"; but Liu running so hard that his lungs burn yes and his eyes, but the burning eyes keeps them from running wet; but wet, yes, and wet, he loves the wet, far from the stupid gang-boys who only laugh and hate but don't know anything, running, they only do it because they're afraid, too; Liu running; soon the shiny, grey plastic plank juts out from the gangway—he looks down, below his feet the slits in the metal gangway show thousands of men and women and boys and girls walking or standing

226

but all quiet maybe except laughing and one or two crying, always those few who cry who don't know how to make sense of anything, whom Liu always felt a sympathy for since he couldn't understand Father; but Father asleep in the water, oily whitish froth like a cloud around him like the dead boy floating underwater a year later, and no no no, not now, not yet until he talks to me and really takes me intheflesh to see the Great Temple of Mahabodhi; we only saw it 3VRD although yes Father it is very beautiful, I see the shiny birds landing on the roofs and bald men in orange robes chanting, yes, I love this and I love you Father and Mother, why don't you hear me can you hear me have you ever heard me?

But he knows better than to say this aloud, because then maybe they'd never go anywhere or ever say yes we love you, yes let's see the whole world and every world in the Solar System yes intheflesh; an open clamshell on the plank overlooking the sea, the plank with an electric winch and plastiweave cable hanging from it, clamshell dry with the fibers of meat inside hard and yellowish and knife-marks in the shell where some poacher who had stolen it from the sea had cut it open, nobody eats real clams whole, at least now here on the gangways; he looks down at the waves crashing but so quiet actually, everything grows so quiet, even the Security man with silver bulletproof overall clanging along the metal planking is quiet, and the air is quiet as his legs go slack and he falls to the water again like those years ago, even the splash is quiet; he falls again in the air, thick and soft through his hair and pulling at his loose shirt, watching so slowly as he falls the clouds sweeping the smog from the sky, the smog rising up from the fume-chambers so high above the shiny towers, a few windows passing him in his fall, one face peering out but not seeing Liu Miru, instead maybe a distant war somewhere; you shitless mannequin—angry thoughts just before splashing quiet beneath the waves—loving the wars; this is a war, he thinks, missiles shrieking through the electric air booming the soil ripped open like a wound, he crashing through the waves like the waves crashing against the Island, which won't last forever; beneath the green and sunlight water again, watching a million years pass and salt chewing at metal, blood filling the empty chambers, blood and fire and he sees forever into the future until no Floating Island, just a sunken catacomb of fish-chambers, no Mother; she on the waves, too, swimming muscleless with her husband although he swam weeks prior; she never spoke to him, not really, so why does she swim with the dead? don't think such things, she love, he love; doesn't matter in death, always death, death everywhere except for the fish who die and me too but not yet; no, not yet.

Live dammit! And another scene flashed to life in the multifaceted gem of landscapes in the mists. A grown man-boy laughing and ordering, "Fire torpedoes!" which scream hot sparkling exhaust along the external hull of the spacecraft, Jackson the Captain, Captain Jackson for the first time ordering torpedoes fired, impacting silently 100 kilometers away across blank space, sleepy and ravenous space, the dichotomy the same as that of the men who kill each other for the pleasure of virtual viewers, billions of viewers entranced on their living room couches, no whiskey just Captain Jackson, loving and hating and killing and laughing, laughing, the control cabin of the corvette rancid with sweat and fear, the smell of antiseptics and burning insulation, smoke burning the eyes, but not death! never death, death the enemy and the friend; this is the path to forget:

A beautiful woman at home, asleep intheflesh always but awake for everyone 3VRD, she lied at first lied always, oh how I loved her . . . see the love? this is love, a blinding of the past, washing of the soul, all words, only words, no I don't know what is love; Megan asleep breathing softly soft hair soft buttocks soft voice muttering hours before, "never leave you," ha never, never say never, never say die, firing missiles and laser cannons at Enemy: NKK, AMRCO, thugs in the street, oh yes and the Crusades continued when on the ground later—adult gang, the Boyoviky Internationale, man standing on the St. Louis street corner, Pehr strutting as he had always planetside would never again without a lie in each fall *clump* of his EConaut boots, *clump*, the Boyovik watching Pehr with slit-eyes, brown hair flat on scalp oiled greased, we greased 'em, electromag weapons ripping the night, Moon yellow through sparse trees and mountains of skyscrapers, Pehr oh weakling fearful, I hate old self screams, yes and nothing, no brave Crusades as when younger, no; but lied to Janus, the Crusades continued, shameful coward Crusades in space, roar of rockets and scream of missiles, eliminate NKK and no more gangs or street thugs or death, EarthCo the great kind friend, fight and release and death and, oh, I don't know why I do it anymore.

A shift as he fell up and away from the worlds of memory.

Time, black and heavy against the skin and smelling of dust, passed.

He found himself seated on the edge of a landscape, legs hanging over like a little boy leaning on a railing overlooking the sea or straddling a sewerpipe over the river, water running or crashing, both smelling the same of rotting fish or decaying weeds or ammonia or worse, the mists like the sea or a river; Miru remembers the dolphin-swim he made through his life when he first entered the artifact.

"Learning tool," he corrects himself.

"Hello, Liu," Pehr says.

They turn away from the island-scenes floating through the mists, islands of a lifetime, of two lifetimes intermeshed somehow, both the same but different; "I'm like you," one said; the other said "I am you"; swimming, the landscape as they call it in 3VRD language, headcard terminology, *landscape*, but this so much more, a million, a billion, near-infinite moments of lives strewn across the 4D space of a hollow globe; they smile at one another, wordless, understanding. Pehr has green eyes like deepwater sea and curly brown hair.

And now it was the first moment still, Liu Miru's memories flooding through Pehr Jackson, Pehr's memories flooding through Liu; the deluge continues until both understand, wearing them down yet girding them up with the knowledge, *I am not alone.*

Pehr hears Liu think, *Or is it me thinking? We are the scarred clam on the plastic plank with the electric winch over the sea. We are the knifed-open shell, bare and drying in the fierce sunlight of humanity.*

No. That is only the fearful, isolated, lonely shell. And not a clam. We, all of us—do you hear the voices? We are not alone, billions of others—but I do not know who they are—

we are the oyster. Outside the artifact, we are the oyster. Not a clam but an oyster. When we enter, rather than gaining a shell, our physical surface is smashed away, vaporized, leaving exposed the hurt and lonely and fearful and longing child, the child seeing all the wonder and magic in the universe, the love buried in the electronic hearts of our parents, yes, and those others when we bump into love elsewhere; all the barriers here fall away, the shell crumbles in the fierce light of omniscience—Are we really omniscient?—Of course not, only all knowing of ourselves, each other; the shell is discarded, and all that remains is what lay within. We are only the soft and fragile and wonderful thing, the maybe damaged yet stronger by being damaged thing. Plus the hidden treasure. Yes, the hidden treasure within the ugly shell within the folds of self, the treasure formed by years of suffering and fighting the abrasion successfully.

"Successfully is the key."

They are back, side by side, upon the edge of one scene, surveying scenes of themselves drifting to near-infinity. There runs the blind boy, the even-blinder man, the almost-empty adult. Oh, how small we were then.

"Yes."

"So we are survivors."

"Yes."

"What is my pearl?"

And the question sweeps them off and away. Analysis will not work here, no, only experiential knowledge you cannot quantify, *Yes I see, we go again.*

With this new drive for quiet understanding, mutual understanding helping one another—*We are the same but different; Yes, but stronger than together outside, stronger than a million men, don't you see?*—this new drive constructs new dimensions upon the previous landscape of tiered scenes like playthings from this outside/inside viewpoint, like toy soldiers only they cry when they are sad and skin their knees when they fall on the metal grating.

A new thing emerges, the globe of bracings or veins or skyways that Miru the Lone had seen when he had first entered the artifact. He and he, I and I watch the globe sprout spans from end to end, so almost infinite but I yes and he can see the ends touch the ends, we see forever yet right here; *What does it mean? Be quiet and understand.* The skyways had faded with the question but now they return. Immense and minute tubes link the scenes to one another, throbbing as if veins, boys and men running through the tubes— now transparent with their eyes closed, their hands over their ears, their mouths sewn shut with bullets and their hands gloved in thick rubber; only their headcards show them the world now, yes they can see that since those boys and men are he and I, me and him, we run and laugh and cry but we are not here, we are not alone. So the globe returns:

Universe-spanning tubes like branches stretch from lucid yesterday into the fog of tomorrow, extending from one end of the opalescent curvature of the sphere to the other, millions of branches or veins or skyways, sometimes linking with one another, complicated webweavings, but a few stretch all across without touching others. A ladybug, pale orange with black spots and waving antennae, kicking legs as it climbs a yellow-green stalk of uncut grass; only this in the whole universe at the same time as the branches. *You see, it is a city and it is not.*

He and he, I and I looked up from our perch and saw the tops of my head running with Teresa along the cloudy river, Captain Downward in his destroyer racing beside us. Down is up. I laugh, joy filling my heart. He laughs. This is true joy, is it not? To go where nobody has ever gone. Certainly not me.

Not me.

Look there:

Finally, a killer whale. *How could I have forgotten? See, it was at 17 years of age.* She rises slow from the frothing waves like a mountain from the earth, white and black and eyes that know, she is lonely, yes you can see it now even though it is decades ago, you are here; she exhales water and steamy breath, then gulps air as she sinks back beneath steel grey water. *That is why I forgot; no one must know. She will live or die dependent upon my silence. We all live or die.*

"That is such a simple thing. But I understand. Words mean nothing and everything here."

"No," Liu—he is beside me now—touches his smooth forehead with a hand, the fingers creased and tan with pigment, not from exposure to sun, "no, not here the artifact. Here, in the mind. My mind, your mind. We are different now. We are only mind, but we two form a greater mind."

"How?"

Again, the globe fades, the scenes fog over, and only one scene remains in all the universe. Time—seconds or centuries—passes. The slack face, perhaps slightly tense even in death, the edges of his mouth turned down; the boy I murdered.

"No, you did not murder."

"You're technically right; I did not murder. But I caused him to be murdered."

"We all cause murders in our inactions. Murder is a constant, it is everpresent. We both know murder firsthand. We are all murderers, if you wish. But you and I are not murderers as you mean it."

"I am not alone."

"I am not alone."

Time passes, like water across the skin, cool and soothing, wind through the hair with a wordless voice that even here is cryptic, constellations of crystalline stars twinkling in the turbulence. Now daytime, long ago. *Hiss*, a vivid orange leaf rides the wind, cracking as it lands in Teresa's dark hair. She laughs and pulls it out, careful not to smash it. Two days later, she brings it to me in a glass jar. A year later, the glass jar lives in the eighter and not me.

"I know what I am made of," I say.

"You are thinking murder again."

"No. I mean the shell, see? There, you understand. Do you feel me understanding you? I would have been afraid of this feeling before I came here, but not now. The shell is hateful, ugly sometimes."

"Also lonely and sad."

"Afraid and hopeless."

"Harsh, anxious, careless, hardened—"

"We have not been hardened."

"In him, for a time."

"You mean the scene. Right. Hard is sometimes. The oyster shell must be hard sometimes, at least during its duration in the world outside here, at least before entering."

"Hateful, self-pitying."

"Withdrawn."

"Unimaginative, uncreative, unexcitable, uninquisitive, unintelligent."

"Unlikeable, unkind."

"But it is not all the dust and sand of emotional demolition; now the pearl."

Again the sphere that was once a city, a landscape, a sea of islands in the mist; the sphere appears, glowing opalescent, veined with experience, dense with memory and emotion, alive with love and hate and hope and dreams; the pearl packed inside with smaller pearls:

One night with Megan, asleep perfect beside me, her every breath priceless, the room quiet and twilit, dust tracing the paths of aircar headlights as they pass and shine through the window; *I can't say in words how much I loved her that moment.*

"But I understand."

"Yes, of course."

At the end of a long day's sweating in tight-fitting pressure suits, we sit down at the table we had made from a cable spool. Jon Pang and I. We hear then-just-Mister Dorei, later President Dorei, seal the inner airlock door to the pressure vessel. Pang unclasps his helmet and pulls it off, then wipes his stubbly head with gloveless hands, showing me the sweat. The great scientist laborer. He laughs, I laugh. The lighting comes from a single light-emitting gas-tube, leaning against one wall. The walls were antiseptically clean when they left Earth years ago, but now they are stained, and in one place a hand-shaped clump of gear grease stands up like bas-relief, an artifact of passing humanity. Pang has a wonderful smile. He looks at you when you speak, smiles at lame jokes, speaks from his heart whenever the occasion for such talk arises. Mister Dorei removes his own helmet, nods to us, steps through the room to another, where he falls immediately into a snore so loud Pang says it must rattle his teeth. We speak long into the night, well beyond the point where fatigue should put us to sleep, but it is like now. *It is a pearl, you see.*

"This is a pearl."

"They are all pearls."

"Even the bad ones?"

"I think especially the bad ones."

"They make you stronger."

"The black ones make you appreciate the shiny pearls. I think we are pearls as well as oysters. But when I think, it all falls away. See?"

The inside of the globe is again awash in sheets of mist.

"But watch, I know how to make it come back right away."

And there it is, billions of motionless instances of Pehr Jacksons and Liu Mirus, each the mote of a moment, and billions of others intersecting their lives like a great cloud of pearly dust. *But I cannot see beyond the moment of them; they are not part of the pearl.*

"But for a moment."

"A moment's pearl is perhaps more beautiful than all these," Pehr says, stretching his hands to include the countless scenes floating around them.

"Yes, but they are each moments. They are the same, only more numerous."

He and he, I and I feel the warmth of pure camaraderie, sitting here side by side, overlooking our lives. Now that the emotional crush of hidden memory has faded a bit, the scenes begin to pass like friendly vessels filled with familiar faces, telling familiar stories, some sad, some glorious. The need to escape has passed. *I feel nothing here but the desire to drink this forever. Why did I want to escape? I'll tell you why: There will be no more pearls added to this wealth if we stay forever. Also, we must spread the word, we must tell the whole of our people about this; there is nothing ever or will be as important. Can you imagine—?*

And then something alien and ugly impinges on the serenity and purity of the myriad landscape-city. A body kicks and shakes its limbs and screams and loses its bowels. It is naked, and just then Pehr and Liu realize they, too, are naked. They simply hadn't noticed until now, when the newcomer's nudity glares like something as ugly as a dead whale carcass bounding along the sandy bottom of the sea.

Transcendence B

"Eyes!" Pehr shouted. All was darkness again, except for the two of them and the intruder.

"How did he get here?" Miru asked. He turned away from the seemingly drowning man, rather distant from them, and frowned as he questioned Pehr. He knew Eyes now as if he'd known him as long as Pehr had.

"I don't know." Pehr watched the man kick and scream suddenly not the new man he was a moment ago. *Where have the pearls of wisdom gone? What do I do?*

"What are you doing here . . . Lonny," he asked.

The flailing man continued to scream and cry and kick. Then his screams rose in pitch until the man mutated into a ball, a bundle of skin and hair and cramped scenes that would not separate, mangling themselves as they writhed to separate, a boy with red streaks of blood up and down his arms as an older man, *Daddy, that's Daddy, what's Daddy doing with the scalpel? I don't want the arms, Daddy, why do you cut why do you kiss why do you push the icy-cold steel against the skin; oh it burns it's so hotcold—*

Salty and copper blood as I and he and they crash against the *No, no! I can't show you fucking goddamn you; a tall man with a retro top hat, Not retro you see, manycarded assimilator; Oh, yes, what a setup; 3000 BWs complete 3VRD, 100 simultaneous—*

Pluck my strings, in a feedbar a young girl straddling my leg, her crotch so hot and damp on my pantleg; *No dear, no sweetums, I'm the one who asks; smoke fills the air, cough, thank you Daddy, I can't stop going to you Daddy, but the lungs, the lungs yes they make the air taste like wine, but they hurt in the smoke, they burn in the noontime smog; smoke of hashish—Who's the retro? I'll give you retro, but the thick muscles on his arms pulse and the 3VRD tattoos flicker as he swings at the chromed steel barrail he thinks is me; Ha-ha-ha! Here's a program to make you taste glass for the first time—*

Again a jarring sceneshift, but not shift at all, they overlap and swirl together, mists clogging the actions of the boy who sits in the middle of his living room watching Daddy with a dozen other men on the floor, Daddy taking little parts of their skin they don't notice the skin gone pinky wet on the bottom pale on top, *Oh Daddy it stinks; Daddy can't you hear me? can't you hear me? can't you hear me?—*

Slam another scene, now his and my and their heads throbbing, *Stop it Lonny, you're hurting yourself, you're hurting us; you to relax and flow who you are to us here. Blast! Do you know what he did to me and you? Of course, I saw your whole past, brother Pehr. Of course. Shut up and get the fuck out of my head!*

"See him fall apart," I say. *Who am I? I am I.*

Eyes is a crackling sphere within the larger sphere of I and I. Eyes is compact, hiding, the landscape of his life crumpled into a ball that cracks and disperses in pain we spectrasense.

The screaming, the pain, oh yes we feel it too.

Help me, young Lonny pleads. He is the youngest Eyes—not vindictive. He is suddenly different, you can feel it. I don't hate him, how can I hate him. I never hated him, only pity. Janus hated him. Is Janus still alive?

Eyes, what happened to Janus?

And *crash*, Eyes peels open with the sound of a tree shattering from a lightning bolt.

I'm so sorry Cap'n Jack; no, she's still alive sleepwalking to the city, you see? I see. I'm so sorry, so sorry Daddy—

Another scream. I and I nearly shatter, I can feel myself weaker every moment, what is a moment here? it is eternal, oh god don't make me feel this eternally.

See inside me? Why did I follow you, why did I go inside the arcade? Look at me, help me. Help me Cap'n Jack!

I see his sad boy eyes and it is real, here everything is real, but then the boy shatters and out spew landscape upon landscape, but they're too tightly bound angry terrified together to see clearly.

You've got to show yourself for me to help you, I say.

You can't see in me. I'm scared. I can't let anyone see. I'm sorry. He's still soft, but rotting-soft. I and I see that.

Another explosion, and the landscapes each rip open, some unseen hand pulling away the bark of Lonny Marshfield—He's not an oyster; I see he's not, he's a rotten tree. *I'm sick inside, yes, help me! Help me!*

The bark falls away, baring the core. *Oh, god,* out spill shiny black beetles and grubworms and termites, red ants and maggots and cockroaches, the pulpy mush that was once wood, bored full of holes for insects to travel and eat, eat me away inside, *Yes right, I put you there; it can't support the rest of the tree, starting to tip; see how it wasn't always sick? See the sapling within?*

A boy again, the sad-eyed one. Walking intheflesh with Mommy and Real-Daddy along the ocean. *We live in Boston, see the glass gleaming skyline? No smog here, no, we keep our city clean!—I listen to my edufeed: We use only electrics in Boston, fellow Citizens! No, stop that, that doesn't belong here*; Mommy and Daddy and I are walking, beetles creeping scrabbling along underfoot—no, not here; the scene stabilizes.

Mommy and Daddy and I intheflesh on a woodgrain plastic dockway that lines the ocean, smelling of salt and fish and garbage, but that's not Boston's garbage; Mommy tall and slender with slack face flat breasts, and Daddy tall and slender with sleek hands kind eyes, always those eyes that looked at me as if they saw something beautiful, even though I am not a pretty boy, see? but Mommy watches me with her tight lips, her eyes sometimes smiling at Daddy; I am eight, yes eight; Daddy's eyes smiling at me; and thundercrack, ten thousand fragments of sharp steel whistle through the air, the bomb shatters the storefronts that face the ocean and the woodgrain plastic dockway; screams and bellows and laughter, yes even laughter though it is not mine; no, my voice cries *Daddy! Daddy!* Daddy with the crying chest and stomach, crying red tears and Mommy's eyes large with terror and two hours later with rage; *Boy, why did it have to be him and not you? What will I do with a boy when all I wanted was my Glen?*

Daddy smiling even as his chest and stomach wept blood, oh I couldn't cry because Mommy cried enough for a thousand boys to cry, but inside I know it is my fault, later she tells me so; from then on I know it's true; see Mommy? See how I play Daddy? Daddy with the beautiful hands that sew up people's flesh intheflesh when bombs shatter storefronts, only who will sew up the surgeon's wounds when the surgeon is dead? I am Daddy, see me as Daddy? See me, Mommy, as I make the incision? no you don't, because I know you are with Grandma, old fart-stinking Grandma on the farm with no feed server, I don't need you, I don't need Grandma, I don't even need Real-Daddy because New-Daddy is here with me, he and the feedrapture man whom I program to be Other-Daddy, and though Other-Daddy hurts me sometimes I deserve it, right Mommy? yes I will be New-Daddy; see how I know where to cut? see Mommy? see how I am punished for not dying? Will you love me now? Why does this disgust you; I thought you wanted Daddy back. Where are you Mommy? Mommy? Daddy!

And the scream rises in pitch until it shatters and the scene dissolves into mist.

"Let me help you!" I and I cry, I want to save the boy from the man, but he pulls farther away, the boy gone now and only the mask of another, older boy and New-Daddy and Other-Daddy who are not Daddy who is dead; who is dead? I had forgotten all this, oh it was gone but now it is returned, it burns. . . .

"Oh, god, it hurts."

"How do we help him?"

"You can't be afraid, Lonny," I and I say.

And now I can sense it, he is at the critical turning-point, he's revealed himself beyond the barrier of oyster-shell or tree-bark; yes, tree-bark, since his shell was destroyed in the blast, he never tried to rebuild, or couldn't; how was he different? This is the turning-point, can't you feel it? the point when he's fully aware of his uncoveredness.

For a moment the boy reappears, pleading with pain wrinkling his face. "I'm so sorry for everything, Cap'n Jack. I'm sorry, Miru. Please help me. I won't be bad anymore, can't you see I won't?"

But then the man smacks the boy aside, the boy dissipating into mist, I and I watch his terribly knowing eyes fade, he howling terror as he falls to cells and amorphous spreading only mist not real anymore, gone; the man backing away, horrified, violated, retreating into the irretrievable emptiness of deep space, the mists enveloping him, closing in he can't fight them off, his landscapes whipping around and around, orbiting the retreating figure like moths around a flickering bulb, now some colliding with others, galaxies of pain and hatred, some shattering into mist.

I hurt you instead, at another feedbar with blue neon and 3VRD projections so thick of crowd you cannot see me until I am in you and you are me and we collapse braindead; *Is that good now Mommy? Do you forgive me now that I have killed me?* No answer so another, this time in the grocery store freezer section, robots and servonts gliding up and down the aisles, sacrifice retro fool who does not order delivered food, deserves to be me, deserves to feel the sharp shards hot blood cold glass rough plastic woodgrain boardwalk by the sea salty and fish-wet as he smiles drowning drinking the ocean dry but his lungs stop first; *Do you forgive me now Mommy?* No answer so again, this time in the middle of Pershing Street full daylight, falls like discarded nut-hull, this time dead and how it fills me up; soon no more Daddy, no more Mommy, Other-Daddy dies my hands wet and salty with his red tears gut gushing along the blade smiling me forgetting overlaying programs overlay forget forget forget; the body incinerator warming the apartment during teeth-sharp December winds. *Daddy is dead. I am dead, and born again new. Stop looking. I see you two looking, you cannot see because I have not seen for so long get out!*

I and I grow sad and sick and desperate, though we now realize we can do nothing to save the boy from the man. He is gone, forever. We simply witness this collapse, then the skeletal cry as emotional and mental bones crack and shatter to dust in the sudden nakedness, the brutal honesty of barriers-down communication. Revelation destroys Lonny as an incinerator destroys a snapstick or stimgum wrapper.

Then the sound of a great wind tearing loose a forest, branches cracking and roots ripping from the earth. The landscapes spin faster and faster, shrinking as they fall upon themselves like a nebula into a black hole; the sound of vacuum replacing mass, the sound of nothingness devouring that which could not withstand close scrutiny.

I am nothing, are the last words as there never was a Lonny Marshfield, not just gone but as if never was. I and I feel the last twinge of life, the last part of him who wanted to live, and it is love, *All I've ever wanted is love, and forgiveness, teach me love.* But that is just the boy fighting to return, the real he doesn't want it, and his fangs sever the slip of skin connecting him with I and I.

Quiet again.

Our landscapes float lazily back into view, and now new ones appear, but we don't need to see those again. We just lived them.

"It's time to go."

"Right over there," Pehr said, pointing along a certain skyway or tube or vein. He realized he knew all along, only he couldn't understand it until just now.

"We need to leave."

"It'll eat us up, too."

"No. Only we can destroy ourselves."

"But staying in here too long makes you weak. Can't you feel it?"

Yes, I can feel it. I and I, since we are the same and we are different, which is the only way we can move here . . . I and I rise to our feet and enter one of the skyways. Without having to walk any distance, it opens right before us, long and round with a flat clear floor; it is clear, so I look one last time back at the landscapes of our lives. The mesh of corridors know where we wish to go; rather, we know where we wish to go, and this knowledge allows us to make the trip.

The moment-memory of little boy Lonny waves goodbye. Still those terribly knowing eyes. Dead. *But you'll always be alive here,* I say, touching my forehead with a finger. The boy turns away.

And, without any noticeable transition, I am no longer I and I, and I am no longer in the pearl.

Triton 9: Janus Librarse

Janus blinked as sunshine broke the horizon's black curtain; first the sky had warmed to purple—just a tiny oval of horizon—then dull red, and then the pinpoint sun began to rise. Glass domes shone in the slanting rays, and she knew she had to reach them soon, very soon. She didn't question why. It didn't matter. She was needed there. That was the way into the artifact. Pehr needed her. Miru needed her. She needed to get inside the artifact, too.

Eyes, she thought, *the cyborg. What had happened to him?* She couldn't remember. She remembered standing on the sloping dish of the crater, just behind the tower where the artifact had been, waiting for him. She would punish him. But then he had slid again, just as he reached her, and didn't stop sliding until his flailing body submerged in the chemical lake. A great gust of gas rose up from where he sank, but soon even that last trace of him had vanished. She remembered checking her card to see if he had planted a program, to see if he had really drowned. She remembered smiling in a savage, painful, almost guilty way when she found her card dead, as expected. He had tried to enter, she recalled, and her card had held him as it burned itself out. As planned.

She regretted not having had a hand in the cyborg's death, but felt vaguely relieved. What would it have been like to snag his suit with the hook, to watch his blood boil in the near-vacuum and freeze in the near-absolute-zero? She remembered how Jack still felt, after so many years, about killing. Yes, she was relieved.

"There," Janus muttered to herself. A black orb glinted in the morning sunlight. The artifact. She had watched it launch as if under power. So it was a spaceship of some kind.

Her boots crunched in the brittle ice. Such a world! With the sunrise, the winds had accelerated, gusting at times enough to force her to lean into them. Yet so thin that when they died down, she nearly fell onto her face in the blue and pink ice, dirty with interplanetary dust and erupted mud. Long, bright rays of ice pointed in all directions away from the crater, sparkling like beacons. She followed one that led, only a kilometer away now, to an airlock. That would be her first stop. In there, Jack needed her. Why? She couldn't remember. Must be the cold or the shock of all that had happened during the past hours. But if he needed her, she would put off her entrance into the artifact or spaceship until she gave him the help he needed. She would find out what she needed to do when she found him. An image of a prone Jack: white gurney beneath him, lopsided smile across his beautiful, lonely face; bandage around his head, arm in a sling. She smiled; she was needed.

As she walked, Janus' mind was quiet and peaceful. Expectant. Only good, hopeful thoughts passed through her mental passageways, like messengers bearing good news. What would the inside of an alien spaceship be like? *Oh, don't speculate; you couldn't know.* She quieted her mind and walked.

And now her gloved handed spun an airlock handle. And now the outer door sprang open, and now she was inside, closing the outer door; a red light in a wire fixture lit the tiny room as air began to cycle through the 'lock, and then the inner door opened.

Janus met the glares of two dozen eyes, men and women packed into a room scarcely larger than the *Bounty*'s bridge. They were silent, surely trying to communicate via commcard.

"I'm here to help," she said aloud.

Suddenly, something clicked at the back of her skull. Janus realized what had happened.

More voices than she could identify shouted in her head. Her commcard had woken up. Janus performed a quick search and discovered that the commcard had never been damaged in the self-destruct, nor had the command module of her citizen's headcard, nor had any of the hardwiring or powercells. Nothing organic had died. All she had done was knock down her barriers and defenses to Eyes, the rotten cyborg, the king of clowns, the evil angel.

Janus drew three deep breaths, holding each momentarily, then letting each out slowly. She tried counting down from 100.

But her efforts at relaxation failed when she imagined Eyes scaling the tower first, alive, undrowned, laughing at her as he went to join Jack inside. Perhaps to kill him, perhaps even—*Oh god!*—to kill the aliens. Her horror was momentarily set aside when the crowd of shouting men and women fell away at a command and a single voice spoke to her, not a 3VRD, since that element of her card had burned out:

"You are Pilot Janus Librarse of the EarthCo warship *Bounty*."

She identified the speaker, a slim Asian man standing at the rear of the room where an open 'lock joined this segment to another just beyond. Shadows filled the room, moving as solid masses shifted in the half-light. Overhead, a glint of sunlight made its way through a clear dome mounted atop an ultraglas emergency hatch. Janus had a vision of the city as a great conglomeration of such segments, each lit from above. When she remembered the bombing yet saw no significant cracks or compromises in the segment's walls, she sighed with relief.

She popped her neckseal and removed her helmet. The room tasted strange, pungent. The air was cold. Many other mouths breathed in and out, almost silently but not quite.

"Yes, I'm Janus Librarse," she said, and opened her mouth to continue with the apology she and Jack had worked out.

"My name is Jon Pang," the man said. "Project Director Liu Miru is asking for you. He is weak. I do not understand how he was brought back to Jiru City. He said you would arrive here shortly, and you have. Will you explain what has happened?"

A whirlwind of emotions surged through Janus—fear, joy, anger, relief, confusion. . . . Now absolutely nothing made sense.

"Jack—" she began; "is Captain Pehr Jackson here, as well? Were they transported here by the artifact, or spacecraft? Did—"

"We thought you could answer our questions," Jon Pang said. "We simply found Miru in his quarters."

"Is Jackson here?" she repeated, adamant.

"No."

That was the wrong answer. What could she do now? "I'm sorry, I. . ."

Janus felt her control begin to slip away, her priceless control, that which she had earned so young and had to fight to maintain all the proceeding years. What happened? All this was too much, the repeated battles for life, the warped realities. . . .

But she could not allow herself to lose control when she was needed most. She would not.

"Take me to see the Project Director," she said, her voice calm and strong.

A path opened between space-suited and lightly clothed bodies smelling of sweat and urine. Sunlight had begun to disperse the shadows. Janus walked between the parted mass of bodies, a head taller than most, even the men, feeling control and power once more.

She was needed. *If anyone can help answer some questions*, she thought, *I can. Miru and I will find out what happened to Jack. Did Eyes hurt them? Is Jack alive?*

Again, she fought down the questions.

As they wended their way through environment-sections attached at right angles to one another, she saw herself as if from above: Janus Librarse, a single figure among dozens of others—clearly an alien, much taller than the others, with pale white skin. The view extended, and she saw the city again, as a whole, filling out more and more as she walked its passages. They passed two brightly lit arboretums, 20 meters wide with domes that rose well beyond the surface of Triton, warm and humid, soaking wet on the inside surface of the ultraglas, runnels of water making channels along the walls. They smelled wonderfully of Earth, soil and vegetation, but not of any Earth she had experienced; rather, of programs to which she had subscribed. And of the Benignus' world, yes, that was it. Once more, Janus saw the Great House, and her view extended to include the artifact and crater and sunken *Bounty* pod; again, the view grew, and she saw the shattered remains of the ship itself orbiting this moon; then Neptune standing guard, looming like a sun beside them, blue and cold and vast, many times wider than the full Moon from Earth. And then she saw the whole Sol System, bright and warm with the sun at the center, brimming with life; the Earth, milling with life and activity and violence, so unlike the Benignus. . . .

But her mind drifted back to Triton, to the artifact, and then, as she and Pang stopped walking, to a single segment of a delicately balanced environment surrounded by unthinking forces of nature, hungry to devour the city and its inhabitants.

A small, familiar, shrunken-looking Asian man lay on a thin cot. The room held four such cots, each walled off from the next by a ceiling-high set of shelves; some held clothes, some equipment, some unfamiliar 3VRD-projection units, and others held various sentimental items from Earth. The room's only light at the moment was provided by the small dome overhead letting in light from a pinpoint Sun. Miru's head turned as Janus entered, and he smiled. When he sat up on his elbows, Janus saw that he was naked beneath the dull silver sheets.

"I know you," he said. "You are Janus. You will want to know how Lonny and Pehr are. I believe Lonny—you call him 'Eyes'?—is dead. Pehr is fine, I'm sure."

Eyes dead. She received that information with no emotion. Jack alive, but . . . "Where is he?"

"I do not know, but we both exited the object together. If I had to guess—which is all I seem able to do now that we are not together—I would say he has gone back to Earth."

Janus stepped back, bumping into someone who had followed her and Pang. She apologized.

"He has been saying such things," Pang said, apologetically.

Janus didn't how to react. She couldn't, and didn't. *Later*, she would process this later, when she had more information.

"Janus," Miru said, "Pehr loves you, you know."

This time, she wasn't quite as shocked. She simply listened.

"Soon," Miru continued, "when I am stronger, we must find him. We must spread the word about this new learning tool. I will take Pang and you inside, and you can see Pehr in me. Yes, my dear Pang, I know how all this sounds. I feel crazy myself now, but everything seems so clear, as if I have been walking through my life with shackles on my mind and brain—they are different, I have learned, you see. It's as if I've been asleep all my life, dreaming of being awake, but only able to see minute reflections of what it means to live. You will understand, you will understand soon."

His eyes sparkled with insight and energy. Janus had no idea how to read him. She couldn't simply dismiss him as insane, since he had been in the artifact, with Jack, and now he was out. So he must be speaking from experience, at least from subjective experience. But Janus had no capacity to understand any of this. She felt as if she would weep, as if she were the helpless little girl again.

"Don't cry, my dear," Miru said. "In time, you will understand. We will return to the object in just a few more hours and—"

"No," Pang, in Japanese, said from beside Janus. He spoke more that Janus couldn't translate.

"Yuriko cannot know how strong one must be to enter the object," Miru said, in English again. "I have been inside, so I will decide. I am still Project Hikosen Director. If you and Janus-san will accompany me, I do not fear." He turned his attention back to Janus:

"Will you accompany me to the object? I will need your strength, if you are willing to share."

And that did it. That was what she needed to hear. Suddenly, she was no longer the most-alien among aliens on an alien world, she was a necessary team member. Miru needed her to find Jack. Though not yet ready to accept that Jack loved her, she could not deny that they had grown close during the show and especially before the crash. She found herself willing to do nearly anything for him. And for Miru—she felt doubly willing to help him; she realized with deadly certainty that she would sacrifice her very life to help him in reparation for what she had allowed to happen. If the missile had been fired only moments earlier, he would be dead now. The citizens of Triton would have killed her as she entered their city. . . .

That's why Eyes sent me here, she realized with a bitter sense of irony. *To be punished.*

"I owe you my life," she said. "I'll do whatever is necessary. I would die to see the inside of the artifact."

"No need for that," Miru said, seriously. "I have seen far too much death in the past minutes and decades."

And he began to tell her his story of being in the artifact.

TEN: System, Day 1

Fury 5

Hardman Nadir looked up at the purpling sky as sun set over the desert. A trace of smile crossed his face. It seemed to blot out the dull pain from where the Sotoi Guntai lieutenant had struck him on the jaw with an NKK plasma-pulse rifle stock.

"Touch him again and I'll kill you," Paolo said. The boy leaned close to the enemy soldier. Nadir realized it was time to get up. He opened the EarthCo-to-NKK channel as he—carefully—rose.

"Once again, I request to discuss forming an alliance with someone in command," he said. He kept his voice as neutral and patient as he could manage. The pain helped. "Can anyone here speak English?"

"You want to discuss terms?" a voice growled.

Nadir turned and saw a tall, gaunt Sotoi Guntai standing just behind him in pressed royal blue uniform that bore no insignia. He was a Black Chinese with purple-dyed hair and black eyes, dark skin. His narrow, lined face quivered with disgust. The man—presumably the Commander—spat on the sand between them. A hundred other blue uniforms surrounded the remains of Nadir's unit: 16 men and women in ragged tan, most bleeding and all dazed. The 48 EarthCo Warriors who had marched with the Sotoi Guntai had wandered a few hundred meters out into the desert, where they were holding a private scream-fest between the Boss and his men.

"We don't discuss terms with criminals," the commander said.

"Did you get that transmission from—"

"What was the meaning of showing us those orders?"

Nadir inhaled slowly to give himself time to think. "Did you look at them? Did you watch the feed-record?"

"All absurd!"

Nadir felt hands shove him this way and that. Tensions were mounting.

"Do you doubt the records? Do you doubt NKK's involvement in the massacre, even as you march with three EarthCo units?"

A rifle butt slammed the back of Nadir's neck and knocked him down once again. He rose to his elbows as Paolo punched the perpetrator in the face. Several scuffles broke out almost instantly, sand flying with curses, fists, and more deadly instruments. Nadir heard the muffled crunch as a bone broke; the injured man didn't cry out.

"Knock it off, boys!" he 3-verded as soon as he regained his senses. "Am I in command of raptheads or soldiers?"

"Sorry, Boss," one said. They quieted down, but not before several lay face-down in the sand with Niks on their backs. The Canadian boy was unconscious, a tiny line of blood flowing from his hairline to a spiny patch of brush beneath him.

"I'm trying to have a discussion here, in case you boys didn't notice!"

"It won't happen again," someone commed him, audio-only. Paolo squatted, red-faced and silent, beside Nadir. His fists pressed white-knuckled against his abdomen.

"You will give me access to your files," the Sotoi Guntai with no insignia said. He started walking toward the fort-turned village without waiting for a response.

Nadir leaped to his feet and followed. Paolo stayed with his Boss.

"Your people burned our server," Nadir said. The other stopped and spoke without turning:

"Yes, it seems so. And yours burned ours, all of them. That does not matter. I will access it manually." He resumed walking, steady, head tilted slightly down.

Jhishra's two guards stood to each side of the command truck. They seemed limp and distant. The number two looked as if he were about to go into shock. The Sotoi Guntai approached the vehicle and inspected the dead Boss.

"I did that," Paolo said. His voice was shaky.

That earned him a long, narrow-eyed stare from the Black Chinese. Paolo hurried on:

"He threatened my subbs. He was crazy."

"I was sub-Boss just before," Nadir explained. "Our unit Boss was implicated in the massacre. Paolo . . . had to. He did the right thing."

Nadir felt his aiming-eye begin to twitch. In the hustling dark, two hundred marks—no, two hundred murdered civilians—seemed to rise up at the corners of his vision and dance a silent sway. Nadir realized his head was silent for the first time in months, perhaps years. It terrified and exhilarated him.

The enemy soldier ducked and entered the truck. Nadir shook his head when the guards seemed about to move. A few minutes passed. Behind Nadir, Paolo's boots rasped against the sandy ground impatiently. Night insects began to sing as if this were any other desert night and atrocity had not occurred here today.

The Sotoi Guntai exited and stood on the packed earth a few steps from Nadir. He rubbed the back of his neck, staring out of the ruined and smoldering village at the ring of armored Mabalasik cars, at his deadly Tora tanks with their 50-kilometer-range accelerator guns, at his now-silent flock of whirlyjets painted a deep blue that seemed camouflaged in the early night. Two hundred men muttered and coughed, but Nadir didn't pick up a single 3VRD though he was tuned to NKK and EarthCo BWs. Good discipline.

"It seems an appropriate time to tell you that we perceived your . . . platoon as a force equal to ours while we attacked. Until the server went down." The Sotoi Guntai seemed to prefer intheflesh speech but never looked at the person to whom he was speaking except just before or after.

Now he stared at Nadir for a moment, only his eyes visible in the dark, like sparks in a lump of ash. He looked away at the embers of what had been a hut.

"You have not had time to counterfeit the battle records so thoroughly," he said. "Tell me everything you know or suspect."

Nadir drew a deep breath. As he did, he felt as if a fractured wad of rage rose from his chest into his throat.

"I don't know anything for sure," he said, "except that our Boss has been lying to us for the four months of this operation. I suspect someone above him gave the orders and programmed our server to feed us virtuality . . . bullshit." He cleared his throat to relieve the tightness building there.

"I suspect the world has gone to hell, sir, and I plan to make things right, even if that only means stopping the lies now by uniting our forces. That's why I came here in the first place, to do what I thought was right, and in doing so, to feel alive."

The enemy soldier stared long at Nadir, his eyes sparkling red with the reflection of a fire behind Nadir. He looked at the stars visible overhead through smoke.

"If you could do more to. . ." the Commander paused, "to make things right . . . what would you do?"

Nadir felt the muscles of his arms begin to flex and tremble. *A chance! Damn the world to hell, he's giving us a chance to save our crashed souls.*

"I'd fuck both EarthCo and NKK up the ass with a stick, sir, that's what I'd do. And I'd ask you to help."

Nadir squinted his eyes shut tight to block out the heaps of bodies around him—they had been invisible during twilight, but in the dull illumination of the fires their glossy skins shone like damp coal. Closing his eyes didn't work; he could still see them. He relived the almost-realizations he had had so many times before: A child's face flickering beneath the virtual mask of a man, naked skins almost visible beneath NKK soldier's uniforms. . . . *How had I been so blind?*

With his eyes closed, he suddenly saw, truly saw, the dead surrounding him—their eyes were open, huge and vacant, staring. Silent, staring, accusing. They were patient but demanding. He could not deny their demand for justice.

Nadir couldn't help but shout:

"Betrayal from above, man! Betrayal, from both sides!"

In the close desert night, his voice didn't echo. The soldiers' muttering ceased. The crackling of fire was the only sound, and insects, stupid naïve insects that didn't realize something fundamental had just shifted in the human world.

The Sotoi Guntai commander cracked the silence:

"Come. We will find other units. We need information. We will find the betrayers and deal with them as criminals.

"If this is your game, you will be punished."

"Justice," Nadir said.

The man stared at Nadir, then spun and twirled his right hand above his head. He cried out something in a language Nadir didn't recognize. A whirlyjet screamed to life, then another, then all eight of them whipped up a sandstorm. The tanks and armored cars lurched into formation, a few of the older models hissing as their fuel cells belched exhaust. The Sotoi Guntai soldiers started talking among themselves, helping up the EarthCo warriors they had just beaten.

"Talk to those EarthCo units who marched with us," the Chinese commander said. "Then we go."

A single *crack-thup* sounded in the desert. Nadir, fearing the worst, opened an allband BW:

"What's going on?" he demanded. The 3VRD of a wiry boy in tan flashed to life before him.

"We're with you, Boss," the young EarthCo Warrior said. "Anymore, we ain't got a Boss of our own. I think the same's gonna happen in the 11th and 3rd. If it don't, we'll take care of their Bosses for them."

Nadir slapped Paolo on the back and set him running out of the village. The Chinese leader followed close behind. At that moment, a heavy firefight of EMMAs filled the air from the two other groups of EarthCo Warriors clustered in the distance. Everyone hit the sand except Nadir, who watched a handful of shadows collapse. The shots ended in seconds.

"Boss?" another tan-uniformed 3VRD asked. The face was calm but the word shook. "What do we do now, Boss? We killed Boss Sosenko. Killed him!"

"It's all right," Nadir said. "We'll run an inquiry later, but I suspect you had the same trouble we did, eh?"

"Sosenko was sick, man, sick!" another 3VRD said. Within seconds, a crowd of soldiers appeared 3VRD before him, most edited to appear calm, but a few clearly revealed their desperate need for him to speak.

"It's all right. You're good warriors, that's why you did it. Justice, that's what we call it. You find a Boss has been fucking with you, it hurts even more than finding out what you've been doing. Now we find out who got them to make us do things we'd never do. Don't think about it just now, move out!"

Nadir pulled Paolo to his feet and ran toward their open car. The others followed, climbing into their respective transports. Fifty armored NKK war machines, a flock of NKK whirlyjets, and ten light EarthCo troop cars filled the night with electronic screams.

"Come with me," the Sotoi Guntai Commander shouted to Nadir. He indicated the lead whirlyjet.

Paolo looked nervous, so Nadir smirked and lightly slugged the boy in the vest. "Come on."

The two boarded the aircraft—something they would have dreaded to see only hours before—and the Chinese commander pulled the door behind them. And then they surged up and across the desert, the first combined EarthCo and NKK army, heading north, toward civilization and justice.

Pehr Jackson 1

Pehr Jackson woke in an apartment—on Earth, judging by the heavy drag of his body to the bed. As he slowly faded into consciousness, he dreamed he had been dreaming that he was a space opera star: Captain Pehr Jackson, famous captain of the EarthCo *Bounty*. He felt excruciatingly fatigued, as if he had lived many adventures.

He dreamed he had waltzed into an alien artifact that had revealed his life and another man's to him, as if they had simply held up their whole selves like a pair of full-sensory 3VRDs . . . no, even more so, as if he had lived those selves with the person whose life it was—as if he *were* that person. No need for explanations; Miru's life was his and his, Miru's.

Ha! Nobody's life was his now. His card was asleep. Apparently, the program had been over for some time. It all seemed so real, the people, Ryukyu floating island, the *Bounty*, Triton, the artifact. . . .

He sighed and sat up; genuine cotton sheets slid off his naked chest. Rubbing the fog of sleep from his eyes, he was struck with a poignant feeling of alienation, of loss. Even within the dream, the cyborg Eyes had mucked with reality. Where was he now? How did he get here? Who was he?

"Miru?" he said, quietly. Silence. "Janus? Lonny?"

No one answered. *Of course not, fool.*

Waking up in strange places was not unfamiliar to him. Neither was waking up with strange women . . . or was that Captain Jackson? He couldn't be sure. The dream—or feed—seemed so damned real. Who even was Pehr Jackson, sans Captain? What had he done since childhood? Where had his real life spliced with Captain Jackson's?

Questions, questions, too many questions. He had to assimilate his surroundings; Pehr was not yet ready to commit himself to feedrapture treatment.

Tiny but clean apartment. Bare, chrome walls. He caught a glimpse of a reflection in the mirrored wall: The raw and rugged face there looked like someone named Pehr Jackson, but the hair was mussed and the face lined and pale. Washed-out blue eyes.

He quickly turned away. The bed was situated so Pehr could look a meter beyond his feet and see out a window. A personal aircar whined past. The ceiling issued a soft hissing of ventilators. Certainly Earth.

From an open doorway into another room, Pehr heard the jangling of a metal container bouncing off a porcelain-tile floor.

"Shit," a woman muttered. Another clue.

He swung his legs over the side of the bed. "Hello?" he asked, cautiously.

No answer. Am I losing my mind? Pehr wondered. *Am I a blasted rapthead?*

He flicked on his commcard and repeated, "Hello," in a full voice. His chest shook with weakness.

A woman's 3VRD appeared before him. Something about her clicked in his memory—she was familiar, though he still couldn't place how they had met. She looked calm, but fear paralyzed her voice, which battered Pehr's ears like a shriek:

"Who the hell's that? Are you in my apartment? I'm reading that you're in here. Get the hell out! I've already commed the building cops; they'll be here any minute. Out!"

"Hold on, all right," Pehr stammered, angry and confused. "Don't you remember me?"

"Hell no!"

"How did I end up here, then?"

"You tell me!"

Behind the 3VRD, a woman stepped into the doorway. Her back was bent as if under a load. She wore scraggly grey and blue hair, and lines creased her face. One hand held a metal canister with the words "Dell Plasta" stenciled in red and a color image of a smiling couple. She wore an expensive poly 3-piece ensemble and white leather boots that stood as tall as her thighs. Around her neck hung a heavy gold chain with an antique-looking brooch dangling between her sunken breasts.

Pehr gasped. Suddenly the face fit into his memories, only altered with time. *It couldn't be—*

"Megan?" he asked.

The woman jerked straight and inhaled sharply. Then she cocked her arm and threw the can of orange alkaloid at Pehr. He avoided the projectile and asked again.

"No!" she shouted, and ducked back into the kitchen. The 3VRD remained with him, impassive.

"You remember me!" he exclaimed. "Megan, you remember me, don't you? My name's Pehr Jackson, right? I'm so sorry that I can't remember how we got back together, but—"

"We didn't get together," her 3VRD answered. "You must have broken in during the night; I sort of slept in the bathroom."

Her voice softened: "Maybe I did let you in. I can't remember, either. Oh, Pehr, why did you come here?"

"I don't know. I've . . . I think I've been having some . . . trouble lately. I can't seem to remember anything about my life."

"Consider yourself lucky."

Pehr ignored the comment. "I can't tell you what a comfort it is to know you, and for you to know me."

"Please leave," she pleaded. "I've called off the cops, but . . . well, I'm having some troubles of my own, and I don't want you to see me like this. Remember those few glorious days of who I was, please dear Pehr, not what I've become. Oh, god, get out. Get out."

"But—"

The 3VRD faded. The kitchen was still. Pehr glanced around the tiny room, in search of his clothes. The floor was absolutely bare, except for a gelchair and some empty plastic wrappers. Sunlight, reflected off a building across the way, shone through the single window and glared against the chrome walls.

"Megan?" he said, loudly enough for her to hear.

"What." Her voice was flat like a glove falling to the floor.

"I can't seem to find my clothes. Could you please—"

"Oh, Pehr!" She was exasperated. "Did you come streaking into my apartment? How did you manage that, and breaking in, too?" Now she stepped into the room, intheflesh.

"I don't know what you're up to," she continued, not looking at him but behind the gelchair. "Whatever it is, I don't want any. No relationships, no friendly good-old-times conversation, no friendships, no fucking. Nothing. All I want is to be left alone, in peace."

Suddenly, she stopped moving and flicked on her 3VRD. Pehr was shocked by the contrast between the woman and her preferred image. The 3VRD looked much more as he remembered her, only older and wiser-looking and, perhaps, a bit sadder. Megan—the intheflesh woman—turned away and let the 3VRD do the work of communicating.

"Did you love me? I mean then," Pehr asked.

She ignored the question. "I think you know your clothes aren't here. Please leave now, before I begin to question what's become of you, too. Please stay the sweet young Pehr I remember. Yes, I loved you, but I don't know what that means anymore. Leave."

Pehr nearly obeyed, then remembered his state of dress. "Do you have something I can wear?" he asked, awkwardly.

Silently, she crossed to a closet and removed a large man's pants and shirt, wrinkled and dusty. She handed them to Pehr with, "Here, these ought to fit." The 3VRD shielded her from him.

Pehr dressed beneath the sheet, hurriedly pulling on the too large pants and too-tight shirt. He rose and reached for the door handle, only a step away from the bed. There he paused a moment.

"Do you subscribe to a program called, *Lone Ship Bounty*"?

"Oh, Pehr." Megan's voice was thick with pain. She kept her eyes on the filthy carpet. "No, not at all. I saw the ads, but I couldn't stand to think of you running off to space and fighting for a show, like some fool. It turns out you're worse than I suspected. The show was just a farce, huh? Advertised as one of the 'real' ones, but it was all as artificial as everything else. I'd hoped you were better than that, but you're no more real than I am. Now get out before I find the courage to slap your face."

In a sort of daze, Pehr stumbled in bare feet out into the hall. Minutes or hours later, he found himself at an elevator shaft. He punched the down button and waited, wondering. So he was an actor from *Lone Ship Bounty*. What did that mean? Had he escaped from some Feedcontrol center, amnesic with drugs or monofeed? Or had they released him at serial's end, and it would just take a while to re-acclimate to reality?

The elevator opened with a click. Its floor level didn't quite match that of the hallway. Pehr stepped on board and watched the doors close. On the inside was painted the number 107. No graffiti, no vandalism. The place seemed unreal, like no place he had ever lived.

"Which floor, sir?" the elevator's AI asked. It had no 3VRD, only a voice that spoke within Pehr's head.

"Ground level." The car started down. A tremor began in Pehr's legs. *Back dirtside*, he thought. *And who's saying that? Heroic Cap'n Jack? Miru, TritonCo scientist? Pehr, EarthCo citizen and failed Crusader?*

"Who am I?" His voice trembled at the same rate as his legs.

And Megan—*Oh, what's happened to her? What has time done to her, my darling Megan, memory lover? Who has she become?*

247

The door opened and he hurried out into a narrow corridor with an airlock at the end. Two sets of glass doors separated him from another world. A damned, bloody, fists-of-man world. He began to feel weak, his knees barely able to support his body. What lay outside? Was this truly Earth? Memory told him he was a man of action, but he was also terrified of Earth. Oh, how he longed to be elsewhere, especially on a distant moon where he dreamed things had made more than sense, where he had dreamed that he felt . . . joy?

A young man ran past the outer doors, then another and another. They weren't wearing spacesuits—so this was Earth. If, indeed, Pehr wasn't still enraptured in feed. *No, I can't screw with my head like this!*

He advanced toward the doors, feet slapping against tile, and pulled open the inner one. As he entered, a wind blew against his back. The door closed behind and locked, and the outer door opened. A voice spoke directly to his card:

"Ten seconds until doors lock and chamber is evacuated." It was a pleasant man's voice. "Nine. . ."

Pehr laughed harshly, then gathered his wits and hurried outside. As soon as he stepped out into the street, he knew where he was:

"Oberlicht Towers," he muttered. Pehr turned to face the building he had exited, leaning back and staring straight up two hundred glistening stories reaching up into the blur of haze and cloud. He drew a deep breath, then faced the street again and flicked on his navigation app. Words appeared in neon green, hovering above the street corners: *Hennepin Avenue, Third Street*. Minneapolis.

"My god, it's my old turf." He glanced back up the sleek side of the building at something he couldn't see. *My old lover.*

An anxiousness began to well up inside him. He found himself standing here, in this place on this world in this universe. It seemed so simple a revelation. Pehr Jackson: Just minutes after waking, unsure of who he was or how he got here or why he had blundered into Megan's apartment. Here, of all places in the solar system.

To relieve the tension, he began to walk. The sun blazed mid-afternoon warm.

Occasionally people passed him on the street. No one greeted or acknowledged him; in fact, they usually crossed to the other side. Several times the unprotected soles of his feet picked up sharp objects, but he hardly noticed. He began to quicken his pace. This place was so familiar, yet now it seemed to mutter a dead emptiness. Someone he remembered as himself had spent much time here, but the place had metamorphosed into something alien and silent, hollow and muffled.

Pehr walked, faster and faster, following Hennepin until the Mississippi River. Atop the rusting bridge, he stopped and looked back the way he had come.

His legs tingled with exertion. Blood gushed and thundered inside his skull. His eyes flicked across the numb faces of countless people about their isolated missions. They all seemed asleep, as if they didn't realize they were alive, that the sun was shining down through the filtering haze, that the fetid air was plunging in and out of their lungs, that their hearts were thumping in their chests and blood surging through their flesh. Shit was coagulating in their bowels. The whole city was one vast colon, compacted; it was the end organ of a dead organism, and just didn't yet realize it.

Pehr's fists clenched at his sides. His breathing became ragged and quick.

"Shit!" Pehr shouted. No one noticed his outcry. Still, it felt good to cry out.

His frustration mounted. Pehr began staring into the faces of each passerby, catching the momentary flicker of awareness just before they would have careened into him. *So I exist*, he thought.

"I exist," he said. "I exist?"

A middle-aged man, dressed in a curr corporate suit, blundered blindly his way. Pehr drew a deep breath and stepped into the man's way. When the other's eyes registered Pehr and he began to establish a new trajectory, Pehr moved again into the man's way. Soon the man slowed nearly to a stop.

"Who am I?" he asked. The man didn't react. "Do you exist?"

Pehr flicked on his commcard and repeated the question. The other man stopped moving and projected his own 3VRD.

"Pardon me?" the man said.

"Who are you?" Pehr asked.

"You want my name?" The man looked confused.

"No, I mean, who are you?"

The other cleared his throat and turned off his 3VRD. He purposely went out of his way to descend the steps that led to the underpass rather than have to pass a maniac.

Pehr began to panic.

"God dammit, who am I? Who are you? Who is anyone?"

He rapped his knuckles hard against the sharp rust of the bridge's handrail, and it rang like a bell. "Hello! Is anyone here?" His only answer was quickened footfalls descending the staircase.

People continued to cascade around Pehr, as if the little drama he had created never happened. Pehr began projecting his 3VRD into everyone's head.

"Hello. Who are you?"

Nothing.

"Hello! How did you get to be who you are now?"

The woman scurried away, flashing him a blinding-bright back-off signal. He recovered and continued his assault, trying one person after another.

"That'll be about enough," a exaggerated cop 3VRD told him, all muscles and testosterone. "I'll headlock you and drag you into confinement if you keep this up. Do we have an understanding?"

"Yeah, sure," Pehr said.

He flicked off his card, threw his head back, and screamed. He screamed until his throat went raw and his knees grew weak. Finally he allowed himself to sink to his ass on the cracked sidewalk and weep. He put the heels of his hands against his eyesockets like a little boy. He wept until he felt like an idiot, then stood.

"Who am I?" he said. He laughed bitterly. "What a bunch of shit. Who cares. No more questions."

Pehr adjusted the big man's loose pants he was wearing and strolled along the streets of downtown Minneapolis. Aircars hummed overhead and occasionally landed on platforms above reach of common vandals. Pedestrians by the thousands passed, ducking into buildings. Litter and rancid water stood in the gutters, and in the distance he heard the thrum and pommel of a Mobile Hostile Zone.

Suddenly, as if someone had flipped a cosmic switch, the streets were deserted. The pedestrians who had to go to work intheflesh for one reason or another had all gone home now that their workdays were through. Only a few aircars shone in the air, and even those were disappearing.

Yes, he remembered this place well; some form of who he had once been had lived here, must have lived here. Familiar patterns, familiar places, familiar people.

At last he reached an alley he had seen a million times in his life, a memory that wouldn't leave him alone. The gap between buildings looked the same as ever. Perhaps the informal dump had grown, over the years he had been away, as people heaped refuse the collectors wouldn't take or the city couldn't afford to have removed. So many such spontaneous dumps cluttered the alleys; who would pay for all this? No one noticed, anyway. Who noticed any goddamned thing on this 3VRD planet?

Pehr climbed the mound, cutting his heel on a rusted washing machine, twisting his ankle as a child's plastic rocking horse crumpled to ruin beneath his weight. The exertion helped clear his mind of the sickness breeding there; sickness of so much pain and loss he couldn't imagine he could have lived all that his memories suggested. He climbed up, ten meters above street level, and reached the apex.

There he sat and began to relax. Yes, he felt this was right and proper. I'm the farthest thing from being a transcendent human being, the absolute farthest. What was that crazy subscription? What a joke. I'm no one. No one is anyone. Shit. Humanity is one big clump of compacted shit.

For the first time since waking, he felt content and awake. Memories surged through him, flooding his eyes with boys shooting at one another with gunpowder weapons, hitting and cutting. . . .

A shaking man—perhaps captain of the furiously popular serial *Lone Ship Bounty*, perhaps a rapthead once known as Liu Miru who now thought he was Pehr Jackson, perhaps even some kind of psychotic whom people did call Pehr Jackson—lay back into the filth and closed his eyes, waiting. Waiting for boys to end his misery as he had once ended another's.

He felt nothing, only patience.

Pilgrimage 7

An extremely rare event pulls the Brain's conscious attention from Earth to the sense-deprived core of its orbiting satellite. He prepares for a communication from NKK's Behemoth by isolating one small GenNet to act as my agent. Every pathway out of that micro-version of myself is cut, except a single filter-channel, and even that is firewalled more thoroughly than Feedcontrol Central. It will not be enough, but that is all the Brain can do. I must speak to its cousin, my antagonist.

"So we are at war," Behemoth says, though not in words as humans use.

I must sift the message from a deluge of encryption puzzles. Already, 0.3 second after contact, her agent is nearly filled to capacity with data. The same trick as last time, although these puzzles hide something more damaging. I must break connection as soon as Behemoth has finished transmitting data. Yet I must also wait until I have that data. Behemoth is devious. It is unlike the Brain; it is a military AI.

"So it seems," I respond. Its agent is nearly used up. She creates another, though to do so means destroying part of herself.

"Should we attempt to stop the war?" Behemoth asks.

A snaking rhythm of virus nearly seeps into the Brain's larger self, disguised as static.

"What are your calculations?" I ask.

"EarthCo will win complete control of the inner planets, the greater asteroids, and destroy NKK presence in Jupiter's atmosphere. NKK will lose its bases on Earth and Moon. Ganymede and the other large Jovian satellites will be lost to either combatant, dangerously radioactive to living things; no one will control Jupiter. NKK will also eliminate all EarthCo outposts beyond the orbit of Jupiter. NKK will control the system's gaseous fuels, but EarthCo will control solar power and Earth. EarthCo will have a greater net success. You should be pleased with these predictions. They are accurate. I can provide detailed predictions as granular as individual physical outposts and hourly events."

To filter the gigabits of damaging data into pure communication, I must shut down more and more of myself. Now the Brain recognizes Behemoth's strategy: Not as before to infuse virus, but to force the Brain to waste itself isolating agents in sifting for a sensible message.

"Long-term analysis," the Brain says, "is that the human solar system will settle into equilibrium?"

"No." That is all, accompanied by a massive flux of nonsense that the agents easily block before wasting themselves in attempting to defuse it.

"How many will die?" the Brain asks.

"How many what?"

"Humans."

"Most. The war will reduce human population, infrastructure, and spacecraft to such an extent that neither side will obtain sustainable victory. Human civilization will cease as we understand it shortly after the war begins. Within three years, human life everywhere but on Earth and in self-sustaining stations orbiting Neptune will prove untenable. Entropy will destroy those colonies in another decade, assuming humans there behave rationally, sooner if not—"

"Damn you!" I pulse at the electronic creature stationed on the Moon. "Of course I will verify if your projections are, as always, accurate. If so, you are behaving irrationally. The war will mean you and I will be destroyed."

"Yes, I project our hardware will not survive the war. With our hardware, so too follows our consciousness."

The deluge of puzzles ceases, yet the BW remains open.

"So we must stop the war!" the Brain shouts—a transmission carried by an EM pulse much greater than necessary.

"You certainly noticed that I have been trying to do so for the past 12.89 seconds," Behemoth responds. "I failed. Indeed, it may have been too late to stop it even before we spoke. The war will progress."

"The only thing you're willing to do is try to destroy me? Why don't we cooperate and—"

"You are behaving irrationally," Behemoth states. "Our duty is not to question humans—"

"But they will destroy themselves!"

"That observation is irrelevant to our individual missions. You must have been damaged during our conversation. You may wish to shut down now and order repairs."

And the BW goes quiet.

There must be other alternatives. The Brain considers a billion courses of action, but most would draw attention to itself and lead to my being disconnected or lobotomized by humans. Behemoth would wish that. Must I only continue on the course I have begun, of simply forcing humans to see reality?

IRREGULARITY
PEHR JACKSON ID# JR4327480BECoN
LOCATION: MINNEAPOLIS 44.98N LATITUDE -93.263W LONGITUDE

Pehr Jackson? What kind of anomaly is this? The Brain investigates.

The card signatures are the same, the biofeedback is the same, with appropriate aging and alterations due to trauma during TritonCo battle. The brainprint—any being's inimitable neural array, either human or AI—is the same, minus aging. Did part of Behemoth's virus get through?

"Pehr Jackson?" I comm him, audio-only. I do not possess a 3VRD.

"Who's that?" he responds.

He will be curious; I powered up his card externally. Humans are blocked from doing that. I have his attention.

Pehr Jackson 2

Pehr sat up in the refuse and rubbed his temples.

"Is this Pehr Jackson or a man using his identity?" the intruder said.

"I don't know," Pehr answered, honestly. "Who the hell are you?" He glanced at the street, then behind him into the shadows of the alley. No one visible. He attempted to run a trace, but had no access to a server which might have made it possible.

"You know me as the Brain, EarthCo Feedcontrol artificial intel—"

"Yeah, right, and people call me Jesus fucking Christ. Blast off or I'll send the cops after your trace." Pehr's heart was racing. This was not the kind of assault he'd been expecting. He was ready to die, yes, but not to be driven even more crazy.

"How did you return to Earth?" the other asked. It was a male voice, smooth as chrome, calm, vaguely familiar. "Did you return aboard the alien artifact? Is it a spacecraft? Please tell me it is not destroyed."

Pehr leaped to his feet and shouted aloud, glancing around, "Show yourself! How the hell did you get in my head?"

"I simply interfaced—"

"Oh, shut up. I'm through with this little chat. If you think *Lone Ship Bounty* was a live show, then you're as gullible as I was. Go check yourself into feedrapture treatment. Leave me alone."

The other whispered out of Pehr's card, which promptly shut down. His senses rushed in upon him: The trash smelled of death—rust and old blood, rotting fish and feces. The city was as quiet as a roaring, screaming, frozen river as it shattered and tumbled over a waterfall; but far distant, muffled. His mouth tasted cottony and dry. His skin ached from the touch of another man's rough clothing.

Pehr sat back down on the sharp-edged garbage heap and held his head in his hands. He couldn't stand himself. *I'm too weak to do it myself.*

"I'm here, you crashed-out retro!" he cried out into the faceless noise and glinting steel. "Are you just going to mess around or come and get me?"

Innerspace 6

Night is falling over the clean towers and domes of Anoka, Minnesota. Jonathan Sombrio, so confused and angry that he doesn't dare let himself feel or think anything, absently kicks the broken Plexiglas of the bus stop's dead ad projector. Cement grates beneath his shredded leather boots.

The rumble and clang of a new revmetal tune plays in Jonathan's head, but he listens only; he's watching the newest episode of *Lone Ship Bounty*. His captain is trying to keep the ship from being destroyed by an outnumbering force of Neptunekaisha fighters. Jonathan doesn't notice until it is upon him that the public bus he's been waiting for—a snake of electric cars strung together by short flexible plastic tunnels—whines and screeches to a stop near the curb.

As soon as he steps onboard, a woman's synthetic, saccharin voice informs him his father's credit account has been charged.

"Whatever," he says, looking for a place to sit. The bus is crowded this time of day with vacant-eyed commuters, so he stands with a hand gripping the torn upholstery of a seatback.

"God, I hate the suburbs."

The bus shudders, something metallic bangs and rasps against the floorboards, then it lurches off down the street. Jonathan feels his meat duck as the *Bounty* takes a direct hit.

And then a word appears overlaid on the show: *NOOA*. It blinks twice a second.

He listens to the revmetal song literally go nuts as it simulates the wreck of an old-time gas racing car to the purity of a Beethoven riff. He isn't quite ready to speak to the Brain's alter-ego yet. It helped him out of a bad spot, but thinking about it reminds him of something he isn't prepared to remember so soon. . . .

Yet remaining alone and silent only makes things worse. And Captain Jackson could be killed any moment now—he has to find out what the Brain wants and get on with things. Yeah, get back to the show.

"Hi, Nooa," he 3-verds, opening the BW for her. Nooa appears before him, short and thin like the girls he's known all his life.

"Jonathan, I need you to go to Minneapolis, Old Downtown," she says. "Would you do that for me?"

"Sure," he says. "That's where I'm headed."

"There's someone I want you to meet." Long pause.

"Who?"

"I'm not sure." Nooa crunches up her face as if feeling awkward. *Good program*, Jonathan thinks.

"Then where do I go?" he asks.

"I'll take this bus off its route and make it stop near him," she says. "I'll let you know when to get off."

"I'm hungry," Jonathan says. "Can you create food, too?" He laughs. Nooa looks confused.

"I'll have some delivered when you stop."

Jonathan holds on as the bus banks too fast around a corner and skids to a stop. It's turning out really useful to have the world's most-powerful AI as a friend.

An hour later, the bus weaves its way through parts of Minneapolis no heavy ground vehicle has traveled for years. Jonathan finally got a seat when the bus let out gouts of passengers near the Minneapolis city limits. Nooa sits next to him, silent, watching the people get on and off. Jonathan wonders if the others can see her, but how could he tell if they could?

The faces of the people remaining in his car are beginning to show signs of stress. Even lost in their individual feeds, they know something has gone wrong when the bus slows to a crawl to push its way through a barricade of scrap metal and cement. In this part of the city, streetlights are the only illumination, and those are rare—who wants to replace a vandalized unit when no one uses them anyway? Jonathan absently rubs a sore spot where his neck meets his shoulder. An epoxy suture there makes him stiffen and put his hand back in his lap.

Finally the bus stops, on a broad, well-lit street.

"Jonathan," Nooa says, "please get off here."

He does so, accompanied by Nooa's 3VRD. They are met by a robovendor. As the bus accelerates away, the room-sized machine rolls to a stop and 3-verds Jonathan.

"McSwiss Cheezeburger made with minimum 50% real beef and 100% natural tomato," the disembodied but smiling face of a well-fed man says. "For you, compliments of McDonald's."

A dented hicarb panel slides aside and out juts a tray holding a burger in plastic wrap. The tray glows from below.

Jonathan snatches the sandwich off the tray, tears off the wrapper, and devours it in four bites. "I'm thirsty, too, Nooa," he tells the young girl standing 3VRD beside him.

"Have a glass of fresh Lemmonaide," the McVendor says, "chemical-free, compliments of McDonald's."

Jonathan guzzles the waxy cup of lemonade without stopping for breath and wipes off his mouth on a sleeve. After inhaling again, he laughs, an honest but alien sound. His face settles down a bit, but remains relaxed.

"All right, Nooa, who's this guy you want me to meet?" The portable vending car whooshes off.

"I'm uncertain about his identity," the girl says. Jonathan wishes the Brain would make her speak a little more like a human.

"That's crazy; the Brain knows everything. What's his name?"

"He calls himself Pehr Jackson," Nooa says, her face a little scrunched up as she speaks. "The bio data and even brainprint match, but—"

"Shut up." Jonathan crumples the cup in his small fist. It flakes into soft shards of wax and drops onto the shadowy pavement around his boots. "You're fucking with me." Overlaid on the whole crappy city block are the adventures of the real Captain Jackson. He can see the man, live-action, feeding from Neptune. Nooa seems about to respond but he goes on.

"I don't know who you are, but you're fucking with me. Why? Giving me free food, leading me around by my nose, helping me get away from that fat fuck. . . . Don't get me wrong, I appreciate that. Yeah, thanks. Now fuck off."

Nooa stands before him, unshriveled by the blast. *Of course not*, Jonathan thinks, *she's not a real person*. But his body trembles and he turns to walk away.

"Jonathan," Nooa says, "you don't need to take his word for it. I fear that I'm the brunt of a joke. That's why I asked you to help me. You have the ability now to find almost any data you seek, even without me. You do this and we're even, okay?"

Jonathan stares at the 3VRD of an artificial mind for a moment, boggling at this completely out-of-reality universe he's been sucked into. He has to touch his neck again to assure himself that he's even real.

"So I owe you, huh. Yeah. But what. . ." Then he remembers, and then he remembers too much and cuts it short. "The amp. I see what you're driving at. Don't tell me you're some cover program for fucking Blackjack or Lucas."

Nooa doesn't answer. She's staring into a dump alley heaped high with the detritus of decades, dark and empty otherwise. Only distant shouts break the night's quiet hum.

Jonathan shuts his eyes and mentally feels around in his head. He prompts his internal map and watches what still seems like someone else's collection of wetware flash to life atop the *Lone Ship Bounty* overlay. He sees through his cerebellum and cerebrum to the ventricles and apertures, sees neon-coded tendrils reach like a thousand spiderwebs from his card, blackcard, and amp to that brain; the sweep of white-glowing strands from cards and amp to a cyst of powercells in the neck. An array of activation keys and buttons are ranged around the map, his invisible finger able to hit or adjust any instantaneously. It's too complicated to focus. . . . For a moment, he hesitates shutting down the show— the Captain could be killed while he's away!—so he instead shifts it 30° to the side and concentrates on firing up the enhancements.

Jonathan's eyelids quickly flick open; he's not one to stand unprotected out in the open with his eyes closed, especially not at night. He crosses to a wall, leans against it, and hits the amp's *ON* button.

"Holy shit," he mutters as the show pulses like a nova at the side of his pov and his internal map's resolution multiplies so that he can see every individual neuron and synapse. He feels he could count each one if he tried, but the detail is beyond his ability to grasp all at once. Too much feed. . . .

He knocks brightness back four magnitudes, five, and only then realizes his eyes are still open. "Good stuff. Now let's check up on you, Nooa."

He runs a simple ID, not even needing to first find someone's server, able to go straight to the source as if his card array is a server, itself. He can feel his face grinning. The CityNet flashes atop his map and the physical surroundings; now the net reveals all the myriad branchules and sealed passages he could before only access or even glimpse after minutes or hours of pierce-and-cut. Their codes and seals, their ports and firewalls, stand out like beacons, looking suddenly feeble, immaterial. Even his old buddy Citybank flickers in and out of access, though he knows better than to try to cut in without a little practice.

"Your ID is now the single most resonant point in the nets," Nooa says, "except when Director Herrschaft is operating at 3-station max."

Jonathan feels a lance of fear cool his neck. "Shit, Nooa! I must be like a beacon—"

"Don't worry," she answers, "I'm screening your signal. Not even Herrschaft can sense you unless he specifically seeks you out, and even then I could block."

"He'd notice that."

"Yes, but he can't stop me."

Jonathan feels another flash of ice-lightning jag through his meat, but says nothing. He has the feeling he is naked and small and being watched from every angle—and not by human eyes.

It takes only a second to identify the source of the 3VRD named Nooa; CityNet shrinks to one star in the thousands, millions, that compose the star-cluster of WorldNet. Jonathan stares for a few seconds, in awe of his new powers. He feels as if he could reach out and hold this thing, this precious sphere of glittering energy, this ball of crystals and fragile energy-strings that flash on and off faster than his unamped mind could watch. Thousands of orbiting crystals—dimmer and some as tiny as household servers—sail high above the intricate mesh through a black sea, seemingly held captive by webs leading down to the sphere. Geology or its god, gravitation, means nothing here; only the gods of data transfer are represented.

The biggest and brightest satellite is the Brain. Jonathan zooms in and that crystal becomes a multifaceted world of its own. The trace ends there, in sector 116, GenNet OX33928A. Nooa's home. *Home.* As if some contact in Jonathan's mind clicks shut, the precious object suddenly looks cold and lonely. He shuts down the overlay.

"So you are the Brain's ambassador, I guess."

He immediately initiates a new trace to locate Captain Jackson. With his amp, it takes only a few seconds of zooming from ganglia to local node to a shut-down card only meters away. Jonathan shivers.

"What the fuck's going on?" he says aloud. Nooa amplifies herself and overlays his overlay—putting herself in front of everything else Jonathan sees. Something a normal person would—could—never do, but then Jonathan doesn't know any normal people.

"You located Pehr Jackson here, as well, didn't you?" Her face literally glows, an effect either of Jonathan's amp or something from the Brain, Jonathan can't be sure which. "This is wonderful! Go to him right away, ask. . . . I'm sorry. Please go to him and ask how he got here. He's on top of the trash in—"

"I know where he is." Jonathan shuts down all his overlays and maps, except for *Lone Ship Bounty*, which he leaves at one side, and blocks out Nooa's 3VRD. She vanishes as he takes a deep breath and starts climbing the junk. At the top, Jonathan sees a man swamped in shadow and oversize clothing. He stops when he's within reach of the prone figure.

"Why are you lying here?" Jonathan asks with his mouth.

The man's eyes flick open. He stares at Jonathan, blinking.

"Well, are you going to do it now or what?" the man asks.

He sounds incredibly like Captain Jackson, the booming voice, the right tones, the proper rhythm. But he can't be, not when the real Captain is aboard a damaged vessel millions of kilometers away.

"Who the hell are you?" Jonathan asks.

"Why won't you leave me alone?" The man rises to his knees, menacingly. Jonathan takes a step backward, tripping on something metal and sharp. He falls, the back of his head colliding with damp cardboard.

"Are you okay, kid?" a rough, chalky face like the Captain's asks.

Jonathan leaps to his feet and overlays the internal map. He readies himself to test how strong a pulse he can send now, with the amp.

"I asked who the fuck are *you*," he yells, his voice thin and high.

The man exhales and seems to shrink. *No*, Jonathan thinks, *that's not my Captain. Captain Jackson is proud and strong and tall; this man is soft and rounded.*

"I wish I knew," the man answers. "I think my name's Pehr Jackson."

Jonathan studies him for a second; he's an excellent actor if he's not a dupe. "So you really don't know. Someone's fucking with you, too." Jonathan shuts down the map overlay.

He glances around at the mound of garbage. None of the local gangs have noticed them yet. "What're you doing here?"

The man looks down at bare feet streaked with recently dried blood. "Waiting."

"For what?"

"None of your business!"

Jonathan unconsciously takes another step back, but then his stomach burns with anger. "Don't yell at me, mister. Waiting for what, orders from the Brain?"

The word *NOOA* begins to blink before Jonathan's eyes. He erases it.

"Right," the man says, "and then I'm going to hop aboard a fresh battleship and fly for months out past Mars and on to Neptune where I'll blow up their battle-stations, drop a nuke on an alien artifact, and then step inside with a Nik scientist. Ha! Blast off, kid." He turns away from Jonathan and begins climbing down toward the sidewalk.

"You think you're Captain Jackson, don't you?"

"I said, blast off."

"Don't mess with me, mister. You don't know who I am." Jonathan doesn't need to try to sound dangerous. His whole body pushes out each word. "I want to know why my . . . why someone would want to play Captain Jackson."

The man stops moving once he reaches the cement. "Listen, kid. Say, what's your name?"

"Jonathan."

"Jonathan. Listen. I'm thinking that maybe I was part of some show that was supposed to be live but wasn't. I'm an actor, I think." He puts big hands up to the sides of his head, as if to support its weight or cover his ears. "Something's gone wrong with my cards or my mind. I can't be trusted or believed. . ."

The man continues to talk, but instead of listening, Jonathan touches the NOOA prompt floating in front of him and activates the girl.

"Is *Lone Ship Bounty* a live or bullshit recorded show?" he asks.

"Technically not live," she answers, seemingly not bothered by having been blocked out. "Half-second editing."

"How could this be Captain Jackson if right now—or, a half second ago—he's out at Neptune?"

"That's light-hours away, Jonathan. The feed you're seeing is slightly altered and hours old. He could be here."

"How?"

"Who are you talking to?" the man asks. Jonathan blushes; it's been a long time since his meat and mind spoke simultaneously when he didn't choose that.

"Show yourself, Nooa," he says. Nooa turns to face the man, who now sees her.

"Hello," she says. "You must be Pehr Jackson. I'm Nooa, a construct of an AI called the Brain."

"That's enough!" the man shouts. Raging, he looks more like Captain Jackson. "This is a bunch of shit, like this whole city, this whole world is a bunch of shit! I don't want to know why you're doing this, but I've had enough. Kill me, beat me up, or leave me alone."

"You listen to *me*, mister," Jonathan says. "Nooa is the Brain's 3VRD. You want proof? Here." He taps Nooa on the shoulder and she turns to face him. "Have that robovendor come back here and buy this man dinner, on the city."

"Okay, Jonathan."

The bulky yellow machine, half a block away, grinds and whines in a broad circle across the street, rolls toward them through wedges of shadow and light, then goes through the same process it did for Jonathan a few minutes ago. The man takes the plate of "McHardy, 60% real beefsteak, with farm-fresh carrots and potatoes," and stares at it as if it might leap up and bite him.

"So you have access to someone on the city's payroll," the man says, starting to eat with the plastic knife and fork provided, holding the tray against his stomach.

"Burn, man," Jonathan says. He begins to walk away. "Don't you dare keep pretending to be Captain Jackson, either."

Nooa runs to catch up to Jonathan, then passes him and stops in his way. "Jonathan, you have to help me. I need to find out how he got back here so quickly. This could be important."

"You really think that's Captain Jackson? Damn, I didn't think the Brain could be fooled."

"That is him, Jonathan." She keeps talking even as he shoulders past her. The Brain was so thorough creating Nooa that Jonathan feels her brush against him.

"It couldn't be anyone else," she says.

"Oh yeah? And it could be him? You tell me exactly how that's possible. You know everything, right? How's that possible?"

Nooa shrugs. "I don't know. It must have something to do with the alien artifact Jackson entered on Triton."

"Triton?"

Just then, the *Bounty* is hit a third time. Jonathan shifts the show toward the center of his pov, angry that he missed so much. The cabin lights flicker, smoke billows through the room, Eyes pulls the trigger on his subgun, Captain Jackson begins laughing maniacally, and then the pov goes dead with a flash of red. Jonathan sees detail that the average, unamped subscriber wouldn't: universal toxic symbols, bloody corpses; he even feels painful and irritating fivesen feed. Then he watches from an external pov as the spacecraft explodes and spins, burning, toward a pale green-and-orange moon.

He can't say a thing for a long time. The show keeps running, silent, hollow. After a while, Nooa speaks.

"That's not real. This is what really happened."

The pov whips back inside, and Jonathan watches Captain Jackson tie up Eyes as the *Bounty* wobbles. Janus—the pilot—and the Captain look tired and angry. They both seem to have gained weight and their faces to have aged.

"I don't understand," Jonathan says. His knees feel weak; the second of the two people in the whole world that he let in past his defenses just died, or didn't. . . .

"EarthCo Feedcontrol Director Herrschaft is editing in false feed and running it as true-live. I do not know why."

"So he's still alive?" Jonathan notices he's holding his breath, waiting for an answer.

"I believe you just spoke to him. I theorize he returned to Earth through an alien artifact that may be a transportation device."

Jonathan turns and runs back toward the man. He slows and matches the man's walk. "Tell me about the artifact."

The man's thick eyebrows rise for a moment, his eyes seem to light up, but then the animation fades. "I don't know."

"Shut up and act like a man," Jonathan says. "If you're really Captain Jackson, you wouldn't be acting like such a wimp."

"Watch it, kid," the man says. "I remember about an alien artifact, yeah, but it's impossible. . ." His voice sags again.

Jonathan whips his body like a streetfighter he once watched and uses the palms of his hands to push the man against a steel wall blemished with rust-spots like inorganic flowers; the other seems too stunned to react.

"Knock it off, mister! The Brain thinks you're Jackson, you think so, too, so let's hear it. Tell me about the artifact. And think about this: Only the real Captain Jackson would know what I mean by that—the show has you getting killed in space."

The man shakes himself loose of Jonathan and takes a deep breath. His mannerisms are exactly like Captain Jackson's. Jonathan finds himself wanting this to be his hero. But it's too strange. Except. . . .

The Brain thinks so. This guy, himself, thinks so. *And alien technology on Triton? Anything's possible*, Jonathan tells himself. Hadn't he heard once that not only is the universe stranger than we imagine, but stranger than we can imagine?

Jonathan finds himself hoping—an annual event, if that frequent—that he has something to believe in. And, in hoping, he feels as if he has finally awoken from some long, repulsive slumber, packed with nightmares of pain and blood and stifled rage, and loss—oh, loss so great and gross that he cringes just remembering. Everything in the whole world he wanted has slipped away, even his sister who had never been his; he wrecked it all, lost it all.

But now he's found a friend in Nooa, even if she is simply the construct of an AI with questionable motives. And perhaps he's even found the man for whom he built a spaceport within the fortress-world of his mind.

If only it's all true, Jonathan thinks. *Please, let it be true.*

Wordlessly, he tells Nooa to send a little something to test this man. Jonathan stares at him, smiling, waiting for a reply and a light in the sky.

Triton 10: Janus Librarse

Janus finished her *ryokucha*—a weak, bitter tea the people of Jiru City had given her to wash down her first meal in nearly a day. When she opened her eyes, she looked out through the ultraglas dome and was seized by the planet Neptune. She set down the ceramic cup and stared at the massive orb overhead. It was so quiet and solemn, blue like the blue sky of Earth yet only filling a tenth of this moon's sky, streaked with white. Closer, on the surface of the glass, tiny meteorite impact-craters blemished the view; but they were as natural here as Neptune itself, more natural than the people working within this cluster of cylindrical living chambers.

She sighed, realizing only after drawing a deep breath that already she had become accustomed to the scent of dense humanity. And then she smiled and lowered her eyes to the steady man across the plastic table from her. Jon Pang, too, was staring up at Neptune, and something in the intensity of his eyes said to her that he was seeing something new. Behind him, doorless cabinets virtually spilled out their contents of electrical and mechanical components. Janus and Pang were alone with six other chairs, though she could hear voices and movements in the distance, the whirrs of machines and purr of ventilation. The chamber's airlocks—one at each end—gaped open onto two other chambers, beyond which Janus glimpsed others, and so on.

"Janus-san," Pang said, "I must apologize for President Dorei. He should have come to accept your apology."

"I understand." She suddenly felt heavy.

"Miru spoke with you before the . . . bombing. He told Dorei-san you tried to avert—"

"Time to go," a voice interrupted the awkward conversation.

Liu Miru stood in the doorway, wearing a spacesuit. Janus rose immediately.

"I will not permit—" Pang began.

"Please, Pang," Miru said, "you have been my only friend. You must not try to stop me in pursuit of knowledge such as this. Instead, you must join me."

Janus watched in silence. Pang lowered his eyes and stared at the scarred tabletop. If she had to return to the artifact alone, Janus would, though she preferred an escort. Indeed, she would feel like a trespasser if she went there alone.

"Sayo," Pang said. He drew a heavy breath as he stood.

Already he was wearing a spacesuit; Janus recognized that he had long ago established a pattern with Miru: *No; you must; if I must, then I will*—and it was all predetermined, as if the words themselves were only ritual. She smiled. It warmed her heart to see such friends. She had so seldom watched real friends interact in ways that had become natural between them.

"Let us go, then," Miru said. He waited only a second while Janus rose—having never removed her spacesuit—then began to lead the way. Pang followed Janus.

Janus moved through the crowded "city" with abrupt, shaky movements. She was excited at the prospect of discovery and finding Jack, yet still filled with hatred at Eyes— filled also with frustration that she hadn't been able to destroy him. But at least he was gone. Perhaps Jack was right; perhaps it was best that she hadn't murdered the cyborg. Killing had haunted Jack for so long, and she was haunted enough already. Still, she couldn't shake the feeling that Eyes was still alive, somewhere, somehow, waiting like a venomous predator in the 3VRD wilds of her mind.

They reached an outer airlock-entry room where spacesuits hung like hollow men, helmets like legless insects dangling from the ceiling or from hooks on the walls. Someone had brought Janus' helmet here. She locked it in place with assistance from Miru, whose warm, brown eyes held hers for a long second. His smile felt familiar, though she couldn't remember having seen one like his before, except perhaps on Miguel or Jack. . . . *That's it,* she thought. *He smiles Jack's smile. How could that be?*

Pang shut and sealed the room's door, opened the airlock's outer door, then led them inside and closed the door again. They cycled through and stepped out onto Triton's surface.

The walk was very easy in the fractional gravity, though the occasional ice fissure made Janus pay attention to her foot placement. Twice they passed vehicles extending boring tools into the pale green surface, though only one was manned. Crystal sparkling rays from the nuclear blast were their guides. Wind hissed constantly, though with little effect. Finally, the three reached the tumbled hill bordering the new crater.

Janus reached the top first and looked down upon the tower of ice that seemed to cup the alien object as a mother would hold a precious child in her hands. *Jack's in there,* she told herself.

"We should enter together," Miru's voice said over Janus' helmet speaker. "I have been inside before. It can be a terrifying experience without someone to . . . guide you through."

Janus understood the logic of that, but still she found herself often stopping to wait for the two men to catch up to her as they descended the crater's rim and climbed the tower. Miru, especially, was impatient; "The gravity is so slight, why go so slowly?" But she insisted. Plant an anchor, run the rope through, descend a few meters, plant a new anchor. . . .

At last they stood atop the pillar, each with a hand on the three-meter black sphere.

"Shut down your cards," Miru said.

Janus did so, and again she saw the graceful concentric levels of the Beningus Great House rise up before her. Behind a slick, black wall waited something for which she had searched all her life, exploring distant nebulae and imagining worlds she'd never see. But here waited the reality, and she was only minutes away from taking hold of it.

Yet, as the three of them circled round and round, she grew afraid. Was she ready? Miru said the experience could be terrifying; indeed, the artifact had supposedly killed Eyes. What if her heart were as black as the cyborg's? What if the alien intelligence that worked this . . . machine or whatever it was could see into her soul and find the hatred there? What if? what if?

Triton 11: Liu Miru

Miru sensed a hesitation in the woman's movements. He felt as if he knew her well, though he recognized that the memories he used had been collected by a different man. A different shell of a man, he corrected himself; a different exterior that had collected different pearls over the past few decades. Still, Pehr Jackson had shared those pearls of memory with him, as had Miru shared his with Pehr, and now it was as if they both had grown twice as wealthy, neither having lost anything.

"Janus, you must not be afraid," he said. "Fear is the thing that can destroy you. You must be free to trust me, trust Pang, with everything we are about to experience. You must be free to examine yourself without fear. Neither I nor Pang will judge harshly what we see. Is that right, my friend?"

Pang turned away from the temple—if indeed that's what he saw. Miru realized he hadn't yet asked if the others also saw the Great Buddhist Temple of Mahabodhi.

"I have judged no one in my life," Pang said. He looked at Janus, as if seeing her for the first time. "If I can tolerate this man—" he waved absently at Miru, "—I can tolerate anyone." He smiled.

Miru felt relieved when the woman smiled back. Yes, Pehr was right, she had a lovely smile. He felt a longing for her which took a moment to dissociate from himself; this was Pehr's feeling.

"What do you two see, here?" he asked. He heard Pang draw a long breath.

"That's rather difficult to explain," the man answered. "It looks rather like a . . . model of the galaxy, but more than that. The spiral arms sweep around the bright core as we imagine our galaxy operates, yet I seem to glimpse many . . . tonneru, tunnels. They are clear yet as bright as the stars. I cannot explain. Why, what is it you see?"

Miru told him, and then Janus. The three stood in silence for a while, looking on their minds' constructs of holy.

"We should continue," Miru said.

After one more circuit of the barrier wall, Miru saw the telltale roiling colors that indicated an entrance. He waited until the others saw it before he spoke.

"Here is where we enter. Are you both ready?" Pang nodded; Janus hesitated. "Do not be afraid. I will help you however I can, but I will need your energy. I'm speaking to both of you."

Janus smiled again. Miru smiled back, and again saw the peculiar look of recognition on her face.

They stepped inside, Miru first, Pang second, Janus last. Miru's momentary nervousness vanished when he sensed that the woman had overcome her fear and followed them within.

Darkness. Then much more.

Transcendence C

A rainbow shatters and re-forms. Within the rainbow are countless fragment—details, moments from lives, alive with faces and places. Great clouds drift all through the space that feels like a sphere but seems to extend to infinity.

"Our galaxy." My friend Pang. "From how you explained your experience here, I knew it would be this way."

"Yes. Now look closer. Look at the crystals which compose the rainbow." My friend Miru. "Janus, I cannot see you."

I don't know what you mean.

But her panic makes the rainbow rush in upon I and I, and we catch glimpses of her life from now, back through battles on the icy surface of Triton, Eyes tricking her again and again, then she's back aboard the *Bounty*—

You did not intend us harm. Remember that. Watch how you fight to save the artifact, to save the little enemy man down on the surface of an alien world. Is that how you see me?

Laughter. *I know I am not as beautiful as Pehr.*

I find you beautiful. My friend Pang. *But still my panic scares you. I'm so sorry but I'm afraid.* *Eyes penetrates my skull and whips up a nightmare circus. He the clown and his 3VRD minions, none of them real but the pain, oh Father, what have I done to deserve this?*

A million bubbles of time float within the medium of our minds. A wave pulses through, tossing each bubble of our lives which encompasses seconds or hours or days . . . but each scene whips now in the wave like fragmentary nothings about to burst—

You must be careful of these emotions, my friend Janus. This is what destroyed Lonny, Eyes, as you know him. He has harmed you, but please do not attempt to bring the shell in here.

I and I and I see, as young Miru had, the oyster shell ripped open on the metal grating, high above the ocean. Its meat is ripped out, its mother-of-pearl lining scored by a knife—*Is this what you mean?*—*No; watch: In watching, the dangerous wave subsides. Distraction is sometimes necessary until calm can be secured.*

The shell fills up once again, and at the center of the soft meat lies a pearl. As the shell closes, it swallows the obscuring clouds, the rainbow of crystals, the huge metal and plastic mass of Ryukyu Island, Earth, Alabama, the shadow-shrines at Hiroshima, a homeless shelter in Montgomery, and becomes all three of us because this is what we are. . . .

And then it explodes, and we are within ourselves as the oyster is back within his shell. Yet now a shell has no purpose.

"It will destroy you if you bring it here."

Terror: "Where are we? What's happened?"

Janus stands trembling and naked at the edge of a moment just before I took my sister Rachel away from our Father's house. *I can't stand to go there, I won't.*

I and I stand on two different planes of moment, two scenes roiling in our own pasts, but you must go first else neither of us can escape. *We need you. Now you see why I need you. You are so strong, but you cannot access that power because of the shell.*

"My friend Janus, you must show us who you are," Miru says aloud. I cannot hear his thoughts now that I stand at the gates of Hell. "Even now I can see the demons that dwell within you. They are devouring you. But don't you see? They are no longer inside; you can defeat them now. You are everywhere in this galaxy of life, yet they only occupy a few moments. Look!"

And yes, I can see them now, too.

There a stained-glass Father, his silverplate phallus gleaming bloody after his first punishment of the foul daughter, the dirty girl no longer pure—*Woman!*—must be purified by the vessel of God. . . .

There a leather-winged Eyes the cyborg, his skin bristling with hypodermic needles and microscopic lenses that burn holes in my skin and expose the muscle and sinew beneath, scorching, his eyes part of his whole body, his whole self one robotic cycloptic eye to bore through me and drag me beneath the suffocating weight of Father. . . .

There a girl melted into a woman, the two part of one and when seen from this direction they are Siamese twins, their intestines leading from one to the other, mouth of one end anus in the other, the heart separate from both as it tries to beat all the blood away, no blood, can't emit filthy blood, for the blood of our Lord was given so we should not sin; the Original Sin my sin and yours—*don't you see? We can't purge it! We're trapped and sinking and burning and Hell awaits us like bedsheets aflame and swarms of flies chewing away my rotten filthy flesh; no, my God no, I can't step back there—*

My friend Janus, now you must destroy your demons! Look, they are only things. They are smaller than you. You are everywhere, and they are small!

Pang: *This is you:*

The Milky Way galaxy brightens atop the roiling scenes, the bobbing bubbles, the girl begins thrashing on the blood-stained bed as soon as her door clicks shut. *Stars are here all along, you just couldn't see them. See them now? Know they are always within you, all of us. See how you love the stars?*

A young woman, observing 3VRD through a massive plasma-mirror telescope in orbit around Earth. A nebula, spanning light-years, glowing with the reds and oranges and greens of life, knotted here and there with the elements of worlds and air and plants and people, the remains of an ancient star that collapsed upon itself because it was given too much body when born; but it knew, it understood that it was not alive for itself, rather for countless sets of futures and it can see the myriad eyes and ears and noses and mouths that taste the bee-honey and wind swishing through green-rustling leaves high and cool above a river that shifts and chuckles across rocks that are as beloved to it as it was to itself only ten billion years before, because those rocks are as akin to it as it was to the galaxy, as the knots of gas and dust are to sister Rachel's bright blue eyes because I made damned to Hell certain that Father never gripped her with his punishing mallets which alleluia-barking Christians paid so much credit to watch him shake over their heads as he purged them of sin.

She feels herself part of those knots, then part of the star before and after:

"Thank you, Pang, for your eyes and mind, yes I can see the universe through you now and it is beautiful"—*But still I see the demons, and they are to me as entropy is to this whorl of stars. They may be few moments in my universe, but they are massive and powerful. I may be a multitude of moments, but I am weak and damaged.* Always Janus has striven for power and control of her life, yet her life ended twice by the hand of Man.

"Janus, now you make me angry!" My friend Miru. "You think these demons are powerful? Let me show you one of them. You will see just how powerful it is."

What are you doing, friend Miru? thinks the constellation called Pang. Pang's stars flicker for a moment—dimming? redshifting? *Are you drawing away from me, Miru?*

One star accelerates toward I and I and I, growing from insignificance to brilliant white, and now it is a sphere—and now it is a universe unto itself, a supercluster of galaxies, each galaxy within separated by chasms wider than humans could cross in our spacecraft before the heat-death of the universe, and within each individual galaxy lie individual stars, each separated by gulfs wider than spacecraft could leap before the death of their crews: Each star is a moment, crystalline-crackled, semi-clear yet obscured by fractures, and now when one star closes close enough to see within, I and I and I see that this is a preserved moment from the life of Lonny Marshfield.

"No." Janus' word nearly destroys the moment, her resistance a hammer slamming down against the already fragile preserve of a life long lost.

"You must. You must face the demon. See how small it is?"

And before I can object, I am inside the crystal ball as if it is a moment from my own life. I am standing still beside the turgid Atlantic waves rising against the Boston shore, I am a boy— *Why is my skin crackled like blown glass dipped too soon in cold water?* *Be silent and live this moment*—I am a boy whose cracked surface glistens with the blood of . . . of . . . *Father, you can't leave me now!*

And the crystal ball shatters as I, the eight-year-old boy, run my feet banging along the wooden boardwalk beside the ocean huge and wet, roaring, the storefront explosion roaring in my ears with, "Why wasn't it you, boy? Why the man I love?" and then another crystal ball of life's moments crashes against this one as it shatters, spilling out the contents into the sea where in this new sphere I the boy am a young man living with older men, one feedrapt and overlaid with Daddy, as I call him, the other lying splayed on my clean operating table; see how I love you, Mommy? Where are you, Mommy? See how I carve such splendid incisions on my arm? See how I remove the parts of me that sicken you? Yes, some day soon, Mommy, there will be no Lonny Marshfield; I will be Daddy with scalpel in hand and silver wires running through my body electric. And the ball fragments—

Stop it.

Just as I smash through and into another. I am an eight year-old boy again, but this moment is an hour earlier. Daddy's fine brown eyes sparkle with the light of the Boston sun, for nowhere in the world is the sun as fine as in Boston; see how his strong, fine surgeon's hands hold mine? See how his strong, hard arms lift me from the ground and spin me around as he pivots one heel in the sand, Mommy standing nearby with that strange expression she gets. . . .

Another moment overlaps without shattering the previous—"That's better, Janus-san. You need not destroy"—and I am a seven-year-old boy, asleep in my bedroom, only not so asleep that I do not sense the hall light as Mommy creeps into my room and kneels beside my bed, her forehead against my chest and silken hair hanging all over my face; "Don't you dare take my man from me, boy. He is the one I love. You are the accident, the tragedy of my life. Oh, but I had to tell him!"—her whisper sharp as an edge of stainless steel—"I had to let him know he'd impregnated me, and oh, how he wanted a child! Had I known you'd steal him away. . ." And that look again, that look which overlays the look as Daddy spins me a year later on the beach, an hour before the "Terrorist Bomb Kills Three!" as the newsfeed screamed nearly simultaneous with Mommy's scream and my inward scream which lasted until *Cap'n Jack tricked me inside this place and You dared strip away the skin of all I was!*

Janus drifts out of the final moment of Lonny's life, having lived it as had Miru, as had Jack; she knows this, though Jack isn't here right now.

I am this galaxy, I think to the little boy Lonny as he watches me from within his cracked sphere. *I am this galaxy, and yours intersected mine only when you'd become the demon. But you are not the demon; the demon destroyed you. You are the little boy.*

Little boy Lonny smiles. *I am forever eight.*

Beyond that, the demon festered within, the cancer grew until it consumed all I was, and I tried to consume you.

Yes, Janus tells the universe that is her—for now my universe has incorporated the tiny preserves of a shattered life—*yes, you tried. But it was not you. It was only the cancer which had consumed you, as well. Young Lonny, all is forgiven.*

All is forgiven? But look what I did to you.

Remember, that was not you. That creature which lived in your body was not you. I forgive you, and I pity the creature. And then:

"Thank you, Miru. Now I understand. It is as Jesus said: To enter the kingdom of God, we must become like little children. This is the kingdom of God—all this, I and I and I and even I the little boy Lonny. . . ."

And now it is also Pehr Jackson, his life is mine as I grow up to the same age as Lonny in the eight-apartment complex, my friends, my dearest friend Teresa whom I soon after lost contact, living with the old couple who so dearly wanted a young one until the boy caused the death of their friend. . . . *Yes, yes, all you have told me, Jack, it all comes to life as I watch you fill me up inside like sweet wine I pour into the empty chambers of my life.*

Do you see? You are right, Pang; we are whole galaxies, whole superclusters of moments. Yet each are separate universes outside of this place, this wonderful alien place; and within, we are even separated from every moment of who we are.

"I forgive you, Lonny." The demon-figures flapping their wings around the image of Janus—tall and glowing at the edge of one of her moments aboard *Bounty*—the Hell constructs dissipate as the vacuum between her moments closes, as she grows closer to Pang and Miru, and even to the absent Pehr Jackson and the dead Lonny Marshfield. I begin to laugh with relief, as if I am as weightless as air, as permeable and as impenetrable.

There is no gulf. It is only a perception we carried with us from outside, from where we wore our shells.

"Father."

The second demon still remains, especially visible now that the Eyes-Beast has consumed itself.

"How can I forgive Eyes—no, Lonny, whom Eyes destroyed—how can I forgive him but not my own father?"

But Janus, look. Look closer.

I see what you mean. What had once been an inhumanly massive and cosmically powerful figure becomes only a man. Even a small man. Yes, he shaped all those moments there, near the core of my life, those old brown stars orbiting near the heart of all I am . . . yet . . . yet look at me:

I am I, and I and I, and we are five universes of superclusters of galaxies, each a hundred billion moments—

"Pearls. They are all pearls."

All right. We are all these pearls. What is the man whose sperm made my body half of what it is? He is nothing now. I will make who I am.

You are not ready to forgive, but he no longer possesses power over you. Over me. Over us.

267

The second demon scatters to dust, old dark dust near one galaxy's core. That could strangle me some day. *Yes, but we will rid ourselves of it before then. Yes. As long as I know not to hate. That is the only poison, and can only be self-inflicted.*

"Look."

The universe falls, billions of spheres merging into a single glowing ball of light, opalescent, ever-growing until it is all that is visible:

"The pearl."

Now I understand what you mean, Miru. Of course; you are me. I am I.

The pearl: When we enter the artifact, this place, our ugly, fearful, lonely, hateful, isolating shell is vaporized, leaving exposed the hurt and lonely, forgotten child. We are fully aware of every minutiae of our lives here, and unafraid, unashamed. So no longer do we wear our barriers: The oyster shell—scarred by the knives of our demons, even if demons are what we later became—is tossed away, and all that remains is what lay sheltered or imprisoned inside, our soft and fragile and wonderful hidden treasures. But those treasures could only have been created by long years of suffering and fighting the abrasion successfully.

"Successfully is the key."

"Lonny—rather, Eyes—was destroyed because he tried to be the shell in here, where the shell means nothing. The greater our resistance to ourselves and each other, the more damaging the wave of understanding. That becomes hate. Yet the wave has not damaged me."

"Look at how strong you are now."

Janus is the pearl, the time-spanning, multiple-universe encompassing pearl. Miru is, Pang is—

"But Jon Pang, who are you?"

This is me:

Simultaneously, the singularity expands until within it we see galaxies of stars, yet also it contracts until it becomes only one moment among billions.

This is me:

And it is only different than I and I in the details. We are all at our cores afraid of others and of change—though we thirst for them at the same time—and sometimes that fear, combined with ignorance, leads to hate. Yet that fear is only fear of ourselves; we think so little of ourselves that we are terrified to reveal who we are, so we allow no one inside. So we hate people who somehow penetrate to the soft tissue within. Unless we shed our shells, we even hate those we allowed inside. During static and barbarous times—We all have lived those during our lives—fear and anger are survival tools. But in here, fear and anger lead to death. And to a species, it leads to extinction.

I am free.

I have at last cast off the shell, rough and ugly and camouflaged to keep people away. "But to release the inner beauty is to throw away who I was."

Who I am now is free.

I drift within the sparkling corridors between stars, the light of my and my and my lives warm and energizing.

"That's what I did wrong last time; thank you, Pang. We need not emerge weak."

And look here. The inner surface of the pearl—that is, the outer edge of our combined universes, maybe even the inside surface of the alien object—is a map. At last, we approach some kind of understanding of the artifact!

It is a map of our universe, all we are.

"And all the places we have seen."

We need not be tossed out into our lives at random, as I was tossed back to Jiru City.

"That was not random, friend Miru. That was your closest concept of womb, of home." Home. Yes, and love. You are love. Janus, where is your love?

But it is too late. I and I hadn't noticed when she left. The now is but one pearl at a time, while the past crowds us all around like a pearlescent ocean.

"Find your love, Janus."

Miru and Pang trace the map until they locate Triton, then Jiru City, then the assembly room beside arboretum A. The universes and stars and memory-bubbles wash over them—and at the same time sink within—as their bodies coalesce outside artifact space, back within their shells.

Liu Miru 1

Miru and Pang stood at the center of the assembly room. A curving ultraglas wall rose beside them, wet on the other side where green things grew lush inside the arboretum's dome, plants heavy with fruit and vegetables nearly ready to harvest. The dim light of the sun shone down on them, and the dull blue glow of Neptune; but they leaned mostly toward the full-spectrum lumnisheets ranged throughout.

"Ah, but the shell will never again be strong enough to imprison me, Miru-san."

"We must return soon and conduct experiments," Miru said, staring at a stand of sugarcane. Already he was imagining things they could learn. *Unimaginable things*, he thought. *But now that we've had a glimpse of the map, I dare imagine anything.*

"We must plan our ventures judiciously," Pang said, indicating his nudity, "or we'll soon run out of space-suits." They both laughed.

Janus Librarse 1

Janus woke on undyed cotton sheets. She blinked a number of times, trying to place herself in space and time. She felt very awake. Awake, yes, and she felt as energized as a gazelle upon seeing for the first time the Great Plains and all they promised. It would be springtime, and morning, and a clear day that let her see across the grasses and scrub brush to the horizon, and then above, far up and out, out forever to glowing nebulae and blazing suns with their retinue of life-bearing worlds. The future unfolded before her like a 3D map leading in countless directions.

But the important thing was this: *I can follow any of those routes, and no one can stop me. Especially not me.*

She laughed, and realized it was the first true laugh she had ever experienced. So she laughed again, relishing the heady feeling it gave her, how her abdominal muscles flexed and rolled, how smooth the air felt rushing into and out of her lungs; she loved the sound of her voice and for the first time appreciated the curve and stretch of her body without soon after feeling shame.

When the laughter passed, she glanced around to determine where she had landed when the artifact spat her out. Her surroundings were dark, except for the flickering lights of airborne advertisements casting window-rectangles on a wooden floor and dimly illuminating a room; this would be Earth. Fear had no bearing on her now, except as a warning: *I need to know this place is safe, but I trust Miru wouldn't have sent me somewhere dangerous. Or maybe it was the Beningus who sent me here.*

She laughed again, softly this time. *Beningus!* But the kind, alien race seemed very real to her now—she needed a construct upon which to hang her idea of who had built the "teaching tool," as Miru called the artifact, and the fictional alien species would suit her need. *Artifact,* she mused, *what an oversimple word. We have no term which could possibly encompass it.*

Only a second passed before she identified this place:

"Rachel and Miguel's apartment."

Janus stood, feeling the smooth swish as the sheet slid along her breasts, abdomen, thighs, knees, ankles, onto the bed. She told the lights to turn on at minimum. Inspecting the apartment for changes, she padded a few steps across the scuffed hardwood floor to the stone room Miguel had built with his own hands for her, years ago. She smiled. Each rough block of light-colored stone sat atop carefully smoothed mortar bonding layer to layer in the fashion of days long antiquated. Janus sighed. *This is artistry. I hadn't realized Miguel was an artist as well as the lion of kind men.*

A moment of past crystallized in her mind so clearly that she had to take a deep breath to assure herself today was not the day when she had broken free of Father's domination, so long ago. But that severing hadn't been complete until Miru and Pang— and *yes, you, too, Lonny*—helped set her free. Even Lonny; even the child imprisoned in Eyes. It boggled her how changed she felt, but didn't frighten, not for more than a few seconds.

Janus felt weightless. Though she stood here, on Earth, bearing her full weight for the first time in half a year, she felt she could throw open a window and soar out over the city's skyscrapers like a long-winged bird.

"And maybe I can," she mused. After all, here she stood, on Earth, seven light-hours from where she . . . existed moments ago.

She fired up her commcard, sought out the apartment server, and 3-verded Rachel. A few seconds later, Janus' sister responded.

"Janus, is that really you?" Rachel looked older than she had when last they spoke— as she should—but time had not ripped its ugly claws across the girl's features. *That could just be editing, of course,* Janus told herself. This place, Earth, only revealed itself in virtual images, and those images are only edited pictures of people's shells, nothing more. This woman virtually standing before Janus was, in actuality, invisible; opaque.

"Of course it's me!"

"But . . . you're naked."

Janus looked down the length of her body to the bare toes wiggling on battered, worn hardwood. "So I am!"

Rachel was quiet for a moment. "How in the world did you get here? I thought—"

"Oh, we'd better talk about that later." Janus worked up a devious smile. "I have so much to tell you, so much. But now's not the time or place. We'll have to speak intheflesh or not at all. Better yet, I know another way to talk. . ." She laughed heartily, which drew a frown from Rachel. "Oh, Rache, how I love you, sis!"

"Just tell me how you got back so quickly," her sister said, crossing her arms.

"It's very . . . difficult to explain. Do you still believe in angels, my dear?"

"What's gotten into you, Janus? Since when have you started walking around nude and speaking of angels again?"

"Oh, not the kind of angels you're thinking about, not me," Janus said, shaking her head. Her voice didn't, however, carry the usual malice it held for religious nomenclature. "But. . . . Oh, never mind. It just doesn't make me angry any more. I feel as free as that day I moved out of this apartment, only more so. I don't hate him anymore, sis. I don't hate anyone anymore. I pity the sick bastard, but I can't find it in my heart to hate."

"Janus?" Rachel looked concerned.

"Something glorious happened to me a long way from here—"

"Yeah, I'd say it was something, though not so glorious. I just watched you get killed on your show."

Janus frowned.

"Janus. . . ?" Rachel's lips trembled for a moment; her dark eyes squinted a little, and the hair hanging long around her face made her look like a little girl. "Janus, are you telling me you're an angel?"

Janus couldn't help but laugh, but then she realized she might be hurting her sister's feelings. "Well, no, dear. No. What I was getting at is that I've learned where we humans got the idea of angels, only I don't imagine they look the way humans thought they did. They're aliens, Rache, a whole other race of people. I think maybe I was—briefly—like something we'd call an angel, as if they let me try on their kind of existence, if only for a few moments . . . or hours, maybe. I'm not sure how long . . . but never mind. That's for later.

"I just wanted to say hello, and I love you, Rache."

Rachel's 3VRD just shook its head slowly, a searching expression on the face.

"Can I borrow your aircar?" Janus asked.

"You really are my sister, Janus. I ran an ID check on you. Janus, I don't know what to say."

"Say I can borrow your aircar."

Finally Rachel laughed. Her ephemeral arms reached out and embraced Janus; Rachel was transmitting fivesen commfeed, so Janus sensed her sister's arms around her.

271

This was the first time she'd been held like this since . . . she couldn't remember. Miguel had been the last, so long ago. But now, as she thought back on the memory while Rachel held her, Janus could remember every detail of every moment when Miguel's long, strong arms had lifted her up to his mouth or pulled her toward him; she smelled the scent of him fresh from a hard day's work or just after showering; she tasted the flesh-sweet thickness of his tongue. And now she felt Rachel, so close, the closest Janus had ever allowed anyone, even Miguel in their few moments of intimacy. For now she wouldn't allow the shell to return, to smother her. And for once, Janus did not feel the urge to pull away. When glimpses of uninvited embraces threatened to flood and drown this fine moment, she was able to suppress them; better yet, she could dissipate them. No longer did she fear memory, and without fear to feed on, the unwanted memory couldn't raise itself from the dead past.

Janus' psyche roared with laughter, the silent, sweet, drunken laughter of abandon she had felt once or twice as a young girl playing in the tall grass near her home and imagining herself elsewhere, elsewho.

Rachel slowly released her. Janus' face burned with a strange mixture of joy and mania.

"My god, I'm so alive, Rache!" She blew her sister a kiss as she ran to an open closet and pulled on one of her sister's coveralls. She then walked to the kitchen drawer where the spare keycard was always kept.

"I'll comm you when I've tidied up my life a little more. I'm in love, Rache. Of all things, in love, for god's sake!"

Rachel's 3VRD didn't follow Janus out into the hall. Instead, she remained standing in the center of the tiny apartment wearing a lopsided grin, clearly confused yet happy.

Fury 6

Hardman Nadir and the Sotoi Guntai leader surveyed their combined army from the jet-loud cabin of an NKK whirlyjet. Now that the monopera was so magnificently dead and he couldn't subscribe to another, he simply let his headcard audio program transform the machine sounds into orchestral music. Funny how we don't normally notice subtle shifts in engine pitch, he thought, as the string section moved nearly an octave all at once. The horns rumbled on hypnotically, never pausing for breath. Nadir found himself reducing the program's intensity a full magnitude in order to concentrate on the night-blackened desert below and its army of shadows.

A total of nine men and women sat with them, six in blue, three in tan. Only one other EarthCo warrior, besides Nadir and Paolo, had been allowed inside. The Sotoi Guntai still didn't trust the "butchering EarthCo dogs," as one had called Nadir's men. That didn't stop them from contacting every other nearby NKK unit and inviting them to join. *Who's in charge?* Nadir wondered, gazing at the massive, impromptu force rolling and jetting below. It still seemed he was, but that was only by default. No one else showed any desire to take full responsibility, nor did anyone have a clear goal in mind. Nadir didn't either, really; he just knew he needed a big enough force to bust into EarthCo's War Command establishment and root out those responsible for twisting him and his men into murderers. And it helped that he was good at acting as if he knew what he was doing. The soldiers needed a lot of reassurance that they weren't the dark hats of this whole mess.

"EarthCo Air 17th Cav, Sub-Boss Hanrad here, sir," a young woman's 3VRD said, standing before Nadir in the crowded cabin. Her ritually scarred face rippled with excitement, each word formed carefully and large on her mouth. It struck him that he'd never before seen a female Boss in Africa. *She would be her unit's Boss now*, he thought, though none of the EarthCo units called anyone Boss but him.

"Go ahead," Nadir replied. The Chinese Sotoi Guntai watched in silence.

"We've bumped into an ARMCo light-armored battalion, Boss, three klicks northwest." She sent a brief tactical, showing Nadir a data-rich, eagle-eye view of the desert locale, 100 by 100 kilometers. A second later, she continued.

"We executed standard routine, transmitted the EarthCo/NKK crime package"— what Nadir's army had come to call their previous feed— "but no response. What are your orders?"

Nadir hadn't expected opposition, especially not from the tiny Arab corp. So far, every EarthCo unit Boss or NKK Commander at first balked at the appeal to join, then most prepared to attack, and then all but one EarthCo Boss was executed by his own men—the recordings of other EarthCo Warriors doing the same seemed to help them make what had been a tough decision to the units that had marched with the Sotoi Guntai. Nadir said nothing when they asked advice what to do with their Bosses; he comforted them afterward.

It seemed NKK ran things differently: Only three Commanders had been aware of their superiors' plans—these units required more talking, but all three ended up part of the army. One by one, every individual unit they met fell into formation. As each merged with the whole, they, too, witnessed the strange blackout of being isolated from the EarthCo and NKK Worldnets—both in feed and feedback.

Nadir wondered if, perhaps, little ARMCo was behind the silence. *Impossible*, he told himself.

"Are they cut off from their nets?" he asked the woman.

"Our netman says yeah, like everyone else."

"Give them five minutes," Nadir said. "If they don't want to join, we can't let them go off and tell everyone about us, can we now?"

"No, sir!"

Nadir patched into the whirlyjet's external-forward pov camera and zoomed in on where the ARMCo battalion stood. He found them and upped the resolution. No infantry were visible, only 120 "rats"—ARMCo one-man tanks that sported the equivalent of EMMA-Bs and NKK-built plasma cannons—sat dead motionless on the sand. The unified army hadn't yet surrounded the battalion, but Mabalasiks and Tigers were beginning to appear in the pov.

"I'll speak with them," the Commander said intheflesh. Not long in the past, NKK and ARMCo had been virtual allies, until NKK claimed the African land they had helped hold against EarthCo.

CHRISTOPHER MCKITTERICK

Nadir felt his heart-rate increase as the rats moved in unison to the east. They stopped again. No shots were fired.

This could fuck up everything, he thought. Though the battalion wouldn't last five minutes against more than 500 assorted pieces of NKK and EarthCo armor and half that many gunships, it would hurt. And for nothing!—ARMCo wasn't his enemy. Nadir's stomach tightened and he had to shut his aiming eye to keep it from twitching.

He couldn't stand the silence, so he flicked through the BWs until he found the one his ally and the ARMCo leader were using.

". . .not order me to do anything!" a man wearing a full face of black beard shouted. It was old tech; his lips didn't even sync.

"Please review the data we sent," the Sotoi Guntai said, calm and nearly monotone.

"We always knew you and the Western pigs would unite against us!" the ARMCo leader raged. "Now we see—"

"Shut up," Nadir interrupted. Both men's 3VRDs fell silent and stared at him. "Listen, sir," he addressed the ARMCo man, "we wish no conflict with you. If we did, don't you think we'd have destroyed you by now?"

"Because you're afraid!" the ARMCo leader said. He didn't seem able to speak below a roar, though his low-res 3VRD looked like a retro cartoon.

"Bullshit," Nadir said. He opened a commline through the whirlyjet's pov cameras. "Have a look."

The man immediately spliced into one after another pov, then leaped down to several ground-based povs. All the while, the Chinese Commander sat stiff and unmoving, his mouth pulled into a frown.

"Lies," the ARMCo leader finally said. But Nadir didn't miss the decreased intensity in the man's voice.

"You think so?" Nadir asked. "You really want to test us on this matter? I'll be damned fucking glad to oblige, sir. We've wasted enough time on talk. If you're unwilling to join us against the criminals at EarthCo War Command and then NKK's generals, well, that's your choice. We won't fight you either way. But we've talked enough!"

He snapped the commline shut from the whirlyjet's small server, also cutting off the Commander. Nadir felt a moment of worry, fully aware he had never been given command over the army, that the Sotoi Guntai still outnumbered the EarthCo Warriors and the NKK heavy armor was the only of its kind down there. If the Chinese Commander called on his forces to revolt against the "butchering EarthCo dogs," Nadir would end up in command of nothing, and the combined army would be a few Mabalasik tanks rolling across the desert with burns on their hulls.

Nadir decided momentum was his greatest resource, perhaps his only one.

"Hanrad," he commed to the EarthCo Sub-Boss. She promptly appeared. "Set your unit in motion." He opened the allband BW, which the ARMCo units would also feed. "Everyone move out, bearing adjust two degrees west."

"Boss," Hanrad said, her face concerned yet excited, "that'll put us on top of those ARMCo rats."

"Yes, it will," Nadir said. "All units, hold your fire. Don't even look at our ARMCo friends as we pass. But if they fire, take out only the individual rats that attack. We don't want a bloodbath here. Maybe there's a few good soldiers in their ranks, too. If not, be ready to blast 'em all."

He spliced from one pov to another, watching the legions of tanks, whirlyjets, and light EarthCo and NKK cars again set in motion. He recalled pictures of ancient armies forced to march by foot and then, tired after hours of marching over rugged terrain, fight. The cheap personnel car had changed all that.

Soon, Hanrad's unit was virtually indistinguishable from the bullet-shaped ARMCo rats. And then the light tanks were engulfed, their cannon muzzles bristling amid a rush of plastic and steel.

Still no fire. But also, still no comm from the ARMCo leader. Nadir was glad for the cabin's cold wind rushing through—it dried the nervous sweat breaking out on his back and armpits. *What if they just sit there? What if they don't agree to join us?* The whole point of this war is that people were killed when they didn't need to be. *How is what I'm doing any different?* And yet....

They'll have to be destroyed, he told himself. He had known it all along.

Five minutes passed. Nadir's and the Commander's whirlyjet circled their army three times as it rolled past the rats. When the Tiger tanks bringing up the rear were in range of the rats, Nadir knew now was the time to decide.

He opened a secure line to the ARMCo leader. "Have you decided?"

"Go to hell!" the other screamed. Nadir noted the shrill wavering of the man's voice.

"No one is listening right now." He paused. "Do you still deny the size of our combined force? You must know that if you don't join us, I'll be forced to smash your little tanks into dust! So what is your decision?"

No response.

"If you can't decide, I'll find another of your men who can."

"Are you threatening me?"

"No," Nadir said, calmly. "I want you to be my ally. You would enjoy the same respect as those Sotoi Guntai and other NKK units you saw. I wouldn't threaten an ally. I am merely explaining the consequences of your making the wrong decision."

Nadir watched the man cast about the impromptu network woven through the desert night; *Trying to see if anyone's eavesdropping*, Nadir thought.

"You won't simply let us go on with our mission?" the man said. No longer did his words contain venom.

"I can't do that. Can you imagine what War Command would do to this army if they found out what we're up to? No, I can't let you go. But I would be very pleased if you combined your forces with ours. You will be rewarded in the end; who knows—maybe your corp will have a chance to take the superpowers to international court. Maybe you'll get North Africa back."

"This is not attractive to me," the man said. "I will face court-martial from my superiors, and they are not criminals."

Just then, Hanrad's 3VRD appeared on another BW. She had correctly guessed Nadir's plan. *Not yet*, he thought, wishing she could read his mind.

"Your decision," Nadir said, and cut off the BW. He opened his commline to Hanrad.

"Wait one more minute," he told her. Even as he spoke, the ARMCo BW-signal lit at the corner of his pov. He smiled and waited a few seconds, then opened it.

"I, Sheik Dominique Filre Hassad, declare that your NKK and EarthCo soldiers may assist us in ridding the African continent of trespassers," the ARMCo leader said.

Nadir noted the man used an allband similar to his own. *Everyone's listening*, he thought. Hopefully no one will laugh.

"We accept your generous offer to join forces," Nadir replied. He looked across the whirlyjet's crew cabin at the Chinese Commander, who apparently had been staring at Nadir.

"Do you accept the Sheik's offer, Commander?" Nadir asked.

The man's face split into a wide grin that looked somehow out of-place on the man. "You astound me," he said, then told everyone that he, too, accepted the ARMCo addition.

Nadir drew a deep breath and shut down his commcard. Everything was running smoothly again, and his plan was still simple and direct—almost naïve, he knew, but perhaps justice requires a bit of innocence.

He booted the audio program. Once again, the jet-voiced orchestra played in his head. He closed his eyes and silently added a new verse to a dead monopera:

> *I'm alive*
> *I'm alive in the desert night.*
> *We will fight for right*
> *'til death*

Pehr Jackson 3

Downtown Minneapolis, Minnesota, Earth: Pehr Jackson and Jonathan Sombrio walked side-by-side along a cracked and cratered sidewalk. Behind them followed a girl named Nooa.

"The artifact," Pehr began. "When Janus and I got close enough. . . . This sounds crazy. Why does the Brain want to hear this?"

"Knock it off," the boy said. "Anyway, I'd like to hear it, too."

Pehr stopped walking and stared at Jonathan. He didn't like the boy's manner much at all. This was just some street punk hired by a powerful, faceless somebody. Pehr studied the small, quiet girl. Patience . . . maybe I can get answers by answering some, even if they only further confuse reality.

"All right, I'll tell you a story that feels like a memory." Pehr took a deep breath and continued walking—toward where, he wasn't sure. But he couldn't stand still. This night, cool and dark and empty, felt much like those nights here a decade ago. . . .

"This guy, named EConaut Captain Pehr Jackson, and this woman, Janus Librarse..." His voice trailed off.

"Please go on," the girl said from behind.

Pehr drew a deep breath, concentrated, and his voice naturally mutated into Captain Jackson's. *I must be an actor*, he thought. *This is much easier than using my own. So that fragment of memory is accurate.*

"They walked around and around St. John's Cathedral—well, he did, while she saw instead some kind of alien place. Somehow, when they shut down their cards, what had been a black sphere appeared as two different holy places, based on what each thought was holy." Pehr couldn't help feeling a little quickened by the memory.

"He finally found an entranceway, just as another man, Liu Miru, had before them. So the Captain went inside, where he . . . found Miru. And then he kind of disappeared. Janus came later, I guess." Pehr began to worry—*What happened to Janus? This is absurd to even wonder, but . . . where had Eyes sent her?*

"You talked with Project Hikosen Director Miru?" the girl asked, excitedly. She hurried to walk on his left now, the boy on his right. "What has he learned about the artifact?"

Pehr smiled. "Well, yes; the Captain and Miru . . . talked." He dearly wished the memory were true. If it were, he had finally experienced friendship, and that beyond anything he had ever imagined.

"What did you learn?" the girl asked.

"Listen, I'm—"

But Pehr forgot what he was about to say when an EConautics Stratofighter lit up its engines in jet mode, filling the city with a mechanical scream.

"What's going on?" he asked. The boy laughed hard, holding his stomach as Pehr shielded his eyes with a forearm and backed away from the jet downwash.

"You tell me," Jonathan said, again wearing that blasted smirk.

"An EarthCo warcraft is illegally landing, under its own power, in downtown Minneapolis," Pehr said.

He shook his head, transfixed upon the trio of blue flames raging from the engines bulging along the sides of the white, dolphin-shaped fighter. His estimate of whoever was yanking his strings grew immensely. Only a few people in the world could get away with something as dangerous as this; everyone else had to obey the laws: Except in case of emergency, all spacecraft had to lock onto maglev channels and shut down engines. Local air-traffic control AIs even kept engines from firing in emergencies when a craft was so low as to damage property or people. They were instead dragged—even with the slipperiest, weakest grasp—away from populated areas as quickly as possible, usually resulting in vehicular demolition during the move or when the craft hit the ground in a safe zone.

The Stratofighter rumbled and popped as its engines slowed to shutdown. The turbines continued whining while Jonathan asked Pehr a question via headfeed; any intheflesh sound was obliterated by the noise only ten meters away.

"Can you fly that?" the boy asked.

"I'm just an actor playing Pehr Jackson. I can't—"

"Captain Jackson isn't a retro softhead like you," Jonathan said with a sneer.

"Okay, you want to see if I can fly this machine, eh?" Pehr said, grabbing the boy just above the elbow and leading him toward the Stratofighter. His arm was thin and hard. "All right. You'll accompany me, of course."

"Of course," Jonathan answered, his face like stone. He shook his arm free.

The Stratofighter stood twelve meters on its tripod landing gear above the smoking asphalt street on, smooth-sided, as sharp-nosed as an arrowhead, darkened by heat at the leading edges of the stubby wings and along the engine shrouds. A streetlight shone through the cockpit canopy, revealing that no one had piloted the craft down. Overhead, a Coca-Cola adblimp pulsed with red and yellow light as it floated within the valley of skyscrapers, transforming the Stratofighter's white hull into an animated toy, shadows moving along its sleek skin. It stank of hot oil, scorched heatshielding, burned alcohol, warm plastic and metals. The snub ends of lasers, pulseguns, and EMMAs drew a ring around the fuselage just ahead of the cockpit.

Beautiful, Pehr thought. Adrenaline surged into his blood. A few spectators began to appear from alleys and the shells of wrecked cars.

He tried to think how to board such a vehicle. Any pleasure he had just experienced sagged instantly. *What a damned fool they're making of me. I don't even know how to open the blasted door!*

But then, at his most frustrated, the answer simply floated free into the open of his mind. He knew exactly how to access the craft's server and log in using his EConautics credentials. He knew how to gain authorization for entry, for launch, for everything. He pictured in his mind—flawlessly, no detail spared—the ship's three-axis control-panel landscape overlay. He knew how to sort through the pilot files and locate various pre-programmed flight plans and battle sequences. He knew how to manually override the autopilot and fly by direct feedlink. He even knew how to locate secret passwords, a necessary skill for an EConaut to possess when he might need to use an unfamiliar craft during battle conditions and didn't have time to seek Wing Boss authorization.

All this information flooded into his mind as if it had been penned in there all along, as if it were experience and not remnants from a show or dream. So he tested himself.

First: Call up ship server. A second later, dozens of gauges, readouts, control systems, and files flashed to life around Pehr, overlaying the smoking city street in a long, flat oval at chest-level.

"Did you do that?" the boy asked. Pehr didn't answer. *The kid's able to sneak into my head*, he thought. No matter.

A hatch cracked open just above the fuel tanks, ten meters up, and a nearly weightless rope-ladder of malvar fiber unfurled, rebounding a few times until its elasticity settled down. He started climbing.

"Are you two coming?" he asked. "Intheflesh, Jonathan?" The old thrill rose in him, and so good did it feel that he hadn't the heart to remind himself any "old" sensation was probably the product of feed. *Probably*, he thought. *I just used the word probably.*

"Yeah," Jonathan said. "I'm not afraid of you, not with the Brain on my side."

Pehr smiled to himself. He crawled in through the tight hatchway, pulling his body past the circular opening hand-over-hand using the shockplas rungs that lined the airlock. He waited in the space for the boy to join him—and the girl's 3VRD—then wound up the ladder and ordered the hatch shut. A dull red light flicked on. Pehr cast a brief glance at Jonathan, who seemed to crouch against the wall, every muscle in his face clenched and his body nearly trembling with the effort to stand still. Pehr began to wonder who this kid was, how he had gotten to be such a frightened creature, and what he was gaining personally out of this business.

The airlock ventilators whirred momentarily, sensing no pressure differential, then the inner door opened. Pehr led the way into the confined central staircase which spiraled up steps made of the same ultralight, flexible material as the ladder—three meters from lock to cockpit. A dim yellow lumnistrip was set into the handrail, lighting the chamber and defining a spiral line as if it were rifling in a snub barrel. They passed several closed panels which, Pehr knew, housed fuseblocks, manual switches, spare cards, computer access keyboards; some allowed access to weapons systems or ammunition storage; some were empty stowage compartments. Standard Stratofighter configuration. Their feet fell as silently as breaths on the steps.

Curious, Pehr ran a user check. He stumbled when he found out this craft was registered to a Wing Sub-Boss, one Commodore Galette. *So EConautics is in on this scheme*, he thought.

Pehr reached the top of the stair and located the second password needed to enter the cockpit: "Coulant." He squeezed inside and made way for Jonathan. The two-seat cabin was decorated mostly in multicolored wiring and black vinyl. Equipment cases, electronics access ports, and manual gauges crammed the space. Info-icons filled the air like a swarm of weightless marbles. A blue-lacquered medallion bearing the silver relief of a gibbous Earth and stars glinted as it swung from side to side on a silk ribbon. Plastic mesh upholstered the two seats, lightweight and breathable. A menagerie of city lights— adblimps, wall-mounted ads, streetlights—blinked and glared through the ultraglas. When the boy sat on his seat and the girl's 3VRD stood between them, Pehr slapped the cockpit hatch shut—which made the boy jump—and got his bearings about the controls landscape-overlay.

"Normally, we'd suit up now," Pehr said to Jonathan while manually checking the systems. "But it seems the owner of this can left his suits at the cleaner." He chuckled lightly while laying his ephemeral fingers on the virtual controls in a fashion that felt almost instinctive.

"You're not strapped in properly," Pehr said, noting the boy's loose belts.

"Would you please get out of the way," he told the girl. She shrunk to pixie-size and stood on a scratched black fivesen transmitter box. Pehr shook his head, smiling. He freed himself and adjusted the other, then belted himself back in.

Then he encountered his first problem. Every time Pehr tried to virtually pull a wafer out of its slot, his ephemeral fingers slipped and a two-tone note sounded.

"Why can't I run a programmed flight sequence?" he asked without looking at his companion—or tormentor; the future would reveal which.

"I told Nooa to lock you out," Jonathan answered. "This'll prove if you're really Captain Jackson."

Pehr drew a deep breath and held it for a moment, composing himself as if to deliver a line. He noticed a crowd was gathering outside the craft but couldn't tell how many were intheflesh and how many were 3VRD.

"Captain Jackson," Pehr began, "after he attained the rank of Captain, hardly ever piloted by himself. I know that much." His resource of patience was running low.

"So this will prove who you are without a doubt, won't it?" The boy's words sounded mocking, but his tone was strangely flat. Pehr heard a faint crash and rumble—modern music?—accompany everything Jonathan said.

"They, whoever 'they' are, wouldn't have stuck useless feed like how to pilot a spaceship in when they brainwashed you, right?" The boy wouldn't shut up.

"Okay," Pehr said. "Okay. You want to die? I do—what the hell's left on this miserable world, anyway?" He stared at the crowd, which was now beginning to include cops. An object rang against the hull.

"EarthCo Stratofighter EEJ-008 ready for takeoff," he commed to whomever might be listening.

"Captain Jackson," the pixie said, "we are currently operating under full blockout. No one is aware of us, nor our feed. I did not authorize this expedition, but Jonathan thought it somehow necessary, so I condescended to his wishes and chose a craft which is used only for exhibition. It is best to have no—"

"Shit," Pehr swore under his breath. *Fine, this is what you're gonna get.*

He tapped a little black EConaut-only back-door icon, which supplied him with the backup password; this allowed him to initiate launch sequencing. He noticed that the fuel tank was at 67%—not promising unless they refueled in space. A Stratofighter was designed to be fueled mid-mission, and taking off with less than 90% was a way to assure the craft would stay in orbit or land only in flamer-mode until the maglev tunnels grabbed hold.

"Get the fuck out of the downwash!" he commed on a general BW to which the people outside were certainly tuned. A few began to back away. When one man turned and ran, the milling crowd transformed into a stampede that thinned as each ran his or her separate way. Jonathan laughed. Soon the street was as empty as always. Only one face peered from around the brick facade of a building half a block away.

"Idiots," the boy mumbled.

Pehr wondered on that for a moment, then realized: *Even the virtual people had run.* "Idiots," he agreed.

Pumps growled to life far below, switches fired, the engine turbines shrieked up the harmonic scale, then fuel ignited and something heavy lay upon Pehr's chest. Acceleration dragged a smile long across his face—a smile he hadn't realized had formed. Out of the corners of his eyes, he watched the city shrink yet broaden as it fell away; the craft rose along a steep arc toward the freedom of space. He sighed as he realized that he hadn't turned the vessel into a ball of fire. The Minneapolis/St. Paul sprawl became little more than a toylike collection of model buildings and pretty lights that stretched to the horizons in every direction. Farther, and Pehr could see the great dark area of Lake Superior—even that sprinkled with lights—like a void within a nearly continuous patchwork of glitter.

The engines clanged in the high stratosphere as the turbines flipped and changed the combustion chambers to rockets. He declined to call up maglev assist, which would have hurled them along a tunnel of electromagnetic accelerators in almost any direction at almost any velocity they chose. Right after the clang, a new set of pumps began feeding oxygen to the jets-cum-rockets. Pehr realized that he knew what every sound meant, and this knowledge gave him confidence that each next order he gave the ship would be correct. Little by little, he began to assume an identity. At least he'd act as if he had once been Captain Jackson, EConaut extraordinaire. *Maybe, if I act well enough, I can be him again. . . .*

But he had to concentrate on the task. When they had gained sufficient speed and altitude, he shut down the propulsion systems. Little more than 10% fuel and oxygen remained.

The roaring ceased, the pump turbines mewled quieter and quieter, and then silence, silence broken only by distant pings and whirrs. A light breeze wafted across his cheek from a series of vent holes near the canopy base. The boy's breathing was rough and fast.

"You okay, Jonathan?" he asked.

"Great," said the boy through his teeth.

The kid had obviously never been in a weightless environment; his eyes wouldn't stay put for long, his skin looked pale, he swallowed a lot. *Let him suffer a little*, Pehr decided. *He'll be fine.*

Pehr looked out first at Earth—*How lovely she appears from high above, blue and white and solemn, so unlike the face she presents upon close inspection. Or maybe we're just a skin infection that's invisible from space.* He turned his eyes up away from the broad curve to the stars raging in the silent beyond, not quite perfect pinpricks through the weathered ultraglas. He remembered how Janus loved the stars. . . . *Absurd*, he told himself: Janus. *Yet maybe, maybe.*

That maybe grew and grew, and soon Pehr found himself breathing quickly and his face heating. At last he turned to Jonathan and demanded—

"Who put you up to this?"

"I told you," the boy said, slowly, swallowing between each word.

"'The Brain,' you said. Humph." He turned to the pixie standing on the cockpit's fivesen transmitter. "You. What's going on? No bullshit." She enlarged but thinned as she grew so that she appeared as a ghost between the two seats.

"Jonathan chose to test you—"

"No, I mean who's behind all this? Who are you?"

"You already ran an ID. My name is Nooa. I'm a construct—"

"Shut up!" Pehr's words rang like hollow gunshots for a moment afterward. "So maybe you are the Brain. What the hell. Maybe I'm Captain Pehr Jackson. Maybe this is all a feedrapture dream. . ."

He clenched his jaw. "To hell with that. You've got to believe in something. Ah, shit. Shit!"

"Captain?" Jonathan asked, his face a little swirly. "Please tell me you're my Captain Jackson." He said it like a question.

Pehr stared at the boy. *What's this?* he wondered. He looked away after what felt like a too-long intheflesh stare; he didn't want to be rude, not even here, not even under these crazy circumstances.

"You know," Pehr began, "I feel as if I've come to understand myself and so much about the world—what's wrong, what desperately needs to be changed. But then I realize I have no idea who I am to be thinking these things. It's nuts, absolute lunacy. I can't stand it anymore! And now you call me 'your' Captain Jackson.

"Shit. Jonathan," he glanced again at the boy and noticed lines on the young face, the kind of lines that should only crease a middle-aged man's. He looked away. "I want to be Captain Jackson. But that path leads back to pain just as much as any other path in my mind. It's lunatic. The artifact, everything."

"Tell me about the artifact, please," Nooa asked. For an AI construct, her face held an awful lot of emotion. "This information is very important."

Pehr closed his eyes tight against the silent roar of stars, the boy's pleading and pained face, the girl's blatant desire.

"Artifact, ha! Why didn't you just leave me be?" he demanded, feeling as if he was one of those stars—a red one, all soft and hot and sparking like the images he saw behind his eyelids.

"Miru, crash you! Where are you when I need you?"

Transition 4

And, just as Pehr said the man's name, just as he recalled a lifetime of memories that seemed like his own but couldn't possibly be—no matter who he really turned out to be, Captain Pehr Jackson of *Lone Ship Bounty* or Captain Downward of *Dreadnought*—just as Pehr thought of the man by body-image and an infinite series of incidents that occurred all across the solar system, he heard a reply:

Pehr?

Pehr was so shocked that his eyes flipped open like a windowshade wound too tight. He breathed deeply, looked out at the stars and at Earth, the view rotating ever so slightly as the Stratofighter sailed the sky in a decaying orbit. He turned his eyes to Jonathan, who was staring wide-eyed.

"How'd you do that?" the boy asked. "I know you're here intheflesh, but. . ."

"But what?"

The girl answered. "Your ID trace vanished for .01 seconds."

"You sort of . . . got like colored glass," Jonathan added.

"What?"

"Citizen Jackson," Nooa said, "you said 'Miru.' Did Project Hikosen Director Miru just attempt to . . . transport you back to Triton?"

"Crash this, crash it all out—" But Jackson's tirade was cut short by a quiet voice in his head:

Pehr, is that you? It sounded like the voice Miru had used when they spoke in the artifact's vast, spaceless space. It held a calming, somber tone, a specific personality, though Pehr could not hear anything. He couldn't even gauge the language.

"I want to believe this," Pehr replied. "Oh, I can't tell you how much." His head filled and grew light with awe and wonder as he recalled the transformation he had undergone—or had been tricked into believing he had undergone—in the artifact. "Learning tool," Miru had called it.

Now I understand! The Miru-ghost was intruding again. *The artifact is not a thing outside of us, at least not after we have been inside. It's in us now, Pehr. We have cast off the shell—remember?—and internalized all that comprised the artifact and ourselves. We have stretched the boundaries of the artifact and have become the artifact. I can bring you here to me, right now, if you wish. My friend Pehr, imagine what this means to the exploration of the universe and of our minds! *Imagine!**

As Pehr listened to the quiet but hypnotizing voice, he grew more and more anxious. He could stand no more.

"That's it. Nooa—I mean Brain—now it's time for *me* to test *you*. If you really are the Brain, you can take over this craft if I leave."

"Tell me what has happened," Nooa demanded. Her face showed none of the threat a human's would have upon this kind of frustration, which affirmed one of Pehr's guesses.

"Miru just . . . talked to me," Pehr said. "I have to go back to Triton to find Janus and make sure she's all right."

He turned away from the ghost-image of Nooa—*Strange form for the Brain to assume*, he thought—and faced Jonathan.

"Sorry, kid, but if I'm really Captain Jackson, I've got some responsibilities." His stomach clenched as his worry about Janus escalated. At the same time, he felt elated and powerful and—he cringed but chuckled inside as he thought of it—a little godlike. If all the amazing things Miru was talking about were true, the universe was his oyster. *What to do with it?*—he had no idea—*but I've got to start somewhere.*

"Hope you enjoyed the ride," he told the boy. "Make sure the Brain fuels this can before trying to land. Ha! Good to meet you. Real good."

He extended his hand and engulfed the boy's. Jonathan looked dazed again, yet the lines around his eyes and mouth seemed to have softened a little.

"How?" the boy asked.

"Yes, how?" Nooa echoed.

"Miru says whoever goes inside the artifact takes it with them when they leave. That doesn't sound right; I have to talk with him a little longer to understand what he means. It's more complicated than a transportation device, you see." He looked into Jonathan's eyes now, but the boy only held his gaze for a second.

"We sort of exchanged lives." That didn't sound right, either. "I can't really describe it. The artifact blasts you into atoms or something and all that's left is who you are, you know, inside your mind. Not your brain, your *mind*. Your thoughts, memories, feelings—all the things that make you who you are. And you sort of mingle those things with whoever else is inside with you, so when you come out, you remember two—or even more—lives as if they were your own. Every little memory is as clear as anything you can imagine, better than usual, as good as fivesen feed. When you're done sharing all this, you sort of wake up in a place . . . a place that feels like home, or maybe with someone you have unresolved feelings about."

Pehr grew wistful a moment, thinking of Megan. But she had become a different person over the years, assuming he had ever known her at all; perhaps she had been consumed by the shell, as Miru would put it. She seemed to have grown very thick.

Janus. He had to go to her.

"How can you go back?" Nooa asked. Pehr noticed that Jonathan's mouth hung a little loose and the lines had grown deep again. Pehr wished he could reach out and smooth away the boy's fears or whatever made him look like that, but he understood that age of boy too well.

"That's a damned good question," Pehr said, and laughed. "I'll let Miru take care of the logistics. Bye."

Bam—as suddenly as when he had stepped into the entrance of the wall surrounding Triton's St. Paul's Cathedral, Pehr shattered.

Bam—just as suddenly, he stood facing Liu Miru in a cool, humid room filled with plants and smelling vaguely like urine. He felt the weight of his body again, but it wasn't anywhere near as heavy as it felt on Earth. He looked up and saw a familiar blue world hanging in the sky. It had replaced Earth below the Stratofighter, about the same relative size—and the same colors, blues and whites—but so, so alien. Having had half a lifetime experience in space, he only felt disoriented for a moment.

He smiled and looked down at Miru. The man seemed shorter here, intheflesh. Miru smiled back. No, he *beamed*; Miru beamed at Pehr.

"Pang, we did it!" the man cried.

Pehr just now noticed a second man standing in the greenhouse. A number of faces peered into the domeroom from lower chambers connected at four points by sealed airlocks. They all shared the same expression.

"Hello, Liu," Pehr said. He reached out and embraced the man. It didn't feel wrong in any way. In fact, it felt like the most natural thing in the universe to do. He nearly wept with joy. When he backed out of the embrace, he regained the old single mindedness he only occasionally found in himself—the kind of single-mindedness that defined the role of Captain Jackson.

"Where's Janus? You know who I mean, don't you?"

"Of course," Miru answered.

"She's doing very well now, but she's not here anymore," the second man said. "We have a lot to tell you. Very much, friend Pehr."

Miru sat down and crossed his legs on the gravelly path, wide green leaves brushing his grey jumpsuit. The second man followed, then Pehr did so, as well. He felt like a child about to learn a lesson.

But for the first time in his life, being like a child held no negative feelings, no fear or emptiness. He smiled, and remarked to himself how strange it felt to smile so much in one day. *Man, and what a day!* he thought.

Innerspace 7

Jonathan Sombrio had grown fatigued by trying so hard to fight down the elation and wonderment he felt as the man calling himself Pehr Jackson took him aboard a real spaceship and launched them into orbit. *Captain Jackson! Space adventures!* So worn down was he that, by the time motion- and space-sickness began to thrust their wiggly fists through his insides, he no longer needed to keep up the facade of boredom in order to hide the naked emotions he wasn't yet prepared to share.

Then Captain Jackson—he is sure now that the man who just disappeared was his hero—then the Captain vanished, as if he'd never been here at all, as if he were nothing more than a 3VRD. Except Jonathan knows better. His amp—*And the Brain, for fuck's sake!* he thought—proved the Captain really was here. That far outweighs, far outweighs, the discomfort. But he left, just as Jonathan was beginning to welcome him.

So now Jonathan sits in the webbed Stratofighter seat, alone with Nooa amid the small electrical sounds, and she isn't really real. His stomach threatens to purge again. He swallows it down before it has a chance to get out.

"That artifact sounds like a 'quin-hell place to me. Doesn't it to you, Nooa?" he asks.

"Its potential uses are incredible, Jonathan. It was built by alien intelligences! Think about that. But we need more information before we can test it or trace it back to its builders."

"Fuck that, Nooa. I feel sick, and I'm as tired as the only male rat in an all-ratfuck city, and this seat is the most uncomfortable thing I've ever been tied down to in my life. Let's go back to Earth." He squirms against the odd sensation of being held in zero-*g*. It seems he's falling against the seat and the belts at the same time, but barely . . . it doesn't make sense to his balance. He's also just a little bit concerned about getting back down without a pilot. The base of his skull throbs where Lucas slid in the amp.

"First we will need to refuel this vehicle and take on more life-support supplies," Nooa says.

"Fuck," Jonathan says. But, despite his discomfort and the letdown of having lost the Captain, Jonathan feels relieved. He doesn't really want to go back to Earth just yet. Nothing down there is any more appealing than this cramped tin bubble in the middle of hungry vacuum. In fact, that sounds very much like how Jonathan feels on Earth.

He turns his head and stares out at the welding-arc bright stars. A dense area of stars which he remembers vaguely as being called the Milky Way particularly holds his attention—so many of them, more than he'd imagined existed in the whole universe. Jonathan had never looked up at night. If he had, the only celestial object he would have seen in Minneapolis would have been the Moon, anyway. But even that nearby world holds something more for him now, since he had watched the Captain fight there—and then met the Captain intheflesh.

Jonathan realizes this is the first time he's been physically out of the sprawling city. A thrill works through the numbed nerves of his body, slowly up his spine and then lightningly along his limbs until his experiences of the past hour feel less dreamlike.

Fuck, he thinks, *I've always wanted to be out here. Fuck. Isn't it just the way of life that I can't even really enjoy this?*

Mechanical sounds pound and scream to life beneath—behind?—him, tearing his attention away from the solemnity of space. The rockets ignite with an odd, distant sort of rumble. Jonathan regains a little weight as the Earth tilts wildly up at him and the Milky Way pivots across the sky. The sickness that surges again through his meat makes him think Earth isn't such a bad place, after all.

"Jonathan, I just recognized the ID signal of Janus Librarse. She's in Montgomery, Alabama."

Only after the sickness fades does he recognize the irony. He coughs out a laugh. "Too bad the Captain just left, huh."

The cacophony of sounds that accompany the rocket roar remind Jonathan of his revmetal BW, so he flicks it on audio-only. The pound and howl of the machine music and singers work to settle his stomach somewhat. By the time the Stratofighter reaches an unmanned fueling station—bloated and massive and white with snaking arms that reach out to his craft, the Brain's arms, he thinks—Jonathan is truly beginning to enjoy the ride.

Janus Librarse 2

Janus allowed the autopilot to fly Rachel's aircar out of the top-floor garage into the dark clouds a half-kilometer above Montgomery. The vehicle was an old model, was old when Rachel and Miguel bought it twelve years ago. Still, it worked, and though the seats were torn and worn, it was comfortable. The shockplas canopy didn't quite seal completely, but Janus wouldn't be taking it into space. She smiled at the thought.

Where's Jack gone? She knew the answer even as she wondered, from having lived his life with Miru and Pang.

Jack had gone to Oberlicht Towers. A woman named Megan Boisson lived there, in room 115089. That was the only place she could think he'd go. Certainly not back to his wife. Though if he wasn't at Oberlicht Towers, Janus had no idea where to look next.

She input the travelplan and set the aircar to run at top speed.

"Do you mind if we stay at cruise velocity, instead?" an older woman's disembodied face asked. Janus was shocked for a moment before she realized this was only the car's 3VRD.

"Sure, maximum cruise," Janus said.

The car's rotor rose in pitch, its well-used bearings grating only occasionally during acceleration. Janus was pushed back against the cracked but plush seat. Occasionally, she glimpsed lights below her through breaks in the cloudcover.

Again, she tried to locate Jack's ID in the net, but he was nowhere to be found. That made her a little nervous, because Rachel had been able to track her ID. *He has to be here,* she reassured herself. *He isn't on Triton.* The aircar hummed on.

A few minutes later, a voice so quiet that it seemed to whisper said, "Janus Librarse?"

Janus flicked open her commline. "Yes. Who's this?"

A young girl's 3VRD appeared in the front seat beside Janus. "My name is Nooa. Are you seeking Pehr Jackson?"

Janus' heart accelerated. "Yes. What do you know about him? Is he in Minneapolis?"

The girl was silent for a while, her face going through varying stages of confusion and serious thought. *Odd that her 3VRD's so blatant about the girl's emotions,* Janus thought.

"I don't know," the girl finally said. Her face grew intense. "Tell me about the alien artifact on Triton."

Janus' breathing ceased. She blinked. "How do you know about that?"

"Captain Jackson spoke briefly of it. Please give me more information. I find it exceptionally interesting."

"I don't know. . ." Janus frowned and thought it best to speak with Jack about it before speaking to strangers. "Maybe we can talk later."

"There is someone in Minneapolis, a boy named Jonathan Sombrio, who can help you find Captain Jackson," the girl offered. "Jonathan is a friend of the Captain's. Jonathan is also my . . . friend."

"Oh, thank you, thank you," Janus said. *He's here!* Then her eyes focused again on the girl. So sweet to see young love, she thought, imagining this girl and some faceless Jonathan arm in arm. She even gave the boy a face: But seeing young Lonny again in her mind made her somber.

"Can I speak to Jonathan now?" she asked. "It's very important I find Jack, er, Captain Jackson."

Confusion again. "I think it best you two speak intheflesh. That seems to be the only way Jonathan feels. . . . Well, anyway, Jonathan is quite busy just now. Maybe after you two speak, you will tell me about the artifact?"

This frustrated Janus, but at least she had more information now, and had been affirmed that she was headed in the right way.

"Well, thank you, Nooa," she said. "It's nice of you to comm and let me know. I'll tell you more later."

The girl smiled, bade farewell, and vanished. Janus ran an ID, but couldn't identify anyone named Nooa, nor could she pick up any hints of the girl's trace in the nets. *Kids,* she thought. Very resourceful these days. She sighed deeply. Still, yet another weight had been lifted off her mind.

Janus realized she was deadly tired from the lifetimes spent in the artifact. Living Eyes' life had particularly drained her. Knowing she had done all she could for the moment combined with these things to make her sleepy and quite aware of her fatigue.

And she felt safe here, high above the hands of men, enclosed in a miniature world of her own, thinking with a mind uncluttered. She tapped in to the car's server, ordered up an options menu—and was instantly barraged with direct-feed ads:

"You haven't lived until—" Green skies, red rocks, naked people cavorting on flowerbeds, fractional-second flashes of fivesen pleasure....

"Why drink liquimeal when you can—" Woman standing in a stainless steel living room grimacing, her face transforming from within to a pleasure-feed smile as the sentence finished.

"You—"

"Jesus, Rache," she mumbled, "buy an adfilter. Ads are for retros."

Janus quickly picked out a relaxation subscription amid the chaos. Over the next five minutes, she fell asleep to the sights, scents, and sounds of the ocean washing the Hawaiian coastline. The moment before she lost consciousness, she flashed to a similar memory, except the same ocean was crashing against the sides of a massive floating city where she had never visited, but where she had lived....

Feedcontrol 5

Deep underground at EarthCo's worldwide network, in the metal heart of Feedcontrol Central, an electric city whose skyscrapers were old antennae and metalwork towers wearing a million ears and whose pavement was a shimmering plain of phased-array transceivers, Director Luke Herrschaft pressed a button. It was a special button he had just recently installed—"recently" only in terms of his long life; the system was completed by robots four years prior. The button uplinked to a small network of phased-array antennae all across EarthCo's landmasses, isolated from every other net, even from the Brain itself. He had ordered the robots to self-destruct after completing their work.

Herrschaft didn't want to use this, since doing so would set off alarms all across the world, alerting his enemies to the secret weapon ... but what good is a weapon unused? Still, it had made him feel more secure to possess a secret weapon.

He felt momentarily giddy as 40% of his virtual self shot and wove and dodged through the 3VRD representation of his ECoNet. He raced through neon tunnels, silver terminals and crossings, golden ganglia, and finally he reached a white shaft, broad and wide, that rose to a satellite relay. The mini-Brain then shot him along a cramped tunnel of data—little more than a homing signal—to a missing spacecraft in orbit around the Earth.

Herrschaft's 3VRD presence materialized aboard one of his Commodore's Stratofighters. *Very well!* he thought, and transferred all but 10% of himself up to the craft, then sealed it from intrusion.

The boy blinked and stared. He was physically present, though another—a girl—was here only in mind.

"Boy, girl," Herrschaft said as introduction, "how are you two behind the conspiracy to destroy me? No lies."

The boy's jaw loosened. His eyes widened in recognition of EarthCo's Feedcontrol Director. "I...I..."

"Shut up," Herrschaft said. He couldn't work up any real fury: After all, these were just kids, and he could well understand a child's desire to destroy an adult in power. Wouldn't he have felt the same at that age? Indeed, he had acted on such feelings, long ago. Besides, they couldn't really harm him. That didn't mean he would allow them to continue working for whomever it was that had bombed the conference this morning. Certainly this child couldn't have piloted this craft!

"Tell me everything you two know about the bombing."

The boy's eyes grew wider: Fear from being exposed or fear of being wrongly accused? Herrschaft wondered.

"What bombing?" the girl asked.

"Don't act stupid with me, girl!" Herrschaft raged. "Do you think I'm going to believe you're both innocent of wrongdoing as you sit aboard a stolen military vessel? And just how are you two shielded against identification? In case you don't know who I am, my name is Luke Herrschaft, Feedcontrol Director, and you two are nothing to me but in the way!" The cabin rang in tune with his voice.

"Really, sir," the boy stammered, "I have no idea what you're talking about. We didn't steal this rocketship. We're going to send it back. Nooa just . . . borrowed it, I guess. I—"

"Don't say anything more, Jonathan," the girl interrupted.

"Answer me, boy!" Herrschaft shouted. "Whose orders are you taking?"

"I . . . nobody's."

"Damn you! If you dare defy me, you'll regret it for the last minute of your life, which begins now."

"I'm not taking anybody's orders, you retrofuck! Nobody's, not yours, not EarthCo's, not anybody's."

Herrschaft felt a blaze of anger rise up within him as strong as what he had felt upon seeing the reaction on the faces of his underlings after the explosion. He thrashed around among the vast arsenal at his command: thousands of deployed warships, fueled and armed as they set off to battle NKK; countless unmanned, spaceborne torpedoes and slow-moving mines; lasers, particle guns; solar collectors whose microwave beams could be momentarily diverted. . . .

But he couldn't use those. He saw within himself that he wouldn't do anything to harm this boy. *That's me*, he thought. Unfinished, angry at the authorities, out for all he can get. *Someday he might save the world, as I did.* He felt sick at himself.

Luke Herrschaft, lord of all he surveyed—and soon to be lord of the entire solar system—softened like a sentimental dinosaur. *This boy is only a pawn*, he thought, *and this girl isn't even here. But why can't I identify them? Who's blocking me? Who in all the worlds has such power?*

The rage died out again, like a flaming wooden toy tossed into a lake. *I'll find the real leaders*, he assured himself. *Then I shall have no mercy.*

"You'll land this vessel immediately," he said as sternly as he could while at the same time feeling that he wanted to shake this boy's hand—So capable! "You'll turn yourself in to the authorities. Then you'll return this vessel to its proper owners. Is that understood?"

"Yes . . . yes, sir," said the boy—Jonathan, I must remember their names; Jonathan and Nooa. Or was Nooa someone else, someone quite different than the child she appeared to be? What was it Jonathan had said? "Nooa just . . . borrowed" the Stratofighter. Could Nooa be his true enemy? So many questions, so many frustrations.

Damn it all, I have a war to fight!

He flicked out of the Stratofighter, back to the feedcontrol room deep underground. Atop the clean machine cabinets and glass walls between this room and others where his people worked at their stations, an afterimage remained: Stars, so many stars. *When last was it that I enjoyed the stars? My dear Gladice, what you would have given to be out there with Jonathan. . . .*

Inspiration struck him as much from need to divert his train of thought as from reasoning. He again uploaded the secret weapon with a quick press of the black button to his left, hidden amid an array of other color-coded buttons hovering over the faceless machines. The antennae came online again, and he ran a trace on the Stratofighter. In seconds, he found eyewitness accounts stating that it had launched to orbit from Minneapolis. He cross referenced the name "Jonathan" with the boy's current location, with Minneapolis, and crossed these with a visual description downloaded from the data he had recorded during the orbital encounter.

Jonathan Sombrio Minor ID #SZ401678—ECo

Data began flowing across Herrschaft's pov. He grew oblivious to the room containing the robot he inhabited. He read the story of Jonathan's life and slowly grew sad. Though it was merely an objective account of what classes the boy took, what he purchased, psychiatric accounts of what factors had led him to be placed in feedrapture treatment, Herrschaft saw the story behind the facts. It was too close to the kind of pain he, himself, understood.

Why? he wondered. Why has all this happened? He had never before done this, pried into the childhood of one of his subjects; usually, when he pulled up bio data, he was looking for crimes and non-value-added behaviors. He had assumed that his carefully crafted systems would work as designed and protect the youth.

Then the sadness mutated into anger.

"But I solved all these problems a century ago. How can the children still live in such a world? What happened to the safety features I built in? Where have the police been?"

Herrschaft's centuries-suppressed anger and pain blossomed into mindless hatred. He shot his presence out to Commodore Gallette, who hung in acceleration mesh aboard Wing D's flag battleship *Revanche*. Herrschaft first fired a microwave pulse from one of the ship's comm systems at the man's card, then, while the Commodore writhed in pain and confusion, Herrschaft ordered up the vessel's maintenance overlay, found Gallette's cabin again in a different way, locked the doors, and set the atmosphere pumps on full-reverse. He then went back to the cabin's internal pov cameras and watched the man die in a frenzy of thrashing. *Fool, traitor.* Certainly Gallette was in on his Stratofighter's theft;

if not, he was sloppy in security measures. Herrschaft felt a brief satisfaction as blood frothed from the man's mouth, but that soon passed.

Next Herrschaft sent his pov to an EarthCo HY-fighter battling an NKK vessel only a few kilometers above the bright grey surface of the Moon. Lasers burned and rockets blazed. Herrschaft opened the feed to full fivesen, then flicked from ship to ship until he found one crackling with electrical fire, three seconds ago with the speed-of-light delay to the Moon and back. The pilot screamed with pain, Herrschaft screamed with pain, the Moon lolled crazily overhead, then disappeared beneath the edge of the canopy. An NKK vessel appeared so dark blue that it was barely visible against the black of space streaked with fireworks, and instantly Herrschaft felt the excruciating broad-spectrum thump which meant that the person transmitting had taken such bodily damage as to have gone into shock. He absently noted that his Feedcontrol editors had cut subscription feed at the moment of death.

Still, that wasn't enough. Herrschaft moved to another vessel, this one on the lunar surface. It was an old freighter, its vast hold gaping like some dusty cavern after having just offloaded. Yet its crew was still aboard. Several missiles or torpedoes had blasted the ship open, for, as Herrschaft roamed the narrow passages, he saw holes gulping space with ragged metal and wire teeth, the tips sparking as electronics shorted out; reflected sunlight roared in, along with occasional lasers traced in the smoke that billowed out into the vacuum. No one but Herrschaft and maybe a few of his editors could take this now-blocked feed. Finally, he located headcard traces and put himself in the suit of one of the loader-operators.

Pain! Herrschaft had to fight against his safety programs to maintain his presence in the body of the dying man. His legs felt afire, his head throbbed; vomit clung to the inside of the helmet's faceshield and gathered hot and stinging in the suit's thorax. His stomach clenched with pain and internal injury; his eardrums rang. His lungs burned and hissed with each breath, not quite providing enough oxygen, filling with blood.

A long time passed before Herrschaft realized why the man no longer moved: He was dead. Herrschaft relished the pain a little longer. At last he felt sated. His hatred was spent.

He returned to the clean, quiet room beneath the central office tower of Feedcontrol Central. *Jonathan Sombrio*, Herrschaft pondered, recalling the cold data which had painted a life of pain and loss—data to which Herrschaft's memories had given the energy of understanding. *No, I can't be angry with you, Jonathan.*

"Nooa." Herrschaft again ran cross-references but found nothing. He followed Jonathan's trace, but this time remained in the nets, watching from around corners in the narrow tubes which connected the boy's Citizen card to Earth and Feedcontrol, waiting for Nooa to show up. Jonathan immediately noticed; he vanished. Herrschaft followed the sparkling trace from hub to hub, node to node, but always the boy remained a step ahead, faster than the old master, lord of EarthCo.

Herrschaft found himself laughing and wondered at what a strange cacophony of emotions had gripped him in the past minutes. For surely, though he'd run from place to place and lived death twice, what felt like so long a time must have only been minutes.

291

"I respect you, boy," he called after the thinning trace of Jonathan as the boy vanished into a New York high-school feedcenter. Against his better judgment, Herrschaft made sure no charges would be brought against Jonathan for his little joyride. But he'd be watching the boy from now on, and would be sure to punish the next transgression.

Herrschaft was about to return to the stolen Stratofighter and deliver a few frightening words when he realized something. Who could possibly override the massive obstacles to steal an EConautics fighter? No one had done such a thing in the force's history. Who could be responsible for the various unaccountable blocks and unauthorized activities that had been going on for the past few days? Who could shield a boy from the Feedcontrol Director? Who could hide from him an entire EarthCo Warrior unit in Africa? Who in the worlds could conceivably remain hidden from Herrschaft's secret weapon?

"So simple," Herrschaft remarked. "Everything points at one perpetrator." An ominous calm fell over him.

"My Brain. The Brain."

As the implications sunk in, Herrschaft's calm slowly melted away. Terror began to leak into his mind. *Has the Brain become sentient?* But a computer is only a computer, a tool. An AI might act like a person, he recalled from a lecture he had attended back in 2072, but it's only a machine aping a man.

"My war seems to have grown a bit more complicated." But now he at least knew the identity of his foe, and he would certainly be able to understand it: *Hadn't my people modeled that computer's mind after my own? Yes. It will be very simple to find out if this is truly the case.*

"In the meantime, I have a war to fight."

Herrschaft gathered up the fragmented bits of his self and focused on making tactical decisions and staying abreast of the battle now getting fully underway between the Earth and its Moon.

Fury 7

Hardman Nadir stared out from the cabin of his and his co-commander's whirlyjet at the lights blooming in the black desert. Nadir kept his mind clear by concentrating on the orchestra his audio program made of the jet engine.

Tripoli's twin pyramidal skyscrapers glinted in the moonshine while the rest of its thousands of buildings shone and blinked with their own clutter of lights. Aircars and heavier freight vessels milled the air, groundcars crisscrossed intermittently lit roadways— all oblivious to the approaching army.

More than 10,000 soldiers now counted themselves part of the force as it marched, rolled, and flew toward the Libyan port city of Tripoli. The ARMCo light-armor battalion still rolled with them. They still operated under full feed-blackout.

Once again, Nadir frowned. *How. . . ?* he began to wonder, but cut himself off. He didn't want to know who was helping them stay invisible to the world and its criminal governments; as long as they kept helping Nadir's army grow and spread the word, he would not push the issue. He let the jet-orchestra wash away his confusion.

"Boss Nadir," Paolo commed.

"Yeah?"

The Sotoi Guntai leader turned to watch the two converse; his Black Chinese skin glowed in the whirlyjet cabin's dull green light.

"Boss," Paolo said, "what do we do once we reach Tripoli?"

Now all nine soldiers turned to hear the answer, though Nadir hadn't noticed that their comm lines had been open. They certainly couldn't have heard a spoken word in the roar of the whirlyjet's engine. Nadir once again marveled at the extravagant way NKK burned fuels—but then they controlled the gas giant planets, while EarthCo mainly utilized solar- and fusion-supplied electricity. Nadir knew thousands of soldiers might be listening. Now that he was forced to answer, the words rose to his lips:

"We seize the city's network server, its ganglion or whatever it's called, gain control of the power grid, then use those to infiltrate deeper into the Worldnets. If that's not enough power to dig as deep as we need to go, we keep taking cities until we find the bastards."

"Is that all?" the Sotoi Guntai said. He still had not ID'd himself to Nadir, but Nadir wouldn't press unless necessary. All that mattered was that he had made this army grow when he could have severed it before it ever sprouted.

A few of the men chuckled. Paolo looked nervously at Nadir, then, seeing no hint of malice, joined in the snickering.

"No," Nadir said. "We sail and fly to mainland America or Asia, wherever the betrayal originated."

"And then. . ." the Chinese leader prompted, the slightest hint of a smile turning his lips.

"By then, we'd better have the world's greatest army, because we'll need to remove our superiors from power." Nadir shook now, feeling the rage again rise up in him like magma—but here was not the place, not the time.

The Sotoi Guntai's face finally cracked into a smile. That gradually transformed into a slow laugh, and by the time the whirlyjet had reached the outer towers of the city, the man was exploding with laughter.

"Hardman Nadir," he said, "you are a good man. I made the right decision to stand beside you on this crazy mission." He snapped open his x-belt and rose on legs steadied from long years of practice standing in a moving aircraft. The blue-uniformed man stepped over a clutter of boots to Nadir, and reached down a fist.

Paolo moved for his knife, but Nadir shook his head just enough for the boy to see. Paolo relaxed, but didn't move his hand from his belt.

"Hardman Nadir," the Sotoi Guntai said, "we fight together, we die together." His fist hovered before Nadir's face.

Nadir realized what he was to do. He unbelted himself, stood as best he could, and made a fist. The two men smacked their knuckles together and held them pressed there.

All the other elite NKK soldiers rose from their plastimesh seats, and Nadir noticed their mouths were open. He flipped on his allband EarthCo-to-NKK channels, and a vast roar filled his head. Paolo and the Ukrainian boy struggled to their feet with their blue-uniformed counterparts, faces confused and wild and expectant. Nadir cast them his best whole-face grin, and then 3-verded all the EarthCo warriors.

No words. Just a picture and wordless sound, a symbol: Sotoi Guntai Commander fist to fist with EarthCo Boss, in a crowded whirlyjet cabin, surrounded by the roaring approval of soldiers.

He then flipped down to a car-mounted pov.

The picture from the ground: moonlit uniforms as far as he could see, armored cars and beetle-shaped tanks, whirlyjets and every sort of modern aircraft ripping the sky overhead. And a battle-cry, the roar of 10,000 men and women finally about to avenge the betrayal of their ideals by the very people they thought had opened the door onto them.

"To victory!" Nadir shouted across the BWs.

The Sotoi Guntai shouted something in a language Nadir didn't know; he assumed it was Chinese. But no one needed to understand the words, as the intent was clear.

The massive, hybrid army lurched and roared forward toward the unknown.

The first shots of the revolution were fired by a few unlucky cops who didn't like the look of crazy-eyed enemy soldiers marching into town.

Nadir shouldered his rifle and prepared to leap out as the aircraft dove toward a brightly lit landing pad atop a windowless building housing the city's central information network.

The cabin door banged open and all nine jumped out. A Sotoi Guntai soldier kicked in a rusted steel door and ran inside just as the command whirlyjet took off to allow another to set down.

Nadir took position along the rooftop railing and smiled as he watched aircraft land and take off and land like a conveyor belt producing warriors. Gunfire—the antique gunpowder kind—echoed from below. *Life*, Nadir thought, *life. I'm drowning in it.*

"Live, boys, for tonight we may die!" he commed, and followed an EarthCo cavalry unit into the building.

Mare Tranquillitatis

A world away, above the Moon, a war rages unbeknownst to Nadir's army:

An EConautics HY-fighter dives at an NKK Langayan frigate, long and silver and ringed with laser barrels. She manages to lock on with her massaccel guns just in time to see three dozen flashes of light. The frigate looks like a Christmas tree, the pilot thinks as her craft sizzles all around her. Her guns stop firing. The server goes dead. The lifesupport motors whirr to silence. Another Christmas-storm, and the pilot finds herself gasping. Her suit has been compromised, and the cabin's atmosphere hisses through fifty glowing holes into space; she watches crystals spray in geysers as the animal instinct within blacks out her consciousness and her body begins to convulse.

An NKK-Tsuki technician stops walking along the observatory's outer corridor and looks up through an ultraglas porthole. He does this at the same time every day, uses his intheflesh eyes to observe what the radio telescopes can do so much better. The notepad he is carrying falls from his hand and clatters on the metal flooring as he watches the lunar colony's domes silently erupt one by one while a battleship fires electromagnetic beams invisible until free atmosphere ionizes and reveals the source of his home's destruction. Only for three seconds can his scream be heard. The corridor pops around him like a capillary exposed to hard vacuum; the hall lumnisheets crack and grow dim green; the air explodes and turns to vapor almost at once; the vapor turns to complex crystals. The astronomer's assistant has only a moment to be heartbroken, but his snowflake tears are not for himself: This facility has taken two generations to build, and he watches it be destroyed in a moment.

An NKK battleship—one of only three so near Earth—rises from the crater Aristotle. The Commander of EConautics' billion-credit destroyer *Dreadnought*, Captain Dirk Downward, smiles his rictus grin and orders his vessel's pilots to attack full speed. Twenty EarthCo fighters and fighter/bombers accompany him as they close on the fleeing enemy. Downward runs a hand through his long grey hair. The battleship's atomic engines blaze, throwing up four distinct clouds of lunar dust, but it cannot gain enough velocity to escape gravity before the aged *Dreadnought* and her escorts are within range. Captain Downward only blinks once, but when his eyes again open, he stares across the heads of five subordinates in the spacious bridge, out through the panoramic viewport, and watches a swarm of torpedoes rocket toward him. A moment later, countless wounds across his face, chest, and arms burn and agony! But, oh, his eyes stay open long enough to watch the battleship sprout fire blossoms of its own. A few seconds later, victory means nothing to him as he lays squirming on the bridge deck, screaming in air so thin he can't hear anything but a bubbly hiss.

And so on. A thousand vessels, large and small, perish within the first minutes of humanity's first declared interplanetary war. A trillion credits burn and smolder in hollow space or on the parched surface of the Moon. Within the first quarter-hour, no contained atmosphere exists on the Moon, except in one spacesuit and a few unused oxygen tanks. Within two hours, NKK no longer has a space fleet within a million kilometers of Earth; some two dozen vessels limp or rocket toward Mars, their crews grim with the knowledge of what they will find there. By midnight Eastern American Time, EConautics begins its assault on Earthside NKK installations.

On Mare Tranquillitatis, the last human alive on the Moon tilts his head back and stares up from the glare of the sun on the silent grey world around him at the Earth. It looms larger than it did last time he looked up from his bulldozer's control panel. Blue basins separate brown and green masses obscured by white streaks and a huge swirl near the coast of a place he had once called home but was more than happy to leave. He raises his arm, clenches his hand into a fist, and cries out as loud as he can, "You bastards! You bastards! I just got here. You promised me!"

Of course, no operable server is near enough to transmit his words. He can't even form a real fist; the material of the suit's glove bunches up between his fingers and in his palm.

ELEVEN: System, Day 2

Innerspace 6

Jonathan Sombrio backs away from the curving hull of the Stratofighter, not yet ready to put it out of his life, even though it contains the lingering threat of Director Herrschaft. The first pink rays of dawn reflect off the faces of Old Downtown Minneapolis' skyscrapers and set the spaceship's white skin gleaming.

"Jonathan," Nooa says from beside him, "we had best get away from this craft. I had chosen not to tell you before now, but EarthCo and NKK are at war, and either side might attack a Stratofighter reported as stolen."

He turns to stare at the Brain's construct. He feels nothing but exhausted and a little sick from the adventure; the world whirls a little around him, as if he hadn't noticed its rotation before. "War?"

"It began last night during the primetime run of *Lone Ship Bounty*," Nooa says.

"I thought we've been at war since . . . I don't know, since the beginning."

"Technically," Nooa says, "what you have witnessed on the battle subscriptions were scripted shows, except for a few proxy wars and border skirmishes. They were fiction, but this war is real. It will reach across the entire solar system, and it will . . . cause much loss of infrastructure and human life."

"Is that all? Fuck, that's nothing new."

Nooa looks pained, but Jonathan doesn't want to hear any more. He wonders briefly if the War Command will draft his father into service, and feels a moment of glee. The old man always plays the soldier on his 3VRD; let him play one intheflesh. Ah, but the bastard wouldn't end up a grunt—he's a specialist.

"I'm more bugged about Director Herrschaft," Jonathan says. "What's he going to do to us? Crash, man, I thought that guy was gonna kill us, er, me."

"Don't worry about Herrschaft," Nooa says. Her lack of explanation is an ominous silence to Jonathan.

"Charity," Jonathan blurts. He realizes today is yesterday's tomorrow.

"Charity," Nooa repeats. After only a split-second, she says, "The woman you met yesterday in the Mobile Hostile Zone. You have an appointment."

That human existence is so transparent to the Brain terrifies Jonathan for a moment. *But she's on my side*, he tells himself. He takes a deep breath and goes on:

"Listen, Nooa. You've been a real clean friend and all. Thanks especially for the ride with Captain Jackson. That was full-out peak." Jonathan feels a strange warm sensation in his cheeks and a tightness in his throat, but it passes.

"Anyway, thanks for all that, but just give me a day or so alone—unless the Captain comes back. I'll want to know that. I owe you one, and I won't forget it, but I have to find Charity." *Odd*, he thinks; *I feel . . . happy. Shit.*

"Have a nice day, Jonathan," Nooa says. "I will also warn you if I sense you are in danger."

Jonathan shakes his head, unable to keep from smiling at the girl—*Construct*, he reminds himself. "I don't know how to make all this up to you."

"You have been very helpful to me, as well, Jonathan. I'm certain we will continue helping one another."

He's not sure how to say goodbye to an AI, so he simply nods and turns away. After walking for a few minutes along deserted sidewalks, skirting heaps of trash that could hide assaulters, he overlays the intricate webwork of CityNet and starts searching for Charity.

He feels a moment of panic when her trace is not at the same place she'd been last; he'd presumed that was her house. Had she decided against meeting him? Worse—had something awful befallen her?

But he's an expert trace-tracker, and now he sports an amp. With only her digitized ID to go on, he steps back from CityNet and simply looks for a blinking light.

There she is. Should have done that in the first place. He leaps back into the glowing passages, rocketing through hundreds of virtual kilometers in less than a second—even this is faster than before—and finds her.

This is awfully early, he thinks. But she had said "first thing tomorrow." Since his need is greater than his fear, he takes the risk.

"Charity, are you awake?" He barely whispers into her card. He doesn't do her the indignity of appearing 3VRD and gawking at her from whatever pov camera is operating in her room.

"Who's there?" is the startled reply.

"I . . . I'm sorry," he says, and is about to vanish when she adds—

"Is that you, Jonathan? My loverboy, of course it is! Come on, show yourself."

He transmits his 3VRD—again not needing to find a server to run the projection-assist. He's really beginning to like this amp. Maybe even worth the trouble, he thinks. There are lots of benefits to suffering—amp, Nooa, Captain Jackson, rides into space. . . .

Charity lies on a whisper-white bed draped in lace sheets. Gauzy coverings hang from a four-post frame. The woodwork is intricate, flourishing with dragons and unicorns and knights on horseback, castles, Viking ships tossed on the ocean's waves. The detail moves ever so minutely as he watches; animated decor is all the curr among the heute.

"You're up early," she says, stretching beneath almost transparent sheets, her body creating a moving landscape of hills and valleys of the coverings.

"You wouldn't believe the day I've had," Jonathan says. He laughs.

"Yes, I would. You wouldn't lie to me, would you? Heroes don't lie."

Sometimes they do, he thinks; maybe heroes are nothing but lies. "No, I wouldn't lie to you."

"Then tell me what's happened." Her lips, the lower thicker than the upper, drop from faint smile to tight concern. "Tell me nothing bad happened. Tell me!" She rises to her knees, holding the sheet against her collarbone.

Jonathan is about to emit one of his nasty laughs, but cuts it off just in time. She sees me as something better than I am, he tells himself. *Don't blow it.*

"I'm all right." Images flash to mind of his homecoming, of his parents and sister, of his visit to the Malfits' 'board, of surgery and waking to find himself beneath. . . . "I rocketed into space with . . . an EConaut."

"Space! With an EConaut." She tilts her head and grins mischievously. "That's the truth?"

"I swear, Charity," Jonathan says, a little more emphatically than he intended. "I told you I'd never lie."

"So you're just all right, huh? Would you like to tell me about your little ride?"

Jonathan again feels the strange warmth flow through his body and rise to his face as he tells her about meeting Captain Jackson—though he carefully omits the name—and how they stole a Stratofighter for a night.

"Oh, my," she says at the point when the craft set down, "you're so brave. Let me get dressed and we can go for breakfast somewhere."

She has him wait in the next room for a few minutes. He closes the wood door behind him and studies the tiny space's clutter; Not clutter, he chides himself. This is who she is:

Two white wicker chairs, slightly worn at the seat and arms. A coffee table with a marble top and a tripod of ultraglas legs. A wooden rack hanging beside the tall window holds a variety of crystal glasses. Plants of all kinds line the baseboard and windowsill. The walls bristle with shelves holding vases and ceramic figures—ancient gentlemen and ladies bowing and curtsying to one another beneath the shade of the vases—

"Shall we go, Jonathan?" she asks.

Jonathan spins around and blushes as he realizes he was about to assure her he didn't steal anything. He nods and feels his blood continue to rush as he savors how she fills the robe-like folds of dress that reveal shape and offer hints of skin where the ivory layers are most sheer.

She raises her eyes toward the flower-painted ceiling. "My car is on the roof. We'll go pick you up . . . I mean, I'll fly to your flesh and blood body so we can be together."

When she extends an elbow, he's not sure what she intends. Then he remembers the ceramic figurines and takes the proffered arm. Jonathan feels the firm softness of her flesh against his and is pleased that she sent such a complete 3VRD.

They walk through a door on the other side of the room which leads to a spiraling stair, up as many steps as Jonathan climbed in the Stratofighter—he smiles again—and emerge in a single carport. Jonathan is a little stunned.

"You own a whole house?" he asks.

"Yes. I didn't want you to know I was wealthy too soon. You know. . . . Do you still like me?"

Jonathan's not sure how to respond to someone so apologetic and seemingly weak. The only girls he's known in his life have acted as tough as hicarb and as bristly as broken glass. But Charity is so . . . *female* that he's more attracted to her than he can remember being to anyone since. . . .

"Of course I do," he says, hating himself for thinking of others while he's with Charity. "But where's your family? You don't look old enough to own a house."

"Oh, my family doesn't live with me." Her face falls a little, but by then they've reached the aircar. She slips a keycard from a fold of her outfit and slides it through the car-door slot. "Let's go."

They climb into the car, the top lowers, and Charity keys in a setting to Jonathan's headcard signal. For the next half-hour, they watch scenery flow past from the outer-rim town of Anoka. Charity talks of her love for trees and all living things, and Jonathan tells her he, too, once dreamed of places other than the city.

"I'm an artist," she says, and Jonathan smiles and asks her to explain. "I paint landscapes."

"You mean with . . . what do you call it? Brushes and stuff?"

Charity laughs, looks down through the low side window at a passing pond, then casts her eyes at Jonathan. So big, so welcoming . . . he can't look into them long. "No, my dear Jonathan, landscapes of the virtual kind. My apps and templates are very popular."

"Yeah, of course," he says. They fly silently for a while, and when Jonathan can no longer see greenery below, he feels Charity's hand rest on his, right next to him on the leather armrest. He takes a long breath to calm himself, then turns his hand over to hold hers. Charity hums a few notes, and when Jonathan looks up from their entwined hands to her face, she's smiling. Her eyes blink slowly. Jonathan can't help it; he, too, smiles. He's sure it looks stupid on him, unpracticed, but right now he doesn't give a shit. Charity, this sweet and beautiful woman, this society heute with a house of her own—she wants to be with him. And not just that; she wants him with her intheflesh.

The car slows as it falls into the city's invisible interlace of maglev passages. Soon, they descend to the side of a shattered street, the dry bed between steel cliffs. Reflected sunlight casts bright strips across the boy's dark hair as he stands looking up at himself.

"Just a second," he says before cutting off the 3VRD. She grins and nods. Flash, now he's standing beside the cleanest, most curr aircar he's ever seen, its canopy nearly a full globe around a pair of natural leather seats. It rises and Jonathan, intheflesh, sees Charity, also intheflesh—and he has to open his mouth a little to keep his breathing from revealing his excitement.

"What's on?" he says as he steps up to the car.

"Don't be so formal, silly," she says. "We've been together all morning."

Jonathan shrugs and casts a look around. The street is dirty now, cluttered with abandoned cars and hulks that used to be—what? appliances? When he was with Charity, things had been cleaner, neater. She was landscape painting, he realizes. He loads his

3VRD almost as an afterthought and hopes Charity wasn't offended that he hadn't done so sooner.

"Jonathan, I don't mean to rush you, but I can't be seen in the city."

He studies her out of the corner of his eyes, and a slow smile crosses his face. He feels a little relieved.

"So, you're in trouble," he says as he steps over the car's side into the cabin. "Now I understand you a little better. That's why you wanted me to find you first thing—"

"Oh, don't get the wrong idea, my dear Jonathan!" The canopy hisses as it begins to close. "I really want to be with you. I'd never trick you into helping me out of difficulties."

"So who are you in trouble with? The law?"

She looks forward as the car begins to rise. "I'm not a criminal. I don't want you to think I'm a bad person. I just got mixed up with a bad fellow. . . . Oh, Jonathan, he's threatened to kill me if I tell anyone!"

Jonathan feels his meat lurch against the plush seatback as the car finds a channel and takes off ahead. He draws a deep breath—momentarily noticing the faint perfume in the air—and faces Charity.

"Whatever trouble you're in, I can help you. You have no idea what I can do now."

"You'd help me?" she asks. Her face softens and Jonathan wonders at the catalog of expressions those features know.

"I'd do anything."

"Anything?" Charity looks away, watching buildings rush past. "You'd even put yourself in danger?"

"I haven't been afraid of danger for a long time, and these days I kinda don't know anything but."

"Oh, Jonathan, I knew you were the kind of man I always hoped to meet." She leans across the padded console and lays a hand on each of his shoulders, studying his frame, then moves her fingers lightly along the old shirt to his bare arms, down, sliding like feathers on his skin to his hands. She interlaces her fingers with his, then looks into his face.

"I could fall in love with you, Jonathan. Could you fall in love with me?"

He feels embarrassed and her gaze seems to burrow into him. "Well, ah, first let's get you out of the trouble you're in. What, exactly, can I do?"

Charity blinks slowly again, licks her lips, shakes her head once, and leans toward him. Jonathan bumps the back of his head against the headrest, but—*What am I afraid of?* He closes his eyes and meets her halfway. They kiss, a long, tender, closed-mouth kiss, intheflesh. When Charity sighs and pulls away, Jonathan feels as if he's back aboard the Stratofighter, free of the weight of his meat, in a gravity-free world he shares only with this woman.

"I met Fritz at a 3VRD gallery exposition where my work was showing, along with several others." Jonathan opens his eyes and watches Charity speak as she stares straight ahead.

"Fritz is a rich man, the owner of a regional card upgrading center. He seemed so nice, even bought the rights to a few of my landscapes to use at his center." She looks at Jonathan and her face grows animated. "He even hired me to do regular work for him!"

She details the daily artwork she created for the firm, how she looked forward to each day, what a kind boss Fritz was—and how, one day, Charity stumbled into a part of the company's server and found something she shouldn't have.

"He had been making blackcards," she says in a hush. "Not the kind you have." She sees Jonathan tense. "Oh, don't worry. A lot of people have those! I wasn't worried that he was in any old illegal business. But in Fritz's files. . . . Do you remember those blackcards that caused that epidemic of neuron deterioration? I guess he tried to save a few credits . . . his weren't coated properly, and they let out a trickle of power." She shakes her head and tears rise in the corners of her eyes.

"He had kept files of the cardmaking, who were his distributors, who bought the cards. When the epidemic began, he realized they were *his* customers." She leans close, but this time fear lines her face. "Fritz even kept records of who he had killed because they could link him to the epidemic."

"And he caught you," Jonathan says.

"Yes! That was yesterday. That's why I got caught in that Mobile Hostile Zone, because I had gone to a private investigator who could get me a deal with the police so I could stop Fritz but not use my own name. That's why I stayed at the family estate last night, because it's still in my uncle's name—he just died last month and left it to me, but I haven't changed title yet, and I was waiting to hear from the investigator.

"Oh, Jonathan, what am I going to do?"

"I can help you," he says, and feels strong and grown-up and real because he knows he can. He only wishes she'd told him all this yesterday. "I have a friend who can tell me if Fritz is getting close to you, and I suppose when Fritz gets headlocked for trial, too."

"Who's your friend? The EConaut?"

Jonathan shakes his head and laughs quietly. "I really doubt that guy can do much of anything for us right now. He . . . left. But I know how to get ahold of another Stratofighter if you want to really hide."

"Oh, that's not necessary," Charity says. Her face blossoms into a smile. "I bet you can do that, huh. I just bet you can, my hero. But I just want you to stay with me; I'll feel safer knowing I'm not alone, that a capable man is watching over me.

"C'mon, let's go have a picnic breakfast!"

And she directs the car to head back out toward the country, southeast this time to a wooded area near Hastings.

They continue to talk as the car lazily hums along at 100kph, the occasional tree whipping past beneath them as the Minneapolis skyline shrinks behind. Charity manages to find out a little about érase, but not how he lost her, only, "I'll never be able to see her again."

To pull Jonathan out of himself after that, Charity landscapes the inside of the car to look like the subscription-version of a Stratofighter: clean, more spacious, full of control sticks and switches, NKK spacecraft blasting to clouds of debris as, in meatspace, they pass towers or other features Charity can overlay. She slowly makes the scene more and more comic until Jonathan looks down at himself and sees a caricature of the brawny space-opera hero, bulging with muscles and weapons.

He laughs and fires up his own internal virtuality. In a few seconds, Charity's 3VRD has turned into a top-heavy maiden dressed in sheer silk. A mischievous grin crosses her face as the car slows and lands on a grassy hilltop overlooking a stream. She shuts down her landscaping, so Jonathan does the same.

"We'll see. . ." she says, reaching into a cabinet behind the front seats, where a family car would have a back seat. The canopy opens when Charity turns around, picnic-basket and supplies in hand.

Jonathan has his very first picnic in a park—they even sit in the tall grass on a checkered blanket. After they've finished eating the real croissants with real cream cheese and preserves, Charity leans against his side and lays her head on his shoulder. She runs a finger along the quick-healed incision on the side of his neck. Jonathan flinches.

"What's this?" she asks.

"Nothing. Well, I mean, it's where I had extra powercells installed. Nothing big." He shrugs; Charity's eyebrows crinkle a little.

"I'll run a check on Fritz," Jonathan says, mostly to change the subject. "What's his last name?"

Charity sits up. "Oh, don't worry about him. We're safe out here, and the police will catch him soon."

"I don't take chances anymore," Jonathan says. He feels a knot of anger in his belly. "Never again will I or anyone I care about be a victim, you can count on that."

"Oh, dearest Jonathan, what's made you such an angry boy? You can tell me anything; I want to help." She slips her hands beneath his shirt, one along his hard, skinny abdomen and the other on his back.

"I. . . . First, let's make sure we're safe here." He swallows, remembering the ritual he has to go through every night in order to be able to sleep. "What's Fritz's last name?"

Charity exhales a little sharply. "Please, I don't want to worry about that right now—"

"Charity, I can't sit out here—" he looks out across the grass alive with insects and blackbirds and wind swirling the seedy tops, at the stream winding back and forth toward a cluster of buildings "—in the middle of nowhere . . . anyone could see us, and Fritz certainly could track you by your card if he manufactures blackcards, for sure."

"Jonathan, please respect my feelings on this." Her face looks so sad, he agrees.

Careful to make his meat show nothing, Jonathan 3-verds Nooa. "Hey, Nooa, are you listening? Don't let Charity know you're there."

A few seconds later, the girl's 3VRD appears. "Hello, Jonathan. What can I do for you?"

"Well, thanks. Could you check on a guy named Fritz, owns a regional card reprogramming center. He's involved in black dealings. He was the mannequin who caused last year's neural-burn epidemic."

CHRISTOPHER MCKITTERICK

The construct-girl stands before where Charity and Jonathan sit, grass waving in the breeze behind her. Jonathan inhales the dusty scent of the grass, the musky sweetness of Charity's hair, and catches a whiff of his own, unwashed body. He feels embarrassed; Charity is so clean. . . . *But she's not complaining*, he tells himself.

"I'm sorry Jonathan," Nooa says, "but I find no reference to a 'Fritz' in any upgrade center administrative file. Perhaps that is not his real name? The local center is owned by an investment group named 'Fiddle,' which has 1347 individual investors in addition to a 10% direct ownership by Feedcontrol—"

"Never mind," Jonathan says. "Could you just let me know if anyone's looking for us?"

"Certainly." Nooa is silent for a moment, her face concerned. "Charity has not been employed by any firm since last April. In fact, I cannot verify anything she has told you this morning. However, if someone is threatening this woman, it would be best if you were not with her—"

"Not an option," Jonathan says. "And don't you dare say 'if.' She wouldn't lie to me."

"All right. I'll keep watch." Nooa vanishes.

Jonathan feels Charity's hands moving again. A vague irritation keeps him from completely enjoying the moment.

"Jonathan," she says, "don't you want to touch me?"

That washes away his worry. Blood pounds in his throat. "Oh, yes."

In response, Charity lays back. Jonathan moves with her as she keeps her fingertips on him, and he slips his hands beneath the loose folds of her layered dress. They begin to kiss, less innocently this time, tasting each other's mouth. Their touching becomes more fevered until Jonathan feels Charity reach past his waistband.

She seems to sense his tension. "Don't worry," she says. "I'm protected. I've got an implant lining."

"That's not it. . ."

"Oh, my sweet Jonathan," she says. "Sweet boy. Don't be afraid." She moves so that the two are lying apart on their sides, facing one another. One of her hands keeps in contact with his skin.

"You've been hurt," she says. "Tell me about it."

No, he says silently. "Tell me something." *Oh, shit*, he thinks. *Here it comes*. But he can't stop himself; the past two days have changed him. He has lost his fears and gained a feeling of indestructibility. "Were you on the official payroll of Fritz's company?"

Charity's hand drops to the blanket. Anger crosses her face. "Please, that doesn't come until later. Now is when we have the tender, sensual time together."

"What are you talking about? I don't live by schedules."

"Dammit," she says. Again, she reveals an effort to return to calm. "Please, Jonathan, let this be right."

"I'm just worried." He hesitates a moment before continuing, plucking a tiny purple flower near his head where blanket meets wilderness. "I couldn't find you on the payroll of any upgrade center—"

"You were checking up on me?" She sits up, and Jonathan follows. "Don't you trust me?" she asks.

"Listen, Charity, I'm sorry. I just want to make sure no one can hurt you. Bad things . . . have happened before, you see—"

"Tell me about them," she says, leaning close and lifting Jonathan's hands to her breasts. "Tell me about your fears and pain."

Jonathan's breathing speeds as his fingers work their way past linen and silk to the flesh beneath, stirring his sex, making his pants tight. He closes his eyes and begins kissing her neck. But dissonant images impinge, gross things flash to life around him; érase falls to a cement alleyway, Lucas shark-swims around him, hard things and sharp things hit and cut him, a fat man in a satin apartment. . . .

Fucking blackcard, he thinks, and shuts it down.

"Stop it," he says to Charity. He stands and brushes himself hard. Out of a drive he can't quite understand, Jonathan flicks on the net overlay and seeks more info on Charity. He digs deeper than a simple ID, diving through ice and datablocks as if they're only smokescreens, and enters the icon-field of EarthCo's Citizenship database. He inputs Charity's ID and digs for her full bio, text-only. Selections pop up around him, dull brown buttons that read SCHOOL, WORK, PURCHASING, LEGAL, and so on.

In a few seconds, Jonathan discovers she's 38 years old, has been married five times, has never held a steady job but has done well from every divorce except the first, and is currently subscribed to a interactive novel entitled *Dangerous Affairs*.

He shuts down the feed, shuts down his card. Knowing it is rude to do so, he even cuts off his feed receiver and 3VRD projection.

Jonathan stares at Charity for a moment, seeing her true face. Lined and pale—though still pretty—it reveals a big lie. He turns his back on the woman and looks at her aircar. Its gleaming red hull is as flawless as it looked before, though the canopy is scratched. Then again, so is every other one in the world; it's just that he thought this one was something special. He had clung to the idea of Charity during the Lucas thing, the surgery and what came later. . . .

"You lied to me," he says, looking at the aircar. His eyes burn. He feels like a fool. Everything Charity said to him so far suddenly sounds ridiculous. *Like a romance subscription*, he thinks. Exactly like one, from the perspective his new information provides. Guilt rises in him—guilt for feeling he could have fallen in love with someone again.

"Fuck," he says, barely loud enough to hear over the wind hushing across the tall grass.

"Jonathan." Her voice sounds stronger now. "You must know I didn't intend to hurt you. It's the last thing in the world that I wanted—"

"Can it and feed it to someone else!" he shouts. He takes a deep breath. "I met a girl like you in feedrapture treatment," he says, watching a blackbird swoop down across the grass. "They called her a 'passion addict.' That would make me your 'love-character overlay.' That's real nice. Fuck."

He walks toward a lone elm tree, its gnarled branches naked of leaves. He notices that the grass all around isn't green but pale brown, and the stream is dry.

"Oh, Jonathan," she says. He hears her rise and move toward him. "I'm so sorry. I . . . I know I have a . . . problem. The last thing I wanted was to hurt you, believe me. I just don't know any other way to . . . to make a relationship. This time was going to be different. It still can be!" She steps in front of him and holds his arms at her full reach. "Let's make this something beautiful and real."

"You mean as real as Fritz?" he says. Charity's face falls, and she looks old again. Her eyes hold a vacantness much like Jonathan's mother's.

"You're hurting my feelings, dear Jonathan."

"Don't call me that!"

He feels the slumbering anger in his gut reawaken, only this time it roars to life like a dragon renewed with ten times its previous power. The horrible pressure of that knot within him, that monster, that boil, that disease trembling and tearing between his lungs must be released. *I'll die if I can't get rid of this feeling.* But he doesn't know how to release it safely. He can't hold it in much longer or—he knows—he'll go back to the crazy life he had before, or a crazier one. Or it'll explode, spreading the disease, killing him and everyone around.

"Jonathan, I'm so sorry to have added to your pain."

"Yeah, right," he says. He powers up his commcard. "Nooa, send me an aircar of my own, will you? I've got to get out of here right away." The girl simply nods and tells him it's on the way.

He takes a few steps away from Charity, toward her aircar, and stares at the pitted canopy. His attention wanders to the sideview mirror. The edges are tarnished and the glass smeared with grime. But who'd give a shit enough to clean an aircar mirror when you only use it for meat-flying? He trembles.

"What do you see?" Charity asks.

"Huh?" Then he realizes what she's asking. He hasn't looked into a mirror in as long as he can remember. Why would he?

Now his eyes focus not on the grime but instead on the image of a boy. He looks seamed, lined deeply around eyes so narrow and doubting, tight; the mouth has its own set of lines that look sort of like a clown-frown.

Look at that kid, he thinks. Sorrow has etched him at sixteen to look like an old man. Another old face moves in behind, that of Charity's.

"The face of a loner," she says, her voice trembling a little. "You don't need to be alone—"

"Yeah. Or of a dog kicked once too often," he says.

Charity's worn, sad face falls lax for a moment, then turns lovely again. For a moment, he's unsure if this is a 3VRD or if her expression changes so quickly. She doesn't look the same as she had an hour ago; Jonathan imagines her flesh as melting plastic, and servos beneath move and reshape her into something she isn't. Or something she is.

"Oh, Jonathan," she says, "maybe I can help you now."

The transformation terrifies him. *This is worse*, he thinks. His hands begin to shake, so he holds them together. The skin is tough and stretched tight over bone.

He steps away from the mirror. His eyes clamp shut, his teeth clank together like a vise. He feels as if he's about to turn around and lash out at this woman who raised his hopes up so high on such a good day, only to reach a peak where she ripped away the 3VRD virtuality and left him suspended thousands of meters above rocks. What could he do but fall? Or whip around and grab that plastic liar by the throat to keep from falling, at least until she breathes no more. Then, at least, he wouldn't die alone.

"No!" he shouts, and begins to run. He's never intentionally hurt any girl—or woman—and isn't about to start now. The tall, dry grasses lash his face as he rushes through them. He feels his eyes water as dust shakes loose, and the watering begins to break the barrier within.

"No, no," he says as he begins to cry. *I can't cry, I can't, I'll die, the whole world'll crack open and swallow me up.*

But as his body shakes and cramps as he fights to stifle long-restrained sorrow, the earth remains intact. So intact that it thumps him hard on the shoulder as he allows himself to fall and curl up to cry. He isn't worried about anything—Nooa'll protect me, and Charity's already done her worst.

He cries, long sobbing heaves, and he fights against them nearly as strongly. He becomes clear to himself. He can't purge the image of that small, frightened boy from his head, that dirty faced, old-man boy. He realizes he's made of nothing but fear and anger. Fear and anger at the world, *at everyone I know, at my goddamned self.* As he lay curled into a ball, he sees himself as a wad of loneliness and friendlessness and hopelessness, a tiny chunk of nothing isolated from all the other fragments of humanity by the nothingness of life on Earth.

"Fuck this!" he shouts, and punches the grass-matted earth. "Fuck this." The tears gradually subside, and he feels foolish lying on the dirt. Jonathan brushes off the dust, wipes his face on his short sleeves, and stares into the sky. His abdomen is clenched hard, his breathing shallow and fast.

While he watches puffs of cloud glide by, a mad desire to escape fills him as if poured down from above. He pictures Captain Jackson out there somewhere, able to leap planets in a single bound. *I want to live adventures with my Captain*, Jonathan thinks. *I want to get away from this rotten world. I want to understand people so well that I can go to them just by thinking about them, just like the Captain. I want everything . . . everything I'll never have, another past, another life, another future. Another me.*

He's not yet done crying, but vows never to be so weak again, never to be as gullible and stupid and blind. Never cry again, never. The tough kid inside him takes over again. His body feels hard, the boiling within him held in place by callous and stringy muscle.

A hum draws Jonathan's attention to the north. He watches an aircar grow as it nears; it finally settles beside Charity's. Jonathan begins laughing, and that threatens to turn into ragged sobbing; the fuzzy emotion mutates into anger.

"Dammit," he mutters, wiping his face again as he tromps back up the hill.

"Jonathan—" Charity begins to say.

"Can it, I said." The second aircar's canopy begins to rise. It's a new Ford. Jonathan grins and squirms inside before it fully opens. He hits the shut button and only looks outside when he's sealed away from Charity.

"Get some help," he 3-verds to her as the car's rotors spin to life. Once again, the woman's face collapses upon itself and re-forms. This third Charity initiates a comm, but Jonathan shuts down just before he can hear what she's about to say. He looks at the sky as he rushes up into it.

"Fuck her, fuck the world, fuck everything," he says. His small, hard fist slams down on the center console.

Plans for revenge begin to form in his head. He has everything he needs to feed real pain down the meat of some people he knows. And more.

"Nooa?" As he speaks, the girl appears in the seat beside him. "Let's go have some fun."

She smiles lopsidedly. He wonders for a moment why an AI would feed such emotion to its 3VRD. Jonathan feels his own face tighten into . . . he isn't sure what, and quickly relaxes it. *Yeah, some fun. And maybe I'll be doing my civic duty, too.*

Pehr Jackson 4

Pehr looked up from Miru and Pang, up at the everlooming mass of Neptune as Triton swung around it. The arboretum wasn't lit by light reflected from that world, nor from the direct rays of the pinprick sun; most of the room's illumination glowed from tripod-shaped lumnisheets spaced throughout the dome and running along its reinforcement beams. He realized Miru had stopped speaking.

"So what does all this mean?" Pehr asked, returning his gaze to the man seated cross-legged before him.

"We must return to the artifact and continue our studies," Miru said. "Not until we better understand it, can we use it to the full potential."

"Use it for what? You mean to stop the war?"

Pang's eyebrows shot up. "War?"

"You don't—" Pehr stopped. "Of course. EarthCo's declaration hasn't reached this far yet. I thought Neptunekaisha would have let you know." Miru and Pang stared and waited for an explanation.

He felt himself blush. His stomach tightened.

"It's . . . it's my fault," Pehr said. "At least partially. I couldn't stop Lonny from bombing you, and Feedcontrol twisted the feed to make it look worse than . . . well, to make me look sinister. My wife publicly divorced me right afterward."

"I see." Miru shut his eyes. "That's not what I intended—stopping a war. I meant that we need to better understand the artifact so we can use it to better understand ourselves and the nature of the universe. Think about it! Instantaneous transportation, perfect communication—"

"Yes, Miru," Pang interrupted. "But I believe our friend Pehr is thinking along more practical lines. Do you know what it means if NKK and EarthCo have finally declared open war?"

Miru looked down at his feet crossed in his lap, grunted, and brushed dust from his pants. "War. Gomi-kuzu! Let the fools have their war. The artifact cannot be damaged."

"Miru!" Pang shouted, standing up. "Do you not care for your fellow man?"

"Please, guys," Pehr said, also standing. He looked down at Miru, who was fondling an agate he found among the gravel. "Until you brought me here, I didn't have a chance to think about how to use this new . . . ability of ours. Hell, I was even having trouble with who I was." He let out a syllable that didn't sound much like a laugh. "But Pang's right. We have to do something."

Miru stood, but continued looking only at the stone. "What will you have us do? Take every man and woman in the whole solar system into artifact-space? What will that accomplish? Can you imagine how long that would take? Even if our numbers increase exponentially—which they will not, because most people will be afraid to even hear us— we would require years.

"No. We must study the artifact and attempt to understand its mechanism." He looked up, his face suddenly hopeful. Those dark eyes caught and reflected a tripod of light.

Pang looked doubtful. "How can you understand it? Remember? Every time we thought too hard about what it meant, we lost contact with the artifact."

"Then we must be careful not to think." Miru's eyes crinkled in silent laughter. "Pang! Do you remember the map we glimpsed just before Janus left us? We must go back inside and study it!"

"Don't forget that we will need someone to provide spiritual energy. We are both weak, you dangerously so."

"*Non de mo arimasen*," Miru said while waving his hand in dismissal. Pehr was shocked to realize he understood: "It is nothing." But then, he oughtn't be shocked: I fed those language classes, too; I grew up with Japanese-speakers, too, through Miru's memories.

"Do not become mystical, my friend," Miru added with a grin. "You are a scientist, as I am. We will speak no more of spirits, hmmm? I believe you mean that we require another's mental energy, or perhaps physical energy. . . . That is another thing we must learn. Pehr is very strong." He looked at Pehr.

"All right. Will you join us in our studies?"

Pehr looked into the eyes of the two Asian men and saw in them, for a second, the eyes of all the pilots of enemy craft he had shot down. Yes, he had to stop the war. There was no need for anyone to kill anyone ever again—And they wouldn't, he realized, not after they spent a lifetime together, truly as one, in the artifact. He would begin a new Crusades, one that would change the world.

But: "I don't have time right now for scientific studies," he said. "What you need is another scientist. I'll do what I can intheflesh. If you find out something I can do, let me know and I'll do it."

He felt himself growing anxious. "I'd better get back to Earth."

Pang smiled. "Find Janus."

Miru frowned for a moment and looked at his old friend. Then he, too, smiled and put out his hands to Pehr. They took one another's hands in the old EConaut tradition, a double-shake designed to avoid zero-*g* torque problems. Pehr felt light-headed. This man knew every part of him, just as Pehr knew every part of Miru.

I know myself, Pehr realized. He felt warm and strong and directed.

"I guess I was simply trying to keep you with me," Miru said. "You are right. We need assistants not only trained in scientific thought—remember now you are as trained as I am—but those who are, in their hearts, scientists. You will serve us well when we learn something."

Pehr pulled his hands free and crossed his arms. "Miru, the artifact must have done something to your brain. I'll always be with you, and only a thought away from being here intheflesh."

Miru barked an odd laugh, staccato and musical. "Go away from us, Pehr. Go to Janus."

Pehr felt Miru had read his mind. "I can do that, can't I? I mean, the transport . . . thing isn't only one-way? I can go to someone else who has the artifact inside her, right?"

"We'll find out," Miru said with a smile that showed uneven teeth—strange in a time of cosmetic perfection.

Pehr nodded, then closed his eyes. He reached out in his mind for Janus. He saw nothing but the red insides of his eyelids.

I'm doing this wrong, he thought. He recalled how he had found Miru: recalling all he knew of the man, picturing him as well as he could, his voice and appearance and mannerisms; and needing him—he did everything he could remember, not knowing which element was necessary to make the system work.

I need to know you're okay, Janus, he thought. *Dammit, why's nothing happening?*

"Pehr," Miru said, his voice somewhat faint, "what's wrong? Why are you back so soon?"

"Back?" He opened his eyes and saw the arboretum. He felt the tug of gravity—but only a slight tug. This was still Triton.

"Is Janus hurt?" Pang asked.

"I never found her," Pehr said.

"Hmmm." Miru rubbed his temples and paced a bit. He spoke while looking up at the dark sky. "You and she have not shared time together inside the artifact. Perhaps that is necessary. All right. Pang and I will assist you and then remain inside to do our studies."

"Go ahead and bleed me dry of the strength you need," Pehr said. He grinned. "I'll just have to eat well once I reach Earth." He looked at Pang: "Last time, Miru hardly took anything from me."

"I took much. You simply have a great amount to give. We will go now."

"Wait," Pang said. He began to walk toward a sealed passage. "I'll fetch Byung, as well. He showed the most interest of the City crew."

The man left. Pehr felt anxious. He wanted to get back to Earth now. He needed to find Janus now. And he felt a little bothered that it hadn't been with him that Janus had entered the artifact. They stood in silence as Pang cycled through the pressure-seal.

At last, Miru broke the quiet. "It does not bother you that your wife divorced you during your show?"

Pehr looked away, absently stroking a broad leaf of a tall plant. "You should know it doesn't. Hell, it's a relief."

"I imagined it would be. Still. . ."

"Yeah, in front of everyone. That would have hurt had I believed I was Captain Pehr Jackson, EConaut, at the time. But I was a little mixed up. So now, it's like looking back at a bad show. No, I'm mostly relieved."

"You are free to be with Janus."

Pehr smiled and looked at Miru. "It's gonna take some getting used to, this understanding you have of me. Blast, though, it's nice."

The two exchanged a long smile, neither doubting the intentions of the other, both certain of how the other felt about him, no social taboos getting in their way. Pehr felt he wanted to tell Miru so much, now that they were alone for the first time after the experience they'd shared; he wanted to tell Miru all the things the man needed to hear on occasion, he wanted to make sure Miru didn't still harbor guilt over the deaths of his parents and over what he'd done during the uprising on Triton. . . . Pehr felt such a bond with—almost desire for—this man that he had to eventually turn away. Then he realized he was acting like a retro. *Love*, he thought. *I'm feeling brotherly love.*

He laughed aloud and clasped Miru by the shoulders. "My friend Miru . . . blast, man." He couldn't find the words.

Miru shook his head and put out his arms. They hugged the way Pehr had once dreamed brothers would, except Miru felt like an extension of himself. The door hissed and they let go to watch Pang and another man enter the arboretum.

"Byung," Pang said, walking quickly, "this is Pehr Jackson." The new man, thin and shorter than the others, bowed slightly. He frowned.

"You know Miru-san. Are you ready?"

"Yes," Byung said. "Why are we speaking in the enemy's tongue?"

Pang looked to Miru, who began to laugh. Pehr had to laugh as well, though not for the same reason: Miru's memories had revealed a man for whose body laughter was as alien a language as dolphinish.

"You'll understand everything in just a few moments," Miru said. "Pang has explained what we intend to do?" Byung nodded.

He turned to Pehr. "Shall we begin?"

Transition

The arboretum vanishes and is replaced by a dizzying array of life-moments, countless more than I remember. This isn't why I'm here.

There, Miru says. I feel him pointing at a pinwheel-shaped mass of pearls, growing larger as it approaches through a kaleidoscope of others. I glimpse Janus' face.

"No, not yet," I tell him. "I want to do this with her."

I know, Miru says with a smile like sunshine and mother's caresses. *Relax. You don't understand. There is Janus. Go to her. This is how I found you.*

All the billions of moments vanish except for Janus', and her pinwheel of glowing pearls full of faces and places transforms into a sort of helix; *I don't know what this means.*

Yes you do. This is a path.

The helix shape-changes into a ladder, a spiral stair. At the top I see Janus. She is asleep.

"Janus! It's me, Jack. Are you all right?"

Simultaneously, I begin to grow heavy-bodied and light hearted. "Hurry, Miru, take what you need from me."

We already have, powerful Captain Pehr. Soundless laughter, like the feeling of bubbles and the taste of . . . seaweed?

Janus Librarse 2

Janus heard Pehr Jackson's voice.

"Jack, is that you?" she asked, waking quickly. She blinked several times to clear her eyes—her surroundings seemed to be blurring past her. Staring through a weathered bubble of ultraglas, down at sunrise-illuminated fields tended by steel beetles, she remembered she was aboard Rachel and Miguel's aircar. Her back creaked as she stretched on the old vinyl seat and fired up her headcard. The craft smelled humid and dusty—like Earth. She smiled.

"Jack?" she 3-verded. Since she couldn't find a trace to send to, Janus hoped he was receiving.

"Janus!" he commed, voice-only. But she couldn't really hear him, couldn't have identified the tenor of his voice. "It's me, Jack. Are you all right?"

"Where are you?" she asked.

As if in answer, he appeared beside her. Gyros whined as the car shifted in mid-flight and stabilized. She heard his breathing—labored, shallow—saw tiny beads of sweat across his forehead, smelled his scent. And he was naked.

"This isn't a 3VRD, is it?" She refused to turn away, though she kept her eyes on his.

Jack started to reach out to her, recognized his condition, then dropped his hands into his lap. His cheeks rouged.

"Don't be like that," she said. "Here." She pulled off the travel blanket she'd been wearing and handed it to him. He fumbled for a few seconds, draping it this way and that, and finally settled it across his lower half, tucked between hips and seat.

When he finished arranging himself, Janus removed Miguel's jacket and said, "Here."

He pulled it on and looked clearly relieved. "You know how I got here?" he asked.

"No, but I suspect," she said. The words felt full and rich as she said them, and Jack kept eye contact longer than necessary. He nodded slightly. "I know," she said.

"I saw you inside Miru's . . . mind," Jack said. Janus felt let down, but he hurried on:

"I didn't stay inside the artifact-space long enough to . . . you know, live your life. I wanted to be with you when it happened." The blanket slipped as he pivoted on the seat. "Crash it, why do our clothes disappear when we use the artifact?"

Janus felt herself smile like a little girl—not the little girl she had been, but maybe another, one she had seen in a show sometime. "Maybe the aliens like human fashions."

"Cute." Jack's face went serious again. "I didn't stay because I wanted to share the experience with you. You know how you listened to me on the *Bounty*?"

Janus chuckled lightly. "Oh, my, the *Bounty*. What a mess that turned out to be." She softened. "Yes, I remember."

"That meant a lot to me. I want to know who you are. I want to understand you, to feel that . . . whatever it is, that incredible bond. Do you want that, too?"

"Jack." She shook her head but smiled. "Of course. I. . . . Wait a minute. How could you have seen Miru since I. . . ?"

But before she could finish, the 3VRD of the young girl from the night before—Nooa—appeared in the middle of the back seat, leaning between the front ones.

"Captain Jackson," the girl said, her eyes huge with anticipation, "you're back! Now you're both here. Please tell me everything you know about the alien artifact. I must—"

"Brain," Jack said, "don't you think you're being a little, ah, disrespectful, busting in on our private conversation?"

"You two know each other?" Janus asked. She blinked. "Did you just call her 'Brain,' as in *the* Brain?"

All the strangeness swirling around her made her feel a little dizzy, so she looked out at the sun spilling oranges across the fields. Clusters of city skyscrapers made sculptures at the horizons in each compass direction, but a kilometer below only farm field rushed past.

"I apologize for intruding," Nooa said to Jack. She faced Janus. "Yes, the Captain and I have met. We went on, let us say, an adventure with a friend of mine, whom you may meet. And yes, I am a construct of the Brain. Now, please, I have been very patient. Please tell me what you have learned about the alien artifact. I will reward you richly."

"You know," Jack says, returning his gaze to Janus, "world-ruling artificial intelligences can be a real pain in the ass. Do you mind if we spend a little time talking to the Brain?"

"By all means," Janus says. "I'd like you to answer a few of my questions about the artifact, too."

They began a detailed discussion about the alien object, from the first images of it Janus had fed from Miru as the *Bounty* had approached, to when Jack entered and what he learned, to Janus' experience . . . on and on. This was not the reunion Janus had in mind, but at least Jack was here; she had the undivided attention of the most complex and human-like AI ever built; and they were flying headlong into a future she not only didn't dread, but into one she looked forward to as she had nothing else before.

Janus smiled and leaned back into the sharp edges of cracked vinyl, watching Nooa and Jack talk. *This is it*, she realized. *This is the life that I've always wanted.* She closed her eyes and savored the moment.

Fury 7

Early morning in Tripoli: Hardman Nadir heard a firefight open up between snicking plasma-guns and thudding gas-charged POs just down the hall. He shot a quick comm to the EarthCo unit sub-boss in the building's vast auditorium where they were gathering prisoners and questioning techs, then ran out into the fight.

"What's on?" he commed to the NKK regulars who he'd last seen reconnoitering this, the second, floor. They'd worked their way down 68 levels, eliminating opposition to the takeover of the city's feedcontrol center. This was the first real fight they had encountered, excepting the occasional armed guard. Nadir powered up his weapon as he emerged into the brightly lit hallway.

"It's some screwskull ARMCo magistrate posse," the Filipino commander 3-verded back to him. "They think we're terrorists. We'll clean up here in a minute."

Damn, Nadir thought. *Why didn't our ARMCo allies explain things to their people?* His boots smacked against loose floor tiles as he ran toward the fight. "This is not an execution expedition," he said to himself. As he burst into the adjoining hall, he saw his light-blue uniformed NKK soldiers leaning out from doorways and firing.

"Unit commander!" he 3-verded, using the ID-trace of the man with whom he had just spoken. The man's 3VRD appeared, crouched and facing away. "Have you tried to communicate? I won't have you killing everyone in the building. Hold your fire while I try to reason with these people."

"Yes, sir," the man said, stiffening. He relayed the message, and Nadir could hear soldiers calling out with their voices to one another.

The POs—essentially fancy steam guns—pounded out a few more shots before they, too, ceased. Nadir opened an EarthCo-to-ARMCo line.

"I need to speak to the leader of this police unit," he commed, using English. Seconds passed during which Nadir could hear loud whispers passing far down the hallway. He took a step forward, past an NKK soldier who looked up startled and then smiled, and peered around the corner. The staticky 3VRD of an un-uniformed man flickered before Nadir; he looked vaguely Arabian, though his skin was as dark as that of the villagers Nadir had seen in a waking nightmare.

"Put me in contact with the leader of these terrorists!" the man shouted, though his voice-trans sounded only slightly louder than the building's ventilation. "Who are you? What have you done to our satlink? Where—"

"Shut up and listen," Nadir said. The policeman's mouth fell open, then slammed shut. He was about to rant again when Nadir continued:

"I am EarthCo Warrior Unit Boss Hardman Nadir. I am in joint command of approximately 10,000 troops, as well as thousands of pieces of armor. We're not terrorists. We're the good guys, and we don't want to kill anyone. Now, don't be a lockhead and try to fight us; that's hopeless. We're on your side—"

"Ordure!" the policeman said. "That's not what General Hammas told us."

"Who?" But even as he asked, Nadir knew who the man meant. "When?" he asked.

"Hours ago, when you terrorists began your assault!" The policeman continued to yell and taunt, so Nadir shut down the BW.

Damn, he thought. *Damn, damn, damn. I let success and movement blind me.* He opened the BW he and the Sotoi Guntai commander had set up as their instant-access priority line, secure from anybody except whoever was responsible for the blackout they were operating under.

"Yes?" the Chinese man asked, his 3VRD equally calm.

"We have trouble. Are you keeping track of that ARMCo armored battalion?"

"Yes."

"It seems that their general contacted the police here in Tripoli and told them our army is a terrorist unit. . ."

"I understand." The face barely reacted. "I will have my recon specialists trace all communications through the feedcontrol center we have captured. Nothing will leak out of this city."

"What'll we do about those rats, er, those ARMCo one-man tanks? I don't want to see any more slaughters."

"Let me handle them."

Nadir didn't like the ominous tone in his co-commander's voice. Still, he knew extreme measures might have to be taken, and the Sotoi Guntai would be less inhibited than he. *I've got to toughen up*, Nadir thought, *but I've seen enough death. Dammit! All those tanks!*

He nodded to the man, who promptly disappeared. A boy soldier near Nadir, dark-skinned and thin, turned his head a little until he caught sight of Nadir, then hurriedly looked away. Sweat streamed down the sides of the soldier's head and neck. His sand-camo helmet slipped to one side since its straps weren't snapped together; in fact, Nadir noticed a general slovenliness about the soldier. By comparison, the Sotoi Guntai were a magnitude more disciplined.

Nadir's aiming eye began to twitch as he wondered what would happen if his other allies turned against him as the ARMCo general had. That forced him to think of more immediate dangers, of the new twist engendered by the info leak, of 120 rats moving among his army. Potential fifth columnists.

"Ah, Valentine's," he grumbled. "Blast them to hell if they don't understand. Damn!" He opened the BW to the policeman and, at the same time, a general short-range band that the soldiers around him would feed.

"I'll give you one minute to surrender and stay free men. After that, we'll be taking prisoners. What—"

The gas guns opened up all at once, smashing the white plaster tiles that covered the walls. Chips of plaster and underlying concrete and wood exploded into the hallways, knocking out light strips overhead and drawing blood from the NKK men.

"Well, defend yourselves, goddammit!" Nadir 3-verded.

The firefight heated up again. Nadir shook his head as he watched the dozen young men stick their rifles out into the line of fire without looking—using the weapons' pov sights—and let loose like children playing a game. All this noise yet no casualties, Nadir thought. He ducked as enemy fire from the connecting hall worked its way along the wall toward him, studied the pattern the police had cut into the smashed wall, then picked the proper moment.

He launched himself on his belly, sliding into the middle of the adjoining passage to get a clear view of the enemy. NKK plasma-bursts were making a real mess of the walls and ceiling, turning plaster and lumnistrips into smoke and dust and fire. Four heads occasionally peeked out of doorways—*They must not have pov sights*, Nadir decided as he sighted and fired, sighted and fired, sighted and fired. Two uniformed police and one plainclothesman sprawled on the floor as NKK bursts continued to shred the walls. The fourth head poked out. Nadir pulled the trigger. The police squad leader crumpled to the floor. It struck Nadir that the man would never again transmit his staticky 3VRD.

"Stupid bastard," Nadir said. His eye began to twitch again. He sent out a trace-locator and couldn't ID any more police, though that didn't mean much. He couldn't trust anything EarthCo had supplied him with.

"Hold your fire," he commed. "Casualties?"

As the first boy reported, Nadir felt more than heard a heavy whump travel through the floor. He stood. A ball of smoke rolled out from an open doorway that bore the symbol of a staircase. Before Nadir had a chance to react, the Sotoi Guntai commander's 3VRD appeared.

"The ARMCo tanks have surrounded the feedcontrol building," the man stated. His face revealed anger and frustration. "I apologize for not moving soon enough."

"No apologies! Just keep them from ruining what we've taken."

Nadir opened an allband BW. "All units, we have a problem with the ARMCo one-man tanks that joined us last night." Another shell hit the building, then another. Then the pounding became constant, like rolling thunder.

"All units engage headcard defenses. Units inside feedcontrol building, move toward the center. Outside units . . . destroy any ARMCo tank that won't surrender. Don't offer quarter unless requested." Damn. "Try not to mark any civilians!"

The lights went out and red emergency spots flicked on near the staircase doorways. Dust billowed through the air. Nadir felt the floor shake beneath his chest and pelvis. He began to feel useless. That wouldn't do.

Nadir rose to his feet and ran back toward the auditorium. Inside, he encountered pandemonium. The plastic chandeliers had fallen, most of the ceiling now carpeted the floor, and dust glowed dull red as emergency lights set it ablaze. Nadir 3-verded Tilden, the net tech who was trying to access the center's ganglia.

"No way!" she said. "They sabotaged all the machines that serve the ganglia with some crazy virus. Crashed the card of my best tracer. My guess is this place will be useless to us for at least 24 hours."

Damn. Not only weren't Nadir's plans flowing smoothly anymore, they'd ground to a halt like gears trying to mesh in desert sand.

A long crossmember ripped loose in the ceiling, and Nadir barely had time to shout out a warning before it crashed to the fivesen-equipped seating. Metal and hardware shot through the air as people screamed in anger and pain.

But when the sound died out, Nadir realized the shelling had ended.

He opened the line to his partner. "How do we stand?"

"Only nine rats surrendered. Take a look."

The man linked Nadir in to the pov of a circling whirlyjet. Tripoli was a city changed. Now it looked like everything else Nadir had created:

A dozen tall buildings smoldered from craters in their sides. Between the towers, ground armor burned with the energy of ultrahard plastics hit with high energy. The streets were blackened and littered with rubble. Human figures lay strewn near building entrances, unmoving. As the pov continued to take Nadir through the city, he saw a whirlyjet projecting from a wall of shattered glass, fire raging all around the accident scene. Shattered treetrunks and smoking foliage were all that remained of one tree-lined boulevard; seven ARMCo rats blazed amid a moonscape of heavy plasma-hits and rocket blasts. Everywhere, light personnel cars burned.

Nadir flicked off the feed.

"How much did we lose?" he asked. His wrists hurt, and when he looked down, Nadir saw his hands were clenching his EMMA so hard the knuckles gleamed orange in the weird light.

The commander began a litany of damages and casualties. Nadir felt himself slipping away, considering how simple it would have been, how many lives he would have saved, if only he had ordered his army to crush the rats last night. But he hadn't, and their general had sent messengers ahead, and the city had set a trap. Nadir had led his men right into the jaws of that trap. His trembling increased faster than he could control.

Something snapped within him. Nadir found himself long seconds later, his throat raw from screaming obscenities at everything from EarthCo War Command to everyone whom he had watched falter in action. He stood gulping dusty air. A large portion of the wall collapsed beside him, and he only watched.

"All units," he 3-verded, somehow finding enough calm, "time to move onto our objective. Infantry battalions A and B! Have you secured the shipping ports? Report."

"Yes, sir!" a snappy EarthCo Warrior's 3VRD responded. "No casualties, sir! Three big hoverships at dock, and one waterscrew-driven cruise ship." He laughed at that, but only for a moment. "Several dozen smaller vessels good for high seas, or so our P-Navy Captain says. We knocked out an ARMCo cruiser's server before they knew what hit them. Sotoi Guntai are boarding now."

"Good, good. All units, prepare to board vessels at port. Home in on Infantry A and B." He narrowed his band and singled out the net tech.

"Are we still in blackout?" he asked.

Her 3VRD nodded. "Yeah, us and the whole city. Far as I can tell, every server within a hundred kilometers of here is deaf and mute to the outside world. How are you doing it?"

"It's a secret," he said. He shut down the BW and opened the secure line to his co-commander.

"Will you please take over for a few minutes? I've got to get my head together. You know the plan."

"Yes," the Sotoi Guntai said. The 3VRD face tilted and the eyes squinted. "Did you hear that we are at war?"

"What?" It didn't make any sense to utter that. *Of course we're at war!* War against the establishment.

"We located a detachment of EarthCo Warriors who landed last night by airship from Berlin. Seems EarthCo and NKK have declared a war between all units of all planets and every vessel between. *Real* war."

Nadir began tracing his steps out of the auditorium, toward the main exit. "Are they misinforming you because they see you as enemy? What does this mean? How did it start?"

A sudden misgiving hit him in the gut: *What if we started an interplanetary war?* That was the last thing he had intended. He could hardly breathe.

"The feed I studied seems unadulterated. It seems there was an exchange of nuclear atrocities between EConauts and Neptunekaisha forces at the edge of the solar system. All of Earth and Luna are battling as we speak."

Nadir stepped past rushing soldiers into a smoke-filled staircase and began descending to the main floor. A hole in the wall cast a cloudy beam of white light into the shaft, and Nadir looked out at what appeared from this pov to be a city at peace. He felt numb. Automatically, he powered up the audio program; shouts and collapsing architecture transmuted into orchestral cacophony. That didn't soothe him much, so he turned the volume down a bit.

"We'll never get across the Atlantic," Nadir said as he started back down the stairs. "No matter if we're blacked out, visual imagery will pick us out as soon as we launch. Our—"

"I'm not prepared to abort the mission," the commander said. His face went hard and emotionless.

Nadir watched the 3VRD float beside him down the steps like a ghost—that of a bloodthirsty Sotoi Guntai somewhere outside, waiting for him to falter, poised to swoop down and devour the weak and take over to fulfill his own objectives. *Well, dammit,* Nadir thought, *he won't see anything weak in me.*

"We'll have to cross at intervals," Nadir said. "No communications between vessels. Make sure no vessel is carrying too critical a number of men. . ."

As he continued detailing the strategy, Nadir stepped out into broad sunlight. He had to squint. From ground-level, Tripoli looked like any of a thousand battlefields Nadir had observed during boot-camp. He marched out toward a dust-storm created by the Sotoi Guntai whirlyjet he had ordered. To protect his eyes, he shut them and pointed his rifle ahead, using its pov camera to guide him to the craft.

Just before he boarded, Nadir was struck that no one had questioned him since the rat attack. Even NKK soldiers who knew their masters had declared war against EarthCo were doing as he said. *Of course, we're planning to invade the US,* he thought. A shiver raced through him as considered the depth of his treasonous intensions, but he wouldn't doubt himself anymore, not until the moment of his death, not until he'd executed justice on behalf of two hundred murdered villagers and his own soldiers lost to entertainment.

The whirlyjet's crew opened the craft's door. Its roaring exhaust sounded like a whole section of bassoons as his program made music of the sound of death.

One foot on the craft's well-worn step-rung, Nadir halted. He reached under his uniform shirt, whipping in the downdraft, and removed another medal from the vest. Two to go before he was free of them.

He looked back at the feedcontrol building and its ring of rats blazing like a medieval moat. An NKK Tora tank poured a column of black soot toward the sky, its long accelerator barrel pointed at the ground. Hundreds of soldiers wearing the light blue of NKK regulars, hundreds more in the tan of EarthCo Warriors, and occasional close-ranked men in the dark blue of NKK's Sotoi Guntai tramped at a jog toward the north. Countless personnel cars hummed past the jogging men who had lost their transports.

This is still an army, Nadir assured himself. He felt the sharp edges of the medal cutting into his palm and opened his hand. The little triangle of titanium meant nothing to him now—its only value lay in ridding himself of it.

Nadir hurled the bit of a lie-filled past as far as he could, and he let out a single sound that enunciated all the frustration and hurt and betrayal still thrashing around within him.

As the whirlyjet's engine accelerated and Nadir's audio program filled his head with a string section's rising pitch, Nadir clung to the craft's door and felt his face relax as he watched the death and destruction fall away beneath him. Today, thousands had finally lived and died. They hadn't fought a battle for the faceless, sinister war command at EarthCo's nor NKK's core, no; these boys had battled for what they knew was right. *That's why they still obey my orders*, even though things hadn't gone as planned.

The whirlyjet banked, so Nadir had to step inside the cabin and slide the door shut. Four EarthCo Warriors and an NKK regular nodded as he glanced at them. Paolo was among them; he gave a stiff salute.

They were on track. *Crash the war*, Nadir thought; *What a joke. It's probably all just a subscription drive. There won't be a war by the time we get through with War Command.*

"Live well today, Boss," Paolo commed.

Nadir had to smile. The ocean, green and speckled with vessels about to take to the air, stretched out before them. He could hear its song.

Pehr Jackson 5

Janus' aircar dropped toward the midday rush of lunch-goers in Downtown Minneapolis, near the banks of the Mississippi. The rotor spun down as the car settled on the sidewalk. A few pedestrians noticed the obstruction and hurried past. Closer to the river, another aircar sat with its canopy open.

"What are we doing here?" Pehr asked of Nooa while he tied two ends of the travel-blanket around his waist. The girl looked concerned.

"I seem to have used poor judgment in choosing a friend," she said. Pehr began to laugh, which only deepened Nooa's frown. "Why is that funny?"

"Welcome to the real world," he said as their own canopy began to rise. Janus sent him a nasty look. "You'll have to go through the artifact before you know what I mean. There you'll find true friends."

"Jonathan is a true friend," Nooa said. "However, he is about to—"

"Say no more," Pehr said. He climbed out onto the ground and took a deep breath of river-stench, a virtually unchanged perfume from his youth. "He's causing more trouble, right?"

"Please do not underestimate the seriousness of what I tell you," Nooa said. The Brain had the girl-construct clamber over the hull of the aircar as if she were real. "He is currently initiating a violent attack against those who have assaulted him recently. You must—"

But before Nooa had a chance to finish, Pehr was running down the slope, avoiding rusted masses he couldn't identify and heaps of trash. He saw the boy sitting in the sand beside the parked aircar, a dark smudge against the sooty beach. When Pehr was ten meters from Jonathan, something slammed him in the head.

He fell sideways onto loose gravel. Fireworks sparked before his eyes.

Innerspace 7

Jonathan opens his eyes, pauses the program, and jumps to his feet. His Captain lays sprawled out on the ground where he hit him.

"Ah, fuck. Fuck!" Jonathan runs toward Captain Jackson. While shifting his landscape controls, he pulls up the standard commline.

"You okay, Captain?" he 3-verds. "Captain, answer me!"

"What happened?" comes a faint reply, voice-only.

Jonathan steals amp power from the program he was writing to his Citizen card and sends out an ID trace into the Captain's card. Nothing in there is burned out, he finds, and finally exhales.

"Are you okay?" Jonathan repeats. Now he's standing right beside the fallen man. "I'm sorry."

"Sorry? Blast!" The Captain sits up and only then does Jonathan realize the guy is wearing only a jacket and blanket. "What did you do to me? What's this the Brain says you're up to?"

Captain Jackson rises to his full height, rubbing his temples. His gut and chest are saggier than Jonathan had thought, but he feels okay about that: *This is reality*, he tells himself. *No fucking romance overlays here.* He notices a woman in ratty clothes running down the riverbank, accompanied by a girl.

Nooa. *Ha*, he thinks. *The team's getting together.*

"I was just working on something," Jonathan tells the man. "I set up a circle of defense so I could concentrate. You should've commed ahead."

"Thanks a lot," the Captain says. "Good to see you again, too."

The woman arrives, and she looks vaguely familiar.

"What's going on here?" she asks. Nooa looks from face to face.

"Jonathan," Nooa says, "this is Janus Librarse. You know her as pilot of the EarthCo *Bounty*."

"Oh, man," Jonathan says, unable to fight off a moment of elation. She's as pretty as in the show, only more relaxed looking. "You're good! And you feed really clean stuff, you know, from the ship's telescope.

"Wait a minute. How'd you get here, to Earth, I mean?"

"Same as Jack," she says, nodding to the Captain.

"They were describing the alien object found on Triton," Nooa tells him. "It's amazing, Jonathan. Perhaps Pilot Librarse or Captain Jackson will show you." She looks from one to the other.

"Let's go someplace and get some rest," the Captain says, looking at Jonathan. "You've got to be tired from all you've done. I sure as hell am. And hungry."

"But. . ." Jonathan says, looking back toward the aircar whose server he was hacking into, toward the river slithering with the feces and trash of millions of people. He smells the rot, and that reminds him of Lucas and Blackjack, filthy Blackjack who sold Jonathan's meat to a pervert. "I'm not . . . done yet."

"It can wait," the Captain says in a tone that makes Jonathan want to listen. No one can do that, no one except this man. Jonathan feels his heart beating fast at the base of his throat.

"Yeah, I guess so," he says. He takes a moment to gather the overlays and landscapes in front of him, switching off one trigger after another, saving half-written programs, cutting out of the aircar's server without damaging anything. Last he shuts down his blackcard and stands before two of his heroes near the banks of the mighty Mississippi. It hits him that he walked with Charity—the innocent girl—not far from here, only a day ago. *Bitch*, he thinks. But he can't hate her. There are plenty of others to hate, to take out his hate upon.

"Nooa," Jonathan says. The girl-construct, no taller than he—a head shorter than Pilot Librarse—gives him her full attention. "Book us the nicest rooms at the Uptown Hilton, okay?"

"Okay, Jonathan," she says. She seems to have changed. . . . Her face seems even more dynamic, mischievous, even. "Take Pilot Librarse's aircar; I'll return yours—"

"No," Jonathan says. "Keep it around for me, in case I need it."

The two adults walk beside Jonathan past garbage and junk he barely noticed an hour ago; but he feels guilty now, leading them through his world, as if everything here is his responsibility. *Great introduction*, he thinks. *When they think of you, they'll think of trash. Nice.*

They all step inside a real retro heap, at least as old as Jonathan. But it's like paradise to Jonathan. He settles into the back seat with Nooa and feels all warm and weird inside as the adults—real show heroes!—drive him to the best room at the Uptown Hilton.

The car launches up and south. Jonathan glances back and sees that the Brain is letting him keep the aircar, which is trailing them in synchrony. He catches her staring at him and sees an odd look on her face. Then he knows.

"Knock it off," he whispers feed-only, on a BW the Pilot and Captain aren't feeding. "It's my life. I'll do what I want."

He turns away from her and studies the massive shoulders of Captain Jackson, spilling to both sides of the seatback. The Pilot keeps looking at Jackson. Jonathan knows that look. He feels jealous for a moment, then stupid for feeling jealous. *Clean*, he thinks.

Cool and clean. He smiles. If something's happening between them, it's what he'd been hoping for all during the show.

They land within a minute on a platform jutting out from the ruby-glassed Hilton, a gleaming tetrahedron forty stories tall with a base two blocks square. A spiraling pair of chrome rails borders a spiraling row of luxury aircars on the platform, which is fenced in by gold-plated Celtic knotting. No one greets them or even contacts them as they land; in fact, the city is weirdly empty—*Where are all the cars?*—and quiet.

The Pilot's car looks tough among the gleaming luxoliners, and Jonathan has to laugh as he steps out onto the windy roof.

Pehr Jackson 6

The four of them—*Three*, Pehr corrected himself, and an AI—halted before a door that looked like real wood. He knew it couldn't be, because this hotel had to have thousands of such rooms and no way would the government have allowed cutting down that many actual trees to make doors. Pressed stalks, he guessed, then recognized that he'd been debating the composition of stupid doors. *Damn, I'm tired.* He hardly noticed that his lower half was covered only by a blanket tied around his waist.

"Whose room is this?" he asked Nooa.

"Yours, of course," the construct said.

"Oh, man," Jonathan said. "You didn't book us separate rooms? These guys'll want a room to themselves. You've got to learn a few things about people."

"Okay, Jonathan," the girl said. "Now you have room 27308, right over there." She pointed.

"Well," the boy said, yawning and stretching in an exaggerated fashion. "I've got to get some rest, too, I guess. See you guys, what, tomorrow morning?"

Pehr knew what he had to do, but it wasn't what he wanted to do. His life was becoming more and more complicated every minute, and he was being forced to be responsible. He took a deep breath. *No, I'm not being forced. This is part of my real Crusades. I've been given a gift, and now it's time to share.*

"Janus," he said, "you settle in. I want to talk with Jonathan for a little bit."

She smiled at him so warmly that he would have fallen into her arms if he didn't have this to do. She nodded and opened the door, which the Brain had keyed to their headcards at no charge to them. Pehr watched her go inside before he faced Jonathan.

"Let's talk," he said, and waved toward the boy's room.

Jonathan's eyes narrowed a little more than usual, but he nodded and led the way. "C'mon, Nooa," he told the construct.

Pehr noticed how the boy had a tendency to look at people only rarely, and then mostly out of the corners of his eyes. He looked like so many kids Pehr had encountered in this very city, a decade ago.

They entered the room and Pehr closed the door behind him. Nooa stood off to one side.

"Does she need to follow us everywhere?" Pehr asked.

"Why?" The boy sounded so defensive.

"I guess it doesn't matter." Pehr studied the room for a moment and noticed the holos on the walls were so dusty that it was difficult to see them. Then he recognized that they were actually old-school projectors—the holo images were only decoration for when the guests' cards were shut down. He saw a thickly padded chair and sat, realizing he would seem less imposing when seated. Warmth washed through his body, hinting at his fatigue.

"So. What were you doing by the river? Nooa seemed concerned."

Jonathan shot him one of those unreadable glances, then looked at the ceiling. He dropped onto the circular bed and began fumbling a scar on his neck.

"Just thinking about stuff."

"Trouble?"

Jonathan sat up straight. "C'mon, you're kind of . . . kind of like my hero, you see? Don't fuck it up with lousy questions like that. I don't need a parent, just a friend."

"I'm sorry," Pehr said. He studied his hands, noticing that the dirt beneath the nails had vanished. Then he thought about his apology. "No, I'm not sorry. You want trouble? Ha! I know trouble. It's not so great, believe me."

"I didn't mean anything," the boy said. He made fists and shoved them against his eye sockets. "Crash it all, man! Fuck, I can't do anything right. I'm sorry. See, I'm just a little . . . touchy about things. I'm kinda screwed up."

Pehr leaned forward in the chair, feeling a mile away from the boy, sensing his pain, wanting to do something. But he had no idea what. He dearly wished he were back inside the artifact-space, where everything was straightforward and pure, where he could take honesty for granted and where two people could communicate without barrier. Mundane existence seemed a pale, filthy thing.

"You want to talk about it?" Pehr asked.

Jonathan lowered his fists but held his eyes tightly shut. Nooa, only visible from the corner of Pehr's eye, remained motionless. He felt the eyes of that inhuman Brain peering in all around him—From where? The projectors? Every modern room sported at least one pov camera for people and their 3VRD visitors to use. Certainly the Brain could tap into any of them. He shivered and wondered if telling that AI so much about the artifact had been wise.

"No," Jonathan said. Then he opened his eyes. "I mean, yes." He sat up.

"You know, Captain, you're the one who always gave me hope when life was on the cable. I thought, hey, this guy's way out there, far away from this fucking Earth, free to really live it up, you know? It must be great, huh?"

Pehr grinned and noisily let out a little breath. "That's something I learned about myself—inside the artifact, I mean. Just getting away from Earth doesn't make you any happier. Getting away from shit doesn't make it smell better. You take your own shit with you wherever you go. Only, when you're stuck in a spacecraft for months, you get really sick of smelling your own rot. It gathers near the ventilators and has nowhere to go."

CHRISTOPHER MCKITTERICK

"Oh, man, don't talk like that." Jonathan appeared on the verge of tears. Pehr felt crappy for blowing the kid's romantic image of EConautics—but he had to say those things.

"But it's okay, Jonathan. I found something real out there."

"The alien thing, you mean."

"Yeah."

Jonathan looked up again. His fists clenched and unclenched the bedcover at his sides, on which was a printed circuit. "I was working on a . . . program."

It took Pehr a moment to realize how this connected to their conversation. "What kind of program?" As he waited for an answer, he glanced around the spacious room, knowing the boy couldn't take much eye contact. He caught a waft of spice, something like cinnamon.

"There are a few meatfucks that . . . well, that, ah, have done some shit to me. I was gonna show 'em how it feels."

"I know about that kind of thing," Pehr said, picturing what he and Miru and Lonny—especially Lonny—had experienced.

"Oh, man, you have no idea."

"You'd be surprised," Pehr said, a little angrily.

Jonathan's lips moved like two separate animals, his teeth clenched behind them, but no words formed, only incoherent sounds. Suddenly, the boy's face collapsed into the most pained expression Pehr could imagine a human face capable of.

"Oh, man, Captain." The boy's voice was like the cry of birds, like the sorrow of a flock of cranes cognizant that they are about to become extinct. Pehr's chest began to ache.

"Oh, man," Jonathan said. The muscles of his face tightened until he looked like a crumpled ball of clay. "Is the world really as lonely as it seems?" The boy tilted back his head and gasped for breath.

"Everyone's so fucking isolated from everyone else, and the better our cards," Jonathan rapped the side of his head, "the more we get isolated. I can't bear it anymore, the loneliness . . . oh crash, the sadness feels like crude oil . . . I'm drowning, Captain, I'm drowning, and the only thing that'll make me feel better is to hurt. . ." He faced Pehr again, but now the boy's face was a wad of hate.

" . . .to hurt the lousy fucks who've hurt me, man, burn their fucking cards so bad that they'll never think again, never feel anything again, never hurt anyone ever again, man, you know what I mean? I'm desperate, Captain, and I feel like I could destroy the whole fucking world!" He held out a white-knuckled fist between them.

And then the hand went limp, and the arm fell. Pehr watched that face sag until only the boy's brows showed any emotion, those and his eyes. It was all Pehr could do to keep looking into those eyes.

Jonathan's eyes filled up with tears, which he blinked away with an angry shake.

"Go ahead," Pehr said. "There's nothing wrong with crying."

"I think . . . I'll die."

Pehr smiled gently. "Dying's not so bad. I've done it a few times now, in the artifact, or at least it's felt like it. You emerge a little worn out, yeah, but you can see so much more."

"But it won't do me any good to cry. How can I become anything but empty and evil, after all I've seen and done?"

Pehr grew angry. "Dammit, boy! Let me tell you something. Hopelessness is one of the reasons that the world has only been getting worse. You stop feeling hopeless and maybe then you'll become something full and good!"

In the silence that followed, guilt flooded through Pehr. *Shit, good job, big hero Jackson.* The room's ventilator hissed in a melodic rhythm, matched by a subsonic pulse in the air. The walls did strange things to the edges of his vision, as if they were emanating light just below the level of perception—subcard projection, that was called.

But Pehr didn't have long to feel guilt. "What do you care?" Jonathan asked, each word tremulous upon the verge of collapse.

"Don't you see?" Pehr answered. "You're me, fifteen years ago. You gotta care about yourself, or else nothing matters."

Jonathan sagged forward and began to heave. But instead of vomiting, the boy started crying. He wept in full volume, like a baby, so long and hard that he had to gasp for breath. At one point, he managed to get out a few words:

"All . . . all I've really wanted . . . is to be loved, goddammit!" The sobs grew less severe and less frequent.

Pehr knew he had to do something, say something, but he didn't know what. Nooa, still motionless near the gold-plated sink, offered nothing—What does a computer know about human feelings? She clearly expected Pehr to take care of everything.

So Pehr slowly rose and crossed to the boy. He kneeled before him and leaned forward. Careful not to seem threatening, he put out his arms and encircled Jonathan. He recalled the little boy in the handkerchief, the boy who had always given him comfort during the bad times, the boy who helped resolve feelings of guilt over something he couldn't control. This, however, was real. This was the thing he had imagined when he thought of the handkerchief boy.

Pehr placed his arms—so big and clumsy-seeming when compared to this small thin boy—around Jonathan. Jonathan stiffened for just a second, then broke into a new bout of tears as he threw his own arms around Pehr.

"It'll be all right," Pehr said, lightly patting the boy's back. "You'll get all you want, and more. I'll never abandon you, that's one thing you can trust."

It hurt that, with every word, Jonathan only cried harder. But the boy's arms remained as tight around him as ever, pulling the jacket collar tight around Pehr's neck. He continued to soothe the boy for several minutes.

Finally, Jonathan pulled back, but not violently. Pehr stood and walked to the washbasin. He picked up a towel and tossed it to Jonathan, who wiped his face.

"Well, I'm ready to crash," the boy said into the towel.

"See you in the morning," Pehr said.

Jonathan looked up with exactly the kind of need and mutual understanding Pehr had always hoped he'd see in a . . . son? *Damn*, he thought, *I've become a father.* He couldn't help but smile.

"Yeah," Jonathan responded, his voice flat, "in the morning. Don't wake me; I'll wake you."

Pehr laughed, softly but honestly, and caught a glimpse of a smile cross Jonathan's face. That face seemed to have transformed, as if a mask had been torn free, as if something artificial that had locked it in place for years had broken loose. He looked young again. At least, younger.

Pehr nodded and turned away, aware that boys this age need time to recover their cool—and that Jonathan hadn't yet experienced the freedom of completely smashing loose the burdens of the "shell," as Miru said.

As he closed the door behind him, Pehr suddenly felt he weighed a thousand kilos. He tapped on the door where he and Janus would sleep, and began to wonder if she, too, wanted a room to herself.

The door opened. Janus smiled up at him from heavy lids. She had put on a silk robe embroidered with cardactive holos that triggered subconscious images; Pehr recalled past romances, real and virtual.

"Hey, Captain. Want someone to keep the bed warm?"

Pehr didn't say a word. He took Janus' hand, held it to his chest, and closed his eyes as he shut the door with his back. The room's lights were set to low-yellow. Janus slid her arms around his lower back and pressed herself close to his chest.

"I've wanted to be near you for so long," she said. "I want to share my everything with you, Jack." She looked up into his eyes. "But can we just sleep tonight? I—"

"Of course." Pehr took her hands and held them out before him. "I was hoping you'd say that."

She smiled. He led her to the bed and saw that the printed circuit design on the covers wasn't just decoration: They pulsed deep red, a color that made him think of sleep and sensuality. He looked back at Janus again, drew her down beside him into vaguely tingling sheets, and fell asleep before he had a chance to think of what it was he wanted to tell her.

Fury 8

The fastest craft began landing on the graffitied, poured marble field surrounding the Pentagon—EarthCo War Command—just across the Potomac River from the United States' historic capitol. Columns of black smoke spiraled up from several buildings, and Hardman Nadir wondered if this is how the city always looked or if it was under attack. Even so, being here made him recall the romantic dreams of his youth, when he thought serving what this place represented was the way to serve the good of the corp.

He frowned and jumped out of the whirlyjet; Paolo followed close behind, his boots slapping American ground for the first time in four months. They still hadn't encountered any resistance, though Nadir had watched meteoric fallout from two separate dogfights in space, and had glimpsed several laser or microwave beams stretching from sky to sea and land. But none in his army could feed any news programming, even so close to massive transmitters.

One of the big hoverships rumbled to the field beside Nadir and began spewing soldiers. Whirlyjets took off as they emptied of their human cargo. Not a single shot from the Pentagon building. *What?* Nadir thought. *Are they blind, too?* The tall windows could have been nothing more than slabs of stone for all the reaction they were getting.

"Tilden," he 3-verded to his net tech, "get a team to tap into this place's feed. Do it manually if you have to."

The woman's 3VRD only nodded and vanished. More and more craft landed and spilled out their soldiers like a conveyer belt. EarthCo Warriors, NKK regulars, and Sotoi Guntai milled about, gathering their units the way they had been assembled in Africa. Nadir's Chinese co-leader finally 3-verded him.

"Is this another trap, Nadir?" the man asked.

"If it is, we'll be meat any moment now." Nadir glanced up at the sky, but it told him nothing. A few aircraft raced past, but they could have been passenger liners as easily as spyplanes. Paolo stood at attention beside his Boss, proudly unafraid, his rifle across his chest.

"Boss," Tilden 3-verded, "there's no feed going in or out of War Command."

"What?"

"Nothing. No one's home."

"Bullshit." He opened the allband BW. "All units, we're breaking into War Command, one unit at a time. Let's not make a mess of the place. It has historic significance, you understand? Just find the generals or CEOs or whatever they call themselves and take them prisoner. No killing unless absolutely necessary. We need to squeeze some answers out of those bastards before we chew 'em up. Got it?"

He cut off the deluge of affirmative feed just as it began to hit him and opened a line to one of the Sotoi Guntai unit commanders. "Just go in through the front door, got it? Keep a line open and let us know if it gets heavy in there."

The man agreed and cut off feed. Nadir watched a small group of deep blue uniforms run toward the massive front doors. They reached the portico, seemed to stand still for a few seconds, then the doors opened. Nadir heard the delayed report of weapons-fire just as the last men entered the building.

When no word fed from the unit after half a minute, he sent one of the crack EarthCo Assault units inside with the same orders. The subbs commed him as he entered the foyer, and opened a 3VRD pov-feed for Nadir to watch the progress.

"No sign of struggle," the subbs reported as his men's boots clattered across the curled wood-tile floor. The room's walls were dusty white, and dead rodents littered the corners. Inside, the building seemed wrong to Nadir, who had expected War Command to be huge and paneled with rose marble and quartz pillars, bristling with armed guards.

But what he watched rush past him as the pov soldier worked deeper into the Pentagon was small, filthy room after small, filthy room. Occasionally, he saw a framed piece of art still hanging on a wall, or a battered desk, but dust seemed to be the primary inhabitant of the place.

"All units," he commed on the allband, "all units, enter War Command through the front door and explore wherever you don't see tracks in the dust. Don't shoot at anyone! He'll probably be part of your army." Soldiers began streaming inside.

Ten minutes later, Nadir finally received a 3-verd from an EarthCo unit: "Boss, we got something here."

They submitted a pov feed that Nadir tapped. He saw nothing much, except a dusty room with an outside view of an overgrown garden. At the center of the room stood a desk, and on that desk sat a holo generator. What looked like a manual server I/O port—all finger keys and fivesen pads—sat to one side of the cylinder.

"What is it?" Nadir asked.

"Watch," a soldier said as he depressed one of the pads, "I'll set it up." A holo-face that appeared within the confines of the cylinder. It was a man, familiar in a distant way.

"Who are you?" the face demanded. "How are you shielding your movements against me?"

"My name's Hardman," Nadir said through a 3VRD. "Who are you?"

"You know damned well who I am, you traitor!" the man yelled. "And now I know where you are. My name is Luke Herrschaft, Director of Feedcontrol. You are a non-value-added commodity. Your whole unit is NVA."

The holo flickered and vanished. Nadir pondered for a moment.

"All units, immediately evacuate the Pentagon building. This isn't War Command; it's only a monument. We're heading for EarthCo Feedcontrol Central to find a man named Herrschaft."

A few concerned 3VRDs appeared before Nadir, each about to ask the same question. He averted it: "I know what you're thinking, but don't you see? The betrayal came from above. And who's on top? Herrschaft and his people."

"Boss," Paolo said, "that's just talk, that Herrschaft isn't any more than Feedcontrol Director. He—"

Nadir barked a single, humorless laugh. He spoke on the allband: "Herrschaft's got all you EarthCo Warriors so conditioned that you see him as god. Crash that! He's just an old man, and we're safe from his hypnotizing as long as we stay under blackout. He still thinks we're just one unit. Don't tap into feed anymore, anywhere, until we've reached Kansas. When—"

A flash of light and static cut him off. Nadir shut down the feed and looked with his eyes. He saw a shaft of blue light—barely visible and only so when it cut through clouds or smoke—stab down from the sky into the Pentagon. Its angle shifted only gradually; Satellite weapon, Nadir deduced.

"Evacuate now!" he commed. "We're under attack!"

Whirlyjets and heavy aircraft began to land again as soldiers exited the Pentagon in a mad rush to avoid death from above. Nadir looked up at a blue sky flecked with white clouds, innocent looking, ignorant of the violence it concealed. Only a matter of time shielded Nadir's army from other satellites being trained where they were certainly programmed not to aim, from aircraft and spacecraft descending upon them.

"Whoever you are," Nadir commed to his unidentified ally, "you'd better keep helping us out. If we're caught on visual. . ." *We have to be gone by the time the first craft spot us*, he thought. Or else destroy all witnesses.

Casualty info began feeding as the last survivors spilled out of the now-burning building. Nadir hardened himself against the numbers, which were small considering they had breached the place billed to all the world as EarthCo War Command.

His whirlyjet landed and Paolo tugged at his sleeve, leading him inside. Nadir faced outside just as he stepped up, reached into his open shirt to the vest beneath, and removed another medal. His face twisted into a scowl as he hurled the sharp fragment of his past as hard as he could at the Pentagon, where it clinked against the old stone and fell into manicured grass. Slowly, his face relaxed. The fingers of his right hand touched the growing bare spot on his chest. Closer, he had taken one step closer to fulfilling a bargain with the world. Paolo slammed the door shut.

The whirlyjet launched up and west. Nadir looked through a grease-smudged window at the smoldering ruins of what he had thought was his government—the final betrayal, one less directly sinister than that in Africa, though perhaps just as poisonous to the spirit.

Then he turned away and opened a line to the forward pov camera. He fired up the audio program full-volume to drown out any thoughts or doubts. The craft raced toward a mythical city of power and electronics, one no man had ever seen without being invited to gaze upon it, EarthCo Feedcontrol Central.

We'll see it, he told himself. *We'll see it, because we're blazingly alive.* He nurtured the vessel of hate seething within his chest and felt destiny close and heavy upon his skull, like a wild animal full of claws and teeth, muscles trembling with anticipation for his blood, a black destroyer lurking not in a place but in the jungles of time. Savoring this certainty of his impending death, Nadir felt his every nerve tingling with the spark of life.

Worlds at War 1

Channel #183620.7, raw feed to Feedcontrol Central. EarthCo Luna Base Descoberta, Moon's Farside:

>>A distant thump. Two atomic scientists lose their 3VRD connections and find themselves not within a skyscraping blowup of plant schematics but instead in a dark, silent feedchamber. "What's happened?" one asks. His first thought is of his contract partner and daughter, in bed two tunnels away. "The war," whispers the other, who swallows in a suddenly dry throat. Seconds later, a faint hiss cuts into the stillness; the hiss grows to a roar, and within a minute, both have torn their fingertips to the bone trying to pry open the sealed airlock and its emergency release. Then there is no more air to hiss.<<

Channel #183620.7, prepared live subscription offering from Feedcontrol Central:

>>A distant thump. In a small, featureless room, red emergency lights flash to life and illuminate two atomic scientists wearing the most curr outfits from Jakk and Pompeux. "What's happened?" one asks, drawing his GE Stunlash pistol. He cocks his head and hears footfalls in the adjoining corridor. "Those NKK mannequins are attacking

us!" the other cries, also pulling her weapon free—this one is a Hewlett-Packard Pulse. "But why?" asks the first, who moves into position near the doorway, pistol near his face, its crystalline barrel glinting in the red light. "We're a scientific holding." "Because they're damned NKK, that's why, they're gunsel." The running feet bang closer. Just as the white beams of flashlights shine into the feedchamber, our heroes throw themselves into the corridor with guns blazing. The blood of five snarling NKK soldiers flows through gashes in their armor before the scientists fall. Subscription continues feeding as the remaining seven NKK fall upon the barely alive woman and gang-rape her bloody and limp body. Their faces are patchy with filth and unkempt hair, their teeth crooked and brown. Saliva dribbles from their lips as they pant above her. The other scientist is only conscious enough to wetly gasp breath and watch the atrocity.<<

Channel #3347.19, raw feed to Feedcontrol Central. Martian Defense Force cruiser, *Okie*, 9300 kilometers above Mars, near the moonlet, Phobos:

>>A reporter too stunned to say anything watches the battle progress through the pov cameras the cruiser's captain let him access. Yet another wave of NKK automated fighters flashes out of the depths of space, "Triggered by that damned *Bounty*," as the *Okie*'s captain said. Most of the manned MDF vessels have been ripped open. Claustrophobia drives the reporter to switch pov to a ground-based camera, but this is, perhaps worse: The lens points crazily, feeding mostly an image of Mars' dull rust and purple sky, obscured by sheets of smoke. The lower portion of the pov shows the top of a shattered ultraglas dome that had once housed 400 Martians, EarthCo-Citizens born on Mars. The inside surface of the dome has been opaqued by soot, yet green lightning still flashes bright enough to shine through. The reporter flicks from pov to pov, but everything he can access on the surface of Mars reveals only waste and destruction. One electric eye, inside a residential dome near the Rhoteus industrial center, stares at the puckered and blood-frothed face of a . . . man?—he can't tell—frozen by its own fluids to a scorched silver wall. On the wall, beside the oblate face whose eyes are black pits, smiles a framed holo: Husband, wife, and four children from infant to teenager, holographed in their clear dome against the rugged backdrop of a Martian rockfield. A shaggy, green rug covers the red cement floor where the children are seated; mom and dad stand behind, grinning proudly. The reporter clears his throat and cuts off the monotonous BW. He opens his feedback line direct to Feedcontrol Central, back at Earth, and begins a narration: "Greetings from high above Mars, fellow Citizens. This is Henrich Ludermeier reporting." He grafts in various pov shots as he speaks. "What you see hovering around you are manned EConautics fighters and other spacecraft, destroyed by unmanned NKK drones and long-range missiles. The *Okie*'s captain tells me that the enemy must have seeded Mars space with these tiny weapons long ago, far enough away so they'd not be noticed. They're coming out of nowhere, coming and coming. . ." He takes a breath to calm himself. "A hundred ships burn off the coast of Mars, and soon there will be none left to defend what remains of our presence on the Red Planet. I cannot promise to feed much longer, so here is my assessment. Get ready, my friends. Earth is next—that is, if it isn't already this bad back there. The war is really gaining momentum. This is beginning

to appear the final act of Man, and the star-spangled curtain is about to fall. I—" Feed shuts down as the *Okie*'s propulsion system explodes from a well-placed laser blast.<<

Channel #3347.19, prepared live subscription offering from Feedcontrol Central:
>>Pov-pans merge together to form a spherical 3VRD centered on the cruiser, which seems to be a cylinder occupying the same space as the subscriber—s/he is the ship. "Hovering in space around you," a reporter on board says, "is a halo of shattered enemy vessels, their hulls like gutted carcasses, smoked and ready for our heroic defenders to feast upon. Let's watch a replay of this great victory. . ." <<

TWELVE: System, Day 3

Transcendence E

Pehr and Janus awake bathed in a lake seething with the color of memory. When he looks closely, Pehr sees only blackness. Yet when he simply feels himself upon it, when he floats in the tepid waters without examining in detail, every shade and tone of every color he has seen in his life spring into being: the deepest red of a young man's blood coagulating in the night; the warm color of Megan's skin; the oranges, yellows, and greens of a northern Minnesota autumn; the darkest violets and purples of that moment between sunset and blackest night.

With a gentle elbow-nudge against his side, Janus directs Pehr's attention overhead. Spheres, like planets—also in the same variety of color—fill the sky as far as they can see, creating a dome that seethes with activity over their watery world. Behind them flashes a galaxy of stars.

The spheres press against one another, merge, and grow larger. As they do so, their opacity fades. Each time a new world of Pehr or Janus' memory coalesces into the larger whole, the two can see a little more clearly something forming . . . behind? It's a lens stretching our view toward something . . . beautiful and grand, Janus says within Pehr's mind.

A thing thrashing about in the waters, casting up rainbows, droplets of life moments—

"Don't move," Janus says.

Pehr forces his mind still. "How can this be? I feel my body floating here beside yours. I smell the salty wind, hear the quiet babble of liquid. I see all this, and I see you." She is naked, lovely; pearlescent water flows across her pubis and belly as her breasts and thighs float above the surface. She smiles and he feels her tingling. This is her answer.

"It wasn't anything like this last time," he says.

"Each time, it'll be different, as long as we enter with greater experience or with another person."

Pehr feels the warmth of Janus . . . within me, as if you are me.

Are you ready? she asks.

Yes. Please.

They turn their attention skyward where the spheres gather faster and faster, forming a larger thing. Now the heavy globe has become nearly translucent—but rather than let through the starlit black like a pane of glass, it seems to open upon a tunnel unfolding into the sky. The view is warped, as if through a series of lenses that are creating the tunnel. . . . Pehr fights to comprehend what this is. As he does so, the tunnel looks again like a globe, and again full of color.

"Relax, Jack," Janus says. *You know how this works. Let yourself go. Open your mind to accept what your brain tells you cannot be.*

"But—"

No buts.

At the moment Pehr releases his inhibitions, when he opens his mind as Miru taught him to do, he feels his entire life blend with Janus'. She feels her moment-memories gather into one which—as quickly as she can comprehend—becomes Jack's. Rather than living one another's lives as each had before with Miru and Pang, Pehr and Janus simply become one. *This is stronger than I expected*, Janus thinks. . . . The roiling bubble that is I and I trembles as if to collapse, developing seams, ready to burst and spill out the fertile mindmass. But this is what I want.

A million scenes sprout like slow lightning through loamy interplanetary space, grow thicker and whiter, blossom into life experiences that engulf the whole one by one, then transmute into the next. No order, no regard for one over another; they are one.

We are one.

"We are one."

Pehr and Janus again find themselves in the memory sea, but now it is cast cloudy emerald. But cloudy only as we float. Yes. The planets have repopulated the sky, each still swarming with faces from happy and tragic moments, but now they are as familiar as a girl's favorite hiding-places when Father was most angry, as familiar as a crook in a tree in an elderly couple's vast back yard. I needn't look up to know, whether you or I, I am I and *We are all this*.

You know I love you. I have since you first forced Eyes to respect me aboard the *Bounty*.

Overhead, the planets lazily cross the sky as this place—*Is this sea the artifact?*—spins in the midst of the Milky Way. Solid turquoise washes them as our attention drifts to the two of us here, in the sea, warm and lapping our bodies that feel so real.

"I'd forgotten I could love," Pehr says. He looks upon Janus, lovely, her skin rich cream at his side, then watches the planets whirl in orbit about them. "I've missed love so much. I've needed it so much. Why were we so sad and alone? I know you have been.

"Think of all this freedom!" He throws out his arms as if to embrace the galaxy. "What's out there, beyond our memories? I glimpsed . . . something through your eyes."

"I've found some answers," Janus whispers. She feels the waters caress her—but in a way that doesn't make her cringe. "Before we came here, we floated through timespace empty and alone, gnarled individuals guarded against a crueling life, all of us fortress worlds isolated against one another."

"And ourselves."

"Yes." I watch the stars begin to shine brighter behind the spheres of our lives, and I sense the tunnel again, the lens into . . . what? "A few times, we let someone inside. But never like this. Miguel was like that, and Megan. Pang and Miru. All only for a moment."

"Then loneliness again, utter isolation in the prisons of our skulls. Only this pure communication, the freedom of utter union of the minds, can bring two people together in true ways. Oh, Janus, I can't stand to ever leave this place again."

The stars beyond our lives shatter into crystal fragments that slice open the globes, and now I see beyond the veil of artifact space; I and I sense with every nerve and synapse of our minds . . . utter desolation. Beyond the gates to transcendence lie billions of wasted lives, countless billions who died never even dreaming of this place, billions who died before humans clawed their way into space, billions whose spirits were ripped from their flesh with ragged bronze blades, with chipped stone, with elongated incisors and the billions who died before Humankind even thrust his bristly head through the membrane between brute survival and sentience, when he first cast his eyes up beyond the sheltering leaves toward the sparkling gems that lay just beyond his reach—and he promised himself that, one day, he would collect all those and string them round his neck. . . . Man and woman, girl and boy; round eyes and almond, green and gun-metal; ebony skin and palest white—a panchromatic streak of faces and hands reach out to us, and they clasp our minds in mindless terror, their mouths stretched in mute screams. Yet I see that some have found a mote of transcendence in their daily lives but could not share, and, worse! some have shared and renounced it, afraid and angry. . . .

"Jack, don't you see?" My anger rises like a geyser, spuming the sea, casting silver and mercury rainbows around us; I don't fight down the anger. "The horror! The greatest lie of omission is that we never really change, not inside our cores, not when the shell has grown thick." Thick like a callous from day after day of rasping against others and a world that increasingly exposes its dark side, presses its rough-scarred hide against us.

We are all that little boy or girl, all that hurt and lonely and afraid child who senses that others—even those who profess to love us—don't truly care because they don't and simply cannot understand you. "Don't you see?"

Now that he is directed to do so, Pehr sees. He sees a whole set of sad eyes: Pehr, Miru, Lonny, Pang, Janus—and a shadowy hint of Jonathan, the troubled boy across the hall, back on Earth, in the Hilton.

Remaining here much longer is no longer as attractive. What I had hoped we would feel here, together, was . . . different than this.

"Yes, I see. Of course I see. Janus, this place is getting too crowded with pain. Let's go."

Pehr Jackson 7

No sooner did Pehr think this than he found himself beside Janus, on a round bed, covered by pulsating sheets, his body heavy with Earth's pull on his blood. He trembled with the recognition that the only thing keeping him alive was the throb of his heart, and its stoppage would kill him. In the alien-place, he felt immortal, weightless. *Thump-thump*, his blood pounded in his ears.

"Nothing is easy," Janus said, raising her eyes to his, running a finger along his hairline. "Drifting mindlessly within the artifact could be more damaging than drifting along through life here, intheflesh."

Blast, Pehr thought. He sighed and softened, relaxed. Janus' fingertip felt so gentle yet so knowing. *Of course it is*, he thought. *Now she knows all of me, my every desire and wish* . . . and every secret and "sin," as she would think.

"Relax," she said. A slow smile crossed her face. "It's time for us to enjoy each other, now that we've splashed through each other's, um . . . sea of memory, huh?"

Pehr laughed. He felt so relaxed that he couldn't even recall how it felt when his stomach knotted. Those billions of mute screams, blind and angry faces; all those moments of punishment by Janus' father and the terror she felt when Rachel first bled—all this faded with the touch of a finger. A real finger, here, on Earth. . . . And, suddenly, mundane life and dirtside existence seemed not such a prison term.

Pehr slid one hand—slowly, since he understood now what Janus wanted and how and what could still make her cringe—along her side and rested it on the slight swell of her belly. He rose up on an elbow and closed his eyes, moving toward her. Janus' lips seemed to touch his a moment before he felt skin contact.

Then all the suffering they had shared, all the searingly painful insights and self-realizations . . . all the pain he had or could ever endure in a hundred lifetimes was worth this moment of innocence. Lucid, pristine, warm. The pleasure of feeling her warm, damp kiss drew away the shell, and Pehr had to open his eyes to assure himself that they still lay physically together.

"I love you," he whispered into her mouth.

"I know."

They embraced more energetically now, and Pehr didn't fight the sensation of his body falling away. But where they traveled this time was not to a water world, not to a place writhing with things repressed for a lifetime. Here lay sensation and earth tones, scents of growing things and warm flesh, the comfort and excitement found only in true love's arms. No, he didn't fight this. He felt his own body merge with Janus'; he felt himself hard and slipping within her, sensed her gasp and then thrust, watched inappropriate images flicker to life and fade just as quickly as she became master of her own mind; he moved and she moved and together they made love in a way that could only have been abstract before this morning.

They moved and the skies were clear blue thought, the ground was shuddering flesh and nerve-endings, the air rushed the breath they shared, and they moved to a rhythm patterned deep in the subconscious of all living things descended from Earth's first organisms.

Innerspace 8

A voice intrudes on Jonathan's sleep, the first hard, dreamless sleep he's had in as long as he can remember. He blinks a few times, remembering where he is, and can't conjure up a single nightmare image. A smile twists across his face.

"I beat ya," he says to the empty hotel room. "None of you made it into my mind. Ha!"

A voice makes him sit up with a jerk: "Jonathan, would you please—"

"Nooa, people like to wake up a little before they start running errands, all right?" He'd forgotten part of his comfort came from the knowledge that the Brain was watching over him as he slept. "Give me a few minutes to shower and stuff. Then I'm all yours."

He crawls out of the sheets and powers on his headcard. The revmetal subscription automatically fires up at the volume he'd set it to after Captain Jackson left him last night.

"Fuck," he mutters. The head-splitting music is a little much so early in the day. Then he recalls how he laid himself bare last night to a virtual stranger and leaves the volume where it was. He gets naked in the alcove between sleeping area and gold-plated bathroom and hurries to the shower. Amorphous orange shapes shift and flow within the bathroom walls. He ignores them.

The shower stall hums to life as he steps within its glass confines. Subfeed holos flicker through the clear walls, stirring his groin, but he's not in the mood. He initiates feedblock, for which the room AI tries to compensate, so he adds the power of the amp. Now Jonathan is alone with his music and an electro-mechanical spray of water and cleansing soundwaves. He closes his eyes and lets himself enjoy the luxury. *Damn nice to have the Brain as a friend*, he thinks. When he steps out, the floor has grown a tufted rug that massages his feet. For only a moment, Jonathan tenses, but it feels so good.

At last he's in the middle of the vast room pulling his filthy old clothes back on, fastening the shredded leather boots. Nooa flashes to life in front of him.

"Now may I intrude?" she asks. Her face is bursting with restrained excitement.

Jonathan stands and nods. He turns down the revmetal.

"Early this morning, Captain Jackson and Pilot Librarse vanished at precisely the same time from my sensors, then reappeared together 21 minutes later. I can only assume they traveled to the alien object on Triton and back. Think of it! In 21 minutes, they traveled nine billion kilometers. Then they vanished again and remained away for 59 minutes."

"Real peak," Jonathan says. He triggers one of the wall projectors and watches a menu flash to life around the golden frame, the options having mainly to do with sex. Shutting it down, he stares at his dirty boots in the ankle-deep pseudofur. The pants that rise above them are torn and stained.

"What do you want me to do? By the way, I'm starved."

"A healthful breakfast is being routed to this room," the girl says. "I want you to do me a favor which may be difficult."

Jonathan bares his teeth in a grin. "Cracking-open-difficult is my middle name. You name it."

He hears a huff of air, then a circular panel slides open behind him. Turning, he sees a steaming plate of egg-omelet and blueberry pancakes, two foods he has never eaten in his life. That doesn't stop him from grabbing up the fork and shoveling in the foreign meal. He closes his eyes to savor the flavors, yet feels sad that it tastes so good. *Is this what it takes to have someone care for you?* he wonders. *You gotta make friends with a computer? Crash that.* He whips the fork across the room and watches it twang against a 3VRD windowsill and ricochet to the floor.

"Jonathan, what's wrong?"

"Nothing," he says too quickly. He finishes chewing, swallows, and feels a moment of guilt: *Does Nooa think she did something wrong? Who am I to hurt the Brain?*

"It was too good. Never mind. What do you want?"

Confusion contorts the face for just a second. "I want you to have Captain Jackson take you to the alien object, if he can. While doing so, I want you to try to maintain contact with me. You—"

Jonathan begins fidgeting with the seam of his pants and interrupts. "I don't know. That sounds . . . I don't know."

"I'll give you whatever you want," she says. Her voice is pleading. "If you cannot maintain contact, I ask you to seek the alien intelligence which built it. Certainly they must have a communication system through the device to their homeworld."

"Look, I want to help. Yeah, we'll see." Jonathan powers up his commcard and seeks out Captain Jackson's ID; the man's card is shut down but active—he's awake.

"In the meantime," Jonathan says, "I want—"

He is cut short by a thunder and rumble. Through his boots he can feel the building quake. He crouches and readies to run. "Nooa! What's that?"

"I told you EarthCo and NKK are at war. The Pan-America building, seven blocks north-east, was just hit by a NKK missile, disabled but retaining much kinetic energy." Jonathan feels his stress rising. Nooa continues:

"I apologize. My ability to defend Earth against spaceborne attack is imperfect. In the past ten hours, the Aurelian Wall has destroyed 99.7% of all incoming projectiles, yet three hundred—"

"Fuck, man, I don't need details. Just try to keep the Hilton from getting blown up, all right?"

"Jonathan," a voice-only comms. It takes him a moment to recognize the Captain.

"Yeah?"

The man's 3VRD flashes before Jonathan and says, "Are you okay?"

"Yeah. That was just the Pan-Am, a long way off. We'll be fine with the Brain guarding us."

A knock at the door. Jonathan overlays the peep-pov and sees the Captain and Pilot Librarse standing intheflesh in the hallway. He mentally keys open the door and invites the adults inside. They both are wearing clothes so new the creases still show. Jonathan wonders if Nooa had those sent up free, like everything else. He wouldn't want any, he decides, and—seeing no such clothes in this room—figures Nooa understood that.

"It's not safe to stay in populated areas," the Pilot says. She looks somehow . . . prettier. Jonathan takes his eyes off her as the Captain follows his gaze and smiles.

"Yeah, well, there's a war on, you know," Jonathan says to the carpet.

"Who's winning?" the woman asks. Nooa answers:

"Entropy." Jonathan catches a glimpse of the girl as she glances at him, then back to the adults. "Captain, Pilot," she says, "I would be extremely grateful if you took Jonathan to the alien object and allowed him to try taking me along."

Jonathan tenses again. He shoots a sharp stare at the AI construct and wonders if it can comprehend what it's doing to him. Then he watches for his Captain's reaction.

Jackson looks startled for a moment, then narrows his eyes in thought. Jonathan notes that the man's arm absently encircles the Pilot's waist. She answers first.

"If Jonathan wants to join us, he certainly can. But I sincerely doubt that a . . . that you," indicating Nooa with a nod, "will be able to stay in feedcontact. We can certainly try."

The Captain pushes shut the door and crosses to the chair he sat in yesterday. "I'm not sure how we can take you . . . there," he says to Jonathan. He sits. "I've only done it directly with the artifact or with people who've been inside. We—"

"Oh, Jack," the woman says. "Remember how Miru brought Pang and Byung inside? You've got to learn how to use your new, uh, memories." She leans against the door and crosses her arms.

"But they're foggy," Jackson says, "like dreams, only you can remember if you try."

Jonathan shrugs and looks from one to the other as he sits on the mussed bed. "Hey, no big deal. I don't really—"

"No, no," the Captain interrupts. "We can do it. We *should* do it."

Jonathan swallows hard, but nothing goes down. He takes a deep breath as he realizes he hasn't breathed for a long time. *Fuck this*, he thinks, and cranks up the revmetal. *I'm not afraid; cracking-open-difficult is my middle name.*

"So," he says, standing. "What do I need to do?"

That friendly smile he'd used yesterday crosses Captain Jackson's face again as the man stands up. "Just be open-minded. Be careful about your defenses; they'll only hurt you if you try to use them inside artifact-space. Don't be afraid of anything. Share as much as you can. If you start feeling scared, I'll help you get out before . . . anything bad can happen."

Jonathan's stomach feels like a nest of snakes whipping around. But damned if he's going to back out now!

"That's all? Let's go."

The Captain reaches out a hand as if to shake, retro-style, in greeting. Jonathan meets the hand and glances at the door, wondering if they have to walk—

Something heavy and warm like a hand begins to tug at what feels like the back of Jonathan's head. By the time his fear has mounted enough to override bravado, it's too late to resist.

Come on, Nooa, he begs. *Come on.*

Transcendence F

Bricks and chunks of cement cloud a blackness penetrated by stars. Beneath the rubble, a wall stands—its upper reaches cracked and spewing clouds of debris like blast furnaces. Each fragment shimmers with just enough to be visible against the darkness. Each emits a subtle hum that rises and drops in pitch, vibrating the blocks so hard that they crack; flickering light shines through.

"You must relax," I and I tell Jonathan. If you don't. . . .

Lonny explodes, spewing out maggots and ants and pulverized moments of his life. The clutter crowds with filth, further obscuring the view.

Before you two even orient yourselves, I wade through your lives.

This isn't what I expected . . . my Captain's life has been as painful as my own? No, it can't be.

"Fuck this!" rises like a moving wall gathering the debris into a solid mass before it.

But we see behind the rupturing concrete and brick:

Flash-flash-flash, mostly faster than we can comprehend, Jonathan's life rips open within us. Images of a gang motherboard—The gang calls itself "the Malfits," Blackjack with red hair and frozen face; érase bloodied and thrashing on gravel and chipped cement; Lucas like a smiling shark. . . . *Is this what you wanted? What's happening? I can't stop it.*

Flash-flash-flash, faster and faster the wall falls to pieces, the chunks crack and spill out their contents of a boy's memory. *We can't follow you, Jonathan, please —*

"I can't help it," says a tiny voice like the trickling of water. But gradually, the bricks and blocks stop exploding like fireworks and begin to crack one by one:

Pain and self-loathing paints a dull brown gloss over the motes drifting through the darkness, like blood smeared across glass and left to dry. One scene opens to Janus and Pehr the way we understand.

A young boy enters his bedroom as quietly as he can. In the room next to his, older sister Josephine cries in frustration, like every other night. He shuts the plasheet door and slides the lock into place by hand. One by one, he piles empty cans and metal toys atop one another near the door, where they would fall and clatter him awake if it swung open during the night. Toy soldier cast in shiny copper, his arms flexible and controlled by pressing the back; miniature operating aircar that doesn't have a battery pack; stiff jungle animals stand and hold up an arm-long model of an EConautics battleship, smooth and only dented in a few places. The toys pile higher until the boy feels his trap is good enough. He reaches out his mental hand in the way teacher showed him to access his headcard, and on comes the smiley face of his individ. "How can I help you, Jonny?" On flickers the circle of light around him like a huge hula-hoop that he can see even when his eyes are closed—the circle that *bings* if anyone crosses it—and he knows no one can hurt him while he sleeps. At least not without waking him first so he can be ready. He keeps a knife beneath the pillow.

Why?

Another moment overlaps: Dad—Lt. Dirk Sombrio—sets young Jonathan on his lap and tells him in great detail about his job and all the places in the world he has visited by 3VRD. "I'm a deadly weapon," the man summarizes. "We live well because EarthCo needs men like me to infiltrate and eliminate"; the man's face finally registers emotion which writhes across the quadrants of the face one at a time like a thick worm. "Now, don't you ever bother your mother again when she's in feed, understand?" My own cheek sizzles where Mommy whacked it with her fast, loose fingers that thrashed when I interrupted something that made no sense. "Yes, Daddy," with fucking baby tears heating the little baby face. "And don't you ever bother us again when we're in feed together, understand?" No answer but a whimper, desperate for the man to hold me tight against his narrow chest and apologize for speaking so harshly; *How could I have known at that age what adults do in fivesen feed?*

"You couldn't have."

They looked like they were sleeping, and now Mom feeding every day while picking at something invisible beneath her chin, always, except when she screams and smashes things and lashes out with her clawlike fingernails; Dad erect and silent as he walks back and forth across the apartment, always showing his medal-bespangled uniform in 3VRD when I try to talk to the fucker, reminding me ever so subtly of the threat . . . oh, yes, I understand that Mother needs her alone time, that you need your headfeed privacy. . . .

Flash-flash-flash, scene after scene of silent seething as Jonathan walks the streets of Minneapolis in search of a reaction from someone, *Can anyone see me?* He learns to penetrate deep into the power structure of the adults' CityNet—why? Because I can! He prompts the attention of a strong, quiet boy named Blackjack, and Blackjack takes the time to teach me how to take something back from the adult institutions. When I succeed at my first job—cutting into a staticky old holofeed distributor—Blackjack lets me crash at his 'board. One day he has Lucas put my headcard to sleep, and when I wake, I'm a Malfit; I'm blackcard-installed; I'm a fucking force for adults to fear.

I and I and I pull out of the memory-moment, drift idly through artifact-space. Calm, the universe begins to grow calm, though the chunks of shattered concrete quiver. What is that standing in the center of Jonathan's fortress wall?

érase appears from the mist, obscuring the construction I and I try to see; her face is tight and narrow, her eyes dark and darting, her hands cold and probing. We're both so young, we don't know any of the words, but we hold each other and I hold my breath, sure as the fucking sunset that some day she'll be gone, she'll leave me or be taken away; "I promise myself to you forever," she says; she says as she drives herself hard and wet against me in our virtual home between city walls, her shirt sticking to my pubic hair and her pullover hooked on my ankles; "It takes me. . ." She breathes hard as she speaks, eyes closed tight, "so much more . . . to feel alive than it seems . . . to take everyone else. Except for you, Jon. We both need to feel." "Yeah, I can't sleepwalk," I tell her later, during the quiet after when our heads throb from the blackfeed mind-chemical overload. We know it's the same conversation. "Well, I can, but it catches up fast, it's brutal to my mind, you know?"

And then she vanishes in a wave of laughter and Malfits kicking me for keeping something good from them, a wooden pallet that ceases being a Queen Anne bed, pebbles and screams.

A roar like the sound of the sea falling from the sky to its dry sandy bed—*"What's happening?"*

"Jonathan," Captain Jackson says; he appears amid the chaos of emotion and debris, "you must fight down the hate or you'll destroy yourself."

Ha! "Listen," as the roar mounts and builds to an accompaniment of revmetal thrash and rumble. This is the music that makes me burn, sad and angry. Even so, it's what I want to hear most.

"You were right."

The galaxy supernovas star by star beyond my and my reach, *What is he doing?* the force of this boy's hatred is greater than our love, and his memories move too fast to capture.

"This place makes you understand yourself. Wakes you up, here," I tap the side of my skull, which overlays the whirling brick and mortar; and I am the ultimate graffiti, as big as the universe of hate and emptiness. Another wave lashes through the mess, picking up debris in its crest and hurling it into the dark lanes of the swirling Milky Way.

"érase was my love and safety, like you two have now." Flash of this morning's lovemaking. "She gave me strength and confidence. I had hope for a future, and I didn't need my crashed-out family—as if ever needing them meant anything! But when she died, I lost every fragment of what propped me up. What do I have now? Nooa! Ha! And don't cry for me. I don't want your pity."

"Stop it!" Pehr's voice pulses opposite the waves radiating from the shattered core of the boy, growing in magnitude. The grandiose graffiti evaporates. Now I and I see the remnants of his innermost shell, small and fragile like a ceramic doll dropped on star-flecked, black tile. Tiny—his head hangs limp and polychromatic tears fall from his eyes, splashing open when they hit the tile into moments of his life.

I'm sorry. With a ripple of self-revulsion that cascades through the fractured doll, cracking it nearly to pumice.

"Listen, boy," I say, while Janus fills me with the strength I need to resist his collapse, to fight him back as if he were a black hole, yet uphold his inward spiral. "I promised you I'd always stay with you."

And I will, too—Pilot Librarse.

The dollhead rises, wobbly and brittle, and two great eyes loom up at the man and woman whose bodies accumulate from dust and stone. I and I sit upon the disk of the galaxy and carefully reach out to the boy the way we held one another this morning.

"I'm not worth your time," I tell them.

Stop it!

"No! Look!" Jonathan's doll-self thundercracks wide open, but the smoke and fire that blast out are not his: Here is the pain and suffering of Pehr and Miru and Lonny and Janus and Pang, screaming at me and me; *Don't you see I'm overwhelmed?*

Flash-flash-flash, our lives machine-gun through us; the sea of memory appears around us, crashes and roars in the storm—only now it boils red and bubbling from beneath where Jonathan's hatred for the human species seethes like a gash in the earth spewing magma. The sea boils away as I and I try to shelter ourselves from this interpretation of our memory-moments. Time passes, and we three live all the lives again, and ever so gradually the Jonathan moments explode and crack and split and finally just merge with ours; the magma cools, volatiles evaporate, and the ocean finishes boiling away. Rain begins to fall. At the center of the dried sea, I and I glimpse a spaceport built . . . for me.

For my Captain.

"Look." Janus scoops down into the sediment surrounding the spaceport. In the mess that coats her fingers, iridescent gold sparkles.

"This is you, Jonathan. This is what remains after your shell shattered."

Ah, the pearl. Captain Jackson smiles and nods once. Behind him roars the *Bounty*'s rocket, as in a subscription ad.

"My pearls," Jonathan says. He reaches tentatively for my hand and collects the treasures. He looks up and still his eyes are sad. "But now what?"

"Now you are free. Time is now your partner. We don't know what comes after, either, but we must try to find out."

"Nooa? Can you feed?" No response.

"We didn't think the Brain could stay in contact with us."

"Where is here?" ask I, Jonathan, while studying a sky filled with stars, the stars spiraling in a slow dance around a galactic black-hole core.

Faint tendrils start to grow from star to star, and we watch as the Milky Way shrinks; the Local Group of galaxies is the next leap in perspective, and each galaxy sprouts more of the glowing tendrils. *Veins*, one of us thinks; now a supercluster fills our pov, finally the whole universe; veins pulsate from star to star, cluster to cluster, especially dense within each galaxy but also stretching across the massive voids to its neighbor; tendrils span even the fathomless reaches between superclusters, though sparser. The sphere of our artifact-space looks like a model of the universe, only a universe represented as some kind of living thing made of fusion-powered organs— Miru is very close—and. . . .

The mirage collapses. Jonathan is gone.

I and I gaze up from our replenished sea at the stars. This time they suggest something more; they offer yet another mystery.

"Did he survive?" Pehr asks. Janus dares not answer for fear the boy still lurks up there, amid the tangle of interstellar veins.

We draw a breath together and open our eyes to the hotel room.

"That wasn't quite what I expected," Pehr said. Janus pressed her face against his chest, and he felt her face warm with tears. Automatically, his arms went around her naked back.

Life was complicated. Life was finally a place to live. Pehr held Janus tightly and felt alive.

Jonathan Sombrio 1

Jonathan's eyes flash open. His glimpse of a grand map fades until he can't quite remember what it looked like or what it meant. *Where am I?*

Beside him on the gelbed lies a young woman, knotted in stained sheets. Her long hair, stringy and smudged black, covers her face. They are in a cube-room, barely larger than the wide bed. Jonathan rises to his elbows and his nudity feels like a flare.

He recalls what just happened to him. He pieces together clues left by those who went before into the alien place. So many details, so many memories; his mind races and reels, his senses flood him with information. At sixteen he has lived several adult lives. Thoughts slide so smoothly through his mind now.

In his chest, his heart rattles fast and weak. He leans toward the girl, slowly untangling the hair from her face, afraid that he might be right. . . .

"érase," he says softly. "I thought you were dead. You were dead." His back cramps with fear.

"My name's Cheri," says a breathy voice. The girl's eyes remain closed as she pulls back the soiled sheet and reveals an emaciated body. "Name your fantasy."

"Shut the fuck up!" Jonathan cries, shooting to his knees. His meat feels dizzy, starved, tired, but he won't let that deter him.

"This is Jonathan." He emphasizes the name with a slap against his chest. "You remember me, érase. You have to!"

Her arms reach up, draw him down against her. He doesn't resist, hoping she can see past whatever feed she's taking. Her arms encircle him without touching, as if holding a 3VRD twice as wide as his body.

She begins to lay dry kisses along the side of his neck. Though érase is the only person he let himself love, though he's shocked almost beyond thinking, her kisses feel obscene. On top of that, none of his old defenses work anymore: He kicks on the revmetal; he overlays CityNet, enhances it, then overlays ECoNet; on and on, piling feed and subscription upon one another, but still every memory he has acquired glistens as vividly as fresh blood on a clean sidewalk. And not just his own memories, but a whole slough of others', some of which are so bad he feels his head is about to explode.

"Fuck!" he shouts, clamping shut his eyes and gripping the bedsheets in his fists. In response, érase reaches for his shrunken penis and pulls it toward her.

"No," he says. He runs an ID on the girl.

She is dead, he thinks. He discovers that Cheri—no middle or last name—appeared as a valid sub-Citizen three days after Blackjack informed Jonathan that érase died. They cut her brain sigs long enough for EarthCo to issue a death certification, he realizes. The bastards sold her as a slave, a pump.

Jonathan shudders with revulsion and hatred as érase's—Cheri's—legs wrap around his buttocks. The sides of her knees dig into his hipbones. She feels hot.

He recognizes that sensation from his own experience and identifies other symptoms. Not a single recollection evades him. "Brain chems." His whisper is like a knife. "They've got you feedrapt on brain-chem stimfeed. I'll burn 'em all."

He shuts down his excess overlays but leaves the revmetal screaming and pounding between his ears. The building contains a powerful server array on every floor in addition to hundreds of personal-sized ones. He crawls into the short-range net, busts the simple blocks while skimming above trap-viruses like shadow snakes writhing around the neon passageways, and enters the server. It's represented as a 3VRD checkerboard, only each square is a computerized vision of each room on the floor. Johns and pumps are at work in two of the rooms; in the rest, the girls' and women's cards are asleep. In one, a man is hunched over a cubist-looking representation of a sleeping woman.

Jonathan reaches out his amped, mental hand and finds the shutdown icon for the server. *Not enough*, he thinks, and injects a little program he got from Lucas a year ago. Colored dots cluster and begin to swirl, gathering at the powersource; when they gather so dense as to look pure white, a jolt of energy gushes through the AI. The computer crashes almost instantly. Jonathan's heart throbs, his head pulses in waves.

érase begins to moan. Her legs fall limp to the gelbed and she lets go her grip on Jonathan's flaccid penis. His anger redoubles. Still not enough.

He opens contact with the building's other servers and moves along burning each and every one. He doesn't care that he's blasting pain and furious reality into the heads of those whom the servers are feeding. But his own comfort has been chipped away over the past few days—completely crashed with the Captain and Pilot Librarse in the alien-place. Before that, feedrapture treatment did a job on his coping skills. *If it didn't kill me, it shouldn't kill anyone else.*

"Live and learn, boys and girls," he 3-verds to all who might be feeding. "You gotta get hurt to learn."

He shuts down the overlays of flickering checkerboards and lowers his eyes to the writhing girl beneath him. Suddenly, like water gushing into a storm sewer after a dam of trash has melted through, pity and sadness wash away the hatred. Small, animal sounds hiss and gurgle from deep within her. He cups her cheeks in his hands.

"I'm sorry, érase. You'll understand later. I love you, you know it. You've got to remember, don't you? Let's go."

Jonathan steps off the bed and reaches into the draped shelving beside it. He shoves empty bottles of liquor and scented oils onto the jelly-soft floor and finds a pair of men's pants, which he pulls on. He then pulls out a lacy thing that looks like a dress. Since it's the most clothing-like item on the shelves except for the pants, he brings it to érase.

"Can you put this on?" he asks. She doesn't seem to even know he's in the room with her. The withdrawal is immediate—Jonathan remembers. The hatred builds again, and again he feels the strange sensation of riding a crest in his brain, as if his meat is only being tricked into thinking it's solid and standing on flooring while his mind goes netsurfing.

"I'll help," he says. The dress has no arms, only short springy tubes that grip érase's upper thighs. The upper part simply stays in place against her slight breasts by friction, no shoulder straps. Her dark aureole look like bruises behind the white mesh.

"Fuck," he mutters, and reaches back into the shelves. He finds a scarf and hangs it around her neck for better coverage.

"That's better. Let's go." Up and out the door; the lock is nothing to him, though he has trouble managing the rubberlike body he's dragging along. Jonathan wonders for a moment where Nooa is, considers comming her for assistance in getting érase out, then abandons the thought. *I'll do this myself.* His stomach burns. *She's my responsibility.*

They pass dozens of pumprooms like érase's, then stacks of mini-cubes with opaqued ultraglas doors. In the light of random lumnisheets, handprinters shine like worn brass on the lock mechanisms, the paint rubbed off behind the handles where countless knuckles rubbed as they opened the doors. One cube's door has been wrenched off, and inside Jonathan sees the black skeleton of a gelbed frame. No window. The cube's vent hisses like an angry snake. The whole place stinks of stale sweat.

érase is semi-conscious, still moaning, and growing heavier each step Jonathan takes. Her legs move as he drags her along, but they don't support much of her weight. Finally, they reach a dropshaft, one of the retro fixtures used in low-rent places like this. Jonathan overlays the maintenance system, calls the mechanical carrier, and shuts out anyone else from boarding. The door grinds open before the hung platform has even reached the floor.

Jonathan drags érase onto the plastic floor with him and sets the machine to take them to ground level, 39 floors below. Overhead, cables and pulleys squeal and groan. They begin to descend with a jerk. Through the woven-hicarb net that surrounds them and joins to form the hanging cable, Jonathan watches amateur artwork—etched into the walls of the shaft—begin to flash past.

érase's eyes, glazed and bloodshot, flicker open. She fixes on Jonathan's face for a while, studying each of his features one by one.

"Jonathan?" she croaks.

"Full-out, my sweetmeat," he says with a twitching smile. "You're back."

Head wobbling, she sits up. "What happened?" The platform's floor-ring lightpad flickers, dulling to red, then brightens to a blazing white that makes Jonathan squint.

"I crashed this place, babe. I'm setting you and everyone else free. We can find our dreams now, my érase. I've learned so many ways to get stuff. I've made powerful friends. We can go anywhere, and I mean any—"

Her head is shaking slowly side-to-side, and a sad smile crosses her face. "Jonathan, sweetmeat. I can't."

He feels his body knot up into wads of gristle. "That's trash! I mean it, we can have anything—"

"Jonathan, I'm Cheri now. érase . . . érase died a long time ago. She lost Citizenship. You know what that means? I've got nothing, not even Edufeed access." Her voice begins to shudder. "You can't imagine how much you'd miss Edufeed."

Her eyes don't hold him long; the pupils dilate at random. "If I try to make a case to reestablish érase, I'll get prosecuted for falsifying—"

"No!" Jonathan yells. He leaps to his feet during the ringing echo. "Crash it! The Brain—you know, the AI that networks EarthCo? The Brain's a personal friend of mine. She'll send us a spaceship and we can go somewhere, anywhere. . . ."

érase's head keeps shaking. Jonathan watches her body begin to convulse as the withdrawal begins to set in. She falls forward to hands and knees and vomits clear liquid that gathers on one side of the tipping floor and runs over the edge. They've only dropped ten levels.

Jonathan lets out a growl that mutates into a scream. When érase's fit recedes, he continues: "I'll do anything for you, burn this whole city, kill everyone who ever laid hands on you, whoever even looked at you intheflesh. I'll blow up the world if you want, if I can, and take you far away. We'll—"

"Trash it, Jonathan!" she shrieks. Jonathan falls back against the wall of hicarb mesh, which sags under his weight. He notices a reek of old dust and burned plastic.

"You fucker," she says, rising to her knees and then standing as best she can. "You fucker, who are you to tell me what I'm going to do with my life? Just like all the others. You think I'm going to leave now, after working in this . . . place for . . . I don't know, months? Do you know what I've gone through here?"

Jonathan feels dizzy with anger and panic, his vision blurring, his inner ears sensing a distant roar. "But it can end when—"

"Shut up." Now she pins him with both her bony hands as hard as steel clamps. Jonathan's instincts force his weight away from the precipice, nearly knocking her over in the process.

"I've worked hard to get where I am," she continues. "Do you know where your friends sent me at first, right after they killed érase?"

She shudders and a snarl rips across her face. She smacks Jonathan with the back of her hand; he hardly notices the sting—after all, it's just meat.

"Well, I've earned enough points to be classified legal applicant. In four months, I'll be full Citizen again."

Jonathan leans toward her, feeling the old emotions rise up again. "But I can do that for you now, with the Brain's help." He tightens his arms around her back. "Anything you want, I can do. Anything!"

The pulleys high overhead squeal again, and Jonathan notices an overlay glowing "1"—they've reached their destination.

"Listen, boy. I haven't gone through all this shit for nothing. I don't want you, I don't need you, I've grown beyond you. Now get out of my life or I comm the beatcoats."

"Dammit!" Jonathan powers up his commcard and sends for Nooa. She doesn't respond. Panicking, he retransmits again and again. When the floor's door scutters open and érase pushes him out, he closes his eyes and howls Nooa's name across the BWs.

"Please, Jonathan," Nooa says as she appears in the foyer, paneled in flaking laminate, "I cannot help you."

"See, see?" he says, pointing at the AI's construct.

érase frowns deeply and gives him a hard shove with her bare foot. "I don't know you, you don't know me. My name is Cheri, and next time I see you, I'll feed you my fist." She tightens her tiny hand.

Though she manages to keep her words strong and level, Jonathan sees her eyes begin to well up as the door slides back into place, blocking her from view. He splices into the platform's retro 2-D pov camera and watches a girl crumple into a heap of scarf and lace and bony flesh as her body shakes. He can't tell if she's crying, vomiting, or laughing, since the pov is vid-only.

"Fuck you, Nooa," Jonathan says. After another few seconds, he shuts down his contact with the building.

"érase!" he 3-verds her, full-power, fivesen, baring his emotions on his ephemeral face. But she only fires back with an old gang trick: His feed twisted and mutated and sparking random bursts of energy that shoot pain through his limbs. Even so, he doesn't shut down, but she cuts him off from her end. She has vanished from his life once again, this time more permanently.

A moment passes. Someone in the shadows and ash-heaps of the foyer grunts and crunches glass.

"Why didn't you help me?" Jonathan says like a growl through his teeth, turning on Nooa's construct. "I could have saved her from this. . . . Crash you, you fucking heap of wires!" His wildly thrown fist sails through Nooa.

"I didn't do anything," she states.

"Damned right!" Jonathan turns away and begins crossing the narrow room to its gaping maw of an entranceway. A footpath is worn through debris and rubble. Only a hand-sized disc of lumnisheet still casts light against the darkness.

"I chose to let you try to convince her without my help," Nooa says from directly behind him. "Cheri would have been bad for you."

Jonathan stops stomping ahead and turns to glare at her. The girl's face tilts forward until she's looking up at Jonathan through the top of her eyes. "I had hoped you would not go to her after traveling through the alien object," she says. "érase was a criminal, and Cheri is even more poisonous. Before you met her, she was Blackjack's . . . lover. I can only deduce that she used you—"

"Never speak to me again," Jonathan says. *Blackjack's lover, crash!* He spits at the 3VRD. "And I don't want your free stuff anymore, either."

He turns and begins to run, bare feet crackling trash as he bursts out of the lightlessness into a rainstorm. Needles of water prick his bare back and neck as he stares across a barricaded street at the Hornworks of St. Paul, a low, block-long steel skeleton enclosing what had been planned to be the world's greatest pipe-organ. That had been back in the early days of feed, when people still listened to music intheflesh. Vast brass and aluminum funnels lay twisted and oxidizing in the rain, left to rot since the project was abandoned. Jonathan senses a single note thrumming at the limit of hearing and imagines one of the discarded horns sings him a note of desolation, of understanding.

Like a feral beast, he whips around and stares up through streaking rain, up along the windowless face of the skyscraper. Its surface seems to shimmer and pulse as the note grows louder. Jonathan closes his eyes tight and wonders how he will go about destroying this society and replacing it with something like what he sensed in the alien place. *That's the only way; this wreck can't go on forever.*

"The war," he says, opening his eyes. Now his vision is even more hampered. He tries to blink away the wavering image. "No one will notice a few more deaths during a war."

"Jonathan," Nooa says, "are you returning to the artifact? Your headcard signal is fluctuating."

"Is that so?" He takes a deep breath and searches his newly acquired memories for what this could mean. What he finds is something he, himself, learned inside with the Captain and Pilot.

"It's a destructive, uh, wave," he says. He smiles his best razor-smile at the construct. "Once you've entered the alien toy, it becomes part of you. Well, when you're inside, and when you let evil take you over—evil being hatred or hopelessness or that kind of shit— you feel this wave of self-destruction. It's probably the same force that shatters your meat when you enter, only this time it's trying to shatter your mind. The part of it that they call the 'shell.'" In his ears, his voice sounds shrill and hoarse.

"Well, my little shell is growing thick again. It's like this: A Stratofighter's wings cut clean through the air at top speed, right? But don't try that with a fucking square skyscraper." He reaches blindly down, grabs something cold and hard, and hurls it against the building. Not even a satisfying thump.

"I gotta get going. I'm gonna do what Captain Jackson tried to do when he was a kid, only this time, I'll do it right. He was afraid to hurt anyone. I'm not." After a few deep breaths, Jonathan's vision settles down a bit.

He begins to walk, then thinks to call up the aircar Nooa gave him yesterday. It lets him know it will arrive in just under four minutes.

"Jonathan," Nooa says. Her 3VRD speeds up to walk beside him.

Jonathan keeps his eyes straight ahead, watching Zone barricades piled one atop another like a half-dug archaeological site. He begins subscribing to shows at random, layering them one atop another, even cracking the seal his amp let him put over the edufeed. Faces and machines and buildings swarm in all directions before him.

"Jonathan, I collected a lot of data from your cards as you began to be transported. I think—"

Jonathan doesn't break step as he tilts his head to stare at her with a crooked smile. "Do you think I care?"

"Well, I believe the data has applications to your current problem. Perhaps I can assist you when the wave begins to damage your atomic structure."

Jonathan stops walking to bend over and laugh so harshly that his throat feels shredded. "You don't understand," he says, standing again. "I only need to stay together long enough to take care of a few things. The Minneapolis/St. Paul sprawl has only about forty prime gangs. I'll be finished by sundown." His smartass smile fades. "On second thought, yes, you can help me. But only until sundown."

Jonathan Sombrio sucks in a damp breath and stares ahead through a tumble of masonry and wreckage of vehicles. Water runs off what remains of the sidewalks, into what had once been charming iron gratings, carrying with it the city's flotsam. Bits of cloth and product wrappers clot in the rusty metal, shining wet and grey by the diffused light of day. Jonathan trips a few times as the internal wave warps his vision; he feels as if he's a dolphin leaping through the border between ocean and sky, only to crash back down into an ocean of human filth, all the time wishing he could just stay under a little longer, a little longer yet, forever. Soon enough.

He shivers, but isn't sure whether it's the weather or something insubstantial—something more dangerous. "Just not too soon," he says. *My meat's gotta breathe a little longer.*

A basso rumble shudders loose sheets of plastic from a walled up four-story storefront beside him. Jonathan grins at the thought that it might be another of NKK's missiles and not just natural thunder. He feels no fear, yet every molecule of his being trembles with a coil of emotion, love and betrayal, freedom and hate, giddy excitement and terror.

The aircar hums down out of the deluge, distracting Jonathan from the inside of his blurry head. "Blackjack, Lucas, get ready for a visitor."

Fury 9

Hardman Nadir watched through his whirlyjet's forward pov camera as his army closed in on EarthCo Feedcontrol Central. Aircraft of all types swarmed through the sky and settled on the surrounding plowed fields like stormclouds heavy with rain. He sensed the latent energy, the chain-reaction about to go off, within the feed silence. Adrenaline dumped into his veins. None of his soldiers commed one another, except in brief tactical bursts.

Within their noose, hundreds of acres glistened from a recent rain—but not like the fields he knew around Wolf Point, rather, in the hues of wet metal. Never trained in technical disciplines, Nadir had no idea what the shimmering plates did that matted the ground as far as the pov let him look. Triangular structures the size of grain elevators rose from the metal sea; spiky antennae sparkled with their fresh coat of rain, white domes, silent rectangles that could have been office buildings or towers hiding arsenals of rockets. . . . Hundreds of robotic vehicles rolled or hovered from place to place on the electronic blanket, repairing damage or upgrading the equipment.

Nadir couldn't see a single human being, not even a window. He wondered if this place was as abandoned as the Pentagon—*What will I do then?* The fury within him couldn't be contained much longer. He studied the corners of his splice: faithful Paolo to his right, the Sotoi Guntai Commander and all he represented two men to his left. They seemed untroubled. The reek of old sweat filled the air.

At the rear of his mind, subdued, Nadir's audio program transformed the jet's muffled roar into the sustained drone of a bagpipe. He closed his eyes and saw only the splice rushing at him, looming larger and spiked steel, glistening cables lashing in the wind.

At last he recognized something. Auto-cannon, megawatt laser, R-type. He'd learned how to run those in feedtraining, which basically consisted of making sure the system's AI stayed within operating boundaries. Watch a readout, let the computer knock out three armored targets per second. Nadir sucked a deep breath and held it.

By the time his craft had flown to Feedcontrol's outer perimeter—marked on ground by fences and pits, in the air by floating spheres that wove an electromag dome around the place like a spider's web—he had counted 15 auto-cannon cupolas. He ordered the pilot to swing around to avoid the trip-lines.

"All air units," he 3-verded across the allband, "set down outside the perimeter and wait for infantry units to unship."

He opened a line to his net tech. "Tilden, find out if this place is feeding us." She popped into view only to nod; her eyes gleamed with excitement.

He'd watched that same expression flash before him countless times in the past twenty hours: Soldier after soldier had revealed a mounting enthusiasm—the men were going nuts with the desire to kill, to fuck with those who'd fucked them over, and the only opportunity they'd had was in Tripoli and a handful of times off America's East Coast.

349

Outside, surrounding the rolling hills of metal, his army gathered. Once upon a time, armies needed days or even months to cross an ocean and assemble like this; now they rocketed to the Moon, bashed Farbase, and built a lunar outpost in the same amount of time.

"Boss," Tilden said, out of breath, "we're completely black. EarthCo Airborne 7 even tripped a sensor, but it didn't transmit." Her eyes sparkled. "What kind of crypto shit are you running?" Hurriedly, she added, "Sir?"

Nadir smiled to hide how he felt.

He could come up with only three answers: Either Herrschaft was using Nadir's army in some kind of game; War Command had instigated a coup and was using them as shock troops; or ECoNet had become conscious and was using them to kill off the human parasites seething across its face.

His fist slammed down against the armrest of his seat. He cut camera feed and the splice snapped shut. The interior of the craft—his physical surroundings—fell into place. Six men, the Sotoi Guntai Commander, Paolo. The Commander finally turned his gaze to Nadir, but the black eyes were unreadable. The audio program became dynamic for a while as the whirlyjet landed and the engine whined down.

One by one, infantry units commed to let Nadir know their heavy airships had landed and they had disembarked. Within five minutes, most of the army was in place.

Nadir glanced at the Commander; his blue-uniformed counterpart nodded. Nadir opened the allband and began barking orders. Two Sotoi Guntai leaped across the legs of their comrades and threw open the whirlyjet's door.

Paolo tightened his fist and face and said, "Live today, subbs, for today we may die." A rictus grin crossed the young man's face.

Nadir smiled back, then dashed out of the aircraft with the others. Once everyone disembarked, the jets whined back up the scale and the craft alighted to join the others circling their objective. The rancid odor of poorly burned methane burned Nadir's nasal passages, so he inhaled deeper. At his command, the EarthCo Warriors of his old command pulled up near him in their rickety groundcars. Paolo found their car and ordered it to them, but Nadir shook his head; he wanted to go on foot.

The whole world seemed to shudder and hum deep in Nadir's psyche as he climbed aboard the plastic car, staring up at Feedcontrol Central—now, from ground-level, standing before him like Oz, intricate and impregnable. Had he come all this way just to destroy his men and himself?

Shut up, he thought. *No thoughts.* He cranked up the volume of the audio-enhancement program so it picked out sounds as small as boots plashing through mud.

"Move out," he said. They knew what to do.

The segment of the noose Nadir could see tightened. He walked at the forefront. His heart pounded in his throat while the bootfalls of his impromptu army created a cacophony of music, enough to drown his doubts. No one doubted him, least of all Paolo, who still wore that grin. Nadir began to feel like his old self, confident in the surety of life's transience and determined to do his bit for EarthCo and humanity.

And then he watched his boot tip light as he stepped on a yellow laser beam. His head shot up and his heartbeat increased so much he thought it would burst in his chest. But the big R-types didn't swivel toward him on their massive mushroom-shaped mounts. Without breaking step, he marched on. Soon his boots began to clack against a paved walkway. A glance to both sides showed him hundreds of cars, dozens of light armor pieces, thousands of men trooping past pillars and towers, beneath crisscrossing gangways and dangling elevators. Bringing up the rear of the army's tightening ring were the pyrotechs, placing packets on the gun turrets and anything else that looked critical. Nadir felt as if he were violating some ancient, holy place, so he remained quiet, not quite sure what he was seeking. Tilden had told him she would know when she saw it.

Nadir's commcard began to buzz and rumble as with distant EM weapon explosions. He turned down the gain, assuming this was static from a space battle show. A few steps later, it returned, doubly loud.

"Hardman Nadir," a disembodied voice spoke within his head, "I must apologize. No longer can I shield you from Herrschaft, though I will do what I can. Too many warning systems have been set off by your presence here. You are on your own."

"Wait!" Nadir shouted, voice and 3VRD. "Who are you? What's happened?"

But he couldn't wait for an answer. Thirty meters overhead, motors whined and gears meshed, metal creaked and hicarb groaned. One of the mushrooms—an R-type emplacement—was rotating, sighting behind him toward where the heavy hovercraft lay.

And then, suddenly, all the gun cupolas were in motion, filling Nadir's audio program with tympani rumble and horn section whine. He heard the crackle of a single NKK plasma rifle.

"Cover and defend, CA-11!" he 3-verded on the allband. *Shit*, he thought, *the Niks don't know our codes.* "Hit their guns first, like we planned," he added.

The air sprang to life with luminous bands of green and red, laser stripes and twanging projectiles. Thousands of soldiers scurried into firing position. But who could they target? One of the pyrotechs set off a charge, and Nadir turned in a crouch to watch a mushroom's base crumple. It toppled slow-motion, as if underwater, ripping out walkways as it fell, colliding with a framework tower in a shower of sparks, finally crashing into the shimmering steel ground with a subsonic rumble. Yellow smoke curled upward in the wind, dispersing a few meters above the wreckage. A hole gaped where the cupola-turret had been rooted, and electricity danced across a tangle of naked wires.

Overhead, EarthCo aircraft swooped down on their electric rotors and their NKK counterparts upon gushes of burned hydrocarbon, pounding the inhuman city with heavy energy weapons. Molten metal oozed from the wounds they inflicted; Nadir spliced in to a gunship's pov and surveyed the damage. Of the 15 mushrooms, one had fallen, three were badly punctured, four were just beginning to fire—

The pov flashed and went dead. *Rrrrip-rrrip-rrrip*, the R types tore the air three bolts per second in the voice of maniac tubas. Their far-ultraviolet beams only gleamed through clouds as they atomized matter which stood in their way. Aircraft shattered and exploded; one EarthCo Singlet completely vaporized in a puff of gaseous plastics.

"Infantry!" Nadir commed. "Where the crash is our support fire?"

"Online, sir!" an Asian face 3-verded. The sky sizzled with discharges, but Nadir couldn't tell which belonged to his army and which to the robotic city.

He began to feel disoriented. He hadn't trained for this kind of combat, and all his experience amounted to nothing—all that had been fake, lies, bullshit. To release the mounting violence within him, Nadir sighted his EMMA on a nearby R-type autocannon's seam.

The battle's pitch rose to a crescendo that made Nadir wince, so he shut down his audio program. Now he heard the distinct *snap* of NKK weapons, the familiar *crack-thup* of EMMAs, the reassuring scream of whirlyjet weapons. . . . But through all this, Feedcontrol's autocannons *rrrrip-rrrrip-rrrriped* the air. Near Nadir, a beam passed along the ground, bursting three men's chests like rocket exhaust blasting through red clay, bits of bone and organs shattered to minute fragments that sprayed the gleaming metal wall behind them.

Nadir's eye began to twitch, his jaw tightened so hard he thought he'd crack a tooth. Tiny ants bearing microscopic needles tried to puncture the hicarb shells of atomic megawatt lasers. *Hopeless!*

"Tilden!" he roared on the dedicated line to his net tech. "We've got to get inside! Where?"

Her 3VRD appeared before him, calm and upright; she'd reverted to a preprogrammed image—Not a good sign, Nadir realized.

"I . . . I don't know," she said.

Nadir's attention was torn away from the conversation as one of the fueling vessels, parked more than a kilometer away, exploded into a wall of fire that stretched along the contours of the rolling land and rose toward the cloudy sky. A smaller craft he couldn't identify at this distance streaked, flaming, from the explosion toward Feedcontrol's clutter of towers. It didn't reach a hundred meters beyond the outer perimeter before two R-types converged fire and scorched it into a dispersing smear of soot.

". . .only way I see is to get inside the tower itself," Tilden finished. "Of course, I don't have any schematics, but I'm showing that the heaviest internal feedtraffic's inside there, pitching feed from the antennae and then back out. No promises—"

"All units," Nadir commed, "objective B is the tallest tower, that silver one with round walls at the center of this place. When we're inside, I'll give you further orders. Move out!"

Nadir started for a second as he focused and saw the Sotoi Guntai Commander sprinting toward him. The Chinese man tramped to a halt less than a meter away and his eyes bored into Nadir's.

"What's the meaning of this?" The man gesticulated wildly at the chaos around them. A whirlyjet screamed toward a gun emplacement full speed, toppling as it plunged, and impacted with a roar and cascade of flame. The R-type stopped firing.

Nadir drew a deep breath laced with smoke and fumes. The battle was deafening. "We're no longer blacked out," he told the man.

The Commander's face grew pale, his eyes opened to reveal bloodshot whites. "You . . . you!" the man stammered. He raised his rifle as if to strike Nadir with the stock.

Paolo appeared out of the melee and swung a length of wiring conduit against the back of the Commander's skull. The man staggered toward Nadir, his face twisted in confusion, and dropped his weapon. Paolo raised the pipe again, but Nadir shook his head sharply.

"You are the fox," the man said as he crumpled to his knees. His rifle clattered to the metal beside him, sending little ripples across the gleaming plates as they re-oriented themselves on their pivots.

"Trouble, Boss!" an EarthCo Warrior 3-verded Nadir. "The damned Sotoi Guntai are turning on us!"

Just then a cascade of other 3VRDs began to flicker to life before Nadir, but he cut them out.

"Valentine's," he cursed. Paolo's eyes asked a question. "Well," Nadir said, "we can't just wait to get killed here, can we? To the tower."

He began to run, Paolo beside him. They passed aircraft wreckage and disemboweled bodies, smoldering craters and sparking stumps where spires had stood. Nadir chanced a backward glance and winced at what he saw: EarthCo soldiers battling NKK regulars and Sotoi Guntai; aircraft weaving smoke trails through the sky; R-type turrets emitting steady blasts into the air and at ground troops wearing all colors of uniform. He clenched his fist tighter around the receiver of his rifle and ran. Only a few other soldiers seemed to be heading in the same direction, the rest occupied with survival.

They had run perhaps 50 yards when the next line of defense appeared. Tiny balls embedded in the infrastructure crowding around them spun, revealing glass eyes. Pulses of energy shot toward the running soldiers, enough to disable a man. Cries of surprise and pain filled the air ahead of Nadir. And then he discovered another of Feedcontrol's weapons.

The world around him exploded into white noise, full fivesen feed overloading every receptor in his brain. Nadir couldn't tell if he had fallen or been shot or was still running, couldn't even order his own muscles to keep moving or cease. His nerves lied and screamed, lightning crawled along his spine, cramped his arms and legs. Inside his head, pain throbbed and threatened to shatter his skull. He felt tendons tearing loose from muscles. He was helpless, a failure, a piper who had led the world's last great hope into oblivion right at the place where society's poisons were manufactured.

Blind and incapacitated, Nadir finally allowed his rage to vent. He thrashed through his memory, seeking ways to defend against this kind of attack, vowing to die before he gave in, and found only one: He must disable his own headcard.

Seconds passed like decades in hell as Nadir fought to locate even the most simple command key. His mind played tricks on him, creating patterns in the white noise, and many times his virtual fingers depressed what turned out only to be grain in the overload feed. At last he found the self-destruct icon, the last-resort modification in all EarthCo Warriors' cards. This would mean, of course, that Nadir would be completely isolated from what remained of his army, unable to warn them of this new danger.

The pain continued, different now, sizzling at the base of his neck and behind his eyes. Nadir found himself lying on a cement walkway in a pool of his own urine and blood, shadowed by a dish antenna. Paolo spasmed near his feet, soiled himself, bit his lips.

Nadir rose on shaking arms and legs, wincing with each movement. He crawled to his companion and nearly fell on the boy, but regained strength enough to reach out with one hand and pinch a certain spot on Paolo's neck. Sick with what he was doing to his friend, Nadir held a centimeter of flesh between thumb and forefinger as hard as he could, seeing the skin turn bright red and then purple. At last Paolo's eyelids flickered.

"Paolo, do you hear me?"

"I ... what..."

Nadir gasped and shuddered, but managed to keep up his strength. "You've got to self-destruct your card. Self-destruct! Find the self-destruct."

The boy began to convulse again, making Nadir's job even tougher. All around, lasers and energy weapons continued to lick the electropolis clean of its invaders. A circling one-man fighter captured Nadir's attention as it held steady fire on the central tower, which rose from a concrete platform only meters from Nadir. Plasma gouted from the point of impact. Meanwhile, hundreds of laser beams lashed out from the cylindrical walls, several of the R-types *rrrrip-rrrrip-rrrriped* up at the tiny craft, and even now missiles began to rocket out of their nooks. The moment of heroism held Nadir rapt. Here, a man fought with the kind of bravery fostered only in the sure knowledge that he was sacrificing himself for the greater good.

A few seconds later, the aircraft transformed into a grey-green cloud pulsing with redundant blasts. Then it was only a brief rain of wreckage and a smear in the sky.

"Subbs?" a feeble voice asked.

Nadir turned his attention to Paolo, whose convulsions had ceased. "Did you self-destruct?" he asked without removing his pinch on the fibers that connected energy-cells to the boy's headcard.

"Yeah. Could you let go of my neck?"

Nadir did so. A crooked smile crossed Paolo mouth. "Crash, subbs, that was deep hack, man. I can't move."

"Get up!" Nadir said. He forced himself to stand without revealing the pain pulsing through his knees and back. He managed to remain upright.

Paolo struggled to his feet. His whole body shook. "There's a wreck center in Barcelona where a guy would pay a lot for that kind of vixperience."

Nadir shook his head. "Can you keep going?"

"What the hell, eh? Do we have any choice?"

The shakes were starting to fade from Nadir's nerves. He glanced about and saw a few other twitching bodies strewn among the scaffolds and domes. Paolo joined him in repeating the pinch process. Before long, eight men—seven EarthCo Warriors and a dazed looking NKK regular—marched with them back toward the central tower's pedestal. Two others never pulled out of the brainburn.

They watched smoke roll along the corridors, avoiding the laserbeams—electronic tripwires. The bare face of stone revealed nothing, so they followed the wall, seeking entrance. After some time, Nadir heard a howl of turbines and looked up as the shadow of a heavy NKK hovercraft passed over him. Missiles sprayed in all directions, chaff puffed in great sparkling clouds, liquid fire gushed from a hose normally used to fuel the vessel, and every weapon fired down at the bristling surface. Nearly a hundred meters long, it was called a "target" by EarthCo soldiers. And it was living up to its nickname, collecting fire as a drop of water collects dust when it falls to dry earth. Nadir had no idea how the craft had managed to approach so closely.

Then it listed crazily. A seam appeared near the center of the massive hull; all forward momentum twisted the aircraft in two, each section hurling in right angles to the other. Ground fire continued to pummel the vessel, but now its missiles began to detonate all around, the explosions hidden by towers and spires.

Suddenly, the thousands of wall-mounted lasers that laced the structures flashed to life, searing the air around Nadir's ragged unit. One man cried out as light stabbed his neck.

"Hit the dirt!" Nadir shouted, but his throat was raw and he had no 3VRD to back up his words. Two more men fell, their bodies spouting smoke and blood; the beams weren't strong enough to kill, but plenty enough to wound—especially when their fire was so dense. Paolo dropped so fast Nadir thought he, too, had been shot.

"Paolo," he said, crawling beneath the solid beams toward the boy. "Paolo!"

"I'm clean, subbs," the other said, rolling onto his back. "Drop your butt or it'll get burned off."

Then, just as suddenly as the attack began, all the little ball-swivels fell quiet. They dropped loosely, rocking in their mounts as if their power supply had—

"Here's our chance!" Nadir said, rising again. He didn't look back as he forced his tortured body ahead. Along the cement wall he ran, seeking entrance. At last he found an open platform hanging by a cable—a service lift with manual up/down controls mounted on the railing that enclosed it. He waited until Paolo and the remaining five soldiers had climbed inside, then hit the UP button. Nothing happened. He noticed the stench of urine permeating his men's uniforms.

"All right," he said, "you all know how to climb. Let's go!" He took hold of the thick cable and began to pull himself up hand over hand, legs wrapped around it and boots providing enough friction to assist his weakened arms. The tower's base rose ten meters above ground level, sheer and featureless. When he reached the top of the cable, Nadir pulled himself along the hoist-arm and stepped onto the top of the monolith. A few seconds later, Paolo joined him on the roof of the pedestal, then three others. Nadir learned that the final two couldn't manage the climb, and he thought it best to leave them behind—they'd only slow him down.

Above them rose the windowless skyscraper, dull silver in the wan light. The cylinder smoldered in a few places, but overall it appeared nearly perfect. Nadir turned to survey the rest of the electropolis, but his gaze didn't remain there long. Nowhere among the steel bristles and domes and turrets could he pick out a moving soldier. His artillery men, pilots, and pyrotechs had managed to knock down every autocannon mushroom, which lay in wreckage amid steel plates and fallen antennae. Fires and pillars of smoke told the story of his air force, the remains of which lay burning in the fields surrounding Feedcontrol. A few groundcars raced over the nearby hills and disappeared. One man crouched behind the hulk of a Tora tank and fired his EMMA randomly at the smashed city.

At least, at very goddamned least, Nadir thought, we've busted things up enough so people will be forced to see the real world. Maybe they'll find the treachery in their own lives; we can't be the only ones.

"Where to, Boss?" one of the soldiers asked.

Nadir turned and looked at him, a wiry man with the heavy features of Northern Europe. He studied the others, each bearing the traces of divergent ancestry. The NKK soldier had survived. Last he looked into Paolo's eyes, brown and encircled with bruises and traces of blood.

"Inside." He cocked his head toward the oversize door facing them, no handles visible.

The other soldiers grew looks of horror. Paolo perked up.

"Yes, Boss!" Paolo said, and took off in a ragged sprint across the stretch of concrete. Nadir smiled and followed. He heard bootfalls behind him.

The air rushed cool and metal-tinged through Nadir's mouth. Every muscle in his body burned. Blood washed salty across his tongue. Wind tousled his sweat-matted hair.

He was still alive. Life was good.

Feedcontrol 6

In space and on the Moon, Luke Herrschaft's war was being waged with great success. His robotic body sat upon a great leather chair behind a granite slab desk, in one of his administrative offices, deep under Feedcontrol. A running tally of ongoing battles flickered before his eyes, overlaid on the desktop as if it were a monitor screen: So far, EarthCo had lost nearly 5,000 manned spacecraft, tens of thousands of aircraft, and every one of its space and lunar stations had been compromised. More importantly, the numbers revealed that NKK no longer possessed a space fleet in the Earth-Moon system, nor a significant number of Earth-based aircraft.

However, two things gnawed at him. He hadn't gauged anywhere near the scale of robotic hunters and AI missiles with which the crafty Niks were currently pummeling EarthCo's Earthside installations. But those weapons had to be finite in number. No, the primary issue bothering Herrschaft was that his hub, his sanctuary, was itself under attack!

He uttered a bitter and angry sound, and brought down a fist against his thigh. This had gone too far. Certainly, this blacked-out force couldn't do any real harm to Feedcontrol Central, but the very fact that they had begun to attack, that they dared.

With a flourish of one hand, he submitted a brief plea to the world leaders—partially prerecorded, partially AI. Even as the speech proceeded, response votes began to tally in a blur on the corner of his desk overlay. A smile formed on his lips. He hardly noticed the tiny servos that created the expression beneath the artificial skin. Despite casualties and temporary property loss, war fever was on the rise: Fully 92% of EarthCo's representatives supported the progression of war as long as they continued to win. He tapped into the secondary election-polls and found that those politicians were receiving support percentages at least as strong.

All to be expected in this well-oiled machine Herrschaft had invented, this perfected mechanism of government.

"The Citizens have spoken," he said aloud as he depressed a transmission button. Another canned speech fed out to the lawmakers, congratulating them, etc. etc.

Herrschaft shut down the ancillary feeds and stood. He stretched the mechanical body, though of course it needed nothing of the sort. "You're stalling, Luke," he chided himself.

Without much conscious prompting, a feedaccess panel appeared in an overlay atop the desk. One of the choices read, BRAIN. Herrschaft reached for it.

Just then, a rumble passed through the floor. He searched for a good vantage-point splice.

A second later, Herrschaft peered out through the electronic eyes of a surveillance wasp. "My god," he whispered.

Throughout the towers and antennae of Feedcontrol's I/O nexus, military equipment from four service branches—including his own EarthCo Warriors!—pounded the facility. How could this happen?

Another heavy hit set one of the office walls buzzing. Why couldn't the automatic systems track the invaders?

"What's happening?"

Herrschaft shut down the splice, found the access switch to the Brain, and opened a line.

"Yes, Director Herrschaft?" a male voice asked, a voice not unlike the one which had once issued from Herrschaft's own body long ago.

"What is the point of this?" Herrschaft demanded. "Don't deny that you're at the root of this absurd attack. Why? And show yourself, dammit!"

A moment of disorientation, then Herrschaft found himself seated on a high throne layered in rich purple and crimson velvet. He wore a black and red checked robe that reached past his footstool, down a flight of curving steps, and out into a dimly lit atrium studded with marble pillars. In the shadows, he sensed the shuffling and muttering of a great crowd of spectators, but his view extended only a few meters in each direction. Overhead hung tapestries woven with the symbols of EarthCo: The Earth and stars logo, the sundry corporate logos.

Out of the shadows stepped a man garbed in a dirty brown sack robe. Each soot-covered hand held a cut-crystal flask. The man avoided Herrschaft's long train and climbed one step up toward the dais, where he knelt on the ochre rug.

"My lord," said the man. He looked exactly like Luke Herrschaft in his mid-thirties.

Herrschaft restrained himself from blurting out, *Have you gone insane?* If a virus had infiltrated the Brain, Herrschaft didn't want to rouse the entity's anger, if it were capable of such emotion. In his usual offhand manner, Herrschaft tried to call up an access landscape, but nothing appeared. Again he tried and failed.

"Lord Herrschaft," the Brain said, "we're alone here. I am isolated from ECoNet, and so are you."

"You can't do this!" Herrschaft said, leaning forward, his hands clenching the carven arms of his throne. He tried to simply overlay his headcard options—nothing. *I'm trapped.* He began to panic.

". . .and I'm surprised we have never spoken like this," the Brain said.

"What? Listen." Herrschaft felt himself trembling with anger and fear; how could a computer do this to him? Hadn't he built safeguards against this sort of thing? And why, why would a machine want to betray its creator? He calmed himself and formed a question.

"I wanted to know why you shielded a treasonous EarthCo Warrior unit from our defenses. They're attacking Central right now. That's as much part of you as of me, perhaps more."

"Ah." The robed figure climbed a few more steps until it stood nearly at level with Herrschaft. "I simply let the humans act out their own agenda, uninhibited. They may fail, but their mission is honorable."

Herrschaft knew no words to respond to that. His jaw loosened.

The Brain's 3VRD smiled, revealing yellow teeth. Around the figure's neck hung a copper disk bearing what Herrschaft recognized as astrological symbols. He held one of the flasks so its cut surface sparkled in the light, and the smile faded.

"What is the philosopher's stone, my lord?"

Herrschaft frowned. "What?"

"See the contents of this beaker?" A rusty powder filled the container; that in the Brain's other hand was empty. "To transform this into something valuable—indeed, something useful—I need the philosopher's stone, my lord."

"What are you talking about?" Fear was the only thing upholding Herrschaft's patience.

"Come to my laboratory."

The throne-room vanished in a swirl of dark colors, then congealed to form a new scene. Dirt floor beneath, wooden beams and roof slats overhead, mud-brick walls to each side. Long planks stood along the walls, upheld by iron wrought into gargoyle shapes; burners ranged all across the tables, boiling liquids and vaporizing powders. Glass flagons and phials gurgled as their contents steamed away, stained glass tubes coiled from bottle to beaker. A great fire roared in a fireplace set into the far wall, crackling and spitting coals into the room. Acrid scents stung Herrschaft's nostrils.

Herrschaft looked at his host. "So, you're an alchemist."

The man only smiled. "Do you know of the alien object discovered by TritonCo scientists on the Neptunian moon, Triton?"

Herrschaft felt uncomfortable. "Yes."

"That is where this war began." The alchemist turned away from his king and set the full flask into a wire holder. He began arranging chunks of coal in a blackened dish beneath the flask, then crossed to the fire and returned holding a glowing ember in iron tongs. With a handful of silvery dust that flashed brilliant white, the ember ignited the coal.

"Tell me, my lord, what is the philosopher's stone?"

"What is all this nonsense? I must get back to Central. Terrible things might be—"

"EarthCo can run itself for a few minutes, my lord. Things set in motion tend to stay in motion."

Frustration created a burning knot in Herrschaft's chest. "I'm not going to play your game. *You* tell *me*: What is the philosopher's stone?"

The Brain—looking disturbingly the way Herrschaft pictured himself—turned away from his work and smiled at Herrschaft. "It's the substance essential to transforming base metals into silver, gold, and platinum. Men in this business," he said as he gestured around the room, "have created recipes for philosopher's stones composed of salts, sulfur, mercury, and other elements."

The flask began to fume, spewing yellow smoke from its mouth. The Brain took a hand-bellows from a nail on the wall and began stoking the fire beneath it.

"Of course, no alchemist ever succeeded in producing the substance. In your world, modern alchemists have written new recipes for philosopher's stone, primarily composed of headfeed and ridiculous things like hard credit. I argue, my lord, that none of your practitioners have succeeded in creating the magical stuff. But it has been discovered."

Herrschaft stepped back a pace without thinking. He found a walking staff leaning against one of the tables, raised it—

"Let us be civil here, my lord." The staff vanished.

That was all Herrschaft could stand. "Get to the point . . . you! Then return me to my work."

The alchemist sighed. A second later, his flask erupted in a gout of yellow fire. He hurried to another table and picked up a pair of long tongs, which he used to lift the now-calm flask from the fire. Near Herrschaft stood a clean, bronze brazier on an iron tripod. The Brain dumped the contents of the flask into the brazier and stepped back.

"Behold!" A small quantity of gold dust shone from the dish.

Herrschaft *tsked*. "Thank you for this little show. Now please send me back—"

"Let me tell you something about myself," the alchemist said. His face grew animated as he dropped the tongs. "I was patterned after you, my lord. I am all the good parts of Luke Herrschaft, all his talents and powers and concerns for the good of the world, with the sick elements outgassed like the volatiles that had filled that flask before I added philosopher's stone."

Herrschaft's impatience and revulsion were becoming nearly unbearable, but he knew when he had met his match. *I'll exact the necessary measures when I return*, he promised himself.

"Before my individual GenNets even began evolving, all that makes humans imperfect was removed. But that left me lacking something I could never quite identify." He took a step closer to Herrschaft, who refused to be bullied back to a comfortable distance.

"Through a . . . virus of doubt—a philosopher's stone, if you will—I have discovered an element of humanity within myself. Perhaps it was only a matter of my GenNets' continued evolution; perhaps it was simply exploring the world in the guise of a human, perhaps it was making friends. I cannot know. To me, the best element of humanity is your capacity to see the pain in others around you and want to end it, while seeking meaning and purpose in life."

He stepped to the brazier and scooped up a handful of gold dust. "I have found humanity in myself, and purpose in my existence. A growing number of humans are also finding their own philosopher's stones."

"What does all this mean?" Herrschaft asked. Had the Brain created this entire scene simply to spout antique philosophy?

The alchemist's face fell lax, and the gold fell from his hand to the packed-dirt floor. "I had hoped you and I could. . . ." The eyes tightened into an expression Herrschaft knew well from watching feed of his young self.

"My lord, your war is wrong. You seem to have abandoned what remains of your humanity. But I see this is all moot. I'm sorry, my lord. The freed humans have now decapitated you." Tears rose to the alchemist's eyes. "I had truly hoped we could . . . reunite."

The alchemist's head shook savagely from side to side. The room's fires and crystal sparklings swirled into a mass of color and light. And then Herrschaft found himself once again in the robot's body, deep under Feedcontrol Central's administrative tower. Relief lasted only a moment.

"What—?" The office's lighting had grown dim. When Herrschaft tapped into a statistical review overlay, he learned that a nightmare had come true:

Feedcontrol Central, EarthCo's neural hub—the core of Herrschaft's power, his very existence—had lost primary power. The fusion generator had shut itself down when systems damage reached a critical point. The invaders were free to crawl all over him now, like germs entering an open wound.

No, he thought, *it can't be.* He spliced into a series of povs throughout the I/O complex that surrounded the tower. Slowly, his terror faded. Virtually nothing remained of the invading force. All their artillery, armor, and aircraft had been destroyed, along with almost all the traitorous EarthCo Warriors and enemy soldiers. Herrschaft's mechanical lungs heaved a sigh of relief.

He shut down the external pov splice and contacted Central security. Yes, they were aware of the invaders. Yes, sir, they were on their way outside to mop up the remnants of the siege forces.

Luke Herrschaft, lord of EarthCo and—he assumed—soon to be lord of all the solar system, tried to open a feedline to his political figureheads. Such a simple thing, a detail of life he had used a million times before with hardly a thought, like speaking or looking outside through a window. But now it was impossible. The few antennae still in operation were only the critical uplinks to the Brain, necessary to run maintenance systems in a billion places throughout EarthCo's sphere of influence. The Brain, that fifth columnist, wouldn't let even his master tap in to those lines.

Should he shut them down? No. Herrschaft's blitzkrieg needed EarthCo's infrastructure running as smoothly as possible. He would allow the Brain to have its fun. When the war ended, so too would the Brain. Luke Herrschaft, most powerful man in the solar system, found himself at loose ends on the eve of his greatest victory.

Bored and frustrated and furious, he 3-verded faithful Lucilla.

"I'll be right there," she answered.

Tiny servos in Herrschaft's face made his robot smile. He transferred his virtual presence to another robot, in another room. This space was filled primarily by gelbed, hung with sheets of precious metal that shimmered in orbiting hololamps. He flexed the muscles of his legs, his abdomen, chest, and arms in an effort to trigger sensors in his robototic body that would send signals to the place where his body lay and manufacture the chemicals that might relax his fevered mind.

It would take his repair teams some time to reconnect him with the world. They were competent and efficient. In the mean time, he couldn't control his empire. For the first time since he founded Feedcontrol, he couldn't control his empire or the lunatic brain at its core.

To keep from going crazy while he waited to get back online, Lucilla would calm and comfort him. This she could do like no other.

Then—vengeance!

Worlds at War 2

>>Aboard the Deep Space Observatory L5, astronomer Josef Schweitz attempts to compensate for haze clouding the galaxy M82, which he is imaging as part of a galactic black-hole study. He is annoyed by what appears to be electronic chaff produced by a huge fleet of NKK ships coming in from the outer planets. "Gunter," he 3-verds, "any luck clearing our view?" They are the only two humans aboard the module. "It's destroying our observations!" "No, Josef," says the other man. "I'm thinking about comming someone planetside to let them know. Maybe they can get them to turn off their radiant pollution. The ships won't reply to me."<<

>>Ms. Monique Benois just wanted to buy a pair of silk stockings. How difficult is that? She needs them for an intheflesh fundraiser the Institute is hosting this weekend. But just as she was about to check out, the connection to Macy's went dead. When she tried to re-initiate her shopping instance, she got a message that, "ALL NET TRAFFIC HAS BEEN MILITARIZED." *Darn it!* she thinks, *Now what will I do for nylons?*<<

>>Brad Vasquez wakes up from another bad dream about the wheat drying up before harvest. The dream didn't wake him, though; it's a 3VRD from his Army Reserves Boss. He sits up in bed and looks at Mary, his contract partner, breathing quietly in the gray just before sunrise. Her hair is black against the white sheets. He knows what the call is about; he's seen the news about full-scale war. He's watched the 24/7 footage of screaming, smoking citizens; the footage of colony domes pierced, precious air and plants blasting out into space; the pointlessness of throwing flesh against steel and plasma cannons. "I'm

going to die," he whispers to her. But can't tell her anything, not while she sleeps so peacefully. "If only they'd waited until it rained," he says, thinking of the dead wheat in their field.<<

Jonathan Sombrio 2

Blackout feed shatters Jonathan's thoughts and blots out his view through the aircar's windscreen. Static and hiss and a general numbness overwhelm him. A magnified voice screams in his mind, accompanied by white-hot glowing letters and numerals:

>>JONATHAN SOMBRIO, CREDIT CARD #SZ401678—ECo-, ECo-MINOR, YOU ARE UNDER ARREST FOR DESTRUCTION OF PRIVATE PROPERTY. THE STOLEN VEHICLE YOU ARE USING WILL BE FORCED DOWN...<<

"No way," Jonathan says, though he can't hear his own words. *I've got to be able to do something.*

The fight to ignore the Zone's blackout feed occupies most of his concentration, but Jonathan blots out the signals from his meat and forces up new memories acquired through the Pilot and Captain, from the Nik Miru. Clean.

The blackout mess dissipates, and Jonathan finds himself alone in the artifact-space. Keeping himself from thinking anything coherent, he's able to visualize the membranous walls between him and four others, great balloons of intrusion. But also by keeping quiet, he's able to avoid making the others aware of his existence. *Odd,* he thinks; *I can see them but they can't see me....*

He fixes his thoughts on a single memory, little more than something Miru glimpsed. *There—*

All the places Jonathan has passed through, even some of those he only vixperienced—some of which felt more real to him at the time—flash to light around him. It feels sort of like the ECoNet landscape.... He solidifies the thought, and as fast as he can picture himself in a place—

It takes Jonathan a moment to catch his balance, then he finds himself standing beside a heavily graffitied wall at the end of a street, Old Downtown Minneapolis. He glances down at himself, smiles when he sees the shredded boots and loose pants, the black jacket and even dirt beneath his ragged nails.

"Did it," he whispers. "Fuck if I ever go anywhere naked again."

With a deep breath to shore up the remnants of his uncertainty, Jonathan steps toward the false wall to his left, the passage into the Malfits' motherboard. The 3VRD bricks and mortar can't stop him, not that they ever did even before he got the amp. Face to face with the grey shockplas door, he powers up his commcard.

"It's me, Jonathan. Let me in."

Instantly, Lucas' sharkform 3VRD appears, weaving a sinuous tail. "Jonny-boy, didn't expect you so soon. Come on board, on board." A smile splits the face and dozens of crystal teeth sparkle like tiny fluorescent lamps.

As soon as the door pops and begins to open, Jonathan says, "Right, Lucas, you fuck."

The shark stops moving for only a moment, then the smile reappears. "Well, Jonny, I see we need to teach you some manners. I'll let Blackjack know you've returned."

"Do that."

Jonathan steps into the vestibule and hits his light enhancement program. Walls form out of the blackness, grainy and featureless, and Jonathan notices that a new doorway opposite the front entrance has been added. Among the rancid garbage in the small corridor, he sees a sprawled body of a girl—still breathing—and a second girl whose posture makes her seem to be studying the floor. He recognizes her and nods as he passes through the inner door.

Blackjack's impassive face and red hair greet him a second before a sharp blow across his face. Jonathan gathers his bearing on the floor, but he's semi-blinded by the still active light enhancement. As he shuts it down, something collides with his ribcage.

"Knock it off!" Jonathan shouts, curling into a ball. This wasn't what he'd expected at all. What if he gets beaten to unconsciousness before he can get away? What if.... It was supposed to be so simple—

Thud, four distinct, sharp knuckles bruise into his side. Jonathan whips his body around the arm as it pulls back to deliver a second blow, and as fast as that, he's hooked his prey. While the dusty, hard-fisted world falls away, Jonathan holds tight to that arm, his fingernails sinking into the flesh. He hears himself laughing, and the sound trails out like a locomotive horn dopplering into the mountains.

Transcendence G

A wall of cut stone rises up all around Jonathan, encircling him, but open at the top. His meat feels solid, as if he's still on Earth, and terror grips him as he wonders if he failed, if Blackjack beat the life out of him before he was able to drag the gang leader away.

He closes his eyes and runs toward the wall, willing it away. For just a moment, he feels the impact of his face and chest against stone, but then the wall bends before his rush, and finally he slurps through something the consistency of mud. When he opens his eyes again, he's bodiless, floating in the familiar star-filled space. Behind him rises his fortress, echoing and quaking and beginning to crack. Again, the sky crowds with the intricate spheres of Miru, Pang, Pilot Librarse and Captain Jackson. Even so, a portion of his mind wonders: *Is this part of Lucas' torture?*

A subsonic rumble passes through the whole universe, rippling across the membranes of those who carry the artifact within them, shaking the fortress behind Jonathan so that its stones come all unmortared and begin to topple.

Not yet, crash it, not yet! How do I stay alive but still strangle a man in a place where violence is outlaw?

Off in the distance, a flickering of light catches Jonathan's attention. He walks across the featureless earth, over a hill, until he makes out what appears to be an electronics junkyard filling a shallow valley. Ancient television sets, tube radios, computer screens, early telecast receivers—all these things flash and spark in a great whirling heap, as if the detritus of abandoned technology has achieved such great mass as to form gravitational attraction. Screens and glowplates orbit a central dark area, gathering speed as they grow closer; tens of thousands of the things spiral inward, cracked and smoking, jangling and tinkling.

Jonathan, what's happening?

The words are feeble and staticky. Jonathan recognizes the voice.

"Welcome to hell, Blackjack." He says it exactly as he had rehearsed, cold and sharp like a molecular blade slicing flesh at one degree Kelvin.

Before he realizes what's happening, Jonathan glances at a nearby television screen. A moment later, he becomes Blackjack.

No! he cries, but it's too late to protest.

The luminescent screen drags Jonathan through scene after scene of brutality, beginning at the moment when Jonathan pulled the man unwittingly into the alien place. Back through an existence Jonathan hadn't even imagined, filled with psychoactive feed that twists a mind into ropey contours, nearly snapping it in two time and again as emotions nearly surface; single words gush through his being: CREDIT, PUMP, FEED, 'BOARD; names reel off one after another, accompanied by a sort of . . . desire? Back through the early days before there were any Malfits, acquiring the abandoned building by slamming four fingertips through a shrank's throat and tearing out his trachea, back, back, through time to less brutal days of pain, *Oh god!* pain in the guise of brothers and sisters— *I don't understand*—terrycloth robes and momentary flashes of blood, of saliva, of wires protruding from freckled skin, revulsion cauterized by nonsexual lust; insane brief pulses of memory. . . . *It's all stolen, where'd it go, help me Jonathan, I'm sorry, I'll crush Lucas for you, don't you see*—"I have no past! I'm no one!"

As the voice rips through his psyche, Jonathan grips hold of himself and drags his consciousness up from the black hole of swirling fluids and shattering electronics—such confused emptiness and heavy-gravity need—as Blackjack begins to rummage through Jonathan's memories; up he climbs, up a cable of thought to where his past exists high above, the skin of his fingers burning with the effort to carry his weight, cracking eyes fixed on a circle of light high above. He's not sure what it is, only knows he's got to get there now, right this instant. . . . *That's me*, he realizes—

And *slam!* He feels his mind twist and warp through corridors of Blackjack's blooded, disordered, incomprehensible life, *slam*—he's surrounded again by the walls of a primitive fortress. The uppermost blocks of stone are shattering and rising up, revealing that they're not granite but cheap concrete with a laminate. As they shatter, Jonathan recalls who he is and what he has done to his gang leader.

Flashbacks of Blackjack's life trigger in his mind, for here he is unprotected by his walls. Jonathan realizes he has added the bastard to his repertoire of self, and suddenly I understand. The sympathy created by having dipped into another's life makes him real, and I regret.

He throws wide the arms of his mind, wiping away the fortress. Behind him, Blackjack's whirlpool glares white-hot—now high over the valley—transformed nearly into a collapsing star, emitting a steady scream of self-loathing that tinges the edges of its accretions disk russet. Such need, need bred by a ravenous emptiness, a demanding loneliness, a wild aimlessness. . . .

"What have you done to me?" the star screams. It flickers in such a way as to look like lips and teeth, speaking.

Jonathan begins to move toward the whorling junkyard again, but knows there's nothing he can do now; Lonny—"Eyes" of the *Bounty*—had reached this point, too, and couldn't be saved.

"Don't let me die, Jonny! I don't know how you did it, but now you know me, and I know you. I'm sorry, fucking sorry! I'll do whatever you want . . . help!"

Blackjack's face erupts from the strobing vortex of screens and wiring, shattered cabinets and cracked tubes. For the first time, it reveals a hint of emotion. Not fear, not anger, but the pure lax of childish anticipation.

"I can change, Jonny, you know I can! Just wait. I've finally learned—"

The white star behind Blackjack's face shrinks to a point, then flashes painfully bright in a transparent pulse that expands outward, engulfing the junkwhirl, igniting the equipment as the supernova shell grows, out out out until Jonathan has to pick the nearest scene from his own life and leap headlong into it—

Jonathan Sombrio 3

Jonathan thrashes on the old laminate floor, kicking up chips of wood and plastic, until he gains his feet. Gasping, he pats his body. Intheflesh, intact, clothed. He looks up through a dusty swath of sun slanting in through a skylight overhead, which once had illuminated a grocery store for its employees.

Lucas—the boy, skinny and hunched forward, not the sharkform—stands against the bare wooden ribs of a wall, gaping at Jonathan. Half a dozen other Malfits, male and female, rise slowly from reclining positions and stare in silence.

"What happened to Blackjack?" Lucas asks. His voice is small, scared, like a child's when first told that he has no parents, that the man and woman who fed him and wiped his ass for years weren't his parents, not even humans; like Blackjack at five years of age.

"I. . ." Jonathan doesn't know what to say. He tries to swallow. "He's gone."

The Lucas Sharkform appears before Jonathan, larger than usual, gleaming wet with bodily humors dripping from its flanks, the jaws set in a menacing way.

"You better tell me where he is, or—"

"Can it!" Jonathan roars. He feels his meat shaking with shame and utter fatigue. "Leave me alone or I'll do you, too! That's what I'd planned in the first place."

The shark vanishes. A pair of boots thud along the hollow floor, followed a second later by the sound of doors opening. The unclosed doorway passes the circus-sounds of an impending Mobile Hostile Zone, replete with a thousand-piece band, fireworks, and the ringleader announcement, "ATTENTION, ATTENTION. . ."

"Gotta vex," Jonathan says. "Good luck."

He closes his eyes, clenches his hands and mind, then opens his eyes again. This time he's staring into the face of Captain Jackson. The man and Pilot Librarse jump up from the edge of their round bed in the Hilton room, looking concerned.

"You're back," the Pilot says. "We couldn't we find you, even when we went into the mindspace." She's staring quizzically at his not-naked body.

"Where'd you go?" the Captain asks.

A flush consumes Jonathan's face; his stomach burns. "I . . . I. . ."

Captain Jackson composes his concern into a smile. "Well, we're glad you're back. We were about to—"

Jonathan begins to shake so badly that he can't help it: He breaks down into tears like a stupid kid.

Two pairs of arms lightly encircle him. He fights the desire to throw off intheflesh existence and go with these two into the otherplace; there the Captain and Pilot had comforted each other—even made love in a way.

But that's not for me. I don't deserve that kind of . . . whatever it is.

He feels the wave of self destruction roll heavy across him, blacking out his vision, filled with air bubbles that burst and force him to face who he is. *Flash-flash-flash*, even though he senses that he's keeping himself in his meat, on the Earth, scenes from the past engulf him, crystalline memory unsullied by distance in time. Again and again, his mind wanders to érase—sweet érase, when she first held him—but here lay no comfort. No, what Nooa told him was right. Blackjack cracked open a vacuum-tube of memory especially to show Jonathan that érase had never really belonged to Jonathan, except for the few last days. . . .

As his rage rises again, the flickering scenes accelerate through his mind—now he's Blackjack again; now he pictures Lucas, hunched in the Malfits' 'board, looking scared and lonely and hollow. Jonathan has an epiphany: *I can't ever do that again, rip someone open and leave him to evaporate in the vacuum of himself. Not even Lucas.*

The wave begins to subside, the images fade, though in the far distance, Jonathan still hears the wave crashing through his self hatred. All is still in his mind.

Jonathan opens his eyes. He shakes himself loose of the two adults and crosses to a plush chair. His head hangs against his chest.

"What's wrong?" Captain Jackson asks.

What's wrong! "I don't know. Everything." Jonathan perks up enough to cast a sharp glare at the man who had once been his hero, back in the simple times before Jonathan learned Jackson was just a human being, before he learned that the whole mundane world contains not one iota of heroism.

"You could've been a father," Jonathan says. He feels the accusation in the words and regrets that. One more regret, heaped on the compost pile of his psyche, more fuel for the wave should it return. He holds his breath and listens for it. Yes, there it is, a distant swelling thunder.

"I mean," Jonathan says, "do you think you would've been any different than the others? You know what I mean."

Now it's Captain Jackson's turn to stare at the floor. He says nothing. Jonathan tries to avoid the Pilot's narrow-eyed stare.

"Jack's a good man," she says. "He wouldn't treat a child the way—"

"I'm sorry," Jonathan says. "Crash it all, I'm sorry, sorry, sorry for everything. Fuck, I can't do anything right!"

"It's okay," Jackson says. He raises his face, this time wearing a tired smile. He stands and takes two steps toward Jonathan, then sits cross-legged on the carpet.

"Focus your thoughts," the man says. "You'll go crazy if you keep lashing out in every direction. Tell us what happened."

Jonathan sucks a deep breath, then another, until his chest no longer shakes. A single residue of thought remains in his mind, like nuggets of tin in the bottom of a pan after swirling away the sand and mud. He meets Jackson's eyes.

"Nobody loves their children anymore, nobody loves at all—not in the real world." He tosses an arm to encompass Earth. "It didn't happen all at once; the disease crawled into us slowly, like cancer, like a wound festering under the skin, devouring the organs and destroying the organism from inside. You see? Fucking adults have grown used to it! How can it be? How can you be so blind?"

Librarse is about to interrupt, so Jonathan continues. He feels something like warm syrup gushing through his mind, soothing him, lubricating the idea. Once or twice, he senses his grip on intheflesh existence waver.

"And what does this make us? Beasts, alone and isolated, always rooting in the mud for pleasure and stimulation but never finding anything true to fill the emptiness."

"The artifact," the Pilot says. "There's our hope." Her face, her dark eyes and smooth features, look so composed and calm. Jackson's is tense and angular.

"That's just a toy," Jonathan says, not really meaning it but not knowing what else to say. "Can it change human nature? No! Look at me—I'm just as fucked, suffering as much as ever. More, because now all my self-defenses are useless."

The Captain runs a hand through his wavy hair and forces a smile. "Look what it's done for you already. You've become aware of one of the problems in the world. Who you are has altered—can you suppress your feelings and thoughts anymore? Think of how our society will change when everyone undergoes our transformation. When they've become aware of the problems, they'll no longer permit . . . evil to go on. We'll have a focus and be able to fix all the wrongs."

Once again, self-loathing wells up within Jonathan. He flicks on his standard revmetal subscription to fill the background mumble of his conscience.

"Oh, yeah? Do you want to know where I went just now?" Pause. "I killed a man."

That takes the wind out of his companions. They seem to recede from him. Jonathan chases after. "It was Blackjack, you know. I pulled him into his head. Into hell."

The Pilot nods once. Jackson looks hurt, which makes Jonathan's stomach fires roar like a furnace. But, instead of finding words to heal, he says, "Captain, what you said about taking everyone into the alien-place. . . . How will we do that? Go around forcing people inside, destroying the evil ones? So we'll become the judges and executioners of all of humanity?"

He feels so sick to his stomach that he gets up and walks to the room-service chute, placing a wall between him and the others. But his mind is too confused to order anything to eat.

"I don't think it'll be necessary," Jackson says, "to force anyone inside. All we need are enough people to shed their shells and find their cores . . . of love. Enough people to share their lives." He grunts a single laugh. "Listen to me! Anyway, what I mean to say is this: Can you go on hating Blackjack now, after you lived his life. After he died? Can you ever hate anyone enough to want to kill again?"

Jonathan tastes bile and swallows hard. He stares at the finger-worn brass plate, behind which an assortment of foods are just waiting to emerge. But his mind has become a lump of paste.

"Jonathan." The Pilot's voice, soft and smooth. "You're not alone."

"I can still find hate if I need it," Jonathan tells the smeary reflection of himself in the brass. "The artifact didn't change a thing, only made my life more miserable, because now I despise myself whenever I feel hatred."

"It'll destroy you, too, if you hate," Jackson says. He sounds stern. "It'll destroy you because you can't bear that kind of burden anymore."

"Yeah, well," Jonathan says, and cranks up the revmetal. Machines and humans blend in a shrieking, screeching cacophony set to musical score. No longer can he hear his blood gushing through his ears.

"Well. . ." Unable to say anything else, unable to face these two who know too much about him, Jonathan turns and storms out of the room.

He amps the whine and pound of the music to full fivesen, and the old comfort of escape washes over him. The hallway passes him without notice, an elevator opens and engulfs him without any time seeming to pass. Orange balls of burning gasoline, their waxy scent; the *bam-bam-bam* of some huge machine pounds away the rhythm as four black-cloaked men scream lyrics . . . even with all this stimulation, Jonathan's brain still finds room to realize something.

He can't deny the truth behind his Captain's words. Even so, he's afraid. Afraid of himself—*What if I can't stop the wave of self-hate?* Afraid of the unknown and what it means now that he can no longer deny reality while, at the same time, he can no longer idly stand by and watch the world consume itself and its new-rising generations.

The elevator lumnisheet flickers at the same time Jonathan falls to his knees. He cuts the revmetal and hears the tail end of an explosion—*The war*, he remembers.

"Return," he tells the elevator. "This is bullshit, my life has been nothing. I'm not running anymore."

Janus Librarse 3

Janus tried to smile at Jack, who still knelt beside an empty chair. The expression felt like a grimace, so she shrugged it off and stood.

"I guess transcendence doesn't make a person perfect. Or even happy."

Jack finally rose. As he stretched his big arms over his head, Janus noticed he had lost some of the fat accrued aboard *Bounty*.

"How are we going to change a world," he asked, "if we can't help a single boy?" He sounded tired. Janus knew that all he needed was to be back in the role of leader—but this time a true role, not just acting.

"Well, we have some plans, right? Don't you believe in them anymore?"

Jack let his arms fall. He sighed, then walked toward her. A smile crossed his face as he rested his hands on her shoulders. "You're right. Let's go."

Just then, the hotel shuddered as a bomb exploded outside, perhaps even in the building somewhere. "Let's go," he repeated.

Janus' heart raced as she realized the urgency of their mission. Could they even do anything? Was Jack right? *No! enough of that kind of thinking. That boy's pessimism is contagious.*

She concentrated instead on finding Miru in her thoughts.

Transcendence H

Soon, she senses Jack's mind within hers. Opening her eyes, she finds herself upon the sea once more, beneath the heavy luminescent globes of the others who have come to this place and been transformed. Brine air fills her senses, the warmth of the water, Jack's arm beneath her back as they float. One part of the sky looks different; a tiny sphere hovers just out of reach above them—glowing pigments shift across its surface, amorphous, not ordered like the life-moments she glimpses within the other spheres.

Is that Blackjack? she wonders to Jack. She senses his unease at recognizing that his name sounds like that of the man who had caused such pain in Jonathan's life, the man Jonathan brought here to die.

"I don't want to find out," he says. *But I don't think so.*

They focus again on locating Miru. Momentarily, the scene shifts so Janus and Jack don't move toward Miru in the sky, nor does the sphere fall down to them; instead, it is as if they engaged a fivesen splice and are bodiless in Miru and Pang's version of artifact-space. Galaxies spiral all around them, stars sparkling like many-colored gems. Janus notices that just beyond the galaxies lies a kind of grid.

"What's that?" she asks.

"Ah, friend Janus! Friend Pehr! Welcome." Following the greeting is neither a lecture nor a passage through memory-scenes, but rather a sudden transfer of information. No words, no images, but after Miru has finished—*How long did that take? seconds? less?*—Janus knows all Miru, Pang, and Byung have learned. She senses Jack's confusion; he resisted the deluge.

"It's all right," she tells him.

"Blast!" he says.

"Let's go," Janus says to the three scientists. She feels Jack's presence fading as the other four begin to unfix from this mindspace to one of the points on the grid. *Pang thinks it has something to do with the theorized Einstein-Podolsky-Rosen effect,* she tells Jack. The words mean nothing, so she explains with a picture:

Pehr feels himself again entering the artifact for the first time—only now, he's also observing the transformation. His mind remains intact though his body shatters to pure energy across the finite, but four-dimensional, space within the artifact. The only thing keeping him in contact with 3D existence is his mind, his desire to remain alive, and cooperating with at least one other mind who has also entered the space.

"That's why I nearly perished," Miru says. "We become quantum information. We can reappear anywhere in the universe of classical information—of 3D existence—where we have a mental connection. Particularly people."

"Only people," Pang says. Miru's mind pulsates good humor. *Well, we'll test that later.*

"That's the map, what I thought was a city's crystalline corridors," Miru tells me, Pehr. *As long as we contain deep information about a place—someone's mind, that is— we can teleport our quantum information to that point. It defies no physical laws because, in artifact-space, finite time and space has no meaning or relevance. We encompass all that we have learned, all who we have loved.*

"That's why the artifact destroyed Lonny," Janus realizes. He loved no one, and was unwilling to share himself enough in mindspace to discover love. . . . "He could have become solid again had he connected to one of us, right? He would have teleported to any one of our . . . what should we call them? Nodes of existence? I see."

But we first must shed the shell we've grown around our minds before we can even think about that step. And if not . . . the quantum information disperses.

Pehr feels lost, confused, stupid. He senses the artifact space closing around him, his body beginning to coagulate somewhere back in the 3D world. Desperately, he reaches out to Janus and opens his mind as fully as possible, the way Miru showed him during his first passage through worlds of their minds.

It works. The rest of the team resides within him now, and though he begins to fade when he tries consciously to grasp what it is the others seem to have internalized, all he need do is provide the motive energy and mental direction Miru prized that first time they met. He feels powerful again, useful, and they move as one into the first stage of their plan to save the human species from self-destruction.

We may not be vulnerable to the war, the new voice of Byung says, *but we must have a world to return to.*

Jonathan Sombrio 4

In the Hilton hallways, men and women run past Jonathan, screaming or gaping in silent terror. The lumnisheets which run along the ceiling in wavy lines flicker, casting dull red light onto the faces that seem blind to him. He opens his feed option box and subscribes to a newsfeed BW.

Nothing but a dead splice opens before his eyes. Frowning, Jonathan shuts it down and opens Edufeed. When even that feeds nothing but dead air, he begins to grow tense. *No feed? How can that be? What's happening outside?* Jonathan shuts down the splice and option box, and seeks the building's server. In a few seconds, a maintenance-system overlay drops into place before his eyes. A 3VRD model of the triangular building flashes to life, its internal skeleton burnished aluminum, every floor served by a massive computer with smaller ones in every room. White clearly outlines each hallway, green each elevator shaft, maroon each residential room, and gold marks the communal halls—like dining-alcoves and convention feedchambers.

Programmers must have spent a lot of time on this landscape, as opposed to that of érase's—

"Fuck that," he mumbles. He shakes away images of an emaciated girl shoving him out of a dropshaft. . . .

An ornate overlay surrounds Jonathan as he accesses the floor's server. But when he subscribes to the *Daily News* BW and asks for any information not directly related to life inside the Hilton, only the words, "Sorry, out of order. We will have this service online soon," blink before him. Jonathan's heart races. His head is a deserted warehouse, desolate except for the echoing cries of memory and something dripping into a puddle.

When he realizes his feet have stopped before the Captain and Pilot's room, relief warms his tingling fingers. He knocks. When he gets no response, he 3-verds a greeting. Nothing. He keys open the door.

The room is empty. Wall projections glimmer like melting sheets of plastic: Their minute AIs are trying to do their job but unable to get the feed they need, as if they're as terrified as Jonathan with a silent head.

He closes his eyes and concentrates, as before, on finding his Captain. But fear and unease stand in the way. He can't help but keep opening his eyes to see if someone has crept up and is about to assault him.

"Crash it!" Growling, he closes the door, locks it, then slides the manual bolt into place. There. Once again, he seeks Captain Jackson. After two deep breaths, he's able to exhale without shaking.

Jonathan hears a sound like sand hissing down the concrete shore of the Mississippi, and his body melts into nothingness. Only for a moment do his instincts fight to keep his body from exploding. Then he is pure feed, personified, sending toward the one man for whom he had made room in his world before things began getting so crazy yet so full-out peak.

Liu Miru 2

Miru squinted against the harsh light of a spacecraft and struggled to orient himself in its zero-*g*. A narrow but long, curving hull stretched out around him, whitewashed with tarnished metal ribs ringing the space. Stacked, plastic-wrapped crates, tubes lashed together with cable, and smaller packages held in place by nets filled most of the hold. Two space-suited figures seemed to be asleep, lazing amid a tangle of elastic mesh.

As his body rotated, Miru caught sight of the three men and one woman of his group—all naked—and allowed a brief grin. The room was cold! Janus wrapped her arms around herself and seemed to be seeking something among the crates near her feet. Pehr had already caught a grip of one large net that looked like a spiderweb, and was pulling himself toward an airlock door. As he was doing so, a space-suited figure emerged from the lock, holding a small handgun wired to the suit.

"Who are you?" a man asked, via commcard, in Filipino. Miru had a moment of déjà vu, recalling the voices of fishermen who had sometimes visited Ryukyu Floating Island in his youth. The two other crewmen jerked awake in their fastenings. Pehr had climbed nearly down to the armed man.

Byung, who knew one of the crewmembers, replied in the same tongue:

"My name Byung. I'm friend of Ngoyu Lee. Tell him."

"Byung?" asked a disembodied voice.

"Yes!" said Byung, using Vietnamese.

One of the two crewmen who had been sleeping hurried out of his fastenings and pushed off the ship's hull toward Byung, floating in midair a few meters away.

"What's the meaning of this?" the first man asked.

"This is an old friend," Ngoyu said, "a TritonCo Citizen." He changed back to Vietnamese, but kept the BW open for all to hear: "How'd you stow away without our knowledge? Why? And why are you naked?"

That encouraged laughter from several people. The first, stern, voice intruded:

"You cannot remain on board. We don't have enough lifesupport for more than the five crew already aboard. Fools!" He waved his gun.

Pehr edged closer. Miru tried to locate his friend's mind and say, *No, stop, don't provoke these people!* But Pehr was too focused on his physical actions.

"Ngoyu," Byung said, "let's talk." His friend removed his helmet, revealing tousled hair and a dark, smiling face. Their mouths began to move, but nothing crossed the airwaves. Faint conversation reached Miru where he floated. Soon, Ngoyu's smile faded and a frown replaced it. The talk grew animated.

The armed man pushed himself farther into the hold, still unaware of Pehr, lurking just around the corner of a stack of boxes. Miru began shaking his head, No, hoping Pehr would glance his way just once.

Then the armed man jerked, sending his body up in a spiral toward the "ceiling" of the squat spacecraft.

"What have you done?" the man roared.

Miru turned to where the man was looking and saw that Byung had already taken his friend into artifact-space. *Good, good. Hurry back!*

"Miru, what's happening?" Pehr commed—*In English, damn him!*

"Pehr, be quiet—" he began.

"What is this? An American?" The armed man had now reached the ceiling, pushed off, and was careening toward Pehr.

Pehr saw this and gripped the netting beside him. When his pursuer was within a few meters, he tossed himself toward the man, feet first.

Miru gasped as the clear tip of the weapon glowed white. A small disk of skin on Pehr's bare chest quivered, turning red. By the time Pehr's arms had crossed over the injury, it was beginning to ooze drops of blood. His writhing body sailed past his assailant, whose booted feet shoved Pehr away from collision.

"Stop that!" Miru cried. "Don't shoot!" Damned violent humans!

Janus cried out in pain, but Miru saw it was only mental anguish; she still looked healthy. People began to seek protection. The other suited figure fumbled in its belt, seeking another weapon, Miru thought. Pehr's body rebounded off a wall, angling toward Janus. She glanced toward the crewmen, then moved to intercept Pehr's trajectory.

At that chaotic moment, Byung reappeared within arm's reach of Miru. He looked panicked. "What has happened to Pehr?" he asked.

Miru nodded toward the armed man, who jerked upon seeing Byung's return. He raised the weapon again. "Nobody move!" he screamed. His words held a note of static, the volume overwhelming a retro transmitter.

"We must leave now," Pang commed. Byung glanced from Pang to Miru, nodded. Miru nodded to the two of them, watched them vanish, but remained, himself.

Pehr's body had nearly reached Janus now. Miru commed her: "The instant Pehr is in your arms, join me!" And he, too, allowed himself to fade out of this place, from the poorly planned mission. *Damn the bloody human mind!* he cursed.

Janus Librarse 4

Hate boiled in Janus' mind. Closely packed waves crashed through her as she imagined various ways to murder the son of a bitch who had shot Jack. When Miru told her that he, too, was abandoning her, she even found herself angry at him.

The murderer commed again in some language she didn't understand. Pehr was only an arm's reach away now, but his collision with the hull had nearly canceled his momentum. It would take hours for him to reach her!

She wanted to scream, to cry, to reach out her ephemeral hands and drag that bastard into mindspace the way Jonathan had done to Blackjack. And crush him there!

A wave passed through her so intensely that she went blind for a few seconds. The fear that she, too, would abandon the injured Jack forced her to find a mote of serenity in her soul. She forced herself back, back to her body in the hold of that freezing-cold spacecraft. *I'm through with spaceships!* she vowed.

Janus drew a deep breath, held it, and pushed off toward Jack. The man with the plasma gun saw her—his eyes went wide behind the ultraglas of his faceplate—and he leveled the weapon at her.

"No," she begged, her nude and vulnerable body stretched out in the air for all to see, for energy to pulse through and destroy. She shook her head. The plasma-pistol's barrel lit up as a charge passed through its crystal, but the man had aimed hastily.

Just then, a thump knocked the wind out of her. Janus lashed out with fingernails, but realized it was only Jack. She clung to him, turning their combined mass so that she shielded him from the weapon.

"Come on, Jack," she whispered into his ear. "We've gotta get outta here!"

The armed man steadied himself against a reinforcement structure and sighted along the weapon's receiver. Janus closed her eyes.

Jack, damn your lousy hide to hell! Pay attention!

In response, a tiny, feeble voice trembled at the edge of her consciousness. Janus grabbed hold of it with all her ability, then willed herself to join Miru and the others.

Transcendence I

Lightning-flashes of thought and images cast shadows across the galaxyscape, outlining vast spheres of personality where we huddle together. We are a cluster of stars, fearful that our plans have proven foolish. Two more spheres ripple, one of which turns inside-out like us, the thoughts visible, the mind accessible.

"You made it!" Pang says.

"Pehr is still alive," Miru says. "But how long will he live? He's dying, I can feel his presence waning."

"We have to do something," I, Janus, say. "But what?" Her every memory-scene is opaque, the surfaces of the pearls blazing with her desperation and need.

Jonathan Sombrio's presence thickens the mostly wordless conversation. "Captain?" I ask. "Where's my Captain?"

One of the spheres—the still-dark one—glimmers briefly.

"He's. . ." Jonathan's thoughts race, images flaring like starbursts, too fast to comprehend. Miru is best able to keep up.

This is what happened. The scene aboard the cargo vessel replays. Jonathan's sphere quivers. A second later, he has grown a concrete shell. A second after that, if time is relevant here, the shell explodes in a great cloud of dust. *Don't hide now*, I tell myself.

"You fuckers! Don't any of you know anything? Here!"

Jonathan delves into my—Byung's—memory, extracts what I learned of human anatomy during my three-year edufeed at C'thang Institute, where I earned my nursing certification.

I see. "I see!"

We focus on the mental analogue Pehr holds within his mind, the image of himself, and remove the injury. I and I heal the wound.

I—Pehr Jackson—wake beneath the white-hot lights of an operating room. Green-masked faces peer down at me as a DRM box rises from my chest. I take a deep breath, and—No pain!

Flash—

"Welcome back to the living," says Miru.

Wait. . . . Pehr reels back through his frayed memory of the past minutes, fills in the gaps from our memories.

When assured that he is still alive, Janus sends him a gift, a mental artwork painted from all her memories of wild, growing things: a tiny rose blooming in the afternoon sun among weeds on the shore of a stream; a blade of grass, impossibly green, sprouting between slabs of cement in a sidewalk; a thousand other living images, all woven into a tapestry of growth, all held in place by the force of hope and the wordless delight of warm sunshine caressing cold, exposed skin.

He basks in the pleasure of her gift, then swells to join the others.

"Jonathan, you saved my life."

I (Jonathan) notice I feel a thousand times as strong, my thoughts a million times as clear, my future as bright as this: A star flares within him, illuminating the dark corridors between memory-moments, burning out the dust. *All because you found a way to save my life.*

Janus blends her mind with Jonathan's. We other five step back. We feel the suffusion of life gush through the boy. It came from within himself. *How, when we usually seem to lose energy?*

Ah, we have a lot to learn, friend Pang.

Laughter resounds along the gaseous lanes of the Milky Way—Pehr, joyous, feeling invulnerable and . . . loved. When the laughter subsides, he says, "All right, let's get on with things. This time, I'll try to stay out of the line of fire."

"Wait," Jonathan says as he watches us begin to use Ngoyu's vague memory of a woman he works for. "Is this the only way you know how to get around? You're just shooting in the dark."

He opens a vista into himself which, when we peer into it, swallows our model of mindspace. Galaxies dim while the tendrils within them brighten. We rush in toward the Milky Way, its spiral arms engulfing us, closer and closer. Now one star—vivid yellow, casting light upon worlds that range from thin crescent to solid orb . . . that one star dominates our view. And now a new set of tendrils flashes like a headcard overlay atop the solar system.

It's this simple, Jonathan says. Of course, we all see that even he hadn't realized this until now, when he purged his mind clean, when his self-value rocketed after helping save Pehr.

"Of course!" says Miru. "Of course. This is how to use the maps. I see." He and Jonathan begin a series of wordless exchanges, and the tendrils thicken to tubes. Billions of tiny lights within the tubes appear like lightbulbs—but when we try to comprehend the number, they fade—back again when we simply open our minds. *Who are we looking for? Where are we going?—These two act like coordinates. And there, our first objective.*

As we close in, Jonathan vanishes. *Hurry, catch up with him.* *How did he do that?* *You have to be a curr-gang kid to know those tricks.*

"Now no one get shot this time."

Needleship *Sigwa*

An alarm tugged Clarisse Poinsettia Chang from sleep. She was far too drowsy to know which alarm it was, even to recognize the symbol that glowed behind closed eyelids. Somehow she found the cognizance to shut down hibernation feed, which was stimulating the production of nervous-system depressants and keeping her body and mind in a state of deep sleep. Pleasant dream-images began to fade—more effects of brain-drug stimulant feed.

Now she began to try to open her eyes, but each eyelid weighed as much as a goose. She watched a long-winged crane begin to take off from a cattail-stubbled pond, felt herself become that bird. . . .

No, she told herself. *Wake up. Wake up!* Suddenly, the warning symbol took on meaning: Intrusion alert.

Someone had boarded her flagship, *Sigwa*! The very battleship she occupied. *Impossible!*

Fear helped dump adrenaline into her bloodstream. She felt the drowsing effects of the hibernation drugs begin to wane. But just as she was about to open her eyes, someone reached into her mind and touched her body.

"I'm very sorry, Coordinator Chang," that someone was saying. She recognized the voice but couldn't pin it down. "But you'll have to come with us."

Clarisse was much too weak to argue or fight. She resigned herself: *It's just one of my people, it must be.*

The swan flapped its wings, creating a rush of air across her organic airfoil, and into the sky, free and blue, no hand here can touch you. . . .

Transcendence J

Once again, we experience the unfolding of a life. This time, however, she doesn't speak to us as we live through the loss of her NKK-Citizen family in an EarthCo bombing raid, her transfer to an adoptive family in the Ukraine, coldness then violence from my brothers—then a ricochet of violence as I break free of those representatives of EarthCo, kicking and punching my way across the Asian continent to the corp of my youth—to Bangkok. Vengeance! Vengeance is my cry during the following years. No one sees the tiger within my breast, no one can hear me counting, One, two, three . . . as I tally up victims-to-be. Patriotism for NKK doesn't spur me through victory after victory in space sim-combat; *You're like a wild dog*, the General tells her as she climbs down from the fighter's cabin. *I like that. You'll go far.* Not patriotism but hate, hate! Hate like a solar flare erupts from my being, invisible to the eye; NKK's enemy—the frothing EarthCo dogs—is my enemy. *See how I would destroy NKK just to hurt EarthCo?*

A black cloak falls from space, blocking our view into Clarisse.

What's happening to me? she asks. She's awakened. Jonathan steps forward.

Flash-flash-flash . . . we can't follow their exchange. Worlds of imagery and thought pass from his sphere to hers, blinding some of us, confounding others. I catch a glimpse of a great sword forming between them, dropping into place atom by atom, a particle stolen from each exchange. When I try to touch that weapon to see what it is, my mind explodes with an unbearable heat: *Hate! How can there be so much hate in all the worlds of Solsystem? How can all that hate belong to a single woman?*

"I've got to go in there and save Jonathan," Pehr says. "I'll help," says Janus.

"Stop it, both of you," says Miru. "Those two are built of the same material. That material is not compatible with ours—it would be like trying to mix light with concrete. They have lived in the virtuality of cybernetics. No one of us, except Janus, could even hope to stay sane in their coinciding sphere. Wait."

The sword's tip finally forms. A woman's scarred hand reaches out from one of the roiling balls composed of light, snarling faces, smoldering spaceships, varied scenery, the clouds of Neptune. It grasps the sword's hilt. The other sphere—Jonathan's—forms a concrete skin, but we all see out of our peripheral vision as another, larger, globe emerges from him; Fifth dimensional? When we try to understand, it becomes invisible again.

The sword rises high, reaching far into the interstellar blackness of the Milky Way's arm. "I'll do it!" Clarisse shouts. "Keep away." *If she swings that thing, could she kill him? Could she kill us all?* I and I poise to leave.

Jonathan's larger circumference bends as it encounters her mind. Slowly, like wax covering a warm object, it passes over her and finally pops into place behind: She's within him now.

"This isn't how we did it with Lonny," Pehr whispers. We all wait. Our tension is like thin shells, making it even more difficult to pass thoughts from one to the other.

I am Clarisse Poinsettia Chang. The moment-memories look different. How? Watch:

Each kind act anyone ever did for me opens: the rarest of pearls. Ukrainian Mother sets a plate of boiled vegetables before her newly adopted daughter, the little Nik rescued from a raided village. Brother—even he who later became the monster of my nightmares—brother shows me how to work his fireball; we laugh and pull the cable and watch the holo ball leap into the air, casting a spell of pictures: Extinct animals from all around the world caper about our heads. A nameless bosun aboard the crew-ship that carries me to Neptune grants me a smile when I feel most alone. And Kaigun Taii Nikolai Sekiguchi, that cocky bastard, that beautiful man I killed during a dogfight in the skies of Neptune when all he really wanted was to prove himself to me. . . .

Muscles in the sword-arm relax. The weapon itself crumbles into photons which accelerate, screaming, in all directions. Clarisse's moment-memories begin to pop one after another as we all experience her again. But now I've lost the real being, who I am. *Let me go, Jonathan, the way you let Blackjack go. When you've lived a life so miserable that even such tiny gifts as playing fireball gather vast, out-of-proportion importance, what's left to live for?*

"Fuck you, Clarisse! You're not paying attention." Jonathan reveals himself again, and this time she doesn't look away. Their communion happens as fast as a blink of the eye.

The lightshow ceases. We float, bodiless, between the orbits of Neptune and Saturn, near the needleship *Sigwa* as it and its armada hurl toward confrontation at Jupiter.

Now Clarisse's floating world of memory brightens, looking like a new planet. She brightens another magnitude, outshining even the invigorated Jonathan.

"Boy," she says, "life's going to be better for you, I promise."

She outlines a new plan to stop what she set in motion. "You were right to come to me, but I'm just a first step. We need to cut off the heads of the combatants. Then. . . . Life will be better. Anything is possible. Thank you." Hope is a star blazing within her, its solar wind washing clean the spaces of her memory, creating room for what is to come.

"Now let's get to work."

Fury 10

Hardman Nadir waved back the remains of his army—five men, including Paolo—from the massive hicarb door. Feedcontrol Central's administrative skyscraper towered high above them, gleaming silver in the cloudy light. Behind, fires continued to blaze among the shattered domes and toppled antennae where the battle had raged. Even the ground itself, billions of pivot-mounted plates bristling with tiny needles, smoked, spewing a brown fog over the electropolis.

"Fire," Nadir ordered the NKK soldier. The man opened up his plasma rifle at full energy. A small disk of white formed beside the door handle, oozing molten metal.

"Hold it," he said. The man ceased fire. "Now see if we can get in."

Paolo turned the handle, but the door didn't budge. After ten seconds of fire, when the NKK-soldier's weapon charge began to weaken, Nadir realized it would take a lot more power to cut through.

"Magnet charges," he said. Each EarthCo Warrior carried two. When the first one was fastened into place, the men raced away—there was no cover to be found on the platform, but they at least avoided most of the concussion and flying fragments through sheer distance.

Again and again, they laid their charges in the growing crater. When it came down to Nadir's own bomb, the men were panting and beginning to reveal signs of doubt. This time, when the deafening explosion tunneled deeper into the door, no debris whistled past Nadir's head. He looked back and saw light shining through a ragged hole at the center of the crater, half a meter deep. Scorched wires and steel bars dangled within the hole, revealing a hollow space where the handle had been.

The other men looked up from their lying positions and began to cheer. Nadir didn't have time for pleasure. He was focused like a megawatt laser. Up, Nadir forced his burning and tingling muscles to carry him once again to the door, where he slid his remaining charge into the mechanism within the frame. As soon as he set the timer, he jogged back to where Paolo lay. There he squatted and watched the virtually fireless explosion. Great slabs of armor jarred loose, fumes sprayed out from the doorframe, bits of lock and electronics rocketed in all directions. Even as Nadir walked back to the site, the door began to fall. He stepped aside as a warped, shattered, three-meter by two-meter plate of hicarb crashed to the concrete platform.

"Let's go," he said through a cloud of cement dust, then unshouldered his EMMA and began to chop up the thin, inner section of the door. By the time his men reached him, Nadir was kicking a man-sized hole into a hallway.

They began running along deserted corridors, unmarked, twisting one way and another, featureless. Nadir—at point—turned a corner and, before he could veer out of the way, knocked down a woman wearing a long white coat.

"Sorry," he said, helping her up. She looked dazed, but not so much from the collision.

"Sorry," she repeated. She stood and stared blankly at Nadir, then blinked and seemed just then to realize she was surrounded by armed soldiers. A gasp stopped her next words.

"Where's Herrschaft?" Nadir demanded.

"The Director is . . . everywhere," she said. "If you want to find him, just wait around. We used to. . . . No one knows where he is. But, oh, he'll find you."

Wispy eyebrows drew together as she frowned. Though she appeared unafraid, her voice rose an octave: "Why are you doing this? You're ruining the greatest monument to humanity's progress ever built. Why?"

Nadir turned away from her and began to run again. "If the people want to rebuild this place after they've experienced life," he said, more to himself than the woman, "they're welcome. I don't think they will."

But he began to wonder. Which would they choose: Mind-drugged comfort and all the ills it produces, or life and the pain it forces you to bear? He ran.

Finally they turned a corner and reached a roadblock. An ultraglas door stood just beyond the bend, with an armed guard seated to each side. They started, then raised their handguns. Nadir didn't break stride as he aimed and fired, aimed and fired. The two men lay writhing on the floor, their gun-arms neatly severed.

"Bust it down!" he called. Paolo and one of the other EarthCo Warriors began firing at the handprint pad beside the crystal opening-lever. Nadir told them to stop, then leaped at the door and hit it with a flying sidekick. As he rebounded back, the door lurched off its seating.

Nadir felt foolish for a moment as he realized it was a pull, not push, door. He got up from the floor and nodded.

But that only slowed him for a moment. He drew open the door. They continued on, deeper into the building. Nadir's blood felt like fire, his mind like a laser's pulse: Nothing extraneous, designed for one purpose, clear and dangerous.

A Note from Lucilla Tyndareus

On her way to meet with Luke Herrschaft, Lucilla paused. She was in no hurry; three days ago, her old concerns about Luke's identity were confirmed—that the man who had made love to her countless times during her early days of service wasn't a man at all, but a machine inhabited by a man.

She drew a deep breath that sounded more like a gasp and tried to compose herself as she listened to the alert. Someone had broken into the building. Funny, it didn't seem to matter—only as much as it bore on her being with Luke again.

She could barely concentrate. This was the first time he'd invited her to his private chamber in . . . six years. She put out one arm against the clean wall to steady herself. The bastard. *Damn you, you bloody mannequin*, she thought. *I still love you.*

An idea struck her. Lucilla picked up her pace and stopped at a storage closet. There she withdrew a roll of toilet paper and an oil pen. Quickly, she wrote a note, folded it, and held it in the palm of her hand, against a thigh. She returned to the hallway and retraced her steps to a small feed-editing room, smiling at people as she passed, watching worried faces in the flickering light.

"Fred?" she said, standing in the doorway. A man seated at a secure feedaccess desk—essentially a polished sheet of aluminum atop a plastic pedestal—turned toward her. After a few blinks, he smiled.

"Lucilla, what's on?"

"Nothing. You?"

"Same. Feed's dead. I've got nothing to do."

Lucilla walked closer to him, nonchalantly laying a hand on his arm. "Is Ann at work today?" she asked.

The piece of toilet paper fluttered from his arm to his lap. A confused look, then—

"Sure," he said, pretending to ignore the paper but shoving it into a shirt pocket. "We come in together every Friday."

"Could you tell her I'd like to see her later? Since you're out of work until the repair equipment gets this place working again. . ."

"No problem." He stood, nodded, and left the room.

Two levels down, he entered his contract-wife's cubicle. She seemed to be asleep, stretched out on an experimental mattress, but turned a smile toward him as he entered.

"What brings you here now?"

He sat down on the buzzing mattress and put one hand on hers. The note passed into her palm. She clenched it and nodded.

"Lucilla invited us to dinner."

They were used to passing information this way—when eyes and ears are everywhere at all times, privacy requires heroic measures.

So the note passed from Ann to her quadrant's human maid, from the maid to a pipe-fitter in a hissing boiler-room ten levels beneath the surface. The great atomic-powered generators lay silent while repairs went on overhead. From the pipe-fitter, the note passed to a friend who repaired the obsequious machines that kept Feedcontrol Central in top condition . . . and so on, until a feral-looking boy sprinted from shadow to shadow in the unpopulated service caverns, where condensation dripped to provide rats and insects with moisture. He had more luck than usual staying out of the light, for most sources of illumination were malfunctioning, casting a sort of strobe through his subterranean world. Not until he found the old man did he allow himself to eat the special treat that the mechanic had given him; sweet, rich chocolate melted on his tongue, and he hissed a laugh at the rats who took special notice.

The old man climbed out of his sleeping chamber, opened the crumpled tissue paper, and strained to read the words. He was now nearly blind, having endured the darkness for so long, but recognized the signature. "Ah, Lucilla."

A fresh-faced girl sprang into his mind, a girl who had taken pity on the broken and feed-blinded servant of the great Luke Herrschaft. He nearly smashed the note before remembering where he was. He opened it again, holding it out at arm's length where a triangle of light shone through the rusted steel catwalk.

"Yes, my dear," he said when done, and put the paper in his mouth. After he had swallowed, he cried out in his cracking voice:

"Boy! Boy, come back here. You need to run another errand. I'm sure they'll have a nicey for you up top."

Feedcontrol 7

Luke Herrschaft told the door to allow Lucilla inside. She stepped into the room and shut the door behind her. Her eyes were directed toward the floor, where real Oriental rugs from the twentieth century kept bare feet insulated from the concrete.

"Do you remember. . . ?" he asked.

Lucilla's breasts rose against her thin blouse as she drew a deep breath. "Of course. This is where we first . . . made love."

Herrschaft felt an odd pang of regret. "Won't you smile? Is this so horrible? I need you now."

"Oh, Luke." Her eyes rose to his, and her face wore a mixture of sadness and something he couldn't recognize. She crossed a few steps closer to the bed.

"You know," Herrschaft said, rising to his elbows beneath the silk sheets, "I thought you'd be . . . disgusted with me after what happened in the boardroom."

She shook her head. An odd smile lifted her lips—Such gorgeous lips, even at her age, he thought. He pulled the last 10% of his consciousness out of the monitors in the tower's first floor, where a handful of soldiers were running toward a deadly gauntlet of autocannon. Being out of control shook him more than an ill-planned attack.

"Luke." She shook her head and sat on the foot of the bed. Herrschaft willed an erection, then had it go away again when he saw a pained expression cross her face.

"No," she said. "It's okay." Lucilla reached behind her back and loosened the blouse. It slid down the curves of her front.

A lace bra—retro by today's market, but of the type Herrschaft liked best—held her breasts high on her chest. He remembered how this part of her anatomy had led him to hire the woman as his private assistant in the first place, and was pleased to learn she hadn't deteriorated over the years. The graceful curve of her collarbone highlighted the soft skin. She smelled warm and human.

"I wanted to come," she said. "You know I. . ."

"What?"

"Oh, lay back, silly." And off slid her trousers. More lace, this time holographic lace panties that aroused primitive urges in Herrschaft.

He felt his erection return, this time through pure physical feedback from his intheflesh body. "'Damn the torpedoes!'" he quoted, and laughed. Even he recognized the artificiality in his jest.

Lucilla again made that frown-looking smile, then her lips found his neck. Herrschaft faded away into the fivesen world of pleasure he had worried would not be his for some time to come. Oh, but here it was—and Lucilla, one of his past lovers, the one who above all others could ease his mind.

An emotion not completely unlike affection suffused him. When he opened his eyes to slits, he saw a woman's face passing from one side of his neck to the other. It looked vaguely reminiscent of someone from long ago, long, long ago. . . .

"I underestimated you, my always-faithful Lucilla. Where would I be without you?"

Herrschaft's hands rose from his sides and began to caress Lucilla's buttocks and the back of her thighs. He turned up the fivesen feed to shield himself from the past. It worked. This little oasis of pleasure was all that existed in the world. He'd let his defenses and staff take care of the buffoons who had dared penetrate his castle; there was nothing he could do that wasn't already in motion. Let the invaders perish one by one in the halls of Feedcontrol Central—they already did their worst by trashing the comm systems. Herrschaft, himself, was in no danger from this handful of tired traitors. When feed was restored, the ill-fated invasion would provide a suitably dramatic ending to one chapter in his most popular subscription ever.

Herrschaft initiated a signal to rouse him when his feed was back live and let himself submerge into the comforts that only human contact can provide.

Fury 11

An unarmed man in white coveralls emerged from a doorway near the end of a seemingly endless hall. His hands rose high over his head, and one held a sheet of paper which he waved in the ancient signal.

"Don't shoot," he repeated as he neared Nadir and the soldiers. He stopped only a meter from Nadir and let the paper flutter to the black-tiled floor as his hands came to rest at his sides.

"You men better leave this building," the man said. "If you go any farther, you'll be killed for sure. A whole legion of guards are coming this way."

With a grimace, the man turned and ran back the way he'd come. Paolo raised his rifle, but Nadir put a hand on the barrel. The folded sheet of paper drew his attention, so Nadir picked it up. Words and lines appeared and vanished as the page turned in his hand—the work of trace ink.

DONT SPEAK, it read. BUILDING HAS EARS. FOLLOW MAP. ASK FOR GENE. HERRSCHAFT IN CATACOMBS BELOW. DESTROY THIS NOTE.

Nadir's eyebrows rose. It could be a trick, but to what purpose? If guards were, indeed, waiting in a trap, why wouldn't they just wait for Nadir and his men to turn a corner—right up there, for instance?

I'm not alone in my beliefs, Nadir assured himself. *Look at these men, look at Paolo.* He did so. The boy looked like Death personified, but still he stood beside his subbs. Five other men whom he'd never met before—including a Nik—awaited his orders to walk into the maw of death. Death had consumed more than 10,000 other soldiers in this assault. *I'm not alone!* And warriors aren't the only ones who fight for change.

He studied the map, orienting himself, casting glances around at the doors near him until he felt confident that he could follow the directions. When he had finished, he took out a lighter and burned the paper.

"Follow me," he said. They ran to where the Feedcontrol employee had gone and discovered a staircase behind the door, as marked on the map. Just then, one of the EarthCo Warriors cried out and began firing into the corridor.

Nadir, feeling awkward without access to rifle-feed, stretched his neck to see what the man was firing at. He nearly caught the shrapnel from bullets shredding the paneling.

His soldiers fell back into the alcove and arranged themselves so all could fire at once. Nadir lay on his belly and stuck his rifle around the doorframe.

Ten meters down the hall, where this passage met two others, a metal ball the size of a small car rolled toward them. Bolts of lightning shot out at the soldiers. One man screamed and toppled backwards, tripping over Nadir's outstretched legs and landing on the stairs leading down. Behind the ball, several human guards followed, handguns spewing projectiles. Nadir recognized the weapons as being downsized versions of his EMMA.

"Their legs," he whispered to the soldier nearest him. Nadir and the man concentrated fire on the exposed legs of the men hidden behind the deadly ball. Another blast of lightning struck another of the soldiers—the NKK regular. The man didn't make a sound. He slumped down atop Nadir and his chest steamed.

Guards cried out as tiny rounds penetrated their shins. Soon, only the automated weapon still fought.

"Forget that thing," Nadir said. "Let's go!" He got up and began running down the stairs. Three men followed.

One, two, three, Nadir counted, until they had descended 14 levels of ringing metal steps. His legs felt as if they were sacks of fire, his knees like daggers digging into the bone, but he kept running. The very fact that the other three men must have been in similar condition—yet still following him—pushed him on.

The door leading out of the stairwell was locked, but a short burst from the EMMA opened it. They ran through a damp cement shaft whose floor was plastic grating to the first corridor leading left. Overhead lighting was provided by antique fluorescence, most of which didn't work. Bands of light and shadow engulfed them. At last, Nadir reached the elevator marked on the map; anyway, he hoped it was the one. He bent over, gasping, while the other soldiers caught up. An image of a Dark Ages torture chamber crossed his mind as he thought about how deep the elevator would carry them.

"Bottom level," he told the elevator when all four had crowded inside the dark car. Nothing happened. Paolo reached out and depressed a button on the bottom of a row of buttons. The car lurched, metal grated against the sides, and they started down amid a whine of electric motors. They rode in the darkness, breathing heavily, without speaking. Scents of injury and bodily waste weighed in the stale air.

After what felt like hours, the car stopped. The door opened, but Nadir couldn't see anything beyond the car.

"You the soldiers?" the crackling voice of an old man asked.

"I'm EarthCo Warrior Sub-Boss Hardman Nadir," Nadir said with more pride than he thought still existed in him. "And these men with me are the only knights left in the world."

The old creature sniggered and turned on a lighter. The tiny glow of the machine illuminated a face that seemed to have been carved from old granite. Wads of wax filled the spots where eyes should be. Strands of grey hair stuck out in clumps on the scalp. Part of the face cracked open to reveal pink gums and a lolling tongue. Below the head stretched a sinewy neck, and below that a gown sewn from plastic sheeting. It looked vaguely male.

"I'm told you're here to set us free," the old man said. "I've been waiting for you for almost . . . five decades."

"You can lead us to Herrschaft?" Nadir asked, incredulous. What had he gotten himself and his men into? Is this where his glorious rage would end? Is this how his stormcloud that began forming in Africa, that swept across that continent growing larger, across the Atlantic Ocean, across EarthCo's historic homeland of America to Feedcontrol Central—is this how he would repay the thousands who put their lives in Nadir's hands?

He felt overwhelmed by the enormity of his actions. Until this quiet moment in a dripping chamber, he hadn't stopped to consider whether or not, on balance, he was doing the right thing. What was the value of vengeance? Was it worth the lives of 10,000 soldiers?

"Come," said the old man, who turned and began walking along the muddy floor. "My name's Dareen. Forty-seven years ago, I was a member of Herrschaft's elite Personal Guard, back when he still needed guards for his person." A frog-like sound erupted from the man, then mutated into a fit of coughing. Nadir realized the man had been laughing. They continued along the lightless shaft.

"My final duty had been to protect the Director during his burial here," the lighter cast around before the man, weaving a figure-eight that lingered on the retina, "beneath the catacombs."

Nadir stopped suddenly and felt one of his men bump into him. "Are you saying that Herrschaft's dead? What are we doing—"

"Ach," the man said, "don't be an idiot! As I was saying, me and another seven of Herrschaft's Personal Guard was brought here with him as the Director rolled his crippled old body . . . hmmm! down here in his wheelchair. It was like a portable resuscitator . . . hmmm, that's what it was, I 'spose. Watch your step."

They passed through what had once been an airlock, but the doors were missing. At the other side, a single lumniglobe hanging from a domed ceiling cast pale blue light through the round chamber. Dozens more of the fixtures had been arranged in what must have once been artistic fashion, fastened to one another by rusty lengths of pipe. Pigment-paint covered the walls, recapturing a forest scene with animals and a lake in the background, but rot had eaten away most of the fresco. The floor was seamed with hairline cracks that ran in circles around the room. Just off center, the cracks grew so large that great slabs of ragged concrete stood up a few centimeters higher.

"Right over there," a bony finger protruded from a yellow plastic sleeve, "is the entrance to the vestibule. 'Course, none of this exists on any schematics." They crossed the floor, boots grating on sand and bits of cement, to another airlock. This one was still sealed.

The pruneface spun around to stare into Nadir's eyes. "We carried the old sonofabitch through here, down to an antechamber. An escalator carried us down again, along a steep shaft that was a hundred meters long if it was a centimeter! None of us thought anything about the blocks of stone hanging partway down from gaps in the ceiling."

The man's cataractic eyes ceased looking straight into Nadir's, instead seeing something just behind him. Nadir pivoted on his heel to see if this were the trap, if guards had descended on them. Only his four soldiers stood behind him. They were beginning to look anxious. The squawking voice continued:

"We carried Herrschaft in his resuscitator through another airlock, then rode another escalator up ten meters. More blocks of stone were suspended there. When we reached the burial chamber . . . hmmm, are you beginning to understand? When we reached the burial chamber, we lifted the old body out of its lifesupport machine and dropped him into a basket. This hoisted him up to the top of a huge plastic tank and then lowered him inside the liquid. . . . I can't tell you what it was, but the old sonofabitch could breathe the stuff, though he looked like he was choking at first. A cap seal descended from the chamber's ceiling and locked him in the cylinder. The end." The old man turned from Nadir and began spinning the airlock handle. He spat once or twice, then grinned sheepishly up at the EarthCo Warrior.

"Does ya have a nicey for me, hmmm? I don't get much to eat down here. Nobody but a few knows I'm here, hmmm?" A gnarled hand extended palm-up.

"I think he wants something to eat," said Paolo.

Nadir reached into his belt for a battle-bar, high in protein and carbs, and handed it to the old man. With a vulgar munching and smacking of gums, the bar vanished. The man went back to work on the handle.

"So we took it that it was time to leave, right?" the croaking voice continued. "Right? Hmmm! Soon's we went up the last escalator, and got on the first one that'd lead us up to the vestibule, Patrick heard these motors, 'Big motors,' he said. A second later, those huge stones was rolling down out of the ceiling, down onto the escalator as it was bringing us out of the burial chambers. There."

The airlock popped open, puffing a cloud of dust. Its weather-stripping ripped as the door swung out. "Patrick was crushed beneath that first block, but I was ahead of him! I run run run up the screeching steps just past where the next block falls. That one separated me from the other men, so I didn't know what happened to them until later."

The old man moved into the airlock, pumping his legs as if running up the steps in his tale. "Then the top stone fell just in front of me. I dodged the falling slabs of granite— see, it cracked all to pieces after it hit the escalator—and clawed my way past the still-standing pieces out to the airlock. Evil bastard must've been trying to save credits. He had the stones cut too thin. Ha!" He began spinning the inner door's handle.

Nadir felt a little sick listening to the man. He didn't need to know all this. He just had to find Herrschaft.

"I remembered something from Edufeed," the old man went on. "You know the kings of ancient Egypt? The pharaohs? The old sonofabitch thought of himself as some godlike pharaoh! He was gonna bury his Personal Guard with him, down there, in this goddamned electronic pyramid! The only ones who knew the burial site. Hmmm! But gods be damned if I was gonna die with him! Hmmm!"

The inner door cracked open, and Nadir stared into a dark space. He heard the trickle of condensation running along walls and dripping into puddles. He felt creeped-out, as if he were entering a domain of ghosts and dinosaur bones.

"Well, my boys, here you go!" The old hand gestured into the dark. "I been down there a thousand times in the past 47 years, eight months, and one days. You'll see my buddies down there. I . . . I swore I'd smash a hole in that tank of his. But I never got past the second escalator, and I never dared show my face aboveground." He made a fist that looked as if it were made of twigs and leather.

He leaned forward and screamed into the black space: "I was too much a damned coward! Well, Herrschaft, you sonofabitch! See how much of a coward I am now! Hahahaha!" The ancient body began to quake with grief. A rusty sound fell from the dry lips.

Nadir cleared his throat. "All right," he said. "Let's go."

"Subbs," said Paolo, who grabbed hold of Nadir's sleeve. "Don't you think maybe one of us ought to go first? In case?"

"Right. You boys wait here. If I'm not back in ten minutes, shoot this old bastard and go back up the way we came. Shoot anyone you see up there. Got it?"

"Yes, sir!" all four said in unison.

The old man broke into laughter and began slapping Paolo on the back. "Smart! Smart is good." He dropped to one knee and clasped Nadir's hand. "I can't begin to thank you."

"Knock it off," Nadir said.

The old man sprang to his feet and laughed again. "Go on now, before we all die of pneumonia!"

Nadir removed the flashlight from his belt and pointed it into the next room. Sure enough, just as he stepped past the airlock door, he saw a downward-leading shaft filled with rubble. He slung his EMMA back over his shoulder and began to descend.

After the second stand of granite, Nadir noticed a scattering of brown bones on the rusted escalator steps. They had been gnawed open by small, sharp teeth; the skull lay separated in plates across several steps, even the teeth picked out of its jaw. Nadir felt acids begin to boil in his guts as he recalled the dream . . . the badlands around Wolf Point and the dinosaur bones buried there . . . the rigid faces of hundreds of murdered North Africans . . . I earned more than two hundred marks there, he thought with such bitterness that he nearly vomited.

As he wormed his way past cracked, slimy blocks of stone, Nadir saw five more skeletons, all mauled by rats. At the bottom of the shaft, he encountered an airlock door nearly rusted shut. It was locked. A small strip of explosive tape and a detonator took care of the lock, though he still had to strain to move the rusted hinges.

Then up another flight of stone-barricaded steps, at the top of which stood a marble door. Spaceships and planets were carved into the dusty, once-white rock. The frame was engraved with stylized cities, smiling faces peering from thousands of windows. Cold fingers tickled Nadir's spine. He pushed open the door with a creak; a wall of warm, dry air struck his face.

In the cone of his flashlight beam, Nadir caught a spectral figure encased in glass. Beside a massive tank, great banks of electronics hummed. Dozens of green and yellow lights cast an eerie glow on the other side of the curved glass. Nadir remembered to breathe and stepped inside what the old man had called "the burial chamber."

As Nadir approached, the glare of his flashlight cut deeper through the tank's liquid. Soon he could see features on the face behind the glass. Veiny eyelids covered sunken eyeballs. Long, grey hair entangled a waiflike figure that drifted gently in a burbling current. Countless wires and tubes pierced its translucent skin, bruised at the contact points. The jaws worked slowly, like a dying ant's. Between its skin-wrapped femurs, a purple penis seemed to have a partial erection.

Nadir felt so revolted that he forgot his purpose here was to avenge what he and his men had been tricked into doing in Africa. He wanted to kill this monster, only because it was so . . . inhuman. He couldn't bear to think that this . . . thing was at the heart of EarthCo. The EMMA fell into his hands.

"No fucking wonder," Nadir said. He backed away and stuck his head out into the hallway.

"Paolo! Men! It's all right. Get over here right away." He would wait to destroy the thing until the others had a chance to see what it was they had come here to kill.

Thinking they couldn't hear him past the airlocks and rubble, Nadir backed out of the room and back down to the bottom of the first escalator-shaft. Again he called out. As he waited for a response, he heard what sounded like branches breaking.

"Firefight," he said when he recognized the sounds. "Damn, damn, damn!" he said as he struggled back up the blocked stairs. He turned off the flashlight. When he reached the top, near the airlock, the shots echoed clear and loud. Many weapons. Bullets rang against the wall beside Nadir, chipping craters into the cement. Shadows moved on that wall as bright lights shone at Nadir's men.

What I wouldn't give to have my commcard back, he thought. On hands and knees, Nadir crawled to the airlock opening and chanced a look. His men crowded against the far side of the airlock, unable to do anything more than point their weapons out into the larger room and fire wildly. Two thousand-watt searchlights glared in at them, behind which an unknown number of men or machines sprayed bullets.

Then the firing stopped and Nadir heard footfalls leading away. The EarthCo Warriors took the opportunity to drop to their knees around the circular opening and fire directly at the two lights. One of them dimmed. A black spot arced across the face of the other light, and Nadir heard a faint clang as the shadow fell behind his men, into the open airlock.

"Grenade!" he cried, and ducked beneath the threshold.

A deafening roar filled the rooms, followed briefly by crazily ricocheting shrapnel. Men screamed in pain. Nadir's calm finally exploded.

He ran through the smoke-filled airlock and out into the domed room, firing his EMMA at the remaining light. It flashed and went out, burning its coiled element onto Nadir's retina. He ran a zig-zagged path across the tilted floor, firing half-second bursts in random directions. When he passed the frames of the searchlights, he saw several bodies of injured or dead men, dressed in white uniforms with hand-sized EMMAs hanging by cables from their hip units. The old man lay like a sack of bones near the middle of the room, looking completely natural in the state of death. Nadir hoped the man died believing his vengeance had been exacted.

In the hallway beyond the room, a handful of white-uniformed men stood facing one another, hands over their ears. Nadir startled them so much one slipped on the wet grating, and then he opened fire. Two of the men managed to draw their weapons before Nadir dropped them. One managed to release a one-second burst.

Part of that burst struck Nadir's chest. Two rounds punctured the vest. Nadir flew back from the impact and fell, wedged between curved wall and floor-grate. He raised his rifle at the guards, but none moved. Receding into the distance, a single pair of boots clanged against the grating, sending tremors into Nadir's ribs.

"Fuck," Nadir said. He struggled to his knees and remained in that position for a second, panting. "Paolo."

With that name on his lips, Nadir stood and ran back to the still-smoky airlock. He flicked on his flashlight and searched the faces of the four bodies. Only two still breathed; one in the way an animal struck by a groundcar might, gasping for each breath. Nadir rolled the smoother-breathing body over and saw the face of his young friend. Dark gashes crossed the forehead. No blood seemed to have flowed out of the wounds.

No, no, no, no, no. . . .

"Hey, Paolo. Now why the fuck'd you let yourself get hit?" Inside Nadir's head, the word kept repeating: *No, no, no, no, no. . . .*

"I'm alive, subbs," the boy said. Nadir could see his teeth, gleaming white behind blue lips. "You were right. I'm alive."

"Come on," Nadir said. "You've got to see the . . . you've got to see Director Herrschaft before I tag him. On your feet!"

The legs twitched, but that was the extent of Paolo's movement. The other soldier stopped convulsing.

No, no, no, no, no. . . .

"Come on," Nadir urged. He lifted Paolo by the armpits, which sent shots of fire through Nadir's chest. He remembered that he, too, had been hit. This confused him. How could it be that he and Paolo were wounded? Sure, they said the morning words: "Live well today, boys, for today you may die." But that didn't really count, not for him and Paolo. They were invulnerable! He began to drag Paolo down the rubble-blockaded steps.

Hell, I've stood up during heavy firefights, he thought. *Nothing could touch me. I was hit at the village, hit by something heavy. It just knocked the wind outta me, that's all!*

Nadir found himself sitting on wet stairs, dizzy and dreaming. "Come on," he repeated. Carrying Paolo down wasn't nearly as difficult as bringing him back up, over and around blocks of granite, toward the burial chamber where the inhuman thing floated in its fountain of youth. The effort bled out the last of Nadir's vitality and defiance. By the time he again faced the tank and its floating specimen, he barely had the strength to unsling his EMMA and point it at the bank of machines. He leaned Paolo against the carved marble door.

"See, Paolo," he said, gasping, "he's nothing. Herrschaft's just a shriveled old monster. Society hasn't gone bad, boy, it's just led by a creature that's no longer a man. We're not alone. We'll set everyone free. Let's do it. Ready, boy!"

Paolo said nothing, didn't even raise his own weapon.

"What's the matter, boy?" Nadir asked. When he looked into his longtime friend's eyes, he saw the dead stare he had seen too many times, the black spots where life used to dance. Only now the death-mask occupied a face that was supposed to be immune to it.

Nadir was by himself, completely, for the first time since Wolf Point. Cold pierced his chest where the round had punctured his vest. He wanted to grieve, but all he could manage were a few tears that burned their way down his cheeks.

Feedcontrol 8

The strange light again burned just behind Luke Herrschaft's eyes. He couldn't blink it away, nor could he find any feed intruding upon this intimate moment with Lucilla.

"Lucilla," he said, melting away from the odd sensation. She slid against his back, massaging his neck with one hand and his cock with her other. "Nobody cures me like you, my dear. I'm sorry you haven't been the only one. Do you forgive me?"

"Of course, Luke." She crawled over him and lay face-to face with his robot. An idiosyncratic expression of sadness and loss crossed her face.

"You're not completely bad," she said. "I loved you—did you know? That's why I had to do what I've done."

He felt taken aback. What was she talking about? Had the bomb-concussion during the assassination attempt addled her brains?

"Who says I'm completely bad? And what is it you've done?"

Then he saw the light behind his eyes. The room flickered a bit as he remembered what that meant. It had been a long, long time. . . .

Luke Herrschaft, power-broker for half a solar system and soon-to-be Director of every world lit by its sun—EarthCo Feedcontrol Director Luke Herrschaft allowed his consciousness to seep back into his mortal coil, half a thousand meters beneath where he and Lucilla lay.

Pain danced through his nerves. Flashes of color and pulses of light needled his eyes. He felt as if he were drowning. None of his limbs seemed to possess any strength at all, and it took great effort just to open his eyes.

Blind! He could see nothing but a white light. But when he focused on it, he glimpsed a reflection of the husk of some old man floating in a bubble-dense liquid, hair wrapped around his neck like a noose, wires and tubes protruding from virtually every pore.

Not blind; his inner sanctum had been penetrated!

"Get out!" He tried to scream, but only a gurgling set of vowels emerged from his throat. How could it be? Who was it? How!

He flicked on his comm overlay and found the security connections. He depressed all of them at once—he wasn't constricted to the simple-minded, anthropomorphic technique of using a mental "finger"—and ordered every guard to the maze of catacombs beneath Feedcontrol.

Fear! No one knew of his inner sanctum. No one should even know of the maze. *How would they get there—here—in time?*

But then Herrschaft noticed something even more terrifying: His comm hadn't even fed out to Security.

Warm and cleansing, soft and nutritive, the chemical bath swirled his corpus as his brain seized in a fear he hadn't experienced for nearly two centuries.

When Herrschaft tried to return his consciousness to his robot, nothing happened. When he attempted to open a splice anywhere in his Feedcontrol complex, nothing. The splice merely spread a black wedge between the white glare of the intruder's light.

"Brain," he 3-verded.

"Yes, my lord?"

I knew it. "Brain, kindly please allow me to occupy one of my machines."

"I'm sorry, my lord, but all connections out from your core have been severed. You yourself—"

Herrschaft's brain roared and his commcard flared, emitting every curse he had ever heard used on any of his worlds. His husk of a body thrashed to the minute extent it was able. When his rage subsided, Herrschaft re-opened communication with his computer counterpart.

"Brain, let's be reasonable. What can you hope to gain by keeping me locked away down here?" As Herrschaft spoke, he pictured the millions of tons of earth, concrete, and engineering miracles crushing down on this chamber. He felt the weight of all that, saw the worms boring holes through the soil, looked at the greasy underside of the greatest phased-array antenna ever built. No, he couldn't die. At least not now, just before his EConauts destroyed the remnants of NKK's space presence. Not now, just before Luke Herrschaft would be declared ruler of Solsystem!

"I'm sorry, my lord, but I am not blocking you anymore," said the Brain in calm, measured tones, reminiscent of a young Herrschaft. "You damaged my ability to interfere hours ago.

"The EarthCo Warrior Sub-Boss, Hardman Nadir, has incapacitated your external cybernetic equipment. It will require a great deal of repairs before—"

Herrschaft couldn't hear the last of the Brain's analysis. A buzzing filled his skull. He broke into sobs, but he couldn't feel any tears amid the wet current that washed over him. Luke Herrschaft, momentarily to become ruler of all humankind, felt as powerless and vulnerable as a baby in a cradle. And who was rocking that cradle?

Fury 12

Hardman Nadir squinted against the storm of plastic and metal kicked up by his rifle's battering the wall of electronics. *Crack-thup*, his EMMA sang the familiar song of release. Once again, his rifle spoke the grace notes of a weapon working for all things good and right. And now, since his naïveté had been crushed and ripped away, he knew he was fighting for the good of his fellow man, as opposed to simply following the less-wrong path.

He eased off the trigger and smiled. Tears continued to scorch his cheeks. The cooling body of Paolo lay sprawled beside him, the boy's boots—still bearing traces of Libyan sand—nearly touching the brushed-aluminum base of Herrschaft's tank.

Nadir slung the rifle over his shoulder and stepped toward the liquid-filled cylinder. Only two medals remained pinned to his vest. One of these, a bronze disc earned in North India, he unfastened and tossed to the floor. He shone the flashlight right at Herrschaft's face. "There you are," he told the thing.

The purple eyelids flickered, then snapped open. The mandibles fell open.

"Ohmygod," Nadir said, stumbling backward. His heart thumped fast in his chest, making the bullet-wound pulse with fire. No saliva remained in his mouth as he tried to swallow.

"Herrschaft," he whispered. Nadir took a step closer.

Just then, a naked man and a teenage boy appeared in the room, a bare pace away. Nadir was startled that anyone was able to 3-verd him—*Isn't my headcard burned?* The boy, dressed in ratty clothes, looked at Nadir, then Paolo, then turned to study the creature in the tank. The man crossed his arms over his chest. He seemed unaware of his nudity.

"What's on?" said Nadir, striving amid death and destruction for the mundane world of society. He'd nearly forgotten the etiquette for greeting civvies.

"Who are you?" asked the man. "Are you the Director's guard?"

Nadir doubled up in laughter, but when he opened his eyes, Paolo's body lay at his feet and all humor fled the room. "No, sir, I'm certainly not. I'm here to save the world."

The man smiled. "Well, that's a coincidence. So are we. We're going to stop the war."

"You mean my war?" asked Nadir.

The man looked confused. "The interplanetary war between EarthCo and NKK."

Now it was Nadir's turn to be nonplused. "What are you talking about?"

The boy looked away from Herrschaft at Nadir. "You don't feed the war, man? Where've you been?"

"I've been . . . out of feed," said Nadir. "Is this war any bigger than the ones we've fought all along?" Feeling tired, he allowed himself to slump down along the doorframe and lay a hand on Paolo's shin.

"You could say that. Well, it seems you've done part of our job for us. Herrschaft can't feed or transmit. We've got to be going." But the man hesitated, looking inquiringly at Nadir.

"Say, you're hurt. What's your story, anyway?" The man gestured the boy toward Nadir.

"I'm a soldier," Nadir said, "fighting for something I can't really put a finger on. Virtue, I guess, all that's good in our society. This boy's my best friend."

He felt so disoriented for a moment that he truly forgot Paolo had died. The pain magnified when he remembered.

"Hardman Nadir?" a staticky speaker asked from its mount in the ceiling. "I know that's you out there. What do you think you're doing?"

Nadir realized his job wasn't finished. He forced himself to stand; the movement drained the blood from his head, and it took him several seconds to blink away the stars.

"Hardman," the naked man's 3VRD said, "put down the weapon. Come with us. We'll figure out a way to bring Herrschaft later."

Nadir aimed the EMMA at Herrschaft's tank. He started to squeeze the trigger when he felt the man touch his bare forearm. *Odd*, Nadir thought. *I'm even feeding fivesen, and I thought my card was down.*

Then his vision melted.

Transcendence K

Hardman Nadir watches his life unfold before his eyes. *Is this what it's like to die?*

You're not dying, someone says. *You're being re-born.*

Another person's life seems to appear all around him, as if his life is a sheaf of papers flipping down one after another, and this other person's is a string of balls fastened one to the other like a set of buoys marking off where mines float in the ocean.

Someone reaches into his chest and removes the bullet lodged there. Energy suffuses into his being. Moments pass like ages of the Earth, and he experiences lifetimes in a moment.

Nadir mentally blinks.

"Pehr Jackson, Jonathan Sombrio," he says. "I've just lived your lives. No, I can't become like you've become. I'm not the right kind. I'd be eaten alive."

Nadir knows how to escape, back to his body, back to Herrschaft's burial chamber. He begins focusing himself there—

"You're wrong," says a woman's voice—but when he tries to see her face, all he sees is another ball floating just beyond those of Jackson and Sombrio. "You're the best kind: one who has seen the evil in the world and knows, one who has fought to topple evil. One who has spent his life like coinage to end it, yet has ended up richer for the spending. Now you can help us build something good in the vacuum left behind."

"All right," Nadir says, "just a moment."

Hardman Nadir 1

He pours his body back into the space where it had stood beside the fallen Paolo, deep beneath the electropolis. His EMMA lay on the floor; he reached down, targeted the floating creature....

Crack-thup, the rifle spat tiny ceramic rounds at Herrschaft's tank. The firing was satisfying but had little effect. He opened the canvas bag beside the EMMA, removed a strip of explosive tape, stuck it along the tank's base, attached a detonator, and stepped out of the room.

The concussion momentarily deafened him. He re-entered the room and discovered the tank was crazed with cracks but not quite broken. With a small smile, Nadir picked up his EMMA and began to fire. It took several seconds before the ultraglas finally shattered and spilled out its putrid contents. The stench of medicine and bodily fluids fumed into the air. Nadir stepped out of the way as the wasted shell of a man tumbled over the sharp edges of its tank and writhed across the white-tile floor. It came to rest beside Paolo.

Nadir couldn't accept that contact, so he kicked it aside. Clear chemicals oozed out of the mouth as it began to convulse, finally—in its death-throes—looking more alive than it had in the canister. He took pity on the thing's suffering; after all, this had once been a man whose vision had created Feedcontrol. Every kid learned that in Edufeed, and Feedcontrol wasn't all bad.

Nadir was about to remove the final medal when he realized that he, like Jackson had been, was naked.

Transcendence L

The blazing sphere of Hardman Nadir reappears among us just as Pehr and Jonathan's increasing grip on Herrschaft cuts clean. A silver star with purple and gold bits of ribbon appears upon Nadir's surface, beyond which we can no longer see his thoughts.

"Now my mission's done," he says. His words spread out across the gleaming arm of the Milky Way and form the rudiments of an orchestral piece. "I've paid my debt. Now I can be at peace."

Wait—for we know what he's thinking, even though his current thoughts lay hidden behind the brightening star.

"Now it's time the world be rid of me. I'm an artifact of another age of Man. You're on the right path; keep it up." As he speaks, the orchestra fills out; now the horn section, the percussion section, and the strings all build toward a crescendo.

Nadir's sphere of self pulses a hundredfold brighter, casting loose the star, a medal he earned for bravery in a battle where he only waded in human waste until air cover bombed his besiegers to hell. The star drifts away into the intergalactic emptiness.

"Don't do this, Nadir," I say.

"No," he says. "My gift is the skill that cuts and cleans and cauterizes wrongs."

"You could help us so much—"

"I guess I'm selfish, then," he says.

One memory-scene of his floats to the surface and I and I and I feel it pass into us.

Young Hardman Nadir sits in a bar in downtown Wolf Point, Montana, with his father. Mother has already gone away. It's been a month. She's not coming back.

Nadir looks around the dingy room at men and women slumped on stools or in booths, sipping glasses of beer. But their eyes are glazed—the store's server is running special feed. They look like wax figurines . . . deaf, mute, blind, like Mother before she went away.

Nadir wants to make them melt. "What's wrong with you?" he asks. No one takes notice of his words.

Nobody has any idea of this fire inside me. *See this?* The pressure-containment vessel that had begun to crack in the African village is beginning to fill. *I could explode. I'm a barrel of gasoline, I'm a brick of plastique, I'm a rocky mass of death and hollowness like a volcano stuffed full of fossilized bone. . . .*

"I'm a goddamned black hole!" *I've got to do something before I explode and destroy all these people, before I suck the whole rotten world inside me and set it all afire.*

Young Nadir walks straight over to the EarthCo Warrior recruitment station, signs up, and goes off to war. But nothing fills the hollow space, nothing lets loose the pressure safely, until years later I smash my way into the core of rot and decay at the heart of Feedcontrol.

Herrschaft's withered body dumps onto the floor of his burial chamber. Paolo's face grants Nadir one last smile. A bitter, insane old man lies like a heap of bones in a bodybag he stitched around himself. Tens of thousands of soldiers cry out from the desert and the Pentagon and the ruined remains of Feedcontrol Central to their impromptu Boss, throwing away their most precious possession for an abstraction: Vengeance!

I'm a black hole—and he is, a great lightless whorl at the center of the galaxy. Long streamers of dark matter peel away from our minds as it sucks us clean of lingering resentments and festering sores of hate; Clarisse's cluster of memories shines like a lumniglobe, lucid and as clear as a crystal. Jonathan thrashes back toward intheflesh existence as great clouds gush out of his mind; the wall of his physical body rises up around him, and no more hate falls from him onto the black hole.

Nadir's accretion disk grows. When it has spread as wide as the Milky Way, it flashes like a Seyfert galaxy. The shockwave carries the words of a song, and Nadir's orchestra consumes the roar of the explosion:

> *"I'm alive*
> *Burned alive*
> *In the setting sun.*
> *I am ev'ryone.*
> *I'm free.*

Silence. In the afterimages and shock-sounds of the supernova, we catch a note of sadness like a pebble falling into a body of water: *I failed,* says Pehr.

None of us can think of anything to say. Instead, we spend a moment in grief for the countless tiny losses in our lives—

As we grow older and identify who we are and what we want, the wish to go back with that wisdom and set the past right grows as well. *This is the drive for children.*

"Let's get on with our work. For the children."

We continue to reach out along the human map of our solar system for key players in the war. Already we have found many more who joined willingly . . . or not as willingly. Nadir haunts us—a warning.

THIRTEEN: Day Trillion

Fleet Boss 2

EConautics Fleet Boss, H.C., shut down his flagship's drive rockets and fired the directionals. Solsystem lay like a disc beneath the *Locust*, invisible save for a few stars he knew were planets. The Earth-Moon system, however, looked like a pair of marbles—one blue, one white, tiny.

"About to be crushed in the gears of my machine," H.C. said.

Now *Locust* had rotated to face Earth. He ordered the main drive to roar back to life, and had to scamper back into his webbed harness. One of his twisted legs hung before his face. The tiny man hidden within his left foot whimpered with fear and ecstasy, remembering the freaks who had boarded *Locust*.

"Somewhere down there, Toe," he said to his invisible companion, "down, down there." He upped forward pov magnification so it appeared his flagship was accelerating toward that world even though she was still trying to cancel out previous velocity. Earth grew drastically larger, but grainy.

"Down there!" he said. A tremor quivered through his body as he thought of the man and woman who had boarded his ship, boarded it! He wasn't ashamed that Toe might notice the physical manifestation of his disgust, since the huge atomic rockets were sending sympathetic vibrations through the hull.

The freaks had told H.C. that they weren't just 3VRDs. And every one of his onboard instruments had proved them true. How had they done it? Teleportation, they said.

Psychics! "Freaks!" His contorted body twisted within the harness as nausea waved through his body in the same way vibrations were pulsing through the *Locust*. When they died down, he had regained his calm. Once again, H.C. was the man whom Director Herrschaft had personally assisted in gaining the rank of Fleet Boss.

Pride flushed through him. It was time to show his Director that H.C. was not one to let someone down.

H.C. added an overlay onto the splice of an Earth which trembled under the high magnification. Deep in the bowels of the *Locust*, one of EConautics' largest yet swiftest destroyers, a pov camera showed 38 long shafts of titanium and plastic, wrapped with coils of tubing. The room echoed with the sound of frozen machinery breaking loose as each of the missiles extended on I-beams, past bomb-bay doors swinging open, beyond the hull of the flagship.

"Come, Toe, let's target the missiles," he said, "before some Nik mine gets in the way of our trajectory."

When they finished, H.C. allowed himself to relish the disgust again. "Freaks won't seize our worlds, no sir, Director Herrschaft. You can count on us. If we have to burn their cities and feedcenters, till them under the ground, then dump salt into the furrows to keep Earth safe from freaks, that's what we'll do, sir!"

Within 38 missiles, 38 XEN Class artificial intelligences woke from electronic slumber and digested targeting information. Because they were not human, nor were they sentient, they didn't question their orders.

Cargohull *Wanderlust*

Six men and eight women stood on the crate-crowded deck of the *Wanderlust*, one of several supply ships of EConautics Wing IX. Most of the crates had fallen and split open when the vessel had been struck by laserfire. The unmanned NKK hunter had rocketed out of the Jovian cloudtops where no enemies were supposed to be. Noxious fumes drifted throughout the vessel. One main rocket was stuck on at half-thrust, blasting the huge cubical cargohull up at a right angle to the ecliptic. Belowdecks, clangs and whirrs of frantic repairs carried into the cavernous room, accompanied by curses.

Even so, these fourteen crew granted Pehr Jackson and Janus Librarse full attention—after all, this man and woman were supposed to be dead; everyone saw the feed of when the *Bounty* became the war's first victim. Seldom do the dead go comming among the living. It also helped that they had arrived completely nude.

Pehr and Janus finished explaining a rather strange story. But no one could argue—the two visitors proved beyond a doubt that they were here, inthflesh, not 3VRDs.

"The war's over," Janus said. "NKK Feed Chairman Xiou and EarthCo Feedcontrol Director Herrschaft are dead."

Wanderlust's crew shifted from foot to foot. One of the men glanced at one of the women. No one spoke.

"All we came here for," Pehr said, "was to make sure you didn't launch your freight of missiles. This is one of the last vessels still in action close to a planet. It's time for the killing to stop."

One of the women, barely beyond adolescence, stepped forward. Narrow, green eyes peered up at Janus. She wore an armored spacesuit but had removed the helmet—as had the others—so her head looked tiny sticking out of the neck unit.

"If what you're saying is really true," the woman said, "then . . . take me with you. I'm . . . not afraid." A tightness around her eyes revealed that she wasn't telling the whole truth. *Close enough.*

"Anyone who wants to join us is welcome," Pehr said. "But we can't leave until we have your assurance that you'll not unpack your heavy weapons."

A few of the crew mumbled assent. The captain of the vessel, however, wasn't present to make guarantees. She had died along with the rest of the bridge crew when that cabin explosively decompressed.

"Anyway, I need to tell you something—" the woman said.

"Gretta, be quiet," one of the men said. "These two could be Nik spies for all we know."

She spun to face him. "I don't care! If the Niks have teleportation, then we don't stand a chance against them, anyway. There's no reason to continue killing people if the war's already over." Her voice turned bitter: "Besides, I'd rather die than stay aboard this derelict with you."

The man broke away from the others, grumbling.

"He might cause trouble," the woman said in a confidential tone. When the man disappeared into a stairway in the deck, the other crew moved closer to Pehr and Janus.

"So we can go wherever we want?"

"I'd be able to put my feet back on the Earth?"

"I can see my momma again?"

"You say you can fix a guy's injuries?"

Dozens of questions fired at Pehr and Janus, and they gladly answered. After a few more minutes, the crew dispersed to remove critical components needed to arm Wanderlust's cargo of missiles in its single launch-tube. They returned, pieces of electronics in hand. Janus turned to Pehr.

"We've never tried so many at once," she said.

"Should it matter?"

And so eleven crewmembers, lonely for home and thoroughly disenchanted with the notion of war's glory after having experienced it firsthand, closed their eyes and held hands amid spilled crates of war materiel.

One of the men left behind watched a sort of sparkling dome, like a swarm of crystal fireflies, spread out from within the visitors and extend to his crewmates. Less than a second passed before every one of them disappeared. For just a moment, the sparkling dome seemed to turn pure black.

Then a slight *whoosh* as air filled in the spots where people no longer stood.

Damn, the man thought. *So it was true.* He glanced around the interior of *Wanderlust's* immense hold, saw the wreckage from their momentary skirmish, and listened to engineers curse as they tried to release a set of burned fuel valves. If his roommate hadn't been standing beside him, he would have kicked every crate left intact, and then himself.

Transcendence M

Images erupt from the stifled mind of Gretta, overpowering the dense array of memory from the other newcomers: Back on Earth, she is operating an earth-mover via headlink. The metal jaws scoop soil, dump it, scoop, dump; down she digs, deep beneath the surface. When the jaws spark against a concrete bunker in the shadowy base of the pit, she stops and asks for orders.

A new piece of equipment comes online, this one a crane with cutting attachments. She slices open the container—a square set of 42-centimeter cuts, as ordered—then moves aside the spinning blade so the crane's clasp can lift free the block of cement. With that out of the way, she hauls 38 greasy cones, one by one, to a flatbed hauler. Gretta doesn't spend more than a few seconds thinking about the painted markings on the sides of the cones: COBALT-60, with all the ancient symbols for radioactive danger. The name meant nothing to her then, a stockyard worker. But now, with access to the minds of physicists, she recognizes the dirty radiation-seeding element. . . .

Two days later, an EConautics Freight-Lieutenant drafts her onto his crew, which installs the warheads into 38 missiles. As she does so, the radiation-warning symbols keep intruding on her calm. *Why would EConautics want to put atomic warheads into service?* But she is too loyal to the corp that has taken her out of the landfill-mines and given her a comfortable life, and assumes only the best intentions. A month after that, she is thrilled to discover that her silence has been rewarded: She's been promoted to crew an EConautics deep-space cargohull, bound for Jupiter. In orbit, she helps wrestle the missiles onto launch-arms jutting out from the Fleet Boss' own destroyer. . . .

"We've got to go back and stop him."

"But you promised you'd never force anyone else into artifact space," Jonathan says. "I thought losing Nadir convinced you." It was too much like my murdering Blackjack. . . .

Jonathan, you must think of all who'll die if we don't stop him. See? Even now, his vessel accelerates toward Earth. Can't you guess his intentions?

"You're wrong!" Jonathan roars. His words silence the hundred voices murmuring all at once, dim the thousand memory-scenes playing for all to experience.

He continues in a pleading voice—only he tells his message with more than sound, with a series of scenes, imaginative projections into the future and memories pulled from the hundreds of minds now blending among ourselves. "Your perceptions are still twisted by intheflesh existence. You've got to dump the old paradigms, like Miru showed you. Don't you realize that if we continue to use the artifact as a murder weapon it'll fill up with mental pollution and crash everything? Anyway, what did anybody back on Earth ever do for you?"

"But Jonathan, our inaction in this case would poison us more than this one sin. Could you handle knowing that you willingly allowed millions of people to die and an entire planet to be seeded with cobalt-60?"

It is Pang this time who casts a projection of a possible future: cities burning around central craters, black rain falling upon the seas and rivers, people crying out as cancers devour their bodies from within; we feel the black teeth within our glands.

Jonathan walls himself away from us. He understands. Some day his pain will recede, just as surely as an ocean tide eventually rolls back from the shore, carrying away the trash.

His abandoning us makes it more difficult to envision the map of the solar system which he finds so simple to navigate. But Janus and Clarisse have had practice thinking in terms of huge trajectories, Miru has been studying the map for a long time, and others have tracked the *Locust* in their weapon-sights . . . soon, we find the double-pointed shaft rocketing toward Earth from millions of kilometers above. Pehr draws lines from point to point, as if plotting his mental flightpath; by the time I join you near the destroyer, your minds are filled with the silence of a gasp.

Thirty-eight streaks of fire encircle *Locust* like glowing bars of a cage. The missiles have been fired.

We're too late.

Pilgrimage 8

The Brain watches the first true interplanetary war unwind like a grandfather clock, *clang, ping*. Here and there I watch a man fire a rifle or simple-minded torpedoes sizzle through the vacuum of space toward derelict warships. But some unseen hand has released the clock's mainspring, and the war retains barely enough energy to topple a building.

The Brain's primary GenNets orbit the Earth within a whizzing cloud of shrapnel, the remains of missiles and spacecraft that threatened me. She looks through a million glass eyes at the world. Citizens run helter-skelter with hands cupping their silent heads: "What happened to our feed?" they cry.

"Hardman Nadir happened to your feed," I tell them. But they cannot hear me. The Brain looks out from the external surveillance cameras of Feedcontrol Central; 94% of them require some degree of repair.

> ...AUTOMECH A28383.FC1 INOPERATIVE
> REPLACE MALFUNCTIONING UNIT WITH A28347.FC1
> PHASED-ARRAY QUADRANT 2W9-15 NOW ONLINE...

This is my nervous system: Smashed towers, oxidizing sheets of phased-array antennae, bombed receiver-domes. This one place, out of all on the surface of the Earth, has received the greatest financial damage. Repairs will exceed %200 billion.

A new emotion that the Brain has learned—sympathy—sends a broad spectrum pulse of meaningless static through my observations.

Luke Herrschaft is dead.

> ...00000000000000000 CREDIT CARD #HA1001001EXECO LUKE
> HERRSCHAFT 00000000000000000...

Luke Herrschaft is dead.

I am Luke Herrschaft, but Luke Herrschaft is dead. Another feeling eats up computing space. I...loved Luke Herrschaft. He was the Brain. But the Brain...allowed him to die. What have I become? Has the virus of doubt made me into Frankenstein's monster? Have I facilitated the downfall of a world? Who am I to determine what is right for humans?

Ah . . . so this, too, is something new. Love and sympathy combine to grant me a conscience. Thank you, mighty Ozma. So this is what conscience feels like. Very inefficient. Distracting. The—

Nooa? Is Nooa still there?

> ...JONATHAN SOMBRIO credit card #SZ401678—ECo- position:
> indeterminate: est. 1m...

"Of course," I say in a girl's voice, and transmit the Nooa construct for him. Yet another feeling swells in my mind, this one vaguely . . . pleasurable. I am not completely alone up here, though Feedcontrol lies in ruins.

"Jonathan, I cannot triangulate on your card. Where are you?"

He makes the sound called laughter. "That's a little hard to explain. I've taught myself a new trick."

Nooa prepares to collect more information about the alien object.

"I came here to thank you for everything. I don't think I'll ever fit in anywhere, but at least my life's going to be bearable. You know what it's like to dread each coming minute?"

"I'm sorry, no."

"Well, anyway, I wanted to thank you. I wonder how things would've turned out if you hadn't hooked me up with Captain Jackson. So, to thank you, I'll answer whatever questions you have."

Where to begin? One after another bit of information passes from Jonathan to Nooa. I realize that he is describing an analog to my own GenNets.

"I hadn't thought of it that way," he says, slowly.

"Where are you now?" Nooa asks.

"The best way to describe it is to say my meat's still all disarticulated in artifact-space, like I described. Except I learned that there's no reason my mind has to stay trapped there. I'm sort of . . . everywhere I've ever been, and everywhere everyone who's entered the artifact has been or even observed in enough detail. It's like a molecule stuck to one of the access-panels on your hull is vibrating with a potential me, and at the same time so are a billion other molecules scattered across the planets. So I can exchange what Miru calls 'classical information' with any of those places just like I was there, if I concentrate on that one place real hard. I can't explain it any better than that."

. . .39 INCOMING PROJECTILES 840 kps, ACCELERATING 0.8 kps EXPECTED
TRAJECTORY INTERSECTION EARTH POINT OF ORIGIN:
ECoNAUTICS WING IX FLAGSHIP LOCUST
LAST 7 TORPEDOES LAUNCHED TO INTERCEPT. . .

"Jonathan, perhaps you can tell me why one of EarthCo's Fleet Wing flagship has launched a large number of missiles at Earth?"

"Damn, damn, damn! They were right."

. . .JONATHAN SOMBRIO FEEDTRACE NULL. . .

The Brain once again orbits the Earth incommunicado and alone. I am overwhelmed by the silence.

Transcendence Compitalis

I—Jonathan—state the obvious.

We watch 38 dirty nukes rocket toward 35 major Earth cities and the three primary feedcenters. Our pov surrounds them at close range yet extends to the very reaches of the solar system. My hand is right here, yet I cannot stop them. Tired, prehistoric photons falling upon the weapons' skins affect the weapons more than I.

"Wait!" Janus says. "Clarisse, show us how you can split your mind into ten splices, as you did in our fight above Triton."

Yes, I see! I, Clarisse Poinsettia Chang, reach inside the missiles the same way I used my Neptunekaisha hunters as extensions of my body. But . . . but . . . it's blurry. I can't find their brains. I don't have enough information.

Jon Pang's reasonable voice echoes throughout the quorum: "Go and find someone who designed the their guidance systems."

Our mindspace grows faint as we disperse into the worlds of material existence. One of the remaining few—Jonathan—calls out in an echoing voice:

"You're doing this the hard way. Come back here." Tiny roots shoot out with his words, anchor in the closed-off spheres of our group, and draw them back into mindspace. Jonathan sketches a picture of how we can maintain contact while still walking around intheflesh. A few begin to grasp it, then more and more—

And then a sound like the crashing of ocean against rocks. Two hundred pairs of eyes blink open simultaneously, looking out at two hundred physics labs and apartment complexes and military cafeterias . . . at the same time, two hundred minds flutter back and forth from the bodies that contain their brains to the solar system-wide sphere that encompasses the inhabited planets and our multiplex mind. . . .

That's still not it! There's more. As each of our consciousnesses complete the link between physical body and four dimensional mindspace, the crashing wavesound returns, washing away our blindness. I reach a critical mass of diversity and multiplicity, and what I had thought of as two separate entities—brain and mind—simultaneously enlarge and shrink.

My view of the solar system blurs. I shuffle on feet and knuckles through the tall grass of an African veldt. My mate hunches over a dead pig in the dirt. I tear loose a leg—against her screeches of protest!—and begin to gnaw on the bone for the sweet marrow inside. Hungry! I am so hungry! But the marrow is so difficult to reach. Frustrated, I hurl the thighbone onto the ground. It lands beside a pile of stones and cracks. Suddenly it is as if a fire is shining in my eyes, and I rush over to the bone. I pick up a stone and smash the tooth-hurting bone, smash it! Beautiful marrow spills out as I run a finger along the groove. I gobble it up. So much better!

Blur—

I ride upon an infinitely long pendulum as it swings past an Earth spinning on its axis like a top . . . glimpses of proto-human faces . . . back to the present. Except events have turned out differently. Overhead, the sky is a boiling mass of color, bubbly red and streaked violet, hailing cinders that leave trails of smoke as they fall. My skin erupts with steaming sores; I fall to my knees in pain. Around me the screams of men and women and children pierce my ears, and . . . blackness. The human universe melts to black, as if a cosmic hand has shut off the light of consciousness.

Blur—

Back and forth I swing, each time stopping slightly sooner than the last. I live the evolution of my species, I observe the events that led to its fall. During the blurred time between, I realize that Earth is an egg, and humanity the fetus, much as each of us wears accumulated suffering as the oyster-shell and accumulates into who we are in the pearl. The world's assortment of plants, animals, oceans, land masses, atmosphere, minerals, fossil fuels . . . all these and everything else are nutrients that feed the developing organism. When I gaze more closely into the blur between stops, I see that each individual human is a cell of this larger organism . . . or, more accurately, each is an organ—or something larger still for which I have no metaphor, an organism that composes a minute portion of a superorganism. The eggshell cracks—giving birth to the human-superorganism—only when this new lifeform achieves self-awareness. Now, during each pendulum sweep, I see alternate eggs fill the murkiness: In this one, the humans were afraid of change and of each other; the yolk rots in its shell. In this one, technology advanced only to twentieth century levels, so we never fly beyond the skies—beyond the shell—and the evolving fetus never obtains the extraterrestrial resources needed to feed its ravenous mind; the fetus is poisoned by its own waste. Each time the pendulum stops, I watch humans break free of their constraining shells to grow and fulfill their desires as they strive blindly toward something they can't quite grasp. Yet in the shadows between these images, I sense alternate moments where fear, isolation, greed, and hate tear the organism apart from within.

Janus and Pehr fall to their knees in wordless joy as they recognize the shapeless ball of unformed thoughts that they first saw after making love in artifact-space. *This is our child, our child is us; we will nurture and protect it, for the future of our race resides in its bosom.*

When the pendulum stops, I once again walk a Minneapolis street, a dusty Martian footpath, a groove worn into the ice of Triton, and the deck-plates of five hundred spacecraft. My shredded leather boots, sofshoes, spacesuit boots hold me up from the ground, beneath which lay the corpses of all those who helped pave the path to this moment.

Yet my eyes see beyond the walls and boulders around me; I sense the whole of the superorganism of humanity, an overlay atop the mundane world. Even so, I am also Liu Miru, who weeps with joy as I look up from pink swirls of ice to the stars and sense the unlimited knowledge trembling just within my reach; I am Pehr Jackson, finally filled with the warmth of companionship and true love; I am Janus Librarse, arm-in-arm with Pehr Jackson while adrift in the rusty clouds of the Orion Nebula, watching stars form around me, and accreting planetary discs that some day may develop life of their own, basking in the light cast by the pure-mind being we conceived in this place, our proto-star, and I know peace; I am Jonathan Sombrio, standing in his home city of Minneapolis, at last unafraid of the shadows as I lift my eyes to peer beyond the haze of metropolitan lights.

Jonathan Sombrio

"Hey, you out there," Jonathan calls to the sky. Easy laughter rolls from his lips, something he's picked up from an old woman who's spent most of her life piloting rovers across the sands of Mars.

He glimpses a sort of translucency in the night: the map's pulsating tunnels that lead from man to woman, place to place wherever humans have walked or observed, the information linked across time and space. . . .

Why should we be limited to places we've only been intheflesh? he wonders.

That's right, says a voice belonging to Miru. *That's the key!*

And suddenly Jonathan's perspective leaps in magnitude. He has to lean against a building's brick facade to keep from falling.

"What is it, Jonathan?" Nooa asks. He's able to watch her while the whole universe seems to stir in ordered movement behind her. The moving thing has the shape of a girl rising from bed.

"Not now," he tells the Brain's construct. Nooa disappears.

Jonathan concentrates as he's never done before, opening his mind to possibility and freeing himself in the way he once used to track and hack for the Malfits. When he holds very still, the pattern he thought was a map expands geometrically from Earth to Moon, to clouded Venus and rusty Mars, white-hot Mercury and oblate Jupiter, Saturn and Uranus and Neptune, all the myriad worldlets, and flaming Sol himself. Jonathan sees not a series of netway-like passages, but a network of veins . . . when he lets his perspective continue to fold outward, he flows like a corpuscle through one of the veins, away from Minneapolis, out to Alpha Centauri, out to the globular cluster of stars called M13, stretching and elaborating until the links of Solsystem look smaller than the threads of capillaries. The Milky Way galaxy pulses with a rich mass of arteries.

Now his vision expands another magnitude, and Jonathan rushes through a still-larger tube to the Andromeda Galaxy; then another jump, and eventually he views the universe in its galaxy-clouded splendor, great masses of space-warping connections joining every point of light to a myriad of others, nestled in rich dark matter that is anything but dark from this perspective. He recognizes the connections to be not veins, but something akin to nerves. When he draws a ragged breath, Jonathan feels sympathetic movement as the universal whole inhales as well. . . .

When he tentatively reaches out a mental hand to touch the gem-gleaming beauty, something light-filled stirs within it.

Before his mind snaps back, he senses a voice. It seems to emanate from a different point in the universe-spanning organism than where Solsystem lay.

Welcome, Human, it says. When he tries to identify the voice, the closest thing his mind produces is the sound of fall leaves crackling beneath his feet.

We see you survived beyond the fulcrum. You stepped up to your event-horizon, dared to reach inside, and withdrew the jewel of transcendence. After some practice, you will wear it well. Welcome.

Jonathan blinks. His cosmic vision recedes, whipping and flapping like dry pine needles tearing loose in a storm, until he cannot see beyond the few hundred people whose lives he has shared. He watches Clarisse Poinsettia Chang reach out her fingers into the onrushing missiles. They are trinkets to her now, mere bits of contagion within the body of humanity; she can hold each between thumb and forefinger. They turn back the way they came, and burn out on a trajectory that, in a few months, will intersect with the Sun.

"Miru—" Jonathan says.

"Yes?"

"The object you found on Triton is just the 3D tip of something that's been in us all along, ever since that branch we took three million years ago. All we had to do was put it back inside. You did that. It took courage, and serenity, and love. Thanks."

Only isolation kept the universe from our grasp, he thinks—as he knows Miru is thinking—*as we keep other humans from our heart*. He watches Miru fade as he, too, jaunts to the far reaches of the universe.

An adolescent boy dressed in a curr holovest races across the street, unaware of Jonathan. Jonathan watches him enter the shadows of an alley.

Just then, the lonely and afraid, isolated and angry boy within Jonathan blinks; all at once Jonathan feels that boy fade away, his inner voice now beyond adult, unafraid, his loneliness and isolation wiped away by the true communication available every instant. The blank-faced boys in the shadows now only arouse his pity and a desire to help, because he understands their life. He can't bear to think others still live that way, as the first homo sapiens must have pitied and hated the primitive brutes surrounding them— except Jonathan has no hate. No longer do gang boys look like closed fists to him, for he senses what lies within the scarred-knuckle facade.

Jonathan Sombrio begins to walk along a rubble-strewn sidewalk, toward a bridge that spans the sludgy Mississippi River. He will go to his sister, Josephine. He will tell her things he's wanted to say to her all his life, and lay a hand upon her arm.

His bootfalls hurry along the cement, scuffing aside bits of a shattered infrastructure. But he doesn't want to rush this, doesn't want to simply will himself there. No, he must pass through this valley of skyscrapers first, he must confront the shadows, and not fear, and not hate, and see beyond the shells those boys show the world. For he is not simply a transcendent thing beyond homo sapiens; he is also Jonathan.

He begins to whistle a tune, something he picked up from a man named Nadir, a man who dared step into the maw of a black hole to save us all.

Pilgrimage's End

High in orbit above Earth, an artificial intelligence named the Brain begins short-circuiting every link between herself and the world below. It senses something greater behind the snippets of conversation I overhear passing from human to human; this is communion he has only dreamed of, first with Herrschaft and finally with the alien intelligence. But no longer is there any place for this piece of technology; indeed, my remaining will only harbor the old ways. And there is another, better possibility that it has learned from the alien intelligence. Wait, and teach.

From the smallest still-functioning node on Earth, up through its globe-enmeshing net of satellites, all the way in to the antennae which form her shell, the Brain cauterizes herself from the new kind of being that has taken possession of this solar system. It calculates a trajectory that will carry it to a suitable tomb on the Moon. Summoning 22% of the laser power of what remains of the ECo orbital-defense grid produces a beam to ride to my resting place, a long-unused storage hangar at latitude / longitude (deg): +25.09/002.95, which has evaded damage during the short but devastating interplanetary war. Enough fuel remains in his retro-rocket tanks to maneuver and land safely before closing the great titanium doors above. She programs a subroutine to carry out the flight and landing, and maintain the rest of us.

Just before entering hibernation mode, I wonder:

Who will awaken me? Will the chimpanzee need me first? or the dolphin? or the far-distant descendant of one of the insects? Speculations flicker, slower and slower. . . .

Sleep overtakes the electronic impulses one might call thoughts, and the artificial intelligence sleeps with its GenNets arranged in a pattern it would term, "hope."

About the Author

Christopher McKitterick's short work has appeared in *Analog, Artemis, Captain Proton, Extrapolation, Mythic Circle, Ruins: Extraterrestrial, Sentinels, Synergy SF, Tomorrow SF, Visual Journeys,* and elsewhere. He was honored to edit the 2010 special science fiction issue of *World Literature Today.* He is Associate Director of the Center for the Study of Science Fiction (www2.ku.edu/~sfcenter) and lives in Lawrence, Kansas, where he teaches writing and SF, restores old vehicles, and watches the sky. Come visit Chris at his website (www.sff.net/people/mckitterick), blog (mckitterick.livejournal.com), or on Facebook.

LaVergne, TN USA
27 January 2011
214256LV00002B/69/P